Ronie Kendig

SHILOH RUN PRESS
An Imprint of Barbour Publishing, Inc.

Print ISBN 978-1-68322-064-0

eBook Editions:
Adobe Digital Edition (.epub) 978-1-63409-062-9
Kindle and MobiPocket Edition (.prc) 978-1-63409-063-6

Cover Design: Kirk DouPonce, DogEared Design

Published by Shiloh Run Press, an imprint of Barbour Publishing, Inc., P.O. Box 719, Uhrichsville, Ohio 44683, www.shilohrunpress.com

Our mission is to publish and distribute inspirational products offering exceptional value and biblical encouragement to the masses.

ecpa Member of the
Evangelical Christian
Publishers Association

Printed in the United States of America.

Main Characters

Zulu One: Annie Palermo
aka Ashland Palmieri
After the tragic mission in Misrata, Annie became Ashland Palmieri, renting a small house on Lake Wapato and working at a sub shop in Manson, Washington. But the intrusion of a handsome former Navy SEAL, **Sam Caliguari**, threatens everything she's worked to build and protect.

Zulu Two: Téya Reiker
aka Katherine "Katie" Gerig
After Misrata, Téya became Katherine "Katie" Gerig, embracing the quiet life of her Amish grandmother in Bleak Pond, Pennsylvania. She's at peace for the first time in her life and is set to take the faith and start a relationship with **David Augsburger**.

Zulu Three: Jessica "Jessie" Herring
aka Jamie Hendricks
After Misrata, Jessie became Jamie Hendricks and fell into many of the vices of "Sin City"—Las Vegas, Nevada. The tragedy in Misrata fractured her psyche, and she could never pull herself back together. She's a computer specialist, and despite orders not to, she continued researching what happened in Misrata.

Zulu Four: Candice Reyna
aka Charlotte Reynolds
After Misrata, Candice became a park ranger at Denali National Park in Alaska, who goes by the name Charlotte "Charlie" Reynolds.

Zulu Five: Keeley Shay
aka Kendall Shine
After Misrata, Keeley Shay became Kendall Shine, a dive instructor on Little Cayman Island.

Zulu Six: Nuala King
aka Nyah Kesebi
After Misrata, Nuala King became Nyah Kesebi, who works at a lodge in the Blue Ridge Mountains in North Carolina.

LTC Trace Weston
Lieutenant Colonel Trace Weston was a Special Forces operator and team leader who assembled the Zulu team. He is now working for U.S. Intelligence and Security Command (INSCOM).

CWO2 Boone Ramage
Chief Warrant Officer Boone Ramage is Trace Weston's former right-hand man. He helped train the Zulu team.

SFC Rusty Gray
Sergeant First Class Rusty Gray is former Special Forces operator who helped train the Zulu team.

Lieutenant Francesca "Frankie" Solomon
Frankie Solomon, daughter of **Brigadier General Haym Solomon**, works for U.S. Intelligence and Security Command (INSCOM).

Houston Plunkett is an Information Systems Specialist working with Trace and Boone to protect and vindicate Zulu.

Kellie Hollister and **Mercy Chandler** are cofounders of the organization HOMe—Hope of Mercy, International—which had a branch located in Misrata, Libya.

Berg Ballenger worked with HOMe. His wife and child died in the tragedy at Misrata.

Giles Stoffel, husband of Mercy Chandler, is the CEO and owner of Spirapoulos Holdings.

Titus Batsakis is the owner of Aegean Defense Systems.

The Lorings (Carl, Sharlene, Cora, and Charles) are a family who have been hiding in Greece and may have information about the incident in Misrata.

Military Terms

ACU – Army combat uniform
AHOD – all hands on deck
Airsoft M4 – tactical Airsoft (paint pellet) assault rifle
BUD/S – Basic Underwater Demolition/SEAL Training
CQC – close quarters combat
DOD – Department of Defense
GIS – Italian Carabinieri Special Intervention Group
Glock 17 – a semiautomatic handgun
HK USP Compact – a compact semiautomatic handgun
HUMINT – Human intelligence
INSCOM – U.S. Intelligence and Security Command
JAG – Judge Advocate General
JBER – Joint Base Elmendorf-Richardson
KA-BAR – type of combat knife
MP – military police
M4A1 – an assault rifle
NVGs – night vision goggles
PIT – pursuit intervention technique/tactic
RPG – rocket-propelled grenade
RTB – return to base
SAIC – Special Agent in Charge
SF – Special Forces
SOP – standard operating procedure
SOCOM – Special Operations Command
SureFire – a tactical flashlight

Overkill –
The Beginning

I

Jessie
Las Vegas, Nevada
27 April – 1950 Hours

Tonight, I die.

A shot cracked the night. Sparks zinged off a Dumpster as she sprinted past it. Blood pounded her temples as she raced through the dark stench. She skidded and slapped her hand against a brick to slingshot around the corner. She pushed off, the texture roughing her palm. She stumbled but caught traction. A split-second glance into the ebony void revealed nothing. The dark alleys of Sin City refused to lift the hem of their darkness, refused to show her who or what pursued her. But she could feel it. Feel *them*.

And she'd never doubted that instinct. Not now. Not five years ago.

"Quit staring," she whispered to herself, her pulse whooshing in her ears. "Go." Jessica Herring threw herself around. Tumbled into a steel bin overflowing with rotting food and boxes. She shoved away, but not before the Dumpster lashed out, searing her cheek with the cut of a flattened box.

It was nothing compared to what *they* would do if they caught her. If she didn't get back in enough time. . . She sprinted down the narrow sliver of space between two multistoried buildings. Splashed the puddles of rainwater. Ducked into a corner for a moment to breathe, to get her bearings.

She peeked out, careful to stay within the shadows, and surveyed the lit street. Cars rolled past, slowing at a red light.

Lights. Lights. Lights. Too many! She'd be spotted.

A large black Suburban lumbered onto the street.

Jessie yanked back, hauling in a hard breath as she flattened herself against the wall. Bricks dug into her shoulders. Chest heaving from the hard run, she rested her head but watched the road at the same time. A breeze scampered across her shoulders, breathing a chill down her spine.

This was it.

Live to survive one disaster, only to die in another.

Right. Because that's just how life worked.

Heavy thuds gave pursuit, hammering. Shouting. Screaming her stupidity for stopping.

Waited too long. The men had caught up, racing toward her from the rear of the buildings.

Jessie eyed the roof of the alcove. Feet on the wall in front of her and arms behind her, she shimmied up. Her leaden legs threatened to defy her attempts, but she commanded obedience. Just had to get back to the apartment. She pressed her spine against the ceiling and prayed this was enough to conceal her. Buy her some time.

Three men ran past her hiding spot, skating to a stop in the open street.

Arms trembling, she waited. *Go on. Keep moving.*

If she dropped now, they'd see and hear her.

Jessie gritted her teeth. Steeled her aching limbs.

That black SUV returned, sliding to a stop in front of the men.

"Anything?" a male voice asked.

"Nothing," one said. Another, "Lost her."

"Find her. He wants her *dead*!"

Feeling's mutual, Jessie thought as her arms bounced under the strain. She slumped, her shoulder ramming into the brick. She only allowed a grunt to escape before catching herself. Waited to make sure she hadn't alerted them to her presence, that there was enough noise with the traffic that they didn't hear her.

The men went in opposite directions.

About time.

Jessie dropped to her feet, muscles taut as she worked to temper the sound her boots made in the dirty alcove where pamphlets, dust, and rock swirled. She shot a glance around before stepping into the open again.

She jogged back to the end of the alley. Banked right and headed in the direction of her apartment. *Slow down. Look natural.* She hadn't been as careful as she'd thought. What had she done to give herself away?

Okay, chatting with Candice was probably a bad idea. But they hid their identity. There wasn't anything to track them back.

She trotted out onto the main street. Too bad she wasn't wearing something she could shed. Change her appearance.

"Church Girl."

Jessie felt the smile before she realized she'd put it on her face. "Hey, Bardo." The African American loping toward her, his pants hanging practically on his hips and his boxers exposed, grinned, his head back in that gangsta way of his. But Bardo. . .Bardo was cool. He looked out for her.

One side of his full lips lifted into a smile. "How my babe?" The thing with Bardo, he considered every girl who walked the streets—those who did it professionally and those who didn't—his. And he looked out for *his.* And right now, even though she'd hooked up with him once or twice in the last couple of years, it was better to be with Bardo and his brothers than to be alone. Hide in a crowd.

Behind her, tires squalled.

She swallowed. Held the question. Gave a sidelong glance, begging God not to let it be them. The beams of the Suburban struck them. Snap!

"You in trouble, Church Girl?"

Jessie spun back to him, widened her eyes.

"Go," Bardo said, brandishing a gun. "We got this."

Hope surged. Then deflated. She couldn't put them in this kind of trouble. "I…they're dangerous, Bardo." She glanced at the SUV—stopped now. The thugs were deploying again.

"Go!" Bardo pushed her behind him, muttering something about someone stepping in on his girls in his 'hood.

Guilt chugged through her veins, as thick and heady as some of the drugs she'd fallen into living in Sin City. Tears blurred her vision as the sound of guns exploded. She jerked with the violence of the noise intruding on the busy night.

The peppering of bullets and the wail of sirens threw Jessie around. She sprinted. Ran her heart out. Prayed—When had she last done that? *Really* prayed?—God wouldn't let Bardo die for her stupidity. Awareness shot through her. She spotted her apartment building. Took the stairs two at a time.

"Is that you, Jamie?"

Her landlady's singsong voice trailed through the hallway, but Jessie hurried. Let herself into the apartment that she, as Jamie Hendricks, had rented two years ago, after her restless journey dropped her in this forsaken city. Forsaken just like her. She slapped the deadbolt. Flung the chain lock. Poor excuses for security, she knew. No wasting time to put a chair in front of it. Wouldn't work. They'd bust in one way or another.

No, she had more important things to worry about.

Spun herself around. Stared at the wall with van Gogh's *The Starry Night* on it. Cheaply printed and bought at a craft store. But her favorite. The heavens were endless, free. That's what she wanted. To be free.

"Yeah, free of this freakin' nightmare," Jessie muttered as she walked to the kitchenette, climbed on the counter, and reached into the thin gap between the cabinet and wall. She gripped the laptop and pulled it out. Turning it over, she verified the burner phone was still taped to it. When a roach scampered across her hand, she flicked her wrist, sending the pest across the room.

Jessie hustled to the window, unlocked it, and pulled it open. Wait.

She glanced at the van Gogh. Then to the carpet. Saw a mark.

Heart in her throat, she rushed to the tufted chair spilling its stuffing and moved it to the wall. Adjusted the table and lamp. Stood back. Assessed it. Craned her neck.

She lifted the Gideon Bible and set it on the rickety end table someone had thrown in the Dumpster.

He'd know, right? He'd know it was a clue.

An ache, a five-year-old ache burned in her chest. Jessie grabbed the Bic pen from the kitchen counter. Raced to the Bible. Scribbled in it. *May it be a lamp unto your boots. . .*

Thud! Crack!

Jessie snapped the cover shut. Dropped it on the table. Raced to the window, laptop beneath her arm. Powering on the burner phone as she folded herself through the small window, Jessie prayed she could make the call in time. She rushed around the landing and down the steps. The call connected. Her boots thudded against the rear parking lot as she heard the thunderous crack of her door breaking. She sprinted across the parking lot.

"Harry's Antiques."

An ungodly force punched the air from her open mouth. Thrust her forward. Face first into a puddle. *Splash!* Only as a strange warmth spread across her back and she realized she was paralyzed, Jessie knew she had been right: *Tonight, I die.*

Annie
Manson, Washington
27 April – 2015 Hours

"Hey, Calamari." Annie Palermo used the back of her hand to brush away the strands of hair that had sprung free from her hasty updo. "Usual?"

Eyes like a brownie—with warm caramel inside—held hers. Samuel Caliguari's grin never left his face when she was around. Even when she called him by the absurd nickname. "You know it." The former Navy SEAL had it going on in all the right places—including his heart. Perfect in every sense of the word: handsome, a dozen inches taller than her own five-five height, short-cropped black hair. A slight cleft in his square jaw. Rugged. Dangerous.

Too dangerous. *He can dig up every secret you're protecting.*

Sobered, Annie focused on crafting his cheeseburger sub, a Green Dot Sub Shop specialty.

"Sam." Owner and manager, Jeff Conwell, emerged from the kitchen.

"How's it going?"

"Good, good."

"How's your brother?"

While the two caught up—as they did every time Sam came into the shop, which was often, and not because of the subs but because of his appetite for Annie—she layered on the lettuce and tomatoes. *No olives.* Her hand slid over the container of black slices and on to the mayo, and. . .slid right back again to the olives. Head down, she stole a glance to make sure he wasn't looking. Eyes on Sam, she dropped one olive onto his sub. Lathered the thing in mayo and marinara. *Ew!* His order still made her want to throw up a little in the back of her throat, but you didn't argue with the owner's best friend, who was a man who'd been trained to kill.

Annie wrapped the sub in paper then cradled it in a red basket with Sam's favorite barbecue chips. She placed it on the tray before moving on to the next customer, guilt hanging over her like a giddy concoction. *Hates olives. We'll see.* She'd bet he wouldn't even taste it. Even the most macho men could be such wimps when it came to healthy food.

Minutes fell off the clock, Jeff and Sam still talking. Annie buried herself in her job. If Sam did notice the olive. . .oh, he'd kill her!

Maybe something needed washing in the back. She headed that way, her ears burning. Only the drone of the evening news and chatter in the small shop made it back to her. She slipped through the back and waited.

"Ashland," Jeff called, using the pseudonym Annie adopted for life in Manson. "Need a hand—"

Metal groaned against vinyl in a massive protest. Clearly the sound of a chair scooting back—hard. "Augh!"

Annie froze, a smile pulling against her effort to fake ignorance.

A long gagging noise came next. As if someone had unleashed a demon out front.

"Sam," Jeff called out. "You okay?"

Coughing ensued. Then Jeff offering to get more water.

A thump against something solid, probably Sam pounding his chest. "An olive—I swear those things. . ."

"You okay?"

"Yeah. Sure."

That was it? Sam just chalked it up to an accident? Was he really not going to figure this out? An ounce of disappointment clunked through Annie. Chewing the side of her lip, she stood just out of sight of the eating area. Telling herself it wasn't a big deal. A joke that fell flat. Might as well get back to work.

"Thought"—hot, quiet breath skated down her neck—"you got away with it, didn't you?" His powerful presence loomed behind her. A vise clamped onto her wrist. Yanked her back.

With a yelp, Annie thudded against his barrel chest. "I have no idea what you're talking about." Had she hidden her smile that time?

"Right." His rich brown eyes bore through her. "You just had this total brain fart and put an olive on my sub."

"There was an olive on there?" Were her eyes big enough to feign ignorance?

Sam pinned her in the corner, thunder in his gaze. "You did it on purpose."

"I have no idea what you mean."

"You put that nasty black olive in my sub!"

Annie tried to feign surprise, but a giggle leaked past her facade. She swallowed the laugh. "I have no idea what you're talking about." But she was laughing now. Hard.

"You think it's funny? I about choked on that nasty piece of crap!" Sam's thunder-and-rain demeanor lightened. "You trying to kill a guy?"

"I had no idea it was so easy to take down a guy your size."

"That is cruel and unusual punishment, ma'am."

"A SEAL who can't handle his olives." She smirked at him, trying— and failing—not to appreciate all the good looks he had going on. "Good to know."

"Give me bin Laden over *bin Olives* any day." Laugh lines pinched the sides of his eyes. "Now. You owe me. . . ."

Annie's laughter, her lighthearted mood, vanished. She straightened, pulling herself off the wall, knowing full well the joke behind his words. Sam had never been quiet about his feelings for her. Six months in Manson and he hadn't given up. But did he know how close she was to giving in? To saying yes to this guy who was relentless in his pursuit of her? Everything in her wanted to try because of him, who he was.

Military hero. Strong. Protective. Funny. He'd never let his dark brown hair grow long but kept it short and tight. Naturally tanned from his Italian side, Sam had the brooding spec ops persona down. Even without tac gear. Bulging muscles and personality, he'd swooped into Manson months ago, buying up the cottage next to his sister's two-bedroom place that Annie had rented for the last several years.

Sam's expression slid from playful to serious. "Just one date, Ash," he said in a quiet, husky voice.

He smelled good. Looked good. Talked good. With one hand on his pec and another on his bicep, she struggled to think past the corded muscles she felt beneath his shirt. "Sam. . ." She barely heard herself as disappointment pushed his gaze down to the vinyl floor. She drew in a breath. "I. . ."

Bobbing his head, he said, "Remember?"

She couldn't help but smile. He'd told her many times not to answer. Until she could say yes. She'd said yes many times—in her dreams. He was never far from her thoughts. Or far from her. He was in the parking lot every night she locked up. Followed her home. Gave her salutes each morning she sat on her deck overlooking Lake Wapato.

Five years she'd been here. Been safe here. But one date with Sam and Annie knew this guy would unglue and unseat every secret, passion, and terror.

"Ashland, need your help," Jeff called from the front.

With a lame shrug, she weaseled out of Sam's grip. "Work calls."

"Hey." He caught her fingers—and her heart.

She turned to him, enjoying his touch. Not pulling away. Not wanting to. But she should. She had to. She did.

He grinned that heart-melting grin. "You can put olives in my sandwich anytime if it means I get to corner you again."

"That's the best you've got, Calamari?"

He didn't even flinch at the nickname this time. Instead, he took a step forward, challenge lurking in those rich eyes. "You want my best?"

Trace
Joint Base Elmendorf-Richardson, Alaska
28 April – 1020 Hours

Brittle and icy, the air in the room mimicked the unsanitized environment outside this theater. Two arcs of tables huddled against the recessed floor in the amphitheater-style room, facing the long, rectangular formation of dignitaries seated on the dais that elevated the dignitaries and senior personnel above the rest. Ten military officers hosting a press conference about joint operations and training under the command of newly installed Lieutenant General Charles Perrault. Beside him sat Brigadier General Haym Solomon.

Lieutenant Colonel Trace Weston sat listening to the drone of conversation. The suggested changes were not unexpected, especially since Solomon had briefed him en route from Virginia. The last several hours had pulled on his patience. He was getting older and had been through enough to hate waste of time and resources. He could be back at Fort Belvoir planning the latest technology efforts, both equipment and personnel. Or digging into the past.

Trace tucked his chin in an effort to hide the yawn clawing through his chest and throat. He blinked and straightened.

"At this time," General Perrault said as he leaned into the microphone, his mechanically amplified voice bouncing off the sound-buffering panels in the ceiling, "I think it would be foolhardy to shift away from our projected troop placements, but technology and the political map demand changes. We can't have a repeat of Misrata."

It felt like an RPG had struck Trace center mass. He stilled. Coiled his reaction into a ball in the pit of his stomach. Let his training kick in. He wouldn't flinch. Wouldn't blink. Not now.

He flicked his gaze to his mentor.

General Solomon's brow creased as he adjusted his microphone—a squawk snapping through the room, silencing the murmurs. "General Perrault, your concerns are understandable. Conflicts will arise. Teams will go in to deal with situations. We act on the best intel we have."

"And sometimes," came the gravelly voice of General Leland Marlowe, "you don't."

"Sorry, I thought we were here to discuss plans for the next phase—"

"We are here to ensure our soldiers and airmen are guaranteed the best chance to return home and reduce the casualty risk to innocent civilians."

"It is our highest mission," Solomon said, his chin raised. "Now, moving on." The general glanced down and slid a folder to the side. "Ah, yes. The TALOS—Tactical Assault Light Operator Suit."

Trace let out a breath—slowly—that he didn't realize he'd held. Misrata. Even now, five years later, his gut still clenched. The screams. Haunted shouts through the coms. . .

Marlowe was behind tossing the hand grenade of Misrata into the discussion. He'd tried to run Trace up the flagpole more than once. As he sat near the back of the room, Trace let his gaze rest on the general's. Waited. And he'd wait however long necessary until the man found his manhood and faced Trace.

Finally, brown eyes rammed into his.

Trace didn't flinch. He schooled his facial features. Wished for the beard he had five years ago. Wished for the modified M4A1. Or better yet—M24 sniper rifle.

Marlowe broke contact.

He had nothing on Trace. Only conjecture. And "my gut," as Marlowe had muttered during the meetings with JAG officers in the attempt to get Trace court-martialed.

Almost five years and Marlowe still didn't know the truth.

Neither do I.

Trace balled his fist.

A vibration against his thigh snapped him out of his fuming. He tugged the phone from his pocket and glanced at the caller ID.

His heart jacked into his throat but not before pounding against a few ribs first. Trace pushed out of the seat, which flipped up as soon as he'd vacated it. He pivoted and started for the doors. An MP nodded and opened the door for him.

Trace hit the TALK button as he swiftly moved down the window-encased corridor. "Tango Whiskey Six." He tried to breathe normally, but this wasn't a social call. They kept their distance, using this number only in cases of dire emergency.

"Bravo Romeo Five."

"What's going on?" Trace shoved through the main door and stepped into the frigid air and pristine purity of the Alaskan tundra, and slid on his cover, shielding his eyes from the glare of the sun and snow.

"They found them."

The words stopped him in his tracks. He shoved his gaze around, making sure nobody had seen him. Irrationally praying he'd imagined those words. "How?"

"Don't know." The voice belonged to Chief Warrant Officer Boone Ramage, the man who had, for nearly three years in Afghanistan and two elsewhere, been Trace's right hand. A man he trusted unlike anyone else. "Zulu Three is dead."

Trace slammed his eyes shut, a rancid taste coating his mouth. He turned, lifted his hand, and gripped his forehead. Adjusted his hat. "The others?" His heart started beating a little faster, chugging through the tragic news.

"Checking now. You're at JBER, right?"

"Yeah." Trace skated his gaze around the joint base where the Army and Air Force trained and deployed from.

"Zulu Four is up there."

Trace heard the words, but his mind had lodged between a pair of sultry blue eyes. "Zulu One." *Annie. . .*

"You can reach Four faster."

His heart punched him—hard. "Right. You'll—" Trace's brain caught up with him. He wouldn't ask where Boone was, but he knew the guy had been on a month-long vacation. More like doing contract work south of the border. He had the brains and the brawn, not to mention the experience covert agencies liked. Though they didn't use the phones often since anything could be located these days, Trace wouldn't give the enemy more ammo. "Five?" He verified he wasn't being followed or watched. Unless a sniper. . .

The hairs on the nape of his neck prickled, anticipating a lethal strike. He quickened his step.

"En route now to Five."

"Good. And—"

"I'll swing back and get Two. I've tapped Gray. He'll give the warning signal."

"Good." Trace climbed into his car, barely remembering the trip to the vehicle. "I'm leaving now. Keep me posted, and I'll do the same."

"Copy that.

Five years they'd hidden them. Five years they'd buried the truth. Five years they'd come up empty-handed on who'd baited Zulu and sprung a deadly trap.

Now he had to get to Four. And One. His pulse sped. His tires spewed dirt and rocks as the car bucked and found purchase on the road.

Racing down the highway, he squinted up at the High One looming in the distance. Denali spread its brutal terrain across the landscape in a menacing challenge. Snow capped the peaks and pines dotted its spine. And somewhere. . .in the thousands of miles of tundra and glacier, he had to find her.

Candice
Denali National Park, Alaska
28 April – 1100 Hours

Candice Reyna climbed out of the Bronco she used as a Denali Park Ranger. Her boots crunched noisily on the snow covering the pine needle–littered path. "Charlie here," she said, using her alternate identity—Charlotte Reynolds, adventurer, wildlife lover—for her life on the lam. "I'm up at the lake."

"Roger that," came the voice of Beth, the ranger in charge of the ranger station. "Brad and the chopper are leaving now."

"Copy." That meant they were still at least fifteen to twenty minutes away. If someone was trapped. . . "I'm going to check it out." She grabbed her pack from the back of the Bronco and started up the path to the hidden lake that had become a hotspot for tourists. At least—for those who knew its location. Hidden and miles from any cabin or free range, it was a perfect spot. In fact, no place on earth matched it for solitude and tranquility.

"Take care," Beth admonished.

"Yep." Nobody knew she'd been through much worse.

Well, nobody on this mountain. Facing the High One each time she worked fueled her. Challenged her. Reminded her that even though she'd been a part of something horrible once, she could redeem her days by protecting this land.

Crazy.

The steep climb up the path gave her legs a good workout. Reminded her how crucial staying in shape was up here, where the air was thin and help a distant hope. She'd been out this way, checking campsites, assisting a family of four with a cherub of a four-year-old girl who'd started showing signs of hypothermia. It never ceased to amaze Candice what people would do. Who would bring a child into this frozen tundra? Challenge Denali on its own turf?

Candice rounded a copse of pines and for a second was caught breathless at the scene before her. The lake appeared out of nowhere, a stark, pure contrast to the dark foliage of the pine trees huddled around it, as if protecting it.

Protecting me.

And they had for the last four years. She'd called this place Sanctuary.

She grabbed her radio as she walked the perimeter, seeing nothing. "Beth, Charlie again. I'm not seeing anything." No broken surfaces. No depressions. No black spots against the white. But there was a small inlet in the kidney bean–shaped lake that hid itself behind some trees.

Candice followed the path around—and stopped. Two trees lay across the path, their trunks snapped. *Strange.* The trees were young but not enough to be bowled over by winds. She'd have to come around the other side of the lake. A bit longer though.

She backtracked and came up around the northern lip. Cold dug into her bones, the biting winds no friend to humans. Which begged the question and sanity of the parents who brought the little girl. She'd like to think she would've been a better parent. More responsible. Sensible.

God doesn't give child killers their own children.

They get isolation. Depravation—of society. Of friendships. Of acceptance. Of forgiveness.

She swallowed, pushing back the memories, and lifted the hood of her jacket. Fur trim tickled her quickly numbing cheeks. Then she saw it.

Candice stopped short. Studied the dark spot. In the ice. She hurried forward, eyes on the frozen lake, feet traversing the treacherous terrain closer to the bank, where snow blurred the point where dry land gave way to ice.

Edging closer, she hunched. Keyed her mic.

A strange pulse shot through her when she saw the body. "Oh God, help me." She tossed down her pack. Yanked it open. Drew out her rope and carabiners. "Charlie here—I've got something. I see. . ." She didn't want to say it. "I see. . .*someone.*"

"Tell me," Beth's voice crackled. "I'm tying in Brad."

"They're half submerged." She lowered her radio and shouted out over the lake, "Hello? Can you hear me?"

"Charlie, don't go out on that ice without a raft or tube of some type." Nearly drowned by the *thwump* of the chopper's rotors, Brad sounded like he was shouting. "Do you have one?"

"No." She scratched her head.

"Then wait for us," Brad said. "We're ten minutes out."

Ten minutes. The person could be dead in ten minutes if she didn't get to them. In fact, they weren't moving. "Hello? I'm Park Ranger Reyna." She roped up and anchored herself to a boulder. She hit her mic again. "No response. I'm going out."

She stepped onto the ice, testing it. When no cracks or pops happened, she scooted out, carefully. "Hello?" The rope draped along her thigh, batting it with each step as she made progress.

Brown hair. Matted. With ice in it.

As if the body had been there a while.

A knot grew in her stomach. This person could've been here for days. "Hey, Beth?"

"Yeah?"

Her foot slipped, nearly face-planting her into the ice. "Whoa." She swung out her arms and steadied herself. "Who called this in?"

"Some hiker."

"Uh-huh." She was almost there. The light blue and black jacket looked bloated. "And why didn't they help?"

"I. . .don't know."

Right. Most people let fear stop them. Candice let fear propel her. She lowered herself to her knees. "Almost there." She reached out with a winter-tek-gloved hand, suddenly terrified of what she'd find.

She yanked back her hand as a memory intruded. Smoke. She could smell smoke.

On all fours, Candice lowered her head. Shook off the thought. No smoke here. Just the snow and ice. *Just snow and ice*, she repeated and reached once more.

Fingers coiled around the collar, she tugged the person back. "Hello? Are you okay?" She drew them up, the weight fighting her. Sodden and frozen, the person wasn't moving.

Bracing herself, she used both hands to haul the person free.

They budged only a few inches. She grunted. Flipped them over. And screamed.

It felt like a caged animal trying to get out of her chest as she stared down. "A dummy." What...? A laugh of disbelief snaked up her warmed breath that floated on the air before her. "Who would—"

She keyed her mic. "I—"

Pain exploded through her shoulders. Slammed her forward.

Red—her blood.

White—the snow.

Black—icy death embraced her.

Téya

Bleak Pond, Pennsylvania

28 April – 1100 Hours

Wind blew in a different direction here. It came softer, warmer. More inviting.

Katherine Gerig wrapped her arms around herself, savoring the breeze that carried across the plain, rifling through the stalks of corn that separated the Augsburger property. The strings of her prayer kapp surfed the breeze. Things were so different here. So much quieter. Better. More peaceful.

Way more peaceful than the life she'd lived as Téya Reiker, a Special Operations combat veteran. Though that life and what she'd done must cease to exist, even in her memory. She pushed it as far back as she could, embracing the new person she'd become.

"Katie?"

She turned on her heels, the simple dress flapping against her legs, compliments of the wind, as she did. "*Ya, Grossmammi?*" She stepped through the screen door and entered the small kitchen where her maternal grandmother shuffled in from the sitting room.

"Is that pie ready, *liewi*?"

Katie bent before the oven and tilted back the door. "A few more minutes," she said, closing it.

White-haired and wrinkled, her grandmother was sturdy and firm. "It will be nice to go with the chicken and fixings, while they go through this hard time, *ya*?"

"*Ya*." Katie gave a sad smile. "Zech and Hannah have been through so much already." It hurt to think of the older couple facing yet another trial after losing their youngest to drowning. "It is good, though, that David

23

has the car, so the family doesn't have to hire a driver going back and forth to the hospital."

At the mention of the Augsburger's second eldest, Katie felt her heart scamper into her stomach. At thirty, David should have been married long ago. To a sweet, compliant Amish girl who'd taken the faith.

"I'll get the rig ready and be right back when that pie is done." Katie stepped back onto the porch and made her way down the steps, searching for the horse. She gave a call, and the mare lifted her head from the field. Katie groaned. In the corn again! Rein in hand, she hurried across the yard to the fence. David's older brother, Isaac, had been irate the last time the mare chewed a couple of ears.

Really, it wasn't the horse. Katie knew that. It was *her*. He, like others in the Amish community, had rejected her, an *Englischer*. She bore her mother's shame, though she'd had no control over her mother's departure.

She slipped the rein around the horse and led her back to the yard, where she hooked up the rig. Her grandmother was there with the chicken potpie and fresh-baked bread. As she set them in the rig, Katie retrieved the pie. They made their way down the road. Though the two properties shared boundaries, the creek and distance made it too difficult for *Grossmammi*, especially with food.

Katie guided the rig down the lane and onto Augsburger Road. Even as the horse drew up to the white clapboard house, Katie felt her stomach squirm. Which was insane!

Miriam Augsburger hurried out to them and wrapped her arms around Katie. "Thank you for coming to my rescue."

Laughing, Katie appreciated the friendship David's sister had provided since she'd moved to the community. "Is it that bad?" She handed the potpie to Miriam.

"Worse! They act as if Lydia is dead!" Miriam muttered.

Pie tucked in the crook of her arm, Katie made sure to offer support to her grandmother as they climbed the steps. When Katie glanced up, her stomach once again flopped. Light brown eyes fastened onto hers like a homing beacon. Black hair curled around his ears, despite the typical bowl cut.

For Pete's sake! She wasn't a simpering schoolgirl. And she wasn't a young, single Amish girl attending Sunday evening singings in the hopes a boy would offer to take her home.

Though, were she honest with herself, she envied those girls with their simple lives. Nothing about hers was simple. Even moving here had complicated everything in ways unimaginable.

"Ah, David. How are you?" *Grossmammi* asked as they reached the final step and she made her way to him, an arthritic hand reaching for him.

David bent and gave her a hug. "*Gut. Denki*, Mrs. Gerig." He lifted the food from her arms. "Let me help you."

"Such a good boy," her grandmother said as he opened the door.

His gaze once more hit Katie.

She breathed in, startled at the way his gaze warmed her.

"Katie," he said, allowing them to enter while he held the door.

She gave a nod, unwilling to trust herself to speak. She'd negotiated exchanges for high-value targets, but around David Augsburger, where everything was simple yet profoundly complicated, she couldn't speak. And yet she had a lot to tell him.

The spartan furnishings provided a calm balance to the throng of people filling the halls and rooms. Katie smiled at the Millers and Schrocks, who engaged her grandmother in conversation, allowing her to deliver the food to the kitchen.

"Tell me that's blueberry," David said as she set the pie on the table.

"I had some canned and thought I should use them up."

Several other women bustled around the kitchen. While her *grossmamm*i had taught her the art of pie baking, Katie wasn't a master of the kitchen. Something anyone wanting a wife should know. Mrs. Hochstetler squeezed past, her ample size pushing Katie back.

Right into David.

"Want some air?"

"*Ya*," Katie said.

"*Kumm*." David tugged her sleeve and led her out the side door. He went to the fence rail and leaned against it, looking out over the fields.

Immediately a breeze wafted across her face, fluttering her prayer *kapp* strings as she joined him. "I. . .I talked with the bishop." She'd never been very good with subtlety.

David stilled, his gaze dropping to the dirt path that led from the steps.

Was he happy? Upset? She couldn't gauge by his expression. Which was like a stone. A wall of granite. "He. . ." The community of Bleak Pond knew about her mother and Katie's past. They just didn't know all of it. And they never could. Which is why doing this. . .setting foot on this path. . .

Katie sighed.

"Are you going to do it?" David squinted against the sun but didn't move. Didn't look at her.

David was the epitome of a dichotomy. Dressed in dark pants, a white shirt, and suspenders, he was every bit Amish. Until you knew that he owned a car and had a license. The elders had made an exception, quietly looked the other way, since David's family had a daughter with a congenital heart defect and needed medical care often.

"He said I could start instructions next month."

David slid his hands into his pockets. Handsome. Very intelligent. Sought after. "That's not what I asked."

Katie wrung her hands. Her pulse pounded, like a cadence. A military cadence trying to remind her of who she really was.

But she's gone. Died five years ago.

"Yes," she finally said with conviction.

David met her gaze. Surprise and relief—or was it something else—surged through his handsome features. "You sure about that?" Now he faced her full-on. "You realize what this means?"

Did he not want her to do it? They couldn't ever court or think of being anything other than an *Englischer* and her Amish friend if she let things stay as they were. And she'd done that for many years now.

"I think I've lived here long enough to understand," she answered softly. "I want this."

"So you believe in God? You're willing to keep to the *Ordnung*?"

"I do—yes." Surprised at the conviction spiraling through her answer, she once more looked to the fields. The expanse. The beauty and simplicity of it all. How had her heart changed so much? She'd hated the rules, the constraints, *the utter rejection*, when she first came. It didn't take her long to realize it wasn't rejection but a fear of the unknown that her presence created. Her mother's shame and past.

But as she and David developed a friendship, him renting their barn for some new horses they'd brought in for breeding, she wasn't as feared or shunned. She had really started winning them over by attending service with her grandmother—more out of necessity to aid the elderly woman—but slowly, as a hunger gnawed at Katie's insides to know more about God. Thankfully, she'd always had a curiosity about her Germanic heritage and learned German when most of her classmates were learning Spanish or French. Though the words were slightly different, she'd been able to translate. And learn.

Now she embraced Bleak Pond as her home. Embraced the safety and security here. Embraced God and the peace that had come with that decision two years ago in her *grossmammi's* kitchen, holding those parchment-like hands.

But would it be enough?

"You realize, if you take the faith, we could marry before winter."

David's words hung on the suddenly still breeze.

Katie couldn't breathe. Couldn't move. Would he really take her? *He doesn't know! You can't do this to him!*

Keeley
Little Cayman Island
29 April – 0945 Hours

Growing up with an overprotective mother and an obsessive father, Keeley Shay could serve as a glow lamp with her fair complexion and auburn hair. As a classic Irish girl, she used to burn to a crisp, then peel and she'd once again have neon white legs.

Until she moved here.

Keeley lugged her gear down the pristine stretch of sandy beach to the dock. A burst of laughter drew her attention to the resort that anchored the north side of Little Cayman. Though she couldn't see the tourists, their noise carried clearly.

Her Bobs plodded softly against the dock, the camo the only indication of her former life. Minus the sparkles. She glanced at her shoes, twitching her toes so the sun caught the sequins stitched across the canvas top, glinting. *"If you'd wanted a signal beacon, I'd have bought you one."* Boone would've had her head for buying something so. . .girly.

Keeley's smile faded. She missed him. Missed her friends. After tossing her gear into the dive boat, she lifted her iPhone from her pocket. Checked the e-mail account. Weird. Why hadn't she replied yet? They had a deal. Reply ASAP then clear the message. Erase the trail.

"More rich kids to entertain today?"

Heart doing a jig, Keeley glanced over her shoulder. She squinted behind her Oakleys, the sun sparkling off the blue-green waters in the distance, and spotted the thick-chested form of her boat captain, Henri. "Corporate execs."

Henri waved, his almost-black skin satiny smooth in the bright sun. "Worse!" Feet sandaled and khakis cut off at the knees, he made his way onto the boat, chugging a container of water. "They all—'Do this, man. I pay, you do it.' "

Keeley still smiled at the way he said *man* as "mahn." He was out of his element here as much as she was, and maybe that's why they'd hit it off so well. "All I care," Keeley said with a laugh as she checked one more time for a message, "is that they pay."

"You and me both, Kendall-girl."

For a second, she hated that she'd fooled this wonderful man, given him a lie for a name. Traded the truth of Keeley Shay for Kendall Shine, a moniker she'd desperately wanted to reflect. But Henri always made her smile, and his laugh reminded her of voices she'd heard in New Orleans each year during spring break. She went below and changed into her dive suit. When she came topside, Henri started the engines. Mixed in the rumbling wake was a familiar sound that tugged her gaze upward.

"Hey, lookie there, Kendall-girl," he said, stabbing a finger toward the sleek white plane descending. "More rich. Maybe we stay busy this week, eh?"

She grinned. It wasn't uncommon for a Leer to show up here, but it wasn't exactly normal either. Most aircraft were puddle jumpers going from one island to another. "Now you can do something for Dorinda?" She joined him at the wheelhouse and slapped his tattooed bicep. "Like buy her a ring."

"Why? She already got more than she can wear!"

Keeley slapped him again.

"All right, I hear you," he said, laughing and protecting his arm.

"Promise me," Keeley said as she lined up the suits and tanks for their gig and checked the oxygen levels. "If we get two more gigs this week— you buy her a ring."

"What is this? Skull Island? You torturing me, Kendall-girl!"

" 'Scuse me," a voice called from the beach. "Are you with Little Dive Spot?"

Keeley shoved her hair from her face as she looked toward the sandy area. Three men stood there in almost matching shorts and tank tops. They seemed comfortable and casual. Well-tanned, well-muscled, and well. . .*everything perfect.*

So why had her spine shut down? Why did she want to reach for the weapon that wasn't there?

"I got this, Kendall-girl," Henri said as he hopped onto the dock. "You are with Tibbo Consolidated?"

"We are." The dark-haired guy indicated to his buddy. "My friend here is a little scared of the water. We thought we could get him over that."

The blond thumped his hand against his friend with a scowl but said nothing. The other man, also dark haired, remained unmoving.

"No worries, man," Henri said as he motioned them onto the rig.

Something in her stomach curdled. Warned her to stay in the wheelhouse. Through the window, she watched as Henri showed the men below to change into the suits and gear up. She eased the boat from the dock and started out toward the favorite dive haunts, her nerves upended. They weren't right. The men weren't right.

But what was wrong?

She couldn't put her finger on it, but somehow they felt familiar.

Before they got too far, she checked her phone one last time. Unfortunately, she'd already lost the signal. Tossing her phone on the chair beside her, she bit back a curse. Curled her hands around the wheel. Told herself to calm down.

"I do not trust them," Henri said as he came into the wheelhouse.

Keeley said nothing. Focused on steering away from the island, navigating around the populated areas. On what she'd do if these men were trouble.

The familiar racking of a slide snapped her around. She widened her eyes when she saw the gun in Henri's hand. "What are you doing with that?"

"Take precautions, Kendall-girl." Ferocity laced Henri's expression. "I protect me and mine." He bobbed his head, those tied-back dreadlocks swaying.

"Do you even know how to use that?"

He laughed. "Kendall-girl, you know me now. You didn't know me then."

Whatever *then* was, he wouldn't tell her. And she wouldn't push his imposed anonymity. Just as he wouldn't impose on hers.

"You feel it, too?" She nodded toward the area where the men were changing.

"How can you not?" he asked as she cut the engine.

The silence proved deafening. As if announcing the end. Their end.

Needing to shake that thought pushed Keeley toward the open sea air. As she moved, a shadow loomed behind Henri.

Keeley reacted with instinct. She elbowed Henri out of the way. Saw the knife coming. She caught the wrist. Yanked, using the attacker's momentum against him. When he came forward, she shoved the heel of her hand up against his nose.

Crack!

The man stumbled back, blood spurting from his face as he dropped to the deck.

Keeley spun toward Henri, who stood wide eyed. "Go!"

He sputtered then shook himself out of the daze. "How. . .we. . .call for help!"

"No time. They won't make it." She manhandled Henri, turning him from the wheelhouse. "We have to take care of the others."

"How do you know to do this, Kendall-girl?"

"Just go!" Over the *whoosh* of her own pulse, she couldn't hear his reply. But he moved. That's all she cared about now—that and getting off this boat alive!

Henri stumbled.

Did the man not know how to—

He went to all fours. Collapsed, facedown on the deck. A dark stain exploded across his back.

Catching Henri by the collar and dragging him backward, Keeley threw herself against the corner of the wheelhouse, searching for the shooter at the bow of the boat. Had to be at the bow or they'd have struck her, too. She peeked around.

Wood splintered, stinging her cheek.

She ducked. Glanced back. Nothing back there except—dive equipment.

As an idea gripped her, she verified the tanks were still where she'd stowed them. If she could. . .

Creak.

She whipped around.

A fist rammed into her face.

Knocked her back. Her vision blurred. Her ears rang! She stumbled, caught her balance as the man rushed forward. She readied herself. When he struck out again, she bent, once more turning the attacker's momentum against him. He fumbled over her. She shifted. Sliced the side of her hand into his solar plexus. Waited to hear that gasp. Then shoved as hard as she could, sending him over the side.

As she pivoted, looking for the third man, she felt something warm trickling down her side. She checked the spot, stunned to see she'd been shot. *When did that happen?*

She clamped a hand over the spot, searching for the last guy.

A silenced Glock 17 slid into her view, followed by the final assailant. Firm grip. Tactical precision. *How did they find me?*

The man leered. "Game's up, little girl."

Oh God. . .help me. Even as she thought the words, she realized the ringing in her ears wasn't ringing. It was a siren.

The man realized it, too. He shifted his gaze toward the roar of a speedboat. Whoever was coming, she didn't know. But she *did* know one thing—she wasn't dying on this boat!

She hooked the guy's knee. Jerked it out from under him.

He went down into a squat but swung the gun at her.

Fire exploded through her abdomen.

Just as quickly, the man jerked and stumbled backward. Jerked again.

Keeley couldn't move, the sudden gush of blood pooling around her. She felt cold. Crazy cold for the sun that shone in her eyes.

Thud!

A shape burst over the side rail. After a few meaty grunts, someone scrabbled up to her side. "Keeley!"

Hearing her real name, she blinked and looked up into the gray eyes she'd known and loved. "Boone. . ."

Pain exploded through her side. She grabbed the spot with a guttural scream. Covered it with her hands, surprised to find Boone's there.

"Hold on, Keeley. Help is coming." He worked quickly. Sternly. Fiercely. It's what she'd loved about him all those years ago. Even as the light began to fade—why was it fading? Had clouds come? She didn't recall a storm warning—she was just glad he was here. She'd be fine now.

"How you doing, Keeley?" Boone demanded, his tone gruff. In charge. Just like the drill sergeant he'd been.

"My shoes," she mumbled.

She went limp. Felt. . .nothing. Her eyes drifted.

"Keeley! Talk to me!"

She blinked. "Shoes. . ." A cocoon of warmth and comfort surrounded her. Boone was close, his breath skidding over her cheek. "Sparkly." She tried to smile. "My. . .shoes. . .sparkle."

Annie

Manson, Washington

29 April – 2130 Hours

Stars of shattered glass. Glittering under a red moon.

Grief pushed Annie down, her shoulders hunched against the memories. Eyes closed to the nightmare that revived itself every year. *Every day.* She gripped the balcony and fought back the swell of emotions. The memories.

Lifting the lighter, she dragged her gaze from the glass-like lake to the six candles lined up on the rail. Annie flicked the striker wheel and aimed the flame at the first wick, remembering. "They. . ."

Then the second. ". . .never. . ."

And third. ". . .existed. . ."

Choking on emotion made her hand tremble as she lit the fourth. ". . .yet. . ." She mustered her strength as the fifth wick caught. ". . .aren't. . ." The flames danced and popped against the wind. ". . .forgotten." Light flared in front of her.

She brushed away a tear that escaped and set aside the lighter. Fighting more tears, she raised her gaze to the sky. To the clouds sliding in and out of the light of the fingernail moon. Screams mingled with the smell of burning flesh.

Annie stumbled back, gripping her forehead. Instinct tried to block the flood of sensory information. She straightened. "No. I *will* remember," she said through gritted teeth. Palms on the banister, she braced herself, preparing for the mental storm coming.

A door thudded closed somewhere nearby.

Annie blinked away the tears, pulled herself straight as a cool wind teased her hair from her shoulders. Drawing in a breath, she hauled up strength she hadn't planned to use today. She blew out a long, slow breath.

"Hey, Sandwich Girl."

At the sound of that voice, warmth ballooned through her. Sam.

Be strong. Be strong. He had X-ray eyes. Able to see straight through her. Right into her soul. She curled her finger around the water glass. "Calamari." Keeping her back to him gave her time to scrape together the fragments of her mental acuity. Finally, she turned, lifting the glass to her lips. "You lost?" She pointed toward the cottage beside hers. "That's your place."

"Not lost." Sam held up a lawn chair. "Thought you could use a chair up here."

Annie couldn't help but smile. Ever since he'd moved in two years ago, he'd looked out for her. Six weeks ago, a storm moved through, destroying the cheap lawn chair she'd set up on the deck. Working at the Green Dot kept her bills paid and groceries in the fridge but afforded no extra for frivolity. Like new lawn chairs. Thing of it was, Sam somehow knew her financial situation. Whether his sister told him or he was just that good— yes, entirely possible—he also tried to protect her pride. "You didn't have to do that."

His thick shoulders bunched, making his neck all but disappear.

"And you brought two."

As if he hadn't noticed before, Sam separated the two chairs and looked at them. "Huh. So I did." He shrugged, flinging that charming smile at her. "That's what happens when they have those BOGO sales. Be a shame to waste them"—he glanced up—"on such a beautiful night."

Why *tonight?* This was the night she spent remembering, honoring. . . . Chewing the edge of her lower lip, she watched as he set up the chairs and eased into one with a contented sigh. Crazy the way the night seemed calmer just with his presence.

But this is the Night of OZ.

Trace
Chelan, Washington
29 April – 2215 Hours

"General, we have a real and deadly threat against Zulu." Trace spoke using his Bluetooth as he hustled from the small plane at the municipal airport. He nodded to a man who handed over a set of keys, then Trace slid into the car.

"Tell me."

"Two of them are dead." Trace revved the engine and headed toward Manson. "I'm en route to One, and Ramage is dealing with Five. We have one unaccounted for."

"Timeline?"

"Less than a week from start to now."

"So it's more than one assassin?"

Trace's chest squeezed. "Looks that way." He slammed the gear down and took the exit ramp. "I need assistance. SOP on both deaths has been sniper."

"I'd be a little late to the party, wouldn't I?"

Trace bit his tongue. Yes. Since he was within ten minutes of the cottage Annie had rented, if something was going down—

His Bluetooth beeped. He glanced at the caller ID on his cradled phone. "Sir, I'll call you back." He hit the END button and connected. "Tell me good—"

"She's alive, but they aren't sure she'll survive the night."

As the engine leveled out at 50 mph, Trace pounded the steering wheel. Who got the lead on the girls? Their addresses. Identities.

"Annie?"

"Not there yet."

"Hurry."

Trace ended the call, words inadequate and anger raging. He powered down through the gears as he hit the winding roads leading through Manson. She couldn't choose a cottage on the main lake. No, had to be more hidden. Harder to get to.

Frustration built. Speed and winding roads working against him, slowing him. Delaying him.

He tried her hidden sat phone again. When it went to the manufacturer's recorded voice mail message, he ended the call. He'd gotten the same message the last four times. Why he thought it'd be different this time, he didn't know. He slammed a fist against the leather passenger seat, a stream of curses flying out of his mouth. Futility coated his limbs, weakening him.

Annie
Manson, Washington
29 April – 2215 hours

"Hey, gorgeous," Sam said, his voice taunting. "You're blocking my view. Could you move, maybe have a seat?" He grinned, resting a hand on the red nylon and metal chair. "Imagine that—there's one right here with your name on it."

Annie folded her arms over her chest and peered down at the wood deck. She pulled herself away from the small shrine and lowered herself into the game chair. Her gaze settled on the row of candles, the wind teasing and taunting the flames.

She missed *them*. What were they doing? Did they think of her, too, on this night? Every year she wondered if they were sitting somewhere honoring this night the way she did.

Not honoring. That was the wrong word. *Considering. Remembering.*

The wind whipped one of the flames out.

Annie sucked in a breath. *Was that bad luck?*

If she believed in luck. . .

Another snuffed out.

On her feet, Annie moved to the rail. Choked back the emotion, the assault the elements held on her frame of mind, snuffing out the wicks on this night of all nights. She relit them. Let out a breath.

A warm, light touch against her back made her flinch.

"Hey," Sam whispered. "How are you doing?" He tucked a strand of hair the crisp lake breeze snapped into her face. "You okay?"

She appreciated his nearness. His tenderness. With a slight nod, she breathed her answer. "Yeah. Just. . ." Lights twinkled over the water as a strong wind swept through the valley-like setting. "Tough night."

Sam cupped her shoulders as he stood behind her. Though she normally avoided his advances—it just *couldn't* happen, no matter how much she wanted it to—tonight his strength, his presence filled a void that had left her cold for the last five years. Tonight she didn't have the fortitude to be alone.

No, it was more than that.

Tonight. . .tonight, she *wanted* to be with Sam.

He drew her back against his chest. Muscles tensed, Annie closed her eyes, chiding herself. Telling her this was a colossally bad idea. Getting close—

His arms encircled her waist, her head cradled against his left pectoral.

She didn't move. Refused to, torn between obeying the rules and the desperation that wanted to explore what could happen with Sam. If she'd been someone other than Annie Palermo, she'd have given herself to him long ago.

But she wasn't that person. Not anymore.

And yet she didn't move.

There were times, she told herself, that everyone needed someone to lean on. God never meant for people to be alone. The flicker of the candles drew her attention once more, and though she'd thought it an intrusion for anyone else to be here during the memorial, it felt right for Sam to be here.

Two of the candles winked out. *The same two.*

Weird.

Sam's jaw and lower cheek rested along her temple. Warm. Scruffy. Smelled uniquely of him—Old Spice. Seemed too good to be true, like something out of a romance novel or chick flick. That skin contact awakened in Annie an ache. For intimacy—not sexual intimacy—just closeness.

I'm so tired of being alone. Of hiding.

When she realized she was leaning into his touch, she tried not to stiffen. Didn't want to offend him. Didn't want to scare him away.

She almost laughed. Was it even possible to scare off Sam Caliguari? He'd been so resolute in getting her to date him for the last year. So persistent.

Soft but firm lips teased the edge of her jaw, the spot right in front of her earlobe that shot darts of warmth and nervous excitement through her. Annie tensed, her mental warnings a distant shout in the thick fog of pleasure.

Sam traced a slow line of kisses to the corner of her lips.

If you do this—

He turned her and gently planted one on her mouth. He hovered just above her lips, his warm breath teasing her more. Again, he kissed her, this time a little longer. Still gentle, but waiting...

"Sam," Annie whispered, eyes closed, feeling electrified. She sounded weak, even to herself. And for once, she didn't care.

He captured her mouth with his as he slid a hand around to the small of her back and drew her closer. Deepening the kiss, he cradled her neck with his other hand. Annie lost herself in the passion, in his strength. Her fingers traced a slow path up his back.

She'd wanted this. For a very long time. To be cared about. To be with someone.

No. Not just someone. *Sam.*

She wanted it to be Sam since he'd first stepped into the Green Dot with his hair still in a military high and tight. Muscles bulging out of his black T-shirt. And his machismo oozing as he caught up with Jeff, the two of them sitting in a corner well past closing. But every time Annie glanced over at the duo, Sam was watching her. Tracking her, like the Navy SEAL he was.

And that was why she'd kept the distance between them.

Because Sam never missed a thing.

And he could never, *ever* find out about her past. Who could forgive that?

Annie hauled in a breath. Drew away a fraction. Stepped back. Hot tears streamed down her heated cheeks. Forehead resting against hers, Sam's breathing was labored. But she couldn't look at him. Couldn't face him—if he knew. . .

A sob snatched her breath.

"Ash?" Hand still around her neck, he used his thumb to nudge up her chin. "Hey. Babe. Look at me."

She shook her head then turned away. Out of his touch.

"Ashland, please." Sam didn't give her personal space back. He crowded in. "Talk to me. What—?"

Before she knew what happened, Annie went flying across the deck. Her head thudded against the wall. Sam was on top of her. "Stay down! Stay down!"

Annie
Manson, Washington
29 April – 2230 Hours

Annie hunch-ran along the edge of the house and ducked around the corner, Sam right behind her. He took point, a weapon in his hand like a magic trick. Where he'd gotten it, she didn't know. Right now, all that mattered is that he could help defend her.

If she could get inside the house, she would dig out her emergency stash. She peered over her shoulder and up at the window in the east-facing wall. Her bedroom window, conveniently blocked from road view thanks to the fruit trees. She reached up and tried it.

Glass exploded, peppering her face.

With a yelp, she dropped back. Onto the ground.

"You okay?" Sam knelt at her side.

Her face stung. She grimaced and reached for the spots—only to feel the prickle of glass embedded in her cheek. She cursed herself for not thinking through trying that window. It was a clear shot from here to the front windows that overlooked the lake. The shooter had anticipated her move.

"Yeah, fine," she spit out. She'd need tweezers to pluck out the glass. But later.

Sirens howled in the distance.

"Finally," Sam muttered. "Just stay down. We'll wait for the authorities."

Annie didn't like that option. They'd want answers. And in a small town, tonight's incident would spread like wildfire. That could reach news outlets.

Rocks crunched and popped to her left, drawing her attention to the road.

Headlights poked through the shadowy tree limbs, probing.

Annie froze, watching the car.

It swung around and parked. Not in her driveway, but across the way. In the ditch. A door opened. A man stepped out.

"Stay here," Sam said, easing in front of her, still low.

Annie bristled at the command. But reminded herself that Sam didn't know the truth about her. Didn't know she had just as much, if not more, tactical experience.

Which is why she didn't listen. She trailed him, keeping to the shadows. Watching. Expecting another attacker. *Hitting me from both sides.*

Though she wanted to ask who'd hit her, she couldn't even go there. Because that would beg the next question. Not, did they know who she was?—but rather, how did they find her? Because if they'd found her, clearly they knew who she was.

The more painful question, however, was—did they know what she'd done? How she'd served as lead on that mission?

"Stop right there!" Sam's voice boomed through the night.

Rocks crunched.

Annie peeked around the tree. Eased to the side, trying to see over Sam's broad shoulder and wide stance. There were too many shadows concealing the newcomer. If the wind would just shift. . .

Annie eased forward.

"Who are you?"

"You the one who called in a shooting?"

Annie's mind tripped and fell over those words. No, not the words. *The voice.* Her heart skipped a beat. Then two.

"Yeah. You got a badge?"

Annie slipped closer. It couldn't be him. She hadn't seen him since. . .

The breeze tugged back a branch, like pulling back a curtain. Light from Sam's floodlight on his cottage speared the man's face. Eyes.

Her breath caught.

Sam snapped his weapon up and tight again. "Hands or badge!"

"Easy," came the voice again. "I left my badge—heard the call and was at my girlfriend's. Raced out of there—"

"Then just keep those hands up." Sirens almost drowned out Sam's voice. "We'll wait it out."

Annie stood beside Sam, who instinctively reached for her. She gave him a reassuring nod, but the whooshing of her pulse made it hard to hear anything.

It was him. Trace.

A flood of fresh grief rushed through her. Followed quickly by myriad memories. But what held her fast, what told her this life, this possibility with Sam was over, was that he was here. That meant she'd been compromised.

As if the bullets didn't tell you that?

An SUV pulled into the driveway, lights swirling. "C'mon," Sam said, tugging her along. "The cops will settle this."

But with one look, Trace conveyed his message.

It was time to leave. She would need to slip away when they weren't hovering.

She nodded as she stepped out of view. The cop quickly ushered her into the back of the cruiser. Sam wanted to find the person trying to kill them. The next dozen minutes happened in a haze, her grief over having to walk away from Sam strong but her will to survive and not resurrect the past stronger.

Or was it? Would Sam understand?

She snorted. Blinked. Looked up and realized she was alone. More cops showed up, rushing to the lakeside part of the house. Time to go. Annie opened the door. Stepped out. Glanced one more time at the house. Saw Sam on the balcony and the distant whirl of lights across the lake where cops pored over the terrain looking for the shooter.

Before turning, crossing the road, and climbing into the black sedan, she whispered, "Good-bye, Calamari."

Téya
Bleak Pond, Pennsylvania
29 April – 1740 Hours

Can I really leave her behind. . .forever?
Opportunity banged on her front door, rattling the hinges, begging her to step from the storm that had been her existence into the quiet safety and shelter of the Amish.

She never thought this would be her life. Never thought she'd ever be a part of this community. It'd be like a thriller writer penning a Mennonite story of love and romance.

There wasn't a day that went by without Katie remembering in vivid detail who she really was before she came to live with her maternal grandmother—*grossmammi*—almost five years ago, a woman dedicated to her country: Téya Reiker. Daughter of an *Englischer* father and once-Amish mother. Army grunt who readily joined a Cultural Support Team to put her linguistic tongue to use. Recruited into the first all-female special ops team. Soldier zealous in her determination to make sure the mission succeeded, no matter the cost.

She'd been driven but not bloodthirsty.

Yet not far from it either.

Katie ladled stew from the pot into ceramic bowls. "Ready to eat?"

Her grandmother shuffled into the kitchen, the hitch in her hip making her limp and move a little slower than normal. Katie turned, smiled at the image before her. At eighty-three, her grandmother still stood almost perfectly straight. No frail, bent woman here. No sir. Not in the Gerig line. She'd learned strength and courage from her grandmother and mom. Well, maybe not as much her mom.

"That smells wonderful." *Grossmammi* eased into the wooden chair as Katie joined her with the bowls and basket of rolls.

Could she leave it all behind? Bury it? Did David need to know, if he made good on his intention to court her?

Nervous jellies flitted through her stomach. *He's too good for me.*

But she wanted it—him, this life.

Her innocence back. Her belief in people.

"You could weigh anchor with those thoughts," *Grossmammi* said as she delicately lifted the spoon to her mouth.

Téya—*no! Katie!*—blinked.

"I think much more happened at Mr. Augsburger's house than my visiting with Hannah." A smile crinkled the soft lines around her

39

grandmother's eyes. "*Ya?*"

Katie felt the truth of that statement heat her cheeks. "*Ya.*" She tried to hide her smile. "I told David I was going to take instruction."

Perpetually cold fingers wrapped around hers. "You have made this old woman's heart so happy." The soft squeeze was firm for a woman her age. "That you have embraced God, that you found shelter with His Son, I could not ask for anything more."

Katie nodded, her gaze lifting to the window. Things—*she*—had changed a lot. Was it enough? But David... "David..." She swallowed hard before setting down her spoon and sitting back in the chair. "He suggested if I took instructions now, we could be married by winter."

A gleam stole through her grandmother's hazel-green eyes. "I lied."

Caught off guard, Katie shook her head. "How? What?"

"I said I could not ask for anything more—but *this* is all I could ask for." She slurped some stew then again shook her head. "No, then of course, I will be waiting for the great-grandchildren!"

Katie laughed. Then sobered. Before she and David could get that far, she had to get him past her former life. "Do you think he'll understand...about...before?"

The smile faded from her grandmother's eyes but clung defiantly—as a Gerig's would—to her face. "If he loves you, he will."

But her *grossmammi* didn't know...not the whole truth. Not that Katie had been in the military, a career that violently contradicted the Amish stance of nonviolence.

Her grandmother squeezed her hand—hard. "That is your past, Katie." Ferocity churned through her grandmother's words. "Let it stay there."

"Should I tell him?"

"I think you must, so there is no appearance of deception, of evil. A marriage is not merely two people living together. It is a commitment and must be grounded on truth—*God's Truth*—and trust. A foundation of godliness makes for a solid structure."

Katie nodded. Though she'd expected the answer and knew it in her heart—David deserved no less than every bit of her. She just wasn't sure he deserved her or the past and the nightmares that came with it. Would David even love her if he knew what she'd done?

She glanced at her food and felt her stomach roil. Lifting the bowl, she stood.

Grossmammi caught her hand. "You will speak to him, *ya?*"

And ruin everything?

I might've done that already, just by being who I am.

"*Ya.*" She dumped her stew back in the pot and set it aside. "I will clean up in a bit." It took every ounce of strength to walk the distance to her room. Inside, she closed the door and slumped against it. *God, You have given me so much more than I thought possible. There is peace here. I'm safe. Please let David understand.*

As she moved to the rocking chair, she stopped. Frozen in the spot as she looked out at the clothesline she'd already cleared. Only, now. . . "No," Katie whispered hoarsely. "No!" She slammed her palms against the window. Heart thundering. She jerked around. Sprinted out the door and down the hall to the back door.

"*Ach*, Katie!" *Grossmammi's* concerned warning chased her into the dusky night. "The storm's coming!"

Wind tugged at her prayer *kapp* strings as she bolted for the clothesline. She slowed until she stood right before it. The red baseball cap. Hot tears careened down her face. She reached for the hat, her hand trembling.

My whole world is trembling!

She snatched it from the clip, which popped and flicked away.

Katie didn't care. She twisted and clenched the ball cap against her stomach. She shoved her gaze to the darkening sky. "Why?" Her face heated from the tears. "Why?"

And just as swift, the grief swept away on the strong wind, and with it came the answer she'd heard too many times: *You don't deserve it.*

Katie returned to the house, closed off. Shut down. Though she noted her *grossmammi* in the sitting room with the kerosene lamp, she continued on to her room. Went in and locked the door. Closed her eyes.

Could she ignore it?

She glanced down at the hat twisted in her hands. Red. Highest threat.

She sucked back more tears as she bit out, "Do not let them get hurt." Her voice was a low growl that echoed the scream of her heart. Then she threw the hat down and knelt beside the bed. There she retrieved the small duffel she'd arrived with almost five years ago. She rested her head against the feather mattress, willing back the grief.

You knew it would happen, so just soldier up like you were taught to.

Katie sat on the edge of the bed, calling good night to her grandmother through the door and waiting until the moon had risen high into its place of protection. She changed quickly. But putting on the tac pants felt like. . .sin. Putting back on the old life.

I DO. NOT. WANT. THIS.

She pulled up the tattered edges of her courage and clothes, slid on the ball cap, then walked out of the house. And out of the life she so desperately wanted.

David
Bleak Pond, Pennsylvania
30 April – 0900 Hours

A misfit for a misfit.

David Augsburger steered the sedan into the driveway of the Gerig property that adjoined his father's and brother's properties. He'd left the house a little earlier than necessary to get to the hospital so he could talk with Katie's *grossmammi*. Ask her permission to court Katie.

Heart full, he eased the car to the side—opposite from where a rig might park. Before stepping out and into this brave new territory, he bowed his head. Thanked God for sending Katie to Bleak Pond so life wouldn't be so bleak. *I just know that I love her. A lot.*

He took a deep breath and looked up at the house. Already he saw movement. No surprise. Katie and Mrs. Gerig were early risers like everything else here. Chores were finished before it got too hot.

"Quit stalling, you big chicken," he muttered to himself as he reached for his hat.

As he slammed his door shut, the sound echoed loudly across the plain. *Odd.* He turned, donned his hat, and started for the stairs.

The screen door punched open.

He looked up, expecting to find an excited Katie, mischief in her hazel-green eyes. Instead, he found a gun pointed at him.

"Where is she?"

Fear whipped through David. Then swiftly came the anger. "What'd you do to them?" Only as he said it did his brain catch up.

"Where's Téya Reiker—or as you know her, Katie Gerig?"

As I know her? "I don't know what you're talking about." He nodded to the weapon. "You don't need that here."

"You're right." The man grinned, a malicious, loathing grin. "Because I'm done here—unless you know where she is."

David looked toward the house. If Katie hadn't been there. . .

"No?"

"If she's not in the house, I don't know."

"Then you're no good to me."

Thwat! Thwat!

Téya
Lucketts, Virginia
30 April – 0900 Hours

Headed south on Route 15, Katie. . .*Téya* barricaded herself from whatever had happened that prompted the coded signal. She'd walked to town in the wind and moonlight and climbed into the waiting King Ranch Ford truck. It'd been a relief to see Boone behind the wheel, but just a temporary Band-Aid on a now-gaping wound. As always, Boone respected her space. He'd never been an intrusive person, until you were out of line or needed a fire under your butt. That's when his drill sergeant personality came out. He'd aimed that at. . .

The girls.

She sighed. Used the toe of her shoe to push her straighter as they crossed the steel bridge over the Potomac and headed into the winding, curvy section of the drive draped in stunning scenery.

But she felt numb to it all.

"What happened?" she finally asked. She wasn't sure she wanted to know, but. . .

"Briefing will happen at the bunker."

In other words, she had to wait longer. Téya nodded and watched the stretch of farmland blur past. They slowed to 35 mph as they hit a small town with a single light on the route. She caught the sign: THE VILLAGE OF LUCKETTS. Antique stores flanked the spot where a light controlled the flow of traffic. . .past a school. An old '70s-era school. Small. Quaint-ish.

Nothing as quaint as Bleak Pond.

Téya dropped her head back against the headrest. *Let me go back, God.* Maybe. . .maybe this wasn't forever. Maybe once they dealt with whatever threat there was, she could go back to David and—

And what, genius? Tell him—"Oh, yeah. I've murdered children and killed people then left your life without a word."

Right. He'd so understand that.

The blinker set and Boone slowed the truck, yanking Téya's morbid thoughts back to their surroundings. To their left, three homes sat back from the main two-lane highway, crowded with northbound traffic. The perpendicular road broke off and curved around, out of sight.

As traffic backed up behind them, a car slowed and flashed for them to cut through.

With a wave, Boone moved through the intersection. They rounded the bend and drove a few yards before he turned right onto a dusty road that led to an—

"Are we going antiquing?"

Boone parked in the barn. "This way."

Right. Mr. All Business.

Téya followed him toward the back of the barn stacked with bales of hay. He hit a lever and a door appeared in the hay. Surprise flashed through her, but Boone wasn't the patient kind, and when he angled his head toward the opening that led to stairs, she hustled through.

About halfway down, darkness enveloped her.

"Uh—"

With a soft hum and dull glow, spiral bulbs came to life. A steel door sat before them. Boone, his large frame and larger-than-life self stepped in front of her. He hit a panel and an access panel slid forward. He punched in a code.

"What? No retinal scan?"

Boone glanced back, his expression unimpressed. "You offering your eye?" The door clinked open. He ducked to pass through, and that's when she was reminded how much taller he was—she didn't have to duck.

But she stopped at what met her gaze.

A dozen paces forward, a grid of tables and computers looked as if they were held hostage in a wall of chain link that snaked cables in and out of the area. Beyond that and tucked in the far right corner, a raised platform that still had tools and uncut wood laid out offered the hopes of what would eventually be a dais. Beside the unfinished area was a half-walled area with a brown collapsible table—the beginning of a briefing room, she guessed.

Boone urged her into the area and punched a code. The door hissed shut, drawing Téya's gaze around. A series of thuds rang out as locks engaged. Then what looked like a blast shield lowered.

"Impressive," Téya muttered.

Boone strode toward the table, where a wild-haired guy sat hammering away, his gaze bouncing from one monitor to another. . .then another. "Houston."

The guy kept working, his mind in the cyberworld as he worked like fire on the keyboards.

"Houston!"

With a jump, the guy blinked but still didn't look up. "What?"

"Houston Plunkett, this is Two."

"Numbers belong in computers." He peered at Téya over his spectacles.

44

"You have a name, I assume."

Boone shifted in front of her. "Not necessary at this point."

Houston pointed to the monitor. "You can tell me or I take two seconds and verify that the woman with you is Téya Reiker."

Téya smiled. She liked this guy. Wasn't intimidated easily. Didn't take Boone's tough-guy grumpiness.

But something about Boone's use of her previous Zulu designation slid warm dread down her spine. She wanted to demand answers, to know why they'd dragged her away from her grandmother and. . .David. His name alone pulled a sigh from her.

"Get her coded in." With that, Boone headed toward the left side of the underground bunker. He motioned her to follow.

No windows. Everything drab and dull. A prison.

How fitting, she thought as they moved around a wall that angled into an area with two couches and a chair. He rapped his knuckles against the first door.

When it opened, Téya drew up straight. Her lips parted as the air left her lungs. "Annie."

Hair in a hasty updo, Annie Palermo entered the sitting area. She wore a pair of black-and-gray pajama bottoms and a T-shirt. She'd always had the perfect beauty—blond hair, blue eyes, killer smile. But her face was dotted with several scratches. She'd been through something.

"Trace is on his way." Boone pointed to another door. "Shower's in there. I'll get clothes for you." He glanced between them then hung his head. While he stood there, the tension thickened and threatened to choke out a sob from Téya.

But those days were over. She'd be what she needed to be, whatever it took to get back to David.

"What about Nuala?" Annie stepped forward, apparently finding her confidence and voice. "Keeley and Candice?" She folded her arms over her chest.

Boone nodded, his voice ripped with something she couldn't remember seeing on the man's face—worry. "Trace'll be here soon. Sit tight."

Seriously? He stalked out of the area, leaving her dumbstruck. Sit tight? He wanted them to sit tight while—

"What happened to you?" Annie asked.

Téya flinched. "What?" She rubbed her temple. "Oh. Nothing—did something happen to you?"

Annie gave a soft snort with a smirk. "Sniper."

"Sniper?" Confusion clogged Téya's mind as she eyed the scratches and cuts.

"I was standing by a window when he tried to take me out."

"Who?"

Annie shrugged, hugging herself. She jutted her jaw toward the main room. "Let's wait out there. They've been pretty shy on information. I'm not going to let him get away with that."

"You mean Trace?" Téya figured their team commander must be out securing the other members of Zulu: Candice, Jessie, Keeley, and Nuala. It'd be good but weird to be with them again. And yet. . .she didn't want to be here. Didn't want to renew these friendships.

Annie moved without answering. As they stepped back into the main area, Boone and his thick shoulders hovered over the guy—what was his name? Austin? Houston!

The blast shield lifted. Locks disengaged.

In walked Trace with a storm of a scowl.

But Téya's mind snagged on one poignant fact. "You're alone."

Trace

Lucketts, Virginia

30 April – 1325 Hours

Trace blew a weighted breath through puffed cheeks as he rested his hands on his belt. "Have a seat," he said, motioning to the various metal folding chairs placed around the underground bunker. Teeth grinding, he shoved aside his rage over this nightmare. *Stick with the facts.* "Téya, thank you for responding quickly to the signal. It probably saved your life."

Her expression slid from stone-cold anger to alarm.

Trace didn't trust himself to look at Annie. They hadn't spoken a word other than necessary instructions to get them from the sedan to the airplane and, ultimately, to this safe haven.

"Look, I won't candy-coat this. It's bad." Trace took a second to order his thoughts. "Three and Four are dead—both compliments of a sniper."

"Same person who hit me?" Annie asked.

"Unlikely." Trace looked at her and felt the cement dividers in his heart shifting like an ice shelf. "Timing suggests multiple agents." *Get it over with.* "Keeley is on life support. Prognosis isn't good. She has twenty-four-hour guard."

"Who?" Annie demanded.

"Rusty Gray," Boone answered.

"Nuala is MIA. Her last known location was abandoned—for a while. I've got Houston and other assets working on finding her."

"But it might be too late?" Téya asked. "I mean—if they—"

"It might be too late, but Boone and I will not stop till we bring her home." Dead or alive. Whatever it took. He'd committed the last five years of his life to protecting these women while he hunted down the person responsible for putting them in the mess in the first place. The person who demanded they scatter and hide.

"Who did this?" Annie's anger was palpable. "How did they find us after all this time?"

"I don't have those answers, but I will find them."

He'd failed them. Especially Jessie and Candice. Maybe even Keeley. Could he find the killer? Find who'd done this?

Oh, he would. If it took his last breath.

Francesca
Fort Belvoir, Virginia
May 2 – 1400 Hours

Lieutenant Francesca Solomon stood in the conference room, watching the Friday afternoon mini briefing by General Marlowe. The three-star had a reputation for being fierce and ruthless in his pursuit of justice. And while Frankie didn't like the man—he had, after all, gotten the promotion that should have gone to her father—she couldn't help but admire his passion.

The same fire burned in her breast.

A fire to find the man who destroyed her father's career. A man who'd turned on the one who'd mentored him and shoved dishonorable behavior in a smear across a perfect, stellar record. Even as the sense of vindication and vengeance pulsed through her veins, she started back toward her cubicle at the U.S. Intelligence and Security Command. She'd worked hard to get her position at INSCOM. One that would not only advance her career but, God willing, restore her father's.

She logged into the secure system and finished up a report she'd recently done on female soldiers in Special Operations. It was a massive undertaking, shifting females from support roles to direct combat. She knew without a doubt there was a breed of woman out there who could hold her own against men in the field. But more often than not, most women couldn't. They simply didn't have the upper-body strength God had given men. In fact, the first round of female Marines failed the physical fitness test, but now women were passing modified test and heading into the world of special operations.

"Hey, Frankie."

Arching her eyebrow, she lifted her head at the offender who dared use that name. But when she met the brown eyes of Ian Santiago, she debated what to do.

Eyes sparkling and flirtatious, he leaned closer, a paper in his hand. "If I gave you something you've really been waiting for. . .would it get me a date?"

She met his eyes, let him think he was winning that date, then plucked the paper from his hands.

"Hey!"

He tried to snatch it back, but her eyes were already gliding across the sheet. Her heart slowed. "Where. . . ?" She snapped her gaze to him. "This is legit?"

He shot a nervous glance around then nodded. "Between you, me, and the paper."

In other words, it could cost him his job.

"Our date?"

If this. . .if this was real, "Friday night," she said.

Even without looking she could see his grin. And immediately regretted her decision. But this—

She stared at the information. LTC Trace Weston had flown to Alaska. Probably went to the same weapons testing conference her dad attended.

Then reports came in that Trace had been in the Seattle area. Shots were fired near Manson, but no fatalities. He'd also been in Las Vegas—and that chick was found dead. It made the news because of the outcry over her death by the community, who'd called the girl a saint. So, had Trace killed again? Gotten confident he'd evaded justice, and now he'd stepped up his game?

Well, so would she.

And Boone was in the Caymans at the same time a woman had been the target of men doped up on psychotropic drugs and nearly killed her. But she survived. In ICU.

This was it. Though she couldn't figure out how or why, she was certain in the pit of her stomach that this—*this*—would be enough to stop Trace Weston, pin that huge, bloody badge of dishonor on him, and free her father.

She punched to her feet and grabbed her purse.

"Solomon!"

Frankie glanced back as she lifted her cover.

"Don't stand me up."

"Wouldn't dream of it."

Ian groaned. "Fine. I'll find another date."

Frankie laughed and headed to her car after signing out. Fighting traffic was insane, but at least she wasn't farther north up near the Beltway. A nightmare! The forty-five-minute drive to her father's estate, inherited from his grandfather, was enough to put a few gray hairs in her jet-black hair and leave her convinced more than ever of Trace's guilt and now possibly more guilt. He was a murderer who walked free and acted like he owned the world!

"Francesca!" Her father greeted her as she entered the den, where he had a fire roaring, though it was nearly the middle of spring. But since Misrata, Libya, he had a chill he couldn't shake.

"Dad," she said as she planted a kiss on his cheek then plopped down on the ottoman at the foot of the chair where he sat reading through some pages. He looked tired, worn. "How are you?"

He chuckled. "What does that mean?"

Right. Brigadier General. One-time Commander of Coalition Forces. "Nothing. Just—you seem"—if she said *tired*, he'd kill her—"worried."

He waved the papers at her and tucked them inside a folder. "Work came home with me." He sighed. "So, what brings you home so early?"

Frankie drew up the dregs of her courage. "I think I found it."

"Found what?"

"The proof we need."

"Proof of what? And *for* what?"

"That Trace Weston is responsible for what happened in Misrata."

He cursed and came out of the chair. "No. We're not doing this."

"Dad, I have it—I have leads that place him in the same states where two former military women were killed."

He barked a laugh. "You're kidding me, right? I would've strung a grunt up the flagpole for bringing me half-cocked information like that!" His tone grew hard as stone and derisive. "You realize that we are in the same state where three men were murdered today—better, they were right here in this city!"

Frankie swallowed.

"Are we to be arrested, since I was in Misrata and now I'm here and three men die?"

"Dad—"

"No!" He stabbed a thick finger at her. "Do not do this again. I told you before—leave this alone."

"Or what?" she spat back, her rebellious streak bouncing into position. "You'll court-martial me?"

His eyes launched 40mm grenades at her. Nostrils flaring, he stood her down. "We will *not* speak of this again. Stay out of his life and his records. Or I will see to it your privileges are revoked!"

The ricochet of that last word hit her chest, bounced back to him, and lodged in her throat.

As his daughter and as an officer, she surrendered. But only in her posture. She would never give up this fight. She would prove what Trace had done in Misrata, murdering twenty-two innocent women and children. Then flushing the evidence right down the drain with her father's career and dignity.

Trace Weston would meet justice. And Francesca Solomon would hand-deliver it!

Part 1:
Collateral Damage

II

Nuala
Blue Ridge Mountains, North Carolina
2 May – 2200 Hours

Unforgiving branches dragged their gnarled, sharp fingers against her cheek. She winced at the slice of pain but plowed onward. Through the brush. Deeper into the darkness and shadows. Fighting branches, fallen limbs, stumps, and her rancid fear. She shoved a branch aside. A green, monochromatic hue guided her. The specter of darkness stole into the mountains, draping the thick, hilly foliage in a blanket of fog.

Three minutes. She just needed three minutes.

Nuala King plunged on, focused on one goal—getting to her spot. Ignored the shouts back at the remote lodge. Shots rang through the still, oppressive night. She refused to allow herself to think about what was happening back there. Whether Coleman Carson would survive the two men who'd shown up at the lodge, acting like hikers lost in the mountains. If the men were both butchers and rapists—would Sonja survive unscathed?

Nuala knew better. So did Coleman, which is why he'd been reaching for his gun beneath the counter as soon as the men shut the door. They'd seen enough hikers and trackers to know the difference.

And she had seen enough special ops soldiers to recognize one. Or in this case, two.

She sailed over a fallen oak. Hit the ground and kept moving liked a seasoned runner. Upward and to the east. She'd done it a million times. Could do it blindfolded, although she'd really rather not. Dark with NVGs made it tough enough.

Each step rammed her heart farther up her throat, strangling oxygen from her. She was getting closer, but if the snapping branches and shouts were any indication, so were the assassins.

Bark and leaves exploded twelve inches to her left.

Biting back an expletive, Nuala ducked and threw herself right. Didn't slow as she zigzagged through the green-bathed terrain. A pair of eerie gold eyes popped up as an animal—Deer? Big cat?—lifted its head. Bolted in the other direction.

Breathing hard now, Nuala dove into the brush and weaved through a thick copse of pines, allowing the craggy fingers to trace her path.

Pushing through the dense foliage slowed her a little but also hid the path she'd taken in the dense litter. As she ran, the slight incline of the hill weighed on her endurance. Altitude pressed on her lungs. But she kept going.

Run or die. Those were her only options.

Needling pines smacked her face, evidence of another gun blast.

Nuala cursed herself for slowing down. But her legs were aching. One thing she hadn't counted on in her three dozen test runs was the adrenaline that sent her heart into overdrive. It sped her but also tired her.

"This way! I saw her!" came a shout way too close.

Almost there. She'd make it. Had to.

A weight rammed into her back. Sent her sprawling. Nuala landed with a thud, twigs and rocks digging into her abdomen and chest. Her head rammed down, pinned.

"Kill her and get it over with."

Using a knifehand strike, Nuala slammed the fleshy part of her hand into the man's side.

He grunted and his hold slackened. Not a lot. But enough. With all her strength, she threw herself to the side, flipping him. Shots exploded the leaves and dirt. Nuala landed on top of the guy, all too aware the other had given up on his comrade and probably had a bead on her.

She coldcocked the attacker. He went limp beneath her.

Nuala hopped up, bullets peppering the area around her. She tossed herself to the side—and saw the cleft. Relief surged through her but also an acute awareness that she wasn't out of this yet. She rolled, avoiding more gunfire, and thudded against the rocky cleft. It was a small overhang at the base of a massive rock formation that dug into the mountain. Moss and leftover nests softened the ground as she crawled into the spot. Back to the chilled rock, she knelt, cocooned in the cleft. The overhang barely shielded her. Groping in the dirt, she watched the footpath. Watched for the second attacker. As she did, she spotted him crouch-running about ten yards away, zipping in and around trees.

Something to her left, farther back, drew her attention. Another man.

A third? Where had he come from? Maybe he'd been waiting outside. Why hadn't she noticed him before?

Keep it together. You can do this.

Her fingers grazed the draw cord. Pulled it. The long rectangular object came free from the dirt and leaves. Nuala tugged open the neck and slid the Remington from the nylon sleeve. Slowing her breathing even as she took up position, she lifted the rifle to her shoulder. Cheek pressed against the stock, she peered through the sight. Zeroed it in. Waited for the man to step into the crosshairs of the reticle.

Vrrrrrooooppp!!

Nuala twitched at the sound of the trap she'd set being sprung. If one got caught up in the trap, another still lurked in these woods. Waiting to kill her. She would not deviate from this mission.

Breathe. Slow. In. Out. In. Out. Like some weird time warp in a movie, she saw the glowing green man step from behind a tree.

In. Out.

Attuned to the wind and the location of the target, she calculated the right settings. *Wind right to left, six miles an hour, hold one-quarter mil left.*

Nuala slid her finger into the trigger well. Eased it back.

The tiny sonic boom signaled the fire.

Glowing Green Guy stumbled backward.

She let out a long, slow breath. Closed her eyes and asked God to forgive her for taking another life. Scooting out of the hiding spot, she eyed the large capture swinging from a Mossy Oak. Weapon up, Nuala stalked toward him, swinging around, verifying they were alone, verifying someone wouldn't put lead in the back of her head.

Nuala skirted the copse of trees, the six set in a circle—the spot she'd chosen specifically for that reason—and watched as the man dangled upside down, both feet in a noose. He used a large blade to saw at the rope.

But then—she saw the swirl along his right bicep and forearm. Her throat tightened. "Boone?" she called.

He spun around, dropping against the net.

She wanted to laugh, but there was nothing to laugh about tonight. *"Boone?"*

"Hey, Noodle." As the swinging slowed, he eyed her. "Thought I'd take a look around."

With a sigh, she walked over to the counterbalance and severed the cords.

"No!"

Phffvvvvvvttt!

Thud!

Groaning and arching his back, Boone lay on the ground.

Nuala stood over him, wishing she felt free enough to throw herself into his arms. Adrenaline bottomed out, and she felt her limbs trembling. "You almost broke my favorite tree."

Boone
Reston, Virginia
3 May – 0630 Hours

Boone aimed the SUV off Fairfax County Parkway and turned onto New Dominion Parkway, easing into the turn lane that would deliver them to Reston Hospital Center.

"I'm not hurt," Nuala said, her pale blue eyes wide and dusted with fear as she stared at the multistoried building ahead. The scratch across her cheek looked angry but not stitch worthy.

"I need a doctor more than you after you dropped me twenty feet onto the hard ground."

"It was seven feet, and you're a big guy." Her gaze traced the hospital, worry evident and strong.

"Relax," he said as he slid the vehicle into a parking spot. "Keeley's here."

Nuala's pink lips parted. Then she closed her mouth, apparently not willing or ready to face the questions that were no doubt plaguing her.

"I need to check in," Boone said. "Then I'll take you to the safe house."

Nuala nodded, her gaze tracking the movement of pretty much everyone in the parking lot, especially the security truck. "Should I come in?" she asked, dragging her attention back to him.

"Yeah." He'd never thought of her as the "easily spooked" type, but the scared-rabbit look on her face made him reconsider. Besides, he wouldn't want her sitting out here. They couldn't trust anyone or any situation right now. Everything posed a risk. A threat.

Nuala, a petite thing at five-four, made his height and size seem monstrous as they walked. Maybe it was just that he was more aware of the difference after five years. Her round, cherubic face didn't help things—she still looked fifteen, though her dossier read twenty-five. He'd always had this big-brother feeling toward her, wanting to keep her safe. Though his instincts said to protect her, Boone knew Noodle could take care of herself. The girl's skills with a Remington had outshone his in no time.

They entered the CICU wing, and he strode down the hall toward the secure area. Nerves on fire after their adventure in the Blue Ridge Mountains, Boone immediately zeroed in on the lanky guy sitting in the chair outside Keeley's room. Rusty Gray, former Army and Special Forces, came to his feet and settled his gaze on Nuala.

"You remember each other?"

They both nodded. The less said here the better. Boone moved to the door. "How's she doing?"

"Same," Rusty said.

"Hang tight." Boone let himself into the room. A sort of dusky feel had fallen over the room with the subdued lights and soft beeping and hissing of machines. Sun poked defiantly past the closed shades and curtain, demanding access to the still form in the bed.

Auburn hair curled around her face, Keeley lay there the image of peace and beauty. He touched the soft strands, smiling as his gaze shifted to her face. "Hey. Time to wake up, beautiful. The team needs you." He wanted to kiss her cheek, but they had an audience—he could feel their gazes boring into his back. "I need you," he whispered.

He squeezed her fingers. "I'll be back later." Linger here too long and they'd start asking questions. Ones he didn't want brought up. Ones he couldn't afford to be exposed. Boone stepped back out and jutted his jaw toward Rusty. "Doctors been by?"

"Not yet," the guy said, his brown, curly hair longer than regs. "But it's early. Nurse was here, said she's doing good. They might downgrade her to the ICU by the end of the week."

With a nod, Boone felt the pressure in his chest ease a little. "I'll be back as soon as I can. Thanks for doing this." He caught Nuala's arm and started moving.

Back in the SUV, Boone headed north on Fairfax County Parkway and hit Route 7, instantly feeling like a trout trying to swim upstream. "Hungry?" he asked, glancing at Nuala.

She shook her head.

"We have a full kitchen at the bunker, but it'll take us an hour to get there in this traffic."

"I'm fine."

This is why he'd steered clear of Nuala. She would seem fine and strong one minute, moody the next. He didn't get it. "Well, I'm hungry after you strung me up." Besides, stress made him crave protein and a good workout. And with the attacks, the murders, and being around Trace and Zulu once more, Boone was sure his BP was up again.

Boone hooked a right onto Countryside and aimed into a drive-thru where he ordered three sides of eggs and three sides of sausage. Before getting back on Route 7, he dug out two of each of the sides and handed the bag to Nuala. "Eat."

"I said—"

"I didn't ask."

Nuala huffed and took the proffered nourishment.

In the stop-and-go insanity of the drive, Nuala drifted off. She'd situated herself so it wasn't obvious, but he could tell by the twitch in fingers that bore the grime and dirt of her incident with the killers at the lodge that she'd fallen asleep.

Boone was glad for the silence, glad she would get a bit of shut-eye before he delivered her back into the lions' den with Trace and the others. The team was in a fight for their lives.

They all knew this day was coming.

But nobody wanted to see it.

Sam
Manson, Washington
3 May – 1030 Hours

"That's the answer you're giving me?"

The deputy sheriff, a beefy guy in his own right without a trace of gray in his brown hair, sighed heavily. "Sorry, sir. We have no leads, no proof—"

"I'm proof!" Sam's anger thumped against his pulse. "I was there. I saw it—I was shot at. What else do you need?"

"Bullet casings, witnesses, *a suspect. . .*"

"What? You want me to hand him to you?" *Bring it down. Easy. Easy.* He huffed then stretched his jaw. "What about Ashland? What about the spent casings in the house where he blew out the windows?"

"Miss Palmieri, you mean? And there were no casings. Our forensics teams swept the place. They didn't find anything."

"Bull!" Sam's heart thundered. "I want Ashland found. I was there and she was taken. She wouldn't have left willingly." *Not without telling me.*

Who was he kidding? Ashland didn't talk to anyone about anything. She had a better vault and internal security system than Fort Knox. "What about Ashland—what are you doing to find her?"

The deputy hesitated and glanced to the side.

"What?" Sam's response came out as a snarl.

"Sir, I'm sorry." The deputy shrugged. "I know you're concerned, but at this point, we have no proof of kidnapping—or that she's even missing."

Sam was not leaving this station without some information, some hint that they would do everything they could to find Ashland. To find whoever had taken a bead on them. "Call my sister—Carolyn Caliguari Jennings. She can verify that Ashland has been living there and she's missing."

Another reluctant expression. "We did."

Sam gritted his teeth, unwilling to trust himself to open his mouth—and snap off this officer's head. He was too used to the "we all come home" and seeing the mission completed even if it meant dying. To suffer bureaucracy when Ashland's life hung in the balance...

"Mrs. Jennings said she found an e-mail from Miss Palmieri stating she was going out of town."

Sam felt as if his veins pumped mud. She left? Of her own will—and she'd told Carolyn but not him? After what had built between them? She...

No. No, this wasn't right. Something was off.

Sam pivoted and stormed out of the building, tugging out his cell. He hit Carolyn's speed dial.

"Hey," came her weary greeting.

"What e-mail? Tell me about the e-mail." Sam slid into his black Camaro and started the engine.

"Wha—? Oh. Yeah, I tried to call you." She hadn't. There were no missed calls on his phone. "It was in my spam folder."

"Read it." Sam hated ordering his sister around, but he needed answers.

"Uh...let me get to my computer." Rustling rattled his nerves as he made his way back to the cottage. "Okay, here: 'Hi, Carolyn. Sorry this will be late notice, but I need some time to get away. If you need to rent out the cottage, I understand. I hope to come back someday.'"

"She didn't write that."

"Sam—"

"When was the last time Ashland e-mailed you...*ever?*"

"I...uh, well, never."

"Exactly. Because Ashland doesn't have a computer or e-mail. She told me months ago she didn't trust what the government could do with them." Sam wanted to curse, but he'd given that up right along with his career in the SEALs. He'd seen enough and heard enough to last a lifetime.

"What are you saying?"

"Ashland was taken." And the authorities weren't going to be any help until he made them do their jobs. "I'm going to prove it and find her, if I have to do it myself."

"Sammy..." Her warning, whiny tone grated on his last nerve.

Sam ended the call and found himself pulling into the parking lot of the Green Dot. He parked and sat staring at the wood deck where he had shared ice cream with Ashland. Many times Jeff had given Sam that "I'll kill you if you hurt her" look, but they both knew Sam had it bad for Ash. His mind drifted to two nights ago. Had they not been shot at and had she not disappeared, he would've called it the best night of his life. She let him into her protected vaults. Not only had she let him kiss her, but she'd responded. He'd known in the heat of that moment that he wanted to marry her.

Not true—he'd known for months he'd marry the girl if she dropped out of her stealth mode of running past his interference attempts.

He climbed out and entered the shop.

Jeff looked up from behind the sandwich station, catching Sam's gaze through a long line of customers. Sam dropped into a chair near a window. Though Fox News played on the monitor that hung in the upper corner, the volume couldn't compete with the chatter and laughter in the sub shop. His gaze caught on the ticker scrolling across the bottom.

. . .NATIONAL PARK —RANGER CANDICE REYNA BRUTALLY MURDERED. . .

Why wasn't Ash up there?

Right. Because the cops think she just walked away from the barrage of bullets and kept going. Sam stretched his jaw and rubbed it. What was going on?

"You Sam Caliguari?"

Sam snapped his gaze to the man in the windbreaker with a news logo emblazoned over the left breast. He gave the guy a look that in his Navy SEAL days would've had the guy running to change his pants. The last thing he wanted or needed was some nosy, microphone-pushing reporter—

"Can I talk to you about Ashland Palmieri?"

Sam eyeballed him. Kept his mouth shut. But the mention of Ashland's name made the gears of his heart grind down into first.

The reporter took the silence as an invitation.

"Look," Sam finally said. "I'm not in the mood—"

"Don't you find it weird that suddenly nobody knows where she is?" He thumbed toward the Green Dot owner. "Mr. Conwell says she hasn't worked in weeks."

Sam shot a scowl at Jeff. Rose to his feet. Crossed the restaurant. He zeroed in on Jeff. "C'we talk?"

"Sorry," Jeff said, nodding to the line. "Too busy."

But he saw it. Saw *something* scrawled all over Jeff's face. "What do you know about Ashland?"

Jeff stuffed a paper-wrapped sub into a bag and handed it to the customer, effectively turning his attention and his back on Sam as he completed the sale.

Sam waited, but his mind drifted again. Envisioned Ash standing there preparing his sandwich. The night she intentionally accidentally put an olive on his sandwich. Her giggles. Her smile. Her breath. Sam ground his teeth together, trying to push those potent memories aside so he could focus.

Jeff wasn't going anywhere. Not with the answers he had. He felt the presence of someone behind him and glanced back. The reporter, who came to Sam's shoulder, leaned in, apparently wanting to hear the conversation.

He hated reporters. They'd never gotten stories about his SEAL team right, though they were quick to splash inaccurate facts all over the six o'clock news. But the guy's questions tugged at the gnawing in Sam that something was really. . .*off.*

"What's your name again?" he asked, angling into the guy's personal space.

"Lowen Miles."

He clapped a hand on the reporter's shoulder and could swear the guy about wet himself again. Maybe his SEAL skills were still intact. "Let's talk." He led him out of the shop and into the parking lot. "What do you know?" Hands tucked up under his arms, Sam worked to keep his frustration down.

Lowen shifted his messenger bag onto his shoulder. "Sh–shouldn't I be asking the questions?" He nudged his wire-rim glasses and managed a shaky laugh. "I mean, I am the reporter, right?"

Sam waited. Told himself killing the guy in plain sight would get him jailed. Then he'd never find Ashland.

"Right." Lowen's smile faded. "Okay, it's just. . .have you heard about the girl killed in Nevada?"

Sam didn't respond.

"What about the ranger in Alaska?"

"On the news."

Lowen nodded. "Yeah. Well, they've all been former military."

Lifting a shoulder, Sam tried to let the guy know he didn't care about other women. Had Ashland ever said she served?

"Was she former military?"

Sam crowded the guy back against an SUV. "Do not probe me for information."

"I. . .I wasn't. She was." He blinked. "I mean, she was in the military. At least, I think so."

"So was I. What's your point?"

Lowen looked up at him, then his expression went blank. "Honestly, I'm not sure. I just. . . someone. . ." He shook his head. "Someone gave me this information. Suggested I look into it."

Sam's radar pinged off the charts now. "I think we should take this elsewhere. Give me your phone."

Lowen handed over the device, his eyes wide.

Sam programmed his number into the phone then returned it. "You know who I am, Lowen Miles?"

The man shifted on his feet. "Y—yes."

"You know what I did for a living?"

He swallowed.

"So just remember that if you do anything that puts Ashland in danger."

"I don't need to be threatened."

Sam flared his nostrils. "Not a threat. Due diligence—to keep Ashland alive till I can find her."

Trace
Lucketts, Virginia
3 May – 1300 Hours

Trace Weston stood in the plywood-paneled room that would someday become his office. For now, it was a box that allowed him to contain his thoughts and frustration. He held the secure phone to his ear, waiting.

"Go ahead," said an older, more seasoned voice on the other end.

"One, Two, and Six are secure. What do you know about Six's assailants?" Elite military experts had slipped into the mountains and retrieved the bodies, hoping to identify the shooters and finger whoever was behind this.

"Mercenaries. No information yet on who hired them."

"Not surprised. Whoever did this wants the girls out of the way, unable to talk."

"Agreed." The general let out a long-suffering groan. "This is a fine bloody mess, Colonel."

"It is, sir."

"One that I do not need, but then again, I'm sure you don't either. Listen, I have teams working round the clock to contain this. Keep the assets there till we get this swept under the carpet."

"Sir, we need to find who did this."

"Yes, we do. But not yet—we can't. Things are too hot. Understood?"

Trace wanted to tear something limb from limb. "Yes, sir."

The line went dead.

Trace lowered the phone. What would he do with three women whose lives had—once again—been turned inside out? Who had found them? Had it taken the person five years to hunt them down? Or was there significance to this timing?

A solid but soft—at least for the guy doing it—rap came on the closed door. Trace turned, pocketing the phone as Boone stepped in. "They're gathered."

What would he tell the girls? They had no answers and nowhere to go.

"Did he have anything to say?" Boone asked.

So, he'd figured out Trace had talked to the general. "Just to stay underground."

"What will you tell them?" Boone asked, bobbing his head toward the partially exposed conference area where Trace saw the remnant of Zulu. Three of the six he'd recruited. Three of the best female operators he'd ever met.

"They already know it's screwed up. Let's just give them what we know and leave it at that," he said as he made his way out of the plywood office.

Trace tucked aside his feelings, his anger, his frustration, and entered the conference area.

"Who came after us?" Annie asked, sitting beside Téya at the table.

He held up a hand to stay the questions. "One thing at a time. First—we do not yet know who came after you. What we do know is that they were mercenaries." Trace pressed his fingertips against the table. "Teams are working right now to contain the situations, to limit any traces that will lead back to you or your real identities."

"I just don't understand how they found us," Téya said.

"We all knew it was just a matter of time." Annie folded her arms over her chest.

"But we did everything right," Téya said. "New name, new identity, new location. No contact with each other or those in Command. Right?" Téya shoved her hair from her face as she looked from Annie to Trace. "How did they find us?"

"The better question," Nuala said, "is *who* found us."

"There are a lot of questions, but give us time. It's only been thirty-four hours." Trace eyed Houston as he lured Boone away from the conversation. "We still have a lot to sort through. For now, we need you to stay here, stay below. I know the bunks are a sorry excuse for beds, but I'm just grateful Boone has been working on this the last few years."

"I don't like this, *Colonel*," Annie said, nodding to his rank patch in the center of his chest. "Congratulations on the promotion."

Trace nodded. He'd been a promising captain when Zulu had assembled. Despite the disaster, he'd been promoted twice, the most recent step to LTC coming just three months ago. His silver oak leaf was something he didn't want to lose. And if what happened with these ladies five years ago resurfaced now. . .

"Nobody likes this," Trace replied. "But it's where we are."

Nuala sat forward, hands on the table. "So, nobody's asked, but I will—we think this is connected to Misrata, right?"

"West," came Boone's terse, quick call.

"I can't see any other explanation," Trace said. "Excuse me." He strode across the room and up onto the dais where Houston had established his place of dominance over the command bunker.

Boone pointed to a monitor. "We've got trouble."

Téya

Where have you been living?"

Téya met the pale blue eyes of the girl who'd been their sniper. "Pennsylvania."

Nuala nodded.

"What about you, Noodle?" Annie asked.

They all smiled at the old moniker. Nuala's Irish name took a beating in a military setting, going from the correct "Noo-lah" pronunciation to "Noodle" very quickly.

"Mountains," the girl said.

Téya chided herself. Nuala wasn't anymore a girl than she was. Hard to believe Nuala was only two years younger when she looked like a high school sophomore, junior if they pushed it. "What about you?"

Annie fiddled with a straw wrapper. "A lake outside of Seattle. Really quiet, pretty."

Twitches of movement in the computer area drew Téya's attention. Something had the men worked up. The WWE could borrow Boone, his size and fight as intimidating as the best fighters. Trace with his all-business attitude scowled at Boone, as he tightened his lips, apparently replying to something the big guy said.

The tech guy hunched his shoulders and shrank away from the two men who had been the mentors and leaders of Zulu.

"They know something," Annie muttered, joining her.

Understatement. Téya left the confines and safety of the conference room, slinking into the open area but sticking to the walls, out of the line of sight of Boone and Trace. She eased toward them quickly, grateful for bare feet in this underground bunker. As she stepped up onto the dais, she saw a news piece on the monitor.

"She *can't* know. It'll only make things worse," Trace said, his shoulder pointed in Téya's direction but his line of sight blocked by the bigger Boone.

"I don't agree with keeping this from her," Boone said. "Everything's messed up, and they need to understand how deadly it is right now."

Peering past them, she eyed the articles on the screens. Téya's heart tripped over the headline: Amish Man Shot; Elderly Woman Missing.

She froze, David's kind face flashing before her mind's eye. Surely it wasn't him. *Please, God, You promised to protect him!* She moved closer. Strained to read the smaller words.

"Téya." Trace shifted, snapping her to the fact he looked right at her.

She met his green eyes. "Tell me that's not my grandmother." Her heart felt like it was pumping peanut butter.

He and Boone shared a look.

It was. David had been shot and her grandmother was missing. This couldn't be happening. *I wasn't there to protect them.* The threat had been closer than any of them realized. "When did that happen?" she demanded.

"Day after you left," Houston offered.

Boone and Trace glowered at the guy.

In other words, whoever shot David had been right on her heels. What if he came back? Téya spun around. Stalked to the bunk rooms.

"Téya," Trace said, a stiff warning in his voice. "You can't leave."

"Watch me," she snapped as she threw open the door to the room she had to herself. On the lower bunk, she stuffed on a boot.

Trace stood in the doorway. "I can't let you leave."

She stomped her booted foot down. "Trace, my grandmother is missing. David—that's who was shot, right? What if they realize he's not dead and go after him again?"

"We're under orders. It's too dangerous to be out there." Trace folded his arms over his chest, a trail of tattoos peeking out along his forearms. "Listen, everyone they tried to kill was a precise hit. These guys don't miss."

"They missed Annie." She slid on her other boot.

"That's because she had help."

She yanked the laces tied. "Exactly." She stamped to her feet. "That's why I'm going back there. They need me."

"Think about it—David didn't take a kill shot because they wanted to draw you out, so they could kill you."

"I would rather take the bullet any day of the year than have someone I love and care about take one." The cadence in her chest felt like an entire platoon on a march. "You can't possibly think it's right to keep me here when they need me."

"They need you *alive*. That's what they'd want."

"If they're dead, they can't *want* anything."

Trace took a step forward. "Téya, think it through. Put aside the emotion and think. I've already called in security detail for David. He won't know they're there, but they will be."

"And my grandmother? What are you doing to find her, Colonel?"

He held her gaze but said nothing.

"She's *eighty-two*. Do you really think she has a chance with goons like that?"

Now, his gaze said everything.

Téya drew up short. "You think she's already dead." She shoved her hair from her face and turned away. Paced the room. "I can't. . .I need. . ." Covering her mouth, she worked to sort her thoughts. Figure out what she had to do. What if Trace was right? What if her grandmother was dead? A deep, strong ache started in her breast. She closed her eyes. "Do you understand what she did for me?" Téya shifted and gave him a sidelong glance. "She *lied* to the elders so I could live with her. She knew I was in trouble and needed help, a safe place. Do you know what the bishop can do to her?"

Trace Weston had been one impenetrable rock since the first day he walked onto the training field after Selection. His sandy-blond hair in an almost buzz cut, his tanned skin, and his green eyes softened the chiseled-from-stone personality that embodied the solider she admired and who made her want to be better and stronger.

And here she was, ready to defy him. She wanted David back. She wanted *Grossmammi* and the farm, the simple, nonviolent life of the Amish back. She wanted peace. "I don't want this," she managed, her throat constricting. "I was glad for the safety of my grandmother's community."

Trace studied her for several long seconds. "But you never felt you deserved it."

Téya swallowed. How did he know that?

"You protect them by staying away."

"How can you say that? He's been shot! She's missing. She can't even get around without"—Téya gasped and took a step back, suddenly remembering—"her cane!"

Trace frowned.

"I can find her."

He frowned. "With her cane?"

"She was having memory problems and got lost a few times, so I put a tracking chip in her cane."

Trace
Bleak Pond, Pennsylvania
4 May – 1000 Hours

Driving through the quiet, quaint town, Trace saw farmers drilling oat or grain seeds with horse-drawn planters. While he could appreciate the simplicity of their lifestyle, he didn't envy them. He didn't want to be out day after day doing chores and the same ol' thing. He liked the adrenaline rush and the adventure of new missions.

Then again, unlike him, these farmers and their families were relatively safe.

Except David Augsburger.

Trace couldn't pretend a small amount of curiosity about the man. He'd gotten under Téya's skin, and that was no small feat. She was a driven, hard-hitting woman.

"Sure can't imagine living in a place like this," said Martin Hill, the tech Trace borrowed from INSCOM to get a facial recognition workup of the man who'd hit David.

Off East Frederick, Trace turned into the parking garage of Lancaster General Hospital. "Let's just get what we need and get out." The longer they were here, the bigger the target on their heads.

They made their way to the main postoperative unit on the second floor. According to their records, David had surgery yesterday for a fractured fibula and to remove a bullet. They stepped out of the elevator and saw an elderly Amish couple exiting a room.

"Guess we're in the right place," Martin muttered as he hitched his gear pack on his shoulder.

Trace kept his eyes straight, not making contact with the couple. He waited till they went into the elevator, then he entered the room.

In a hospital gown and strung up to an IV tower, David Augsburger looked like an average Joe. A brace over his bed kept his leg elevated. Weights provided a counterbalance to keep his leg up, and the pulleys provided traction. Trace knew that pain all too well.

"I already talked to the police."

Trace entered the room, stuffing his hands in his pants pockets. "We're not with the police."

67

Suspicion crowded the man's expression, seeming to darken the bruise around his left eye.

Trace wanted to put him at ease, but he had little information he could dish out. "I'm with a special branch investigating your incident and that of Mrs. Gerig and—"

"Katie." The way he said her name showed his affection for Téya/Katie. "They're both missing. Please—you have to find them."

"Yes, sir. We plan to, but we need your help." Trace indicated to Martin. "My friend here works in a criminology lab." Not quite the truth, but close enough. "He's an expert on reconstructing faces from descriptions."

David nodded, but the suspicion hadn't yet left his face. "You want me to tell you about the man who did this to me."

Trace nodded.

"Look," David said, glancing to the window where medical staff and patients moved up and down the corridor. "I'm not sure—"

Trace leaned in, placing a hand on the man's pillow and forcing him to look up. "You care about Katie, right, David?"

He swallowed.

"So, I need your help. Tell him what you saw. Give us something to go after whoever did this. Whoever took Mrs. Gerig and Katie." He hated deceiving the guy, but he could not know what happened to Téya. She had to remain permanently MIA.

"Okay," David said with a shaky voice.

Martin swung the bag onto the food tray and unzipped it. "Okay, this will be pretty painless."

Téya
Somewhere along the Maryland-Pennsylvania border
4 May – 1345 Hours

"In position."

The coms report of Nuala brought Téya's head up from the live feed she'd been focusing on. Listening to. Hearing David's voice pressed against her composure. Anger and hurt churned through her. Too many things angered her right now: being forbidden from seeing David; making sure he was okay; someone going after those she loved; and her own stupidity putting *Grossmammi* in danger in the first place.

Pushing back the tears proved harder with each minute she spent sitting in Boone's oversized truck. Téya looked toward the three-story building a quarter mile away where Nuala had taken up her position on the roof.

"There are three—nope. Four—*five!*" Houston went silent for a second, and Téya glanced back at him. "Yes, five tangos. Make that four. I think the fifth—lying down—is most likely the old lady."

Téya glowered at the tech geek.

Boone glanced at Annie then Téya. "Ready?"

After a curt nod, Téya slid on the hat and did a press check on her Glock. She adjusted the bulletproof vest before climbing out of the truck. They used the shadows and patches of grass to conceal their movement.

"Looking good," Houston spoke through the coms, watching them from one of his drones.

Boone led her up the side of the building, lowering himself to a hunch-run. Téya followed his lead, and Annie trailed, watching their six.

"I have joy," Nuala said, indicating she had a line of sight on one of their targets. "He is alone and outside."

"Take the shot," came the deep, husky voice of Boone.

Hustling up to the side steps, Téya felt her heart skip a beat. Irrational as it was, she wondered what would happen if her grandmother got mistaken for a target.

A firm pat came to her shoulder as Annie said, "She'll be fine."

Téya drew in a steadying breath, grateful for the friendship and familiarity with Annie. They'd been able to read each other's thoughts and predict moves since they joined the team.

"Tango down," Nuala called.

They stacked up on the door, ready to breach. "Going in," Boone said, his gray eyes hitting Téya then moving past her to Annie. He held up a gloved finger. *One.* Then another. *Two.* And a final one. *Three.*

He stood and rammed his heel into the door.

The steel flung open.

Téya pushed upward, weapon at the ready, and entered. She swung right, tracing the wall and scanning. Behind her, she heard Annie moving away from her. Boone stepped in as Téya flanked left and pied-out. Their beams crossed.

Téya spotted the paneled-off area and indicated that direction with two fingers. The others followed as she swept into what turned out to be a narrow corridor. *So much for one big open space.* Houston needed to update his description skills.

She moved decisively but cautiously. Down about twenty paces, a doorway gaped, begging for them to enter its ambush. At least, that's how it felt.

Annie's pulse sped. Her grandmother was in there. *In who knows what kind of pain.*

They'd need to draw out at least one more of the targets. Téya lifted a fist and stopped. Bending down, she lifted a crumpled soda can. She tossed it down the hall. It clanked and thunked noisily.

Téya shifted to the right wall, pressing her shoulder against it. Waiting. Listening. No cheesy dialogue. Just the soft crunch of boots. Whoever had taken her grandmother expected them to come after her.

A gun slid into view, held steady by two hands.

The next second seemed to take forever as Téya anticipated neutralizing this guy.

Boone slid past her, dwarfing her.

Like lightning, he grabbed the guy's weapon. Wrapped a beefy arm around his neck. Clapped his large hand over his mouth. Pressed against the back of his head. And dragged him out of sight.

The guy went limp in Boone's arms. He laid him against the wall and strapped on plastic cuffs. Boone gave a nod.

Téya eased up to the doorway, Glock up and ready.

A pat came to her shoulder. She pushed into the doorway.

Tsing! Tink! Tsing!

She dove to the side as more shots rang out. On the ground, she searched for the shooter.

"Taking fire!" Annie spoke through the coms.

"No joy," Nuala said. "I have no joy."

Téya's stomach tightened—the shooter had her grandmother and Nuala couldn't get a line of sight on him. *It's up to me.*

Remembering the layout, where they'd seen the tangos and her grandmother on the thermal scan from the drone, she made her way to the opposite wall that was perpendicular to where the tango held her grandmother. When she made it to the corner, she squinted through the dim light available but had no better view. In fact, a four-foot wall a few feet from the tango concealed him.

Téya crouch-ran along the wall.

"Téya," came a whispered warning from Boone. "Easy."

She stretched out along the half wall, her knees digging into the dirt as she held herself out of sight.

"Why don't you come out?" Boone's deep voice echoed through the large space. "Save everyone some work and pain."

"Not happening."

The man's voice sounded close—closer than Téya imagined. *Must be on the other side of this wall.* Téya traced the plywood structure. She couldn't just fire through it since she didn't know where her grandmother lay. A stray shot could kill her grandmother or just anger the guy.

She knew what she had to do. Téya used every stealth skill she had and turned onto her butt. Boots touching the wall, she gently tested them against the steel. Held her weapon in a cradle grip.

Blew out a breath. Closed her eyes. Imagined the setting. Imagined success. *God, help me.* She thrust herself backward. Landed on her back. Eyes took a split-second to adjust. She saw the man. Fired twice.

He slumped to the ground.

Téya hopped to her feet, weapon still trained on the guy.

Behind her, Boone and Annie ran toward them.

After verifying the guy was dead, Téya went to the corner where her grandmother lay in the corner, whimpering. "*Grossmammi.*"

Wizened eyes widened. "Katie?" came her whispered disbelief.

She gathered her grandmother into her arms, holding the eighty-two-year-old trembling frame close. "You're okay now."

Slightly gnarled fingers gripped her shoulders. "You are a *soldier?*" Fear. Disgust. Shock. They all tumbled through the face Téya loved. Soldiering, violence, war were all the antithesis to the Amish community. To what her grandmother believed in.

"Let's move," Boone ordered.

Annie was at her side, and together they helped her grandmother to her feet. They started for the door. Boone went ahead, still sweeping with his weapon as they crossed the open area. At the corner, he found the guy he'd knocked out. Only now he bore two bullet holes to the head.

Boone cursed. But started moving again. "Nuala, we have a shooter. He killed our hostage."

"Roger, shooter spotted." Nuala's calm seemed preternatural. Scary calm, and her skills never failed. If someone met the Barbie-like girl on the street, they'd never know she was a top-notch sniper. "Target acquired. Rooftop."

An explosion of glass erupted inside the building they'd just left, followed by a heavy, sickening thud.

"Shooter down."

"Literally," snickered Houston through the coms.

"Quiet," Boone snapped then turned to Téya and Annie. "Let's move." Once in the truck, Boone pealed away, the truck fishtailing as they did. "Stay down!"

Bending over her grandmother, who curled into Téya's lap, Téya protected her. Prayed they could get out of here safe. They remained down for several long minutes. "Clear," Boone said ten minutes later.

Téya turned to her grandmother. "Are you okay?"

"Yes," *Grossmammi* said, her voice strained.

It's because of me. Because she knows the truth now. Téya placed her hands on her grandmother's. They rode in silence for the next thirty minutes until Boone pulled into a mall parking lot. He eased alongside a Pennsylvania State Trooper's vehicle.

Téya shifted on the seat. "*Grossmammi*, nobody can know you saw me today. Do you understand?"

Green eyes so like her own stared back. Studied. Tracked down to the tactical vest. The weapon holstered at her right hip.

"I know you don't understand," Téya said, the guilt strangling her. "And I'm sorry. But—my life is in danger. The men who took you, want me. Do you understand that?"

Her grandmother nodded.

Téya looked out the heavily tinted windows to Boone talking with the officer. "That trooper is the one who found you—that's what you must tell anyone who asks."

Concern—no doubt over having to lie—creased the wrinkled face.

"I'm so sorry I put you in danger, to ask this of you. But it's very important. For both of us. For David. For everyone in Bleak Pond."

Grossmammi patted her hand firmly.

The door swung open. "Time," Boone said as he held out a hand. "Ready, Mrs. Gerig?"

Annie
Lucketts, Virginia
5 May – 0915 Hours

Annie wasn't sure which was worse—the immediate aftermath of Misrata or right now. She'd never forget the instant they discovered what *really* happened at their hands. The devastation. The deaths. Trace believed Jessie would crack, and by the evidence spread out before them—the contents of her apartment—he was right. Really, it was a miracle that they hadn't all lost it.

Even now, bile rose to her throat as images of those bodies—the small, frail bodies burned in her mind's eye.

"Okay, listen up," Trace said as he and Boone hauled in several boxes and set them on the operations table. "We all know the mind Jessie had—she was a strategist. An analyst."

"And an obsessive one at that," Annie put in as she left the couch and joined him.

"Right. So, it'd be no surprise that she disobeyed orders and tried to find out who was behind Misrata. And since she was hit first, I'd wager my career she found something." Trace's jaw muscle twitched as he waited for Téya and Nuala to join them.

"How'd she die?" Téya asked, her stony facade thicker than ever.

Trace studied them, and Annie could see his thoughts, could see him working out if that information would be beneficial or diversionary. "Sniper shot."

Nuala straightened. "So, she died instantly."

Trace nodded. "If you feel anything that I'm feeling right now, then you'll want to dig through these boxes. They're from her apartment. I have to get back to INSCOM for a meeting, but I'll be back tonight. Let's find some answers."

Swallowing, Annie shook off the dread. Going through her friend's things was as creepy as seeing her body in a casket—which, thank God, they hadn't done. Jessie would be buried quietly and anonymously—since they were, according to government records, already dead. It grated on her nerves that Jessie and Candi wouldn't have full rights burials. They'd earned it.

But then again, they'd *earned* the anonymity when they attacked a warehouse full of ammunition. What they didn't know was on the other side of that warehouse, twenty-two orphans and caretakers were waiting out the night for their new residence.

Awkward silence rang through the operations center as she, Nuala, and Téya pored over the boxes, files, every scrap of paper found in Jessie's Las Vegas apartment. Things had changed. *They* had changed. A lot. Nuala had always been quiet and reserved but uncannily focused. Téya and Annie, however, had been close and raucous. Livewires, Boone had called them.

Téya seemed even more reclusive since the mission with her grandmother and boyfriend. Though Annie wanted to comfort her, the words—even in her head—sounded shallow. *Sorry* didn't quite make up for the harm caused to someone you loved.

"What's he like?" Annie asked, pretending less interest than she felt.

Riffling through a stack of papers, Téya hesitated then resumed her perusal.

Okay then. "Words are cheap, but—"

"You're right. They're cheap." Téya tossed the file down and moved to another box farther away from Annie.

"You're not the only one who lost in this attack," Annie said softly. Not to be confrontational, but they needed perspective. Had to remember the greater mission.

Téya didn't respond. She squatted at a box and thumbed through some items.

"What about you?" Nuala said, her eyes curious. "Did you find someone since. . .?"

Sam's handsome mug leapt into her visual cortex and forced a smile. "Yeah." She laughed. "I have a knack for trouble—he's a Navy SEAL."

Nuala's eyebrows raised. "Seriously? How'd you meet him?"

"I worked at a great place called the Green Dot Sub Shop. Sam's friends with the owner." She dug through a box of clothes. Slinky, sparkly clothes. "Please tell me she used this to blend in," Annie said, holding up a skirt. "This looks more like a tourniquet than a miniskirt."

"Um," Nuala said, lifting something out of a bin. She held out her hand.

Annie stared at the syringes and elastic bands.

"Did she get into drugs?"

"Jessie struggled after Misrata." Boone appeared out of nowhere, his expression stiff. "She couldn't keep it together or cope with what she'd done."

Téya straightened and glared at Boone. "What someone forced us to do."

"Easy," Boone said. "I'm not blaming. Just giving the facts."

"So," Nuala said, tossing the syringes down. She planted her hands on her hips, looking at the boxes. She turned a circle.

"What?" Annie asked.

"I'm just wondering—Jessie wasn't just a brilliant strategist, she was a computer geek."

"Everyone knew she loved her devices," Boone said.

"Then where are her computers? Laptops? iPads?"

"I thought that odd, too," Houston called from the command dais. "Especially since I can track a bit of traffic back to her address. Utility records do not show she had Internet, but all she needed was a mobile hotspot or something and she'd be up and running."

Boone glanced back, standing as he always had while training them, hands on his tac belt—appraising. "You sure about that?"

"About as sure as I can be without getting hold of her device. In fact, I suspect she and Keeley had been in contact."

Annie tensed. That was one of the cardinal rules Trace placed on them when they went into hiding—no contact with anyone in their former lives, especially other Zulu members. Jessie had sent her a message a couple of times, but Annie hadn't responded. As cold and heartless as it felt at the time, she believed it too dangerous to have those dots connected. If Keeley and Jessie were communicating. . .that could explain why they were hit first.

Boone lifted his phone and started toward the soundproof briefing room.

"What do you make of that?" Téya asked as she eased up next to Annie.

"Trouble."

"So, you had a boyfriend," Téya said quietly, waiting for Annie to look at her. "What happened to—"

"It ended." New tension knots bunched at the base of Annie's shoulders.

"Listen up," Boone's voice boomed through the bunker.

Nuala snickered as she stood behind the two of them. "He says that like he's still our drill sergeant."

"We're heading to Nevada."

Nuala
Las Vegas, Nevada
6 May – 0830 Hours

The Citation Sovereign delivered the team smoothly to the North Las Vegas airstrip, avoiding the overly busy McCarran International. Nuala watched as the sleek craft glided to a stop. A black Ford Expedition EL waited. As soon as the stairs were deployed, the driver's side door of the SUV opened. A man in a navy suit stepped out as Boone hustled down the steps of the aircraft. They shook hands as they pulled into a shoulder pat/hug.

When Zulu reached the tarmac and huddled up, Boone made introductions. "This is Dan Baker. He's an FBI slave now."

Normally, those three letters would put Nuala on the run. And not for the first time. She shot a look at Boone. Was he crazy, bringing in the feds? Weren't they trying to hide from men like this?

"*Slave* is right," he said, his gold eyes hitting Nuala then Annie but back to Nuala. He gave her a once-over then grinned. "Boone-Dawg, you been holding out on us. Keeping the beauties to yourself."

Nuala shifted under the attention. Among this group of soldiers, she'd never been the one to get singled out, unless she'd done something wrong. Weird that someone would take an interest in her, not Annie or Téya.

Boone laughed. "Dan is going to get us into Jess's apartment. We'll go in. He's buying us a few hours. Trace will join us soon, but we need to make it quick."

Houston lagged behind, three different equipment bags slung over his shoulders.

Dan backed up and reached for the door. "Ready?"

They piled into the vehicle, Boone up front with his buddy. Nuala sat behind Boone, watching the city slide by, wondering what Jessie had seen in this crazy city. Too many people. Too many buildings. Too many drugs and deaths. Though she hadn't been especially close to Jessie, Nuala wanted her back. The brunette had provided balance to the team.

As they delved deeper into Sin City, Nuala did her best to pay attention to routes, dead ends, hiding locations. *Always have an exit strategy*, Trace had said more than once.

Twenty minutes later, the Expedition slid up to an apartment building. Paper, cigarette packs, and beer bottles cluttered the path up to the four-story structure.

"You've got to be kidding me," Annie voiced Nuala's thoughts.

Jessie had always been meticulous about her bunk space and apartment before Misrata. She'd lived *here* after they all split up?

They climbed out and headed into the building. Dan held open the door while they trailed in, Nuala last after Houston with his gear. She felt Dan's hand on her lower back as he stepped in behind her. He brushed past her with a wink.

Nuala tucked her chin, the heat of embarrassment filling her cheeks.

"Landlord is in apartment 100." Dan walked down the hall and rapped three times on the door.

The door creaked on its hinges as a graying, older lady answered. Hair frizzed, she wore a polyester dress and flip-flops. Though she looked like a throwback from the '70s, she didn't have the flighty, lazy look in her expression. "May I help you?"

"You Mrs. Higginbotham?"

She touched her messy frizzy hair as if it were coiffed, clearly taken in by the smooth-talking and charming man at her door.

Dan lifted his badge from his belt. "Dan Baker with the FBI, ma'am." He unfolded a piece of paper. "I have a warrant to look through apartment 312."

Dawning broke out over her plain face. "Oh. Jamie's place."

"That's right," Dan said, with a smile that poked a dimple into his left cheek. "Can you either let us in or give us a key?"

"Oh sure." She squeezed into the hall and produced a ring of keys. Her gaze swept over the five of them. "You girls knew Jamie?"

"No, ma'am," Annie spoke up with a fake Southern drawl. "We're just here with Agent Baker."

"Oh." Mrs. Higginbotham seemed a little more nervous now but headed toward the stairs. As she climbed, she said, "That Jamie—she stuck to herself. Real quiet but real nice, too." She clucked her teeth, her false teeth. Dentures? Who did dentures anymore? Why not implants? "Just can't figure why someone would go and do what they done to that poor girl. Don't make no sense."

Huffing by the time she reached the third floor, the woman slowed her pace but not her dialogue. "She never brought no boys around, but she was a favorite. Everyone was always sayin' hi to her. And she helped anyone who needed it. Once, Bert Thompson couldn't get his fancy smartphone to work and she helped him. Sweetest thang, that girl."

Nuala traded knowing looks with Annie and Téya. That was Jessie all right. But it pained, twisted her insides, to think of her being gunned down in an alley.

"A'right," Mrs. Higginbotham said, unlocking the door and passing the key to Dan. "There ya go. Be real kind and bring that down to me so an old woman doesn't have to walk three flights of stairs again?"

Dan gave his agreement as Zulu entered the apartment.

Nuala was first in. Anticipation of what she'd find met with shock. "It's ransacked." She stepped over a scrawny metal lamp and moved toward the futon that had been sliced open, batting bleeding out.

Nuala slid toward the back wall that held a small counter, sink, and a two-burner stove. A microwave sat on the counter. Nuala recoiled when she saw something black skitter out of sight.

"Not exactly the Hilton." Dan Baker stood behind her, a hand resting on her shoulder to steady her. "Take it you don't have to live with those things."

"Not in peace anyway," she said.

He laughed then turned to the apartment. "Looks like someone beat us to it. When I was here the night she was killed, the place was messy, but not like this."

"I'm not seeing anything," Houston said as he looked around. "No cables, no Internet lines."

Nuala walked the seven-hundred-foot efficiency, careful to avoid touching anything. Though the grime and disarray lingered, so did evidence of the strong woman she'd known. Jessie had a thing for all things Africa, so the tribal mask, the carved giraffe, bespoke the soldier who'd felt she was fighting for freedom.

"I don't think we need twenty minutes, let alone two hours," Annie said. "There's nothing here."

Nuala didn't agree. There was something...*something* they were missing.

Francesca
Fort Belvoir, Virginia
6 May – 0915 Hours

"Sir, a word?" Lieutenant Francesca Solomon stood at the door of Colonel Liam Stevens, her commanding officer.

He looked up over his reading glasses as he lowered the file he'd been holding. "Come in."

"Sir, I believe I might have a lead on an unsolved murder that happened a few years ago."

Colonel Stevens sat back. "Is this Misrata again?"

Frankie ignored the squirrels running rampant in her stomach. "Yes, sir. But—"

"Solomon, when are you going to let that go?"

"When justice is served, sir. I believe I have a new lead, one that could solve this and bring down the man responsible."

"You do realize the difference between justice and vendetta, right?"

Frankie swallowed at the insinuation. At the same time, she took courage from the fact he hadn't threatened to throw her out of her job. "Sir, a week ago, a woman in Las Vegas died. Official cause of death was an overdose. But I talked with the coroner and the body went missing."

"Happens more often than you might believe."

"True, but the person who signed for the deceased's effects was one T. Weston."

"You just aren't going to leave the colonel alone, are you?"

"Sir, I just got—" No, she couldn't let him know she'd been tracking him. That wouldn't work in her favor. "I got word that Weston is back in Vegas. I believe, sir, he's there to cover up what happened."

He pinched the bridge of his nose. "And what? You want to go there?"

"Yes, sir."

"You realize if I let you do this and anything goes wrong...Lieutenant Colonel Weston can have formal charges brought against you. You see that, right?"

"Sir, if we keep looking the other way, nobody's going to see anything."

He groaned. "Okay, fine. Go. But so help me—if you don't get something, don't ask me for another inch on Misrata again."

Trace
Las Vegas, Nevada
6 May – 1120 Hours

Trace had landed three hours ago. Spent one hour with some friends at Nellis AFB, putting out feelers, asking them to check around. Never hurt to have more boots on ground. He'd gone over surveillance footage back in Virginia, but being here again, remembering Kingston's body in a bag. . .it made him hungry to stop whoever had unleashed this vicious game against Zulu.

He climbed the creaking stairs to the third floor, rapped on the door to apartment 312, and entered when Boone answered. "How's it going?" His first thought that Jessie needed better housekeeping habits was quickly replaced with the revelation that her place had been overturned.

"Painfully." Boone angled around. "Not exactly much to inspect, but Houston is taking his time, inspecting every square inch with his tech."

On his knees, Houston scooted along the floor, holding a wand to the back wall, moving slowly and methodically.

Trace hit the gaze of a man he didn't know. "You must be Baker."

Dark-haired and solid, the suit came toward him. Extended his hand. "Dan Baker. Nice to meet you."

"Trace Weston."

Baker grinned. "I know. Don't imagine there are many of us who don't know who you are, sir."

Trace ignored the comment. Didn't want to go there. Too many memories. He looked at Téya, Annie, and Nuala. Though he wasn't that much older, he felt like a protective father. And one of their number had been murdered here. Made him want to wrap a steel vault around the whole team. "What'd we know?"

"Not much," Dan said. "Official cause of death is overdose."

"Which would explain the tox reports." He hated that they had to leave the girl with a paper trail that defiled her character, but it was imperative they cover that she'd been hit by a sniper. That would draw attention they didn't need.

Boone watched over the girls, too. "Not much room to clear." He glanced at Trace. "Think we should pack it up?"

"No computers?"

"Nope," Houston spoke from where he sat on the couch, a laptop perched on his legs. "But. . .this is. . .*weird.*"

"What's that?" Trace moved into the room, begging the guy to give them something.

"Well, there are a ton of radio waves exploding around this place, yet"—he waved his arms around the apartment—"we have zilch. No computer, devices, phone, nothing."

"What does that mean?"

Houston shrugged. "Beats me, Boss-Man, but I'll find out," he said, never looking up from the laptop. "I'm checking lease information to see who her neighbors are."

"F. Thompson, R. Wright, J. Heller, and D. Nadler," Annie said.

Trace looked at Annie, feeling an old swell of emotion.

"What the. . .?" Dan asked. "How'd you know that?"

"Mailbox labels when we entered," Annie said, as if her attentiveness was no big deal.

"Right," Houston said. "Neighbor on that wall"—he pointed to the one where a cheap impressionist print hung—"is Heller, J. Across the hall. . .well, that doesn't matter, because the signal is too strong to be over there. I think it's the one that shares the wall."

"I'll check it out," Annie said.

"I'll come with you," Trace said, unwilling to leave any of them alone at this point in the game. They stepped into the hall and Annie knocked on 313.

"Unlucky thirteen," Annie whispered as they waited. The hall light seemed to form a halo around her blond curls. "Guess nobody's home. We can talk to the landlady. She was very helpful earlier."

Trace nodded and followed her down to the first floor, letting Annie take the lead. She gently knocked. When the door opened, the woman on the other side smiled.

"Hi, Mrs. Higginbotham."

"Did you get locked out, dear?"

"No, ma'am. Actually, we were wondering about the tenant in apartment 313."

"Oh, Jennifer Heller. She's not around much, but she sure is nice." She wrinkled her nose. "Not sure why she rented here. The girl looked like she had enough to get a nice place, but I wasn't going to turn down good money."

"Do you know where we can reach her?" Trace asked.

The woman straightened, adjusting her dress, as she smiled at Trace. A coy smile spread over her face. "I didn't see you before. Are you an FBI agent, too?"

"A consultant working with Special Agent Baker," Trace corrected her, wishing to shift her attention back to their question.

"They sure do grow them handsome, don't they?" She giggled to Annie.

"Ma'am," Annie said, her tone a bit more terse. "Do you have a number we can use to contact Miss Heller?"

"Oh—ya know? I don't think I do. She promised to come back and give me one, but she never did. And she told me back last month that she'd be gone for a few weeks."

Annie nodded. "Thank you, ma'am."

Climbing the stairs, Annie slowed, giving him the chance to move beside her. Eyes narrowed, she chewed her lower lip.

"What are you thinking?"

They reached the top before she answered. "Just. . .maybe it's—"

"What is it?"

She shrugged. "Jennifer Heller."

"Yeah?"

"Jessica Herring."

Trace saw her point. "Same initials."

"Jessie loved things like that."

"You think she might've rented 313, too?"

Annie scrunched her nose. "Maybe?"

He glanced around to verify they were alone and unwatched. "Let's find out." The place was borderline run-down and he doubted there were high-tech locks. A simple use of his credit card freed the door.

He drew Annie in and shut the door behind them. Spotless. Spartan. A few decent pieces of furniture. First thing he noticed—no pictures. At least, not of people. There were safari images. Prints of still life, but nothing to give him a clue. He went to a closet and opened it. Standard fare. Traditional dress. But only a half-dozen pieces.

"It was Jessie," Annie said, her voice alive.

Trace turned and found her holding up a flyer of a tribal exhibit. Emblazoned across it in white letters was the word *Zulu*.

"And look!" Annie pointed to an old-fashioned telephone on the counter. Her face brightened with a big smile as she lifted the handset from the cradle. "She had this favorite movie that she always talked about, quoted lines from. In it"—she was dialing numbers—"the hero wired a safe house to—"

Pop!

Trace reached for his weapon at the noise behind him. He aimed his weapon at the closet, wary.

Annie hurried past him. "I knew it!"

"Wait!"

She shoved aside the hanging clothes and pressed both hands on the wall. It slid to the side, out of view.

"You're kidding me," he muttered.

A second later, the other side of the panel slid back. Boone grinned back at him. Held up a Bible. "She left me a love note," he laughed. "Said it'd light my path. . ."

81

Trace shrugged. Okay, so the two rooms were connected via the closet. By why? He glanced back into the cleaner apartment. They were too small to hide anything. The kitchen cabinets. . . Three large strides carried him to them. He cleared them. Turned around. *What am I missing? Why would she need two apartments?*

"Baker had to head back," Boone said as he joined him in the cleaner apartment, walking the perimeter, glancing out the window, then turning back to Trace. "What gives with this?"

Trace shook his head. It made no sense. *C'mon, Jess. . .talk to me.* His gaze traced the walls, the ceiling, the— "Hold up." His gaze hit the closet again, remembering the other apartment. "Was there a closet. . .no, there wasn't. Only a table with a Bible."

He stalked back to the closet. Thrust the clothes to the other side and stared at the left side wall. After unhitching his SureFire, he traced the corners and floor. He pressed his fingers to the middle of the left corner.

Click.

Trace stilled, feeling the wall move beneath his fingers. He looked up, noticing only half the wall moved. He pushed a little harder. It swung back. Light snapped on. Trace crouched, bending in half to fit through the opening. He straightened to his full height, his gaze hitting an unbelievable sight.

Francesca
Nellis Air Force Base, Nevada
6 May – 1300 Hours

Wheels down. Frankie's nerves thrummed as the plane rolled toward the gate where they'd deboard. She was close. Closer than she'd ever been to putting the Misrata tragedy to rest. Bringing justice to the children so needlessly and callously murdered. Cutting the legs out from under one of the most arrogant soldiers she'd ever encountered.

She stepped onto the tarmac, the unusually hot day sending heat plumes warbling over the blacktop. She tucked on her sunglasses.

"Lieutenant Solomon?" An airman stood beside a black sedan. "I'll be your driver while you're here. We're ready when you are, ma'am."

"I need to talk to the local authorities, Airman. Can you take me to the FBI field office?"

"Yes, ma'am."

The ride to the John Lawrence Bailey Memorial Building on West Lake Mead took twenty minutes, thanks to a lack of heavy traffic. The airman delivered her to the front door and went to park the vehicle. Frankie entered the building and showed her ID. "Lieutenant Francesca Solomon with U.S. Army Intelligence and Security Command. I need to speak with the special agent in charge, please."

She waited, refusing the opportunity to sit. Her nerves, her anticipation of resolution sending spurts of adrenaline through her legs.

"Lieutenant Solomon?"

Frankie spun as a woman in standard FBI attire strode toward her, flanked by a man in khaki slacks, a navy blazer, and white shirt. The guy was hard not to notice with his height and unusual gold eyes.

"I'm Assistant Special Agent in Charge Gloria Lopez. The SAIC is offsite right now. Can I help?"

Frustration squeezed the muscles at the base of Frankie's neck. She wanted the top dog to deal with this, not an underling. But time was of the essence. "Yes, that'd be fine. Can we go somewhere private?"

Special Agent Lopez led her to a room where the three of them sat around a long table. Frankie was sure the agents did this to emphasize their position and authority. The Army kept everything small and cheap.

"Ten days ago, a woman died here. Her record of death"—Frankie slid the death certificate across the table—"states she died of a drug overdose."

Lopez, her short hair curled softly around her ears, smiled. "I'm afraid that happens all too often here. Girls come looking for a big break, and they get one, but not the kind they hoped for."

Frankie stemmed her frustration. Already being placated. She glanced at the male agent sitting quietly. He hadn't introduced himself or said a word yet.

"I believe this girl did not die of an overdose. But I can't prove that because her body went missing."

Lopez tilted her head, concerned. "You know this how?"

"I phoned the coroner and asked for more information, but she couldn't provide it because she couldn't locate the body."

"Maybe just a mix-up."

"Possible," Frankie admitted, "but I have another scenario in mind. While you do not have the clearance level necessary for me to share everything, I can tell you that a case I'm working on involves a tragedy that cost twenty-two innocent children and women their lives. I believe the man responsible for those killings to be behind this woman's death."

Lopez straightened. "And this man's name?"

"Trace Weston. He's currently a lieutenant colonel in the Army."

"Then, isn't this a JAG problem?" the man said casually.

"Yes and no. Right now, he is here in this city. I need your help to find and stop him," Frankie said.

"We have protocols," Lopez said.

"I know. That's why I came prepared with this." Frankie handed over a faxed letter from the FBI Director, a favor General Stevens called in to make sure they didn't hit unnecessary dead ends.

The man shifted. "Where is he?"

Frankie felt herself grimace but swallowed it. Couldn't show a weak bone here. "Honestly, I do not have that information right now, but—"

"Miss Solomon—"

"Lieutenant."

Lopez gave a placating smile. "Lieutenant Solomon, I'm afraid this is a little out of our area of expertise. If you have a solid lead, a place we could start, then—"

"The victim's apartment." Frankie shifted. "I'm not asking for a full SWAT force, just a few agents to escort me in and look the place over. If Weston is there, I will take him into custody."

Trace
Las Vegas, Nevada
6 May – 1330 Hours

"Now this is what I'm talking about!"

As Houston squirmed into the three-foot-by-eight-foot cubbyhole in the wall, Trace couldn't take his eyes off the wall-to-wall clippings, photos, articles, and grease boards that swam around the shelf that ran the length of the wall. Four systems lined up at chest height had streaming data.

"What is on the systems?"

"Algorithms, feeds. . ." Houston bent his knees as he leaned from one side to the other scanning the monitors. "And I have no idea what else. It'll take. . .*weeks*, if not months to decipher this." He focused on one laptop. Then moved to the next. "I. . .I think I'm in love."

Trace ignored the geek. Stared at the walls covered with information. News clippings of the building burned down—half the walls missing, steel supports bending at unnatural angles, flames roaring against the black of night. . .There in full color was the tragic night they'd all lived with for the last five years. Hidden from.

An article clipping, printed off the Internet, showed the bodies of the eighteen children lined up and covered with white sheets that bore dark stains of the deaths.

God, help me.

Trace stepped back, as if he could put distance between that horrible night and the truth.

Despite every explicit order and command, Jessie had disobeyed. She'd been researching Misrata. His gaze hit the ceiling. Scrawled in big black marker: *I Want My Life Back!*

"Behind you," Boone said, from the other end of the crawl space.

Trace shifted around. A presentation board nailed to the wall. A Venn diagram. Names. Pictures. Yarn stretched out to the walls perpendicular to it, connecting locations on a map.

"What is it?" Annie asked from the other side of the wall. There hadn't been enough room for all of them, and Trace had no idea what they'd find, so he didn't want them in yet.

"Everything," Boone muttered. He whistled and shook his head. "She was a serious head case."

"As in she analyzed everything." If anyone could've solved what happened, it would've been Jessie. And she'd apparently been trying to do just that.

Pictures of the girls—*where* had she gotten those? He'd wiped everything off the Internet to insure they had a clean start in their new lives. But now, they stared back. Condemning. Accusing. Jessie. Candice. Keeley. Even Annie, Téya, and Nuala, though they were alive—their teammates were not. And lives were still in danger.

He had to get out of here. *Get out. Now.*

Trace bent and ducked through the cubbyhole. Annie was there, her expectant green gaze riveted to him. He could only shake his head as he moved to the Heller apartment. The air conditioner kicked on with an annoying buzz. He lowered himself to the cream vinyl sofa and perched on the edge, forearms on his knees.

Was this why they died? Had Jessie's curiosity, her insatiable tenacity—one of the very reasons he'd hand-picked her for Zulu—been what had gotten her killed? He couldn't imagine her doing all that research, searching all those names and locations, and not arousing attention.

How'd we miss this?

How had she hidden her trail? He had an entire team dedicated to monitoring electronic intel for any sign of her. They didn't know why he wanted her found. It'd been his way of making sure they all stayed off the grid. If they'd chatted, he would know. He made sure.

And now, now she was dead. Reyna was dead. And Shay. . .

Cool air swirled as someone joined him. He flinched as Annie perched next to him. She touched his arm softly. "You okay?"

"No, I'm not okay. Half the team is dead or dying." He gritted his teeth, steeled himself against her presence.

She sat for a few minutes without speaking. "Her data wall is pretty impressive."

"It's pretty stupid." Trace didn't intend to be mean, but— "Did she seriously think she could find what an entire branch of the Army couldn't?"

"I think. . .Jessie wanted vindication." Annie rubbed her knuckles, swaying gently. Nerves. She was nervous around him. "She had this theory"—her voice went soft—"about who was behind feeding us the bad intel—"

"We all had theor—"Trace snapped a look to Annie. "How do you know she had a theory? That she wanted vindication?"

Her fair complexion went crimson and she yanked her gaze away.

"Crap!" Anger pushed him to his feet. "You were in contact with her, too, weren't you?"

Annie stood. "Listen—"

"Do you people not understand the meaning of 'no contact'?" Have I spent the last five years of my career dodging bullets and ambushes by investigators for you six to sink the ground beneath my feet?"

Annie scowled. "This was *our* lives, Trace! We killed children. We lost everything we had and everyone we knew and loved. Do you have any idea what it's like to start over?"

"At least you had the chance to start over. You would've been behind bars for life or dead, if I—" His phone rang and he ripped it from his belt. Glanced at the caller ID. He turned away from Annie, more than ready to end that conversation. "Weston."

"Colonel, it's Baker."

Trace pivoted toward the hidden room. "What've you got?"

"You have military intelligence heading your way, Colonel. Might want to vacate. They just left here."

"How long?" Standing in front of the window, Trace eyed the street.

"Five mikes," Baker said even as three black vehicles slid around the corner.

Trace hung up. "Boone!"

"Yeah?" he called from inside, but the sound of crunching told him Boone was moving.

"Company!"

"What about all this. . .stuff?"

"Tear it down," Trace said, remembering the Styrofoam boards Jessie had mounted all her research to. "Take it with us."

"Uh," Houston whined. "I need at least fifteen minutes to get the systems packed and—"

"You have two," Trace warned, watching as the task force assembled by the vehicles. He turned to Annie and Nuala. "You're smaller. Get in there and pull that stuff down." He unholstered his weapon and moved to the window.

Boone stalked across the apartment to the kitchenette. There he dumped the trash on the floor and stalked back to the room with the can. He packed it with items from the space. "Move, move, move," Boone said. "We're eating time, people."

In the walls, Trace heard the grunts and clenched his teeth as the task force streamed up the sidewalk and into the building.

"They're inside," Trace called. "Out, now!"

Téya received three boards stacked. Annie crawled out, dragging a stack of boards that Nuala slid toward her.

"Window," Trace whispered, pointing to the one that looked out on the fire escape.

Nuala emerged with a stack of papers, and Boone all but pushed her out.

"Quiet, quiet," Trace hissed.

Even with the relative silence they operated under, they might as well have had a bullhorn. As Annie and Téya slipped out the window, Trace heard movement in the stairwell. He hurried to the door and peered through the peephole.

A tactical team swarmed up the stairs like a disturbed anthill. He bit back a curse.

He glanced over his shoulder and waved Nuala toward the window. Three down. Now Boone bent to pick up the bin—and Trace saw into 312. "Close the panel!" he hissed.

Hands full, Boone hesitated.

Trace threw himself around the big guy and eased the panel back into place. Even as the soft snap of the plywood resetting, he heard feet moving on the other side.

Boone muttered an oath.

Trace held out a hand, silencing him. Then gave him a questioning look.

"*Bible*," Boone mouthed.

Trace closed his eyes. The Bible had Boone's name in it. A clear connection to them. Trace waved him out, toward the window, giving him a signal not to worry about it.

"That's so strange," a woman's voice—the landlady!—filtered through the wall. "I never saw them leave. Oh, wait. Maybe you should check 313. They asked about her, and while I haven't seen Miss Heller in weeks, maybe she was there. They might be chatting."

This time the curse slipped free.

Boone gave him a wide-eyed look.

Trace waved him out. Backed up two steps. Gently pulled the closet door closed. Tugged the clothes back into place.

Houston was half out, dragging a box of computer stuff.

"Back," Trace gave a stiff whisper.

Confused and sweating, Houston frowned. "But—"

"*Back!*" Trace forced him back by pushing in after him, dragging a shoe box up to the corner with him as he did.

Behind him, Houston dropped something.

"*Quiet!*" For a second, Trace thought of killing the guy. He had a better chance of surviving without a green grunt like the geek. But that wasn't an option.

Several thuds against the door stiffened Trace's spine as he worked to tug the panel back into place. Only it wouldn't budge.

"How strange. Would you like to see inside? I'm really—this just doesn't make sense."

Had he made a mistake? Hiding in here? Would it have been quicker to escape out the window? Maybe by himself, but Houston never would've made it.

Trace tugged hard on the board. Over his shoulder, he nodded to the bulb hanging overhead. "Light!"

Darkness doused the crawl space.

Feet moved around on the other side of the wall. The panel came free. Trace clicked it into place even as beams of light probed the other side.

Trace drew back and aimed his weapon.

III

Francesca
Las Vegas, Nevada
6 May – 1500 Hours

He'd been here. Right here. In this room. Francesca Solomon stood with the FBI agents and their tactical team. Moving only her eyes, she took in the apartment. The clean but outdated kitchen with a small brass-and-glass table and two chairs. A pleather sofa. Goodwill-looking coffee table. The bed with no headboard and what looked like a Walmart quality bedspread. Simple, cost-efficient.

Sage. She could smell sage with a tinge of something musky. A man's cologne or that body wash stuff her brothers used.

"Ready?" Special Agent Baker asked, giving the room a visual sweep. "Unless they're hiding in the walls, I'm guessing you missed your man."

Frankie eyed the agent as she strode toward the closet, following the trail of body wash scent. A SWAT member was there but shifted out of her way. She stepped in, eyeing the ceiling, walls, and floor. The smell was stronger here. "Right here," she said.

"Come again?" Baker joined her, pressing his shoulder into her back to peer into the closet.

Annoyed and wanting to punch the cocky agent, she shoved backward. "He was here."

"Right," Baker said from behind. "I'm pretty sure we established that possibility."

"Not possibility. Fact." She envisioned herself sparring with this guy, taking him down the way she had her brothers. Dosing him with humility. "Mrs. Higginbotham identified the photo of him."

Baker shrugged, nodding. " 'Kay. He was here. Now he's not." He looked at Lopez. "And why are we still here?"

Assistant Special Agent in Charge Lopez lifted her chin. "We can set up surveillance on the building. If he comes back, we'll know."

"Surveillance." Frankie sighed, turned a circle. It wasn't like he could be hiding anywhere, but to have been so close... They must've just missed Weston by minutes. What did he come back for? Quite a risk. What evidence had he found, ripped out of their hands by mere seconds? "I'll surveil the building tonight. I'm not letting him get away a second time."

Trace

Paper-thin walls made it easy for Trace to hear. Why? Why'd it have to be Francesca Solomon? He wanted to lean against the wall but didn't trust the flimsy building material to not creak or pop, giving away his location. He owed Baker a steak for playing dumb about his location. For ribbing Solomon, making her tenacity seem foolish and ridiculous.

If she was going to watch the building. . .it'd only be one person. She couldn't cover all possible exits. That worked in their favor. What *didn't* work in their favor was waiting till nightfall. The team would have to hang out at the tarmac for his return.

Hold up. If the team went to the airport—he and Houston would have no way to get back to the airport. And they had the equipment. He wanted to curse. Trace pinched the bridge of his nose as they stood in the darkness, listening and waiting as Solomon and the FBI cleared out. Once he heard the door close, he pressed his watch. The timepiece lit up: 1515 hours. They'd have to wait till dark. Not just first dark, but late dark. Enough time for her to get bored. Believe there wasn't anything to monitor.

"They're—"

Trace clapped a hand over Houston's mouth. Using the illumination of his phone, Trace mouthed, "*We wait. Four hours.*" He wouldn't put it past her to be sitting on that sofa all night.

Houston's eyes bulged. "*Four?*" he mouthed back, clearly distressed at having to stand in the box of a closet for that long.

An hour into their wait, legs aching and air stale, Trace wondered if they could push their luck and sneak out now. Right. And have her standing there with her weapon trained on him? Victory in her brown eyes? *No, thanks.*

Creaking in the first apartment, 312, stiffened Trace's spine. He held up a finger to his mouth, warning Houston they had company. Solomon must've gotten anxious. Glock up, he aimed it at the wall.

Creak. Groan.

He trailed the noise. They were right in front of the access panel in 312.

A soft scraping barely made it to his ears. When the sound registered—the panel sliding back—Trace's pulse jack-hammered. He tensed, holding the weapon firm. *I'm not going down without a fight.*

Creak.

Pop!

Air flooded into the area. A face appeared.

Adrenaline exploded through his gut. His finger curled back just as the face registered. "Boone."

"C'mon," he whispered. "She's parked out front. Has been since the others left."

"How'd you get in?"

"Roof." Boone grinned and stepped back. They gathered the computer equipment, closed the hidden room panel, bent out of the closet into a darkened 312. Boone secured the hidden panel and put the table back before they slipped out the front door. *Walking right out the front door.* But instead of going down, they went up and onto the roof.

Boone scurried over to the far left and soared over a narrow alley between the two buildings onto the roof of the other. He turned and waved toward them.

Houston shook his head. In a hoarse whisper he said, "I can't throw this stuff."

Trace took it from him, shifted the contents, then turned to Boone. With as much care and deliberate direction as he could put into it, he tossed the box to his buddy. The box soared over the opening as Houston gasped. Something flung out and clattered against the tar roof, teetering on the edge. Boone caught the box, the contents jarring noisily, as he stomped a boot on what had flown out—a tablet that now dangled precariously beneath his large foot.

With a jump, Trace threw himself over to the other building then spun and snatched the tablet.

"Nice," Boone whispered then nodded to Houston, who looked as if the jump spanned a dozen feet instead of a few. Finally, the geek worked up his courage and lunged over. They all hurried to the fire escape and made it down the south side of the building.

Trace hopped to the ground. "Where's Solomon?"

With a nod, Boone said, "North side of the other building. We're safe."

Slinking along the shadows of the dense apartment buildings, Trace followed Boone out across the parking lot.

"Trace Weston!"

He didn't have to glance back to know it was Solomon. Trace shoved Houston forward. "Go!"

Boone grabbed the equipment and broke into an effortless sprint, Houston directly behind him. Trace lagged just enough to give himself time to provide cover, should they need it, but not enough to get left behind. They sprinted down the parking lot, weaving among cars and working their way to a rear alley, abutted by more buildings. They slipped down one darkened, smelly alley.

"Weston, stop!"

They dove around a building.

The black SUV roared up next to them. Boone dragged Houston into the vehicle, carrying the box as if it were a piece of paper. Trace hopped in after them, diving over bodies. They lurched into motion before the door shut. Giving him a perfect glimpse of Francesca Solomon as she broke out of the alley.

Annie

Lucketts, Virginia

7 May – 0900 Hours

Annie stuffed her plate and utensils in the dishwasher and closed it. She wiped down the long brown table that looked like something leftover from a church. But it worked for their needs. After washing her hands, she made her way to the command area. Utilizing a corner of the bunker on the raised portion plus a makeshift wall Boone had nailed together, Houston reassembled Jessie's data wall.

Leaning against the back of one of the computer stations, Trace folded his arms as he stared at the information.

Annie said nothing as she stood to his left, eyeing the chaos that had some sort of logic to it. All of Jessie's stuff did. But whether anyone else could make heads or tails out of it was another thing altogether. There were names, some with photos, others without. Images of buildings. Cars. Multipage articles.

One picture drew Annie to the board—a woman in her midtwenties. Taped together with what looked like a more recent picture. Beneath it read: KELLIE HOLLISTER/HOME. No wonder it'd drawn her attention. Kellie Hollister was one of the founders of Hope of Mercy, which had a branch in Misrata. HOMe–Misrata had been in that warehouse. The children they were protecting were the same ones Zulu had unwittingly killed in their first and only mission.

"What do you see?"

Trace's voice pulled her around, startling her. She'd forgotten he was there. Those green eyes still held strength that made her feel weak. In more ways than one.

Annie turned back to the data wall. "Chaos," she said. "She never gave up on finding who set us up. Unlike the rest of us."

"You gave up?"

Steeling herself, Annie cast a look over her shoulder at him. "Didn't you?"

"Not for a second." Resolute. Formidable. Trace Weston hadn't changed. He flicked his gaze to the wall again. "See anything interesting? Something that stands out?"

Annie let her gaze traipse over the accumulation of five years of Jessie's research and analysis. *Hollister. HOMe. Children. Misrata. Khalifa al-Zwawg. Ballenger.* There were so many, but none of it felt unique. "Not really. I mean—she has more depth to her research than any I could've come up with." Annie stuffed her hands in her back pockets and bunched her shoulders. "But what's important. What's not?" She shook her head then met his gaze again. "You? You said you haven't given up for a second. Is this familiar?"

"All too," Trace said, pushing to his feet. He came to the wall. Pointed to a name. "Hollister fell off the map after Misrata. After CID and DIA interviewed her, she vanished. I'd like to find her, hear her story myself. Ballenger—his wife and kid were killed that night."

Annie frowned. "Wife? I thought only orphans were there." She'd seen Ballenger's name on the list and on numerous news reports, but she didn't recall anyone being married or having a child there.

"We need to find him. Hear his story, too. We need to find them all. Start over. Fresh eyes. Fresh ears." Still handsome and still in charge.

And she still hated him. Annie took a step back. Reminded herself what he'd done.

Trace

Eighteen children, four women. All dead at the hands of a unit he trained. A unit he led. A mission he organized. General Haym Solomon had tasked Trace with putting together the all-female special ops team. Suggested it was time to make history. Trace had nearly killed the general point-blank after the failed mission, but Solomon had too much of his own fury over Misrata to have been guilty. Someone up the chain, someone neither of them knew, had entrapped those women. Set them up to take a massive fall. Sent them to the slaughter.

It'd been his fault—he led them into the trap. So, he led them out. Secured safe passage. Ferreted Zulu to safe ground. Got them new identities. New lives. Bought time for him to hunt the truth. He just never thought it'd take five years.

Five years and you still don't have answers.

And what he'd done to Annie. . . She still hadn't forgiven him, and he'd known back then she wouldn't. He'd accepted that. It was worth the price.

Trace's phone belted out a rock version of the national anthem. He answered the call. "Weston."

"Returning your call."

At the familiar voice, Trace excused himself and strode to the briefing room. "Yes, sir," he said as he sealed himself in the soundproof room. "Sir, we were in Las Vegas. Searching the apartment of Jessica Herring."

"Did you find anything?"

"Yes—some systems. . .and your daughter."

General Haym Solomon muttered something under his breath.

"Sir?"

"What does she know?"

"That I was there."

"She identified you?"

"Yes, sir."

The general sighed. "I'll handle it."

"I'd appreciate it, sir. She's in a position to create a lot of trouble for me and mine."

"I said I'll handle it. Now—what'd you get?"

Trace looked back to the data wall and struck gazes with Annie. Something inside him cinched. He shoved his gaze to the ground. "A puzzle, sir. It's going to take time to decipher."

"Do you think Kingston figured out anything?"

Trace scratched the side of his face, thinking about the yarn, the markers, the plethora of information. "No telling. She had a. . .unique mind."

"Keep me posted."

When the line went dead, Trace stared at the phone, the searing memory of his failure that night burning hot and cruel in his mind. He'd failed them. All of them—the team, Boone and Rusty, who'd helped train Zulu. And even Solomon.

Should've seen that trap coming. Should've given them thermals to verify the building was empty.

It should have been empty. They'd been there that morning. Saw nothing and no one.

And Zulu showed up that night to wipe out an illegal weapons cache that had been harvested from military "excess." The weapons should've been destroyed. Instead, they found their way into a warehouse in Misrata, Libya.

Now. . .now Zulu was depending on him again. This time to stop whoever was trying to kill them. In order to figure that out, he had to find the answers to a puzzle he hadn't been able to solve in five years.

Lieutenant Colonel, five years, and still no closer.

Might as well eat a bullet.

Francesca
Alexandria, Virginia
8 May – 1800 Hours

Wisdom and prosperity were supposed to go hand in hand with the Solomon name. So why was she struggling with both? Prosperity she'd readily trade for success in actually *catching—securing* Trace Weston. But wisdom would go a long way in taking him down.

Frankie sat in her crossover, thinking. Regretting that she'd failed yesterday. He'd been right there. Slipping through her fingers like water.

Movement at the front door of her father's home drew her attention. Frankie's heart jolted at the sight of her brother. She lunged out of the car and darted to the porch. Launched herself at Paolo with a laugh.

He caught her, crushing her to himself with those thick arms.

"What are you doing here?" she asked when he set her down.

"Had some meetings, had to liaise with the Brass."

Frankie held his shoulders, assessing. She saw something in his brown eyes that worried her. A heaviness. "You okay?"

He guided her into the house with a nod. "Fine."

She glanced over her shoulder. "Liar."

He grinned. "Okay. You tell me yours, I'll tell you mine."

Touché. They both knew they could not divulge information on missions or intelligence they were working on. "You always knew how to shut me up."

Chuckling, Paolo weaved his way through the ranch-style house to the back. "They're on the patio. Dad's grilling."

"When is he not?" Frankie glanced through the French doors and spotted her dad talking with—"Who's he with?"

The guy had a high and tight, broad chest, and deep tan. His left arm was cradled in a sling. He seemed to have an easy laugh and the rapt attention of her father.

Paolo leaned his shoulder against the door as he faced Frankie.

"Buddy of mine. Go easy on him."

"Easy?" Frankie frowned, noticing her brother's friend was pretty easy on the eyes. "I don't even know him."

Arching an eyebrow, Paolo opened the door. "Just remember what I said."

Curiosity tugged at her as they stepped into the cool evening, the thick smoke of the grill seeping out. Paolo's friend stood with a bottled water in one hand, his other stuffed in his jeans' pocket. His gray shirt accented his blue eyes and tanned complexion. Casual yet confident, he talked with her father, but his gaze strayed to Frankie. Took her in.

He met her gaze once more before he nodded, apparently in response to something her father said. "That's what I told the commander."

"Imagine that didn't go over too well." Her dad chuckled as he lifted the lid of the grill.

Smoke plumed out, chasing the oxygen up over the roof.

"No, sir." He smiled, and again he looked at Frankie.

Her stomach squirmed. She was used to attention. She got a lot of it, even in uniform. But it felt weird to get this in front of her brother and father.

Paolo punched his shoulder. "Brent." He leaned in and whispered something to his friend that made the guy pull up. Something, Frankie was sure, that had to do with killing off guys who stared at his little sister.

"Ah, Francesca," Daddy said as he turned and held out his arm to her. He never failed to put differences behind them. To show his unconditional love, even after they came close to ripping off each other's heads. She wished she could do that, but she had too much of her grandmother's fiery Italian temperament.

Frankie slipped in and hugged her dad. "What masterpiece are we having this time?"

"Steaks and shrimp." He planted a kiss on her temple. "You've met Paolo's buddy?"

She faced the man, feeling a bit of warmth as she met his blue eyes. "No," she said as he extended his hand. "I'm Frankie."

"Brent W—"

"Hey, heard you were in Vegas," Paolo said, shouldering into the greeting. "D'you win the jackpot?"

"Ha. Right. Like I had time to hit the casinos, or would want to." Frankie tucked some hair behind her ear.

"Work?" Daddy asked as he sipped a glass of sweet tea.

Frankie skirted a gaze around the three men, sensing a wave of tension lurking just beneath the surface. She wanted to share with them what happened. Nearly catching Trace. But she knew better. "Yeah." Instead, she shifted around, tucked a leg behind her, and eased into the oversized patio chair. "Where's Mom?"

"Resting," Daddy said as he started for the house. "I'm going to grab a few things."

Leaving her alone with Paolo and Brent. She squinted against the remains of the sun settling over the fence behind Paolo and Brent, who'd already fallen into a conversation. Great. Home with four people and yet. . .alone.

Frankie pushed out of the seat and went into the house. She squeezed between her dad and the cabinets to get a glass of ice water.

"Was Vegas about Weston?" Daddy asked, not looking at her, but working on assembling the shrimp onto skewers.

Glass almost at her lips, she hesitated. "Yeah."

"I take it you didn't get what you were after."

Frankie took a sip then rested her hip against the granite countertop, watching as his nimble fingers worked the food. "He was there, but I wasn't fast enough."

He shook his head, gave a soft snort, then lifted the tray of shrimp kebabs and started for the backyard without another word. Again, leaving her alone. She slumped back and thumped her heel against the cabinet. Why did he not care?

"Hey." Paolo entered, his dark hair shorn and his beard trimmed, but the intensity he'd always had remained in place. Especially right now. "What'd you do?"

Frankie rolled her eyes. "I didn't do anything."

"He's mad."

"Then he shouldn't have asked."

Wariness crept into her brother's eyes. "Asked what?"

"Why I was in Vegas."

Behind her, she heard the door but didn't dare look. Didn't want to face her dad's disapproval again.

"And why were you there?" Paolo had that tone, the one he'd taken as oldest kid. Folding his arms, he leaned in.

"He was there. Trace. I went to catch him. A girl was murdered—"

"Frankie."

"Don't do that to me, Paolo. I did my job, and that includes Trace—"

"*Frankie.*"

"No," she snapped, pulling straight. "I'm tired of you and Dad climbing down my throat. Trace Weston needs to be brought to justice, and I'm going to see that it happens."

"What if he's innocent?"

The unfamiliar voice pulled her around. She looked over her shoulder at Brent. He was handsome but didn't have a clue what he was talking about. "Oh, he's guilty. We have twenty-two bodies to prove that."

"*Francesca!*" Her brother's voice boomed at the same time Brent said something and stalked toward the front door.

It wasn't her brother's remonstration that shocked her. The three words that she heard—*thought* she heard from Brent—had stunned her. A door thudded, and Frankie felt bad for upsetting Paolo's friend. Though she wasn't sure how or why. What did he care?

Paolo stalked around the corner and scowled at her. She'd sworn as a ten-year-old that he killed her kitten with that look. Daddy said Duke had some disease, but she never believed him. "You're unbelievable."

"Did he just call me a coldhearted b—"

"You should be grateful that's all he did." Paolo ran a hand down the back of his neck.

"Why? What does he care about my case? He got all worked up—"

"He's Trace Weston's brother."

Boone
Reston, Virginia
9 May – 1100 Hours

The soft beeping and hissing of machines greeted Boone as he stepped into Keeley's room. She lay there, unchanged—well, maybe a little more wan than last time he was here, but nothing could make her look bad.

Rustling fabric drew him around. He stuffed out a hand to Rusty and gave a nod. "How you holding up?"

"Good," Rusty said, his voice low but not a whisper. He held up a book. "Keeping the brain busy." He raised his eyebrows toward the TV hanging in the opposite corner. "News, History Channel, and Military Channel fill in the gaps when things get too quiet."

"They have that up here?"

Rusty smirked. "Not hardly. I rig up my iPad to the TV and stream via my Wi-Fi." He lifted a shoulder in a shrug. "INSCOM's footing the bill since I'm tasked on guard."

"Smart man." Boone hauled in a deep breath and shifted his gaze to the woman who'd stolen his heart years ago. "When you come back to the bunker, you'll have to show us how to do that. All we get is soaps and the public access channel."

Rusty's expression faltered.

Boone tilted his head. "What?"

Rusty glanced down at the book. "I'm. . ." He squared his shoulders. "I'm not coming back." Bending the edges of the book together, he seemed sheepish. A description Boone never would have connected to Rusty. "I told Trace I can't do this. Not again."

"But the girls—the team. We need you." Boone surveilled the hall beyond the windows as he talked. "They're in real danger. Someone's hunting them. We need your help—"

"No." Rusty lowered his head. "I did it once, Boone. But after what happened, after those kids. . ." He gave two long swags of his head. "I just can't go there again."

Boone wanted to wrap his fingers around the guy's neck and squeeze till he saw straight. Saw right. "You're bailing on them."

Rusty met his gaze evenly. "I gave my notice. You don't have to worry—I'm here. I'll watch over Keeley. But after she's gone"—when Boone reacted, Rusty held up a hand—"*discharged*, I meant. When she's discharged, I'm out."

"Never saw you for chicken." Boone couldn't keep the snarl or the anger from his voice.

"Honestly," Rusty said, his blue eyes sparked with determination, "me either. Misrata changed things. . .changed me. Decision's been made."

Did he need to remind the guy he'd signed up to be the handler for two of the girls? It hit Boone then—Candice had been Rusty's "student." He'd trained her, mentored her, just as Boone had trained and mentored Jessie and Nuala. As Trace had done with Téya and Annie. "Did it get personal for you and one of the girls?"

Rusty snorted. "Intensely—we lived and breathed war with them for the six months they were Zulu. Since then, I've lived, breathed, dreamed, eaten that tragedy. It's with me everywhere I turn. Every snooze I take." He scratched the side of his face. "I'm not looking to add ammo to the nightmares, y'know?"

Boone knew. He knew very well. But leaving the team. . .abandoning them in their time of need. . .it just seemed wrong.

"Don't give me that look," Rusty said.

Boone held up his hands. "Hey. Your call."

"But you think it's wrong."

"You don't want or need me to answer that." Boone grunted. "Do what you have to, but thank you for holding out till Keeley is better. I can focus on the team, on figuring out what's happening, knowing you're here with her."

"Did it get personal, Boone-Dawg?"

He smirked at Rusty for throwing the question back at him. After giving him a backhanded swat on the shoulder, Boone said, "Get some rest."

Alone with his thoughts and Keeley, Boone moved the chair to the side of the bed. Pressing his knuckles against the mattress, he leaned in and pressed a kiss to her forehead. "Hey, beautiful. You can come back to me any day now, ya hear?"

He settled into the chair, lifted the book from where he'd tucked it into the small of his back beneath his belt and jeans, and started reading—but not before double-checking that nobody was listening. If this got back to Trace...

Boone cleared his throat and flipped to chapter five. "'In the course of time, Mr. Earnshaw began to fail. He had been active and healthy....'" Boone shot a furtive glance to the windows then to Keeley. "Can we skip the death and failing stuff?"

Probably not. Keeley was fastidious. Attentive to detail. Just as Jessie had been with that crazy data wall. Had Jess figured out anything? He sure hadn't, and that was the burr under his saddle. Someone had found the girls despite meticulous, laborious efforts to hide them. And he and Trace weren't any closer to figuring out who was behind it all.

"'...he grew grievously irritable. A nothing vexed him. ...'" Boone grunted. "You and me both, Earnshaw."

Arlington National Cemetery
Arlington County, Virginia
10 May – 0615 Hours

Sunlight stretched over the rows of headstones, caressing the arched tops with loving warmth as it reached for the two men on the road that wrapped through the countless rows of heroes' headstones.

"The world is a different place. Our country is a different place today than when I signed up forty years ago, Haym." Wistful and soft, the voice of the four-star general settled quietly amid the thick dew covering the field of green.

Haym Solomon nodded. "Changes every day." His gaze trailed a sleek black sedan gliding along a road, slowly. Solemnly. As it should be. "But one thing remains the same."

The four-star grunted. "The hearts of the warriors willing to defend this great country."

Hands folded behind his back in a sign of respect and, in a way, submission.

"We chose this as our meeting ground for a reason." The man glanced to his right and met Haym's gaze. "Remember?"

"I do."

Chest drawn up, the four-star let out a long breath. "So we never forget that we are dealing with lives. With heroes' lives. So that we remember every time we consider sending them out, they might not return to the homes that sent them off." He gave a nod to the fields that dignified the lives of those who'd made the ultimate sacrifice. "They could end up here."

Somber and depressing. Frustrating. Would that he could put a defensive shield around each warrior who stepped into harm's way so those back home didn't have to. Protect those willing to take a bullet for those too cowardly to even acknowledge the enemy.

"But I take it you're not here because you wanted a philosophy lesson." The four-star stabbed a finger toward the Lincoln Town Car waiting at the end of the lane and started walking.

A subtle but powerful way to say Haym had only a few minutes. Time to dispense with the pleasantries. "It's happening—they found them."

"We knew it was only a matter of time."

"I'd hoped for more time."

Laughter bellowed across the serene setting, almost upsetting the mood. "Don't we all." He pointed to the white headstones engraved with rank, name, birth date, and date of death. On the back, perhaps what branch the hero served. What combat theaters they'd seen. "I'm sure every one of these men and women would've asked for more time."

"I have two more bodies to bury."

Gray-white eyebrows, thick and springing up over the rim of the four-star's glasses, raised. "And the person responsible?"

"Still out there."

They reached the car as the driver stepped out and opened the door. "Time for containment, Haym."

"Yes, sir. We'll need—"

"You have whatever you need. Just keep me updated and get this resolved. It's been hanging over your head long enough."

"Thank you, sir." Haym hesitated. Debated the words sitting on his tongue.

"Well, go on. I've got to get to work."

"Sir, respectfully—"

"Bah. Don't start with that crap. Just give it to me."

"Sir." Haym mustered the dregs of his courage. "If they found them, then—"

"I see." With one leg in the car and his hands resting on the top of the door frame, the four-star squinted toward the rising sun. "We have a problem." He clicked his tongue. "I promise you, whoever or however this happened, they will not be able to betray anyone again."

Téya
Lucketts, Virginia
10 May – 0830 Hours

Scooting back and resting against the cement wall, feet up on the edge of the bunk, Téya savored the time alone. Grateful there were enough bunk rooms that they could each have some privacy, and yet. . . If Candice and Jessie had lived. . .well, they'd have to cozy up. Which she'd gladly do if it meant bringing them back.

But that was just it. They couldn't come back. A heavy darkness hovered over them now, the threat of death a constant. But the threat to their loved ones proved oppressive. She could handle getting shot at. *She* signed up for that. But *Grossmammi* and David. . .

She unfolded the piece of paper and stared at the picture of David in the hospital. Leg elevated and IVs digging into his arm, he looked. . .awful. In pain. His smile was gone. The lightheartedness that had always drawn her to the man, nowhere to be found.

What have I done?

Closing her eyes, she rested her head against the wall. Tried to remember the good times. The time of the quiet life that was by no means easy but had a simplicity to it that drew her in like a heat-seeking missile.

She snorted at the comparison. Thinking about Amish living and she uses a violent analogy.

The mattress shifted under a weight, snapping Téya's eyes open. "What. . .?"

Annie sat at her feet and tugged the paper so she could see it. "Stole it, huh?"

Téya lifted the picture. "Copied, actually." She shrugged. "They took him away from me, so this is my recompense."

Annie's brows flickered, as if in question or concern.

But Téya wasn't up to discussion. Folding the paper, she slid to the edge, next to Annie. "They find anything?"

"Hey." Annie's voice grew firmer. "You do know you're not the only one who lost their new life, right?"

"Did your boyfriend get shot and beat to a pulp?"

Annie eyed her, blue eyes twinkling. "No, Sam would've put his SEAL skills to work and taken them down."

"Yeah?" Téya pushed to her feet and stuffed the picture in the back pocket of her jeans. "Well, David's a sweet, hardworking farmer. He didn't deserve what they did to him."

Annie stood. Touched her arm. "None of us deserved what they did." Determination hardened the lines around her lips. "Our job is to make sure it doesn't happen again."

"And how do we do that if we don't even know who we're after?"

"We keep looking."

Téya didn't know whether to nod or shake her head. Instead, she pushed past her friend and combat buddy. "I need some fresh air."

"Remember, stay out of sight," Annie called.

"Thanks, Mom." Téya flinched at her own sarcasm, but she wasn't in kindergarten. This wasn't her first rodeo, to use a cliché. She'd been through combat. She'd been in war. She didn't need Annie smothering her with rules, remonstrations, and chiding. In fact, she didn't need or want that from anyone.

She slipped through the narrow passage and climbed the stairs.

"Téya." Boone's voice reverberated off the steel. "Where you going?"

"Topside."

"Stay out of sight."

"No, I thought I'd go dance in the middle of the road." Téya grunted as she pushed her way outside. A cool breeze wafted across the rolling hills. She took in a deep, steadying breath. And let it out, savoring the country smell. *So much like Bleak Pond.* The cows, the pastures, the sloping landscape. . .

She heard the door creak open behind her and knew she'd been followed. Téya stalked toward the barn, desperate for some solitude. The realization struck her funny. Growing up and even when she first joined the Army, she'd thrived on the camaraderie. Craved companionship. Had the five years in Bleak Pond quieted something in her?

Dimness embraced her as she stepped onto the soft bed of hay. She blinked, adjusting to the reduced amount of light. To her left, she spotted a ladder nailed to the wall and leading to a loft. Perfect. She climbed up and walked to the farthest corner. Through the slats she could see Boone standing in the doorway. *Please. . .just go away.*

It took awhile, but he finally did. And Téya savored the solitude. Tried to quiet the churning within. The grief that she caused David to get hurt. Would he ever forgive her?

You're a soldier! He'll get over it.

But she hadn't asked for this life back. She'd wanted Bleak Pond. Wanted the slower pace, the. . .innocence.

Though she spent hours in the loft, Téya didn't find the peace of mind she sought. Only one way to find that: talk to David.

Climbing down, she scoffed at her own thoughts. Right. Going back to David? He'd never speak to her again.

Maybe if she explained things. . .begged his forgiveness. . .

But then she'd have to come back here. At least until those responsible were found. Which could be years.

No, she couldn't wait that long. She had to talk to David. Explain things to him. Then he'd accept her back. Forgive her for leaving him. That could take months. Would he understand? If she was completely honest. . .would he be that forbearing?

Téya weaved between the vehicles parked inside the barn. . .and slowed. She glanced at the older model truck. Maybe. . .maybe she didn't have to wait after all.

Unknown Location
10 May – 0900 Hours

They hid. And they hid well. But he was better. Nothing like a game of wits when the odds are so evenly stacked. Annoyance cluttered his mind and his ability to function like a rational being. He glanced at the Patek Phillippe on his wrist and grunted. Already the tenth of May. Crowding the schedule a bit with three of them still alive. One mostly alive. That would be remedied.

He lifted the brandy snifter and crossed the penthouse, staring out over the city through the wall of glass. Sipping, he took in the heady aroma of the brandy, the smell of oak and caramel. With that not-so-subtle fire that spreads through the stomach. He also took in the progress.

Correction: lack of progress.

At least he was doing better than Solomon or his lackey, Weston. The two had been chasing their tails since Misrata. He chuckled. A shame, that. Though he'd give them an A for effort. They had failed. Miserably.

That suited him fine. But really, he'd expected more. More fight. More drama. More pressure. Instead, he'd worked channels and connections, recruited hackers, bribed underpaid government workers, and gotten exactly the information he wanted. Needed. The names of the team members who'd come to shut him down.

Imagine his surprise when the names turned out to be all women.

Who does that? Who sends women in to kill children?

He sniggered. Not that they realized they were killing children, but weren't women supposed to have some maternal instinct to *protect* the little menaces?

But he'd had enough. Enough of their ignorance. Once he'd gathered the final name, he'd struck. It wouldn't have done to hit them as they were discovered. The dopes wouldn't have put the puzzle together, that they were targeted. It would've seemed random.

Had it looked as such, they wouldn't be hunting him. And where was the fun in that?

Now, things had heated up. *The game, as Sherlock liked to say, is afoot.*

Most essential when targeting your enemy is to *know* your enemy. And he did. Boy did he ever know his enemy. More than they'd ever realize—and when they made the discovery, they'd be ashamed.

He turned and walked to the guest room. Scanned the walls. In other rooms hung paintings by Delacroix, Runge—and his favorite, a Regency and Medieval painter: Leighton. But here, in the second guest room hung prints by. . .the copier. Fax machine. U.S. government. Images of the women who'd destroyed what should have been a lucrative venture. Women on whose hands he'd painted the blood of innocent children. Women who would die in due course.

Four left now. One was an easy fix. A wrong concoction in her IV and bye-bye Miss American Pie. But the others. . .they were alert to his mission. Wary of contact. Except Téya Reiker. He nursed another sip of the brandy, savoring the fire as he peered into the one-dimensional green eyes. A beauty—not as pretty as Annie, but her beauty wasn't skin deep—it was her heart. The fire in her, much like the one sliding through his belly from the liquor. Téya. Yes, she would be next, he was sure of it.

The gray phone rang, drawing him from the thoughts of revenge and retaliation. It sat on the table amid a myriad of papers, the virtual imprint left behind by the ladies. That phone wasn't a social call. It was a *promising* call.

Finally.

He set down the snifter and lifted the phone. "Good news, I hope."

"You were right. She's here."

"See? This is why women shouldn't be in the military or on the front lines. They can't disengage their hearts." Lighthearted laughter tugged at his heart—it was too easy. Far too easy. They didn't have a prayer. "You know what to do."

Téya
Lancaster, Pennsylvania
10 May – 1400 Hours

He'd been out cold since she entered his room. Téya did something she'd have never done in Bleak Pond—she held his hand. Strong, calloused hands that were no stranger to hard work. In a way, they'd both been outcasts among the community. David with his license and car. She with her past.

"I wish I could have told you," she whispered. Tears blurred her vision as she thought of how that might have gone down, telling him she had been a soldier, that she'd belonged to an elite team of female soldiers who were the first to take a SOCOM assignment. A team with incredible talent.

The door clicked open. Téya set David's hand down and slipped her hands to her side as she met the gaze of the nurse.

"Are you family?" the nurse asked, moving to the IV tower, checking the levels, then recording them.

"Yes," Téya lied—though it wasn't a whole lie. David said they would get married. She was his fiancée, of sorts. Besides, she knew the nurse wouldn't talk to her otherwise. She glanced at David, his wavy black hair framing his handsome face. "He's sleeping. Is that common with a leg injury?"

"There are his ribs, of course," the nurse said as she used a stylus to enter his vitals. "But it's his lung that's giving him fits. We upped his pain meds so he could rest. He hasn't slept much since being admitted."

"Lung?"

The nurse nodded, frowning.

Right. Téya should've known about the lung—whatever it was. "Sorry. I just thought he was improving."

The nurse tidied his blanket as she bobbed her head toward the leg in traction. "His leg is doing better than expected." With a smile, she lifted her tablet. "I'll leave you now."

As she watched the door swing shut, Téya's fingers found David's. She lowered herself to the plastic chair beside the bed, her forearms stretched over the gray blanket as she lifted his hand to her cheek. "You're the best man I've ever known. . . ." And yet, she still had doubts that even with all his firm beliefs in God and the Bible that he could forgive what she'd done. He'd overlook her leaving him, probably, but killing children?

Grief-stricken, she pressed his hand to her forehead. *I want it back. All of it. Innocence. My life with you. . .*

The tougher side of her, the side that had seen war, fought terrorists, told her to gut it up. Voices outside snagged her attention. She spotted David's brother coming down the hall. On her feet, Téya squeezed David's hand one last time. "I *will* be back."

With that, she ducked out of the room and headed to the left, sliding on a baseball cap. Three lefts landed her at the elevator. She pushed the button, ear trained on the conversation down the hall.

"Family?"

Téya's pulse jammed at the words David's brother spoke.

"I'm the only family here right now."

"I'm sorry. The young woman said she was family."

The doors hissed open and Téya lunged at the escape. Inside, she pressed the LL button and then hit CLOSE. It wasn't closing. She hit it again as another woman stepped in, punching the basement button.

As the doors closed, a man rushed into the steel trap. At least it wasn't David's brother. She jabbed the button again. Just as the two steel panels severed her view, she noted a blur of dark clothing. *That* was David's brother.

With a quiet expel of breath, she felt something. . .strange. Wrong. Heat spilled down her neck. The man who joined her. She glanced back at him. "What floor?"

Dark eyes flicked to hers. "Lobby. Thanks."

Right. Same floor. He had dark eyes, but the nonchalance in his expression. . .it seemed forced. Or fake. Something.

Feeling that tingling sensation of danger prickling the back of her neck smacked Téya with a heady dose of realization. *You are really stupid.* Running from Trace and Boone, the two men most able and willing to protect her sorry self.

When the doors slid open, Téya pressed the button to hold them open and smiled at the man. "Go ahead."

After a curt nod, he exited and banked left.

She waited a few seconds then stepped into the lobby. A quick glance to her left revealed him standing at the information desk, talking to one of the volunteers. Téya quickly went right and ducked out the side door. With a determined step, she made her way toward the truck she'd hot-wired. Breathing came a little easier as she put one more parking row behind her. More distance between her and the hospital. She used the reflective surfaces of vehicles to verify she was alone. She turned toward the truck and—

Crunch.

A weight clamped onto her shoulder.

Téya swung around, hooking her left arm over his, making it impossible for him to get away as she hauled the heel of her right hand into the side of his neck. He stumbled, disoriented. Unwilling to give him a second to regain his balance and determination, she laced her fingers around his neck and yanked him toward her, pinning him as she thrust her knee into his groin.

With a hard shove, she sent him stumbling backward, giving herself an escape. Sprinted toward her truck.

A shot cracked the quiet day. Sparks flew off the truck. Téya ducked. She knew hot-wiring the truck would give the guy too much time to take her out. She had to do it first—neutralize the target.

Weight plowed into her. Shoved her into the window frame of the door.

Pain exploded along her cheekbone. The man threw her around, slamming her spine against the truck. His forearm jammed her throat, he brought up a weapon.

Despite her instinct to protect her throat, she stabbed her flattened hand into his side.

He curled in on the spot, responding to the pain and moving his arm.

Knowing he'd correct his mistake quickly, she used his momentary disorientation against him. She drove a hard right hook into his temple.

But he caught it. Blocked and threw an undercut into her stomach.

Shouts echoed in the distance, but no way she'd look away from this guy. He meant to kill her. She wasn't going to become a body in a morgue. Not like Jessie and Candice.

The thoughts vaulted adrenaline through her veins.

With a growl, she curled her hand into a fist, forefinger knuckle aimed out. She drove it hard into the spot just below where his ribs met. She hit him again. And again. Determined to nail his solar plexus.

He punched her head, knocking her sideways.

Recovered, Téya threw a jab for a liver shot.

The man crumpled with a hideous groan.

Téya threw herself into the truck. Hot-wired it. Slammed it into gear and punched it forward. The door flapped open. She reached for it. Red-hot pain exploded through her side. Struggling against the fire in her side, she tugged the door shut. Shoe against the gas pedal. Pealed through the parking lot. Vaulted onto the street. She narrowly slid through a yellow light. Gunned it for the highway. Had to get back. . .

She hissed as her hand clamped over the side where sticky warmth oozed out.

Trace is going to kill me.

Annie
Lucketts, Virginia
10 May – 1800 Hours

"Any word on Téya?"

"Negative," Boone said as he studied printouts Houston created from the data wall they'd taken from Jessie's apartment.

Annie stood over him, hands braced on her hips. "Aren't we doing anything to find her?"

"Like what?" Boone flipped a page, his gaze never leaving the information. When she didn't reply, he finally looked up. Set aside the stapled stack and leaned back, holding his hands out to the side. "She wants to flee, then she flees. I can't stop her, nor can I predict where she's going."

"I can." Annie crossed over to the dais and tapped a picture.

Boone shook his head. "She wouldn't be stupid enough to go there."

"It's not about *stupidity*," Annie said, folding her arms. "It's about her need to protect someone she cares about."

Boone nodded to Houston, apparently relaying a silent signal or message because the guy's fingers flew over the keyboard.

"You protect them by staying away." Trace entered the room, looking like a swift-moving storm. "That's how you show your concern for them."

Annie's heart thumped a little harder. "Is that how it works?"

Trace gave her a look, one she knew all too well. One she'd always hated. "See, to *normal* people, you show your love and concern by being there, by supporting them through the bad times, by doing everything you can to make sure they aren't harmed."

"It'd be nice to live in a normal world," Trace said, "but we are immersed in one of conflict and combat. You signed on the dotted line, or have you forgotten?"

Blast the man! "Yes, I did. Téya did. But Sam and David didn't!"

"Sam?" Trace's expression cut through Annie's defenses. "Is there something we need to know?"

"You need to know that while we might be soldiers, we're also women. We fight hard and we don't give up, but we also don't abandon those we love."

"Are you in communication with Sam?"

Annie closed her eyes and snorted. "This has nothing to do with Sam. This is me explaining that Téya had good reason to go to David."

"No," Trace said, stalking away. "No reason is good enough to draw more attention and harm to an innocent civilian. And if she's there, that's what she's done." His expression went dark. "How do you think she'll live with it if, by visiting him, she gets him killed?"

Annie knew in a black-and-white world like the one Trace and Boone lived in, that hypothetical question made sense. But why couldn't he see or understand what it was like from their perspective? "Our entire lives were upended. Ripped from us. Again."

He gave a curt nod. "Noted. But you want to keep living. You want those you love and care about to keep living, right?"

Annie studied the floor, wishing—just for once—Trace would get it. That he'd understand where they were coming from. "We're not wired like you."

"Look," he said, coming closer. "I get it. I know what you're thinking. Probably what you're feeling, but if you're going to make it, if you're going to survive this very personal attack against you three, then you have to stop thinking with your heart. You have to think strategy."

When she looked up at the board, she saw Sam's name. Wondered what he'd say. Probably exactly what Trace said.

"Annie," he said, his voice low and close. "We aren't trying to cow you into this. We're trying to solve the puzzle, stop this from becoming a massacre."

She bobbed her head, covering her mouth. "I know," she whispered, feeling raw. "It's just—"

"Got her!" Houston's proclamation severed the conversation. "Oh, crap."

Just like that, Trace was all business. "What? What've you got?"

"She's in trouble…oh man." Houston clicked a few buttons, and what he found splashed on the full-wall screen.

Grainy footage, a bit hard to take in with the size covering the whole back side of the dais. Téya running across a parking lot. Getting into a scrap with a man. Getting free and hopping in the truck.

"She got away," Annie said, an acute sense of relief rushing through her body.

"Not quite," Houston said. "Traffic cams. Look."

The footage showed Téya in the blue and silver Ford truck cruising along the highway. Then a black sedan racing up behind her.

"When was that?" Trace demanded.

"Right now. Traffic cams are live," Houston said.

"I want you to erase whatever trail of hers can be found. There can be no record of Téya being there. Got it?"

Houston bobbed his head, his golden-brown nest of curls wagging beneath the fluorescents. "Yep. Got it."

Hurrying toward the door, Trace called, "Feed that to my phone." Then he looked toward his buddy. "Boone."

"Right behind you."

Annie started for the door to join them.

"No." Trace stopped at the door, accessing the security panel. "Stay here." He barked that at her as if she were a dog. Trace met her gaze. "Do we hand them two Zulu members?"

Why did he always have to make sense? And why did he always know what she was thinking?

Before she could respond, give him a piece of her mind, he was out the door.

"Things haven't changed much between you two, have they?" Boone quipped.

"I've changed plenty," Annie bit back. "It's him, stuck in his ways, who hasn't changed."

Boone chuckled. "Men rarely do." And he was gone.

Boone

In his Raptor, Boone barreled out of Virginia and headed north. It only took ten minutes to catch up with Trace. Using his Bluetooth, he called him.

"Houston has them passing York now," Trace said without introduction. "You have eyes on them yet?"

"Not yet. Then again, some of those areas are right through towns and roundabouts, so speed is limited. We should intercept them around Gettysburg."

"Tire spikes."

"Too much traffic. Do a PIT maneuver."

Boone nodded to himself. "Copy that."

"I'll do the PIT. You get Téya."

The hour drive to Gettysburg did nothing but ramp up Boone's nerves. He verified with Houston that, thanks to traffic and small-town congestion, Téya and her troublemaker were still north of him and Trace. He took an overpass and waited on the southbound on-ramp behind Trace.

"Okay, guys," Houston said in a distracted voice, no doubt watching the satellite feed. "They're about two minutes out."

Trace's car pulled back onto the road, and Boone followed suit. They took up a lazy speed, watching their rearview mirrors.

A few seconds after they'd merged into the light traffic, Boone saw his dad's old pickup barreling for all it was worth down 30. Right behind it, a dark sedan. Nerves thrumming, he waited. Waited. . .as the old Ford grew closer.

"Trace," Boone said, watching the rearview and noting the swirl of blue and red. "They've got company."

"Copy. I'll handle him if needed," Trace said. "Just get her home."

Grinning, Boone said, "Roger that."

Téya roared past them just then. Not two seconds later, the black sedan. Immediately, Trace interjected himself and Boone followed. The *whorp-whorp* of the sirens told them the cop wasn't happy. But it was for his own good. Boone slowed, pulling even with a red Prius chugging along in the right-hand lane, effectively blocking them. He toed his brake, watching Trace make his move.

Trace pulled his vehicle alongside the black sedan so that his front wheels were aligned with the rear of the guy's car. Gently, he made contact. Then a sharp turn into the guy's car.

The black sedan's tires lost traction. Started to skid.

Trace eased his vehicle to the right, continuing in the direction he'd taken for the pursuit intervention technique.

Swerving around the black sedan, Boone watched it overcorrect. "Idiot."

The car went airborne. Flipped once. . .twice. . three times like a freaking gymnast. It slammed with a sickening crunch-thud into a cement construction barrier. The cruiser angled toward the accident, no doubt a higher duty to check for injuries.

With the way the car wrapped around that cement, the cop would need a body bag. Boone accelerated and pulled in behind Téya, flashing his lights. "We're clear, but the cop probably got my license."

Téya's vehicle swerved. She corrected. A few seconds later, she was veering off again.

"I'm on the access road. I'll be behind you in five. Just make sure she gets home."

"Roger that. . .I think something's wrong with Téya." Boone scowled as her car almost left the road. He revved the engine and pulled alongside her. He glanced over into the truck and saw blood smeared over her face. Alarm shot through him. Motioning for her to pull over, he relayed the information to Trace.

"I'm coming up on you now."

Boone followed Téya off the highway and onto a service road. She smartly pulled onto a dusty, rural road before stopping. He rammed his truck into PARK and flung himself out of the truck.

At her door, he yanked it open.

Téya grimaced at him, holding her side.

"What happened?"

"He shot me," she said, her words thick. "At the hospital."

"That was two hours ago!"

"*Cha-ching!* The man can count," she said, a sheen covering her face. "It's not bad, but it hurts."

Trace joined them.

Téya flinched at the sight of Trace. "Here to bawl me out?"

"You don't know the half of it," Trace said before tapping Boone's shoulder. "Pack the wound and let's get moving. It's getting dark, so we have less chance of being seen. Stick to the speed limit."

Boone retrieved a first aid kit from his truck and pressed gauze into Téya's wound before helping her out of the truck. Arm hooked over his shoulder, she stumbled back to his vehicle. Dusk bathed them in an amber glow as they pulled back onto the service road, then the highway, and headed south toward Virginia.

"He was there," Téya said. "Right there, waiting for me."

Boone nodded, hearing what she wasn't saying. They knew enough about her to know where to hit. To predict her moves. "Now you know why Trace said to stay at the bunker."

"Just had to see him."

"Was that visual confirmation worth almost dying for?" Boone hated to be tough on her, but she needed to wake up. "Or getting him killed?"

Tears slipped down Téya's cheeks.

Trace
Fort Belvoir, Virginia
11 May – 1340 Hours

"I'm not surprised you called."

Trace settled into the seat at the white-draped table, shifting his gaze around the high-class restaurant. "They are right on us. I need help to stop this. To end it."

General Haym Solomon nodded as the waiter delivered a glass of water then took his order. "And he'll have the same."

Trace wasn't hungry, but there was no use arguing with the general. "Sir—"

"Relax, relax. You'll ruin your digestion."

"It's already ruined. They nearly killed Two."

Haym scowled. "I thought you had Two."

He'd stepped right into that. "She's struggling with the situation. She was very close to an Amish farmer who almost died because of her."

"Aren't they all farmers?"

Shoulders deflating, Trace huffed. Why wasn't the general taking this seriously? "Sir, I'm not sure you understand."

Haym's expression hardened. "I understand far more than you can imagine, Colonel."

Put in his place, Trace lowered his head and chose his next course of conversation. How to impress upon the general that this had to end. They needed a break. More assets. More intelligence behind this.

"You think you're the only one working on Misrata, but you're not. I've got plenty to lose in this deadly game, and trust me," he said, his breath coming in heaves, "we all want the dirtbag behind this brought down. You don't need another conversation with my daughter to remind you of what this has cost me, do you?"

Trace gave a half shake of his head, frustrated.

"Before you get all morose, I need you to know two things."

Trace met the man's bushy-eyed gaze.

"First, I've canceled the task force."

Jerked upright by that piece of news, Trace scowled. "You wha—?"

"On the heels of that, I've put together a cover team. Each member handpicked. Each person I know personally." Giddy victory soared through the general's face and tone.

Unsure whether it was a good thing or bad thing, Trace nodded. "But why. . .why would you cut the original team? They have knowledge—"

"They'd grown blind to it. Stale." He waved a hand. "Nothing worse than stale meat or vegetables." Again, he seemed very pleased and amused with himself. "They had been staring at the data for so long, they weren't seeing it."

"I can relate." Trace roughed a hand over his face.

"It's time to kick things up a notch."

"Beyond time." Something about the way the general said that registered with Trace. He tilted his head to the side. "Wait—what do you mean?"

A man joined them at the table, sliding into the seat across from him. Vague recognition flickered through Trace's mind as he met the man's brown eyes. He frowned, studying the man. Waiting for someone to explain what was going on. He certainly wouldn't continue this discussion in front of—

"You remember my son, Paolo."

Tension coiled in Trace's gut. He tightened his lips. "Sir, I—"

"Paolo's on the new task force."

Bouncing his gaze between the two, Trace tried to pull his brain out of the vat of oil that had just fried it. "Sir?" Trace eyed the guy who had to be close to his own thirty-seven years. With his father's Italian blood and the Solomon strong features, the guy could hit the cover of *GQ* and never lack for attention or money again. "Aren't you—isn't he a SEAL?" Though he wasn't wearing his tactical gear and sweating like a horse, he was the same guy Trace had worked an op with years back, wasn't he?

Paolo sat comfortably in the chair, his button-down shirt crisply pressed and starchy white against his deeply tanned skin. "I am."

"You're enjoying this," Trace said, a growl in his words, but he didn't care. "Sir, with all due respect—"

"Which means with none."

Trace huffed. "Sir, I've lost two members of the team. One more is in critical condition, and their attackers almost took out a fourth. This is not a game. Their lives are not pawns on a board."

General Solomon leaned forward. "Aren't they, though? Someone is eliminating them one by one." Ferocity laced his words. "For what reason?"

"The end game," Paolo put in. "Something has changed recently that made this person go after your team."

Trace considered the man who voiced a thought he'd had many times. "Or, he finally figured out where the last one was."

"C'mon, that's as unlikely as—"

"A SEAL helping a Green Beret?"

Paolo grinned. "We're on the same side, ultimately."

"Are we?"

"Whoever is hitting your team," Paolo said, his voice quiet, his gaze focused, "is hitting them now because their existence jeopardizes something important to this individual."

Trace raised his hands. "Okay, fine. Assuming you're right, how are we supposed to find that out?"

"I'm already making headway. I have access to files and situations neither of you do."

"Why? Because we're Army?"

"No, because you're immersed in the mess. You're being watched." Paolo's gaze slid past Trace and locked onto something. "Trace, I want you to get up right now and walk to the back of the restaurant. Find an exit. Do not look back."

Trust. This is where it came down to trust. He'd trusted him seven years ago on that operation in Kandahar.

"My sister just walked in."

Trace
Fort Belvoir, Virginia
11 May – 1445 Hours

Had they set him up?

Trace's nerves vibrated as he slid into his dark gray Dodge Charger and started it. He pulled out of the parking lot and headed back up toward Reston. He'd hit Route 7 and narrowly avoid rush hour. Either way, there'd be traffic. And lights. Lots of lights. But he was too much a miser to take the tollway. He hated the congestion of the Beltway, but once he hit the Dulles toll road, he'd get home faster. He'd talk to Boone.

Traffic on the Beltway slowed as cars exited for Route 7. Trace shifted over a lane and accelerated. As he did, he noticed a small hybrid darting in and out of traffic. Gaining on him.

Right. A puny car against his Charger? What was the point?

He sped up and hit the far left lane, occasionally monitoring the hybrid as they sailed through Sterling, Ashburn, and Leesburg. When they hit 15 North, traffic slowed to a crawl as the major routes converged outside the outlet mall. Trace glided into the far left lane.

A dozen or more cars back, the Prius did the same.

Just as quick, he dove into the far right, taking the exit ramp for Business 7. Swung up and around then made his way through the quaint and congested downtown Leesburg, hating the 25 mph limit. When he wasn't in a rush, he could appreciate the small-town-ness.

Okay, no. He couldn't. That's why he lived closer to the Beltway, not out in the middle of nowhere like Boone. Country life suited his friend. Not Trace. He liked townhomes and condensed living. Easier to get to places. And quicker.

He turned right onto Catoctin then swung into the strip mall shopping center. With each thump of the speed bump, his gaze slid to the rearview mirror. By the time he aimed toward the Pei Wei, he spotted the car.

Well, if they wanted to follow him, they could waste a few hours.

Francesca
Leesburg, Virginia
11 May – 1545 Hours

Where are you going?

Frankie slid her Prius into the parking lot in front of the PetSmart, watching as Trace walked into the Pei Wei Asian diner.

Seriously? Wasn't it a little early for dinner—and he'd just left her dad at a restaurant?

Well, considering she must've scared him out of the restaurant, she guessed he might be hungry. But she wasn't overly convinced that he'd been sitting at the table beside her brother and father. The table was set, but Paolo said the man had just sat down.

And neither of them recognized him?

What? Did she have *idiot* stamped across her forehead?

Gripping her steering wheel, she banged her head on it. Why? Why would her dad meet with Trace? Clearly not to get a confession out of the guy. And Paolo—after the way he chewed her out and she humiliated herself in front of Trace's brother?

Great. Right. That would be so great for Trace to find out and hate her more. Forty boring minutes later, Trace emerged and casually walked to his Charger.

Poised, ready to figure out where he and Boone were hiding, she shifted into DRIVE. Trace pulled away from the building and then glided in front of another strip mall in the same parking lot. Straight toward Plaza Street.

She let a car pull between them so she wasn't obvious. He turned right on the street—what was it? She strained to see the sign at the corner. *P* something. She followed the blue car and eased into traffic. Only, as she did, Trace drove back into the parking lot.

Frankie looked to the left, afraid he'd see and recognize her. Or had he already realized he was being followed?

She eased back in, hoping—praying—he hadn't noticed. He glided into a stretch of the parking lot that sat empty and parked cockeyed. As she slowly drove by, she eyed him without turning her head and saw him talking on his cell phone.

"What?" she muttered as she went to the end of the parking lot, which brought her right back to Pei Wei, and turned right. "You can't multitask?"

When she glanced back, her heart jolted. He was gone! She nailed her brake. A car behind her honked. She waved them around, searching the parking lot. There! Heading back onto Main Street!

"Shoot, shoot, shoot," Frankie growled as she whipped her little car around and gunned it for the street. Pealed in front of an oncoming delivery truck and rushed to the intersection. She took a risk and jumped in front of a red Mustang, who also honked at her. She didn't care. No way would she lose Trace.

She'd been trying for the last two months to catch him. And then after narrowly missing him in Vegas… "It's on, Trace Weston."

Trace
Rural Northern Virginia
11 May – 1600 Hours

He had to hand it to her—she could handle her car pretty well. But it was borderline comical watching her little car dodging potholes and slowing at hairpin turns. She had good driving skills, but that car fought her. Where had she learned to drive like that?

"I'm not losing her," he spoke through his Bluetooth to Boone. "Can't lead her to the bunker, so I'm going to head back to Reston."

"You sure? I can come out there."

"No. I don't want her knowing why I'm out here."

"Roger that."

A couple of miles ahead, a small white car lumbered down the country road. The distance between them was closing quickly. The oncoming car prevented Trace from passing. He slowed, glancing in the rearview mirror, tightening his lips as he saw the Prius gaining.

"I'll get back out there later, or tomorrow."

"Copy."

The call disconnected as the oncoming truck passed them. Trace whipped around the white car. Another car came over the crest, heading straight for Trace. He bullied his way over, the white car laying on its horn hard. Brakes squalled.

Trace saw the Prius swerve and slow. She was trapped. Not quite as fearless as he believed. Which was good. Told him she had her limits.

He would never convince Solomon's daughter he wasn't responsible— at least, not in the way she believed. As Zulu's commander, he was ultimately the one on whose shoulders blame rested. But he hadn't killed those children.

She was tenacious, Francesca Solomon. Tenacious and bullheaded, just like her father.

Trace slammed the brake on, powered down, and took a right. Arching tree branches stretched over the road, shadowing the car. Making it more difficult to see. To anticipate. This was good—he'd really put her skills to the test now.

Francesca

"Oh come on," Frankie said as she slowed and whipped through the next turn. Though she had defensive driving skills, as well as evasive driving techniques, she wasn't driving a car with an engine that could handle the insanity that ensued following Trace.

He knows. He knows I'm following him.

Sunlight poked through the overhead branches, giving her momentary spots of blindness. She had to admit—it was beautiful out here. She could appreciate the setting, the beauty, but she'd never live out here. Too far from the excitement and the energy that she thrived on.

"Okay, *where* are you going?" she growled as they made two hard turns, one after another. "You're toying with me, aren't you?"

Just as he'd been with Misrata. Evading at every turn. Evasive at every question. The man had no honor or integrity. He wasn't worth her time, but she would not let that stop her from bringing justice to the families of those workers. She would destroy his career just as he'd done to her father.

The image of Trace's brother leapt into her mind. The guy was handsome, not as much as Trace, but he had that same Weston look. Brent had clearly been affected by Trace's actions. In a twisted sort of way, she felt sorry for the guy—to have to live under the shame of his brother's actions. To possibly be naive enough and believe Trace was innocent. She snorted.

She knew what it was like to feel the scorn of the world. She'd borne a lot of that after the fallout of Misrata, after her father stood before committee after committee, investigation after investigation. His promotions stalled. His positions shifted.

Sunlight glared through her sunroof, momentarily blinding her. Frankie squeezed her eyes and looked away—but then squinted through the windshield and ducked to block the light.

A movement on the side of the road.

She saw it.

A deer.

It leapt with all the grace and elegance God had designed it with.

Right into her path.

Frankie yelped and yanked her steering wheel to the right.

Hit a rut in the road. Spun on the gravel. Lost traction. She turned in the direction of the spin. But a heavy thud threw the car to the right. Dipped down. And she went sailing. Flipping.

Frankie screamed.

IV

Francesca
Rural Northern Virginia
11 May – 1700 Hours

Warbling sound banged against her eardrums, pulling her from the heavy fog. Darkness—no, light. Bright light. Hot. *Too bright.* Moving her head only brought a spasm of pain. She cried out.

"Easy."

Something pulled on her body. Tugged. Tearing and scraping hissed through vague coherency.

Her legs dropped.

Jarred, she cried out again.

"Sorry," the voice spoke.

Disoriented, Frankie tried to open her eyes. Struggled against the colossal pull on her brain. On her body to sleep. To surrender. No fight. Too weak.

Garbled noises raided her mind. Mingled with crushing pain. Shoved her deep behind the veil of awareness.

* * *

Rocking and vibrations wormed through Frankie's body. She dug through a haze of pain and disorientation, surprised to find herself lying down. Bright lights glared down at her, poking through her corneas. She winced and shifted her gaze to the right. A wall of clear cabinets revealed...*medical equipment?* At her shoulder, a man sat in a chair, adjusting something. *Ambulance. Why am I in an ambulance?*

Pulse jackhammering, she tried to look around but her head wouldn't move. Gentle pressure held her head in place, forbidding movement.

"Hi there. Welcome back," the man said. "Can you tell me if you're having trouble breathing?"

She swallowed, frightened. "N–no. What happened?"

"You were in an accident. Can you tell me your name?"

Drowning in fear and uncertainty, she nudged aside the adrenaline burst and focused on his question. "Francesca Solomon." She wet her lips and tasted blood and...ash? No, couldn't be ash. "What's wrong with me?"

The EMT made some notes then checked her vitals again. "Are you in any pain, Miss Solomon?"

"I. . ." Mentally, she probed her body. Her leg, her side. . .head. "Yeah, some."

"Is it isolated in one area?"

"Mostly all over. My head—feels like someone hit it with a hammer."

"That would've been the road. You have a concussion, thus the brace. We need to make sure you didn't injure your neck when your car rolled."

Rolled. Yes. The blur of trees. Road. Dirt. Grass. All blended into a terrifying concoction. The thuds, the cracks, the pops. . . They echoed in her ears as if it were still happening. As if the world tilted and somersaulted. But there was something else. Something her mind kept shutting off and refusing to let her see.

The EMT shifted.

"What are you doing to me?"

"I've set you up with an IV catheter, a bag of fluids, and I'm monitoring your heart rate, blood pressure, and oxygen saturation."

She had no idea what that meant. No idea why she was here. "I don't remember. . ."

"Take your time." He sat beside her. "Your body's been through some serious trauma. It's in preservation mode right now."

No kidding—it was like a blank canvas with unreal barriers. Come on. She had to remember something. Obviously, she'd been in her car. But where? *Why did I. . . ?*

Trace.

Frankie closed her eyes as the memories of chasing him down that country road splashed across her visual cortex. Flooded her with the distinct remembrance of her bullheadedness that wouldn't let her back off or slow down. The glittering sunlight peeking through the trees arching over the road, forming a natural canopy. Trace's dark gray Charger charging through the country. Being blinded. The—"Deer. There was a deer."

The EMT gave a soft chuckle. "Those things cause more accidents around here than you'd believe. Know a guy who's been hit by ten over the years. We call him Venison Magnet."

The memories rushed on, uncaring of the way they made Frankie's body tense. Made her wish she could vanish back into unconsciousness. It hurt. It hurt too much to think about it.

Crack. Thud. The sound of something ripping. The deafening silence that ensued when her car came to rest, right side up. A hissing noise. . .a dribbling. A—

She flinched. The memories vanished. Left a gaping void.

What. . .why couldn't she remember anything past the silence? Did

Trace just leave her there? "Was there a man at the accident?"

The EMT swam into view again, a small frown on his tanned face. "Man? Was he involved in the accident?"

"If you mean, did he cause it—no." *Involved* depended on what the EMT referred to. Trace had been involved all right, but not by his own doing. Well, maybe—she grew convinced he figured out she'd been following him. But it was her fault for even trying to catch him going back to his secret lair, to find out where and what he was hiding.

"A man called in the accident, but there wasn't anyone there when we arrived."

Trace just left me there? Why did that surprise her?

"Then again, we were only a couple of miles from the scene, so we came up on you pretty quick once the call came in." He winked at her. "Good thing we were out protecting the town."

She shifted, anxious to be rid of this boxed-in environment and the words, and the confusion. An irritating feeling nagged at her lower leg. "My calf. . ."

"It's burned. Second degree, would be my guess."

"Burned?" She tried not to let the panic douse her. "There was a fire?"

"Your car caught fire. Good thing you dragged yourself free or this might have had a different ending."

Frankie stilled. *Dragged myself?* She had no memory of that.

Should she be worried? Was it normal to have missing pieces of memory?

The sway of gravity tugged on her as the ambulance rounded a corner. A few minutes later, it slid to a stop. Beside her, the EMT prepped her gurney as the rear doors opened. Another EMT did something, and she felt the gurney slide forward. She eased into the darkening day amid the bright lights of the emergency room. They wheeled her into the hospital. Frankie couldn't suppress the fear, the sense of panic. Had she injured herself and she couldn't feel it?

What would her dad say? And Trace—if she was laid up, would he get away. . .again?

"Crash victim, female, age twenty-six. Concussion, second-, possibly third-degree burns to her leg. Possible bruised ribs. Right arm is swollen, possibly fractured."

Frankie lay staring up at the panel lights that swam overhead as they delivered her into the ER. Ashamed and afraid of what she might have done to herself, she closed her eyes. She just wanted justice.

A voice in the distance, in a blanket of black, called to her. "*Francesca!*" A blur. A large, shadowy blur. Creaks. Cracks. Pops.

Boom!

"Francesca!"

She whimpered, seeing the blaze. The flames. The roaring, crackling flames! Dancing and closing in on her. Hot, so hot! The heat and pain overwhelmed her.

A figure loomed through the flames and warbling plumes of heat. The door swung open. Hands reached for her. Hoisted her out. Spoke to her. Spoke over her cries and moans. Dragged her backward. Out of the searing reach of the fire.

She went down. Images flashing in and out. Trees. Sunlight. A face, shadowy and blurry.

Boom!

Frankie snapped awake.

"You okay?" Her dad stood over her, holding her hand. "You were whimpering. I didn't want to wake you—they said to let you sleep, but I didn't want to wake the whole hospital." The laughter in his voice didn't reach his eyes, which bore the concern she heard tinges of in his voice.

Disoriented yet again, she breathed a heavy sigh that was filled with relief. . .and grief. She squeezed his hand. "The fire. . ."

"They said you got out and collapsed."

"No," she whispered over a dry, hoarse throat. "Someone pulled me out."

"Who?" Her father frowned. "Nobody was there."

But someone *was* there.

Trace
Lucketts, Virginia
11 May – 1750 Hours

"She's a problem."

Trace gritted his teeth.

"We have to get her to back off," Boone said, his gaze focused downward.

Searing pain lit through his hand and arm. Trace pushed up. "Augh!"

Boone glanced up. "Sorry." He went back to applying a liberal dose of burn cream.

Grinding his molars, he stared at the pinked and blistered flesh lathered up as Boone carefully wrapped it. Never would he have left someone in a situation like that, but he'd watched until he saw the EMTs. Backed into the woods till they were on scene and treating her. Then he cleared out before anyone saw or recognized him. Hiding like that went against everything he knew and believed in. But that woman. . .

Pressure sent a spike of pain through Trace's arm. He flinched and cursed.

A smile tried to take over Boone's face. "Sorry."

"You don't look sorry," Trace grumbled and withdrew his bandaged arm.

"Maybe you should've left her. . . ."

Trace moved to the kitchen area and drew out a jug of orange juice. Holding his burned hand to his chest, he retrieved a glass then filled it. "You know better. We don't work that way." He took a sip then set the glass down. "She's a pain in my backside, but it doesn't mean she deserves to die."

"You know I didn't mean that. Things would just be a lot easier if she'd get off our backs." Boone folded his large arms over his chest. "Don't know why she's so hell-bent on you being guilty."

"Haym took a fall. She needs a scapegoat." He tossed back the rest of the juice then shrugged. "Lucky me."

"Was she okay?"

"Breathing, vitals were normal." Trace didn't want another death on his conscience, but he was pretty sure Solomon wasn't in a near-death state. "But she needs to be dealt with."

Boone grinned.

"Not like that," Trace said with a chuckle. He knew his buddy too well—Boone wouldn't want her killed. But she was seriously endangering everyone with her tenacity. Tugging out his phone, he headed to the briefing area.

"What happened to his arm?" came Annie's voice just before he closed the door.

He hit the general's number and waited for the call to connect. How many times and in how many ways could he tell the general to get his daughter off their backs without becoming insubordinate?

"I know what you're going to say," General Haym Solomon said. "So let me save you the trouble. I'm at the hospital."

"Then you know what happened?"

"I can imagine."

Trace felt obliged to ask, and curiosity—his own peace of mind—demanded he follow through. "Is she okay?"

"Bruised ribs, burned calf, and a concussion, but she'll be fine."

"I'm sorry. I hope she recovers quickly."

"Thank you."

Silence gaped. As it lingered, Trace hesitated taking the conversation in the direction it needed to go. This man was not only his commanding officer but a friend. A friend with history. They'd been through the fires of combat, steel sharpening iron.

"Sir, if I hadn't seen her following. . ."

"But you did. . .thank the Lord."

Trace rubbed his forehead. "I admire her tenacity, but Zulu is an area she can't be tenacious with."

"She won't get to you."

"It's not me I'm worried about, sir. The girls—the team. They're in enough danger, and they're being hunted." Trace lifted his head and exhaled. "What if the killer takes a bead on your daughter, sir? What then?"

"I hear you, Colonel. But let's tone this down a little."

"Tone it down?" Trace stretched his neck. "From what? From a flipped, burning car to. . .what? Lead in the head? Because if she keeps looking in places she shouldn't, one day she's going to look in the wrong hole—and it'll be the wrong end of a sniper rifle."

"Give me time to grieve and worry over her, will you?"

Trace slumped against the table, defeat clinging to him. "Sorry, sir. I just think. . .she needs to be stopped. You've promised us you'd take care of this."

"Come Monday morning, she won't have a job."

Trace lifted his head.

"She's being put on leave. Suspension of all security clearances until further notice. It's the best I can do, and believe me, that's taking more political capital than I had. I'm owing some serious favors."

"I wish we could just convince her I'm not guilty, not the way she thinks I am."

"Frankie's like her mom in that once she gets an idea in her head, it takes an act of God to convince her otherwise. Hang on," he said, then the phone went muffled for a while. After several long minutes, Trace wondered if the general had forgotten about him.

"Okay, I better go," the general finally said. "By the way, how's the burn?"

Trace hesitated. How'd he know about that? Did his daughter remember Trace hauling her semiconscious form out of the car?

General Solomon sniggered. "She said someone pulled her from the burning car. I figured it had to be you."

"Not sure what gives you that idea, sir."

Another chuckle. "Your character, Colonel Weston. Your character. We'll be talking. . . ."

Trace ended the call and sat against the table. He needed progress. Some serious progress on solving this thing. They were having their backsides served to them on a silver platter by someone determined to end them.

"Hey," Boone said, pushing into the room, a laptop in hand. "Check this out." He slid it onto the table and palmed the surface. After he loaded a video, he straightened.

Trace glanced down and bent toward the screen. A news reporter talking to. . .

"Samuel Caliguari."

"In the full interview, he promises not to give up till he finds her. That he believes there's something bigger than a kidnapping going on."

Anger rumbled through Trace's gut. Whoever had blown the covers on Zulu created a windfall of trouble. First Solomon's daughter. Now this guy.

Boone stabbed a meaty finger toward the monitor. "That right there is a problem. A big Navy SEAL problem."

"Between him and Solomon. . ." Shaking his head, Trace dropped into a chair.

"I think it's worse," Boone countered, his gray eyes lit with fire. "This guy is a SEAL. They're trained to—well, to do what we do. West, we gotta get a leash on this guy, or he could very well bring this whole thing down. Then the girls will be sitting ducks."

They're already sitting ducks. That's what it felt like. That's what he felt watching three of them get taken down.

"How?" Trace didn't mean to be confrontational. He pushed to his feet and paced. "You said it—he's trained much the same way we are. What am I supposed to do? We've already shut down as much as we can. They aren't looking for Annie."

"But *he's* looking for her. Couple his squid tendencies with a man in love—"

"Love?" The word punched a hole in Trace's gut.

"West, anyone can see it in his eyes."

So much had changed in five years. Then the girls were young, ambitious, and not looking for beaus or to settle down. Today two of them had relationships that compromised good sense. Téya going off on that wild chase to see her Amish boyfriend. Trace scratched his head over that one. Téya had been the hardest-hitting woman he'd known, with enough drive and determination to knock any of his Green Beret buddies off their feet. She wasn't a Wonder Woman type. Téya had been more Lara Croft. Refined but no woman to mess with. Annie was a little softer, a little more focused, but just as tenacious.

"If we could get him on our side," Boone mumbled.

Trace scowled.

Hands up in surrender, Boone shrugged. "He has the skills and he knows how to use them. Just saying it'd work in our favor instead of against us."

"No." Trace executed the idea before it had a chance to take on a life of its own. No way would he have a Navy SEAL breathing the same air, protecting the same girls, especially not Annie. "His attention would be divided. He'd be too focused on Annie, not enough on the others."

A gentle knock preceded a, "Hey, I . . ."

Trace pivoted, slapping the laptop shut at the same time he faced Annie as she entered. But by the look in her eyes, he'd been too late.

Annie
Lucketts, Virginia
11 May – 1820 Hours

"What is that?" Annie's heart beat in cadence with a war march. She saw it—a reporter talking with Sam. And he looked ticked. Handsome, but ticked.

"Annie, did you need something?" Trace asked, standing with his hands on his belt. So like when he wore ACUs and a tac belt. Except he had the addition of a bandage on his left forearm and hand.

Anger stirred the second she realized he would try to hide it. Try to dismiss it. "What was that, Trace? And don't tell me 'nothing.' I saw you two." She glanced at Boone, who kept his head down as he sat in a chair, forearms on his knees. "Neither of you looked happy. And right now, neither am I. Tell me what it was."

Braced for a standoff, Annie held her ground. Trace's green eyes held hers. She saw a lot there, a lot more than most people would see.

His anger—but there was a lot of that since they'd been hit. His dislike—she'd talked to him as an equal, not as her superior. Truth of it was, she wasn't sure where she stood on the organization chart considering she'd been Ashland Palmieri, not Lieutenant Annie Palermo, for the last five years. His frustration—things were clearly out of control and there didn't seem to be any tendrils to grab onto to bring this mess back into something manageable. But there was something else there, something she couldn't sort.

Annie stepped into the room, letting the door close behind her. She folded her arms. "What is that? Was it a video?"

127

Trace slid his gaze to Boone then gave a curt nod. "Sam's doing interviews."

Annie blinked. "Interviews? About what?"

"You." Image of calm, cool collection, Trace leaned back against the table, the laptop behind him. When they'd first met, he terrified her because she could never read him. Experience taught her how to read him. "He's stirring up trouble about your disappearance."

Sam. . .stirring up trouble. "That doesn't surprise me."

"But it should concern you." Trace gave her that look, the one that knotted the line between his eyebrows. "If he keeps this up. . ."

Outrage spiked through her. What? What was Trace going to say? "Then what?"

"He's putting your life in danger, Annie. Téya and Nuala's, too," he said, nodding beyond the room to where Téya and Nuala stood watching them. "All of us. If he digs, if he shouts loud enough, someone's going to listen. You'll never be safe from the assassin's bullet."

"We'll never be safe as long as we don't know who we're running from," Annie shot back.

Lips tightened, Trace just watched her.

That's when it hit her. "Is Sam in danger?"

Trace still didn't answer. Didn't respond. Just stared.

"It's not an unrealistic question, Trace. You saw what happened to Téya's boyfriend and grandmother. What if something like that happens to Sam or to Jeff."

Boone raised his head. "Jeff?"

"The Green Dot's owner. A good friend—he's a good man, Trace. They both are, and I'm not going to—"

"You're not going to what, Annie?" Trace's expression darkened. He'd never liked threats or perceived threats.

His words were a good signal that she was getting too emotional. And of course she was. She'd been a civilian for five years. She let Sam in, only to end up back here, yanked out of his arms and life with no possibility of reconnecting until they stopped whoever was behind it. "Look," she said, rubbing her forehead. "I just don't want him to get hurt."

"I thought you were worried about the sub shop owner, too."

"I am." Her heart skipped a beat when she thought she recognized the green-eyed monster in his gaze. Their team commander had never been emotional. To the contrary—he often came across as coldhearted.

"He has to be dealt with."

Case in point.

"Let me talk to him." As soon as the words were out, Annie knew how they'd sound. How Trace would respond.

He laughed and stood. "Right. I just spent every last resource and connection hauling you back here to keep you alive, but you want to walk out in the open for a chat with your *boyfriend*."

Annie drew up at his words. At the ferocity. Rankled, partially by her own foolishness and the other part because of Trace's raised voice.

"No. You're not going out there. You're safe here."

"I'll be safe talking to Sam—"

"Do you seriously believe that?" His face reddened as he leaned toward her. "Weren't you with *him* when the sniper tried to slam some lead through your skull?" Nostrils flaring, he walked to the other side of the table, pacing. "No, you need to stay here."

It was hard to hear. Harder to hear the way he said it. But she knew he was right. Knew going to Sam was a risk.

Only when Boone shifted did Annie remember there was another person in the room. He stood and walked to the door. Then looked at Annie. "He's a SEAL. Sam will be fine."

"If Trace doesn't kill him first," she muttered, half joking.

Boone gave a nod then looked to the team commander and left.

Trace blew out a breath. Shook his head. "We've erased your identity in and around Manson. You don't exist there anymore." Back to her, he touched the table with two fingers. "I called in some favors, and I'm sure nobody will admit you were there."

"Except Sam. And what you're doing—that will just make Sam more determined to find me."

Trace gave her that stern-browed scowl again. "For his sake, I hope that's not true."

Hating to talk to his back, she swung around in front of him, staring up at those green eyes that once held powerful sway over her. She didn't trust herself to touch him. Or close the limited gap between them. "Trace, please. What do you want? Would you walk away from this? For the last five years after we were set up, did you walk away from trying to find out who did this?"

"It's different. They hit my team. *Hurt* my team. Broke laws. Murdered. It got real personal."

"For Sam, it's personal, too. Because of me." It'd taken her two years to let the guy in, to open up and accept that she liked him, too. Her past, her relationships, and Misrata had kept her heart and feelings locked in a box. She'd never been prone to emotional outbursts or typical female hormonal rages, but after Misrata, she was even more disciplined in guarding her feelings.

His gaze met hers then ricocheted off. "I don't have any options, Annie. He could get us all killed."

She touched his arm. When he stiffened, she lowered it. "Can you wait? Just. . .wait for him to—"

"Get bored and give up?" Trace narrowed his gaze at her then pointed to the laptop. "Does that look like a guy who's going to get bored?"

Annie turned to the table and slumped into a chair. Fingertips pressed to her face, she fought the frustration. "You can't just kill him."

Silence dropped like an anchor, leaving her alone with her thoughts and grief. Sam was a good guy. She had to convince Trace. Just. . .how? How did she turn this around? Defeated, she lowered her hands and looked up.

She sat alone in the room. Annie pushed to her feet and spotted Trace crossing the room. Boone hollered something to him, but Trace kept moving. In a few large strides, Boone was at the door, scowling. "What happened?"

Nuala
Lucketts, Virginia
12 May – 0130 Hours

Darkness laid in wait. Haunting. Daring. On the prowl.

Nuala shrugged and leaned her cheek against her sniper rifle. Prostrate on the rooftop, she too waited. In trembling. It was wrong. Something was wrong. She felt it in the warm, sticky air. In the oppressive gloom that coated the city.

Green washed the scene before her, bathing the warehouse and other structures in a pale green shimmer. She traced the reticle to the right, along the tree line that guarded the city and its inhabitants. There sat Zulu, ready for the mission that would establish them.

Téya and Annie huddled near an old, rusted-out truck twenty yards from the warehouse. They had point. Back and over a street, the rest of the team waited inside an empty storefront. But. . .it was weird. They weren't there. Yet they were.

Nuala rubbed her eyes and looked back through the scope. There again. Gone again.

Ghosts.

They were ghosts. A sudden rush of cold air down her spine startled her. Nuala shuddered, firming her grip and reverifying her range to target. Something floated into her sight. A skull. A hollowed-out skull with strips of clothing for a body. The face shifted, becoming that of a small child.

130

Riveted to the ghoulish, midair dance, Nuala couldn't tear her gaze from the scope. Yet everything in her railed, shivered, demanded to be free of the terrifying image. She pushed back, but it felt as if something had permanently secured her face to the rifle. The droning tick of a timer pounded in the back of her mind.

No.

Finally, Nuala pried free. When she looked around, panting, her clothes drenched in sweat, she found. . .nothing. Only a cold night smothered in the pale light of the moon and distant fluorescent streetlamps. No ghoul. No childish-skull-thing.

"Sitrep, Fire-eye."

Fire-eye. Hearing her call sign jogged her out of the moment of terror. Trace wanted an update. Right. *Focus.* With a stuttering breath, she lowered herself to the ground again. She took up her position again. Her limbs shook as she adjusted the dials. She momentarily switched to thermals and traced the building.

Spotted Téya and Annie slipping into the warehouse, setting the charges. Wiring it up. Candice and Jessie hurried through, clearing their area. Moving on target with their projected timeline. They'd be clear in a few mikes. The building would be gone. And Zulu would have saved the day from terrorists.

But something, some darkness hung over a portion of the warehouse. Blotted out her view. Black. Jet black. She scanned left. Found the girls. Bright yellows and reds mingled with some blue.

Nuala slid right. Black. Jet black again.

She adjusted a dial. Slowly, the black began to fade. Lighter. . .lighter. . .gray. A little more. *Keep adjusting, you'll miss your shot.* She turned it again and—

Lined up, row upon row, she spied children on beds. And they were singing. But they were asleep. No, they can't be singing. *How can I know they're singing?*

Just as the question flooded her mind, she realized she could see the children, as if looking through a glass rather than through thermal imaging.

This doesn't make sense.

A child sat up from the bunk. Black hair hung in perfect ringlets. Her dress was yellow and fluffy with tiers of ruffles. Pretty yellow ribbons and beads in her hair. She smiled up at Nuala, as if she peered up the wrong end of the scope.

Heart thundering, Nuala froze. That's not possible.

"Fire-eye," came the terse voice of the team commander. "Sitrep. Over."

"Uh. . ." Her voice trembled and cracked as she stared through the scope at the perfect brown eyes that gazed back with utter affection and adoration. "Fine. All clear."

No! It's not clear! There are children in there!

As if she were two distinct persons, a war erupted. One that told her to order the team to abort the mission, save the children. The other that seemed ignorant of the children, so hyper-focused on the mission and success that it ignored what it saw.

"Roger that," Trace replied. "Stay sharp. Ten mikes."

Ten minutes. The children had ten minutes.

Nuala blinked, easing away from the scope and the image of the girl in the yellow dress. She looked down at the dirt. At the rocks. At the. . .blood!

She yelped and shoved backward onto her rear end, hands braced at her side. She checked the spot—but it wasn't there. No blood. She stared hard, shoving her palm against her temple. She was losing her mind.

What is going on?

"Five mikes," Trace called. "Eyes out, everyone."

No! The children! *Have to get the children out.*

Throwing herself back to the weapon, she adjusted. Sat right. Had to tell them. Had to warn Zulu. Her friends would save the children. They had to.

"How we doing, Zulu?"

"Alfa and Tango, almost done," Annie said.

"Charlie and Juliet all clear," Candice radioed through.

Nuala keyed her mic. "No! Stop. Listen—"

"Good. RTB and let's move!"

"Wait." Nuala's throat felt five sizes too big. Drenched with adrenaline. "Stop! It—"

"Copy that. Charlie and Juliet RTB."

"Copy."

"Tango and Alfa en route now."

Why couldn't they hear her? Why were they ignoring—

Something poked her in the cheek. She flinched and turned to find out what was pricking her. Her heart jumped into her throat at the severed coms cord. A strangled cry gargled up her throat.

Unable to breathe, unable to move, she sat in horror as a high-pitched whistle shrieked through the night.

BooOOOooom!

Amid the yellow ball of fire rose screams. The screams of children. They took form, ghoulish, childlike skulls in shredded clothing.

Flying right at her.

"*Noo!*" Nuala jerked forward.

"Hey hey hey." Arms came around her.

Nuala shoved them away and scrabbled backward. Pain thudded against the back of her skull and she blinked. Blinked again and found herself staring at the concerned faces of Téya and Annie.

Relief detonated in her chest.

Followed by a squall of grief.

She dropped her face into her hands and cried. Comforting arms wrapped around her as sobs wracked her body. Hauling in a deep breath, she detected a fruity scent that proved somehow calming and reassuring. Nuala burrowed into the warm embrace of a friend, wishing the images, the nightmare could be bleached from her mind.

Eyes burning and puffy, she straightened, unsure how long she'd made a spectacle of herself. Palming away the tears revealed how hot her face had become. Gave her a vague knowledge of how splotchy her cheeks and eyes must be. "Sorry," she sniffled.

Hugging her knees, Annie sat beside her. "No," Annie said. "It happens to all of us."

Disbelief spread through Nuala. "Seriously?" She looked to Téya, who sat backward on the rolling chair in front of the bunk. "You have nightmares?"

They both couldn't meet her gaze. But she saw their pain. The grief.

"I would do anything—*anything* to make that day go away."

"We all would." The strong bass voice startled them all, pulling their attention to the door, where Boone, dressed in sweats and a T-shirt but barefoot, stood holstering his weapon. "It was one messed up day." He nodded to them then to Nuala specifically.

Her heart did a jig as his gray eyes met hers. The angular jawline. The thick neck and shoulders. But the eyes. Boone's eyes. . .

Thanks to the flush from crying, Nuala knew he wouldn't see the blush creeping into her cheeks as his eyes lingered on her.

"Need something to rest?" he asked, his voice deep and quiet. Caring.

"No—" Her voice croaked on the word. She cleared her throat, embarrassed. "No, I'll be fine. That. . ." She lifted a shoulder in a shrug, not wanting him to worry about her. Wanting to be strong like Téya and Annie. Neither of them had cried out in terror since they'd come to the bunker. "The nightmare wore me out. That's all."

He wasn't buying it, she could tell. But he also wasn't the type of man to embarrass her further. "No shame remembering what happened." Boone gave her a curt nod. "Get some rest." And he vanished.

No, there wasn't shame in remembering the past. There was shame in not being strong enough to stop it from controlling her mind. And *that* shame was reserved for Noodle-Brain. *Me.*

Téya
Lucketts, Virginia
12 May – 0630 Hours

Sleep clinging to her heavier than a dew-drenched blanket, Téya trudged from the bathroom to the small kitchen area. She started a pot of coffee then dug through the fridge for something. Emerging with a single-serve yogurt, she yawned so hard it made her ears pop. At the six-foot table, she tucked a leg under herself as she sat in the chair and hooked her other leg up and propped it on the edge.

Peeling back the foil of the yogurt, she heard someone else shuffling in. Annie appeared around the corner, her blond curls perfect. "You make me sick," Téya muttered as she stirred the yogurt, churning the fruit on the bottom. "Oh my gosh—you're already dressed."

Annie stopped and frowned. "Of course I am." Her gaze skated to the briefing room.

Téya smirked. "He's not here. Won't be today."

Cheeks pinked, Annie went to the pantry. "Who?"

"You two really went at it yesterday. What was that about? Old passions revived?" Téya snickered as she spooned the first bite into her mouth.

Annie popped her on the back of the head.

"Hey!" Dropping the yogurt on the table, Téya scowled. "It is too early in the morning for that abuse." She lifted her breakfast again. "Especially when I'm hitting the mark."

With a bowl and box of health-nut cereal, Annie joined her. "You're not even close."

Wagging her spoon at Annie, Téya couldn't help but rub it in. "You've always been a bad liar."

Annie rolled her eyes then poured her cereal and milk. "Sam is nosing around, trying to find me. He went on a news show and said he wouldn't give up. Trace wants to neutralize him."

Nearly choking on a blueberry, Téya coughed. "He said that?"

"No," Annie said as she returned the box to the pantry and the milk to the fridge. "He said Sam had to be dealt with."

Mouth full of yogurt, Téya laughed. "And you took it he meant to kill your hunky boyfriend."

Annie glowered. "What else would he do?"

"Get him arrested? Shut down his accounts. Blacklist him."

"He's a SEAL, not a spy."

"There's a difference?"Téya nodded and pointed. "Oh! There is—this one's gorgeous. Am I right?"

Annie smiled.

"What's the scoop on him? Name, rank, and serial number, girlie."

After swallowing a bite, Annie shook her head. "Tell you and the whole world knows."

"All I have to do is ask Houston."Téya grinned. "He's sweet on me." They both laughed and Téya leaned in. "So. . .dark hair? Blond?"

"Dark."

"Brown eyes? Blue eyes?"

"Brown."

"So he's the opposite of Trace. Was that intentional?"

Annie's frown vanished. She stood and went to the coffeepot, where she poured a cup for herself.

Touché.

Téya felt a bit of prodder's remorse, but the questions had been killing her since the fallout with Annie and Trace yesterday. She went to the counter and bumped her hip against Annie's.

"Sorry. I guess that was uncool."

"Very." Sipping from the mug, Annie met her gaze to let her know she wasn't mad then returned to the table.

But there were questions. A lot of them. With her own coffee, Téya sat back down. "Did you hear from him after—"

"No." Annie scooped more cereal into her mouth, clearly ending the conversation.

Thwarted again, Téya knew it was a talk best left for later. "What do you think of Noodle?"

Annie shrugged. "She'll be fine. I spent the first year with more nights of terror than nights of sleep." Taking another bite, she seemed to be forming a fortress around herself.

They'd been close since day one, but Téya had admired Annie from that moment, too. Cute, tanned, blond, and so incomprehensibly focused. Where Téya loved a joke and giggle, Annie wanted discourse and theology. Brainy stuff. Where Téya loved combat boots, jeans, and a T-shirt, Annie almost had that FBI thing going on with her slacks and blouse. Elegant, classy, beautiful to Téya's tomboy comfy-ness.

Hiss-click-click. A deep groaning rattled through the room.

Lights flickered on in the command and data areas as the access door creaked open. Houston with his wild golden-brown Jheri curl hair stepped into the bunker. He flinched, looking over at them. Then smiled. "Morning, ladies."

Téya eased back in her chair and waved as she glanced at the clock. "A bit early, isn't it?"

Shifting on his feet, he nodded. "Uh, yeah." After flashing them another smile, he hurried to his bank of systems.

Annie and Téya laughed and finished their breakfasts. Within ten minutes, Boone emerged, wafting an Old Spice scent through the steel trap.

Téya glanced at the access door then at Boone. He'd been *right there* last night when Nuala woke up screaming. "Where are you staying?"

Boone made himself some coffee. "In the house."

Tilting her head, Téya looked to the ceiling. "You mean someone can live in a ramshackle place like that?"

"Hey," Boone growled as he turned. He blew over the rim of the mug. "That's my grandfather's house you're talking about."

"It *looks* like a grandfather's house—a great-great-grandfather's house. I thought it was condemned."

Boone placed his large hand over his equally large pectoral. "You wound me." He slurped as he moved toward the table and dragged a chair out. "I'm renovating it." He took another long drag of his coffee and breathed deeply. "At least, that's the cover we're using."

Annie shifted to look at him better. "Are you really renovating it?"

His shoulder bounced. "When I can. I've got plans to make a secret egress from here to the house, and vice versa. Thought it'd be good cover for any foot traffic—ya know, like Houston coming/going all the time."

"Could we help?" Annie asked. "With the renovations. I love doing that sort of thing."

"Uh," Houston called from the data area. "Are you forgetting the whole 'out of sight' thing?"

Annie looked to Téya. "Once Boone gets that egress tunnel done, we can slip up there and work. It'd be a nice break from the monotony of this drab place."

"Hey now," Boone protested. "I worked my hands to the bone building this kingdom."

"Kingdom," Téya said, teasing as she cleared her coffee mug, yogurt container, and spoon. "You need a dictionary."

"Oh crap," Houston muttered as the keys surrendered beneath his racing fingers.

"Houston, we have a problem?" Boone asked, sniggering.

"Ha. I'm amused," Houston said as he worked, not looking up. "Like I haven't heard that before."

Boone smiled as he stepped backward over the chair before shoving it back to the table. "What's going on?" He crossed the room.

Téya started to join them but saw Nuala standing in the opening to the lounge area. The girl looked as pretty as ever with her olive complexion and pale blue eyes and all that dark, wavy hair tumbling around her shoulders. It just wasn't fair—even with partially puffy eyes from crying all night, she was still cheerleader cute.

"Might want to grab some coffee before Boone drinks it all," Téya said, winking at Nuala.

"Thanks," her friend managed.

Hushed whispers between Boone and Houston snaked into her awareness, but she focused on the cutie. "Did you manage any sleep?"

Rubbing the back of her neck as she reached for a cup, Nuala shook her head but said, "Yeah. A little."

"Shakes 'no' but says 'yes.'"

Grunts and hissed words drew her attention to Boone. One hand on Houston's desk, he was punching a number into his phone.

Houston sat, arms crossed as he chewed on his thumbnail. His gaze slid around, hit Téya, widened, then ricocheted off.

What. . . ? "What's going on?"

Boone turned toward her, his expression grim.

Téya lifted her chin, feeling the color drain out of her face. *Grossmammi. . .*

"It's David," Boone said. "He's been rushed back to the hospital."

Annie
Lucketts, Virginia
12 May – 0700 Hours

She'd never considered herself empathic or overly sensitive, but Annie would vow there was an electric cord between her and Téya, connecting them to each other's pain. Rigid, hands fisted, Téya stood unmoving.

Annie mirrored her. Afraid one wrong move, one wrong word would send Téya sprinting out and stealing another car.

Boone, big guy that he was, must've seen it, too. He drew himself straight, a formidable sight. Cool air swirled beside Annie as Nuala sidled up on her right. Nobody dared move.

"Téya. . ." Boone said, lowering his phone.

The tallest of the three remaining Zulu members, Téya held up a hand. Then seemed to slap the air. She pivoted. Met Annie's gaze, and that cord between them zapped. Annie nodded toward the rear lounge.

It was ridiculous, the stress. The fear. The trauma.

Téya bypassed the lounge area and went into her room. When she didn't shut the door, Annie followed her in with Nuala. They sat in quiet for a very long time. Téya lay on her bunk with her feet on the plastered wall, staring at the upper bunk.

Annie sat in the chair and Nuala hopped up on the desk. Nobody had desk supplies or a computer. In fact, Boone and Trace had taken their phones, so what use the desk did, she wasn't sure.

"They trained us," Téya said slowly, purposefully. "They trained us to be soldiers, elite soldiers. To protect. To fight for those who can't."

Annie swallowed, knowing where this was going. Knowing Téya was sensible enough but needed the room and freedom to talk this out.

"And David. . ." Her voice went raw. Choked. "He's the best man I've ever known. So kind. So. . .*forgiving*." She lifted her hands in surrender. "I can't go see him, and I can't do anything to protect him. *My* presence puts him in more danger." She flipped onto her side, propped on her elbow. "So what good am I? What is the purpose behind that training when we are hiding here like scared little hens?"

"I kill people," Nuala whispered. "One shot, one kill." She sniffed. "People look at me and think I'm still in high school, but I've been in combat, fighting for freedom. Freedom we don't get to have."

Annie rose, wrapping her arms around herself. An incredible amount of tension and raw emotion roiled through the room. She could relate, knowing Sam was digging himself into a grave. But this talk. . .

"Don't get me wrong," Nuala said. "I know what I did in the Army was justified and necessary, but. . .there's nothing like people looking at me thinking I'm prom queen and me knowing what I've done. What I've had to do. And now"—she shrugged, her eyes glossing—"I feel like I'm being punished. Maybe I should've let those men kill me."

Annie spun toward her. "No." Determination ignited in her belly. "Listen, I know—know what you're both feeling, because I'm living and breathing the same pain. I can't do anything to warn Sam off, and—"

"Is that what you and Trace argued about?" Nuala asked.

"Basically." Annie wouldn't mention the rest. "The point is—it's a choice."

Rolling off the bunk, Téya stood, hands stuffed on her hips. "A choice? You think I have a *choice*?"

Hand up, Annie tried to hold her friend off. "Just hear me out."

Téya grunted. "Ya know what? I don't want to hear you out. I'm sick of this. Sick of my whole life being a lie. Of feeling guilty for not coming clean with David. For even stepping into his life!" Téya shoved a hand through her long, light brown hair. "I did this to him! To the best man I've ever met. A man I could never be worthy of—and he's in critical condition in the hospital!"

A heavy blanket of depression and sadness weighted them all. Nuala with her normally lighthearted demeanor, Téya with her bubbly personality, and Annie. . .she'd never felt so close to losing the reins of control. She returned to her chair. Sat and stared at her shoes.

"This sucks." Téya slid down the far wall and hugged her knees. "I don't know who I am anymore."

"Me either. Nuala died that night in Misrata."

"We all lost our souls on that mission," Annie agreed. "Jessie and Candice felt the same way."

Téya frowned at her, as did Nuala.

Annie sighed. "Jess sent me e-mails. I never replied to them, but I read them."

"Why didn't you reply?" The hurt in Nuala's voice was strong.

"Because. . ."

"Annie's someone who follows the rules because she believes they're there for a reason," Téya mumbled.

"Well, they are," Annie said, feeling defensive. "Trace said no contact. I was afraid replying would betray my location or somehow betray hers. I wasn't willing to take the risk and put more lives in danger."

"You always call him 'Trace,'" Nuala said. "Not 'commander' like the rest of us."

No, she was not getting sidetracked by that conversation. Annie stood and paced. They had to change this whole thing. Had to turn it around. But it felt like trying to turn a ship in a raging sea. "We have to do something."

Téya lowered her hand from her face and eyed her. "What?"

"They won't let us leave," Nuala said.

"I know. And it drives me crazy, but they're right. We need to stay low, let the storm die down. But. . ." She massaged her temple as she paced.

"Jess." Téya climbed to her feet. "Jess left a mountain of information."

"Yes, we've been staring at it for the last few days."

"What if. . .what if she found something and that's why she got killed?"

Annie tilted her head, hesitating. "I. . ." she said, drawing out the single word. "That's a leap."

"But it's possible," Téya said. "We need to study her schematic. Convince Trace to let us investigate."

"But we can't," Nuala said. "They want us to stay underground—literally."

"I have an idea."

Francesca
Fort Belvoir, Virginia
12 May – 0900 Hours

"Morning, ma'am."

Frankie produced her Department of Defense ID card and continued through the gate in her rental car, grateful base stickers weren't required any longer. She accelerated, feeling the twinge of pain in her calf from the bandage that kept her leg protected from infection. She had two stitches in her cheek and was gulping ibuprofen to mute the pain in her side from the bruised ribs. She wasn't here to work—just to get her things. She'd requested a few days off after the accident to get herself in a car and her body time to recover. But she needed her files.

She parked and headed toward the building. She swiped her card over the access panel. The light blipped red.

Red?

That was weird. Frankie swiped it again.

Red.

The scanners must not be working right. She peered through the glass door into the first floor, feeling the throb in her leg. Not a soul in sight. With a grunt, she fished her phone out of her purse. She scrolled to Ian Santiago's name and hit the CALL icon.

She lifted her phone to her ear, watching through the door in case someone passed by.

The line connected.

"Ian," she blurted as the mechanical voice registered.

". . .sorry. Your service has been suspended. If you feel this has been made in error, please contact customer service to resolve this issue."

Frankie snapped the phone from her ear and glanced down at it. "What? You have got to be kidding me." She rapped on the door a few times, but the hall remained empty. She banged again. "Come on. Someone—"

Ah!

Oh.

An MP came around the corner, suspicion gouged into his face.

Great. She waited, plastering on her nicest smile, shifting her weight off her right leg.

The MP opened the door. "Can I help you, ma'am?"

She held up her card. "It must've demagnetized."

Unconvinced, he stepped outside, being sure the door closed behind him. "Do you have ID, ma'am?"

Frankie wanted to groan and chew out this soldier. "Yes." She dug her ID out again and handed it over. "Lieutenant Francesca Solomon." She pointed to the building. "I work here, but my card's not working."

He held a hand to her, guiding her backward. "Let's step away from the door, ma'am, while I call this in."

Chewing him out would only make it worse. *It will only make it worse. It will only make it worse.* No matter how many times she said the words in her head, she couldn't calm herself down.

". . .a Francesca Solomon here, seeking access to the INSCOM building." He rattled off her SSN and her ID number.

"Access denied," squawked a voice.

"No!" Frankie shook her head. "I work here. That's a mistake."

"Sorry, ma'am."

His radio squawked his name then, ". . .ordered to escort her off base immediately."

"*What?!*" Frankie couldn't contain her outrage. "Are you freakin' kidding me? Do you know who I am? Who my father is?"

"Frankly, ma'am, I don't care. I have my orders." He pointed her to the parking lot. "Do you have a car?"

"Wait," she said. "Do you have a phone I can use? I'll call my CO and get this cleared—"

"Ma'am, I'm trying to be nice here. I can let you walk, or I can cuff you and haul you out of here."

Frankie drew back, only then noticing the small crowd forming down the sidewalk. Flashbacks of what happened to her father forced her to comply with the order to leave. She drew up her courage, glanced at the specialist's name patch, then started walking. "You'll regret this, Specialist Buzard."

He said nothing but escorted her to the red compact rental car. As she tugged out the keys, she remembered he had her DOD ID card. "My card." She held out her hand.

"Sorry, ma'am. They ordered me to take it."

"What?! That's my job—my ID. I can't get into my office without it."

"Reckon that's so—but I don't think you have a job anymore, ma'am."

Furious, Frankie toyed with grabbing it from him, but she saw his hand move to his weapon holster. She stamped to the car and climbed in. After starting it, she deliberately pealed out of the spot, whipping toward him as close as she could. She wouldn't hurt him, just give him a good dose of what he made her feel right then.

"Augh!" she groaned, her side aching from the way her own foolish driving whipped her around. Once clear of the gate, she felt her nerves thrumming. She so needed a Chick-fil-A Cookies & Cream shake. She hit the highway then veered off when she spotted the red-and-white sign. Pulling up to the speaker, she rolled down her window.

"Hi! Welcome to Chick-fil-A. How can I serve you today?"

"Yes—I need the biggest Cookies & Cream shake you can give me."

The speaker laughed. Probably mocking her. Frankie didn't care. She needed a fix. After totaling her car, burning her leg, losing Trace, and now—whatever was happening at Belvoir—she needed *five* of these things.

After getting her total, she eased up to the window and handed off her card. She brushed back her long, black hair, desperate for a breeze, for a break.

"Sorry—the card's not working. Would you like to try another form of payment?"

Frankie stared at her. How could her card not work? "Can you try it again?"

The teenage host held up the card and gave her a sympathetic frown. "Sorry, I did."

Stunned, Frankie took the card and dug in her purse and found a five stuffed between receipts. She handed it over, shaken. What was happening? Shake in the cup holder, Frankie pulled away from the restaurant, numb.

As she made her way home, she couldn't get rid of a daunting feeling. The phone. . .the access card. . .credit card. . . It was starting to read like a bad spy novel. She reached for her phone, a second-nature move, only to lift it and remember she had no service.

Bling!

Her gaze slid to the light on her dash. Gas. She needed gas.

"No way," she muttered. Weren't rentals supposed to have a full tank? With the way her luck was going, she probably couldn't get her credit card to work either. No, she wanted to get home and call her dad.

Running to Daddy.

Well, who else would she run to? She didn't have anyone else. Frankie parked along the curb, grabbed her purse, and hoisted it. The strap broke. "Are you—?" Rage shot through her. "For the love of—augh!" She snatched the black bag and tucked it under her arm as she lifted the shake.

She slid out, angling to clear the door.

When the lid popped off the cup, ice-cold ice cream plopped onto her leg. Frankie screamed. Stood next to the car, staring down at her pant leg. Kicked the cup with the remaining shake. Slammed the door. Trudged up to her front door. She aimed the key at the lock.

And froze. Wood splintered along the jamb. The door hung open.

Trace
Lucketts, Virginia
12 May – 1000 Hours

After verifying a dozen times that he wasn't followed, having taken ridiculous routes to get to the barn of the bunker, Trace hustled down the steps into the secured area. He coded in and the door swung open. Good thing Boone had been bored in life and worked on this place, or they wouldn't have anywhere to hide the girls. Keep them out of sight and out of trouble. Though he'd known for a while he couldn't keep them down here forever. They needed to solve this nightmare. Which is why he'd been shooting scenarios, working angles. Something—there had to be a solution.

Across the room, working at the workstations set up in an X pattern, Houston and Boone looked up at him.

"Any more word on Augsburger?" Trace asked as the door thunked closed behind him. Locks engaged with a heavy thud and hiss.

"Still critical," Boone said. "Family found him unconscious. No visible injuries. Doctors aren't sure what happened but suspect he might've had an internal injury they missed. They're doing blood panels, but the results aren't in yet."

"And Shay?"

Grim-faced, Boone bobbed his head and shoulders. "Stable. Vitals are normalizing but still critical."

"What—"

Boone snapped to his feet, his gaze locked on something behind Trace.

Trace pivoted. Saw a form moving forward. When he didn't recognize the person, he drew his weapon. "Stop right there."

The scrawny guy stopped, eyes wide beneath a mop of shiny black hair. Houston's muttered curses whispered through the place as he shifted to a safe location.

"Boone?" Trace wanted to know how this happened.

"Got me," Boone said.

Sidestepping the table, Trace closed in. "Hands up!" The guy's compliance didn't alleviate the dread sinking through Trace. He'd been in the back. With the girls. *Where are they?* "Annie! Téya!" He shoved forward, his finger moving to the trigger. "What were you doing back there?" How'd this guy get in here? Trace sure didn't want to have to shoot someone in here. That'd be a bad mess to clean up, both with the Brass and literally.

Boone said nothing but edged in from the right to flank the kid.

How in blazes did the kid think he'd get out of here alive? *How did he get in?*

When the kid didn't speak or move, Trace knew it was time to take him down. "On your knees! Now—on your knees."

"Trace."

His mind bungeed around the voice. Around the eyes. Felt like he'd been sucked into some wigged-out vortex. Brain warring with what his eyes saw, Trace didn't trust himself to so much as flinch.

The kid lifted a hand to his head.

Trace firmed his grip. "Don't move."

With a quick swipe, the kid gripped a clump of the ebony strands and tugged back.

"Stop!"

The black hair fell away. Something spit from the kid's mouth. Now, instead of the kid, Annie stood there. She stared at him with a vacant expression, her demeanor shifting.

Trace lowered his weapon, his mind blank as if it'd had a massive nerve block. Slowly, Téya and Nuala emerged from the lounge area and stood slightly behind Annie. A defensive posture if he ever saw one. "I don't understand." Anger vaulted his confusion. "Do you know how stupid that was? I could've shot you!" The realization made his head light. Almost shot Annie. . .

"It was a risk." Annie fiddled with the wig, never removing her gaze from his. "But one we felt we had to take."

He holstered his weapon. "Why?"

She looked to her sisters-in-arms and then back at him. "You trained us to be soldiers. To fight. You did a good job, carefully selecting us."

Arms to the side, Trace waited. He was being trapped. Could feel it. But he wasn't stupid enough to step in it. *Or maybe I already did.*

"So you know us." Her voice remained calm and strangely quiet. "Though we're each different in how we handle stress, we're all fighters. We won't take some things sitting down. Including this."

Wariness crowded into his tension. "Including *what*?"

"Being kept here under lock and key."

Trace opened his mouth.

Annie held up a hand. "You walked in here, into what you believed was a secure bunker, and you thought there was an intruder. Right?"

No way would he feed this frenzy.

"You drew your weapon on me, convinced I was trouble." Annie smiled.

"What's your point, Annie?" He hated getting played. Hated that whatever point she thought she'd made, it was going to work against him. Silently, he begged her not to force his hand. Or will.

"We want to help solve the puzzle. Actively."

"How's that?"

Annie held up the wig. "We'll go disguised for now." She pointed to the wall. "We need to start with Jess's notes. The names. Interview, investigate."

Though he hated to admit it, she might be right. With disguises, they could go out there and triple the efforts he'd made. Go over stuff he'd studied a thousand times, but with their fresh eyes. With their experience of being on the other end of the mission.

"There's been too much collateral damage," Téya said, stepping into the conversation. "It's time to put all of our wits and knowledge to work."

"We just want redemption," Nuala said. "To prove that we aren't the cold, calloused killers we were made out to be."

"Redemption," Trace repeated, eyeing them.

They stood staring at him, expectancy in each of their eyes. He ached that the other half of their team was missing, that he hadn't been able to protect all of Zulu. Six amazing women who'd taken on the daunting task of being Special Operations soldiers. Who'd succeeded and kicked some serious butt in the field. Now they were his team. His responsibility. Annie with her formidable tenacity. Téya with her forthright fervor. Nuala with her focused resolve.

Formidable. Focused. Fervent.

God help the man who tried to get in their way.

Trace turned and went to the command station.

"Trace, you can't say no or ignore us," Annie said, apparently following him to the dais. "We can do this. Trust us."

"Keeping us kenneled here is not going to go well," Téya added.

"I'm ready to climb some walls, so let those walls be the ones the traitor put between us and the truth," Nuala said. "I'm ready to end this. We all are. Aren't you?"

Trace studied Herring's data chart. The names. The places.

Annie hovered at his elbow. "Please, Trace. Don't hold what happened between us over this time."

He scowled at her. "Is that what you really think of me? That I'd kill an innocent man, that I'd punish someone because—" He snatched a picture off the data wall and thrust it at her.

Annie frowned at the picture, confusion etched into her face. "What?"

"Kellie Hollister," he said, tapping the image as he looked at the others. "Cofounder of Hope of Mercy, International. We found her."

Nobody spoke. They seemed as confused as Annie.

Trace grunted. "Well, I thought you ladies wanted an assignment." He rested his hands on his tac belt. "You're going to Denver to find out what she knows."

Annie
Denver, Colorado
14 May – 1325 Hours

Four and a half years had passed since Kellie Hollister was last interviewed regarding the ministry of HOMe—Hope of Mercy, International. It'd be interesting to see the difference in her testimony then and now. Annie had read and reread Mrs. Hollister's accounts of Misrata, and not without a great deal of nausea and anger.

Annie climbed out of the dark blue Ford Escape and adjusted her lightweight sweater.

On the other side, Téya stood at the bumper eyeing the building. "Quite a place."

"Maybe someone donated it." But even as Annie said it, her gaze hit the cars in the parking lot. Lexus, Acura, Infiniti. . . "Maybe not."

Téya laughed as they strode around the fountain and made their way to the glass and steel structure. Another fountain tossed light-colored streams of water in a dance choreographed to some classical piece. "Must be some good money in orphanages and shelters," she muttered as they approached the front desk.

Annie showed the guard her ID. Or rather, the fake ID Trace had gotten her. "Angela Pennington to see Mrs. Hollister."

The guard took her ID, motioned for Téya's, then took them both and made a very hushed call. He replaced the receiver in the cradle then lumbered to his feet. "Step through the scanners, please."

Annie resisted the urge to look at Téya—they'd both wanted to take weapons, but Boone warned them that security would not allow weapons on the premises. Although they really didn't expect trouble, sometimes it came to them anyway. Like Misrata. Like Manson.

Sam.

Annie cleared her throat as she waited for the elevator, working to calm her nerves. She wasn't Annie Palermo with curly white-blond hair. She was Angela Pennington with a short brown crop. Téya, on the other hand, had a more drastic change, wearing the black wig that had convinced Trace to let them start working on the case rather than being sitting ducks. But the wig wasn't the drastic change. It was the dress uniform—skirt, pumps, and a blouse, that had startled even Annie.

"Stop staring," Téya said once they stepped into the elevator.

Annie smiled. "Sorry. It's just so. . .*not you.*"

On the fourth floor, they were greeted by another security station. Two sentries stood by the double doors, while a third stood and smiled at them. A flirt. "Morning, ladies."

Projecting an air of indifference, Annie presented her ID.

The guard took her card and swiped it on something. Annie's heart gave a little start. Would it work, being a fake? Where was that data being streamed to?

A bleep sounded, and he returned the card. "Thank you." He did the same with Téya's and it, too, cleared. Trace had been more thorough than Annie expected.

"This way," the guard said and started *away* from the double doors. Away from the stark, poignant black-and-white poster-sized photos of third-world children. Group shots. Children playing games. Children crying.

Annie frowned at Téya. "Where. . .?"

He smiled and pushed through a panel that looked like a regular part of the wall. The heavy release of a lock hissed at them as they passed through the opening.

"Good morning, Miss Pennington." A woman stood there dressed in a sleek dark gray business suit and silk blouse. Annie couldn't be sure, but those pumps sure looked like Cole Haans. She'd eyed a similar pair awhile back, bemoaning her ultra-small paycheck and funds. With a blunt, inverted bob, the woman's salon-perfect hair seemed especially dark against her pale complexion. "Miss Ritter."

"You must be Kellie Hollister." Annie accepted the woman's hand and gave it a firm squeeze, cringing at the weak handshake she got in return.

"Indeed I am." She motioned to a round table by the wall of windows. "Please, let's get started. I have a lunch meeting."

They were seated so the sun streamed straight into Annie's eyes and made a halo out of the woman's coiffed hair.

"As was explained on the phone," Annie began as she scooted her chair in and crossed her legs, "we're taking a fresh look at this tragedy. We want justice for everyone."

"For the children, of course," Mrs. Hollister said as she flicked her hand, the sunlight throwing a blinding flash off the rock on her finger.

"Of course," Téya said.

Annie tensed, hearing the sarcasm in her friend's tone. "Would you please share what you know about Misrata?"

"Well," Mrs. Hollister said, threading her fingers and resting her hands on the glossy table. "As it states in your report, we'd had trouble with the local officials. They were extorting us to stay in the building we'd been in. HOMe didn't have the funds to pay both the bribe and the new lease cost. We had one day where we had nowhere to stay but had eighteen children, four staff, and a spouse. The warehouse was far from cozy or appropriate, but it was a desperate situation and time. And it was only for one night."

Annie switched the legs she had crossed. Hearing this story just ate her alive. The chances. . .the probability of these events colliding were astronomical, and yet—they did.

"We got the bunks set up in the area that had running water and just bedded down." Mrs. Hollister went stiff, her gaze dropping to the table. "They weren't supposed to be there," she whispered, her green-blue eyes glossing. "I didn't even know for two days afterward. . ."

Numb as streaks of warmth washed across her shoulders, Annie feared the moment this woman would uncover the ruse. Realize that Annie had been in the warehouse that night. That she'd set the charges, unaware of the children. Who hadn't been there an hour earlier when she'd cleared that building.

"You didn't know?" Téya straightened and cocked her head. "How is that?"

"It was normal not to hear from a team except once a week, especially if things were going well. I hadn't heard from them, but I assumed things were sorted." She pushed back from the table. "Again, that's really all I know—well, that and the fact that I had to answer to Libya for the death of eighteen children and four caregivers."

"Four?" Annie glanced at her notes. "I thought there were five adults."

"There were. Four were HOMe staff, the fifth was a. . .spouse." She lifted her chin, a haughtiness drenching her put-together persona. "I would *never* have condoned that, had I been aware. One of the orphan girls who had aged out stayed to work at the center. She married a man and they lived at the center." She jutted her chin toward their paperwork. "His name is Berg Ballenger. You'll probably want to talk to him next."

Annie scanned her notes. "It says his wife and child died in the fire."

"Yes. Again, that was against regulations for a married couple to stay with the children, but the Misrata administrator authorized it— temporarily."

"Who was that?" Téya asked. "The administrator, I mean."

"Michelle Campbell."

"The survivor," Annie muttered.

"Yes." There went her stuck-up jaw again. "She narrowly escaped. I'm not sure how. You should talk to her."

"Do you have her address? Or one for Berg Ballenger?"

"I do." She nodded to the guard who stood behind and to her left. "I never felt Michelle quite gave us the whole story."

The door clicked open and a slender, petite woman gave a nod to the HOMe cofounder.

"Sorry," Mrs. Hollister said as she stood. "That's all I have time for. I do hope you can put this thing to rest."

Annie made her way to the door. "Oh, we had trouble locating. Mercy Chandler. Do you know where we can reach her?"

"No." Iciness oozed out of Mrs. Hollister as she lifted her purse from a drawer in her desk. "I do not. She hasn't been a part of HOMe for a long while."

"But you kept her name." Hope of Mercy. . .named for Mercy Chandler.

"We kept everything but her and—" She froze, as if she'd made a mistake. "If you'll excuse me."

Téya
Denver, Colorado
14 May – 1500 Hours

Back in the rental, Téya tugged out the slip of paper the man handed her. "I thought that guy was her 'man in black.' Couldn't believe how he just did her bidding."

"There's a lot I couldn't believe," Annie said.

"Yeah?" Téya used the burner phone and pulled up the maps app. She plugged in the addresses.

"Don't you think they're a bit too wealthy?"

"*A bit*? How about *a lot*? Besides—there's something not right with that woman."

"What she told us matched perfectly with the files."

"Except her tone and body language." Téya lifted her phone and showed Annie the map. "Campbell lives a half hour away." She pointed to another spot. "That's Ballenger's last known, which is only a couple of blocks over."

"That's convenient."

"Yes and no. Our flight leaves in three hours. Think we can tackle both in that time?"

Annie winced. "Maybe."

"Then let's split up." Téya held up her disposable phone. "We have communication, and I can hoof it over to Ballenger's then meet you down the street at that burger joint."

"You're going to walk to Ballenger's?" Annie arched an eyebrow.

Téya frowned. "Yeah, what of it? I'm not out of shape."

"But you are in heels." Annie started the engine. "I'll drop you at Ballenger's then head over to the Campbells'."

"No, seriously. I'm a big girl. I can handle myself. If anything, I can use these suckers to fend off attackers." She grinned and opened the door. "See you back at the burger joint."

Téya crossed the street before Annie could object. It was silly really, but Téya just seriously needed the time alone. She hadn't been this crowded for quiet space in years.

Five years.

And in Bleak Pond, besides the noises unique to simple Amish life, it wasn't too different from being in the country. Most of all, it was quiet. Save the peals of children's laughter. Or the neighing of horses. A sudden pang struck her—she missed those sounds. Missed the evenings of quiet spent sitting on the porch doing needlework.

Téya snorted. Needlework. Who in their right mind would've thought she could find pleasure in doing anything with yarn other than strangling someone with it?

Gruesome thought. She cringed, knowing *Grossmammi* would give her that look. The one that held disapproval and yet never withheld love.

After another block, she turned left and headed down the street, searching the buildings for address numbers. On the other side, a vacant field had been fenced with several signs that read KEEP OUT. With each step, Téya's unease grew—and so did the dilapidation of the homes.

"So, woman in heels and expensive business suit strolls down crack neighborhood," Téya muttered to herself as she rounded a corner, "looking for"—her gaze hit the building—"Oh snap."

Annie
Denver, Colorado
14 May – 1530 Hours

Annie climbed the steps to the rundown Craftsman-style home with its wide, angular columns flanking the path to the door. Peeling paint revealed rotting wood and possible termites. She extended her pointer finger toward the cracked, yellow-brown doorbell button.

She pressed the doorbell. But she heard nothing. She craned her neck. Did the bell even work? After a few seconds and not hearing any movement inside, she jabbed it again. That time she heard the sound of a sick, dying doorbell chirp out its chime.

"I'm coming, I'm coming," someone called from the other side.

Chains slid back. Locks clicked back. The interior door swung open.

Through the screen door with its metal, dingy scrollwork, she saw a man. He stood there in gray sweats and a stained tank top. "Yeah?" he growled.

"I'm looking for Michelle Campbell."

The grumpy facade melted before Annie's eyes. But just as quick, he scowled. Squared off. "Yeah, what for?"

Annie held up her ID. "I'm Angela Pennington with the Department of Defense. I just wanted to ask a few questions."

He pushed open the screen door. "I'm Tim, her husband. Well," he mumbled, "I was. C'mon. I ain't afraid to talk to no one."

Gingerly stepping into the home, Annie stifled her automatic recoil against the dirt and the smell. Stale odors of cigarettes and something...lemony created a heady cocktail, hammering Annie's sinuses.

"Sorry about the mess. I didn't want to change anything after Michelle left." He cleared newspapers off the sofa. "There. Have a seat."

He plopped in a leather recliner that seemed to have a permanent impression of the man's body.

Perched on the edge of the sofa, Annie forced herself to think. "Left? Are you two separated?" That sounded so much nicer than "divorced." Semantics went a long way in placating people and convincing them to talk.

The man looked at her as if she'd lost her mind. "Separated—guess you could say that. She's dead."

Annie jolted at the revelation. "I. . .I'm so sorry. I had no idea." She riffled through her file. "There's no record of that here."

"That's because nobody's been around since then."

"Was she ill?" Annie felt terrible for even asking. It didn't matter how she died.

"You're here about that Misrata thing, aren't ya?" The scruffies rimming his chins caught the dim light of the swing-arm lamp.

"Yes, Misrata. I just wanted to—well, I'd hoped to hear what she knew," Annie said as she tucked a brown strand behind her ear and felt the wig shift a little. She tensed and chided herself for forgetting she had one on.

"Everything she knew she told them. She sure hated that Hollister."

"Mrs. Hollister, the cofounder?"

"Yeah, she wouldn't give Michelle the time of day after she returned." The man clucked his tongue. "For cryin' out loud, she had burns all over her arms and legs, and they wouldn't help her get medical care. They wouldn't even talk to her."

A bitter taste glanced across Annie's tongue. She pushed her attention to the files.

"She had nightmares and needed help, but they wouldn't even acknowledge her." He shook his head, his chin dimpling beneath the brown and gray stubble as he fought off tears. "She couldn't take it no more, so she swallowed a bunch of pills while I was out of town for work."

"For work?"

"I was working for a software company. But after losing Mich. . ." He hung his head then thumbed away a tear. After a long sniffle, he met her gaze again. "You look like a nice lady, Officer."

Annie couldn't bring herself to smile, though she tried.

"Please—promise me you'll find out what happened. Who bombed that place and burned those kids to death. Who stole my wife from me."

Legs trembling, Annie struggled to her feet. "I—I will." Good night! The person responsible for his wife's death was right in his own living room. What would he think when he found out? "Thank you for your time," she managed around a very dry mouth.

Stiff and poised so she did not give herself away, Annie hurried to the car. She climbed in. Her vision blurred, but she blinked it away. Forced herself to drive a few blocks. Tears streaking down her face, she pulled into the nearest shopping center and parked.

Gripping the steering wheel tightly, she pressed her forehead against her hands. Fought back the squall of grief, guilt, and anguish.

She would do anything to erase that night. To rewind it and *never* enter Misrata. She slammed her hand on the wheel. She was so sick of innocent blood being spilled. The children. The staff. Now Michelle in a suicide.

Shuddering for a breath, she sat back. Stared out at nothing, seeing everything from the past. That night. The fire. The smoke...the smell.

She batted the tears away, angry again. Some psycho painted Zulu's hands with the blood of those innocents, and she was going to take him down in the biggest way possible.

Boone
Lucketts, Virginia
14 May – 1600 Hours

"Any word from the girls?"

Boone looked up from the report he'd been reading. Nuala entered the coms area as if walking on eggshells. "Not yet, but they're not late, so I'm not worried." He went back to the report, an intelligence brief dated from the time of the Misrata incident.

"I'm glad the commander let them go." In her words he heard the wistful desire to have gone with them.

"You'll go next time."

"Maybe." She slid into the cubicle that had been set up and assigned to her. It'd been another of Trace's attempts to let the girls feel productive, not like prisoners. "How's Keeley doing?"

Boone stilled, hating that people kept asking about her. Well, not that they *asked*. It was how they asked—like if they spoke too loudly, it'd be bad news or something. As if she were already dead. "Same." It was the only answer they needed. The only answer that kept them from asking more questions.

Bing!

Boone ignored the chime from Houston's station.

Bing!

Bing-bing!

"Uh," Houston said, his mouth dangling open. "Oh, we are so dead."

"What are those noises?" Nuala asked, coming out of her chair.

"Alerts. I have them on each of you."

Bing!

"No," Houston shouted. "No more. Stop!"

Bing-bing-bing!

"Holy—good—no—" He turned a pale face to Boone and shook his head. "This is some serious trouble."

Houston hunched over his keyboard, watching monitors, his fingers flying. Curses and other oaths singed the air.

Boone was out of his seat. "Easy, easy." He leaned over the guy's shoulder, a hand braced on the tall chair. "What's happening?"

"Hang. . .on," Houston said as he struck a few keys then clicked. "And—there it is." He looked over his right shoulder to the wall they'd turned into a massive screen.

More than twenty—*thirty?*—pages were spread on the screen, landing on top of each other as if someone dealt a deck of cards. Dozens of social media sites. What was the. . .

"Son of a. . ." Boone couldn't believe what he saw. On every site, there was now a campaign page labeled:

Help Find Ashland Palmieri!

And there, in the right-hand corner was a picture of Annie in all her wild-haired glory.

"This is so bad. I mean—this is good in reverse, ya'll," Houston said, his voice squeaking. "This is popping up on every site I can think of, and probably on ones I can't."

"Who did this?" Boone demanded. "Never mind—can you take them down?"

"Well, yes. But it's going to take time."

"Do it!"

"This is *insane*." Houston grimaced. "Every site. . .even the ones I think wouldn't have this—*bam!* It's there."

"Who's that with her?" Nuala asked, coming up next to him.

The very guy Boone wanted to get his hands on. "Sam Caliguari."

"The hunky Navy SEAL guy?"

"You sound way too pleased," Boone growled. "You know what that could do?"

"Yeah, get her killed. Or him."

He pointed to another picture. "Houston, who's on the right with her in the other photo?"

"Uh. . ."

Boone watched as the cursor moved to that image and clicked, and a dotted line formed a box around the man's face. A drop-down menu appeared and clicked off before Boone could read the options.

A few seconds later, Houston popped another photo on the screen. "Jeff Conwell. Owner of the Green Dot Sub Shop where Annie worked."

"I want to know who did this." Boone's phone belted out the national anthem, the ringtone he'd assigned to Trace. He lifted it and answered. "You seeing this?"

"I may just make good on Annie's belief that I'd kill that guy."

"You think it was him?" Dumb question, but Boone would rather have proof before he lobbed off the guy's head.

"Who else would it be? I'm on my way there. Have you heard from the girls?"

"Negative." Boone glanced at his watch. "They should be on the plane. I'll verify that."

The call ended and Boone stalked to Houston's station. "Anything?"

"I have to manually remove every one, which means hacking into each site. It will take time."

"The origination?"

"As far as I can tell—all from the same site: Manson, Washington."

"So it was Sam?"

"If I can verify the IP address. . ." Houston scanned back and forth. "Uh, the address doesn't belong to Caliguari." Houston shrugged. "He probably hired someone to do it."

Bing! Bing-bing!

"You're kidding me," Houston shouted. "I am going to nuke this guy!" He did this growl thing that reminded Boone a lot of one of the *Three Stooges* characters.

Bing!

Houston gaped. "I *know* you didn't! Dude, I am sending a nuke so far up your—"

"Houston," Boone snapped, aware of Nuala covering her mouth. If it weren't so serious, he'd be funny. "Get the sites down."

"It'd be *easier*," Houston snarled, "if I just accidentally launched a nuclear warhead at him." His eyes moved as his fingers flew over the keyboard. "But since that would be rude, maybe if I just snuck in"—he craned his neck—"his back door. . .and. . .killed. . .his dog." Houston sat up. "Okay, I think. . .*think* that will keep his trigger finger quiet for a while."

"What'd you do?"

"Sent a virus into his system, crippling him from sending anything out. That should give us time to get those sites down and report his address so the site will ban him."

"You can get someone banned with one e-mail?" Nuala asked.

"I never said *one* e-mail."

Boone shifted closer. "Can you ghost an e-mail?"

"*Psh*," Houston said with a scowl. "Of course I can. Who do you—"

"Send him an e-mail from Annie." Boone gritted his teeth, knowing she'd hate him for this. "Something to the effect of, 'If you care about me at all, please stop trying to find me.'"

Annie
Denver, Colorado
14 May – 1700 Hours

The burger sagged in the red plastic basket next to the fries, untouched. Old memories of her late mother chiding her for not eating all her dinner nagged her conscience, so she lifted a fry and munched on it. Annie sat at a perimeter table, chin propped in her palm as she watched out the windows for Téya.

Half hour late. Nothing to *really* worry about. But worrying, she was.

Téya appreciated consideration, so Annie couldn't believe her friend would willingly be late. She wasn't a punctuality fiend—*no, that'd be me*—but she would consider it rude to be late. Especially thirty minutes.

But she was walking.

In heels.

Then again, what if she'd just gotten enthralled with some new revelation Berg Ballenger had? What if right now, Téya was solving the whole riddle?

Annie lifted her food and dumped it in the trash and headed to the rental car. She climbed in and made her way toward the address. Surely she'd come across Téya walking. Or limping in those pumps. The thought almost made her smile. The thrill of Trace saying they could buy new clothes was lost on her feisty friend when she saw what he insisted they order. Not the trendy jeans and baby-doll T-shirts Téya loved. But work attire. Slacks. Blouses.

"You put him up to this, didn't you?" Téya had accused her with a mock slap.

Annie *had* been grateful for new clothes.

Someone walking across the street caught her attention. Annie's hope flared—then died when she realized the woman had light brown hair. Téya's natural color.

Annie sighed. "Where are you, Téya?" she murmured as she drove down the street and slowed. . . She came to an empty lot. No building.

Strange.

Must've taken a wrong turn. She pulled into the lot and opened the navigation app on her pay-as-you-go smartphone. Working from the address the guy at HOMe had given them, she punched in the address. To her frustration, it said she was at the right place.

Annie glanced at the buildings surrounding the vacant lot. An apartment complex on the right. And on the opposite side, the back of a large store abutted the parking lot. So, if there's no building. . .no address where Ballenger lives. . .

Where is Téya?

She entered the memorized number for Trace and pressed TALK.

"What's wrong?"

How did the man always know? "I can't find Téya."

"What do you mean—how did you lose her?"

Annie gritted her teeth. "We split up—"

"I told you—"

"Chew me out later. She's missing. I'm about to miss our flight. What do I do?"

The line went silent, and Annie realized she'd overstepped. Their history had to stay out of the mission.

"Sorry," she bit out. "I'm just. . .the flight is leaving."

"Forget about the flight. We'll get another." The phone went muffled, but she could hear him talking to someone else. "Okay, listen," he said to her. "I'm going to—"

Crack!

A thousand tiny spiderweb cracks snapped across her windshield. Annie flinched, staring at the glass.

"What was that?" Trace demanded.

As his question boomed in her mind, she saw the hole on the right side. "A shot," she said, dumbstruck. Adrenaline exploded through her. "Someone shot at me!" she shouted as she tore off down the street.

"Get out of there. *Now!*" Trace barked.

"But Téya—"

"You can't help her if you're dead!"

Part 2:
Out of Nowhere

V

A fist flew at her face. Téya swung out of the way, but not fast enough. The meaty paw connected with her chin. Snapped her head up. Made her stumble backward. Even as she stumbled, she swung out with a front round kick. Aimed for the vague shape of the body that had taken form in the building whose only inhabitants were spiders, the shadows, and the musty stench.

That is, until she smelled *him*.

As she came down from the kick, she leaned in and threw a hard right into his side. *Crack!* The move would've shut down a lesser man. But this guy had as much training as, if not more than, she did. He growled through the obvious pain from the broken rib then lifted his elbow and rammed it down against her shoulder.

Téya grabbed his arm, yanked it behind him, and shoved him against the wall.

With a head butt, he freed himself.

The bloody warmth that signaled a serious nosebleed and one, if not two black eyes by morning, slid down her lip and chin. She bounced back a couple of steps in the narrow hall to regroup. If she let a nosebleed and wracking pain stop her, this guy would kill her.

Light pushed through narrow slats of boards barring a window and darkening the shape of her attacker. As she started to weigh her options, his possible moves, she detected a slight change in his posture.

She blocked left just quickly enough and brought the heel of her right hand up and straight into his neck, connecting with a meaty thud. A *whoosh* of air knocked out of him as he went sideways. He dove in and she used his momentum against him, caught his arm and yanked him farther in, bringing her fist into his nose as she did.

His knees wobbled.

With a jump front kick, she drove him backward. His hand flashed out, thumping against the wall as he tried to hold his balance.

Téya jumped and kicked again, her foot snapping his head back. She landed and pivoted, determined to get out—alive.

Her ankle caught.

She face-planted. With a grunt and shaking the momentary brain stun—*what happened?*—she pushed up with both arms.

Pain exploded across the back of her head. She dropped against the floor, hard.

Shouts from somewhere in the building warbled in her head.

The attacker yelled something.

Shots erupted.

There's two of them! Her chance of success just plummeted. Time to get out of here. Get out or die. From the corner of her eyes, she saw her attacker look toward the other end of the hall. He took two steps in that direction.

Téya lunged the way she'd come, scrabbling for traction as she ran. She skidded around a corner, hobbling to stop from slamming into the wall. Behind her, she heard the pursuit of her attacker. She wasn't stopping. Wasn't giving them the chance to cut her life short. She saw the door she'd come through, the one hanging askew, and bolted for it. The thumping of her feet on the old wood floor echoing the frenetic pace of her pulse.

Heavier thuds gave chase. Closer. . .closer. . .

Téya threw herself at the door. It flapped back. She went sailing over the rail. Down the three-foot drop to the dead grass and dirt. Though she stumbled, her fingers trailing along the scratchy terrain, she kept moving. Aimed for the trees, oddly thriving in the dead neighborhood. She dodged in and around the trunks, expecting to feel a stabbing pain in her back any second. Sprinting, she aimed down the block, regaining her bearings. Her sense of direction.

Gotta find Annie.

Panting, she didn't slow. They'd catch her. Any second now. She was sure.

She veered left, heading back toward their rendezvous spot. Ahead she saw a blur of red—*Annie!*

Téya gauged her location. Remembered the map. If she went east one more block and cut north, she might catch her. Lights. Please give her red lights. With renewed hope, Téya bolted in that direction. Defying her rubbery, tired limbs, she ran faster. Pushed harder.

Pain stabbed the bottom of her feet. "Augh!" The fresh injury slowed her.

A glint of red between two buildings warned her the time window she'd figured was closing. If she missed Annie. . .

Unheeding of the pain, she darted down an alley.

A form rose from the side, clumsy—drunk. She pushed around

the vagrant and kept moving, knowing she'd have to soak her foot in antibacterial goo for weeks after this venture. She rushed out into the open and stopped, glancing left.

No Annie.

Right.

No Annie.

"No." Téya turned back in both directions again, frantic. "No no no." Defeat enticed her to step into its embrace. She wanted to scream. Shout for help. But that would only draw attention she didn't want or need.

Tires screeched behind her.

She pivoted. Saw nothing. But then—the whirring of a car flooded her ears. The red compact slid backward into view, having bypassed the street. "Annie," Téya breathed and limp-ran in that direction.

Annie whipped the car onto the street.

Téya jumped in. "Go," she said, pulling the door closed.

It was difficult to see through the shattered windshield, but Téya didn't care. She went limp in the car as Annie drove them to safety.

"What happened?" Annie asked, her gaze sliding up and down Téya.

Still panting hard, Téya shook her head. Too hard to talk yet. She pointed to the street. "Go." That's all she cared about. Getting away. Living. *Not* dying at the hands of those two lunatics.

"I see you got rid of your heels." Annie shot her a wry grin and handed her some tissues, nodding to her nose.

Téya had almost forgotten about the blood—but the swelling made it impossible to forget the head butt. "Two men were waiting for me." Once her breathing and heart rate stabilized, she lifted her right foot onto her knee to appraise the cut that had almost crippled her, and winced.

"Berg?" Annie cast her a worried look.

Téya shook her head. "Doubt it. This guy was trained, lightning fast, thus"—she motioned to her nose—"this. He was skilled. Do we know anything about Ballenger that says he was skilled like that? I thought he was just a guy working at the orphanage."

"No, nothing. But we can't rule him out," Annie said as she lifted her phone. "I haven't seen you look like that since your first go-round with Boone."

Bristling, Téya nodded to the shattered artwork. "And the window?"

"Soon as I pulled into the parking lot looking for you, someone shot at me."

"I don't know how I missed a shooter." As Téya used the vanity mirror to dab away the blood on her face, she realized the wig sat askew on her head. The part running toward the corner of her eyebrow. "Cleared that whole building looking for Ballenger, just in case he was there hiding out." She bunched her shoulders. "Now that I say that—I realize how stupid it was to walk in there. I was on my way out when the guy came out of the shadows."

"Trace," Annie said into her phone. "I've got her, we—" She snapped her mouth shut, nodding. "I know. We are—" Her nostrils flared as apparently Trace interrupted her again. "Agreed. We're heading back to Hollister now. Bye." The words came tumbling out and she ended the call, dropping the phone on the dash. Dropping? More like *throwing*.

Dare Téya ask? "Did you two—"

"We're going back to Hollister's."

"I kinda figured that out on my own. Thanks."

Annie's lips flattened. "Does he really think we can't take care of ourselves?"

Téya eyed her friend and combat buddy, and knew no matter what she said, it wouldn't help. "You think Hollister knew—or that she set us up?"

"How could she not?" The sneer was evident in Annie's voice. "*She* gave us the address."

"Well," Téya said, checking the swelling and mess the guy made of her face in the vanity mirror, "then I'm ready to return the favor her handyman delivered."

Annie
Denver, Colorado
14 May – 1720 Hours

"You set us up!"

Annie placed a hand on Téya's arm, trying to calm her. They stood in the parking lot of HOMe, where they'd intercepted Mrs. Hollister from escaping.

Kellie Hollister stood defiant. "I did no such thing!"

"Funny how two skilled thugs show up at the exact building on the exact day you send us down there," Téya said. "Took a shot at us"—she swung a hand toward the vehicle—"as you can see by the windshield, and tried to shove my nose through my gray matter. And you seriously expect us to believe you had nothing to do with that?"

Annie again tried to quiet her, this time with a look, too. "Mrs. Hollister, the place you sent us to is abandoned."

"Look," the woman said gently, "I am truly sorry for your injuries, and for what happened to the car, but I *promise* I had nothing to do with it.

That was Berg Ballenger's address. On the advice of my attorneys, I never visited the location, so I can't say what is there or isn't there."

"On the advice of your attorney?" Annie asked.

Hollister sighed. "After Misrata, Berg wanted nothing to do with us. He tried to sue us for wrongful death, and it was getting really ugly, but then he vanished." Her finely penciled-in eyebrows knitted as she hunched her shoulders. "I may not want to dredge up the past and revisit that nightmare, but I certainly wouldn't knowingly send anyone into a dangerous situation."

Somehow, Annie believed her. At least as far as this went. And what proof did they have to the contrary? That this woman had ulterior motives or ill intent toward them?

"Thank you," Annie said. "We'll be in touch again."

Téya glared at her before turning and climbing back in the car. "I can't believe you let her off like that," she muttered, buckling in.

"We have no proof."

"No, we only have fists and bullets flying at us."

Trace
Lucketts, Virginia
17 May – 0915 Hours

"Find him," Trace said as he stalked away from Houston. "He's your top priority."

"He's not here," Houston said, pointing to his bank of monitors. "I've looked since they got hit. He's. . .just gone. No forwarding address. No pings on his SSN. I've tried variations of his name—he's just not there."

"He is there." Trace clapped his shoulder. "Do whatever it takes."

"Do I have to be quiet, keep it discreet? That makes it harder."

"I don't care if you have to scream—just scream anonymously."

"Scream anonymously," Houston repeated, his gaze locked with Trace's. "Riiight."

The national anthem belted out, and Trace lifted his phone from his pocket. "Weston."

"I'm here. . .I think."

Trace smirked. "Give me a second." He strode toward the girls' bunk rooms and rapped on the doors. "Rise and shine. Get dressed. PT clothes."

A collective groan rose from behind the three doors.

"You realize we're not in the military anymore, right?" came Téya's loud complaint.

"Wrong attitude," Trace said with a smile. "Five minutes. Command

165

area." With that, he headed through the tunnels and made it topside. There he found a sleek black Suzuki GSX1 300R Hayabusa parked beside his Charger. A beefy guy wearing a T-shirt and jeans secured a flag-and-eagle screen-printed helmet. "Quade."

The guy turned and grinned. "Weston." Then he frowned. "You look old."

"About two years younger than you."

Quade Henley laughed, caught Trace's hand in a firm grip, and gave him a shoulder-bump-pat greeting.

"Have any trouble finding it?"

"More than I'll admit."

"Followed?"

"Yeah, but I killed them." Quade didn't miss a beat with this sick humor.

Trace laughed, shaking his head. "If you only knew how funny that wasn't."

"Don't worry. Witnesses will report that actor did it." More times than not, Quade was mistaken for the actor/wrestler Dwayne Johnson. The guy had a quick mind but an even quicker fist. "So, you need me to do some CQC training with a team?"

Trace nodded toward the secret passage. "C'mon. I'll explain on the way down."

Quade hooked his arm, stopping them both. "Hey." Intense eyes probed Trace's. "You okay, man? Seriously—you look tired. Stressed."

Nothing like having your longtime best friend call it straight. "Yeah. I'm okay. But it's bad."

With a hesitating bounce of his head, Quade slowly released him. "Of course it is—you called *me*. You hate the way I train grunts."

Zulu sure wouldn't appreciate him calling them grunts, but at this point, they were beyond platitudes and stroking egos. "We might disagree on methods, but you get results." Trace started walking. "We *need* results. Two of them were hit hard the other day. They are being hunted." He hustled down the narrow set of stairs to the concrete bunker.

"Hold up," Quade said, ducking as he went. "Hold up."

Hand on the final security measure, Trace turned to his friend, the lone bulb twinkling overhead.

"Is this..." Quade swiped a hand over his mouth. "Is this...*them*? The team you—"

Scowling, Trace said nothing but released the final door. His buddy knew better than to ask that. To go there.

They stepped into the somewhat brighter bunker. Zulu stood there, arms folded, eyes bleary, wearing gym shorts and shirts. Téya's messy and spunky ponytail reflected the girl's spirit. Annie's wavy blond hair looked like she'd had a fight with an electrical socket, and her expression mirrored that. As he'd come to expect, Nuala looked poised and put together, as if she'd been awake for hours. She probably had been.

"I haven't had a cup of coffee yet, so if you expect *nice*, you came to the wrong bunker, Commander," Téya said around a yawn.

Trace ignored the way his friend gawked at the girls. "After what happened to Téya, I felt it was time to regroup. Get some refresher training under our belts and face this threat head-on."

"Do we know the threat yet?" Annie challenged.

"From the looks of her face," Quade injected himself, "you don't. And as your commander said, it's time to regroup. My name is Quade Henley."

"Henley's an expert in close-quarters combat and krav maga."

"Street fighting. I took that already," Téya said.

"Not the way I teach it," Quade boasted.

Fire roiled through Annie's expression. "But he's *not* a part of this team. And that means he can bring trouble."

"He won't," Trace countered, heading off her objection.

"Where exactly are we training?" Téya asked, her eyes narrowed.

Trace led them out a side door and down a narrow tunnel beneath the stairs. There they found another room. Cement floors and walls, a couple of lights, and mats secured to the center. "Boone intended this for a recreation room, but defense is more important right now."

The others moved around the room, straight to the red-and-black floor mats. Last in, Annie hovered near the entrance with him. She turned to Trace. "You're kidding, right?"

He frowned. "About making sure my team is the safest it can be? Absolutely not."

"We don't know him," she hissed through a breath. "How can you bring a stranger—"

"He's not. I know Quade better than I know most of you."

"He's a newb to us."

"Don't let him hear you call him that." He tried to lighten things up.

"How can you do this? You won't let me talk to Sam or Téya to David, yet you bring in—"

"Enough." Trace drew in his anger and frustration with a long, controlled breath. "Enough. Trust me on this. For once in your life, *trust me*."

Her blue eyes blazed. "I did that once. It didn't turn out so well."

The words were very well placed. "You're still alive, aren't you?"

"I—"

"Hey. Blondie."

Annie's anger flared as she turned to Quade.

"Maybe you've been out a little too long, but when your commanding officer gives an order, you obey it." Quade gave Trace a look that said too much, that he didn't understand why Trace hadn't put Annie in her place. That said he was smart enough to figure out the rest if he spent some time on it. In essence, Quade had read through the blood-covered pages of their past.

Trace turned and left without another word. Feeling beaten and whipped, he sat on the iron steps leading to the upper level. Roughed his hands over his face. He'd failed the team. Failed Zulu. Failed each and every girl. Now he had to protect them, train them, prepare them for an enemy he couldn't even name. An enemy who had somehow taken a bead on them.

Why not me? Why hadn't he been targeted? And Boone. There had to be enough intel for them to figure out he and Boone were implicated. This situation was an exercise in futility trying to figure who rode their backs. And being around Annie again.

Trace rubbed his knuckles, conjuring up memories and images he thought he'd smothered years ago. She'd been promising, young, idealistic, naive—beautiful. Hiding Zulu, hiding her, had cost him everything. And she would never forgive him. He'd accepted that years ago, but hearing her hatred, hearing the venom in her voice was something he hadn't been prepared for.

"This doesn't look good." Boone's voice boomed through the stairwell as he descended from the upper level.

Peeling himself off the stairs, Trace sighed.

"Let me guess—Quade didn't go over too well with them."

"It'll get worse," Trace said as he stepped toward the command center. "They just started."

"When do you want me to brush up their firearms training?"

"Tonight. We can't afford to be soft on them. Whoever wants them dead is hitting them for all they're worth." Trace planted his hands on his tac belt. "How's Shay?"

Boone's face brightened. "Good. Doc said she's made a lot of improvement. I'm looking into bringing her back here, setting up a bed."

Trace frowned. "We can't bring a nurse or doctor in here."

"I can take care of her."

"No." Trace started for the briefing room. "I need your attention on Téya, Annie, and Nuala, not babysitting."

"Look, I know you don't care—"

Trace pivoted on his friend. "What I don't care for is that you crossed the line. I knew it was happening. But it didn't interfere with your job performance, so I kept my nose out of it. You violated code and got intimate with her. Now it's compromising your position."

Boone's face went dark.

Trace huffed. "Look, really—I don't care if you two ran off and eloped. What I do care about is keeping Zulu alive and taking down this piece of dirt trying to nail their coffins shut."

"Same here," Boone said.

"But Shay...?" Trace shook his head.

With a narrowed gaze, Boone held out his meaty arms. "What are you asking...?"

"Not asking. Telling." Trace swung open the briefing room door. "Shay's not coming here. Too complicated and too risky. Leave her there. When she's ambulatory, we'll give her a bunk. Until then—she's best situated with medical staff."

Téya

Lucketts, Virginia

19 May – 1645 Hours

"C'mon, ladies! Pain is weakness leaving the body!" Quade Henley barked as he paced the "workout" room like a rabid dog.

"I'll give you some pain," Téya muttered as she did her fortieth sit-up. Sweat slid down her forehead and into her eye, burning.

"What was that, Freckles?" Quade went to a knee, leaning into her face as she continued her repetitions. "Think your attacker is going to—"

Téya's fist shot up at his nose.

Quade caught it. Twisted and turned, flipping her onto her stomach, then hooked her hand behind her. "How'd I do that? How'd I get control of your body?"

Ignoring the pain it'd cause, Téya swung her free arm backward, her elbow catching him in the side of the head. Knocking him off balance.

"Good, good," he said, hopping to his feet and clapping. The guy gave new meaning to *rolling with the punches*. "Never give your opponent an opportunity. Read their body language, watch their eyes."

When she reached fifty sit-ups, Téya lay there on the mat, staring at the ceiling. Anger and a sense of futility roiled through her. She did not want to be here in this cement coffin. Didn't want to be engaged in acts of violence.

"All right, ladies. On your feet," Quade shouted.

"You realize we're only a few feet away, right?" Nuala struggled to her feet. "Screaming doesn't make a point any better than a normal tone of voice."

Quade considered her. Then Téya and Annie, who grouped up around their teammate. "Hit the trail."

Téya fantasized about throwing herself at him. Of conjuring up some psychic powers to make that lightbulb smash into his head. Anything to get this guy—

"Moove it!"

Topside and jogging a barely existent trail through the woods and around a creek that bordered the property, Téya gritted her teeth. "I'm going to kill him."

"I'm ready to take my knife to Trace for bringing this guy in," Annie huffed out, her blond curls matted to her head with sweat.

"What is with that?" Téya wet her lips and swallowed to quench her parched throat.

"Don't know," Annie breathed. "But does Trace really think this will do any good?"

"Can't outrun a sniper bullet."

"Speaking of sniper—where's Nuala?" Annie slowed to a fast walk, pushing her damp strands off her face. "If Trace can bring in this goon, why not Sam or David?"

Téya felt her stomach clench at the mention of David.

"Sam's a Navy SEAL—or was."

"Move it, ladies. Walking's for wusses." Quade's voice boomed over a megaphone.

"Seriously?" Téya glowered. "Why not take out a billboard announcing where we are?"

"Guess he thinks we're far enough out to be safe." Annie resumed her run.

When they made it back to the bunker, Quade was there waiting. "Since you took your sweet time, do another lap."

"Are you—?"

"Argue and I'll add more."

"Who do you think you are?" Téya demanded.

"The guy trying to keep you alive." Quade stood firm. "In ten seconds, you'll be doing two more laps."

"This is bull," Annie said.

"Ten. . ."

"Where's Nuala?"

"Nine. . ."

Téya drew up her shoulders. Inched forward.

Annie hooked her arm. "C'mon. We can use the fresh air."

Even as their feet padded across the inches-thick litter of fall and spring left in the field, they heard Quade say, "Clear your heads and come back ready to fight."

"That's a promise," Téya hissed.

But as she ran this time, she let her mind drift to David—was he doing better? Had he recovered from whatever sent him to the hospital? Her heart and mind were tangled up in the conflicting messages her heart telegraphed. One to stay away and keep him safe. The other to rush to his side.

"Does it get to you?" she asked Annie.

"What?"

"That we put them in danger?" She dropped out of the jog, hands on her hips as she walked, sucking big gulps of air. "I mean—that's why we were ordered to never return to our family or friends, right? So we don't." She swallowed hard, wetting her lips. "But we get close to people and put *them* in danger."

Annie said nothing for a few minutes as they did a fast walk-jog. "Sam. . ." She sighed. "I staved off his attention for two years. Finally gave up and gave in. And *that* night, the sniper shows up."

"Think he'll give up?"

Annie lowered her gaze. "I. . .I don't know. He's like a pit bull when he gets an idea, but at the same time, I don't know how much I meant to him. If I was just a challenge."

"*Laaaddies,*" Quade's voice taunted.

"I am truly going to kill him," Téya said as she started jogging again.

"What about David—have you heard how he's doing?"

Téya shook her head. "I'd rather not think about all that—I'd rather figure out where Berg Ballenger is, who was behind beating the tar out of me, and ultimately, who set us up in Misrata."

"Wouldn't we all?"

"How did we not have the information about Ballenger but HOMe did?"

"Maybe we weren't supposed to have that," Annie suggested. "Maybe she let something slip that shouldn't have come out."

"She admitted they were breaking rules letting Berg stay there with his wife."

"Child bride, sounds like."

"Maybe that's why. Maybe HOMe knew it wouldn't look good if word got out."

They finished the mile-long lap, Téya's rubbery legs threatening to pitch her to the ground as she made her way to the barn. Coming down the stairs, they encountered Boone, who was carrying a platter of burgers and hot dogs.

"What's that?" Téya demanded.

"Burgers," Boone said, a bit of sarcasm to his words, then he took the rest of the steps two at a time.

"Are we invited to the barbecue?" Annie asked as she continued down.

"Only if you hurry. I have a big appetite tonight."

Downstairs in the showers, Téya slammed her door shut. Who were they to beat them to a pulp then act as if this were any ordinary day on the farm? As if they were just lazing about? Ordering them to work their muscles into oblivion while the men drank beers and ate burgers. She scrubbed herself clean in the shower, dressed, then stormed out into the command area.

Only the top of Houston's curly hair was visible in the dimly lit area. Téya hit more lights, which yanked up the guy's head. "Are they still up there?"

Pencil in mouth, Houston stared. Dropped the pencil. "Who?"

"Boone? The Torture-Master."

Houston blinked. "Wha—"

With a grunt, Téya severed his reply. Irritation clawed up her spine. "Have you seen Nuala? She went missing after Henley's torture session."

"Nuala? I thought she was with you."

"It's a sad thing no one knows where we are," Téya groused. "Because nobody'd ever know if they came in and killed one of us."

"Now, that's not fair—I'm very busy here."

Yeah, busy with a whole lot of nothing that had gotten them nowhere. Futility and frustration soaked Téya's muscles. She'd had it. Had enough of this. It was over.

Trace

Thwack!

Shoulders squared, black hair shorn close, Quade stood ramrod straight, staring out at the field, then lowered his Airsoft M4 and lowered himself to a chair, muttering.

With a smirk, Trace grabbed a bottled water from the cooler, ignoring the thirst at the back of his throat for one of the brown bottles Quade supplied for tonight's barbecue.

"Going light tonight?" Quade asked as he eyed the sweating water bottle.

He'd shared more than a few beers with Quade back in the day. It had been a way to relax, to let go of stress and forget what they'd seen and done in the field. But he'd felt himself slipping. . .slipping into the arms of a fierce seductress known as alcoholism.

Trace took a swig of the water and watched Boone flip the patties over. "How are they coming?"

"They hate me," Quade snickered, sitting in a lawn chair, a pair of binoculars in hand.

"If they didn't," Trace said, "I'd wonder why I brought you."

"Right?" Quade's grin shone with pride. "They're good. I'll give you that."

"But?" Trace heard it coming. Tried not to feel irritated with the criticism, because he knew they'd gotten sloppy. Five years hiding, stifling their once razor-sharp skills, made the girls vulnerable.

"But they can be better." Quade took a swig and set it down, peering through the binoculars. He came to his feet. Lifting his Airsoft, he aimed.

Trace tensed, gaze roaming the field lit only by the orange streaks of the setting sun.

Quade fired.

The next several seconds stretched into one of the longest minutes Trace had experienced in days. When only the wind answered Quade's shot, Trace let out a breath he didn't realize he held. "Nice try."

With a grunt, his buddy dropped back into the chair. Took another gulp of his drink.

"Okay," Boone said, "I think—"

"What is going on here?" Téya demanded as she appeared out of the barn with Annie. "I thought we were lying low? Staying out of sight."

Quade tipped his bottle at her. "You are supposed to be lying low, Freckles."

Trace scowled at his friend. Was he *trying* to tick off the girls?

"Look, you," Téya hissed.

"Trace," Annie cut in, her expression stone cold. "We'd like an explanation."

She'd always been tough. Straightforward. Bordered a little on insubordinate as they grew more. . .*acquainted* with each other. He watched her, waiting.

Her nostrils flared. "You will not let Téya see David. You block me from talking to Sam. Yet you bring him"—she stabbed a finger at Quade—"to sit out here, drinking beer and goofing off."

Boone delivered a platter of cooked burgers. Quade was right there, undeterred about Annie and Téya's objections.

"Seriously," Téya said. "Are we supposed to learn how to outrun sniper bullets? Because if I remember correctly, that's how Candice and Jessie died. I'm not imagining all the laps in the world around this godforsaken place would enable us to do that."

They were ranting. Upset. Neither of them had wanted to come back. Though he hadn't interacted with them, he knew what they'd been up to. Kept tabs on them. On every piece of communication or significant event in their lives. Jobs. Moves. Major purchases. He had to so he could catch anything that might draw attention to them.

"Ah, ha, ha-haaaa," Quade said as he dressed his burger.

The ambivalent attitude was one intended to anger the girls. Make them see him as a source of their problem. Get them to hit hard and not give up. It worked well on most grunts. But these two ladies weren't grunts.

"So help me," Téya said, glowering at Quade, "I will shove that thing down your throat."

Thwack!

The sound startled everyone, including Trace. He stilled then saw the paint that had exploded all over Quade's shirt, face, hair, and burger. He dropped it with a curse, lunging to his feet.

Téya and Annie frowned, confused, as they looked around trying to figure out what was happening.

But Trace knew. And smiled.

"Show yourself," Quade shouted, his face red and his vein throbbing near his temple. "Show yourself!"

The girls turned in the direction he shouted. Boone's chuckle seeped into the darkening night as grass shifted just inside the yard's perimeter. The blades rippled and rose. . .up. . .up.

Pride spiraled through Trace.

Dressed in a ghillie suit, Nuala removed the head covering she'd created from local vegetation to conceal her movement. With an Airsoft sniper rifle slung over her arm, she stared back, a hardness in her eyes Trace hadn't noticed before. The same kind darkening the eyes of her teammates.

A raucous applause broke out as Quade started laughing. "Well done, young lady! I'm impressed."

"Thank you," she called as she crossed the field and set down the gear. She straightened and looked at Boone, who grinned unabashedly. "I had the best instructor."

"I showed her a few things, but Noodle has skills that can't be taught."

Quade made a puking sound. "Y'all are nauseating with all this sappy stuff." He slapped Boone on the shoulder. "Brother, I need another burger. Seems this young lady poisoned it."

"Just because we care about and look after each other—that isn't a bad thing," Téya snapped.

"It is when you're in the field and it compromises your decisions," Quade countered.

"Well," Annie said, her voice quiet but her tone deadly. "You don't have to worry about that where Trace is concerned."

Her words sliced through him like a knife.

"He was always a tough mudder," Quade said. "Singular focus to the team and the mission. Kept personal feelings out of it, which is why he's where he is now." Surprisingly, admiration glinted in the man's eyes as he looked at Trace. "Isn't that right, Colonel?"

Trace set down his water. "I think you've had too much to drink. You're going soft."

"You should've seen this guy when we were in Iraq." Quade launched into a tale that was very exaggerated and puffed up his own role in the takedown of some notorious Taliban leaders.

Hanging back with a burger, Trace watched Annie. She hated him. He couldn't blame her. He'd made a decision that had kept her safe. One, it seemed, she would forever hold against him. But what was she worried about? She had that Navy SEAL to keep her cozy.

They'd never be on friendly terms again. He'd hurt her after Misrata. And once she found out about the SEAL…that he'd hurt her again…the pit of hatred would be deep enough to bury him.

Appetite lost, Trace chucked the burger and the hope that she'd forgive him.

Sam
Manson, Washington
19 May – 1645 Hours

Rock music blazed through the night as Sam stood on his deck, hands shoved in his jeans pockets as he stared at the small tan cottage. More accurately, the one that had set his life on a collision course with a quiet, demure woman who'd intrigued him from the first day he saw her sitting on that deck. The sunrise had created a halo around her golden-blond hair that looked as messy and windswept as any model.

Sam glanced down at the object in his hand. A gold circle, just like that halo. But not just a halo, a promise.

"Where are you, Ash?" He tucked the ring away and turned, roughing a hand over his mouth and down his neck as he slumped against the railing. Okay. Enough. He wanted answers. And they were coming as efficiently as a jammed M4.

Sam climbed into his Camaro and headed to the Green Dot. There was something about Ashland Palmieri that had quieted his soul. Getting out of the SEALs had been the hardest decision he'd made, but the back pain and hypervigilance that never went away convinced him it was time. That and the mission that cost him three buddies, who left behind a girlfriend, two wives, and four children.

When he arrived in Manson, he had no intention of sticking around longer than the summer, longer than the time it took to get a gig with a private security contractor. But then Ashland all but dared him to figure her out. Not directly. She was too private for that.

But was that need and demand for privacy *more* than just being a loner?

He parked near the Green Dot Sub Shop deck and strode swiftly inside. A line snaked back six or seven customers deep, but he went around them. Straight to the counter.

Jeff came around the corner with a tray of freshly chopped lettuce. His light expression vanished as he met Sam's gaze.

"C'we talk?" Sam said, making sure his tone warned Jeff this wasn't an invitation.

Jeff hesitated, his gaze tracking to the food bin propped against his green-and-yellow apron, then gave a curt nod even as Sam walked back outside. He leaned against his car and waited, hands in his pockets. The safest place for his fists right now. A few minutes later, the Green Dot owner emerged, sans apron.

"Why'd you lie to the reporter?"

Jeff held his ground. "Wasn't a lie."

"You said she hadn't been there in weeks."

"Yes," Jeff said, "and mentally, that was true."

"I'm not following."

"Easy," Jeff said, holding up his hands.

"I'm not tracking. Ashland considered you a close friend and you—" Sam shook his head. "I'm not sure what you did. But not talking to me, hiding things from that reporter—how does that help Ashland?"

"It keeps information about her contained. You should know about that."

"Contained?" Sam cocked his head. "Why do you think it needs to be contained?"

"Think about it. Think about what you told the cops."

"How do you know—" Sam bit off his question. Jeff knew everyone in town and they knew him. This was his turf.

"You said a pro sniper took hits at you both. Then Ashland vanishes after a man nobody knows or has seen around town—and that's something for Manson—shows up." Jeff thumped the back of his hand against Sam's shoulder. "Put that lethal brain of yours to work. Doesn't it sound a lot like she might be in trouble?"

"Why do you think I'm trying to find her?"

"What if finding her is what puts her in danger?"

Sam hesitated.

"Look, I don't know half the stuff you do with your experience, and I'm certainly no cop, but this sounds a lot like a witness relocation thing or something." Jeff edged in. "You're not the only one who cares about Ashland and wants to know that she's okay."

I don't just want to know she's safe—I want her safely back with me. Sam tugged his hand free from the pocket and rubbed his forehead. "None of it makes sense. Cops find nothing. I can't find anything."

A car whipped into the parking lot and Sam automatically tensed. He glanced over and saw Lowen Miles emerge from the silver vehicle. "Hey, I was headed out to your place but saw you here."

Sam started forward. "You find something?"

"Yes and no." Lowen handed him a paper. "First—remember I told you someone tipped me off, said to look into the women who were killed?"

Sam nodded, vaguely recalling that.

"Well, that person called again." He slid a piece of paper to Sam. "Two more names to look into. One's in Pennsylvania, one in Virginia."

Sam's head hurt. More questions, but no closer to finding Ashland.

"Annnd," Lowen said, producing yet another paper. "Remember those sites you created—'Help Find Ashland Palmieri'?"

Unfolding the paper, Sam cast a furtive glance to Jeff then to the paper. His eyes raced over the words, dragging his mind through a quagmire of muddy panic. Leave her alone? A minute flicker of betrayal slithered through him. Why would she. . .

No. This couldn't be right. Conviction stabbed him. "She didn't send this." As the words left his mouth, the conviction deepened.

Jeff was at his side. "What is it?"

He shoved the paper at his friend as he focused on Lowen. "Did you trace it?"

"Tried," Lowen said, adjusting his sunglasses. "It bounced all over the place like a racquetball. Never seen anything like it."

Sam nodded. "Proves it wasn't her."

"How's that?" Jeff asked.

"Ashland didn't even have a computer or laptop."

"Maybe she had hidden skills," Jeff said, but Sam shot him a scowl and Jeff held his hands up. "Just mentioning possibilities."

"How are those pages doing?" Sam was ready for some progress. Ready to get Ashland back. Whatever it took.

"Good, good. We've got well over 500k on the Facebook one—but then someone complained or something. Said we were spam or porn or some lie. We got shut down, but we appealed it. It'll be back up by the end of the day."

"Half a million?" Jeff asked, his eyes rounding. Then he looked at Sam and went still, his gaze dropping to the parking lot.

Agitation wound through Sam. While he couldn't explain it, there was a massive knot of irritation in his gut, and it needed an outlet. He tried to keep it from hitting Jeff. But that look. . . "What?"

Jeff met his gaze for a second. "Ah, it's—"

"Just spill it." Sam heard the impatience in his voice and drew in a calming breath.

"I was just thinking"—Jeff nodded to Lowen—"this page on Facebook. . .it has a picture of Ashland?"

"I gave him the one of me and her at the Fourth of July fireworks show."

Jeff drew up and gave a half nod. "Ashland's picture. . .half a million people seeing it—if we explore the possibility I mentioned, that she's intentionally hiding for some reason—"

"You really believe that?" Sam didn't want to. Didn't want to believe Ashland would hide, not from him. Not after what they'd shared. Not after she let him into her protected zone.

Staring at the picture for a few more minutes, Jeff finally grunted. Then shrugged. "I don't know. I just would hate to be putting her in danger by bringing attention to this."

Sam turned away, exhaling hard. He scratched the side of his face as he paced. Thought through the possibility. How would they know? "If she's not hiding, then she's in danger. How can you expect me to just sit here?"

"Don't."

Sam frowned. "Come again?"

Again, Jeff looked to the reporter and his friend. "You posted that page and then got the e-mail, right?"

The two men nodded.

"I see where you're going," Sam said, his mind spinning possibilities. "Ask for proof that Ashland's the one telling you to back off."

An idea took root. "I have a better idea."

Trace

Lucketts, Virginia

21 May – 1645 Hours

Ridiculous. Trace sat back in the chair at the briefing table and tossed down his pen. Despite the litter of papers strewn across the brown surface and the years of work he'd put into discovering who had been behind Misrata and who was still targeting Zulu, he had nothing.

Either he was entirely incompetent or. . .

They're just better than I am.

And Sam Caliguari. Like a cancerous tumor on Trace's back, the guy just wouldn't go away. He'd sent a message that read normally, but something nagged at the back of Trace's mind. Warned him Caliguari was testing the response. Trying to verify Annie had sent the e-mail, no doubt. He lifted the printout of the e-mail and read it again.

My only concern is for your safety and well-being. One word will reassure me and I will step off. Answer this—olives: yes or no?

They hadn't answered. They couldn't ask Annie what it meant because she didn't know they were warning the SEAL away. And she'd be ticked off with Trace if she found out. Considering how things were going, that was the last thing they needed.

Back to the mission. To the task at hand. His radar was homing on Berg Ballenger after the attack on Téya that left her with a broken nose and black eyes. Hollister sent them to an address she'd never visited. At least, that's what she said. Trace had Houston monitoring every bit of data and all calls in/out of that organization. He'd even had the tech geek dig through old records. Nothing smelled rotten.

Except Berg Ballenger. Where was he? Why had he dropped off the grid? That smelled fishy.

Trace pushed away from the endless pile of nothingness and stalked out into the command center, straight to Houston. "What'd you find on Ballenger?"

Boone looked up from a nearby system and adjusted his ball cap. "You look ticked."

"Sick of not having answers," Trace admitted. He jutted his jaw toward Houston. "Well?"

"Uhh," Houston said as he pulled up files and splashed them over the wall screen. "Not much. One passport photo—the one you gave me is the only one."

"No renewal?"

Houston shrugged. "Not that I can find."

"What did you find then?"

"I found out that his parents were Robert and Penny Ballenger. His mom's maiden name was Eddington. She has a brother named Bertrand." Houston looked up at Trace through his eyebrows. "That is an interesting man. A businessman with a lucrative stock portfolio. World traveler."

"How does that help us?" Boone asked.

"Guess it doesn't, but Eddington's passport has some interesting stamps."

"Yeah?"

"Morocco, Greece, Paris, Palestine"—his gaze locked with Trace's—"Libya."

Though his heart kicked, Trace wouldn't read into that. "Lot of businessmen travel there. What else?"

"Nothing," Houston said. "The trail dies after the last U.S. stamp."

"Point of entry?"

Houston pulled up the image of the passport stamp.

"Denver," Trace muttered.

Boone pushed back, his boots tipped on the toes as he held his hands behind his head.

"Nothing after that. We've known that for years, right?"

"Why would he vanish?" Houston asked. "It's not like someone was deliberately trying to kill anyone. What happened in Misrata was an accident. No need to run, hide, or conceal your identity." Houston leaned back in the chair, causing it to squeak.

"Unless you had something to do with it."

Houston shot him a look. "Dude, seriously? Berg Ballenger?" He pointed to the screen. "The guy was what? Twenty-four when Misrata happened?"

"An accountant fresh out of college," Boone said, repeating the information they'd hammered into their brains over the last five years, no doubt.

"He married a Libyan orphan who'd aged out, according to Kellie Hollister." Houston shook his head.

Annoyance chugged through Trace. He knew every option to what happened in Misrata. And he knew every counter-option, every reason why the option couldn't be right.

He rubbed his eyes. Needed a shift in focus or some miraculous breakthrough. "What about Pennsylvania?"

Houston gave him a quizzical look.

"Erasing Téya's digital footprint. . ."

"Oh. Oh, right. Yeah, I did that, but. . ."

"But what?"

"Well, there was this"—Houston wagged a finger at each of the three monitors on his left—"image at the hospital in Pennsylvania. It's been bugging me."

A grainy picture of a man in a baseball cap talking to a doctor appeared on the screen.

"Why would that bother you?" Tech geeks were good, but sometimes they were anal. And wrong. "Don't waste your time—"

"I. . . It just seems. . .familiar."

"What? The hospital, the doctor, or the guy?"

"Yes." Houston came up a little straighter in his chair, his head angled to the side. "Yes," he said more firmly. "That's it!"

A frustrated groan begged Trace to give it release. Instead, he waited. Guys like Houston—their brains worked in ways he couldn't fathom. Didn't want to fathom, but he was grateful for them because they made connections that were otherwise missed.

"Keeley."

Warm anger splashed through Trace's gut, making him wary. "What about Shay?"

Houston's fingers flew so rapidly it sounded as if several people were typing at once. "Look look look," he said, glancing from one monitor to another. "Yes! I was right."

Trace saw the security footage of the hospital where Shay was recuperating. A half-dozen people sat in a waiting area. "What? What am—" And he saw it. Saw the same guy. Same clothes.

"I review the footage every night, just to review who's been in and out of Keeley's room and the ICU ward." Houston tapped on the shape of the guy. "He's there, too. Tell me that's not creepy. What's he doing there?"

"Can you zoom in?" A buzzing began at the back of Trace's brain and washed down his neck.

"Even better. Here you go." Houston ran a program over the face. "Connecting it to facial recognition right—"

"No need," Boone said.

Anger sparked through Trace. "Sam Caliguari."

"He's close, West." For Boone's face to telegraph the concern Trace felt was not a good sign. Things had progressed beyond a salvageable situation. "What do you want to do?"

"He has to be dealt with."

"Arrest? Persuasive negotiation?"

"Whatever it takes."

"Hey!" Excitement snapped through Houston's voice. "Look! Ballenger. . ." His eyes were wide as he stared at the monitor.

Trace moved toward him. "What?"

"Ballenger left a message. I have that voice-to-text on that number Annie and Téya left with Hollister. Ballenger just left a message on it."

"What's it say?" Boone asked.

"He says he'll meet them—but in. . .75004 Place. . ." Houston's voice trailed off as his fingers took over. "It's a hotel. Hôtel-de-Ville, Paris."

"Paris?"

Trace and Boone looked toward the lounge area where Téya stood, watching them. How long had she been there? "Ballenger left a message agreeing to meet—but in Paris."

Téya crossed her arms as she drew closer. "That's intriguing. Kellie Hollister had an invitation on her desk for a benefit gala—for HOMe. In Paris."

"When?" Traced asked.

"The twenty-fourth."

"Friday," Boone said, meeting Trace's gaze. "Think we have time?"

"Seriously?" Téya said with a cheeky grin. "I'm going to Paris, right?"

Nuala and Annie emerged from the bunk rooms. "Who's going to Paris?"

Francesca
Leesburg, Virginia
22 May – 1030 Hours

The town had its charm, its history, and its more than fair share of historic homes. And narrow streets. But that's about all Frankie would give it. Though it wasn't her speed—*especially* with the 25 mph speed limit through the blink-and-you-miss-it-downtown—Leesburg held one benefit: it wasn't a big city, so finding Trace Weston should be easier than trying to track him down in a place like DC or New York.

After making a couple of rounds through the congested downtown, she headed north on King Street and back onto the country roads she'd given chase to the always-scowling Weston. The man even looked mean with that knot line between his intense greenish eyes. Thin lips always in a flat line didn't help.

What would he look like if he smiled?

"Probably scare off any nearby children," she muttered as she kept a slow, normal pace through the countryside, her gaze constantly to the side. Silently, she begged the deer to stay off the roads so she could stay on the road.

Frankie explored a few side roads that she hoped would lead her to some hidden, secret facility. His hideout. Brushing her black hair from her face, she groaned. "Where are you hiding, Trace Weston? It's not like you're Batman and have a bat cave."

Or did he? Well, not a *cave with bats*. But some underground place.

She sure hoped not. If he was underground, she'd never find him. Not without access to some serious satellites and technology. Neither of which she had access to since she still didn't have a job.

" 'Extended leave of absence,' " she mimicked what her boss told her over the phone. " 'Take time. Rest. Recover. Get a clear mind.' " Frankie rolled her eyes as she guided her Toyota Camry rental off the dirt road. Her tires caught purchase on the cement and pulled her onward. She made her way to the village of Lucketts and turned right onto Old Lucketts Road past the antique shop. She eased her car around the slight bend and pulled into the volunteer fire station.

She parked out of the way and headed inside.

"Can I help you?" a voice called from the side of the building.

Frankie turned, her long black hair whipping into her face as she spotted a man wiping his greasy hands on a rag, the hood of a car engine up behind him. "Yeah, I'm looking for—"

"Prius."

Confused, then stunned as well as markedly embarrassed, Frankie stood mute.

He grinned, tucking the grease rag in his back pocket. "I'm Landon R—"

Air brakes hissed on the road, a large delivery truck breaking for the sharp curve before the stoplight, startling Frankie and momentarily drawing her attention from the man. When she glanced back, he was holding out his clean hand. "I was the EMT on duty that day."

Color heated her cheeks. "Not my most shining moment."

He grinned, his blue-green eyes sparkling in the morning sun. "Just glad to see you up walking around after an accident like that."

"You and me both." She tucked her hair behind her ear. "Hey, I was wondering. . .did you ever find out who called in my accident?"

He shrugged, pursing his lips. "I never went looking." Landon studied her for a few seconds then thumbed toward the building. "There a reason you're asking?"

Think fast, Frankie. "Well. . ." *A little faster.* "Remember you'd mentioned I pulled myself clear of the fire?"

He gave a slow nod.

"I didn't—in fact, I think someone pulled me out."

Landon gave a low whistle. "Ah, I see—and you want to thank this hero for coming to your rescue."

Relief flooded Frankie that she didn't have to add any lies to this dialogue. "You understand."

"Well, the police report would log whoever was on scene."

"Yeah, it didn't list anyone, but I wondered. . .would the 911 record list who called in the accident?"

"Well, it'd give the number if it was open, but it's not uncommon for a number to be blocked. That would've shown up on the report, too." He thumbed toward the building. "But we can ask Irene."

Hope lit through her. She had to play dumb about Trace's name for now. Landon led her inside and found the dispatcher, Irene. The woman had very short hair, cut stylishly. But her stocky build and fierce disposition made Frankie's insides churn.

"Hey, Irene. This is the lady whose car flipped and caught fire last week. Is there a record of who called it in? She wants to thank them. Can you check to see who called in the accident?"

"Now, Landon, you know full well that would've shown up on the report."

"But what if it didn't?" Frankie asked, trying to insert herself and stop Landon from getting in any trouble or perpetuating lies.

A skeptical look flitted through Irene's tough expression. "If a call was made, it'd be logged, whether from an identified, listed number, or a blocked number."

"Blocked?" Frankie repeated.

"Yeah, some people have to block their numbers for security reasons."

"The report didn't mention a call at all."

Irene frowned. "That's unusual. Let me see. . ." She turned to her computer and started typing. "What date?"

"Eleven May," Frankie said.

A few more keystrokes and Irene's gaze darted over the monitor. "Okay, yep—here it is. A 911 call came in at 2:08 p.m. from. . ." She sat back and smiled at them. "A blocked number."

"And there's no way to find out who it belonged to?"

"Oh, there's a way," Irene said, "but you'd need a compelling reason to go digging through the phone records. And that's not something I can do here."

Disappointment slowed Frankie's pulse and pushed her shoulders down. "Oh. Right." She managed a fake smile. "Of course. Thank you for looking."

"Sure, no—"

A voice squawked through the radio, and Irene turned abruptly away from them.

Landon leaned in, and Frankie knew this was her time to exit.

"Well, thank you both."

Back in her car, she sat there staring at the dash. She did not crawl out of that car on her own. She was certain of that. She'd checked the bottom of her shoes and saw the scuff marks that would only come from being dragged across pavement.

Did Trace pull me out?

"Ha," she said with no small amount of sarcasm. "He'd throw me in, not pull me out!"

Boone
Lucketts, Virginia
26 May – 1300 Hours

Sittin' in church on a chair hooked to his mother's, Boone sat forward, his forearms resting on his knees. His parents had raised him to have loyalty to God, family, and country. His family were true-blue patriots in the deepest sense of the words. But after all he'd done and seen. . .coming each Sunday—when not deployed—he sat here with one thing on his mind: *God, make me whole again.*

Today, and the last few weeks, he sat here begging God for Keeley's life. Wondering if he could take things a step further if she survived, re-integrate into her life and heart. After Misrata, he steered clear of her to keep her safe. A move that almost killed him. But when she woke up. . .she'd go back to the bunker with the rest. Could they pick up where they'd left off? Make good on the relationship he hinted at with words that made her eyes glitter with hope? Words he'd had no business uttering, but the heat of passion made a man do foolish things.

After service, they headed back to his parents' home on the property adjacent to the one he'd purchased where he'd built the bunker that harbored three vital American assets. Three women who had government and black ops organizations hunting them.

And here he sat at his family's table eating fried chicken and mashed potatoes on a calm, pretty Sunday afternoon.

The screen door to the back porch slapped, drawing his attention. Boone grinned at his little brother, who made it to the table in three large strides. "Thought you were on call."

"I am, but I'm not missing mama's fried chicken for the world." Landon grabbed a biscuit and poured himself some sweet tea. " 'Sides, it's my lunchtime."

"Can you have a seat with us, Landon?" Mama lowered herself to the chair and set a napkin in her lap.

"Just for a few," Landon said as he set the walkie-talkie on the table.

"Has it been quiet up there?" Daddy asked from the head of the table.

"For the most part," Landon answered. At twenty-four, he had made the family proud becoming an EMT. Boone's kid brother talked about going to medical school someday, but he'd hated school enough to stay away for a while.

"The whole town was abuzz with that accident—ya know, the one where the car burst into flames."

Boone lowered his gaze, his pulse skidding into his ribs.

"Yeah, speakin' of that," Landon said as he heaped potatoes onto a plate. "The lady came by the station a couple days ago."

"Was she pretty?" Dad asked, winking at Landon.

Boone struggled to think around his panic. This was Solomon's daughter they were talking about. The woman who'd been hunting down Trace and him. "What'd she want?" Boone tried to keep his tone neutral.

"That's the thing of it," Landon said and took a swig of tea. "Firefighters thought she'd dragged herself free of the burning car, but she says someone pulled her out."

"Who?" Mama asked.

"She has a theory that the man who called it in is the one who pulled her free." Landon took a couple of bites of chicken before washing it down with more tea. "But then the guy vanishes before we can get there—and we were less than two minutes away."

"Why would he leave?" Mama asked, scowling. "You'd think he would want to make sure she was okay."

Landon shrugged. "Not my problem, but I sure didn't mind her showing up again."

"Did you give her your number?" Daddy said with a chuckle.

"Actually," Landon said with a mischievous smile, "she gave me hers.

OPERATION ZULU: Redemption

Said if anything unusual came to light—"

"Unusual?" When Landon's gaze hit Boone, only then did he realize how his question sounded. He gave a one-shouldered shrug. "What could be unusual? She flipped her car—there are accidents out here all the time caused by deer." He met his little brother's gaze. "That's what the news reported, right? That she swerved to avoid a deer?"

"That's right."

"So what are we missing?"

"The mystery caller, I guess," Landon said. "Either way, I don't plan to call her. Something felt off, but I'm not sure if it's her or something else."

"Maybe someone named Melissa Sue."

Landon's eyebrows flung up. "Melissa?"

"She asked after you at church." Mama smiled, looking well younger than her sixty-plus years. "A mother knows, Landon Ramage. You've never been able to hide things very well."

"This isn't a family of secrets," Dad declared. "We keep things open and honest."

"Well, most of us do," Landon said as he shot Boone a look. "Anyway, Melissa is a child. She's only seventeen."

Though something in Boone itched to get out of the house—maybe the fear that he'd give away his knowledge of the situation, that Trace was the one who'd pulled Frankie free—but he didn't have anywhere to rush to. No one to protect. He glanced at his watch. Trace and Zulu were en route to France right now. But with Frankie snooping around, maybe he should steer clear of the bunker.

Trace
Paris, France
27 May – 1400 Hours

A white envelope slid beneath the door of their hotel room landed Téya at the café on Rue de Renard. The busy street, just around from the metro, was a perfect tourist stopping-off point for lunch. And by the crowds, the perfect place for a covert encounter.

"Not exactly how I wanted to visit Paris," Annie said softly through the microphone to her friend and Zulu team member sitting at the café across the street.

"But we're here," Téya said with a grin as she scooted her salad around on the plate. "How long do I wait?"

"Until he comes. He delivered the note. We wait. Stay on task," Trace

187

warned from his hidden spot where he sat with Houston and Annie, monitoring the situation. "Noodle," Trace said, using Nuala's nickname/handle. "Sitrep?"

"In position and set up," Nuala replied.

Trace couldn't resist the urge to glance across the square to the Saint-Jacques Bell Tower where she laid in wait with her Remington precision sniper rifle, a recent acquisition he'd managed to finagle. Even her sharp shooting skills didn't ease his concerns. They basically had a triangular set up, and though he would've preferred a fourth team on the north side of the café, their limited resources and the covert nature of this mission required they make do.

But something just didn't feel right.

Trace stood with his arms folded over his chest, one hand scratching the side of his face. This is what they did—tactical missions. Covert operations. They weren't spies, but in this situation, they had to perform like them.

He keyed his mic. "Keep your eyes out. Take no risks. This meet smells rotten."

"Not everyone has something bad up their sleeve," Annie whispered.

"Just remember—he was there the same night we were," Trace bit back. "Hollister said he lost a kid and wife. Might be looking for someone to pay back."

"I have joy," Nuala said, indicating she had a clear line of sight on Téya at the café. If the situation arose, she'd neutralize Ballenger.

"Copy that," Trace said.

Quiet settled through the coms as another ten minutes fell off the clock. Téya ordered a ham and cheddar panini with potato wedges, all to buy time and look like a tourist. "Holy cow," Téya muttered. "There's a whole school of teens headed this way."

No sooner had she said the words than the area was flooded with over a hundred teens, marching north along the sidewalk.

Trace tensed. That cut their ability to see Téya. "Noodle—"

"No joy. I have no joy," Nuala replied.

Trace balled his fists. "Téya—"

"I thought there were two of you," a male voice crackled through the hidden mic in Téya's fashion ring shaped like a giant flower.

"There were—she's back at the hotel puking up her guts. Too much revelry in Paris last night. We were so excited about finally getting to talk with you."

"So, you're irresponsible."

"Stay calm," Trace intoned. "He's testing you."

"Actually, no. My friend isn't a drinker. In fact, she's allergic to alcohol. We ordered a virgin Long Island Iced Tea and the waiter screwed up the order. Now." Téya's tone went dark. "Anything else you want to know about us before you decide to cut the bull and talk to me?"

"Easy, easy," Trace said. But Téya—this is why Téya was sitting out there and Annie in here. Téya knew how to take the bull by the horns. Besides, he was not going to sacrifice both of them if this was a trap.

"I'm sorry," the man said.

The teens were finally clearing out.

"I have joy," Nuala radioed.

Trace could breathe a little easier as Houston announced he had a good facial image and was running it through recognition software. "Start the stress analysis," Trace said.

"Roger," Houston said, activating a software program that would monitor the stress in Ballenger's words so they could hopefully steer this conversation and prevent it from going very bad.

"So, why are you hiding?" Téya asked.

"You know about Misrata, yes?"

"Of course."

"Well, my wife and child were killed in the bombing."

Trace cringed at the words. Though it was accurate, it was also painful. "Why didn't that information ever make it into the official reports?"

"Who are you? I mean, I know you gave Hollister a name, but I think we both know it's not your real name."

Trace's chest squeezed. "Noodle, stay on here." He glanced to Annie. "Be ready." This was going downhill already.

"What you need to know is that I'm trying to get behind the truth of what happened in Misrata." Through the feed, Trace watched Téya lean forward at the table, sliding her salad plate to the side. "You want justice, don't you, Mr. Ballenger?"

Nice. Put the guy on the defensive. Make him think she wasn't buying the story.

Silence dropped on the conversation, and though Trace felt the tension knots tighten in his shoulders, he studied Téya. She didn't look stressed, and the vocal analysis didn't reveal stress.

"Should I—"

"No," Trace said to Annie. "She can handle it."

"If you wanted justice," Téya continued, "why vanish? Why go into hiding?"

"Have you been shot at, Miss Ritter? Anyone ever tried to kill you? Is that why you're using a false name?"

"How does he know that?" Annie's voice pitched as she swiveled toward Trace.

"He doesn't." At least, Trace hoped he didn't. But the readouts weren't showing stress. "He's still testing her."

Beside him now, Annie covered her mouth. She turned to him. "Can we get to her fast enough, if. . . ?"

She knew the answer to that. They were at least thirty to forty-five seconds away in a full sprint. Bullets could reach their targets in a second.

"I'm former military, so of course I've had someone shoot at me. And I'm sure they weren't shooting to say hello. They were shooting to kill, so I have had someone try to kill me." Téya remained unperturbed. "What can you tell us, Berg? Why did you hide? Where have you been? Or should I leave now so you can make up more questions to delay?"

Ballenger went silent. The bustle of the city droned on around them. She pushed to her feet.

"Wait."

"That was a spike," Houston said, pointing to a screen that had the stress analysis in thermal imaging. "She hit a nerve."

"Okay, Téya," Trace said quietly into the mic. "You hit a nerve. Tread carefully but keep going." He watched as she resumed her seat, exuding confidence.

"I hid because after my family died in that warehouse, I went to Tripoli where I managed to lay low for a while. One night at the hostel I was staying at, someone attacked me. Gave me a wicked knot on the head and left me for dead—then burned the place down."

"I'll want to verify that."

"I don't care if you verify it," Berg growled. "Everywhere I go, they're there. They're hunting me. I fled to Europe for a bigger hiding ground."

"So that's why we couldn't find you."

"Using my dead uncle's name helped me stay hidden."

Dropping back against her chair, Téya shoved her long brown hair from her face and sighed loudly. A sign she was still in control but frustrated. "This isn't making sense, Berg."

"I'm glad you see it that way."

"Listen," Téya said as she leaned forward again. "I went to your last-known address in Denver and got the crap beat out of me."

"Denver?" Berg frowned. "I haven't lived there since before. . ."

"Kellie sent us there."

Berg let out a loud bark of a laugh. "Kellie Hollister?" He shook his head. "That's your problem right there. She's the cofounder of Hope of Mercy. You know that, right?"

"I do."

"Do you also know that the only person I ever gave a forwarding address to was that very woman?" Ferocity deepened his words. "Funny how I give her my address and suddenly I'm attacked. Within two weeks of every communication with them, I was attacked. When I confronted her about it, she denied it. Said it wasn't her. But who else could it be? Look, I don't have all the answers, but I know a few things having lived inside a HOMe facility. Mercy Chandler—whom Hope of Mercy was named after—was having an affair."

"With whom?"

Ballenger shook his head. "I never was able to find out. But I believe that man is the reason for Misrata. She starts sharing a bed with this man and suddenly HOMe is in all kinds of money and has sway in locations they couldn't ever breach before. I believe"—he glanced around, swiping a hand over his face—"I believe they were hiding weapons in the buildings. Moving them at night."

Thankfully, Téya didn't respond. The weapons, they'd long known, were the initial reason Zulu had been sent into that mess in the first place. The DOD knew the weapons were illegal and wanted them destroyed. Zulu verified the weapons and the location. But how Ballenger knew about that. . .

"Ask why he believes that," Trace prompted Téya.

On the monitor, he watched Téya look out over the road, quiet and thoughtful.

"If you don't believe me—"

"It's a lot to take in," Téya said. "Weapons—why would you think weapons?"

"One night, I heard a noise outside the warehouse, and I went to investigate and saw these trucks. That night—it went up in flames."

"That's a lie," Annie said.

Trace held up a hand.

"I'll need to research what you've said. But. . .I really appreciate—"

BooOOOOooommm!!!

One minute Trace had a clear line of sight, the next second all he could see was smoke and fire.

Téya
Paris, France
27 May – 1500 Hours

Ears ringing, smoke choking her lungs, Téya lifted herself off the ground.

A gritty taste filled her mouth as she mentally probed her body for injuries.

"Go," a man's gruff voice growled in her ear. "Get out of here!"

Téya blinked, recognizing Berg's voice, thick with warning. Someone grabbed her. Hauled her to her feet. About to shake free, she snapped back to the present.

Berg's eyes seared with meaning. Dust and ash coated his dark hair and smeared his face with lines made dark by sweat. "They found me. Get out of here! Go now, or you're dead."

"Contact me later," she said, gripping his arms.

With a nod, he thrust her away from the café.

Téya stumbled, her only thought to get back to the safety of her team and Trace. Wading through a quagmire of chaos, disorientation, shock-riddled tourists, and a glut of vehicles, Téya made her way south. Away from the café. Away from Berg.

Weaving around cars, she pressed a finger to her ear and felt a sticky warmth. She glanced at her finger and found blood. "Zulu, this is Zulu Two."

Nothing. Only the ringing. The explosion must've damaged the coms piece. Which meant the explosion was close. Not so close that it blew off a limb, but. . . *Enough that I could've been the target, too.* She was running again, this time down Rue de Renard.

Going back to the team could draw the enemy.

Téya stopped cold, her body pumping adrenaline and heat through her in overdrive. Her gaze surfed between the tree limbs straight to the pristine length of the Saint-Jacques Tower. She wouldn't bring trouble to the team. They'd had plenty already. She made a sharp left. Stumbled down Rue de Rivoli, in the opposite direction, praying Nuala saw her. Ducking, afraid her dirt-streaked and bloodied face might draw attention. Praying she'd let Trace know where she'd gone. They couldn't be seen together. Not here.

Behind her, she heard crunching.

Téya glanced in a window of a shop, saw her own image—definitely bloodied and dirty—but focused behind her. Just as she looked, a shadow blurred out of view. Her heart kick-started. Someone was following her.

She lowered her head and started walking again. *Just stay calm. Act calm.* She had training. Quade had put them through Torture 105 with his training. *You can handle this.*

The soft padding of feet behind her spilled heat down her spine, the rush of adrenaline soaking her limbs. Fight or flight kicking in, she quickened her step, though she told herself not to. She scanned the road before her and decided on an alley up ahead. Make it there and she could make a run for it. Get around the corner and just sprint.

One. . . She passed a white super-compact vehicle.

Crunch.

Whoa. That sounded closer.

Two. . . She saw a black blur in the car window.

Forget three. Téya banked right, straight into the street. A car screeched to a stop. "Sorry," she said lightly. Trying to keep the panic and awareness from her voice, she skipped around the car, narrowly avoided a second, then rushed up onto the sidewalk.

No more tire screeches or horns honking, so maybe whoever followed, wasn't. . .

A flurry of French came from behind her.

Téya glanced back. Parisians could be so—

The man in black ducked.

Téya jerked around, terrified. Not only was he still following, but he'd closed the gap. She hurried her steps. Angled toward the building where she'd targeted the alley. Skipped a step—and a heartbeat.

Easy, easy, Trace would say.

But Trace hadn't just survived a bombing. Wasn't being chased by who-knows. . .

Téya felt the surge of adrenaline spike as the opening grew closer. She wouldn't even count this time. She was just. . .

Téya threw herself in front of a crowd of people and dove into the alley. Darkness dropped like a blanket on her, but she sprinted forward anyway. In a hard run, she made it to the end of the alley in a matter of seconds. Only one route presented itself—left. She bounced off the wall and ran fast.

She wanted to curse when that juncture also ended, feeding her to the right. At least she had an opening. Then a left, that dumped into a small square. An exit to the right and left. Téya froze for a second, trying to work out her route. Figure out which way—

"Oh forget it!" she raced toward a small archway that veered to the left. She could smell the water, a strong, pungent odor in this city. She ran. Rounded a corner.

A cement wall slammed into her chest.

She bounced backward, her breath knocked out of her.

Coughing, Téya rolled, agony squirming through her as she fought for air. It was then she saw the booted feet. Followed the black pants up to a black shirt. Corded muscles. And a face of fury.

She hadn't hit a wall.

The man who'd followed her hit her.

He grabbed and yanked her up off her feet.

Blinded by pain and groping for air, she struggled to think. Then oxygen flooded back. She swung her arm back then aimed for the side of his throat.

He blocked and nailed her with one of his own.

Again unable to breathe, she dropped to her knees, straining for air. Feeling her temples pound. She wobbled to her feet.

But the man shoved her forward.

Her head hit the wall. Bounced off. Stars sprinkled across her vision. Téya braced herself then threw her head backward.

But he deflected. Moved away.

She stumbled backward, her feet pedaling too fast. She flopped onto the ground. Anger lit through her. She'd been one man's punching bag already this month. *Not happening again.* In that split second, Téya took in her surroundings. His position. She swung her legs to catch his.

He hopped back—and laughed.

Indignant, she flipped onto her feet.

His punch nailed her jaw.

She spun, gritting her teeth and tasting the blood his hit caused. His hits came again. And again. Driving her back. . .back. . .

Water!

She heard it now—the river. Heard the lapping against a wall or rocks. Smelled it. Felt the dampness. He was going to knock her into the water, no doubt hoping she was unconscious. She had to control this. Own it.

Téya dove to his right and straight into a roll. She came up and spun around.

His booted foot flew at her face.

Crack!

Téya fumbled her footing. Scrambled backward, not wanting to fall.

And he was on her. Forearm crushing her windpipe, he slammed her against the wall. Téya's training flew out the window in the instant she knew he intended to kill her. Right here. Right now. This wasn't a punishment. She fought for survival. Fought to live.

She grabbed onto his crushing arm and pried it back as hard as she could. She wouldn't remove it. Just a little air. That's all. Craning her neck for even the smallest particle of air, she met his gaze.

Wild. Fury. Singular focus.

Head down, his light brown hair shaded a face marked by rage. And a tattoo on his left cheekbone, just below his eye. Those eyes. . .roiling and untamed.

She struck with her left fist, aiming for his head.

Losing oxygen, limbs heavy, she knew her punch went soft.

But it angered him more. He shouldered in, pressing harder against her throat.

Téya whimpered. Hated herself for it. He would not defeat her!

He growled something, words that were unintelligible to her. French? She met his gaze again. Churning brownish-green eyes.

He said something else. Then something more. Then, "Who are you?"

A siren wailed nearby.

Her attacker growled. Stepped back, a large fist around her throat, pinning her to the wall. Téya whimpered again, clawing at his hands to free herself.

He held up a phone. Aimed it at her. He pressed something to her face. "If you want your friend in the tower to live, I suggest you run." He dropped the item, shoved her—though she had no room to give beneath his force—and sprinted off as the *nee-eu nee-eu* of a police siren roared past the opposite end of the alley.

Téya collapsed to the ground, coughing. Gasping and hauling in greedy breaths of air. By her hand, she saw a syringe. *"If you want your friend to live. . ."*

Nuala.

The syringe held a vial of amber-colored liquid.

Antidote.

Trace
Paris, France
27 May – 1520 Hours

"Where is Téya?!" Trace roared at Houston, who didn't dare look up at him.

"I don't know. She went the wrong way. I didn't have surveillance equipment prepared for that!" Houston sounded like he was squealing.

"Why didn't she come back here?" Arms wrapped around herself, Annie paced the small room they used for the recon location.

"Noodle," Trace barked into the coms again. "Noodle, talk to me." He snatched off the headset and threw it down.

"Dude, I told you—something happened with that explosion. We lost radio communications. Doesn't make sense but we did."

Trace started for the door. "I'm going to the tower!"

"But Téya—"

"She's AWOL. King is the only one I can verify is still alive."

He stepped out into the sun and his phone rang. Trace glanced at the caller ID as the door behind him opened.

"Trace, wait." Annie came out of the safe house.

He didn't recognize the number, but few people had it, so he answered. "Weston."

"Trace," Annie said from behind, her words colliding with the caller's.

"Nuala'siintrouble.Gettohernow.Hepoisonedher."

Trace froze. Blinked. The words untangled themselves. With an intake of breath, he lurched forward. Then turned back to Annie. "Go back. Help Houston clear out. Meet at the extraction point."

Her face went white. A barely there shake of her head.

"If we don't make it, just go. We'll follow."

Annie shook her head harder.

"Go, or our lives are on your head!"

She went back. Trace bolted across the street, through the square. He leaped over shrubs. Hustled down a sidewalk, almost toppling a baby carriage thing, and kept going. He threw himself through the opening to the tower. Hauled himself up the stairs two, sometimes three at a time. "Noodle!" he shouted. Looked up the spiraling steps but saw nothing.

Exhaustion and fear weighted his limbs, but he wasn't stopping. He used the walls to pull himself faster. Rounding the last curve, he grabbed the wrought-iron rail. Propelled himself to the lookout.

Saw Nuala slumped to the side.

Trace skidded over to her, dropped to his knees. He thrust two fingers against her neck.

Nuala's eyes snapped open.

"Nuala, stay with me."

A trembling, wobbly hand came up. Then thumped to the ground. A feathered tranq dart rolled out of Nuala's hand.

"Son of a—"

A gurgling sound came from her throat.

"Nuala, stay with me." Trace laid her out. Heard the hiss of breath escaping through what sounded like a pinprick opening in her throat. He pressed an ear to her chest, listening to her heart. Noticed her lips were going gray. Her pulse was erratic. Slowing.

Crap! What could he do? He started compressions and breathing, but knew with the poison—whatever it was—in her body, this probably wasn't going to work. But he wouldn't give up.

Thuds below alerted him to someone coming up the stairs. It'd better not be whoever had tranqed her. Trace plucked his weapon out and set it beside Nuala's hip for easy access. So help him, if anyone but Téya came through that doorway. . .

Feet thudded. Grunts. Coming fast.

Whirl of black and purple. Then Téya burst through the opening.

A syringe went airborne toward him.

Trace caught it and slid it into Nuala's hip and pressed the plunger. Glaring at Téya, he kept doing compressions on Nuala. "What happened?"

Slumped against the wall and holding her knees, she gulped air as if trying to drink from a fire hydrant. She straightened, holding her side, and swallowed. Her face was cut, bruised, and bloodied. Her fists bore the telltale marks that she'd fought back—and hard. "I was foll"—desperation for air choked off the word—"followed from the. . .café. A man tried to. . .kill me. Sirens scared him. . .he gave me that and ran."

Nuala writhed and cried out.

"Easy," Trace said. "Easy. You're safe." He guided her into a sitting position. "Just—take it slow."

Nuala held a trembling hand to her head as she leaned against the wall. "Whoa, my head hurts. What happened?"

Holding up the tranq, Trace supplied the answer. But he wasn't worried about that. Not directly.

"Did you recognize the man who attacked you?"

"No, and I'm really sick of men attacking me." Téya grunted, watching Nuala. "What happened to chivalry?"

"We need to get out of here." Trace knelt beside Nuala, who was slowly regaining a healthy color in her lips again. "If we assist, can you walk?"

Nuala nodded faintly. "Whatever they did to me really sapped my strength."

Supporting her between them, Trace and Téya helped Nuala down the stairwell. Trace had her equipment slung over his shoulder as Téya gave her support. Trace phoned in. "Bring the car."

"Leave it. Come get Noodle. Two and I can pack up the rest, get a cab. Noodle needs to see a doctor."

A cab pulled to the curb as Téya and Trace guided Nuala there. Annie hopped out to help situate her friend.

Trace caught her arm. "Get to the hotel. Contact Boone for a safe house—they can get Nuala the medical help she needs."

"What about you?" She blinked. "And Téya?"

"We'll grab the gear and go back to the hotel. We may need to rendezvous outside France."

Her eyes were wide with understanding and fright, but she nodded, handed him a set of keys. "The van." Then climbed in and left.

"C'mon," Trace said as he headed back to the monitoring site. They grabbed the gear and loaded the rest into the back. They had little time, and this equipment had to go back to the safe house, along with their weapons.

Trace's phone rang again. He tossed a box into the van then yanked out his phone. "Weston."

"Trace, someone trashed our hotel room," Annie said.

He dropped his gaze to the ground. "Get out."

"We're at a coffee shop."

"Okay, I'm going to give you a number. You call it, then do whatever they tell you. Clear?"

"Yeah," Annie whispered.

He heard the strain in her voice, and it mirrored what was building in him. After he gave her the number, he told her not to worry about him and Téya. "We'll find our way out. Rendezvous Plan B."

"Right."

Trace hung up, not trusting himself—he'd break rank when it came to Annie. Do anything to keep her safe.

"What's wrong?" Téya asked.

Pocketing the phone, Trace turned. "Cover's blown. Hotel was trashed." He hoisted a box into the van. "We're on our own."

"A tattoo," Téya suddenly announced as Trace squatted beside a steel case, securing the locks.

"What?"

"The man who followed me—he had a tattoo. On his left cheek, below his eye."

"What was it?" Trace lifted the heavy camera and stacked it on top of two others, wedging it to be sure it didn't fall and break while they were clearing out.

"I. . .I'm not sure. He was kind of off his rocker. I think he took a picture of me—I guess he has a trophy case of those he beats up or kills," Téya said, coiling up an endless sea of snaking cables. "A moon, I think. And a star."

Trace froze. Hands on the steel case, he stared at it. He straightened. "A moon and star. You mean a star-crescent?"

Téya smiled. "Is there a difference?"

"Yes. A big, important one." He grabbed a pencil and drew the star-crescent then held it up. "This? Is this what you saw?"

Téya frowned, her unease evident. "Yeah, I guess. Why?"

"No guessing, Téya." Trace snapped the picture and stepped forward. "Is this it?"

"Yes. That's what I saw."

Trace cursed. Pivoted. Punched the van a couple more times as he cursed. He turned. Ran his hands over his shorn hair then held his head.

Téya watched, her face ashen. "What?"

"We have to get out of here." Even as he said it, he moved. "Now. Move!"

"What?" When Téya got scared, Téya got angry.

Trace went to close the van doors. All this equipment. . .it'd slow them down. Make them easy targets. "We have to leave the equipment."

Téya yanked his arm around. "What aren't you telling me?"

He held her eyes and let out a heavy sigh. "That man—the man who tried to kill you? He's not just some guy. He's called The Turk."

Téya's smile wavered. "Ooooh," she said, her sarcasm wavering like the smile on her lips. "That sounds. . .scary."

"Should be. He's one of the most terrifying assassins known in the covert world." Trace clicked his tongue and gave a lone shake of his head. "I'm surprised you're alive right now."

"But. . .but he—"

Holy—the sudden thought struck him like a bolt of lightning, singeing his confidence and electrifying his fear. "Téya."

She stilled, her face blanching.

"You said he took a picture?"

Her smile slipped.

Trace cursed again, God forgive him. He kicked the tire of the van. Kicked it again.

"Congratulations," Téya said, "you're scaring the crap right out of me."

"He took your picture to run it, to get a facial recognition and find out who you are. He didn't leave you alive, he left you to take care of later. It means you interfered with his agenda." Trace ran a hand over his head. "Leave the gear. We have to leave. Right now."

"Why?"

"Once you're on The Turk's map, he wipes you off."

VI

Téya
Paris, France
27 May – 2020 Hours

Darkness chased away the light of day, immersing Téya and Trace in shadows that bred fear and danger. Though they'd been on the go since the tower, Téya's mind had not stopped racing. Nor her pulse. Acute awareness of her mortality flooded her with hypervigilance. Kept her alert to those around her. Fear that The Turk might discover her awoke a side of Téya she didn't know existed. A side that thrived on the state of hypervigilance.

"You okay?"

Téya blinked at Trace. "What?"

He angled his head and considered her. "You're tense. Like a primed det cord."

"I'm fine."

"Get him out of your head," Trace said. "Don't let it eat at your confidence."

"It's not." Téya gritted her teeth as she pushed through a thick throng of tourists disembarking from the metro. "I'm just. . .mad."

"About?"

Uncertain she could put it into words, Téya muddled through the feelings. The memory of his fury-filled eyes boring holes into her wouldn't go away. His lightning-fast strikes. The inability to breathe beneath his muscular arm.

"That he beat up a woman?"

"I couldn't care less about that. I'm just ticked that I couldn't stop him." She hunched her shoulders. "If that siren hadn't wailed, I'm not sure I'd be breathing this rank, Parisian air."

Trace nodded. "Good, let it get you mad. You'll be stronger and better for it next time."

"I don't want a next time." But she did. She wanted to settle the score. Prove she wasn't a weak nobody some jerk assassin could level with one blow.

"Here." Trace banked right into a multistoried townhome. But instead of climbing the half-dozen steps up to the front door, he cruised down between the two buildings. The stench of rotten food, waste, and a musty smell she couldn't identify closed in around them, making the darkness and walls feel closer, heavier. Suffocating.

He stopped at a boarded-up window and glanced both ways.

Confusion settled in on Téya, drenching her body with exhaustion. "What—are we lost?"

Trace gave her a sidelong glance then stepped forward and rapped on the boards.

Closing her mouth, Téya realized how little she knew or understood. About this mission, about Trace, about the deadly covert world.

A hollow crack made Téya jump.

Trace stepped back when the boards—as an entire unit—swung inward. "Zulu Actual sent by the Gryphon."

A pair of eyes, wreathed in darkness and shadows, peered out at them. Dim light cast a sheen across the person's nose and cheekbones. They seemed masculine, but she couldn't be sure for the poor lighting. Some traumatized part of Téya half expected the person to lunge out and attack. But she'd be ready. Never again would she be caught unaware. Or taken down so easily.

"In," the person said—definitely a man.

Trace and Téya slipped through the small opening created as the man stepped out of the way. A blanket of black dropped on them as the slat door slammed shut. Téya stilled, her ears groping for sound, her vision for sight.

"This way," said the man.

Only then could she decipher the form of the man from the other shadows. Trace followed without hesitation before Téya had taken her first step. They wove through a series of halls, and she couldn't help but wonder how the man had gotten to the door so fast after Trace knocked.

Surveillance.

Made sense.

Before a steel door, the guy looked over his shoulder. Directly at Téya. His gaze lingered there, not with admiration. Not with attraction. With. . .disdain.

Téya forced herself to stand straight. To not cower.

"There a problem?" Trace asked, stepping between her and the operative.

"Yeah," he said, nudging open the door then waiting for them to enter.

Despite the subtle ambiance and quiet, the room they stepped into buzzed. Three other men worked at computers planted in the middle of the area. Wire lockers barricaded walls. Two rooms abutted the space and sported cots but little else.

The man who let them in strode to an empty station. He swiveled the monitor toward them. At what she saw, Téya drew in a breath and froze.

Another expletive escaped from Trace. He lowered his head. In disappointment? Anger? It wasn't her fault the image of her being beaten up was on this computer.

Was it?

"You're all over the board," the man said, his Parisian accent thick. "Getting out of Paris will be challenging. Getting out alive. . ." He arched an eyebrow as a woman walked up to him and handed him a packet and left, but not before giving Téya a long look.

Téya's stomach squirmed. She turned to Trace, about to defend herself when Trace silenced her with a quick shake of his head.

"That's right," the man said as he dumped the contents into his palm. "Listen to Slayer. Follow him close and maybe you'll live through this."

"Slayer?"

"Don't ask questions," Trace muttered as he took the items the man handed off. Passports. IDs. Money. Credit cards. What looked like theater tickets. Probably alibis.

"They expire in three days," the man said.

Trace nodded as he passed Téya her bona fides.

"I can't help but wonder," the man said, his brown eyes assessing, "what you did to tick off The Turk."

Téya cast a furtive glance to Trace, who stiffened.

"You know what," the man said, "I don't want to know. If you're stupid enough to cross paths with him, maybe you shouldn't be living."

"Wrong place, wrong time," Trace snapped as he pivoted and caught Téya's arm. "We need to get going."

"You'll take the Eurostar straight to London."

"Isn't that obvious?" Trace asked.

"Absolutely, but there's no faster way to get you out of the country. The SNCF—French railways—have too few connections." The man shifted. "The train leaves in an hour. Don't waste time, especially out in the open. And I suggest you stick together," the Parisian operative said. "He'll be looking for her alone."

Téya thought about that. "Unless he saw—"

"Agreed," Trace cut in, his expression more severe than ever.

"I've contacted your people. They'll be waiting in London."

Trace hesitated. "You contacted—"

"It's better your voice and your identity are not logged here," the Parisian interjected. "That's why I took the liberty of getting your passage out of here."

"That's. . .generous," Trace mumbled.

"Not generous." The Parisian's brown eyes hit Téya. "We're merely looking out for our own interests here. We don't need the trouble of The Turk."

"In other words"—Téya felt her courage returning in full force—"you want me out of your country."

"Can you imagine the PR nightmare that will plague Paris if an American woman is murdered in cold blood on our streets? Or the frenzy that will ensue in the covert world that an ignorant woman was targeted and hit by The Turk on our soil?"

"Your concern for my well-being is touching."

He smirked. "This goes well beyond you, Miss Reiker."

Téya drew up at hearing her name on his lips.

"There are operatives and operations that have been working quietly, secretly, who will flee if they get wind of The Turk's presence here. Operations that will automatically be deemed compromised because of him."

"If he's so bad, why hasn't anyone stopped him?"

This time he sneered. And Téya knew she'd crossed the line.

Trace hooked her elbow. Held up the bona fides. "Thanks. We'd better get going."

"Indeed," the man intoned. "Slayer, I would remove her quickly before her ignorance and quick tongue incur more damage."

Trace nudged her away, into the corridor they'd come through earlier. "What—"

"Walk, don't talk." Trace's grip tightened on her arm, almost painfully, as he guided her out of the building. Back through the slat-board portal and into the dank alley.

Téya jerked her arm free and spun to him. "What—"

"Not now, Annie."

She blinked, her mind bungeeing on the name. "Téya. I'm not Annie."

Trace frowned. Swiped a hand over his mouth then shifted closer. "The train leaves in an hour. It's a forty-minute walk."

She shrugged. "Plenty of time."

"No, because we need to scout it, make sure we're not being followed and that the station isn't being monitored."

"But we should count on that, shouldn't we? I mean, if he's after me, then he'd watch all possible exits."

The fold between his eyes pinched into a knot as he gave her a sidelong glance.

"Right?"

"It's what I'd do."

"And you're Slayer? How did—"

"Not now." He gave her a fierce look. "Let's get you changed and out of Paris first."

Trace
Paris, France
27 May – 2310 Hours

Trace could not have designed a more perfect nightmare. What were the odds that one of his elite female operatives would cross paths with The Turk? And not just cross paths. The Turk had followed her. Somehow seen her as a threat.

"Act casual," Trace said, catching Téya's hand in his and praying she didn't misinterpret the move. "We're a couple."

Gratefully, the 5'9" woman didn't hesitate. They cleared the ticket area, and he walked straight toward the platform where their train to Calais waited. Even as he moved with ease, he remained watchful, scanning the sides of the station. Looking for anyone *not* moving. Anyone on the hunt. Anyone watching them. . .*too casually.*

"Hard not to think of Jason Bourne," Téya said as they made their way around the cluster of umbrella tables littering the walkway.

Trace frowned at her.

"The sniper. . .in the train station."

"That was Waterloo," Trace said. "And as long as you don't panic and make a break for it, we'll be fine." He meant it to be funny, but the intensity rolling off Téya was almost palpable. "Relax."

The terse eyebrows and taut lips softened.

Then Trace stiffened. Saw a man in a baseball cap. He'd seen him back at the entrance. Trace diverted to a small café and got in line.

"What are we doing?" Téya asked, her voice low. "They just announced our train."

"Ordering hot dogs." He stuffed a few bills in her hand. "I'll be right back."

"No," Téya hissed and went rigid.

But Trace slipped away into a crowd of tourists standing near the café. He worked his way through them, marking the target with each maneuver. Keeping his eyes on the target. Wishing for his team, for backup. Easing his way around the upper platform, Trace ignored the gnawing in his gut as the target closed in on Téya. He resisted the urge to rush. To move too quickly and draw attention.

The target entered the eating area but remained enough on the perimeter for Trace's plan to work. He rushed up behind the target, slipped an arm around his neck, and applied pressure. The man struggled for a few seconds as Trace increased the pressure, not enough to kill the man, but knock him out.

As the man went limp, bystanders noticed them. Trace met the eyes of one man. "Help," he said, wrapping an arm around the man's shoulder and easing him into a chair. "He was sick—dizzy. Call for the police!"

Almost immediately, people surrounded them.

"I'm a doctor," one woman said as she knelt beside the target, checking for a pulse. "What happened?"

"He felt faint. I saw him sway," Trace said, shifting to the back of the crowd that pressed in. In a few steps, he was clear. He rushed to where he'd left Téya by the café with the yellow and red umbrellas.

But she wasn't there.

Panic lit through him. He spun. Scanned the area. Nothing but tables, umbrellas, people, luggage, and workers. Branches rustled hard in one corner.

Trace's heart climbed into his throat. *Téya!* He threw himself in that direction, skidding around the corner as Téya slammed her foot into the stomach of someone, who doubled over her leg. Caught it. Drove Téya backward.

Overhead, he heard the station call for their train. Five minutes.

Trace slammed a hard right into the man's temple.

He flung to the side, his head bouncing off the wall. The guy dropped, stunned. Disoriented. Clumsily struggled to all fours.

Trace spun Téya toward the stairs to the platform. "Go go!"

Téya
Paris, France
28 May – 0015 Hours

The metal stairs rattled beneath her feet as Téya sped down them to the platform. Trace was two steps ahead of her, but she was gaining fast. She jumped, skipping the last three steps, and ran to the train car. Trace jolted to a stop and she bypassed him, but he caught her hand and tugged her back. She swung around and into the Eurostar train.

Trace moved with purpose through the train, though he wasn't running any longer. That would attract too much attention. But she appreciated the decisiveness with which he moved. Shouts outside drew her attention, terror gripping her as she saw the man who'd broadsided her, knocking the hot dogs out of her hands. The fight-or-flight adrenaline coursed through her, had never really left her, actually, since the encounter with The Turk.

But there was her attacker. Almost at the bottom of the stairs.

"Trace," Téya hissed.

He glanced back. His face darkened.

"If you'll please have your seats," a train attendant, or whatever they were called, glided toward them in a navy uniform and bright scarf.

Shouts outside the train stilled the commotion. Téya watched in stunned disbelief as a half-dozen SWAT officers swarmed the platform, surrounding the man who'd attacked her.

"A little excitement," the attendant said. "Well, we're going to be behind schedule if you don't take your seats. Your tickets?"

Trace pulled them from his back pocket.

"Ah, yes. Business class. Right this way," she said, guiding them farther forward on the train. Two tall, tan-ish seats with coral headrests huddled up to a table facing each other.

Trace guided Téya into the forward-facing seat and then took the rear-facing, his gaze locked on the altercation.

"How. . .the SWAT team?"

With a slight shake of his head, Trace let out a breath. "I don't know."

"Think the Parisian who helped us—"

His stormy gray eyes hit hers. "Parisian?"

"The man at the safe house."

The side of Trace's lips quirked up. "He wasn't Parisian."

Téya sat back, too exhausted to be angry or whatever it was she felt. Sorting through the emotions would be too difficult right now. "Fine. But I want answers."

His left eyebrow winged up.

The attendant returned. "Will you be eating?"

"Yes," Téya said, refusing to let Trace answer because he'd probably say no. "Do you have a sandwich?" She shied away from looking at him as the attendant explained their options. Téya chose the ciabatta ham sandwich. As expected, Trace passed.

Once the attendant moved on, Téya leaned back, her brain leap-frogging from each incident. The safe house. The Turk. The bell tower. The Turk. The train station. The Turk. And Trace. He knew an awful lot for him to be a Special Forces soldier and now colonel. "How did you know he was The Turk?" Maybe Trace knew too much. With his tanned face and dark blond hair, he always struck a handsome pose, but there had been something about his bearing since the first time she met him that made him seem unapproachable. Intense.

Even now as he studied her, held her question hostage within that interminable expression, the knot between his eyebrows thick and forbidding... Was Trace more than just Zulu's team commander, a former Special Forces soldier then officer at the Pentagon? *Who are you?* "Why did that operative at the safe house call you Slayer?"

"I've seen my share of field work," he said, as if answering her unspoken question. Now he looked sad. Or maybe thoughtful. She couldn't tell which.

That was it? That lame answer was all he'd give her?

Right. More questions. As if what Zulu was dealing with wasn't enough. Should she now question Trace's involvement in everything? Something about that question roiled through her stomach. He'd led them and protected them. Gotten them to safety.

What if it'd been all part of some colossal plan?

Téya let her attention drift out the window to the blurring landscape. At night there wasn't a lot to see but scattered lights once they left the city.

Paris. She suddenly had no desire to go back. It held no appeal anymore. Had all that really happened? The notorious assassin trying to kill her? Throwing her name to the wolves to make sure she didn't leave Paris alive? Why? "It doesn't make sense."

When Trace didn't respond, she looked at him and found his eyes closed. Disbelief speared her. Who could fall asleep that fast? He didn't want to talk to her? Fine. She wouldn't get answers. Just the very real threat of dying at some unsuspecting moment because she'd set off a time bomb named The Turk.

Curiosity and fear strangled her ability to sleep. She lifted the throwaway phone and went to the search engine. There she typed in The Turk. Scanned the results. Most were about a chess robot, but she noted a few conspiracy theory sites. One blog caught her attention. A woman reported having been in the wrong place at the wrong time when a man with a star-crescent tattoo descended on a quiet evening. The woman's fiancé was murdered—shot to death. The Turk cut a six-inch gouge into her neck and left her to die.

A shadow loomed over her.

Téya sucked in a hard breath.

Trace glowered. "What are you doing?" He growled as he snatched the phone from her hand. He dropped back in his chair, eyes locked on her as he tore apart the phone. "For someone afraid of being found, you sure are making it easy for him!"

Francesca
Alexandria, Virginia
28 May – 0930 Hours

It was one thing to temporarily suspend her job. She *might* have broken some rules. *Might* have been obstinate about that. But to disrupt her entire life—phone, utilities, and her credit—was going too far. Enough was enough.

Frankie stalked into her father's house, bypassing the kitchen, den, and bedrooms, and stormed right into his office.

His graying head came up, expression startled, then he smiled. "Francesca dear!"

"Do not 'Francesca dear' me, Daddy."

His smile wilted. "Excuse me?"

Being upset was one thing, but disrespect never had a place in their home. "I want my life back." Her heart thudded with the anxiety. "Please. I get your point. You want me to leave him alone. You don't want me digging. I get it. Okay, maybe I was even wrong to pursue it, but to get me suspended and destroy my very name with creditors and—"

"What *are* you talking about?"

Anger ratcheted through her. "Don't do this, Daddy. Don't play Top Secret ignorant with me. Please—just reinstate my utilities." She leaned over the desk, lifted the phone from its cradle, and slapped it down in front of him.

Shock riddled his expression, and she hated it. But she'd never been so desperate. "Please. Call them. This isn't fair." Tears burned at the back of her eyes, but she willed them away. She'd never used them to get what she wanted before, and she sure wasn't starting now. Francesca Solomon might be many things, but weak and silly she was not. "It's one thing to reprimand me through work. But to shut down my whole life—I can't get gas. I can't even get a new car because of what you did to my credit score."

Her father stood, a scowl digging into his handsome face. "When did this happen?"

She blinked. "Daddy." The tears were coming, but with every ounce of her willpower, she pushed them back. "Don't do this. Don't play dumb with me. You *know*—"

"I don't." His chest heaved, a sign of his effort to contain his anger.

Or frustration. He waved her to a set of wingback chairs sitting in the morning sunlight. "Let's talk."

Frankie remained where she stood. "Talk?" Was he serious? How could he *not* know? "You are the only person who even cared that I was tracking down evidence on Trace, so feigning ignorance is not going to work."

Well, a few others knew, but they didn't have the power or the means to shut down her life like this.

Or did they? Had she once again underestimated her enemy? She shoved her hands into her long black hair and trudged over to the chair and dropped into it. "You're *seriously* serious? You didn't shut down my life?"

"Why would I?" His tone bordered on preposterous.

"Because I've been investigating Weston."

He went to the edge of the burgundy leather chair, elbows on his knees. "And you think because of that, I'd"—he lifted his hands in question—"hurt you like this?"

"You're a general. It's what you do—protect national secrets and all that."

"No," he said, vehemence scraping his tone. "I am your father first. Look, I won't pretend or lie to you—I was in on the decision to suspend you."

Frankie recoiled.

He tilted his head. "You operated beyond the legal boundaries of your job, Frankie. That puts not only *you* at risk but your commanding officers and, ultimately, the Air Force." He readjusted on the seat. "I appreciate your passion to redeem my name, but"—he shook his head—"it's not necessary."

"It is! Your demotion hurt your reputation, it hurt your pay, it hurt Mom, and it hurt us kids. You know how hard it was to walk with my head up and continue on while the entire Misrata thing plagued our lives?"

His brown eyes held hers but he said nothing.

"But I was not going to let that disaster, that *man* ruin my life, too."

Her father's eyes narrowed a bit. "Is that. . ." He scooted to the very edge of his seat. "Is that what this is about, Frankie? You? How it affected and hurt *you*?"

"No!" Her heart felt as if it would burst out of her chest, startling her. That and the squeak in her voice. "Please don't turn this on me, Daddy."

"I'm not, Frankie, but I just do not understand your vendetta against Colonel Weston. Especially since I"—he placed a hand on his thick chest—"have let it go. Do you understand how this thing is poisoning your life? Your friendships? What about your encounter with Trace's brother?"

Frankie swallowed. "That wasn't fair. I had no idea who he was."

"But you maligned Colonel Weston's name in front of someone you believed a stranger. He was not here to defend himself, and your accusations have no foundation," her father said, the veins in his temples bulging. "I need you to understand your actions are reflecting on me."

Frankie straightened. "On you?" She blinked. "What do you mean?"

"I've heard more than once that I have a loose cannon for a daughter. My own superiors have questioned whether I am the fuel behind your fire."

It felt as if a golf ball had nested in her throat. "I. . .I just want your name cleared."

"And hunting down another officer, a very fine one, and damaging his name. . ." Meaning tweaked the edges of his eyes. "You know what it feels like to have your life shut down wrongly. Is that what you want done to Colonel Weston?"

"I want him to pay for what he did."

"What if he didn't do it?"

"He did!"

"Show me the proof, Frankie."

She dropped back against the chair, petulant and mad. "Why do you do this? Why do you always defend him? After what he did to you?"

"What *you* believe he did to me. How many hearings have there been, Frankie?"

"Three."

He held up a hand. "Three that *you* are aware of."

"What—"

"How many found Trace guilty?"

She gritted her teeth.

"How many?" he repeated, his tone gentle but firm.

Her father might as well be pulling molars. "None," she bit out.

"And you think with your limited access to the case files, to above Top Secret information that you do not have access to, that you, an analyst, can determine his guilt?"

"He was there. There was proof that he had a team in that area, and—"

"Yes, but so did three other special operators." He pressed her fingers between his palms. "You don't have all the facts, and you never will, to seal the case against Colonel Weston. Because it doesn't exist. I've known and worked with Trace for a long time. He is not responsible for what happened in Misrata. I had the great misfortune to be attached to the situation because of my position and tasks assigned me."

Frustration wove a tight cord around her chest, making it difficult to breathe. She wanted to lash out. Wanted to cry. Wanted to hit something. Then *it* hit her. "You did it again." She groaned and pushed to her feet and went to the windows. "You turned this on me, made me look like the bad guy."

"No, I'm only trying to get you to leave this alone."

"Why?" She spun back toward him, surprised to find him only a few feet away. "Why don't you care about your name and reputation? Does it not bother you that there's no resolution? No closure for those families? For us?"

"Of course it bothers me. And my reputation will prove itself. It already has to a degree. Those who know me know I'm innocent of the charges related to Misrata. The only reason that happened in the first place was because they needed someone to blame. A scapegoat."

"Augh!" She whipped around, stabbing her fingers into her hair, curling them into fists and letting out a groan-squeal. So incredibly unfair!

"Does. . .does the fact that Trace refused your attention—"

"Ugh! You have got to be kidding me." She glared at him. Her brothers had tried to rub her crush on Trace in her face for years. She had outgrown that crush as quickly as she had her junior high training bra. "That was ten years ago, long before Misrata."

As a family friend, Trace often hung out with her brothers. Played basketball or football. He'd been handsome and intense even back then. She'd been sixteen, wearing braces, and awkward as she stepped into womanhood. He hadn't given her the time of day. Her crush had crushed her. Especially when her brothers figured out their kid sister liked their friend. They'd been merciless, taunting her.

"Yes, of course," he said with a smile. "I admit for a few years, I'd hoped something might develop between you two."

"It did—it's called disgust." She pushed her hair out of her face. "And it makes me sick to my stomach that he was right here, in our home, your friend, and then this—"

"That should be another reason you should believe he's not responsible. Trace is not only a good officer, he's a good friend."

Daddy's been drinking the Kool-Aid.

Arguing with him would only prove futile. She had to be more cautious, more secretive about her efforts to get to the bottom of this. "Look—I said I'll back off, but I want my life back."

"I'll have it looked into. I can't make promises about your job. That was out of my hands. I only advised. But I'll get someone on the other things. Where are you staying?"

"At my house."

His eyebrows winged up. "Without utilities?"

Frankie gave a one-shouldered shrug. "I know how to camp out."

"You mean you were too proud to ask me for help." He chuckled. "Same thing."

David
Bleak Pond, Pennsylvania
28 May – 0930 Hours

Stretched across the rear bench seat of the large pickup truck, David Augsburger placed a hand on his cast and another on the back of the front seat for balance, wincing against the potholes that peppered the road back to the farm.

"You okay back there?" his *Englischer* friend Tom asked, checking him in the rearview mirror.

"About as much as if someone was hammering my broken leg."

Tom snickered. "Sorry. Road's rough."

Still, the leg pain was nothing compared to the hole in his heart. She hadn't come to the hospital this time either, though he wasn't sure why he thought she would when she'd up and left without a word. Still. . . "Would you mind if we made a stop?"

"Let me guess—the Gerigs'?"

"Just thought I could see how Mrs. Gerig is doing."

"You mean, find out if they heard anything about Katie?"

David leaned back against the corner where the door and the seat met, his head on the cool window as he stared out over the fields. "Think I'm crazy?"

"Of course ya are—you chose to stay in Bleak Pond."

With a snort, David smiled. *Rumspringa*, the Amish way of giving young people the opportunity to taste life outside the community and determine if it's the life for them before committing to it. Tom had met his wife, an Amish girl, during her time away, and the two fell in love. When it came time, she chose Tom instead of her people and community. Tom could've taken the faith and joined, but. . .while he liked the people, he'd often said it wasn't the life for him.

David understood. There were many times he wondered why he'd come back. His sister, Lydia, was the official reason. Though he felt some of the older elders were too hard and too traditional, David believed in the community, in the simplicity of living.

Tom and Mary had compromised. They married and moved to the city right outside Bleak Pond. She was supposed to be shunned, but the family quietly saw her once a month. The elders and bishop looked the other way, just as they had for David with his car and driver's license to help with his sister's medical needs. David had begun to hope that his decision to stay had been the right one, especially once Katie showed up.

She was so unlike anyone he'd ever met, so determined to get things right, to shed her old self. Over the years she'd lived with her *grossmammi*, she had developed into a very fine young woman, a perfect woman for any Amish man.

No, not *any* Amish man.

Me.

And now. . .

Tom guided the truck down the road toward the Gerig house. Even now, David could imagine Katie out there, her sandy brown hair peeking out of the *kapp* she'd worn out of respect for their community and catching the sunlight as she did her chores.

The sudden jolt of the car coming to a stop tugged David from his revelry. Heart heavy, he let Tom help him out of the truck. Situated on his crutches and still weak from whatever had knocked him sick, David stared up at the old farmhouse.

"Want me to go in with you?"

"No, it's okay. Thanks, but this should only take a minute." Careful with his leg, he hobbled up the path to the front porch then negotiated the stairs. He rapped twice on the door.

It took a few minutes, but finally shuffling feet approached the door. "Who's there?" came the suspicious, cautious voice of Katie's *grossmammi*.

David lowered his head, staring at the cast as he called, "David Augsburger, Mrs. Gerig. I just wanted to see how you're doing."

"*Ach*, gracious." She pushed open the door and held it. "*Kumm*, David. How is that leg of yours?"

"A bit heavy," he said with a laugh as he worked his way to the sofa. Sitting, he placed the crutches to his right. "How are you doing, Mrs. Gerig? Are you—"

"Fine," she said. "Just fine. God's grace gets me through each day without Katie." Sadness lined her sweet face.

How could Katie do this? Just up and leave? Put them in danger? He itched to ask her grandmother if she knew the men who attacked them, but the police report said she didn't. He didn't need to hear it for himself and cause her more distress.

"Mrs. Gerig, I don't mean to be rude," David said as he pushed forward with the big question at the back of his mind, "but do you have any idea why Katie left? Just vanished without a word?"

"*Ach*, she left word. She apologized," her grandmother said, her smile flickering as eyes that had seen a lot seemed to be dancing around something.

"Right, but—it was so sudden. And she didn't explain why?"

A weak smile tugged at the weathered face. "I guess. . .I guess she was a lot more like her *mamm* than I realized." She looked frail with the afternoon light filtering through the curtains.

The community knew of Katie's mother, the elder Katherine, who had up and run off with an *Englischer's* son. It wasn't even her *rumspringa*. She wasn't old enough. It'd devastated Mrs. Gerig and put her husband in the hospital. . .only to have him die. Some said it was a broken heart, but the doctors said it was cancer in his lungs.

But right now, the grief David noted in her face was fresh. A new wound. Gaping over a broken trust. Mrs. Gerig had allowed Katie into her home, spoken to the elders and bishop, and then Katie does this. . .

Even David felt betrayed by her. How many times had he defended her to his brothers? To his own *daed*, to whom he'd spoken of courting her once she took the faith. They'd all warned him no good would come of his care for her, though they accepted her into the community. He argued that she was a good person. That she wanted to stay.

What a fool.

"Well," David said, lifting his crutches, "I should be going. But if you need anything, Mrs. Gerig, please know you can ask me. I will help any way I can."

"*Gott* bless you."

David thought *Gott* had blessed him when Katie came to Bleak Pond. "*Danke*. If you hear from her. . ."

"You will know," she said, patting his shoulder as she shuffled to the door behind him.

Annie
Lakenheath AFB, Dover, England
28 May – 0930 Hours

Atlas did not bear half the burden Annie saw on Téya and Trace when they entered the private hangar. Sporting two bruised eyes and a split lip, Téya stiffly crossed the open area, her shoulders sagging, hair stringy, and clothes rumpled. Trace. . .well, he had come out unscathed. But his expression reminded her of the night in Misrata.

Annie stood from the brown, six-foot table where she, Houston, and Nuala had been waiting for the others. "There's a change of clothes back here," Annie said as she led Téya out of the main area into a walled-off space where a bench, two sinks, and two showerheads waited.

Without a word, Téya slumped onto the bench and stared at the floor.

Annie didn't dare ask if Téya was okay. She didn't look defeated. But Annie had taken it as burden. She now realized that wasn't right either.

"He marked me," Téya muttered. "Fed my picture to every agency and who knows where else so I'd be killed."

Annie swallowed. "The assassin?"

An almost imperceptible nod as Téya lifted her gaze to the shower area.

What could she say? In truth, there wasn't anything. "Why don't you shower up and change? I'll keep watch."

Annie stepped outside the shower area and leaned against the wall. They'd heard through a liaison who delivered them here on General Solomon's orders that Téya and Trace had been attacked after leaving the safe house, but that's all they were told.

Shoes scratched on the floor—coming from the main hangar area. Trace came around the corner, roughing both hands over his face. When he saw her, he let his hands fall away. He jutted his jaw toward the showers. "She okay?"

"I. . .I don't know." Annie folded her arms over her chest as she leaned back against the plywood wall. "I thought she was down, but I think. . .I think once she works past that numbness, she's going to be fiery."

"When isn't she?" Trace let out a long, heavy sigh as he stretched his jaw and placed the heel of his hand against the spot.

Only then did Annie notice the discoloration. "What happened? The liaison said you two were attacked."

He nodded and eased back against the wall. "They were waiting for us at the train station."

"Who?" Annie angled toward him.

"Anyone and everyone who needed to make a quick buck." Trace flexed his hand, his knuckles forming scabs. "The Turk sold her out, and some greedy killers took the bait. Surprised we didn't have trouble on the train. Contained environment—perfect place to take us out." He looked at his hand and stood there for a while.

"You okay?"

He blinked and met her gaze.

Annie willed herself not to look away, but the tightening in her belly fought her. Things had once been different between them, but then... Six years ago when she first met the legendary Special Forces operator, she was convinced he could move heaven and earth. While she would still follow him to the grave and beyond, Annie knew to guard her heart. The only thing important to Trace Weston was the mission.

Correction: *success* of the mission.

He broke eye contact. "Yeah. Fine, just could use some rack time."

"Trace—do you..." She wavered in asking the question because the very nature of it implied weakness, and he never wanted to consider that. But she was spent. "Do you think we have a prayer to find out who's behind this and stop it before one or all of us end up dead?"

He scowled at her.

"You've been hunting this person down since we parted ways, haven't you? And we have no answers, no more than the night we made the decision to go into hiding."

Trace shifted his gaze away and down.

Annie moved closer and lowered her voice. "If you haven't been able to find anything—how do we have a prayer? Candice and Jessie are dead. Keeley..." She wouldn't put her friend in the grave before her time. "Every lead turns into nuclear waste. Now Téya is on the hit list of an assassin."

"Hey." Trace faced her, closing most of the gap between them. "Don't do this, Annie. We're behind, we've been knocked down, but we'll get a break. We'll find this piece of crap and end it, end him." He leaned forward. "Every move, every attempt they make, is something we can use to track them down. They will make a mistake—if they haven't already—and we will find and seize on that."

This...*this* is why she'd fallen for Trace years ago.

His hand reached for her hair but stopped short. "I will do everything in my power to protect you, Annie." His gaze landed on her lips. "I promise."

Safety and security had always been found with Trace Weston. Then things changed. "You made that promise five years ago, and then you vanished." Annie pried herself from his spell and turned.

Téya stood there, wet hair dangling darkly around her face and dripping dark spots onto her blue T-shirt. Her gaze flitted from Annie to Trace then back.

Annie froze.

"Done with the shower?" Trace rolled around Annie as if he hadn't just been about to kiss her. "They brought in some food. Make sure to eat," he said to Téya. "Globemasters don't have onboard catering."

But Téya was still staring at Annie.

Once Trace moved out of sight and the shower started, Téya came forward. Taller than Annie by four to five inches, Téya looked down at her. "What was that?"

"That was Trace being Trace." Annie rubbed her temples then considered her friend. "Did the shower help?"

"Well, now I'm tired *and wet.*" Téya almost smiled, her pink lips pretty against her tanned complexion, something Annie envied about her friend. While Annie had blond curly hair, Téya had sandy-brown, straight hair. Where Annie's complexion was a fair-to-golden, depending on sun exposure, Téya had a pretty, slightly freckled darker complexion.

"This assassin thing..."

Téya's eyes narrowed and she chewed the inside of her lower lip. "Am I stupid for wanting another run-in with him, another chance to prove he can't kill me?"

Annie tried to bury her laugh but failed. "Yes, that's stupid."

"Why?" Arms folded, chin up, Téya demanded an answer.

"I didn't mean anything about *your* abilities, but that man, if Trace is right—"

"The safe house told me I was stupid for crossing paths with him." Téya tied back her hair with a grunt. "As if I willingly did it. Where was he? Why did he come after me?"

They made their way back to the brown table where their mostly cold food waited. "Do you think he was at the café? Maybe somehow he thinks you were involved in the bombing?"

"What if he bombed the place?" Téya gingerly lowered herself onto a chair.

Annie frowned. "You hurt?"

"He bruised a rib."

"What if he's been monitoring Ballenger?" Nuala offered, placing condiments in front of Téya's burger and fries. "What if he followed him there, thinking he could find out something about Ballenger, just like we did?"

"And I'm the lucky duck who sat eating a salad, nearly getting bombed, then chased by an assassin." Téya sighed then stilled. "What happened to Ballenger?"

"We lost him in the panicked crowd."

"You know," Téya said as she lifted her burger. "I'm really beginning to hate Berg Ballenger. We get sent to his supposed home, and I get beat up. We go to Paris and I meet him, then I get beat up again."

"You think Berg is doing all this?" Houston asked, his fingers poised over a laptop keyboard again.

"It sure is starting to feel that way." Téya bit into her burger.

Trace emerged, clean and terse as usual. "If it looks and smells like a rat..."

"Then get a rat trap." Annie scooted forward in her chair and leaned on the table, facing away from Trace and toward the others. "I mean, c'mon. There has to be something."

Téya threw down her burger. "I have no appetite, not when some psychopath is trying to get me killed and someone else is trying to annihilate my sisters-in-arms."

"What do we know?" Nuala said, her pale blue eyes alive. "We know that we went to Misrata to hit a weapons cache."

"An illegal cache," Trace corrected, "made up of U.S. military weapons that were reported to have been destroyed."

"Who signed off on that?"

"A supply clerk," Trace said. "He was cleared. As was his boss and his boss's boss."

"And the boss's boss's boss?" Nuala asked, her expression serious, though Annie wanted to laugh at the ridiculous phrasing.

"Andrew Goff. Unaware of the situation, and also the one I believe initiated the investigation in the first place."

"Unaware?" Annie asked incredulously, turning to Trace. "And he got away with that?"

"You want to accuse a three-star? Think you could keep your career if you did?"

"Who was it?" Téya asked.

"Wait—why haven't we heard this before?" Annie scowled at Trace. "You have information and haven't shared it with us?"

"I have information that is not tenable," he said as he threaded his fingers and rested his arms on the table. "What I have are disconnected pieces and a hefty dose of reality that if I move around—"

"We have to throw mud for some of it to stick," Annie said, her agitation with Trace rising. "How can you keep this from us?"

"If I start flinging mud on the wall, the only thing that's going to stick is my butt—right up the flagpole." Trace placed his fingertips on the table as he stared at each of them in turn. "I need you three to trust that I am doing everything I can to end this attack on your lives. That I have not gone one day without searching, investigating, or hunting some element related to Zulu or Misrata." He skated Annie a sidelong glance. "No matter what some might insinuate."

"I believe you," Téya said. "It's just...hard to take."

"What is?" he asked quietly.

"Everything connected to Misrata, to those children we killed." Téya looked down. "And after all this time, we have no better leads? And now, I have a professional assassin—a very *well-connected* assassin—trying to kill me."

"That may not be related to us," Trace said.

"It's very related to us," Téya argued.

"I only meant that most likely there is no connection to Misrata, to why the team is being hit now."

"Think someone has political aspirations?" Nuala offered. Her olive skin made her appear much younger than her twenty-five years. "And they were afraid we'd come out of the woodwork?"

"Is it possible that whoever is behind it thinks we know who *he* is?" Annie asked.

"Plausible," Trace said with a slow nod. "But the timing—there aren't any elections coming up. You were all going about your business without ruffling any feathers. The hits feel. . .strategic."

"What threat were we?" Téya asked. "I would've been perfectly content to stay in Bleak Pond with David."

"Manson met my needs," Annie admitted, her thoughts bouncing to Sam. . .who felt, strangely, a million miles away.

"I felt lost," Nuala said plainly. "I didn't fit in anywhere, and the nightmares made it impossible to be in a relationship or get a roommate." She shrugged, her expression bland. "I'm glad to get this figured out. Maybe a resolution will bring healing."

"Ballenger seems to be our best bet," Trace said.

"Best bet?" Téya frowned. "He's brought us nothing but trouble."

"Which means he's a hot spot. We keep digging. We don't let up."

"The three-star general," Annie said. "Can we know who he is?"

Trace eased back. "I'll consider it, check with Solomon."

"Yes," Téya said, picking at the burger. "What about Solomon—Francesca Solomon, I mean? She's been stirring up trouble, right?"

"Her father is dealing with that. She's dog-headed like you three but barking up the wrong tree."

"Maybe her digging will unearth something we need," Nuala muttered.

"Too bad she's not on our side," Annie said.

Trace snorted. "Not happening. Look, we get back to the bunker, and we dig as hard as we can into Ballenger. He gave us a name and information we can work to verify."

"Someone up this chain of command knows something," Annie said. "It's time to apply some pressure."

Sam
Manson, Washington
28 May – 1230 Hours

The familiar and oddly familial smell of the Green Dot brought Sam a measure of comfort as he held the door for a family of four exiting with their food. Sam gave a nod to Jeff before sliding into a seat at a table opposite Lowen Miles.

Sun glinted through the thin blinds, forcing Sam to adjust them.

"What'd you find?" Lowen asked in a hushed voice, his tone giddy.

"Wounded women." Sam rapped his knuckles against the table. "The one in Amish country is from there—lived with her grandmother. Was dating—"

"They don't date. They court."

"Whatever." Sam scratched the back of his head. "The girl in the hospital outside DC has a twenty-four-hour private guard. I can't get in there."

"But Otto can," Lowen said.

The guy's slick smile made Sam want to punch him.

A sandwich tray slid across the table and stopped in front of Sam as Jeff joined them. "Back from your hunt?"

"Obviously."

Jeff eyed him. "By your attitude, it didn't go so well."

"Waste of time," Sam said.

"But both women were wounded the same day."

"And two kids contracted measles in LA on the same day and ended up in the hospital. Doesn't mean they're connected." Sam felt himself leaning forward, invading Lowen's space. "It's called a coincidence."

"Then why would someone tip us off, give us their names?"

"To divert attention." Jeff shrugged. "Sorry, I tried to warn you—"

Sam pounded the table with his fist. "I'm sick of this. I want answers. I want to know where she is."

"What if she doesn't want to be found?"

"I need her to tell me that."

"No," Lowen said. "I think we're still missing something."

"Yeah. Kinda figured that out, genius," Sam said.

Light swung into the Green Dot as the door flung open. A man stumbled in, hair askew, shirt inside out, and papers clutched to his chest.

"Otto?" Sam was halfway to his feet when his cyber-genius friend spotted him and scurried toward them.

"You're not going to believe this." Otto dropped the wad of papers onto the table. "You told me to look into those ladies, right?"

Sam's pulse thumped in anticipation. This could be it. "Yeah. . .?"

"Well, I did." He scrambled to dig through the pile he'd just dumped. He snatched up one then two, then a third. He laid them out.

Though Sam's irritation was high, he looked at the three. "Dossiers?" he asked, noting the picture, the vital statistics. . . .

"Of a sort. I mean, I put them together. They aren't official records. If you go to Las Vegas, Alaska, or the Caribbean, you won't find these documents. I just thought—"

"Otto," Lowen snapped.

"Right. Well, check them out. Closely."

Sam, Jeff, and Lowen each took one. Sam had chosen the girl in Las Vegas—Jamie Hendricks. Saw her birth date, her school records. Medical records.

"What's your point?" Jeff asked as he swapped dossiers with Sam. "I'm not seeing anything."

"Exactly," Otto said. "Their history is perfect. Too perfect, especially for someone who ended up on the street doing drugs."

Squeezing into a chair, Otto hoisted a tablet onto the table and slid it over to Sam. "Look up her high school yearbook."

Sam frowned. Glanced at the name again then tapped it into the tablet.

"Go to yearbooks. It's there."

So Sam did. Dug through the classes and found her. He shrugged.

Eyes gleaming, Otto took the tablet back. "So, I noticed something weird in the picture. Pixilation was off or something. I dug in and got a friend to check it. My friend says the picture isn't original to the page. The color and pixels are different. So my friend went to the school and looked at a copy of the yearbook—a real copy." Otto handed over a piece of paper. "She's not there."

"Amish girl is a little harder because they don't think it's right to take pictures or something," Otto went on, "but running her face through recognition software, something popped up." He had this sinister laugh that almost made Sam's skin crawl. "Facebook can be a jealous boyfriend's best friend."

The geek had better not be talking about me.

"Someone posted this high school picture."

Sam stared at the picture, his mind revving.

"If she's Amish," Otto asked triumphantly, "why is there a high school picture of her from New York?"

"I see where you're going, but there could be very simple explanations. Maybe Amish girl went to visit friends in New York? Maybe her parents were ill or something and she had to stay with an aunt or uncle for a short while." Sam wouldn't jump to conclusions.

"But I'd think she'd be more likely to stay with Amish friends or relatives within the Amish community than to send her out into the world."

Otto tapped the picture. "Look closely. Amish girl is wearing a work uniform. She wasn't just visiting. She *lived* there. Worked at a pizza joint. Really?"

"They're not against hard work," Lowen said.

"The comments indicate the girl is named Téya Reiker."

Sam, Lowen, and Jeff said nothing.

"What about Vegas girl?" Otto went on. "Her yearbook picture?"

"Maybe Vegas girl was accidentally left out of the yearbook but they added her in digitally once the technology became available," Sam conjectured.

Lowen nodded. "I've seen that happen."

"Oh, come on," Otto cried, tossing up his hands.

Sam wagged a paper at him. "Look, this is good information, but it's frayed. And not enough to string together a realistic theory or to mobilize."

"What if I told you Ashland Palmieri doesn't exist?"

Sam eyeballed the guy.

"Beyond the information on her record, there is no other record of her anywhere, except here in Manson." Otto motioned to Jeff. "How did you pay her?"

"With a check. Twice a month."

"Where did she cash it?"

"Stamp on the back when they're returned says Manson Community Bank."

Otto gave a knowing nod. "All local. All know her. Outside of this community and outside that vital records information, she doesn't exist. No credit cards. No phone bills. No car."

And I thought she was just environmentally conscious.

"Look," Sam said, feeling as if he sat on the verge of a huge breakthrough related to Ashland, but. . . "This broken data trail gets me exactly *nowhere* in recovering Ashland."

"I think we should be careful," Jeff said. "Her disappearance is really solid. If she's still alive—"

Sam stiffened but said nothing.

"Whoever is hiding her," Jeff continued, "whether she's doing it or someone else, it could be very dangerous to find her."

"Dangerous to whom?" Lowen asked.

"Any and all of us." Jeff remained calm.

"Or her," Sam put in.

"So we give up?" Otto asked, his voice squeaking.

"No, we continue hunting but we stay low. Off radars. Whatever trouble found Ashland, we don't need it finding us."

"I'd like to know who tipped us off about those girls," Lowen said. "I can almost feel it—there's a connection here."

"Agreed."

"Otto," Sam said. "Check into that Amish chick, the other name that showed up."

Otto nodded. "Already working on it."

"I've got to get going," Lowen said as he stood. He lifted the picture of the Amish girl and stacked it in with his stuff.

Was that an accident, him taking the picture?

Lowen tucked it away. The move seemed deliberate and bothered Sam.

"Hey," Sam said, "d'you mind leaving the picture? I want to go over it."

"What?" Lowen asked, his expression almost blank. Rehearsed.

Did he really want to do this? Sam came to his feet, knuckles on the table as he nodded to the papers sticking out. "We need those."

"Oh. Right." Lowen's laugh was hollow. Fake. "Catch you later."

Sam sat down, watching Lowen exit the Green Dot. Something was. . .off about that guy.

"A problem?" Jeff asked.

"Don't trust him," Sam admitted.

"He's a reporter," Otto said with a laugh. "It's probably better that you don't. Anyway, I need to jet. I have *real* work to do. You know, the kind that gets *appreciated* by those who ask me to do it."

"Those people probably pay you, too."

Otto sniffed. "I have to leave someone to do all your dirty work."

Sam almost smiled. "Thanks, Otto, I mean it. We're getting close. . . ." And yet the closer he got, the farther away he felt from Ashland. Or whoever she was. Or wasn't.

He and Jeff watched as the geek hurried to the counter and ordered a sandwich before leaving.

"You doing okay?" Jeff asked.

"Yeah, why?"

"Haven't even touched your bacon cheeseburger sub."

Sam glanced down at the sub.

"Need to add an olive the way Ashland did?"

With a soft snort, Sam shook his head.

"So, traveled to Pennsylvania and DC and got pretty much nothing. Then our powwow with the others only adds confusion. Quite a winning streak."

"And to top it off"—he tugged a ticket out of his pocket and flung it on the table—"I got a ticket."

Jeff chuckled and lifted the paper. Something metal clattered across the table.

Sam's heart vaulted into his throat when he saw the ring. He slapped a hand out to stop it, but—

Jeff beat him to it.

Hand on Jeff's, Sam held his gaze. "Leave it." Warning heated the words and Sam's temper.

"You were going to propose?"

Arlington National Cemetery
Arlington County, Virginia
28 May – 1430 Hours

The noonday sun stood sentry over the Marine guarding the Tomb of the Unknown Soldier. He paced back and forth, meticulous and precise in every step, every twitch of every muscle as he carried that M14 rifle, handmade by the Tomb Guards. He marched twenty-one steps south, down the black mat laid across the Tomb, then turned and faced east— toward the Tomb for twenty-one seconds. Upon completing that, he pivoted north, changed the weapon to the outside shoulder and waited twenty-one more seconds. The Guard then marched twenty-one steps back down the mat. Then faced east for another twenty-one seconds before he turned south and changed the weapon yet again to the outside shoulder and waited another twenty-one seconds. Never twenty-two nor twenty.

Always twenty-one. The highest military honor—the twenty-one gun salute.

As that Guard stood fast over a fallen soldier, Marine, airman, or sailor until the changing of the guard, so the brigadier general who waited by the fountain would stand guard over the lives of the Zulu members.

The four-star general joined him at the fountain, his eyes hidden today behind a pair of aviator sunglasses. "A lot of hands are digging into your mess." He kept his voice low, no doubt out of respect for the setting. For the dead.

"Indeed," the brigadier said. "Too many, but I think we can bring it under control."

"Do what you have to. There is a lot more involved than your remaining three gryphons and their handlers."

The brigadier pulled himself straight at the mention of the code name for the female operators. The legendary creatures with the body, tail, and back legs of a lion; the head and wings of an eagle; and an eagle's talons as its front feet were known for guarding treasure and priceless possessions. Just as the female special operators would be doing in protecting U.S. interests abroad.

"Understood."

"Do you?" The four-star snapped toward him. "You seem very cozy with the commander. And you look the other way regarding the INSCOM analyst's meddling. And what of that Navy SEAL?"

"They are all digging in the wrong areas."

"But they're digging. And it only takes one of them hitting a fault line to bring the entire mountain down. That *cannot* happen. Things are too tenuous right now." He let out a ragged breath. "Six years and it could all come crashing down."

"Could, but won't. We'll get a collar on this."

"We are too close to shutting him down. You realize that, don't you?"

"I do." Gunfire cracked the air, a funeral ending with the startlingly loud gun salute. They stood silently, respectfully, until the quiet returned.

"I want them shut down—the meddlers."

The words were not as innocuous as one might believe. This was no ordinary phrasing. This was the four-star's way of telling him to neutralize the threats. But he wasn't ready to kill curious people, people who cared about someone and wanted the truth, wanted justice. "Sir, I can contain this." Though he wasn't sure he could. He'd tried. Hard. "I've already made inroads in blocking their access." That much was true. Rerouting searches. Providing false hits. False information. He had an entire team watching the movement of those in Manson and Washington, and Francesca Solomon in Alexandria. "The colonel is aware of the threats."

"I can't have this unload on him now. Not after all these years. We're too close." He faced him and patted his shoulder. "You weren't afraid to make the hard calls in Afghanistan. Don't be now."

"No, sir."

"Whatever it takes. Whatever you need."

Boone
Reston, Virginia
28 May – 1630 Hours

"Her vitals are fine, have been for the last week or so," the female doctor in the white lab coat said as she stood in the hall with Boone. "Overall, things are looking good."

"Then why is she still unconscious?"

"That's a question science can't answer. Her body is repairing itself, and often, the brain after a traumatic injury will also contribute to a reparative 'downtime.' At this point, only Keeley's body will know when it's time to wake up."

"So she *will* wake up? Is that what you're saying?"

"I. . ." She hedged.

"Okay," Boone said. "Understood."

"I'm sorry."

"I'm a soldier, ma'am. I've seen men die."

She touched his arm, her dark face filled with compassion. "Seeing one of your buddies die is not the same as seeing someone you love die."

"Maybe," Boone said, adjusting his ball cap, "but it's not far from it." He gave her a curt nod. "Thank you, ma'am." He had no idea if she believed him. And he didn't care. Because Keeley wasn't going to die. She'd pull through, just as she had when that chunk of metal hit her when the warehouse blew in Misrata.

Boone navigated the hallway, which was more congested than normal. At the far end, he spotted Rusty. No matter how long the guy had been here, how many nights he'd put in, Rusty always stood ready. Alert. Prepared. There had to be a way to convince him to come back and help Zulu.

Rusty shook his hand. "The doc tell you?"

"What, that she's sleeping on the job?"

Rusty smirked. "No, I meant about the general."

Boone frowned. "What about him?"

"He was here a couple of hours ago, asking about Keeley, about her prognosis."

Now why would the general come down here to check on her? They'd given him detailed reports, including copies of the doctor's notes, her charts, and Boone's personal comments. "Did he say why?"

"No, just asked, went in, and stood with her for a few minutes. He did ask if she'd been moved since coming here."

"Moved?"

"Yeah, dunno. I told him she'd been downgraded from CIC, then he left."

"General Solomon?" Boone's mind couldn't get past their CO coming in here and asking questions. Did he not trust them? Was something going on? Had a threat or complaint been lodged?

"Yeah. No mistaking him."

"Was he alone?"

"To my knowledge," Rusty said with a nod.

Thinking, Boone stared through the window to where Keeley lay. It didn't make sense. "Unsettling."

"Never met a soldier who wasn't unsettled when a general came through."

"Hooah," Boone muttered. Then he remembered a quirk about Trusty Rusty. He paused, glanced at the man he'd grown to respect pretty fast. "What do you think?"

Amusement tweaked his blue eyes. "I think he's weighing options. She's been here a while. We've already had one person snooping around."

"The SEAL."

Rusty nodded. "I'd like to think I don't miss much, but what if I have?" He angled his head to the side, toward Keeley's room. "What danger is she in, if I didn't catch something?"

Balling his fists did little to calm Boone. "Anything else?"

Again, Rusty smiled with his eyes. "Have you thought of relocating her to the bunker? Doc says she's okay, that this coma. . .they don't know how long it'll last, so can't she be monitored at the bunker?"

"I don't have medical skills like that."

"Find someone who does. Pay them."

"And compromise the bunker?" Boone shook his head.

"How much more is compromised with her exposed to a constant stream of medical staff and strangers. It'd be much easier. What about that house you're restoring?"

"Only the lower level is ready. I'm bunking in what should be the laundry room."

"Does it have a living room?"

Boone eyed him, his heart ramming against his ribs. "You're saying bring her out there."

"Not saying anything."

Now Boone smiled. "Trace won't let me until she's ambulatory. You should come back to the bunker and help me convince him to do it now. Heck, just come back to the team, Trusty."

Taking a step backward, Rusty lowered his gaze.

"What would it take, Trusty? You sit here and babysit Keeley. What's different about going to the bunker and babysitting the others?"

"They're active. She's not."

"But you're top dog at threat assessment. You have instincts unlike—"

"I'm not returning," Rusty said, finality in his words. "Sorry, sir. No disrespect intended."

"I'm not a 'sir,' not anymore. I just wish you'd reconsider. We need you."

"Appreciate that. I do. But this. . ." A distant expression took root in his eyes. "I've seen too much and don't want to go there again. Not when it's in my control."

He wouldn't try to guilt the guy into helping them. Boone gave a nod. "Understood."

Rusty frowned and looked over Boone's shoulder. "Who. . .I don't recognize that nurse."

Alarms blazed in Boone's mind. Without hesitating, he threw himself at the door. Broke through and lifted his weapon. Swept the room and found the male nurse standing at Keeley's bedside. "Step away!"

"What?"

"Step away. *Now!*"

"You're kidding—"

"So help me, if you do not move now I will put lead between your eyes!" The male nurse took a tentative step back, glancing at Keeley.

"Hands where I can see them," Boone said. He didn't trust this guy. "Don't move!"

The man whitened. "Holy cow—I'm not. I'm not!"

Sidestepping, Boone gave himself a clear line of sight on the man as he stared down his weapon at him. "Hands. Where I can see them. Nice and easy."

Rusty moved past Boone and plucked the badge from the nurse's uniform. "Stay here."

"Uh," the nurse said, hands in the air as he nervously looked at Boone. "No problem."

"I'll check it out," Rusty said.

"We haven't seen you here before," Boone said, accusation in his tone and words. Vibrations tremored through veins, hot and thrumming. Ready for a confrontation. He'd been waiting for this moment. Waiting to catch the pukes who'd put Keeley here. He knew they'd come back to finish her off. Just didn't expect them to take this long.

"That would be because this is my first day at Reston." He didn't look but midtwenties and like he might wet his blue scrubs. "I worked at Inova Loudoun for the last three years."

Boone kept his weapon down, but he was ready. "We weren't told of new staff."

"Why would you be?" the nurse asked, but his gaze hit Boone's Glock. "Who are you that you are notified of personnel changes?"

"I think the weapon explains why I'm notified," Boone said.

Rusty and the head nurse, Cora, rushed in. "He's clear."

Boone gave the guy a once-over then holstered his weapon. "Nobody enters this room without prior authorization."

"I'm sorry," Nurse Cora said. "We faxed the paperwork in, but—"

"We didn't get it." Boone glared at Rusty. "I'll be back."

Once he made it to his truck, Boone dropped against the seat. Closed his eyes. Swiped his hands over his face. He'd been so ready to take that kid's head off. What bothered him more was that the male nurse walked right past him and Boone hadn't paid attention.

Keeley's life is in my hands, and I let her down.

Annie
Lucketts, Virginia
29 May – 0830 Hours

"Pain is weakness leaving the body," Téya muttered for the umpteenth time as she pushed up from the floor and slapped Annie's hand. Then down again, repeating the phrase yet again, then lifting to pat Annie's other hand.

Beside her, Annie ignored the trembling in her own limbs. Should she be worried about Téya? The fiery woman had more fire than ever. But this. . .this wasn't right. It felt dangerous. Téya hadn't been the same since returning from Paris, since her encounter with the assassin.

Annie struggled to lift herself back up to complete her forty-eighth push-up. She paused, gathering from the dregs of her strength. To her left, Annie shared a look with Nuala, whose brown hair lay plastered to her head with sweat and from the sparring helmet she'd worn ten minutes ago. They both shook their heads, neither of them able to huff through their workouts as easily as Téya. While Annie had an athletic build, Nuala was the smallest of the three. Jessie, when they were together and she was alive, had been the tiniest with her size 2 waist, but she held her own. They all had, but none as fiercely as Candice or Téya. And that was amplified now, after Téya's run-in with The Turk.

"C'mon, ladies! Your attacker won't wait because you're tired," Quade Henley shouted, though he stood only five feet away. "Isn't that right, Two?"

Téya's expression went stone cold as she completed another half-dozen push-ups as if they were her first.

"See, One? That's how it's done."

"Why don't you get off her back?" Dropping against the mat, Annie rolled onto her back. "In fact, give us all a break. We've been at this for over an hour."

"What will your enemy say, One?"

"He'll say I smell too bad to fight." Annie pulled herself off the mat and started stretching.

"Get up! Get up and give me a mile," Quade shouted at her, his face twisted in anger.

Grateful for some time out in the fresh air, Annie headed topside. Even as they entered the cement stairwell, she heard the impatient fingers of rain outside. Great. Exhausted and wet now. They stepped into the ominously dark day and beat the path through the woods and muck to complete their mile.

Téya glided past them.

"She's not human," Nuala huffed out as they crossed the creek.

"She's driven," Annie said then fell silent as she and Nuala maintained a steady, albeit slower running pace. They returned to the bunker sopping wet and with rubbery legs.

"Suit up," Quade barked as he clapped and waved them back into the makeshift gymnasium. "Give me twenty pull-ups."

Annie slowed, but she wasn't giving him anything but a piece of her mind. "I'm not your dog. I don't obey barked commands."

"No, but you're a soldier—"

"I'm not, actually," Annie said, her chest rising with a heavy breath. "I'm a woman snatched out of the life she created when someone tried to kill her. I didn't ask for or want this."

"Well, too bad, because you've got it," Quade growled, his voice gravelly.

Téya slowly came to her feet, dusting off her hands as she walked around inhaling and exhaling.

"Tell you what," Quade said with a vicious grin. "I will get off your back when you can take me down."

Annie blinked. Was the tank-of-a-guy serious? Even as she studied him, she noted that Téya turned toward them, a dark glint in her eye.

Hands on the back of her hips, Nuala asked, "Take you down? How?"

"Any way you can." His voice grated along Annie's nerves. "But I promise you—I will make it as hard as I can. I will not be soft. I will not go easy."

"When?" Téya's question had the air of challenge, the same one that lurked in her hazel eyes.

Quade turned to her, his black hair slick with sweat, his navy T-shirt ringed with stains around his pits and neck, making the shirt stick to his buff body. All reminders that he had strength and power Annie could not dream of possessing. Which made her nervous for Téya, who was taller than Annie, and more athletic, but still a slight woman compared to the oaf.

"When can we challenge you?"

Quade grinned, and Annie realized the guy wasn't half bad looking. Not as charming and sexy as Sam, or as intense and raw as Trace. Quade held his own attractiveness. "You want it now?"

"Yes," Téya said without hesitation.

"Let's do it." Quade motioned her onto the mat in front of him.

Annie felt herself step forward, knowing the pent up frustration fueling Téya's motivation to confront Quade. She had to stop her friend. "Te—"

"No," Trace's voice stabbed the tension.

Annie swung toward the entrance, where Trace stood in a tactical shirt and ACU pants. Though he seemed to wear the same terse expression every minute of the day, Annie saw past that. Saw the uncertainty and protection slipping past his tough facade. So, he was worried about Téya too.

His green gaze slid to Annie and held for a second, then to Téya and Nuala. "Shower up. Command room in fifteen." He stepped back then said, "Quade."

"Guess it's your lucky day, Two. Your commander saved your hide from a heap of embarrassment."

Annie snapped to Téya, who seemed ready to blow as the gruff PT instructor strode out of the room after Trace. "You have some shower gel I can borrow?" Annie asked, knowing full well she had an entire bottle in her locker.

A tremor raced through Téya as she slowly. . .very slowly dragged her gaze to Annie. And it was as if Téya looked straight through Annie, until she blinked. "Sorry. What?"

"Shower gel?" Annie shrugged. "I ran out."

Another blink. A long hesitation. Then, "Sure."

Once Téya headed out, Annie and Nuala gave each other a "that was close" look. Annie let out a long breath through puffed cheeks as she followed Nuala to the bunk rooms. After grabbing a clean change of clothes, Annie went to the showers.

Ten minutes later, dressed and dirty clothes put in the laundry room, Téya bumped Annie's shoulder. "Thanks."

"For what?" Annie asked as she stowed her toiletries in her locker.

Téya leaned past her and reached into the metal cabinet. She held up the bottle of gel. "For distracting me."

Annie tamped down her smile. "Huh. Wonder where that came from."

Trace
Lucketts, Virginia
29 May – 0930 Hours

"You're kidding, right?"

Trace considered his friend, who'd showered in five minutes and joined him here. "I'm not." He motioned to the phone. "He just called me. Wants them in the field."

"Have you even paid attention to them lately?"

"What does that mean?"

"They aren't here"—Quade tapped his temple—"mentally. They don't want to be."

"Once they hear what we're doing, they'll be in."

Quade sat back with a grim demeanor, shaking his head.

Trace wasn't worried. They were his team. He'd picked them. He'd trained them.

"And I'd be worried about Two."

He didn't need anyone to tell him that. The Turk had gotten into her head, or worse—her heart. Poisoned the woman's mind with fear and a thirst for vengeance. And yet Trace had mixed feelings about his concern. This is what he'd always imagined Téya to be—strong, fierce. Facing danger head-on. She'd been great before, but he knew she had *brilliance* in her. She just hadn't realized it yet. No, he wasn't worried. She just had to learn how to hone and manage that acid roiling through her. Téya Reiker had spent too many years hiding behind "nice" and what she felt others wanted from her. She'd worked too hard to fit in and live life anonymously.

But getting her from point A to point B was a delicate process. Push her too hard and she'd crack, which is why he'd intervened with Quade's hard-hitting tactics. But if he didn't push her at all, she'd slip away into a shell of herself.

The door opened and the three women entered. With them came a fruity smell, no doubt their shampoos and body washes. He could immediately pick out Annie's jasmine-scented gel. Stronger than usual today. In hand, each had a snack and water bottle.

As they settled in, Trace could only pray he'd been right about this team. About their resilience. "I appreciate the way you've been putting 100 percent into the training and PT."

"Did we have a choice?" Annie asked.

"Absolutely." Trace wished the turbulent seas between them could calm. "Considering your situations, it would have been understandable for you to push back, resist the attempts to strengthen you."

"In other words," Quade said, "you could've made yourselves miserable."

"I've been in touch with General Solomon. We both believe you're ready to return to active duty."

"Return?" Annie sat forward, all her defenses raised like the hackles of a dog. "What do—we were deactivated! Kicked out of the Army."

"No. Deactivated—yes. But you were never dismissed or discharged."

"This is a joke, right?" Téya asked, her thin eyebrows knitted. "My entire life has upended—again! I gave up this life and embraced my grandmother's way of life. The only reason I'm here is because you said I needed to be safe. All I want is to settle this then go back to Bleak Pond."

"Me, too," Annie said. "Er—I want to finish this fight then get back to my life in Manson."

Not exactly how he expected them to react, but he wouldn't let them derail the plan. These woman had it in them to fight. He wouldn't have chosen them otherwise. They'd been too long in warm, soft safety.

"I'm fine," Nuala said. "I've wanted to be in the military most of my life. Misrata ripped my dream away, so I'm glad to get it back."

"You're serious?" Annie stuffed her hands on her hips. "We're still active?"

Disappointment chugged through Trace that the only one ready for the fight, wanting the fight, was Nuala. That they were all but shirking off his hard work. "How do you think we've been able to keep you hidden? If you'd been discharged, you would've been on your own."

"Maybe it would've been better that way," Annie said with a shrug.

"Right," Trace said, an anchor of disbelief sitting on his chest. "Because you would've had so much more success avoiding the sniper's bullet. Oh, and your SEAL boyfriend—would he be alive now if you'd stayed?"

"I'm in, sir," Nuala said. "All the way."

Trace nodded. *That* was what he'd expected and hoped the others to say. For the quietest and youngest to speak reason—that was a shock, too.

Outside the briefing room, Boone strode into the bunker, spotted them, and headed their way. He stepped into the room.

Nuala straightened and her gaze hit Boone. Almost instantly, her cheeks pinked. Trace glanced at his friend then back to Nuala, who had now lowered her head. Since when did Noodle have a thing for Boone?

"Welcome to the debate," Quade said, holding his arms up.

Boone didn't frown, but his expression wasn't far from it. "What's going on?" he asked Trace.

"I was about to explain to them that Solomon has a tip about Misrata, but One and Two decided they aren't interested in serving anymore."

"Interested?" Boone gave them a look that seared. "You signed up—this isn't about *interest*. It's about duty. And it's your gig—I'd think nobody would be more interested in the truth than those being held responsible for the deaths of twenty-two innocent civilians."

"Do not get self-righteous with us," Annie said. "We've had our lives dissected, disassembled, and then ripped apart again."

"Hooah." Boone didn't seem to care. "Welcome to the Army. Think my life has been simple since signing up? Think any soldier who's lost a limb or come home with invisible wounds like TBI or PTSD didn't have their lives ripped apart? And you think you can just walk away because it's getting hard? What about Keeley, up there fighting for her life? How would she feel knowing her sisters-in-arms are back here whining about it being too hard?"

"That isn't—"Annie snapped her mouth shut. And good thing, too, for the ferocity in Boone's expression.

"Six?" Boone placed a hand on Nuala's shoulder. "You're in?"

Now the girl's face went beet red. "I am, sir." Nuala swallowed. "Sniper is all I've wanted to be. Glad to be a part of the team."

Boone smiled at her. "That's my girl."

A nervous smile flitted across her face as she ducked, clearly torn between the praise Boone gave her and the loyalty to her friends. "Not doing anything special, sir. Just what I love and what I signed up for. I'm glad for the diversion. Being a civilian was boring."

"Regardless of whether we like it," Trace said, cutting into the awkward tension, "you *are* soldiers. Solomon's office got a break—there's a lead on a family in Greece, the Lorings, who can give us some answers about HOMe. But they are in hiding. Priority one is securing their safe exit from Greece."

"After this, once Misrata is settled, I'm out," Annie announced.

"You're out when the Army says you're out," Trace countered.

Anger writhed through Annie's face, but she said nothing.

"I'm not trying to be a jerk about this, but you signed a legal, binding agreement to serve. You haven't fulfilled that obligation."

"If you're going to hold us to that, then I want to speak to a JAG officer, to determine my rights." Man, once Annie got fired up, she was like a heat-seeking missile.

"I'll inform Solomon." He tried to shrug off his disappointment with Annie. She'd been a very different person and soldier five years ago. Then again. . .so had he. "For now, bed down. Flight leaves at zero dark thirty." He headed out of the room, anxious for some air that wasn't thick as mud and laden with tension.

Where had he gone wrong? Doing everything in his power to protect her—them, and it gets thrown back in his face?

He hustled toward the kitchen area, desperate for a drink.

"Hey."

A weight on his arm pulled him around, and he found himself facing Annie.

"What was that?"

"That's what I'd like to know." He extricated himself from her hold and opened the fridge. Orange juice. Apple juice. Skim milk. Soy milk.

The door flapped shut and Annie wedged herself in between him and the metal box. "What is with you pulling that stunt about us being obligated?"

"No stunt. You are."

"I never expected you to stoop to such a low level and—"

"Since when are you scared, Annie?"

"I'm not scared."

"Then why are you running?" Trace leaned down into her face. "The Annie I knew would've faced this head-on and with a baseball bat. The woman standing in front of me wants to slink back to some isolated community with a slick Navy SEAL and play house."

"Just because I found someone—"

"Did you? Or were you just desperate for company?"

Her hand struck hard and searing across his face. Annie gasped, covering her mouth.

The spot where her hand hit stung, but Trace nodded, knowing for that much anger to erupt, he'd hit a nerve. "Thought so."

Francesca
Alexandria, Virginia
29 May – 1310 Hours

"Hey, beautiful. What can I get ya? The usual?"

"Hey, Mick." Messenger bag slung over her shoulder, Frankie tugged out her wallet and flashed her best smile at her favorite barista. "I think today I'm going for the biggest skinny french vanilla latte you can do."

"Living on the edge, eh?"

Frankie smiled. "Need the juice." Her dad had made some calls but only managed to turn on her utilities. He gave her some money to get gas and food. A neighbor had pity on Frankie and gave her a Starbucks gift card, which was nice since she didn't have Internet back yet either.

There were strings she could pull that would make it all go away via hands more powerful than even her father could manage, but Frankie wasn't going there.

As she moved to the end of the counter to wait for her drink, her phone rang. She glanced at the caller ID then answered. "Hey, Dad."

"Just wanted to update you," he said.

"Okay."

"Utilities are back on—water, electric, gas," he said. "But the others are going to take awhile."

"Did you have any luck finding out who did this?"

"Not yet. But I'm working on it." Noises carried through the line, a grunt, then he said, "I've got to go. I'll talk to you later, Angel."

She smiled at his old nickname for her. "Okay, Dad. Thanks."

Mick slid her drink toward her and winked. Frankie smiled her thanks and looked around the coffee shop.

Armed with her caffeine and determination, she planted herself in a quiet corner away from windows and traffic and pulled out her laptop. She might've told her father she would leave Weston alone, but she hadn't made any promises about Boone Ramage, Weston's right-hand man. Interesting thing was that Ramage had bought an old farmhouse in Lucketts. The very location where she'd crashed. Was Weston visiting his friend? Or was something more sinister happening there?

Sinister. *This isn't a Batman movie, Frankie.*

An hour's work today, combined with the several she'd spent over the last couple of days, only netted her his work history, which he'd so kindly posted on LinkedIn, and renovation permits for an old home in his name. Boone entered the Army at eighteen and had served until an injury medically discharged him in. . ."Huh." Frankie eyed the date. "A month after Misrata. Fancy that."

And having a father as a general and her work in the months leading up to Misrata, she knew very well that some soldiers were written out as discharged, but their service had not been terminated. They'd gone black.

Is that what Boone had done?

Or was the back injury so bad that he couldn't serve anymore? He just didn't seem like the type to walk away. But. . .she'd had enough. And never in her life could she have imagined that day would come. Not with the fierce competition she had with her special ops brothers. Three brothers. One sister. All serving. She didn't want to be the wuss. Getting drafted through INSCOM for some dark-cover operations seemed like the perfect way to prove herself. Her abilities. Until some situations and personnel made her feel like she'd been standing on quicksand instead of the firm ground of morality and patriotism.

With a shudder, determined to leave those memories in the past, Frankie directed her energy, her attention to the photographs and files—in particular, Boone's house. Built in the late 1880s. Once served as an antique shop till a fire gutted the upper level. Ramage's family owned the surrounding property, and now he owned the farmhouse and its property. She'd asked a friend who lived in Point of Rocks, Maryland, to stop by and take pictures of the house.

Frankie studied them now. The two-story home with front porch looked largely restored. At least, on the outside. The roof had been replaced. Windows and doors seemed new. Having updated her condo's bathroom, she knew the pretty penny all this work must have cost. Where was he getting the money?

"Check for bank loans," she wrote in a notebook.

The plat map showed that the house sat on thirty-plus acres bordered on the south by a tree-lined creek. That bed of water separated his land from his parents' hundred. Convenient. He could do whatever he wanted and nobody would be the wiser.

Of course, she'd been someone who'd seen an evil plot behind every curtain.

And she'd lost her job, her utilities, her credit rating, her car. . .

Frankie slapped down the laptop. Palms on the top, she rested her head on her hands. What was she supposed to do? She wanted to respect her father's wishes. Wanted to believe he wasn't hiding something from her, but he'd never been so curt and tight-lipped with her. That told her he had concealed things.

Or was he just trying to stop her from digging a bigger grave?

Which way was up? *Who's on First?*

She whimpered. *What am I supposed to do?* Frankie sat up, flipping her black hair out of her face. Her heart jackhammered—a man sat at the table with her. "Varden," she hissed.

Thirty-five, brown hair, chiseled jaw, and yet so common anyone might mistake Eli Varden for a decent human being. She had. And it'd been a fatal mistake.

"Franny."

She shivered, the feel of his voice icy against her eardrums. "What do you want?"

He leaned over the table, folded his arms on her laptop, and probed her gaze.

Frankie steeled herself. Gritted her teeth.

"You're digging up stuff on Trace Weston."

"Actually," she said, feeling triumphantly defiant. "I'm not."

A smile that didn't make it to his lips pinched his eyes. "You're right," he said in that smooth baritone that had coaxed more than information out of her. "Now you're digging into Boone Ramage."

Frankie's pulse tripped over his words and the fact that he always seemed to have one up on her. "What do you want, Varden?"

"What happened to calling me 'sexy'?"

"I grew a brain," she spit back.

He laughed.

At the counter, Mick watched over the espresso machine, giving her a silent "do you need help?" signal with his raised eyebrows.

"You're drawing attention to yourself," Frankie said, knowing this was a sore spot for the operative.

"Nobody ever notices me, you know that." He lifted her drink and took a sip. "Now *you*, on the other hand. Guys notice you as soon as you enter a room." He grinned. "I sure did."

Frankie ripped the laptop out from under him and stuffed it in her messenger bag. "I'm done with you."

"I have proof your dad is connected to shutting down your life."

Frankie hesitated. And she cursed that weakness. Cursed Varden for stepping into her life again. "What do you know about anything, Varden?"

"I know he was ordered to suffocate your will until you broke."

Trembling, she packed up the papers. Secured her bag. How did Varden even know about that? "What? Are you spying on me?"

"I've never stopped."

Bile rose in her throat. "I left the agency. They cut me free."

"Free is a relative term, Franny."

She grabbed her bag and scooted her chair back.

"Don't draw attention," he said, his tone filled with warning.

"What do you want?" she hissed.

"I want you to talk to a man named Samuel Caliguari, a former Navy SEAL."

"Why would I talk to a squid?"

Varden only gave her a thin-lipped smile. "He's on a hunt. I think you should join that hunt."

VII

Trace
Athens, Greece
31 May – 1310 Hours

Sprawling and stunning against the backdrop of the Aegean Sea, the golden-plastered property sprawled over a rich green carpet of grass. Even on the screen, the place screamed wealth and beauty. "The estate is owned by Giles Stoffel." Trace stared at the multimillion-dollar property and shook his head. Was it built with blood money?

"You'd think he'd be a prince or something with a sweet piece of land like that," Boone said, leaning against a credenza. Ankles crossed and arms folded over his chest, he exuded a confidence that Trace appreciated. It'd taken a lot to convince Boone to leave Virginia—to leave Keeley, especially knowing she could come out of the coma any day—but the team had to start acting like a team. That meant they all had to gear up and get their hands dirty. Besides, Trace could tell by all the woodwork Boone had done on the main house at the bunker that he was getting bored. The man had warrior in his blood.

"Why are we looking at this place?" Téya eased onto the edge of an overstuffed chair where Annie sat. "I thought we were here for the family, the Lorings."

With a nod, Trace uncapped a bottled water. "The Lorings are priority one. But Spirapoulos Holdings has come up a few times in my search for the Misrata architect. While rumors abound that they aren't averse to black market purchases, there's little proof, if any."

"But you think they're connected to what happened? The weapons we saw and verified in Misrata?" Annie seemed shaken.

"The weapons that had vanished and were never recorded in the arson investigator's notes?" Téya opened a package of Oreos and dumped two in her hand before offering the rest to Annie, who refused, and then to Nuala, who readily accepted them.

Gulping water did little to help Trace voice his thoughts. He heaved a sigh. "I do. The relative wealth and thriving accounts of Spirapoulos Holdings when most of Greece is poor and flailing give me cause to wonder what's funding their success." He set down the bottle then moved to the small coffee table littered with a pile of papers. He lifted one and sent it around the room. "Jessie had a slip of paper with *Spirapoulos* written on it."

"Coincidence?" Nuala said, shrugging.

"Unlikely, but the probability does exist." He slid his hands into the pockets of his slacks, his 'uniform' for this mission. "Since we are here, Annie and I will do some looking around the estate and do some recon on Spirapoulos while Téya and Nuala head into the Roma slums to find the Lorings."

"Slums?"

"Boone will shadow you, but we want it to look like you're on your own. The Lorings are hiding for a reason, which means they're unlikely to easily trust strangers.

"Don't worry," Boone said. "You'll never be out of my sight."

"The slums are. . .tragic." Trace had entered a similar situation in Russia once, and it left an indelible impression on him. "It's not just a slum like you might find downtown somewhere. It's an entire city—a large city, filled with third world conditions. Trash, disease, crime."

"I think that's his way of encouraging you to get in and get out." Annie's wry comment brought nods all around.

"It is. But I just also want you to be prepared." Trace held a hand over his balled fist. "Remember entering Misrata, the poorest of the poor?" he paused to intentionally meet each of their gazes. Hope they had strong memories and stronger constitutions. "I recall how it tugged at each of you."

That night was as clear as if he were watching a movie. Zulu had stolen into the city and headed straight for the warehouse, while he and Boone stayed a mile out, monitoring their position and progress. Thanks to the use of helmet cams and mics, he'd been able to track reactions. Children, faces blackened by filth and dirt, clogged their path. Begged for money. Food.

"They shouldn't be out this late," Nuala said.

"Out? They have no 'in' to go to," Téya countered, her tone hard, a trait he'd seen often with the tough woman when she got perturbed.

"We have to do something." Jessica wanted to play good Samaritan.

"Get in, get out," Trace replied through the coms, trying to redirect the team back to their mission.

"Okay." Trace broke free of the memory, noting the others had gone quiet. Probably lost in the same past tragedy that nearly sucked him dry. "Two and Six, head out with Boone, who will recon and feed me updates. Houston will stay here, monitoring all of us." He met Annie's gaze. "Ready?"

She stood and held up a finger then moved to the bedroom she'd shared with the other two. In the five minutes before she returned, Boone,

Two, and Six left. Houston went to work setting up a station near the window—"better Wi-Fi and view," Houston had explained—and Trace slid on his suit jacket. He checked his sat phone for any more updates from Solomon but found nothing.

"Okay," Annie said.

Trace turned—and stilled. She wore a light gray pantsuit that made her eyes seem. . .big. Innocent. That was good. It'd work in their favor at Spirapoulos. But the updo and her tangle of gold curls against her neck… maybe that was too far. Too mature. Too alluring.

He remembered slipping his hand around her neck and tugging her closer. . .

"What?" Annie asked, glancing at her attire. "I thought it was a good compromise—business yet casual. No skirt to distract."

Thing of it was, Annie didn't need a skirt to be distracting.

"It's fine," Trace said, gathering his nerve. "Houston, you have the fort."

"Don't worry about me, Boss. I'm good." Houston spoke around a breadstick.

As they headed into the hall, Trace steeled himself. A quick dart of panic stabbed him. It'd be the first time in over five years he'd been alone with her. But that shouldn't matter. This was business. They had a mission. This time wasn't pleasure.

Stepping into the elevator ahead of him, Annie moved as a woman of confidence and means. She would nail the gig, posing as a potential investor. But no matter what Trace wore, where he went, people pegged him as military. A soldier. It wasn't something he could turn off. Not that he wanted to, but in times like this, the mission demanded he *not* be a soldier—in appearance.

The doors slid closed. Silence gaped like a foghorn, buzzing his nerves. Not even elevator music in this steel trap.

"You look nice," Annie said with a smile. "Not every day we see Lieutenant Colonel Trace Weston dressed in a slick suit.

"Same could be said of you," he deflected.

"What? That I look nice or that it's not every day. . ."

"Both." Safe answer. Wouldn't get himself in trouble. Not with them heading into an important meeting.

Annie wrinkled her nose and faced the door. "You should've been a politician."

Trace snorted. "I'd kill everyone who didn't agree with me."

Her soft laugh did crazy things to his breathing. They'd always had a natural camaraderie. One that had gotten them in trouble. The best trouble he'd ever experienced in his life. A trouble he now couldn't afford. "Once we get in there. . . ," he said, leaving off the rest for her to fill in.

"I'm Natalia Policek, daughter of Anton Policek, a Russian billionaire turned diplomat," Annie said, not missing a beat as she recited her cover story. One she carried well even into the third-floor offices of Spirapoulos Holdings.

"And how did you hear about us?" the wiry little man asked.

Trace tucked aside his irritation, immediately recognizing by the cubicle-style office that this man was not high enough up to serve their needs. They'd gone over this at the hotel, rehearsed what to do.

Annie turned to Trace, her face not quite pale but definitely distressed.

Now it was his turn. In as thick a Russian accent as Trace could muster, he demanded, "What is this? A joke? Ms. Policek comes here to make significant deposits and investments, and you expect her to deal with a minion? Someone who does not even have an office?" Trace raised his voice, higher with each word, until several workers around them stalled their productivity to gape. "Insult!"

"No." The man came to his feet, waving at Trace. "Please. Let me call my boss." He gave Annie a sympathetic look. "Would that be better?"

"I am sorry for my bodyguard's anger." She managed a weak smile. "It is just his job to protect, you know?"

"I must advise, Ms. Policek, that you not speak here. It is too open. And this man—his clearance is not high enough. You could jeopardize everything. The danger—"

Wide-eyed, Annie looked around, playing the part. "Oh. . .yes. . .I think you are right, Mr. Volkov." She gave the wiry man a shaken expression. "I'm sorry. We must leave."

"Is there a problem here?"

Trace smiled inwardly as he turned.

"Mr. Christakis," the wiry man said, scuttling forward. "This is Ms. Policek."

Christakis—the CFO. Perfect.

Annie lifted her chin, staring down her nose at the man. "I am here to make investments, yes? But I cannot do it"—she waved a hand dismissively at the maze of cubicles—"in the open, where so many ears listen."

"I am Mikalos Christakis, Chief Financial Officer of Spirapoulos Holdings." Debonair and slick as snot, Christakis had turned the charms on full force with Annie. "Would you come to my office, and we can discuss your options?"

Annie beamed at him like a schoolgirl. "That would be wonderful."

Téya
Athens, Greece
31 May – 1330 Hours

A pregnant woman squatted at a massive heap of trash, picking through the stinking, rotting refuse. Two children, who couldn't be older than three, played with a white, oval disc. The littlest draped it over his head and wore it like a necklace. The elder giggled.

"Please tell me that's not a toilet seat," Nuala said, sounding as if she might puke up the lunch they'd eaten before heading out.

"Okay," Téya said. "It's not."

"You're lying."

The pregnant woman called harshly to the two children.

"You told me to say it." Téya's gaze was stuck on the pregnant woman. What future did she have to offer her child?

On her feet now, the woman held a few remnants of dirty, torn clothes and what looked like it might be a half-rotten orange. She glared at Téya and Nuala, who gasped.

"She looks like she's barely eighteen," Nuala whispered. "*Tell me* those aren't her kids!"

Disapproval and defiance shone in the woman—no, the *girl's eyes*. The woman spouted something, but when they didn't respond, she huffed. "What do you want?" she snipped at Téya. Her broken English was filled with hatred and defensiveness.

As good a place to start as any. Téya took a step forward. "I am looking for a family—"

"Think money can buy you one?"

Téya blinked at the acidic words. "Their name is Loring. The husband is named Carl."

After tucking the goods she'd harvested from the trash heap, the girl grabbed the children's hands. "I don't care what his name was—no way would I help the likes of you." With that, she stomped off, down what Téya had thought to be more trash. It turned out to be a path.

"That went well," Téya muttered. She sure hoped this wasn't going to become a pattern here, but she had a feeling these people wanted to protect their privacy and lives as much as she did outside the slums.

"I'd feel so much more comfortable watching from a rooftop."

"What? Not appreciating the unique scent of the slums?" Téya sighed, brushing a loose strand of hair from her face.

Across the way, down through a narrow alley blocked from this side, a cluster of people stood around talking. Around what might have been a gas station at one time, stretched torn, grungy canopies over makeshift tables and propped-up crates. A man, his drab gray jacket missing a large section in the back, offered a man on the other side something as he lifted a—fruit! A market. What better place to eavesdrop and ask about a family.

"C'mon," Téya said to Nuala and started walking, away from the trash heap.

Nuala was with her, eyeing the surroundings. The sheets of metal, clearly torn from other buildings, were propped together and tied with rags to form a new structure. Téya couldn't bring herself to call it a home. Didn't want to believe people lived in squalor.

"Sure gives a new perspective," Nuala muttered as they navigated the tangle of streets and alleys until they wandered into what was a clearly marked-off area. The market offered partially spoiled fruit and vegetables. Clothes washed and hanging from cord, but with frayed hems and a hole here and there. Used goods. Their own flea market. Only here, she was sure there would be fleas and other forms of pestilence. She chided herself for wanting to dig out a bottle of hand sanitizer from the bag she wasn't carrying. These people deserved respect and kindness as much as any human did. She did not feel pity for them, but rather anger—anger that anyone had to live in filth.

"Act like you're shopping," Téya said, moving to one table where a vinyl purse lay. She lifted it. "If you have to buy something to get someone to talk, then do it."

Already wandering past her, Nuala motioned to a black belt hanging from the ripped canopy. "May I see that?" she asked the seller, who gladly lifted it, rattling off in a quick tongue the benefits of the *fine belt*.

"What do you want here?"

Téya started at the hissed words and glanced to the side. The teen mom stood beside her, hands balled into fists that she pressed against her hips. "I told you," Téya said, acting calm. "We are looking for a family. The Lorings—Carl and Sharlene, and their twins."

"Nobody will tell you anything, and once night comes, they will kill you," the girl said, her lip curling. "Unless they decide to keep you." The girl put her hand to her swollen belly, her meaning quite clear.

"We will leave before then," Téya reassured her.

"You should leave now," she practically growled. "Already, they talk of the two pretty, rich girls. You do not think we notice, just because we are poor?"

"I think you're afraid to talk because you think it will bring trouble," Téya said.

"That is what I said!"

"No, they won't bring trouble to me," Téya corrected. "You're afraid it will be trouble for you."

The girl's dull eyes went wide. She took a step back.

Téya pushed her attention to the woman behind the crate pallet that served as a table and lifted the purse. "How much?"

The teen girl slapped it out of her hand. "Leave! Now!"

"Ten euro," the woman said.

Téya hesitated, glancing at the woman then the purse. "That's a lot."

"Do not say you were not warned," the teen girl said. "It is on your own head if you are hurt!" And with that, she spun and scurried away.

Folding her arms over an ample bosom, the woman narrowed her eyes at Téya. "It is fair!"

Lifting the money from her wallet, Téya hesitated. "I am looking for a family—the Lorings. They are friends of my family, and I got word they were living here."

"I know of no one with that name, and it would not cost you ten euro if I did," the woman said.

Relinquishing the money, Téya smiled her thanks. A gnawing in her stomach telling her this search could take months, not the two days they had to solve this riddle. The Lorings were key to more information, something Zulu needed desperately to put the torment of Misrata behind them. For Annie to return to her Navy SEAL hunk, and Téya to the quiet life with David Augsburger.

What would he think of this, her digging through the notorious slums of Greece for a refugee family? *If they wanted to be found, they would be found. Leave them.* That's what David would say.

But leaving them to their own efforts was not an option. Sprigs of weeds and tufts of grass thrust upward between the sidewalk cracks as she made her way past a building with only two walls. Chunks of brick and mortar littered the path, making the trek both dangerous and frustrating. Crumbling sentries standing guard over broken people.

Ahead, Nuala laughed as she twirled with a multicolored scarf tied around her waist. Three dark-skinned women, adorned with bangles, necklaces, and scarves, danced to a song plucked out by an aged man.

Téya's heart climbed into her throat—gypsies!

Quickening her steps to match her heartbeat, Téya rushed their way. "Sister," she said, breathing relief and exasperation into her voice. "Where have you been? We must go!"

A man emerged from between two thick, old rugs. "She stay with us."

Téya met the man's gaze, working out whether she should be stern or laugh. "She is a favorite with her pretty pale eyes and her dark hair, but our father is marrying her to a rich prince. If she didn't come home, they would raze this whole area."

With a speculative gaze, the man considered her words, a hint of fear in his hesitation. Finally, he waved a hand.

Téya caught Nuala's elbow. "Walk. Fast." They wove in and out of alleys, Téya aware of the danger.

"They knew something," Nuala finally managed. "One of the girls— she went inside their wagon—"

"What wagon?"

"There was a wagon behind the soiled tapestries." Nuala shook a hand. "Anyway, she said she saw twins, new to the area."

"That's all?"

Nuala shot her a look. "It's more than we had before, and it's hope that we aren't putting up with this foul odor for nothing."

They walked the dirty streets that were piled with bags of trash. As they stepped off what remained of a curb, Téya felt something brush against her leg. When she first glanced down, she thought a kitten moved next to her.

Nuala screamed.

That's when Téya saw the pink, segmented tail twitching. A jolt of disgust ripped Téya straight. "Ugh!"

Nuala clapped a hand over her mouth, fighting a giggle as they both rushed away from the large rat.

"Food! Do you have food for me?" a little boy with dark eyes and dark hair ran up to them and grabbed onto them, clinging as if his life depended on it. "Please, I am hungry. You are rich. Give me money!"

"No," Téya said firmly, prying him off. "I don't. I'm sorry." She nudged him in the other direction, but he simply rolled against her push and flung himself at Nuala this time.

"Tenacious, aren't you?" Nuala said, her voice trembling.

A shout went up at the other end of the street. And when Téya glanced in that direction, she saw it wasn't a street but an alley. A chill scampered down her neck.

"*Not* reassuring."

Téya turned to her friend, ready to yank the boy off her. But he was gone. "Where'd he go?"

"Away, which is probably where we should go if that scared him."

"Probably," Téya said. The sky had not darkened yet, but it wasn't far off. The words of the pregnant teen echoed in her mind. "I guess it's—"

"Téya." Nuala's voice was filled with quiet dread and warning, pulling Téya around. Her face had gone white as she stared down the alley.

"What?" Téya shrugged, glancing between Nuala and the alley. "I don't see—" But then she did. And panic ripped through as what she'd taken for shadows and darkness coalesced into a thick band of scraggly men.

Téya started backing up. "Nice and slow," she said, catching Nuala's hand.

But the crowd rushed them.

In seconds, they were surrounded. Men pushed at them. Taunted them. Touched them.

Hand tightening around Téya's, Nuala punched one of the men. Fifteen against two. Not fair. Boone—where was Boone?

Though terrifying, Téya's mind registered that the men weren't *hurting* them. Who cared! They were jostling them. Forcing them to move away from their intended course. A frenzy of excitement, shouts, and trilled yells suffocated her ability to think.

Someone grabbed her hand. Téya jerked it back and tried to nail the perpetrator with a glare, but there were too many. She wasn't sure who touched her. Who grunted in her ear. Who pushed between her shoulder blades.

White-hot fire seared the top of her right hand.

A man caught a fist-hold of her hair.

Téya yelped as he yanked hard. She clamped a hand over his then jabbed her elbow into his gut. Kneed his groin. She couldn't even see Nuala for all the chaos. Her feet tangled and she went to a knee, hand protecting her skull against the wild insanity.

Shouts went up.

A hushed gasp fell over the crowd.

In a split second, the men were gone. Sprinting down the narrow alley.

"Let's go," Téya said, catching Nuala's hand again and running in the general direction of the way they'd entered.

"Think Boone scared them off?"

"How? He isn't here." Her scalp and hand still burned. Téya shook out her hand against the burning that mirrored the one in her scalp.

Nuala sucked in a hard breath and stopped short. She took hold of Téya's wrist. "*What* is that?"

"Two, Six!" Boone's voice boomed through Roma slums.

"Thank You, God," Téya muttered, searching for their protector, but

Nuala wagged Téya's wrist she was holding.

"Téya, look!"

"Hey!" Boone grunted as he jogged up to them. "What are you waiting for? Move!"

Scowling, she tugged free, her irritation from the day's events getting the better of her. She flicked her hand, the stinging as fresh as the moment—and she saw it. Saw the burn on her hand. Not just any burn. The contents of her stomach threatened to free themselves from her stomach. The star-crescent.

Sam
Manson, Washington
31 May – 1330 Hours

He hadn't been in the cottage in over a month. The night they'd shared a plate of nachos and watched a marathon of the science fiction flick *Firefly*. She sat on the sofa, legs crossed and a pillow in her lap, insisting he was out of his mind to watch a show about space cowboys and demented cannibals. But she stayed, laughed, and cheered the characters on. That was the thing about Ashland—she'd give anything a chance.

Even me.

"Can you grab the glasses?" his sister, Carolyn, asked as she carried a box of linens to the back bedroom. "I want to give them to Goodwill and get a new set for the tenants."

Lifting a glass from the cabinet, Sam frowned and looked toward the hall. "Tenants?"

His sister reappeared, her sandy-blond hair pulled into a ponytail. She winced and hunched. "Yeah. . .meant to tell you. I agreed to a six-month lease for a writer who wants to come up and get his next novel written."

"You rented the place?"

"Look, I know for you, Ashland is coming back."

"We don't know otherwise."

"Sam, I know you liked her. And I know you're trying to find her, but Paul and I must have someone paying the bills on this place. Things are too tight for us." She touched his shoulder. "I'm sorry. We are within our legal rights to do this."

"What if I pay?"

Carolyn sniffed, then she must've noticed his expression. "You're serious."

The thought of anyone else living here. . .

249

"Sammy, that's..." She tucked some hair behind her ear. "What if you can't find her? It could be months or longer. I can't let you do that. I know you mean well, and I know you want to find her."

"Why would she leave me?" Had those words come from his mouth? Sam pivoted and reached for another glass in the upper cabinet, knocking the one in his hand to the ground. Glass shattered across the floor.

Carolyn jumped backward.

"Crap." Frustrated with himself and the situation over the cottage, Sam held out a hand to his sister. "Leave it. I'll get it cleaned up."

"I'm really sorry, Sammy."

He nodded and retrieved the dustpan and broom from the small closet in the narrow hall. Sweeping the chunks into the dustpan, he tried to shed his sense of helplessness in with the dirt. It did about as much good. And hadn't he learned in BUD/S that every minute was a choice? *His* choice.

He set the pan down and palmed the counter.

Leave the whole situation alone?

Or hunt her down like the SEAL he was?

His gaze hit one of the chunks of glass. A smudge caught his eye. Sam craned his neck to the side, allowing the light to hit the piece from a different angle. Not a dirty smudge. A fingerprint.

His heart backfired as the questions again plagued him—pursue or abandon?

Holding the piece as if it were directly connected to Ashland herself only heightened his sense of duty. The insane conviction that he was to protect her. He'd wanted that since she took his order at the Green Dot that first day he'd arrived.

Sam moved out onto the deck and tugged his phone out of his pocket. Dialed. Put the phone to his ear as his gaze bounced over the sparkling waters of the lake.

"'alo."

"Otto, Sam."

"You ask me to do complicated things, yet you feel the need every time you call to tell me who you are. You don't think I know this already?"

"Otto," Sam said, more terse this time. "Can you run fingerprints?"

Hesitation clogged the line. "I have a feeling I don't want to know why you're asking that, but yes—I can. And I can even read caller ID."

"I'll be over in ten." Sam pocketed the phone and stepped back into the cottage. "Hey, I'll be back in an hour."

Explaining why he was leaving would give her the opportunity to condemn his efforts, chastise him again. He didn't need that. When he pulled into Otto's driveway, Sam stared at the Jeep already parked. Jeff. What was Jeff doing here?

Sam headed to the front door, which swung open as he strode up the path. Jeff gave him a nod. "What's going on?" Sam asked.

"That's what I'd like to know." Jeff closed the door and, with it, shut off most of the natural light.

A thrum of electricity emanated from Otto's living room, where artificial light cast from a ton of monitors glared back at him.

"Look, man," Otto said, as he pushed up his black glasses and shifted in the oversized leather executive chair. "You just had that sound, ya know? The one like you're on a mission, and when you're like that. . .well, it scares me. I don't want to go to jail—"

"Jail?" Sam scowled at the two of them. "What do you think I'm asking? I just want fingerprints." He held up the glass. "Otto said she didn't exist, so let's find out who does. Running fingerprints isn't illegal." When neither man moved, Sam felt as if someone had tapped a det cord and he'd blow at any second. "What?"

The Green Dot owner stretched his jaw. "You know the deputies found no fingerprints of hers at the cottage."

Sam shrugged. He didn't know but also wasn't surprised.

"It's probably not hers," Jeff said.

"Nobody else has been in that cottage since that night."

"Except you."

True. Sam had been inside, but he hadn't touched anything. "The print is too small to be mine." Sam roughed a hand over his face. Turned to Otto and held out the piece. "Just run it. Please. I won't ask anything else of you."

Otto glanced at Jeff.

"Since when is the sub shop guy mayor of Manson?" Sam's anger rose and crested on a tide of roiling frustration.

"I'm not," Jeff said. "I just don't want you to vanish, too."

Sam swallowed. Understood the implied threat. Ashland had vanished. "You think if I run this, I could end up just like her." And though the itch at the back of his brain told him she was still alive somewhere, it wasn't out of the realm of possibilities that she had died. He could end up in the grave, too, if they ran this. He lifted his chin. "I'm willing to take the risk." A nod to Otto. "Run it."

"All right then," Otto said. "It'll take a couple of days."

Sam backed toward the door. "I'll wait on your call." And before Jeff could pepper him with more questions or doubts, Sam left. They'd long been friends, and more times than not, Jeff was right. A wise man in his own right, Jeff had counseled Sam through many dark days. But not this one. Jeff wanted to play it safe. Sam wanted to play it straight—and hit whoever took Ashland head-on.

Jeff would call it reckless.

Turning back toward the lake house, Sam spotted a brown sedan in his rearview mirror. Definitely not a car from around here. Maybe a tourist. Or a rental. He shrugged it off as he turned right.

A glint behind lured his gaze back to the mirror. Brownie was still behind him. No big surprise. Going through town, there weren't many main roads, so it wasn't uncommon to travel the same route. Passing the Green Dot, he kept his eye on Wapato Way Road, but his periphery homed on Brownie sedan behind him. When he hit Wapato Lake and headed past the casino. . .

Brownie followed.

Sam tightened his hand on the steering wheel, eyeballing the side mirror. There was no way someone could already know about the fingerprint. So. . .who was on his tail? He had to shake them before they trailed him home.

He hit a right on Roses Avenue and slowed.

Brownie came around the corner.

Sam whipped his car around. Flung open his door. And drew his Glock. "Out of the car," he yelled. "Get out!"

Francesca
Manson, Washington
31 May – 1415 Hours

Though she was following a Navy SEAL, she had no idea Samuel Caliguari would tag her so fast. Biting back a curse, Frankie slid the car into Park. Hands up, she eased out of the rental.

"Hands!"

She lifted them higher, her heart thundering as she stood beside a field of grapes. A flicker of temptation had her sprinting away from him through the vines, but that would only get her shot in the back.

"Who are you?" Even yelling at her and his face scrunched into a tight scowl, the man was get-out gorgeous. "Why are you following me?"

"I just want to talk," Frankie said, swallowing a big ball of dread.

"Bull." He was within a few feet of her now. Close enough for her to see the tat crawling out from under his T-shirt on a very large bicep. "Talk? That's what phones are for."

"Fair enough, but there are some things that need to be said face-to-face."

"Yeah, like get in your car, turn around, and don't come back."

Frankie stiffened. Just like her brothers, he was dismissing her. "I just wanted to talk to you—"

"About what?"

"Trace Weston."

His expression didn't change. At all. Great. He didn't know who she was talking about. He wagged the weapon toward the car. "Get in," he said, his words carrying the very breath of anger. "Leave and don't come back." He kept moving forward, pressing her backward. To the car. *Into* the car.

"No, listen—"

"Leave now and you walk out of here alive. No promises if I see you again."

"I just wanted to talk to you about Ashland Palmieri."

This time he flinched. Seared her with a scorching glare. Yet he remained unmoved. Undeterred in his laserlike focus on his mission: making her leave.

Or was this a chance to convince him to work with her?

He rapped on the hood then motioned to the road.

Again, her choices split her down the middle—get out and say she wasn't leaving, something she would've done to her bullheaded brothers. Or turn around and head back into town. . .and find Sam later. Maybe the second time would be the charm and he wouldn't have that gun.

No, he'd have it. And she had a very keen awareness that he would use it.

So. Time to regroup and restrategize. For a second, she considered spitting out that she wasn't easily scared off and she intended to return, but no sense in warning the guy.

Trace
Athens, Greece
1 June – 0730 Hours

Perched on the edge of the bed, Trace sat with his fingers steepled and pressed to his face. Up till after three, they'd come up with exactly nothing on Spirapoulos, though the name was on Jessie's data wall. They'd read files and articles over dinner then at a midnight eat-in with pizza and Chinese. The intensity of his desire to put Misrata to bed had swelled to a colossal peak, layered with thick coats of frustration and dead ends.

A soft flutter of movement forced his eyes open.

Annie stood on the threshold, more casual this time in jeans and a light blue sweater. "You okay?"

He straightened and nodded. "Sure."

She slipped into the room and onto the arm chair next to the dresser. "That's Trace speak for 'It sucks, but I'm gutting it up,' I believe."

She always did know how to read him, look past what he said to what he didn't say. Though she was nine years younger, there was a similarity of minds that had drawn him to her. But that wasn't a conversation for now. Or ever.

Trace pushed to his feet and trudged to the window. "Christakis didn't seem to know anything."

"We didn't exactly give him a chance to show us that," Annie said.

"Three hours dropping hints and he never bit." Greece was beautiful and yet it wasn't. Though the early morning sun climbed into the sky, a certain gloom hovered in the distance. It contaminated the mission and his mood. "We're wasting our time here."

A gentle touch against his back made Trace jerk. His gaze snapped to Annie, who stood at his side. Her blue eyes so blue. Her skin so golden and soft. "I've never known you to give up so quickly or easily."

It'd be so simple to touch her. To break the promise he'd made five years ago. "When one meets failure enough, he's quick to recognize it when it's staring him in the face."

Annie's eyes widened and her lips parted.

What surprised her? What had he said— "I didn't mean *that*." Though *that* had been a failure, too, though he did everything right. Though it was the right thing to do.

Her face flushed and she pulled her gaze away and down.

Way to screw it up again, Weston. He turned back toward the bed and lifted his phone from the nightstand. Anything to shield himself from the hurt in her expression. But he couldn't. Just as Annie read him, he could do the same. And there were images of her burned into his mind that he'd never be able to shake.

"Why did you do it, Trace?"

If he faced her, told her the truth. . .what would it change? Trace gritted his teeth. But he was tired of the failures. The letdowns. He felt like a punching bag.

"Commander!" Houston shouted from the main sitting area.

Coward that he was, Trace seized the escape. "Yeah?" he said, heading out of the room, but not before he heard Annie's frustrated sigh. "What's up?" Stepping into the living area seemed to ease the weight on his chest. The openness gave him room to breathe.

"So," Houston said, "I've been running the names and faces that came up during your visit to Spirapoulos."

Give me something. . .anything. Please. One hand on the guy's chair and a palm on the desk, Trace leaned in. "Right. Last night you said there wasn't anything there."

"I know. There wasn't."

Trace's frustration knotted his patience. He tightened his lips.

"But thanks to that handy spy-bot y'all set free, I went through and ran facial recognition over the people who have been in and out of the building."

"Have you slept at all, Houston?" Annie asked, arms folded as she stood in front of him.

"Sleep, who needs sleep when there's Red Bull? Anyway"—he waved a hand—"about twenty minutes ago, someone showed up at Spiro. And the software matched him almost immediately."

"With whom?"

Houston pulled up the footage. Stopped the frame on a tall, dark-haired man who walked in confidence.

"A power player," Trace muttered.

With a grunt, Houston produced a picture on the monitor. "You could say that." Another click and an entire portfolio appeared. "Titus Batsakis, owner of Aegean Defense Systems."

"ADS," Trace said, his gaze hitting the banner with Jessie's data. He pointed to where three bold letters shone clearly: ADS, right next to the single word Sheba. "She was on to them."

"The news gets even better, ladies and gentlemen," Houston announced and brought up another image. This of Giles Stoffel, Titus Batsakis, and a woman at a very ritzy gala. "That"—he flicked the woman's face—"is the one and only Mercy Chandler, now-wife of"—he produced another document, this a wedding license—"one Giles Stoffel."

Annie moved to Houston's right shoulder. "Wait—that lists Mercy Kennedy."

"That would be because Mercy dropped her last name when she opened HOMe," Houston said, showing a birth certificate with the name Mercy Chandler Kennedy.

Trace let out a long whistle, scanning the document. "Guess that's why we couldn't find her, but you'd think the government could figure out something like that."

"I wouldn't have if I hadn't been using this new program a friend and I put together. It's wicked cool—takes the face in question then zips through online photos and shows the matches."

Trace patted Houston's shoulder. "Nice work."

The beep of a key card swiping the electronic lock box drew Trace around. He set his hand on the weapon holstered at his back as Boone thrust open the door, holding two large bags. Téya and Nuala also carried bags. "Not as good as gyros," Boone said with a laugh, "but maybe they'll convince the natives to talk."

Trace frowned.

"Bread and cheese," Téya explained. "We needed some ammo to get them to talk."

Maybe that gloom hovering on the horizon was starting to break up. "Good thinking."

"What?" Téya wrinkled her lightly freckled nose at him. "Praise from the commander?" She brushed hair from her face. "I might faint." Her hand bore a red, angry mark.

"What happened to your hand?"

He'd rarely seen it happen, but Téya blanched. Then gave him a weak smile. "Flat-iron fight." She turned to the bags. "The smell of this stuff is making me hungry." She lifted out a round loaf and sniffed longingly at it. . .her burned hand sliding into her pocket.

Nuala laughed. "I know you and gluten, so leave it alone or there'll be none left to bribe the people." She set it with the others.

Téya looked stiff. Nervous.

"Téya," Trace said, his tone demanding she come clean.

She stilled, then her shoulders slumped as she met Nuala's gaze then Boone's. He nodded at her. "Yesterday," Téya began quietly, "as we were trying to leave, we were set upon."

"Not really set upon, but more. . .ganged up on," Nuala corrected.

"They came out of the alley and just crowded us. In the end they didn't harm us—"

"Just scared the tar out of us! And when we caught up with Boone, that's when I noticed the burn on her hand."

Trace went to Téya and lifted her hand. Saw the mark of The Turk burned into her flesh, right below the knuckle of her index finger. He wanted to curse. Punch someone. "You hid this from me?"

Tugging her hand back, Téya flashed him a glare. "It means nothing."

"It means *everything*," Trace shouted. Poked a finger in Boone's direction. "We'll talk about this later."

"What?"

"You knew?"

"Trace—what could we do? If she keeps it covered, nobody will know."

"I need to know!" he growled the words. "Do you know what that means?"

Boone said nothing.

Son of a gun. Trace snorted. "You knew and weren't going to tell her?"

Téya's expression fell. "What? What are you talking about?"

"He's marked you, Téya. Wherever you go, anyone who sees that mark and recognizes it will alert him. They won't kill you, but that's about where their kindness will stop."

"This is insane." Téya swallowed hard. "If he was there, if he knew I was there, why didn't he just kill me then?"

"Because it's on his terms. When he's ready, when the time is right, he'll take you." Trace bit back a curse.

"I'll have it burned off."

Trace snorted. "Every man in that slum knows who you are, knows The Turk has claimed you." He balled his fists. "You won't get anything out of anyone now."

Téya's face reddened. "I'm not giving up. Not when we have a chance to find someone. If you want to write me off, fine. Write me off. But I'm going to go in there and hope that at least one person will defy him."

"Don't be so naive!"

"Hey," Annie's quiet, calm voice slid through his turbulent mood. She held his arm and tugged him back.

Trace turned to her, caught her upper arm. And froze. How many times had he done that when—their eyes locked. He patted her bicep. "I'm good," he said, his voice hoarse and thick. Extricating himself, he returned to the desk. Noted Houston's embarrassed expression. Trace half turned to the others. "Houston found something." He gave the guy a slap against the shoulder as he moved past him. "Tell them."

"I. . .uh. . .right. So." Houston cleared his throat. "With the bugs and bots planted at Spirapoulos, I made some facial matches."

Behind him the story unfolded. Trace used Houston's time of explanation to get himself back together. *I am never going to survive this.* Not with Annie there at every turn. She had this way of dousing the fire in his gut. Made him weak—in the knees and in the eyes of others.

Shouldn't have expected to cross lines and come away unscathed.

The phone rang. Silence dropped on the room as Trace turned and eyeballed it. Nodded to Houston who waited for instruction.

The techie lifted the phone. "Office of Miss Policek. How may I help you?" Houston nodded and murmured a few *uh-huhs* as he typed up information. "I'll be sure to let her know. Thank you for calling."

Trace wandered back to the desk. "Well?"

Face bright, Houston grinned beneath that wiry mess of curly hair. "That was the executive assistant to one Giles Stoffel extending an invitation to a benefit dinner tonight at their private estate in Salamina."

Téya
Athens, Greece
1 June – 0915 Hours

Jamming on a pair of fingerless gloves worked better to hide The Turk's branding than a bandage that would draw attention. Téya had, however, applied burn cream and a bandage before donning the fashion trend.

"Seriously think that will work?" Nuala asked, eyeing her skeptically as she hoisted the brown paper bags into a better hold.

"My question is whether the bread will work." Already tired of the attention and irritated with the assassin bent on ending her life, Téya wandered past the market—in the opposite direction of the mob who'd ganged up on them yesterday.

A little girl seemed to peel from the grime of the buildings, her pants and shirt the same grimy shade of the dirt. Though she couldn't be more than four or five, she seemed to have a preternatural sense that they had something good to offer.

"Aw," Nuala said, reaching into the bag and drawing out a roll. She gave it to the girl.

"Okay, I'm all for humanitarian compassion, but you realize we have to buy information with that."

"We show them we aren't here to harm them," Nuala said, as she gave the little girl a warming smile, "and they'll trust us."

"We are American and obviously so." Téya took in the surroundings, the women watching suspiciously from alcoves and open doorways. "They're never going to trust us."

"Don't be such a naysayer."

"And Trace called *me* naive." The words had cut through her swifter than anything else—even the mark of The Turk. She'd never been naive. Her life was fat on abuse and hard knocks—no way could she squeeze into the skinny, narrow-minded space of naïveté. A teen boy, who couldn't be more than fourteen, walked up to her, unabashed.

"Those free?" he asked in a gruff tone.

"No," Téya said. "The cost is a pound of niceness."

The boy didn't move. Probably weighing whether she was serious or not. "We have eight mouths to feed."

"Eight?" Téya wasn't necessarily surprised that someone would have that many children, but she did question the sincerity of this boy's assertion. He seemed a bit too confident, maybe because his claim was a lie. And who would refuse a family of eight a loaf of bread?

He lifted a shoulder. "Maybe it's only five, but when there's that many mouths, it seems like eight because we get so little."

Téya relinquished one of the bigger loaves to him, and the teen darted off.

"I know everyone thinks I'm naive and gullible," Nuala said, her voice soft, wounded. "I just prefer to think the best of people. There's enough bad and negativity in the world. Is it okay if I prefer to see and hope for sunshine?"

Chastised, Téya realized that while she never had the sweet personality Noodle possessed, she did have that same outlook once. A very long time ago. "Yes, yes, it is okay." Shame on her for falling prey to Trace's dark outlook. And yet she couldn't blame him. If she'd seen everything he had, life would probably seem pretty bleak to her as well. She didn't blame him. Couldn't. He'd gotten them through so much. His intensity and ability to see things that were dark and dangerous protected them more than once.

She dug out some wrapped cheese and a loaf of bread, the bag crumpling as she did, enabling her to detect a woman hovering in a cardboard and stained-sheet shelter. Two children clung to the woman's legs, and her belly promised another mouth to feed soon. With a tentative smile, Téya walked toward her and extended the food. "A gift."

The woman scowled and turned her head away but kept her eyes on the food.

"Take it. I ask for nothing," Téya said, "but we are looking for a family—friends—the Lorings. A husband named Carl and his wife, Sharlene. They have two children."

Snatching the food so quickly that Téya jumped, the woman retreated, a sun-bleached towel dropping over the makeshift doorway.

It went like that for the next hour, Téya and Nuala pacing themselves and rationing the food that went way too fast. Three more times Boone met them at a street with more bread and cheese. When he popped the trunk, the smell of yeast assaulted her senses. Téya's stomach growled, but she would not allow herself any food until they had a lead on the Lorings.

"How's it going?" Boone asked as he closed the trunk and passed the last bag to Nuala, who seemed a little flushed.

Flushed? It wasn't hot outside. Not yet anyway.

"Thanks," Nuala said, her gaze flicking to Boone's face, then down, then back.

Holy crushing operatives! Hadn't she gotten over the big lug after all this time? Surely with the way Boone doted and crooned over the ailing Keeley, Nuala would know better. But here she stood, her confidence wobbling it seemed.

"Any progress? Tips?" Boone asked.

"Just that we're filling some bellies but not exactly making friends," Téya said, remembering the talk with Noodle about being positive. "We're making an impact, I'm just not sure it's the one we're after."

Boone tossed his chin toward her gloved hand. "How's the hand?"

"Fine." Téya had to ask, "Why didn't you tell Trace?"

Boone smirked. "He had enough things to work out. The mark doesn't affect us here."

"Doesn't affect us?" How could he say that? "Trace said it could entice people to attack me—if I'm down, I can't search. That affects us."

"Actually," Boone said, "I disagree. I think the burn is The Turk's way of saying if anyone but him touches you, they're as good as dead, too."

"*Too.*" She nodded in disbelief. "Thanks." It wasn't a question of *if* The Turk would kill her, but *when.* So reassuring.

Nuala touched Boone's thick bicep, probably to let him know his words weren't comforting. But she quickly removed her hand. "I don't think that's what he meant. Just—"

"It is what it is," Boone said with a thick-necked shrug. "Ignorance gets people killed."

"Wow, don't placate me, Ramage," Téya said. "Wouldn't want me to worry or anything."

"Hey, I call it like I see it."

Téya thumbed back toward the Roma slums. "We're going back to the wolves now. It's safer in there." She gave him a wry grin.

Nuala hesitated then smiled up at Boone. "Thanks for grabbing the bread for us. Bye."

With a nod, Boone—oblivious to the girl's charms—said, "Meet you back here at eight."

"Unless you hear from us before," Téya said. "And we're grabbing dinner before we go back. I'm starving!"

They'd no sooner turned the corner than a group of children surrounded them. Reminding herself to breathe, Téya told herself the brand wasn't burning again. That it was her imagination reacting to the mob scene—even though the mobbers were half the size and were excited, not angry, to see them. But there were so many this time.

"I guess word got out," Nuala said. "Maybe word will get to the Lorings...."

"I sure hope so," Téya said, taking in the dirty, pleading faces. "How do we know they aren't siblings?"

"We don't." Nuala started passing out the bread.

Téya couldn't help but marvel at how the youngest member of Zulu held no reservations about this. And why should they? The kids were hungry. The parents were without money. Téya really had to get herself together, remember what was really important in life.

But we have to find the Lorings.

They worked their way through the slums, growing strangely and disgustingly accustomed to the stench and filth. Strike that. Téya would never be accustomed, but it wasn't as bothersome as it was yesterday.

When she turned, she met the eyes of a boy who looked to be fourteen or so. Intelligence and shrewdness lurked behind those brown orbs. "You've already received a loaf today," Téya said, a teasing note in her voice. "We have to spread the fun, don't you think?"

Another lazy lift of his shoulder. "I want two loaves—"

"Two?"

"And a thing of that cheese you got in that bag."

Bold teen. "Sorry, but—"

"I can take you to them." His words rushed out.

"We have the loaves here"—her mind caught up with his more likely meaning—"wait." Téya leaned in, glancing at Nuala, who had gone still. "What do you mean? Take us to whom?"

"You look for the Lorings, right?"

Trace
Salamina, Greece
1 June – 1430 Hours

With an hour-long drive from Athens to the Stoffels' seaside estate in Salamina, Trace and Annie geared up—that is to say, he donned a tux and she a slinky navy blue dress that made a man's mind wander—and headed out in the hired limo. Hair done up, makeup expertly applied, and poised to perfection, Annie looked every bit the heiress, especially with the leased jewels gracing her long, slender neck and the teardrop earrings teasing the line of her jaw.

Trace kept his gaze out the window, knowing he'd be in trouble if he stared.

"Reminds me of Sydney," Annie said, her gaze locked out the other window.

He looked at her, surprised at her words.

Twirling the huge rock—another lease—on her right hand, she shook her head. "I shouldn't have said that. I'm just nervous. A lot depends on me getting things right." She finally brought those blue eyes to his. "Let's go over it again."

She didn't want to go over it. She wanted to avoid a conversation with him. "You wanted to know why I did it?"

Annie clenched her eyes tight. "No. Please. Not now, Trace. I can't. . ." She blew out a ragged breath and turned her attention to the world passing them by. "Things can't always be on your terms." The words were soft yet sharp, the dagger thrown exactly where she'd intended it.

Sitting back and once again fixing his gaze outside the limo, he said, "When we arrive—" His secure sat phone belted out the national anthem. He lifted it from his left breast pocket and glanced at the screen then answered. "Go ahead."

"Boss-man, it's me—Houston."

Trace waited.

"I've—there's some disturbing things happening."

Patience was a commodity he didn't have right now. "Well?"

"Sir, I'm. . . Annie's picture is floating the underground."

"The what?"

"We tech geeks have a lot of back channels and sites. Her picture's out there."

Trace sat forward, his knees practically in his chest. "Out where? What are you talking about?" His gaze hit Annie's, and her face registered the same concern.

"I think Stoffel's checking out her story, about being Policek. I mean, he's digging deep."

Hand over his mouth, Trace closed his eyes. "Please tell me her ghost life will hold up."

The seconds that fell off the clock felt like minutes. . .*hours*.

"Houston," Trace said with warning.

"I don't know," he finally admitted. "We put up enough that it would look solid if done by an entity like the FBI, but he's going to the underground. We live to find the holes. I can't make any promises, Commander. I'd go in with the very real possibility they know she's *not* a billionaire's daughter."

Annie
Salamina, Greece
1 June – 1630 Hours

"What?" Several feet of distance sat between her seat and Trace's as he rode with his back to the glass that separated them from the driver, and she was grateful for every inch. It stopped her from going to him.

Trace made another call. "Need you in Salamina...as soon as possible." The conversation went on and he thumbed his lower lip. That was his stress sign. "No, I need you here." He nodded. "Okay."

After he tucked away the phone and scratched the side of his face, Trace looked at her. He always struck a handsome pose, even when he wasn't trying. He had a strong, broad forehead with a perpetually terse brow. Though his hairline had begun to recede, there wasn't anything old or unattractive about Trace. Except his walls, especially the one that pushed them apart and separated their lives.

"Stoffel's looking into you," Trace said quietly. "But they're digging—deep. Possibly deeper than we faked."

She struggled for a breath, as if someone had a chokehold on her neck. "What do we do?"

"You go in there and hold your head high. You're Natalia Policek, spoiled brat of Anton Policek." He swiped his hands out as if smoothing a sheet. "Nothing's changed."

Annie studied his face. His eyes. The line of his mouth. Set of his jaw. Trace believed she could still pull this off, so she would trust him. "Okay," she managed.

He rapped his knuckles against the window, and it rolled down. "Drive around for a bit."

After they were alone with their words again, Annie asked, "Why?"

"Boone's on his way. I want to make sure he's in place before we go in."

"In case something goes wrong."

Trace said nothing.

A bitter taste filled the back of her throat. "You sure—about this?" she asked quietly as she folded her arms around her tummy. Mustering her own courage, she nodded despite the dread pooling in the pit of her stomach.

Trace hunch-walked across the limo and sat on the bench beside her. His arm went across the back of the seat as he held her gaze. "A lot has passed between us, some pretty rough things, I confess, but I'd never put

263

you in a situation I couldn't get you out of."

"Things happen," Annie whispered, looking into his gray eyes. "Things out of our control."

"And that can happen every day of every year." His hand came to her cheek, her stomach jolting. "But in a mission"—his thumb stroked her cheek—"I'd die before sending you in if I thought it was crossing the safety threshold."

Annie moved away from his touch, hating the way her body betrayed her. He had this way of convincing her, making her believe he was capable of almost anything. Of believing *she* was capable.

Twenty minutes later, the limo eased to the front portico of the estate. The driver opened the door, and after a nod to her, Trace climbed out. He stood, blocking her view, acting every bit the bodyguard. Finally, he shifted aside and held out his hand.

Annie took it and stepped from the darkened interior. Her second step went a little wobbly, nerves turning her limbs to jelly. Trace steadied her, his gaze still sweeping the area.

When she looked over her shoulder, Annie's breath was stolen. The sprawling green lawn vanished. And beyond it, the pristine, inviting waters of the sea.

"Miss Policek?"

Annie pivoted, turning awkwardly in heels on a cobblestone drive. A man stood just outside the door, another behind him held the door. "Forgive me," she said to the suited man as she traversed the eight steps to stand before him, then took another gander at the blue-green waters. "I was just admiring the view."

"Indeed," he said. "If you will come this way, please."

With Trace behind her, she moved into the house. Resplendent crystals threw light across the foyer's golden marble floor. A gilded rail guided guests from the lowly position of the entrance to the grand extravagance of a large open area that she could only think to call a ballroom. And yet there were richly adorned sofas scattered around the room, as well as elegant floral arrangements topping white-draped tables around which older guests sat chatting. Most, however, stood in huddles, their conversations hushed and discreet.

This could take all night.

She wasn't even sure where to start. *Remember, you're a billion-heiress.* Right.

"Miss Policek?"

Annie swirled, intentionally let her floor-length gown flutter. She kept her chin up as she met Spirapoulos's CFO. "Mr. Christakis. How nice of you to arrange this little tête-à-tête."

He gave her a languid smile as two men appeared beside him—and she recognized them both from Houston's info dump this morning. "Miss Policek, I'd like to introduce you to the CEO and owner of Spirapoulos Holdings, Mr. Giles Stoffel."

Annie extended her arm, all too aware of Trace moving in, as a bodyguard would when several men joined someone as supposedly rich and powerful as she was. "Mr. Stoffel," she said with a pitched voice. "It was generous of you to invite me to your benefit tonight. I was pleasantly surprised when they told me of the invitation." The man with Stoffel, his brother-in-law, shifted closer several times, clearly intent on meeting her. That girl radar went off, the one that she and most every girl out there had, to alert them to a guy's presence. Sort of like when a lure is dropped in the water and all the fish scatter—and that's exactly what she wanted to do, scatter.

Instead, she gave him a coy, sidelong glance though a bitter taste rose in her mouth.

"And this is Titus Batsakis, owner of Aegean Defense Systems," Christakis said. "Now, if you'll excuse me. The prime minister would like a word."

"Of course," Annie said, perfecting her accent as she turned to the ADS owner. "Defense? You deal in weapons?"

"Not just," Titus said as he lifted two glasses of champagne from the tray and handed her one. "We have many branches, including electronic and virtual training. . .we manufacture farm equipment and large machine tools."

Annie rolled her eyes at the last few. "Droll," she said with a sufficiently snotty tone. "My father, he started building farm equipment, but he said the real money is in weapons."

"It's interesting that I have not heard of your father, and I'm very familiar with weapons builders around the world," Batsakis said, his dark, beady eyes roaming over her. "But had I suspected he had such a beautiful daughter, I would have met him sooner."

That made no sense, but she laughed anyway. A small tremor raced through her when his arm slid around her waist. "Mikalos says you wish to invest?"

"*Da*, my father gave me one-tenth of my inheritance, and if I can double it before my next birthday, he will give me all of my inheritance now. But if I cannot, or if I lose, then I will get nothing."

Trace appeared with what looked like a cocktail and handed it to her, taking the champagne. He gave her an intentional nod, one that the ADS owner wouldn't see, and moved away.

"What was that?" Titus asked, sounding indignant.

"Sorry," she waved a hand dismissively. "I cannot be trusted with champagne, so Mr. Volkov keeps me stocked with cocktails."

His dark eyes assessed her.

Annie wondered if they'd gone too far but sipped the drink—one that was apparently nonalcoholic by the taste of it—and intentionally moved her attention toward the balustrade that spanned a large, gorgeous second-story balcony. "A beautiful view. I'm not sure I'd ever leave this quaint villa if I got to see that every morning and evening."

"That is what I tell Giles often," he said, admiring the view—her. Not the landscape.

"You live here, too?"

"More than Giles," he said with a laugh. "My sister is in residence here, but Giles's business often takes him around the world."

"I love traveling the world," she said, finding more truth in those words than she realized she felt. Maybe it was just five years wrapped in the solitude of Manson. She'd been in Paris, Germany, London, and now Greece. . .

"Your father," he began again. "What was the name of his company again?"

Unease squirmed through her. This is where it began. This where his doubts bred or died.

"Mr. Batsakis," Annie said with a teasing reprimand to her words, "Please—do not bait me. We both know you were digging into my personal files the last twenty-four hours. If you cannot remember the name of my father's company, then perhaps I will be better off doing business elsewhere." She looked out over the view again. "Somewhere with water, since I find it so relaxing."

He gave her a leering smile. "You are an incredible, forthright woman."

"I find it serves no purpose to be otherwise."

He stepped in, his hand going to her waist. Men were so primal, trying to physically possess anything, including women. Over his shoulder, Annie did not directly look at Trace, but she was sure his lips were moving as he stood alone in the corner. No doubt talking to Houston.

"Excuse me, Mr. Batsakis," a waiter said as he approached.

Titus turned, his expression growing dark. Very dark. Frightening.

"Forgive the intrusion, sir," the waiter said as he lowered his head in deference. "The prime minister and Mr. Stoffel would appreciate a word."

With a disgusted sigh, he straightened his jacket. Met her gaze but only long enough for her to see the fury. "I must see to them. I won't be long, dear Natalia."

Annie smiled her consent for him to leave. "Don't be gone too long. I bore easily." And with that, stirring her virgin cocktail, she wandered away. . .toward Trace, guessing he had a message for her.

She feigned interest in a massive portrait of a half-nude woman, something she would really never understand people fawning over.

"Something's wrong," came Trace's quiet voice.

"Agreed," she said with a smile.

"You want out? We can make that happen."

His words about not putting her in a situation that would jeopardize her stilled her. "Would you leave?"

When he didn't answer, she looked in his direction. Trace was staring at her—intensely.

She saw it—saw the turmoil behind his silence. "When you recruited us, you promised you'd never make a gender-based decision."

"This isn't about gender," he hissed, stepping closer. "This is about a piece of slime pawing you. If he gets you alone. . ."

Annie swallowed. Mostly because she knew what he didn't say. But also because of the jealous rage clouding Trace's face. "I'm an operative. Let me do my job." More ferocity filled her words than she felt. Had he heard the tremor in them? Her uncertainty?

His nostrils flared as his lips went flat. He gave a nod and slowly blended back into the crowd. Something about watching him vanish like that left a sickening dread in the deepest part of her soul. He'd vanished like that once before and what dawned next proved to be the blackest time of her life—utter isolation from everything and everyone she loved.

"You like it?"

Annie jumped then laughed as she smiled up at Titus. "You startled me."

"You seemed rather focused," he said. "My brother's decorator chose the piece. I'm not fond of it. I prefer impressionistic works over realism."

"As do I," she said.

"Come." He motioned to the balcony. "I could do with some fresh air."

"Is everything okay with the prime minister?"

Hand on the small of her back, he guided her onto the balcony. "In politics, is anything ever okay?"

She arched an eyebrow at him. "True. Wow," she said as she rushed forward. "It is beautiful!"

And it was. The far right provided a breathtaking view of the water, which spread out in a foamy kiss from the cliff's base. To the left and opposite a meticulously manicured lawn rushed up to a copse of trees that grew denser the farther up they went.

But the water...

Annie sighed. She loved the water. It's why she'd chosen Manson—the lakes and river. Quiet. Solitary.

"You like our Salamis Bay, I see."

"Is that what it's called?" So odd. To have the freedom and expanse of the sea before her and the dense barrier of the forest behind. "I never knew there were forests in Greece."

He laughed. "Most people who haven't visited tend to think that way." His hands slid up her back, caressing.

Gross!

She had to be strong. Turn this into her corner. "So," she said as she peered up at him. "What do you think—?"

"I think you're quite beautiful." He was leaning down to kiss her, and she fought a shudder.

Annie steeled herself. Then put her hand to his chest. "I'm sorry, but you move too fast."

Out of the corner of her eye and close to her face, she saw a glint of something metal. A sharp pinch at her neck.

Her vision swam.

Trace
Salamina, Greece
1 June – 1730 Hours

"Houston, what's going on?"

"It's crazy. The whole freakin' board is lighting up." He let out a moaning groan that wavered, evidence of his not wanting to believe this. "Get her out of there, Trace. Get her out now."

Trace pivoted toward the balcony.

An explosion of light and smoke erupted directly in front of him. Screams and shouts stabbed the air. Training threw him through the smoke fog instead of away from it. He cut through into the open, his eyes burning as he scanned the balcony. The *empty* balcony!

"Houston," he subvocalized as he hurried toward a set of stairs he hadn't noticed before. "Where is she?"

"Uh..."

"I need help now, Houston."

"She's...she's gone, Trace."

He cursed. Hit the bottom step and turned a slow circle, drawing his weapon. He spit out a few more expletives. "Find her!" he hissed.

"Where is the bodyguard?" a man demanded.

Trace slammed himself against the wall, staring up at the upper balcony.

"He came out here."

"Find him and kill him!"

Sam

Manson, Washington

1 June – 0730 Hours (PST)

Sam hit the trail, jogging around Wapato Lake a couple of times to burn off the frustration. Days and still no word from Otto on the print. And thankfully, no men in black showing up to cart either of them off to prison.

His Bluetooth signaled a call and he connected. "Caliguari."

"Sam, hey, it's Nolan. Just wanted to touch base about Colombia."

Sam dropped out of a run, squeezing his eyes. *Shoot. Completely forgot about that.*

"The plane will be there tomorrow at 0800."

Pacing the path, Sam wrestled with the decision. Tomorrow. *I can't.* But he had to if he wanted to keep paying his bills. If he ever wanted another gig. One thing he knew about Nolan Patterson was that he didn't appreciate last-minute cancellations. "Right. Tomorrow."

"Is there a problem?"

If he didn't go, he wouldn't be working for Dynamic Security Solutions ever again. Or any other security firm with military connections. Nolan would ostracize him. Sam looked around the lake. Tomorrow—he didn't have anything planned. Still waiting on those prints. "No, not a problem." He swept the sweat from his face.

"Good. This VIP asked for you by name, so if you screw me on this—"

"I'm good." Had to be. "What do I need to know?"

He resumed his jog as Nolan rattled off the information, including the pickup, drop off, and connections. The contact. The VIP. "We'll supply what you need. Just be there at the airstrip first thing. Clear?"

"Crystal." Sam crested the incline and trekked around the vineyard. He ended the call, cursing himself for losing track of time and commitments. A week in Colombia routing sweaty, cigar-smoking, foul-mouthed drug lords—maybe it'd clear his head.

My head isn't clogged. He just had to find Ashland.

But the more he thought about it, the more he began to wonder if walking out of Manson had been her doing.

No. He wouldn't buy that. He'd have to hear that from her own mouth.

Sam made one last circuit, determined to reset his mind. Get mission minded about Colombia. Expectations. The VIP was an American attaché who had more power in his little finger than most U.S. seal-embossed dignitaries held. At least, with the Colombians. And often—with Sam, too. The gig often entailed security as the attaché made his way into hostile territory and Sam made sure the guy made it out alive and intact.

As he jogged back down Wapato Lake Road toward the house, he slowed. Something was off. Sam cast his gaze about, searching for the trouble. And then he saw it—the car. The same one he'd confronted last night parked in his driveway.

Fifty yards out and his Bluetooth buzzed again. "Caliguari," he said as he moved to the side of the road, walking as a portion of it rose.

"Sam. Otto."

Sam stopped. "You have something?"

"Um, yes."

The words made Sam's heart thud hard against his ribs. "Ser—"

"But not what you think."

Should've known better. It was then the panic in the guy's voice registered. "What's going on, Otto?"

"I've been trying—trying to get it back."

"Get what back?"

"The results."

Sam shook his head. "Otto, you're not making sense."

"Nothing makes sense about this!"

Holding up a placating hand—to whom, he wasn't sure, because Otto wasn't here to see it—Sam squatted, his gaze on his house. "Easy there, big guy."

"Listen, Sam. They know."

"Who?"

"If I knew that, don't you think I'd tell you?!" Otto was shouting now. "They know we're searching for her. That print—I think we've set off a firestorm, Sam. My computers are fried. Everything is locked up with some vicious virus." Breathing hard, Otto gasped. "Be careful Sam. I think they might be coming."

"You're overreacting," Sam said, more to reassure himself than to quiet Otto.

"Yeah, well two big black SUVs are pulling into the parking lot right now."

"Get out of there!" Sam jerked around, nervous for the tech geek.

"Duh, genius. I'm not there. I left as soon as they fried my systems.

Just keep your eyes out."

"Thanks. I'll do that. Stay safe."

"Yeah, you too, though I think we're beyond that."

Sam started toward his house. Had to get a few things before the MIB thugs showed up on his doorstep. Including getting rid of the nosy woman, whoever she was. Or...was she one of them?

He entered the gravel drive.

The car door swung open and the dark-haired bombshell stepped out. "Listen—I know you said to leave."

"I also said I'd shoot you if I saw you again," he said as he slid the knife into his hand. "But all I have is this knife. And not a lot of time."

"Then I'll talk fast."

On second thought, he didn't have time for this. Not if the thugs were already at Otto's. "You get a pass today," he said and stalked to the deck. He tugged back the sliding glass door and went to the bedroom.

"Thank you. I won't take much of your time—"

Sam spun, lifted the Glock from the holster strapped under the counter. He aimed it at her. "What're you doing?"

"You said I got a pass."

"Yeah, as in I wouldn't kill you." He waved the gun to the door. "Now."

"I need to talk to you about Ashland Palmieri."

"Never heard of her."

She nodded to his living area, to the credenza by the wall. "That photo says otherwise, along with all the interviews you gave."

"Know what? It's your funeral." Sam turned around. He went to the bedroom and tugged out a rucksack. Nolan said he didn't need anything, but with the MIB squad coming, Sam might have to lie low for longer than a week.

"My father is General Haym Solomon," she spoke from the hall, standing by the bathroom. "Five years ago he was tasked with sending an SF unit to Misrata."

Libya. Yeah, so?

"Something went very wrong. Twenty-two women and children died in a warehouse the team hit. I believe the man leading the mission, then–Captain Trace Weston, is responsible."

"Great. Congratulations." He squinted at her as he stuffed a couple of tac shirts and pants into the bag, then pushed past her to the bathroom. "What's this got to do with me or Ashland?"

He grabbed a new bar of soap and his shampoo.

"I believe Ashland was part of the team that hit the warehouse."

Sam straightened and stared at her. Hard. "Ashland."

She nodded, her wide brown eyes confident yet wary.

Slinging the ruck over his shoulder, he stalked forward. "Five years ago."

She nodded again.

"That alone tells me you're barking up the wrong tree. Women weren't in combat roles like that five years ago, so that tells me you have no idea what you're talking about."

"Zulu."

Sam frowned. "What?"

"That's the name of the team that hit the warehouse. It was said the team was the last thing anyone would expect." She planted her hands on her hips. "Wouldn't expect females on a special ops team, would you?"

"No, because they weren't legal." He nudged her aside and reached for the picture she'd pointed out earlier. After removing the back, he slid the picture free and tucked it in his back pocket. "Now, I don't know what you think you might know about Ashland, but unless you plan to answer a lot of questions under the threat of electroshock therapy, I suggest you leave." Sam swung open the door.

"Are you threatening me?"

"I'm warning you, Miss Solomon."

"How'd you know my name?"

"I read minds," Sam said, his irritation growing.

"Ashland's real name might be Annie Palermo."

"Come back when you have something stronger than pea soup to feed me." Sam waited for her to exit then locked the door, something that felt futile once the suits arrived.

"What will it take for you to listen to me?"

"A hundred years."

The long blast of a horn drew his attention around. At the other end of Wapato Lake Road, he saw a caravan of black SUVs. *Crap!* Sam ran to his Charger and tossed in the sack.

"What's going on?"

As he slid in, he said, "If I knew that, I wouldn't be running." Sam revved the engine—she'd parked him in. "Go!" he shouted to her.

She raced to her black sedan and backed out.

"C'mon, c'mon," he said, revving the engine. She'd barely made it onto the road when he let 'er rip. The tires spun and rocks spit out, pinging the car. He didn't care. Not now. The Charger roared back.

He spun the wheel left and let it straighten out, then rammed it into DRIVE and gunned it again.

A black Suburban tore up the road behind him.

Adrenaline ripped through his veins.

It seemed like slow motion. The six-point-six seconds it took his car to rev up to sixty felt like minutes, with that SUV growing larger and larger in his mirror. Sam pushed his driving skills. Spotted Woods Road. Aimed for it.

He downshifted to take the turn, ignoring the big vehicle.

The roar of an engine blazed through his ears seconds before a deafening crunch. A horrendous impact rammed the Charger to the right—off the road. Sam's head cracked against the windshield. The car came to a dead stop.

Silence and ringing warred for his hearing. Warmth sped down his temple. He groaned, shaking off the stun of the impact. He reached for the steering wheel, a haze filling the car from the deployed airbag, and then his gaze hit the half-dozen suits surrounding the Charger, weapons aimed at him.

Defeat pushed Sam's hands into the air that still reeked of the powder from the side-curtain airbag.

Téya
Roma Slums, Greece
1 June – 1815 Hours

Her heart skipped a beat. "You know them?"

"No, but I know where they stay."

Could they trust him? Normally she could tell with kids and teens when they were pulling her leg, but this young man. . .he'd learned a lot living here. She couldn't read him.

Nuala held Téya's gaze, question curling her dark brows.

They really had no choice. If they didn't follow him, and the Lorings really were there. . . But following this teen. . . Flashes of the mob last night and the searing pain of the mark. Téya drew her chin up. "Two loaves," she agreed.

"Cheese, too." He held out his hand.

"And the cheese—but only after you show us where they're living."

He hesitated, glanced over his shoulder at something behind them. Though she scanned the distance, the windows, alcoves, shadows, she saw nothing. Finally, he gave a nod. "A'right then."

With half a bag of bread and one chunk of cheese left, they trailed the kid through the passages. He moved through the spaces like a pro, no doubt having grown up here and discovered all the ins and outs.

As they neared the far side of the slums, her apprehension grew. Taller buildings towered over them, blocking light and seeming to hold them in the fist of danger. Shadows skittered around them, half of the movement from fluttering sheets or wind gusts that snapped up cardboard and metal roofs. Each snap elicited a flinch or jerk from Téya. Noodle wasn't faring any better.

"This is getting creepy," Nuala said.

"Getting?" Téya searched for a familiar landmark, but being closed in on all sides with tall buildings and cement, she shrugged and shook her head, as if she could shake off the chill that had nothing to do with the cooling day. This was like falling deeper and deeper down a rabbit hole. Though she tried to keep her bearings, Téya could feel those cords of control turning into the thin tendrils that defied her grip.

Ahead, dark-headed John continued on without hesitation. She wasn't sure if it was comforting or discomfiting that he knew where they were going and she didn't. If it were Trace or Boone ahead. . .yeah, good. But this kid? The one bribing them for bread in exchange for vital information?

"You sure you know where they live?" Téya mentally reached for her weapon, knowing she *would* use it if they were faced with an untenable situation. Whether she'd use it on the teen. . .she couldn't imagine doing that. Not unless he held a weapon on her, too. Of course, she guessed Trace would argue information could be a weapon and he was holding that on them.

This is crazy. I am not shooting a kid. Not tonight. Not. . .ever. She already had the blood of eighteen children on her hands.

Téya skidded her gaze to the shadows, shoulders tense, anxiety high. Every crinkle of paper or tink-tink-tink of a soda can dancing down an alley made her want to reach for the HK USP Compact.

"John, I'm losing confidence in you," Téya said with warning.

"You're not the only one," Nuala said, her pale eyes tracing rooftops. "Wish I were on high ground."

"I wish I were back at the hotel eating the parmesan steak and shrimp special." As if echoing her thoughts, her stomach growled.

"Not sure how you can think about food right now."

"It's comforting."

"Okay, that you can eat food for comfort and be that thin makes me sick," Noodle said.

Téya shrugged. "High metabolism." She turned a circle, checking their six, as they walked. "Johnny?"

"It's just around the corner" the kid said.

"What's your name?" Téya asked, stepping carefully around a shanty that looked like one breath could bring it down.

"John."

"Right," she muttered. "Let me guess—your last name is Smith."

He threw a grin over his shoulder. "How'd you know?"

"Great." Nerves fractured, Téya considered heading back. They'd been walking for forty minutes already. The setting sun hid behind the buildings making it darker. Batman would do well here.

"Just ahead," John said.

Téya studied the buildings a little more carefully, plotting courses to safety. Searching for trouble. They rounded one more corner, and John stopped and thumbed to a brick building on their right. "Third floor. Maybe fourth."

Four floors? Taking in the building only stirred more apprehension. Téya tilted her head back and let her gaze trek up the levels. Ha. Four floors would be easy. There were six here. . .well, on one side. The other had been wiped clean of half the floors. Unease slithered through her stomach when she saw the way half the building leaned to the left. The other half seemed to be pulling to the right. If they went in, their weight alone seemed like it could offset the balance and bring it all tumbling down. The stoop seemed the stopping point for fliers and boxes in various states of decay. It didn't look like *anyone* had been through that door in months, if not longer.

"You sure this is the right place?"

"Now why would I lie to you?"

"Two loaves and a block of cheese," Téya muttered. Nobody had been here. Nobody *was* here. *He's pulling a fast one. . .* "That's your thirty pieces, huh? John, there hasn't been anyone in this building in a long time."

He grinned. "That's what they want you to think."

With a hefty sigh, Téya looked at Nuala. "Don't give him the food till I come back."

"Now that wasn't the deal. I said I'd take you to them—"

"And you haven't." Téya motioned around them. "You took us to a building. I don't see the family we're looking for. And until I do. . ." She shrugged and navigated the swamp of papers, fliers, bills, and boxes.

This isn't right. Nobody's here.

But Noodle's comment about believing the best in people niggled at her. Pushed her past the rank, dank entrance. "Smells like something died in here," she called back to Nuala, who stood on the street, watching and clutching the bread bag.

The foyer stretched pretty far back, so far in fact that she could not see because of the darkness, though she could make out a few doors nearby.

Stairs sat straight ahead then banked left and up over her. Easing her SureFire out, she also lifted her HK. The familiarity of this scenario—Denver—coiled around her. She'd come out of that with two black eyes and too many bruises to count.

Fool me once, shame on you.

And then The Turk chasing her down in Paris.

Fool me twice, shame on me.

Which was why she was going into this armed and ready for the fight. "Johnny, you'd better be right," she called. Over her shoulder. Then up the stairs, a glimmer of light at the top gave her a fragment of hope. "Carl and Sharlene Loring?" Her voice chased the cold shadows.

Swallowing, Téya moved to the stairs. Her boot hit the first step. *This is not right.* Alarms blazed in her mind.

"Téya! He's running!"

She threw herself backward and out the front door.

Nuala was pulling herself off the ground. "He barreled into me and took the food."

"I don't think so," Téya said, holstering her weapon as she spotted him racing around a building. She sprinted after him.

Down one alley and up another. Hustling down a flight of steps that belonged to what might have once been a nice little park setting. He sailed over a half wall like a track star. Téya was closing in on him.

"Johnny! Stop!"

He went left and vanished behind a building marked JEWELRY OUTLET. The kid was fast. He disappeared into a building.

Téya's stomach clenched as she followed him through the lower level of a shopping center that had been converted into another market. He topped a vendor's cart and Téya jumped over it. Someone shouted as several women screamed, but Téya wasn't giving up this pursuit. He was going to answer some questions and he was *not* getting that food. Enough was enough. She wasn't taking this lying down anymore.

Light shot through a dark hall, and she realized it was an exit to the outside. She darted that way, the hall, seeming endlessly long. When she broke into the open, she slammed into a wall less than three feet past the door. She groaned and stopped to get her bearings. Right was a dead end. Left. . . She bolted that way and it brought her out onto a main road. A half mile or so away, she thought she could see Noodle jogging out from another street.

Téya spun. Grunted and slapped a lightpost. "Augh!"

"Lose him?" Nuala's voice carried faintly from down the street.

Hands on her hips, Téya turned circles, searching. "Johnny!" she shouted long and hard. He'd pay. For taking the food. For duping them.

"Hey," Nuala said, trotting up to her. "We should get back. It's getting dark."

Téya nodded, looking around and realizing she had no idea where they were. Darkness meant trouble. And they were alone. "Stupid kid."

"Actually, I'd say he was pretty smart. Capitalized on what we needed and wanted."

"It was rhetorical, Noodle."

"Sorry. I was *trying* to be funny."

Téya coiled up her anger and nodded. "I know. Sorry, just—"

Crack!

Throwing herself around, Téya gasped. "Gunshot!"

Boom! Crack!

"The kid. . ." Guilt chugged through her. She'd never forgive herself if that kid was shot for bread and cheese. "C'mon!" Téya raced in the direction of the shots. A fence that towered over them by at least five feet confined the slums and poor to one side. She trailed that fence, listening, her hackles rising as she moved.

Tires squalled.

Téya rushed forward, certain of her course now. She burst out into a wide open area—a rear loading dock for a warehouse of some kind.

Adrenaline exploded through her when she saw a man aiming a weapon at a white Land Rover. Just under the belly of the vehicle, she saw shoes. John. The person wasn't aiming at the SUV, but at John. *He's going to shoot him.* What was this? A street war? Had the bread and cheese gotten John into trouble?

Téya pulled out her Glock and took aim.

Shouts alerted the glut of men to their presence.

A weapon swung in her direction. Someone sprinted out from behind the vehicle, racing toward a building—*John!*

In her periphery, Téya saw the man fire at the teen. Then she registered Nuala aiming and firing. A man stumbled out of the shadows and onto the ground. *Where did he come from?* The other three ran toward the vehicle. But the one she'd sighted didn't. He aimed. Fired.

Téya's heart jammed. He was firing at John! She sighted. Eased back the trigger. The man crumpled. The van spit rocks and dirt as it sped down the alley, out of sight. Téya wanted to unloaded her weapon on it, but it'd be futile.

With a pat on her arm, Nuala rushed toward the fallen, her weapon ready. The girl was indefatigable. Until she slept. Tonight, Noodle would have nightmares.

Téya trotted forward, her pulse racing. "John?" she called out.

Nuala checked the man who'd fallen out of the shadows. "He's dead." She dragged him back into the shadows.

"What're you doing?"

"Buying us time," Nuala said. She tossed her jaw toward the other. "Him?"

Even as she knelt, something near the alley caught her eye. The bag of bread and cheese. She nodded to it. "Check on John."

The man lay curled away from her, but she saw the dark circle spreading over his back

Careful of the wound, she turned him—and froze. Not at the wound. Not at the dark stubble lining the jaw.

Only one thing stopped her—the tattoo of the star-crescent.

Part 3:
Hazardous Duty

VIII

Sam
Altitude: 34,000 feet
Unknown Date and Time

Cold steel bit into his wrists. Sam shifted where he sat—*which is where, exactly?*—and felt the cuffs make another greedy imprint on his arms. He gritted his teeth, noting the sound of chains scraping against metal. The vibrations worming through his entire body and the deafening roar of massive engines combined with the hollowing of his hearing warned him he was on a plane. In fact, his fourth one. If he'd been counting right. Then again, could be the same plane refueled and they'd placed him in different locations to confuse him. Aboard the first aircraft, he'd been strapped into a cushioned seat. They'd progressively gotten worse from there. Now, he'd been placed on a Globemaster in a strap seat on the uncomfortable-as-possible transport.

They'd cuffed him on scene, stuffed him in the SUV—but not before he spotted a glimpse out the heavily tinted windows of Solomon's car hidden down the road. As soon as the door closed, he'd been hooded and taken to a chopper—a private one, he guessed—that ferried him to an airstrip. Nobody talked to him as they secured him into that first seat.

He knew two things from this little seek-and-find game: One, they didn't want him knowing his location or destination. But this wasn't the first time Sam had been a hostage. He had survival skills beyond most men, probably even more than those holding him. And two, patience would deliver him to whoever was behind this kidnapping. Patience would help him connect the dots of this incident to Ashland.

Ash. . .

Faced with the very real possibility of seeing her again, maybe even face-to-face, fear streaked through him. Stabbed his confidence. Mutilated his courage.

What if she didn't want to see him again? What if she was some sick psycho who used men and loosed them?

Sam snorted and shook his head. She might've been able to hide her real name, but there was so much about Ashland she hadn't been able to hide. The meticulous attention to detail that spoke of someone aware. . .*very* aware of her environment. Of threats. The hunger in her eyes for companionship and understanding. The way she responded to his kiss. *That* wasn't faked, not simply because she'd kissed him back or *how* she'd done that. But because of the heat of passion in her face. That wasn't something a person could fake.

Distinct and obvious, the descent pushed aggravation through his veins. Would this stop be one of many more? He'd tolerated a lot already, but his fuse wasn't endless.

Tires screeched against the tarmac, jolting him forward as the engines and the reverse thrusters slowed the aircraft.

Ashland. . .sure hope you're at the end of this journey. The thought of her *not* being there lit that fuse. All he'd put up with. All he'd endured. The punches. The way they'd walked him into a wall more than once.

As the craft taxied, boots thudded across the steel floor.

Sam stilled, focusing on his environment. More than one person coming. His mind played a quick mini-movie of him yanking free of the chains and breaking some noses then sprinting off into the sunset. Right. That would work in Hollywood. Not so much in real life. As the plane quieted, the chains around him rattled and a heavy whine filled the air. He guessed that a rear-loading door had been opened.

Grabbed by each arm, Sam was hauled to his feet. It was too much to hope they'd remove the hood. They guided him, steel vibrating through his shoes as he shuffled like a maximum security prisoner. No light filtered through the hood, so he used that to guess darkness had fallen. The familiar whine of a rear-loading tail filled his ears.

"Step," someone said gruffly.

Sam went a little more tentatively and felt himself on a decline—the ramp he'd predicted. Shards of light stabbed through the fabric. Not sunlight, but bright lights emanating from certain locations. Had to be dark.

"Watch—"

Sam struck something. Tangled his feet. Hands chained to his feet, he pitched forward unable to break a fall. Hard grips yanked him backward, along with a chuckle.

He had the distinct feeling he'd been tripped—intentionally. Clenching his jaw, he pulled himself straight. *For Ashland. I'm doing this for Ash. . . .* Wind tugged at his clothing and pressed the hood against his face.

"Where is he?" someone shouted, his voice muffled by the dying engine noise.

"He'll be here," the man holding Sam's right arm said. Voice gruff. "Eyes out."

"Spend too much time and there will be questions. Can't stay much longer."

"You will if you want to get paid."

"Since when have you been someone's lapdog?"

The hand around his bicep tightened; the talkative guy was ticking off the thug.

"Hey," someone said just before Sam was guided to the right. The engine noise quieted some more, both as they cut it off and as the distance grew.

The hood was yanked off, along with a clump of hair that felt like fire prickling his scalp. Sam winced and cringed then immediately devoured his surroundings. Yes, it was dark. Sun had gone down. Lights on the tarmac revealed things that stepped into its beams but shadowed that which stood between Sam and the source. Taking in everything, he did his best to gain orientation. In the distance a smattering of multistoried structures stuck out of a semi-mountainous terrain. Thick copses of trees lined the hills. Far away but still visible, a hillside was lit up with golden lights. Sam's gaze rose to the top of the mountain that towered over the rest to the ruins.

No way. The Acropolis? *What the heck am I doing in Greece?*

Téya
Roma Slums, Greece
1 June – 1840 Hours

There was something strangely beautiful about this man. Of course, mostly because he lay unconscious at her knees. But with his dark hair and stubble lining what looked to be a strong jaw—not to mention the curious star-crescent inked on his left cheekbone. . .

He moaned and shifted, his brows knotting.

Téya pressed her hand to his side, eyeing the puddle forming beneath him. *I am so dead. I shot The Turk.*

Nuala's gasp drew Téya's gaze up. The girl's pale wide eyes echoed the panic banging through Téya's chest. "We have to get out of here."

Swallowing hard, Téya glanced down at the assassin. It didn't make sense. He stood out in the open. "I can't leave him here to die."

"Yes, you can. He would've left you. In fact, he almost did." Nuala squatted and caught Téya's arm. "C'mon. If his people come. . ."

"How many assassins do you know who work with people in the field? They have a mission. They take care of it." Téya couldn't move. Couldn't stop staring at the man who'd plastered her face all over the underworld to get her killed. And here, she'd taken him out. "I can't leave him here,

Noodle." Her words hardened her resolve. "Help me get him up."

"What? No!" Nuala knelt opposite her. "Are you insane? We leave him. *Now.*"

"No."

Nuala tugged her back. "John. We have to find John. Remember? And we have to get out of here. It's almost dark."

"If he dies, his life is on my conscience. His blood on my hands." Téya flashed her eyes at her friend. "You realize what that means? How many people will be after me *now* if he dies?"

"We have no car, no way to get him out of here." The voice of reason, Nuala only told the truth, but it angered Téya that her friend wanted her to walk away. "And think about it—Trace will kill you himself if you take him back to the hotel."

Right. So not back to their hotel. That shortened the distance necessary to transport him. She had combat medic skills, so. . . . Téya scanned the buildings beyond the ten-foot fence. Barely visible was a store of some kind. Next to it loomed an office building. Behind it, another building peeked out, its brick darker, older. Fire escapes. A blinking sign hung on the corner, flashing a price and THE AEGEAN HOTEL.

Perfect.

"Help me get him up." Téya moved to his head.

"Are you *insane?*"

"Yes," Téya said. "I just shot the assassin who tried to have me killed, and now I want to make sure he doesn't die."

"So he can finish the job he started in Paris?"

Téya cradled his head against her shoulder as she slid her arms under his. "So I can find out what I did to make his hit list."

"Right," Nuala said, moving toward his legs. "Because he's just going to tell you that. There's no chance he'll wake up after you save his life and put a bullet in that pretty, stupid head of yours."

Téya glowered.

"Fine. But I'm not bringing flowers to your funeral."

"They'll only die anyway." Together they carried him down the alley toward a section of broken-out fence. Backs aching, arms quaking, they hurried across the street. Almost to the curb, Téya spotted a police car coming toward them. Her heart hammered as they scurried into the shadows of the building.

The cruiser slowed and a bright beam of light exploded, shattering the darkness. Téya sucked in a breath as they pressed into a doorway.

"Ugh. His blood is sliding across my arms," Nuala whispered with a tinge of disgust.

The cruiser moved on, but Téya's arms were rubbery now. "Stay here. I'll get a room then come back."

Nuala's eyes widened in the dark alley. "*What?* No way. I'm not staying with—"

But Téya sprinted off. As she rounded the front of the building, she checked her clothes to make sure she wasn't covered in blood. A small smudge at the bottom of her shirt glared back at her. Quickly, she tied the corner in a knot, like some '80s throwback, and stepped into the lobby.

Thank God Trace and Boone insisted they carry their passport and money. Contingencies. . . *Bet Trace wouldn't see this coming.* Téya went to the barred window, having to press closer than she'd like as a couple tangled in each others' arms and mouths stumbled past. Suppressing a shudder, Téya asked for a room. "First floor, please—if you can."

The man eyed her. "What you doing on this side of town this late?"

With an impish smile, she shrugged. "You know. . ."

"A pretty girl like you shouldn't be here. You want me to call you a taxi?"

"No," Téya smiled. "I'm meeting someone."

He clucked his tongue. "You are too good for him if he makes you come here."

Okay, dude. What's with the lecture? Can I get a room or not?

He slid the check-in book across the eight-inch ledge. Téya used her left hand, which would be messier than her right and illegible, and signed. Handed over the money in exchange for the key, along with lectures on taking more pride in herself and not ruining her life on a loser who'd bring such a pretty girl to a place like this.

She hurried down the hall and slid the key into the door on the right. Inside, she rushed to the window. Though the window had locks, they weren't *unlockable*. Well, not technically. Téya kicked the lock free of the jamb and slid open the window. She climbed out and ran down the alley.

She came around the corner and found herself staring down the business end of a weapon. Arms up, she met Nuala's pale eyes at the other end. "Easy."

"I could kill you myself for leaving me here." Together, they hauled the assassin to the window and propped him against the wall. Téya climbed through. "He's losing too much blood," Nuala said as she crawled after them.

Laid out on the bed, The Turk hadn't moved, blinked, or groaned.

Téya checked his pulse. It wasn't thready yet, but the guy was out of it like a cement block. "Put the dresser in front of the door." She headed for the bathroom. "I have to get some supplies."

"What?" Nuala hiss-shrieked. "You are *not* leaving me with him again."

"Tear the towel into strips and tie his hands."

"There's no bedpost, Téya!"

"Be creative," she said as she once more slipped through the window.

"You're covered in blood."

Téya glanced down as she ran to the small convenience store she'd seen when they crossed the road with him earlier—right before the cops spotted her. Shoot. The red smudges over her shirt weren't indicative of gross bleeding. She had to come up with an idea fast. She stepped into the store. The clerk immediately eyeballed her with a worried look.

Téya grabbed up alcohol, bandages, a pair of scissors, and a sewing kit—along with a few boxes of candy and drinks. When she dumped the items on the counter, the clerk didn't move.

"What?" Téya asked, her gaze catching a tower of name-engraved multitools. She turned it as if looking for a particular name and picked the one that said David. She placed it on the counter, too.

"You need this much, maybe you should go to doctor." The clerk's English was enough for conversation but not for grammar Nazis.

Téya shrugged. "I can't afford to take my eight-year-old to the doctor. Good thing I was once a nurse, huh?"

The clerk started ringing up the items. "You are young to have an eight-year-old."

Téya grunted. "We all make mistakes. Not that he's a mistake."

"Right," the clerk said, who couldn't be more than eighteen himself.

Téya paid for the items and hurried back toward the hotel. As she rounded the corner, a glint slowed her pace. Cops. *Keep moving. Act normal.* She shifted the bag in front of her to hide the blood. If she went in the back, she'd really draw the attention of the cops. Going through the front. . .

The desk clerk eyed her. "I did not see you go out."

She shrugged. "Guess you were busy." She left him with his mouth hanging open and hurried down the hall, cursing herself when she remembered she'd told Nuala to put the dresser in front of the door. She rapped quietly. "Noodle, it's me."

A heavy scraping sound preceded the metallic *shink* of locks being released. The door opened. "What are you—"

Téya pushed in, cutting off her friend and the words. "Lock it back. I had no choice—the cops were on the streets still. Let's hope my lies to the store clerk were believable enough." She dumped the contents on the dresser once it was back in place in front of the door, then turned.

And froze.

"I know. . ." Nuala said with a grimace in her tone. "He came to. I had no choice."

A bright red knot rose on his head. But what really caught her attention was the fact that while Téya was gone, Nuala tied The Turk's hands out to the sides, connected to wall-mounted lamps. But she'd also torn his shirt and tugged it away from the wound near his quite-toned abs and pecs. A bloody towel sat on the wound.

"Tried to stem the flow," Nuala said, "but answering the door. . ."

Téya nodded. "Had to go around front. Cops would've been suspicious." Téya spread out the crude, limited supplies. "Sterilize the blades of the pocket knife." She dumped three sleep aids into a bottle of water and lifted it to his lips. Though out of it, he still swallowed, a natural instinct. With that she went to work, cleaning the wound, probing it.

The knife wasn't razor sharp, but it would do. She used it to gently dig out the bullet. The Turk moaned, arching his back. Sweat mottled his forehead, beads forming in and around the tattoo. She cleaned the wound, the alcohol sliding over his bloody injury.

He let out a howl, head coming off the bed. His eyes snapped to hers.

Her pulse ricocheted off her ribs as his wild brown-green eyes focused on her. Widened with a *You!* message.

Téya pressed her hand against his injury, nausea roiling through her, knowing how much it would hurt him.

He growled then his eyes rolled back into his head. They couldn't risk that happening again, so she quickly went to work stitching then cleaning and bandaging the wound.

Exhaustion tugged at her limbs and mind as she scrubbed his blood from her hands—in more ways than one. By saving his life she kept her hands clean. Maybe she could buy her own life with this idiocy. She stared at herself in the mirror. This was stupid. *What were you thinking?*

She hadn't been. She'd reacted. Something. . .something stirred in her. Something she couldn't explain. Didn't want to explain—because it didn't make sense. After scrubbing up, she stood in the doorway drying her hands.

Nuala stared at him. "It's practically a résumé, don't you think? All those scars. . ."

Impossible not to notice. Some were marred messes that reminded her of the film that covered warmed milk as it cooled. Those were probably bullet wounds. Other marks were clean strikes, like from knives. He had a wicked scar across his right abdomen that seemed like it could've been life threatening. And the one over his shoulder and up the back of his neck—she'd like to know that story.

No, she wouldn't. She didn't want to know anything more about this man. Despite the tug of curiosity and compulsion to know more about him, she had to sever this connection.

"What do we do now?" Nuala said. "Boone will be panicked that we didn't come out of the slums."

With a nod, Téya tossed down the towel. "I gave him something to help him sleep. We'll leave him here and return in the morning."

"Trace—"

"Will never know." Because if he did, he'd kill her himself. Besides, this was between Téya and The Turk.

Annie
Salamina, Greece
1 June – 2310 Hours EEST

A hard jolt to her back sent Annie sprawling in the darkness. She hit pavement, scoring her hands and knees.

"Up, move!" someone behind her snarled.

From her position, she glanced forward, squinting against the lack of light. A long, dark tunnel stretched beneath the estate, leading—she had no idea where. They passed several doors, and at one in particular, a gust of air—*fresh air*—swept her hair across her face.

Her head still throbbed, and she had no delusion that they had drugged her, despite Trace's attempts to protect her. Shouts and screams carried distantly as she floated out of consciousness, her mind crying out for Trace but knowing it was too late.

A strange thrum carried through the cement walls as they descended deeper into the belowground area. Like the constant hum of air-conditioning units. Large ones. Whatever enclosed this space—was it completely cement?—blocked sound. Which meant calling for help wouldn't do any good.

She'd given up on that hope long ago. If the broken pieces of memory surrounding her capture were right, Trace probably fled the estate. Though her vision had ghosted quickly, it'd taken her mind a while longer. And in those precious seconds, she'd heard gunfire and shouts. If Stoffel and Batsakis were so thorough as to rout her true identity, they wouldn't have left a stone unturned hunting down Trace. Now the question was—had Trace escaped or was he a prisoner, too?

"Find him!" The fragment gave her hope that Trace's black ops skills had gotten him to safety.

Now. *My turn.* Annie wandered through the storage room, eyeing the pieces. She lifted a hefty candlestick and tested its weight. Her stomach turned, knowing she could crack a skull, even kill a person with the right strike.

Him or me.

She knew that's what it came down to, though keeping her a prisoner made her wonder what intentions they had. Nothing good, that's for sure. And sticking around for them to dig information out of her brain, break her will so she'd betray her friends—

Not happening. She'd memorized every detail as they'd pushed her into this room. Every door. Every access point. Cool and damp, the underground cellar served as the perfect place to lock Annie away. The ruse of her fake identity clearly hadn't worked. But what, exactly, had Stoffel's people discovered? Did they know her real identity or just that she wasn't Natalia Policek?

She paced the cement floor, eyeing the pieces that lined the shelves. A door led into a deep cellar filled wall-to-wall with wine. Another held random accent pieces that were likely switched out during different seasons. As she took in the shelves, she couldn't help but believe that they spirited her away because she wasn't Policek. *They don't know who I am.*

If they had known, they wouldn't leave her with so many options to take them out. The brass candlesticks were a prime weapon. Hefty enough to knock out even the stoutest of men. Then again, Trace had taught her how to use a pen as a weapon. Straight into the carotid artery of any attacker, and she'd be free.

But, she didn't need them dead. Just immobilized. Ignorance would be their saving grace. Having lost friends and watched those children die, Annie placed a high value on life and preserving it. Including her own.

Voices carried down the cavernous space.

Annie rushed to the door, candlestick in hand. Spine pressed to the chilled surface, she focused on controlling her body. Adrenaline could make her choke. Or mess up. She had one shot. At least two men were coming—she could tell by the chatter.

The heavy arched wood door swung inward. Annie sidled up alongside it, candlestick to the side.

A suited man stepped in.

Another grunted something.

Annie swung up and down, carrying the most momentum with her. The brass weapon cracked against the man's head, a sickening vibration rushing up her arm at the impact. He dropped like a lead weight.

Behind her, she heard a gasp. Annie pivoted away from the noise but also into it, giving herself safety from a strike but enough room to make her own move. The man brandished a gun.

Again, she swung in and upward, dislodging the weapon from his hand.

His eyes went wide.

Holding it like a baseball bat, Annie swung a third time. Hit the guy in the temple, and immediately regretted it as blood spurted. Struck her face with its sticky warmth. Her stomach roiled.

No time to be sick. No time!

Dropping the candlestick, she grabbed the man's gun. She bolted out the door, taking in the corner perches. Cameras. Just as she expected. That meant time was ticking down before she'd have a big mess on her hands.

She sprinted to the door where the air had pushed her hair into her face, and tugged. Locked. She glanced around. This was her only chance to get out into the open. She tried kicking it, but without her heavy boots, it was futile. She took aim at the lock and fired once. Twice. Again, she thrust her heel against the door.

It budged.

She kicked again and it flung open.

Annie rushed through the door and went right, grateful for the cement wall at her back. One less perspective to cover. Weapon down, she stuck to the shadows of the overhanging wall and eyed her surroundings. The three-story home towered over her on the left, interior lighting creating the effect of a floodlight over the entire patio area. A massive wall to her right. Dense forest beckoned to her, but it was at least thirty yards away. Though she wore the dress, she would just hike it up and sprint.

If it weren't for the open courtyard. The *lit-up* open courtyard, where stately wrought-iron furniture huddled in groups amid shrubs, trees, and ornate flowers. An illuminated fountain tossed sprays of water in arcing directions beneath what looked like it might be a Grecian god. The quiet conversation of the water might possibly be enough to cover the slap of her feet against the pebbled terrace.

Home. Terrace. Wall.

Guess that leaves me one choice.

The terrace. Cheeks puffed, she blew out a breath. Okay. Here goes noth—

Laughter spilled from french doors on the first level of the home. Guests dressed in gowns and suits filtered out onto the terrace.

Seriously?

Wouldn't the guests have gone home already? Who'd stay here after hearing shots and explosions? Annie wasn't sure how long they'd held her, but it had to be nearing midnight. And of course, thanks to the excitement earlier when they'd taken her, guards took up positions around the terrace.

Annie remained in the shadows with her path to freedom blocked. To get out of here without being noticed, she'd need a distraction.

Sam
Unknown Airstrip, Greece
1 June – 2310 Hours EEST

The guy on his right—head shaved bald and arms built like a tank—tugged Sam forward as a blue SUV pulled to a stop fifteen feet away. The random lights of the airstrip made it hard to decipher anything within that vehicle. Passenger-side door opened, a man stepped out and started toward them. He had short-cropped light brown hair with a receding hairline. All the same, the guy looked thirty-five, maybe forty at most. Though the late hour cast shadows over the man's face, it only added to the grim, terse expression he wore. Ticked. How Sam knew, he couldn't be sure. But that anger combined with at least two concealed weapons that Sam could detect—one beneath a lightweight jacket and one at the ankle—put Sam on edge.

The way he moved, head up, gaze swiveling to take in their surroundings, identify threats or trouble, the grim set of his mouth and jaw, the way he homed in on Sam without reservation. . .this guy had military written all over him. Usually that worked to Sam's benefit, able to connect on a brothers-in-arms level. But with the way he stalked toward them, staring—no, *glaring*—Sam knew there was nothing brotherly here.

"He say anything?" the new guy asked the man on his right.

"Not a word, Colonel."

Military—yeah, pegged that one. Being called a colonel didn't mean the guy was still active duty. Active or not, he wasn't in uniform, so this was either an unofficial mission or worse, unsanctioned.

"Just sat there like a good Boy Scout," the tank-like guy said.

The colonel raked a gaze over Sam, his green eyes both assessing and condemning. "Too busy trying to figure out what's going on."

Sam felt naked the way this guy could read him. And angry—he'd surrendered too much control to them. Had to swing some power back into his court. "Thinking you could fill me in."

"Might want to stop thinking before you hurt yourself." The colonel turned slowly, his irritation evident as he took a few steps away. "Let's go."

Tank tugged him toward the vehicle.

291

No. It wasn't happening like this. They weren't going to get the luxury of him going quietly. Not anymore. He had a theory to test. A question burning his mind. In a defensive posture, Sam moved his right foot back.

Tension cracked the air.

Tank shifted. "Hey!"

But Sam trained on the leader. "Annie Palermo."

Lightning fast, the colonel spun around. His fist drove into Sam's jaw. The strike whipped Sam to the right. Out of the Tank's grip. Though pain spiked through his face and neck, Sam rolled with the momentum and stayed on his feet—barely, thanks to the chains. Straightening in the face of the attack, he gave a grin, one he knew would stoke the fires of contempt, and ignored the warmth sliding down his chin and neck.

The driver's side door of the vehicle now hung open, a Dwayne Johnson wannabe standing there in the beam of a massive lamp. But Sam kept his gaze on the colonel in front of him. The man he would guess was none other than Trace Weston, the man Francesca Solomon mentioned. The responsible party, and that he'd riled the man gave Sam a sick sense of pleasure. "Hit a nerve, *Colonel*?"

The man launched at him.

Barreled into Sam. Knocked him backward, his chained hands unable to lift for defense. Another hard right drove straight into Sam's cheek. With a sickening crack, Sam's head bounced off the tarmac. Spots sprinkled through his vision as the man's fist loomed again. Fiery pain exploded in Sam's side.

"Hey, hey!" someone shouted.

The colonel was dragged off him by Tank and Wannabe.

Sam curled onto his side to haul himself up. White-hot fire blazed through his side, filling his lungs with painful breaths. The man might've broken a rib. On one knee, he wobbled but steadied himself. Spit the sweet, metallic taste from his mouth—blood.

More shouts and angry epithets flew. Sam closed his puffy eye and glanced up at the trio. Even as he stared at the colonel, his eye swelled, partially blocking his view. The colonel was out of control. Was this how he led? Sam sneered at him. If Solomon had been right, it wouldn't take long to bring this guy down.

The colonel tugged himself free and stretched his neck.

Pressing his right arm against his side, Sam pushed to his feet, struggling for a breath that didn't hurt. Having gained some control of power with a few words gave Sam new courage. "Where is she?"

The colonel rubbed his hand. "You piece of dirt. So obsessed with your need to have her, you never once thought about the danger you put her in!"

Sam stilled. Swallowed, assessing the flimsy information he had. It renewed his concern for Ashland. For her safety. "So she *is* in danger?"

"Not here," Wannabe said to the colonel, who spun on his heels and stalked to the vehicle.

Wannabe came toward Sam, who tensed when he reached forward.

Sam moved a foot back, ready to fight again.

"Easy," Wannabe growled and held up something. A key. He motioned to the chains. "Unless I need those on you."

Sam's gaze skipped to the colonel, who now stood at the vehicle, watching. "Only if you want him to kill me."

Wannabe smirked. "Not a bad idea after the harm you've done."

"I only wanted to know she was safe."

"So you put her in danger to find out." Thick-necked and barrel-chested, the man shook his head. "I think you spent too much time in the water, Frogman."

Trace

The guy even smelled like a squid.

Trace balled his fist as Boone escorted Caliguari to the vehicle and set him directly behind the driver's seat. Once they were under way, Trace knew he had to chill out enough to deal with this guy. Hands trembling from the rush of adrenaline, he worked to calm himself. It'd felt good—too good—to beat the daylights out of Caliguari. But he wasn't proud of losing control. *When's the last time that happened?*

"Ashland's in danger?" Caliguari sounded more penitent now, contrite almost. But Trace knew better than to answer that question as they pulled onto the highway.

Bringing the SEAL here had been more to tie his hands, but there was a fraction of hope that he could help. Yet Trace couldn't bring himself to talk to the guy. Knew Caliguari had baited him. And Trace bit—right into the guy's face. Annie would have a field day with that.

"Look, *you* brought me here."

Trace's secure sat phone rang and he grabbed it, identified the caller, and answered, relieved to avoid the SEAL in the backseat. "Go ahead."

"Hey, Houston here."

Trace waited.

A nervous chuckle carried through the line. "I forget you know that already. You know everything, probably before I think it. I mean, not that you have psychic powers—"

"Houston," Trace snapped, betraying how little patience he had left.

"Sorry." Houston cleared his throat. "Right. Anyway. Uh, where was—oh yes. Their security radios are dead silent."

Trace frowned. "That's unusual." Chatter had been hot and heavy while they were in there.

"Very. So I've been hunting around and I've found some phone chatter. Not registered to anyone we know but a truckload of what are probably throwaways. Mostly texts. They aren't traceable to names, but the locations are pinging right off the Stoffel estate. They're using coded phrases, but I'm pretty sure—I mean, it's my guess. . .a pretty educated one, if I must say so—"

"Houston," Trace warned.

"I'd bet my pay they still have her there at the estate, but I think they're planning to move her."

"Can't let that happen. We'll be back in ten." Trace ended the call and felt Boone's gaze on him. "They've gone radio silent. But he thinks she's still there."

"Wait," Sam said, pulling himself forward. "You talking about Ashland?"

"No." Trace hated the guy. Hated his guts. Besides—her name was Annie.

"Look, you dragged me halfway across the world," Caliguari said with a growl. "Why else would you do that and then cut me out now?"

"To get your hands out of the boiling water you stirred around her life." Trace glared at the guy, the late hour preventing him from getting a clear picture of his face, but Trace didn't need light to feel the anger and hatred.

The feeling was mutual. Trace could kill the guy. Right now. And never regret it. "Did you seriously think plastering her face all over the Internet would *help* her?"

"It got your attention." Caliguari wasn't repentant.

"And it also caught the attention of individuals trying to kill her and others under my protection."

"Zulu."

Trace's pulse skipped a beat. Angered him. He couldn't really be that stupid, to keep throwing stuff in Trace's face and expect to live to see the morning, could he?

"Let me fill you in on something, Squid," Boone said as they exited the vehicle and made their way into the hotel. "You don't know this man the way I do, and right now, if he decided to do what's going through his mind, your body won't be found."

"So, it's a good thing I'm fighting for Ashland, since he's so dangerous."

Trace jerked back to the front. Balled his fist.

"You are one stupid man," Boone said.

"In the last six years," Trace growled, "I have protected her from more than a punk SEAL too high on his own juice." Trace pulled in a hard breath, forcing himself to cool off. "If you ever expect to see her again, you're going to climb off that high horse and get square with some facts."

Caliguari gave a slow nod, his chest dragging in what looked to be a heavy breath as he shook his head and smiled. Finally, he glanced at Trace as Boone guided him into the elevator. "So she *is* safe." He splayed his hand and pointed down. "Here. She's here. That's all I wanted to know."

"This isn't about you!"

"I just needed to know she was okay."

"You played Russian roulette with her life!"

Caliguari shifted a foot closer. "Ashland vanished on a night when a sniper took shots at us." The guy was quick with the smirks. "But then, you know that, don't you?"

Trace didn't owe the Squid anything.

"I knew Ashland wouldn't just up and vanish. Not after what we shared. She wouldn't do that to me. She was too nice and too considerate."

Boone laughed.

And made Trace smile. The guy had a very romanticized notion of Annie. "What she is, is a highly trained and skilled operator, chosen by top Brass for black ops missions."

The man considered them, his expression priceless. Uncertainty warred with disbelief. "How. . .?"

"It doesn't matter how. You just need to understand what she is and what you screwed up with your little love campaign." Mentally, Trace chided himself for letting his disgust seep into the conversation. "In fact, your social media stunt is the reason she's missing right now." It wasn't true, but it felt good to throw the dagger into the guy's heart—if he had one.

"Wait." Sam came to his feet. "What? She's missing?"

"We need you to leave it alone, stop stirring the waters."

Caliguari hesitated. Seemed to think over the demand. "Tell me why—what's this all about?"

Trace studied the carpet that rushed down the hall toward their suite. Chewed the agitation of opening this conversation. He cast Boone a questioning glance and found his buddy just as uncertain about moving forward.

"What you need to know," Boone said as they entered the suite, "is that for reasons that cannot be revealed at this time, she went into hiding. For her own safety."

Caliguari nodded. "That's why she came to Manson."

Trace nodded. "It's time for you to stop making trouble. You really want to help her by doing that?"

"If it means protecting—"

"That's not your job," Trace bit out as he stalked toward Houston and thrust his jaw toward the monitors as if to ask if the guy had anything new.

Wide-eyed, Houston nodded as he stared at Caliguari.

"You said she's missing, but you know where she might be." Sam's gaze never left Trace. "Let me help."

Grinding his teeth made his jaw hurt, but it was nothing compared to what was happening in his chest. Trace stalked the hotel room, his mind a mangled mess of rage and panic. It'd been hours since Annie was taken, and now he had to deal with the SEAL, with letting the guy help them locate Annie. He knew it was an obvious solution. But he'd do anything to stop the inevitable, stop them from being reunited.

"On the couch," Trace barked at the Squid. He glanced at Houston. "Nothing?"

"Not yet," he said, glancing again at Caliguari.

"Boone, check it out." His head hurt from the exertion of keeping his rage below the surface. Trace stormed into the bathroom and washed the blood from his knuckles. He scrubbed and felt a pressure building in his chest. He gripped the sides of the sink and stared down at the red-tinged water swirling down the drain.

That man represented an end to everything Trace had worked to build and protect. He was the epic sign of his failure. Annie wasn't here. That jerk was. The one who didn't deserve her. Who risked her life for his own pleasure.

"You okay?"

Trace's gaze rose to the mirror, where he spotted Boone hanging back in the doorway, arms folded over his chest. "I want to kill him."

"You almost did."

"He doesn't deserve her."

Boone's eyebrow winged up, and only then did Trace realize what he'd said. What he'd allowed to slip out. Though he knew it wasn't a secret to Boone what happened before Misrata between him and Annie, the truth had never been vocalized.

"He put her life in danger. Exposed her to the very people trying to find her." He straightened and dried his hands on the towel. "A man who can't see past his own need for selfish desires doesn't deserve the woman he endangers. Bringing him here—"

"Why *did* you?"

Trace threw the towel against the sink. "I don't trust anyone else to keep his hands out of the fire."

"But bringing him *here*. . ." Boone scratched his jaw. "Trace, if you didn't want them together, why bring him to Annie? Is this. . .?" He stepped in closer. "This is about what I said—about having him on our side."

Trace didn't want to own up to it. Didn't want to voice his intentions.

"I thought you hated the idea."

"I do," Trace breathed with a hiss. "But it's better than having him gunning for us and exposing our locations and identities."

"Is it?"

Trace leaned back against the sink, hands braced on either side. Quiet gave him room with his thoughts—too much room. There had been so many things happening, so many things going wrong, that Trace made a split-second decision to corral the SEAL and tape his mouth shut. Now, once they recovered Annie, the two would be together. And it'd gut Trace.

"Why'd you let her go?" Boone's question was quiet, respectful.

Surprise jerked Trace up. How had Boone known?

With a slow nod, Boone sighed. "Thought so."

Shame hung Trace's head. The ache was fierce. And raw. And still bleeding. One drowning him in a sea of regret. He pushed to the surface, away from the truth, and came to his feet. "We've got work to do." He left the bathroom and strode into the living room.

Caliguari sat on the sofa with a bag of ice pressed to his cheek. He wasn't watching Houston, because the monitors were blocked from view. "You won't get the answers you want," Trace said.

Carve a hole in his heart, because he could not—*would not* ask the SEAL for help. Hands fisted, Trace met Boone's gaze then pulled out of that silent dialogue before it could get started.

"Great balls of fire," Houston exclaimed, drawing Trace's attention.

"What?"

"No, literally—a great ball of fire." He lifted a remote and turned on the TV. "Look. News—massive explosion in Salamina."

Trace checked out the footage and immediately recognized the three-story seaside estate.

Houston grinned and pointed to one of his stations. "It's the Stoffel estate."

What did it mean that there was a fire? The footage wasn't from a news crew, but witnesses on scene, judging by the shaky, bad quality of the video.

"We need to get out there," Boone said.

"Is that where you think Ashland is?" Caliguari asked.

"You mean Annie," Houston said, then his jaw went slack. "Oops. I did not just do that."

"Annie," Sam repeated. Then huffed and shook his head.

Yeah, good dose of reality for the SEAL who thought he knew the woman he loved.

"Solomon thought that might be her name."

Trace glared at the SEAL. "Solomon?" General Solomon wouldn't give this guy the time of day. But the other one, the serious pain in his prickly backside...

"Francesca Solomon showed up right before your goons snatched me."

"Son of a—" Trace bit off the curse and met Boone's gaze. "I'm going to have her muzzled."

"She's dangerous," Caliguari said.

Surprise stilled Trace.

"She knows a lot and isn't careful with that information."

"Oh, you mean like you and your social media campaign."

"The information I promoted was already out there. I just amplified it."

"That's true," Houston piped up, nodding.

Trace snapped a seething look at the wiry-haired geek, who ducked.

"She has classified information she's spouting off. At least, *now* I know it's classified. But let's get on task here." Caliguari moved to the computers where Houston worked. "Why are you interested in this estate? Was she there?"

"Three hours ago, she and I were on a mission there," Trace said, giving only information that was necessary. "After what we believe was a diversion they used to separate us, she vanished."

Something sparked through the guy's brows, but he quickly diverted his attention. "If this estate is where Ash—Annie was, then she's in trouble with that fire."

"Negative," Trace said, resenting the way the guy tried to step in and take charge. "If she's there, that fire doesn't mean she's in trouble. It means she set it."

Boone planted his hands on his belt like a proud uncle. "Just like we trained her."

Caliguari double-checked the footage playing on the TV then slowly nodded. "A diversion?"

"Or a signal," Boone said.

"What's around the estate?" Caliguari asked Houston.

"Houston," Trace said, warning the geek not to give the guy any information. "There are forests to the west and the sea to the east."

"Not the sea," Caliguari said. "The forest—she went to the trees."

"She's an excellent swimmer," Trace countered.

"Maybe you forgot," the SEAL said, "that she and I lived on a lake. Ashland loved to take a swim, but she often found the water too chilly. She preferred to sit on the deck with me and watch the sun go down."

Trace held the man's gaze—a power struggle. Most of what he said wasn't necessary information. This was territorial dialogue. Caliguari reminding Trace he'd spent the last few years with her. That he knew her. Knew how to anticipate her.

But he didn't. Caliguari knew Ashland Palmieri. Not Annie Palermo.

Caliguari smirked. "Besides, there's nowhere to hide on the open sea, and the longer she's out, the more tired she'd become. Either way, we need to get there."

"We?" Trace echoed.

Assured and unrelenting, Caliguari glanced around the room. "You seem a little shorthanded for a rescue op."

Boone cleared his throat and waited for Trace to look at him. "Two and Six aren't back, and I haven't heard from them."

Trace hesitated. "Houston, anything on the scanners about them?"

"Negatory."

Two and Six were behind schedule but not in apparent danger. Sometimes an op ran long. But Trace felt the tremor in the waters they'd stirred. Could something go right for once? "We don't have time to worry about them right now," he said. "We have to get up there and secure One."

"We'll need a chopper and thermals."

"On it," Trace said.

"Let me help." The Squid looked entirely too hopeful.

"Not on your life," Trace growled. "You'll stay here—"

"Don't be stupid. I'm trained and I have the same objective—"

"No." Trace felt like an oil tanker parked on his chest. "No, you don't."

"You want Ash—Annie back safely. Right? I'm not the enemy here, Weston." Caliguari held out his hands in a placating manner. "I swear— I'll play by the rules. I'll do whatever you ask if it means I see her again and know she's safe."

I should just kill him and get it over with. It'll be less painful.

Francesca
Alexandria, Virginia
1 June – 0915 Hours EST

Sitting in her small corner at Starbucks, Frankie clung to the delusion that she could hide from whatever and whoever had so brutally taken Samuel Caliguari. Even now, the memory forced her to gulp back the adrenaline. She'd never seen anything like that. Hiding in the open garage of one of his neighbors, she'd watched the scene unfold.

Watched Sam rip his Charger onto a side road.

Watched the first of the Suburbans broadside him in the turn. It'd looked like a freight train ramming a sedan. It slammed his car into a ditch, the Charger sitting at a steep angle. By the time the dust and smoke cleared, three more vehicles surrounded him. Men in head-to-toe tactical gear swarmed into position, their weapons trained on Sam.

Through the cracked rear windshield she could see Sam moving slowly.

Two of the tactical team pried open the driver's door, almost having to lift it straight up because of the steep ditch. Sam climbed out and was immediately set upon. They shoved him face-first into the dirt. Hooded and cuffed him then dragged him to one of the SUVs.

Who were they?

She tried Sam's cell number again, though she wasn't sure why. He hadn't answered any of the previous fifteen times she'd attempted it. Frankie stared at her computer and phone. Varden had sent her to Caliguari, then the handsome SEAL ended up getting arrested.

No, not arrested. She'd searched local authorities to find him and nobody had even heard of him, and the sheriff there in Manson said no raid had been conducted.

So, what is going on?

Was it Trace?

Seriously, how much power could one man have? Who was the force behind Weston? She'd toyed with calling her father, but after Varden's comments about him, she'd been left with more doubts than a loving daughter should have.

Dad always put the military first. She hadn't just known that, she'd *lived* that from childhood. It was no surprise then that his three sons would take a similar path. She had gone into the Air Force, not because she wanted to be like her father, but because he'd never liked that military branch and derided it much the way colleges did their fiercest rival. But taking the intelligence route—she'd done that because he'd been combat. And she wanted to show him she could make her own way in the military without Daddy's golden glove greasing up the flagpoles the way he had for her brothers.

A familiar form strode toward her, and Frankie quickly closed the open files on her laptop as he slid into the seat across from her. "Varden."

"A bit of unfortunate luck with Caliguari, I hear." The beady eyes reminded her of dials on a laser scope, adjusting, calculating for a precise hit.

"So it seems." No way would she let him know how much this mess affected her.

"I think we hit a sweet spot if that drew Weston out."

Keeping her face neutral, she processed his belief that the colonel was behind the hit on Sam Caliguari.

"Did you talk to Caliguari before they took him?"

Frankie turned the silver fashion ring on her thumb as she considered the man. She'd been a fool years ago to find Varden attractive. It wasn't his looks—tall, dark, not-so-handsome. It was his power that had drawn her like a moth to the flame. And telling him what Sam said wouldn't compromise anything. At least, she didn't think so.

"You're wondering if you can trust me," Varden said, leaning on the table with his forearms.

"We were all trained to ask that question, often and repeatedly with every target and asset," Frankie said.

"You have to imagine I know more than you."

"You'd like me to imagine that." Frankie shifted in her seat, pushing into the neutral space he was already invading. "But you came to me, Varden. You sent me after Sam." Why? What had he hoped to accomplish with that? "Why didn't you go yourself?"

"The man I work for is too powerful and in too delicate a situation to dirty his hands."

"Ha." Frankie scoffed and dropped back against her seat. "Lazy answer. And a lie."

Those black eyes probed her. His lips went flat and his brows tugged together.

Good. About time she'd managed to tick him off. He'd done that to her more than once in the years they worked together.

"What do you want?" Varden asked.

Frankie's heart flipped. "Me?" She closed her laptop and folded her arms over it. "*Me?* I don't want anything except the truth about what happened in Misrata. You knew that the day you had me shut down and turned out."

Varden glanced to the side as a bubble of laughter erupted near the coffee bar. He was annoyed to say the least—with the noise, with her. Maybe even with Misrata. Or Trace Weston. "I can guide you to the information, but I can't give it to you."

Well, that was juicy. "Why?" She had the good sense and insatiable nature to question everything.

"I have another name for you."

Frankie arched an eyebrow and huffed. "You gave me Sam, and he knew nothing."

"He knows more than he realizes."

"Doesn't matter now, does it?"

"Find Boone Ramage." He tapped the table. "Find him and you find a tenable trail that will lead you right back to Weston and this mess."

"Are you—" Frankie bit down on the tongue-lashing she wanted to unleash. She'd had Boone on her radar since day one. "He's a dead end, Varden. I've tried—"

"Seems to me you talked to a good-looking EMT in Lucketts."

Unease slithered through Frankie's belly. She should know better than to be surprised by anything Varden said or did. But she suddenly felt like she had strings attached to her arms and legs and should start talking to a cricket.

"D'you catch his name?"

She hadn't. At the time, it hadn't been important.

Varden winked. "See you around, beautiful."

As he strutted out of the coffee shop, Frankie grew sick to her stomach. Varden had said her father shut down her life, but she wondered now if the culprit behind all that was in fact Varden and his overlord. She also knew in that instant that they'd been following her, tapping her phones, and had probably bugged her apartment, too.

She had this crazy, uncontrollable urge to take a stainless steel pad and scrub her body down in a hot shower. They'd tagged her. Somehow they tagged her and were monitoring her every move.

Annie
Salamina, Greece
2 June – 0115 Hours EEST

Annie cursed herself for not thinking to wrap her feet in something protective before escaping the storage area. Forest litter and debris dug into her soles as she pushed up the slope. Though not a steep grade, after the night's adventures, the hill was enough to sap the remnants of her strength. But she'd been hiking for well over fifteen minutes. Pressed against a trunk, she took a breather and glanced back through the trees.

She'd blown a propane tank and it'd lit up the night like Fourth of July in Manson. When the tank detonated, ladies had screamed and rushed in all directions. Annie seized that chaos and sprinted around the terrace, clinging to the javelin-shaped shrubs and ornamental hedges to get out of sight. At most, she knew she'd only have a handful of minutes before they realized she'd escaped.

Though the fire still raged and spread to one level of the home, the flames looked small. Like a hearth fire instead of a blaze. She regretted that it had done so much damage to the property. That hadn't been her intention.

Distant but strange, a sound filtered through the trees, tickling her awareness. Leaves rustled. The fingers of the branches seemingly brushing the sound closer. And then it hit her—dogs. Barking. Howling.

Hauling in a panicked breath, Annie shoved onward. Where the heck did they get dogs? Twigs and rocks pocked the soft pads of her feet. She plunged through the trees, catching the trunks and using them to propel her onward. Though she ran and pushed herself, she wanted to collapse. Give up. The fight for her life had taken a ridiculous turn. In the mountains. . .in Greece. . .barefoot.

Only you, Annie. Only you.

If she could find a creek or small river or lake, she might lose the dogs. But the chances of that were slim. What other recourse did she have? She'd seen the impressive snouts of tracking dogs work in Iraq and Afghanistan with the military working dogs. She'd seen a gorgeous Belgian Malinois catch the scent of explosives buried a couple of feet deep and save an entire unit. How was she supposed to evade the nose that knows?

Legs weak, she stumbled. Pitched forward into the grass and rocks. *Just want to sit. . .for a minute.* She slumped against the ground, breathing hard, her pulse whooshing across her eardrums.

Keep going. She had to keep going.

Annie pushed herself up.

A bark trumpeted success. He was close! Too close.

Tripping over a gnarly root system, Annie whimpered. Pushing up on all fours, she glanced over her shoulder. Saw something moving through the dark shadows. Dogs. They were right on her.

On her feet again, she ran. Dodged fallen trees. Avoided root systems. Rocks that threatened to snap her ankle.

But she heard them. Heard the dogs' barking and snapping. She looked back. Saw them. Springers. Labs.

Panic stole her breath.

A dog flew from the side, a blur of glowing eyes and fangs. She scrabbled backward, terror ripping through her as the powerful jaws dived at her.

A blaze of fire and torment tore through Annie's right ankle. She cried out and kicked at the dog, whose thousand pounds of jaw pressure crunched against her flesh and dug into her bone. Hot tears streaked down her face, the agony numbing her brain, shutting her down.

Annie fell backward, clamping her teeth against a primal scream. Her fingers fell against something cold and hard. She glanced through tear-blurred eyes and spotted a hefty rock.

Bite intact, the dog growled and jerked.

Tearing the muscle more.

But the beast wasn't trying to eat her. His mission was to take her down until his master arrived. *Sorry. Not waiting.*

She brought the rock down against the dog's snout.

He yelped but didn't release.

Tenacious bugger. She hit him again. This time, she must've nailed him right. He yelped and broke away. Annie jerked her mangled foot toward her, grinding her teeth against the agony.

To her surprise, the dogs broke off. Sprinted away from her.

She didn't know what happened, but she was glad for it. Glad for the relief. Reaching down to the hem of her navy-blue dress, she searched for a frayed section. Caught one. And tore. Ripped a length off. Adrenaline must be thick in her blood right now, because she almost couldn't feel what had to be agonizing pain in her ankle.

Bending over, she wrapped the silk fabric around her leg a few times. Growling through the pain, she tied the ends, the final cinch exploding a searing pain. Her stomach heaved, bile rising against the torment.

Though she worked to calm her body, resist the bile, it surged. Annie threw herself to the side and retched.

Swiping her mouth with the back of her bloodied hand, Annie whimpered. *God, I have nothing left. Please, I need. . .* "Trace," she whispered.

The thought of him—powerful, confident him—filled her mind. Nine years her senior, he'd had this magnetism that had drawn her right out of boot camp. She'd seen him at Bagram over the months he worked with Special Forces Command. She'd watched him as he hung out at the

USO with his buddies. Laughing. But when he wasn't, he was intense. Handsome.

Reminded Annie of her older brother, who'd paid the ultimate sacrifice for his country the year before she joined.

But that was then. This was now. Trace. . .he'd cut her heart out and served it up with a fresh batch of loyalty to their country.

She dug her fingers into the ground, forcing herself to muster the strength and courage to work around the pain and fatigue, to get on her feet and get moving, to prove to Trace she didn't need him. She would seriously be talking to him about hazardous duty pay.

Using the tree, she dragged herself up onto her feet, unable to put pressure on her right ankle. Testing it only threatened her waves of sickening bile.

The resonant sound of an inbound chopper stilled her. Drew her gaze to the sky. She couldn't see past the canopy, and she could only pray they couldn't see her. She'd need to hide. Find shelter for the rest of the night.

Téya
Athens, Greece
2 June – 0255 Hours EEST

Téya slipped into the hotel room, glancing around. A single lamp on a sofa table cast warm light over the space. Houston's computers hummed quietly, spotlighted by a swing-arm lamp. Odd that he wasn't sleeping near his systems the way he normally did.

And that Trace and Boone weren't around.

"It's too quiet," Noodle whispered, exhaustion dripping through her words.

Téya lifted her weapon and motioned Noodle toward the room they'd shared with Annie while she went to the men's suite. The door stood ajar and the room dark, empty. Then light skidded out between the bottom of the door and the carpet.

The door opened.

Téya snapped the weapon up.

Houston stepped out, straightening his shirt. When he looked up, he let out a strangled cry that sounded like someone wringing a cat's neck.

"Houston," Téya breathed, lowering the gun. "Where is everyone?"

He shook a finger at the weapon. "Those things kill people, you know." Houston moved past her back to the main room. "And the others are trying to find Annie."

"Annie?" Stuffing the gun in the holster at the small of her back, Téya followed him. "What happened?"

He grabbed a bag of M&M's Salty and Sweet from the desk and dropped into his chair. "They took her right out from under Trace's nose."

Téya's irritation at his tone grated on her. "You really need to grow some respect for our commander."

"Sorry." He popped some pieces into his mouth and chewed. "He's my boss, not my commander. And he was seriously ticked. Of course, things went downhill when they brought the Navy SEAL here." Houston shook his head, his springy curls catching the light. "I tried to tell them that was a bad idea, but do you think they listen to me?"

Nuala joined them. "What SEAL?"

"The SEAL, the one Annie hooked up with. You know—Sam Cal-something."

Téya widened her eyes, glancing at Noodle. Things had really turned upside down since they'd entered the slums.

"And the commander wasn't happy that you weren't back."

"We weren't happy," Noodle said as she took a seat beside Houston and reached for his bag of Salty & Sweet mix.

Houston paused, mid-chew, to watch her, and Téya couldn't help but notice a bit of awe in his expression.

"How long has Annie been missing?"

Houston grinned as he took back his bag, dumped out a handful, then held out the bag for Noodle to have more. Again with a goofy grin.

"Houston." Téya's exhaustion brought out the worst in her. She snapped her fingers. "Annie."

Houston blinked. "Right." Shifted in his chair. "What?" His face had gone crimson, but he still managed to steal another look at Nuala.

"You realize she can take your head off from a mile away with a single shot, right?" Téya couldn't resist teasing the geek.

Houston frowned at Téya. "You know that's not funny, threatening people with sniper shots to the head just because I can appreciate beauty."

"Appreciate is one thing, dear geek," Téya said as she leaned over his shoulder. "Going full-out fan-boy is another. Now." She squeezed his shoulder. "Annie?"

"Annie's been missing since 1730 hours," he said, all business and glaring at her. "About an hour ago, an explosion at the same estate made the news. Trace, Boone, and the SEAL are headed out to meet up with a contact who is going to chopper them in and see if they can find Annie." His nostrils flared. "Anything else, Your Highness?"

Amused, Téya met Nuala's smile with one of her own. "That's perfect,

Houston. Now, we have no problem."

"Except that you're lame."

Téya frowned at him.

"That joke. It's lame. I hear it all the time. It's old. Burnt to a crisp."

Nuala stood, bent toward Houston, and pressed a kiss to his cheek. "G'night, Houston."

"Okay, now that was just. . .unfair."

Nuala stood over him. "Why?"

"You're mocking me. That kiss meant nothing to you."

"Oh, you're wrong," Noodle said. "It was done with my sincerest thanks."

Hanging his head dramatically, he waved them away. "Go, go. 'You mock my pain.'"

Noodle laughed as she backstepped toward their suite. "'Life is pain, Highness.'"

Houston's face lit up. "Be still my beating heart—a woman who knows the classics."

Téya groaned. She was missing something but she didn't want to know what. "Noodle, let's go to bed. We need an early start."

"Yeah," Houston said, his expression suddenly very serious. "Where exactly are you going? I've got orders." His jaw went slack. "Trace is going to kill me." He lifted the phone. Dialed. "Two and Six arrived safe." Houston nodded. "Will do." He hung up. "Commander says to stay put till they get back."

Téya saluted and entered the suite, closing the door behind them.

"Just let me get three hours," Nuala said as she dropped on the bed.

With a smile, Téya stretched out on the other full-size mattress, grateful Nuala knew there wasn't a prayer Téya intended to stay put. As she stretched her arm over her face to cover her eyes, she caught sight of the burn. When they got stateside, she'd go to a doctor, see if they could clean up the skin so it wasn't so obviously a brand.

Like a predator, sleep dug its long, sharp talons into her mind and dragged Téya from consciousness. Images of fires and children and the slums and burning pain in her hand, then staring at the business end of The Turk's weapon, his brown-green eyes glinting in dark satisfaction that he'd found her. And now, *now he'd kill her.*

He touched her shoulder.

Téya grabbed it, twisted the wrist and swung her opposite arm up and over, pinning them.

"Ow!"

Téya blinked, the bedroom coming into focus and the nightmares slipping away, as she found herself holding Houston's arm. She shoved him away, furious. "Why are you in here?"

Rubbing his arm, Houston scowled. "You have issues, Two."

"My name is Téya. Why are you in our room?"

He cast a glance toward Noodle, who was still asleep.

"You sick dog," Téya snarled, imagining him watching them in their sleep.

"Oh, grow up," Houston said. "She cried out in her sleep. I. . .I got worried."

Téya swung her legs over the edge of the bed and glanced at the digital clock. 5:58. She was so not a morning person, but waking up and finding the geek hovering over her— "Go." She stomped as she caught his shoulders and pushed him from the room. "Out. Now."

"Okay, okay. Relax. I just wanted to make sure you two were okay."

"She's a sniper, remember?"

"Right," Houston said.

Téya closed the door and turned.

Noodle sat perched on the edge of her bed. "I had a nightmare again, didn't I?"

"I think Peeping Houston just wanted to watch you sleep."

A small smile tugged Noodle's face, clearly not believing it.

"Shower up. I need one, too, and I want to be out of here in fifteen."

Noodle complied without another word, her countenance haunted. Though there was no cure, Téya wished she could get hold of something that would heal Noodle's mind. It was one thing to deal with drama when you had created most of it yourself. It was another to watch a woman as sweet and gentle in nature get ripped apart from the inside out by something out of her control.

Twelve minutes later, hair still wet and tied back, Téya strode into the main area. "How're the commander and Boone doing?"

"In the air. And grumpy. No sign of her yet."

"We're heading down to the cafeteria," Téya said, noting Houston was distracted with the mission at hand. "Need anything?"

"Nah, I'm good," he said, as he adjusted something then glanced at a monitor.

Téya nodded to the door, and Nuala made for it. They were in the hall, the door almost closed, when Houston shouted, "Hey! There's no cafeteria in a hotel—and Trace said to stay put!"

Laughing, they hurried out of the hotel and back onto the street. Adrenaline thrummed through Téya's body. She skipped a step as they made their way back toward the slums.

"Think he's awake?" Noodle asked.

"Maybe," Téya said, her stomach clenching. "I gave him sleeping aids in his water, but who knows if that will keep him under at all." She hated herself for remembering how toned his abs were and the larger version of the star-crescent over his left, well-defined pectoral.

"Wouldn't he flee?"

She wanted to say nobody with that injury would flee. Maybe stumble out and collapse from the pain. But this wasn't an ordinary person. This was The Turk. "I hope not. He needs to answer a few questions."

"What if he doesn't speak English?"

"Then he's not a very good assassin."

"What does speaking English and killing people have to do with each other?"

"To integrate into someone's life to figure out how best to kill them, he'd need to master the language." In theory, at least.

"I don't have to speak any language but sniper for a kill shot," Noodle said, panting as they walked. "And would you *slow* down?"

Téya rounded the rear of the hotel and jogged to the window. She hesitated at finding it open. Hands on the ledge, she hauled herself inside. The smell of something burnt snagged her senses first. Then the silence.

"I thought we closed it," Nuala came in after her. "Whoa."

The room had been meticulously rearranged. Bed made up. No sign of blood. No stains on the carpet. No bloody towels. In fact, new ones hung in perfect array on the plastic silver rod. Téya took in the cheap, framed print. Not a trace of dust. "He scrubbed it."

"Didn't want to leave evidence we could use to track him."

"We don't need to. Everyone knows who he is—The Turk."

"We know what he wants us to know," Noodle said as she went into the bathroom. "The last time this bathroom was this clean was probably ten years ago."

A rap against the door put Téya's heart into overdrive. Nuala reappeared and gave a curt nod. They were ready. Téya went to the door, not daring to look through the peephole and end up with a hole in the head. She yanked open the thin barrier.

Disheveled and drawn, the bearded man looked as surprised as Téya felt. "Are you Miss Reiker?"

Her heart spasmed, and her mouth went dry. She couldn't move. How would he know her name, her *real* name? She hadn't used it in Greece at all. Which put this man on the deadly side of the Richter scale.

With a nervous glance down both ends of the hall, he pushed a large hand through a mop of tangled, dirty-blond hair. "I don't mean to be rude, but can I come in? I–I'm not safe."

"Tell me who you are first." She said, easing her weapon to a visible position.

His gaze went to the weapon. "H–hey. Easy now. . . ." He licked his lips. "You're looking for me. I–I'm Carl Loring."

Trace
Somewhere over Salamina, Greece
2 June – 0515 Hours EEST

Sitting on the edge of the Black Hawk, boots dangling in the predawn air, Trace used his thermal scope to scan the forest below. Boone and Caliguari were scoping the terrain as well. Three pairs of eyes were better than two, though Trace hated having the guy with him.

Hated that it was possible Caliguari would find her first.

The thought pushed Trace to pay attention.

"I've got something," Boone spoke through the coms. "Chopper's two."

Trace looked to his left where the chopper's two o'clock position lay. Sure enough, a handful of heat signatures—small ones—raced over the ground.

"Goats?" Caliguari said.

Trace shook his head. They were too agile, moving too fast. "Dogs," he countered. "Hunting party."

"Yeah, and One is the quarry."

That's when Trace saw it—a heat signature alone, about a half mile away from the dogs. "Toomer, take us half klick to your three."

"Copy that," the pilot said as the bird swung in that direction.

Trace zoomed in on the position, but the image had vanished.

"What'd you see?" Boone asked.

Maybe he'd imagined it. "Not sure," Trace said, scanning, agitation growing. She was out there. Had been for hours. Daylight was on the horizon, which put Annie's odds at being recaptured higher. "Lost it."

"Hang on," Toomer pulled away and came back at a different angle. "There's an incline. If someone's hiding in the cleft. . ."

As they raced up the slope one more time, Trace spotted the signature again. "One o'clock."

"I see it," Caliguari called.

"Can we put down?" Boone asked.

"Negative," Toomer said. "No room."

310

Trace harnessed and hooked up to the steel rings riveted to the floor of the chopper. Just before he stepped off, he looked over and spotted Caliguari doing the same.

Sam

Hot in his gloved hands, Sam fast-roped out of the helo. Wind fought him, its needling fingers tugging at him as he made the rapid descent. He landed with a soft thud and went to a knee, his M4 sweeping the area. Weston hadn't been pleased about Sam having a weapon, but he also hadn't been able to argue against it. The man hated Sam, and it felt very personal.

Sam wasn't worried. He had no ill intent here. His only mission and purpose was to find Ashland and make sure she was okay.

Then kiss her senseless.

The trees were quiet sentries on this Greek island, providing cover against the moonlight and the early morning lightening of the sky. He saw no visible threat. "Squid clear," he said, hating that he had to use that term, but it was a concession. If it meant finding her. . .

To his right, he spotted the colonel kneeling behind a large boulder. He signaled Sam forward. Moving along a dense copse of saplings, Sam hustled toward the rendezvous point—the location they'd spotted the heat signature. No way of knowing if it was Ashland, but it'd be a long shot if it wasn't her.

Thwack! Thwat!

Heat seared across his shoulder. From behind. Sam hurtled himself over a fallen limb and scrabbled up against the decaying wood. "Taking fire." He gritted his teeth, refusing to admit he'd been nailed. Hand near the spot, he eyed it. Blood glistened under the moonlight, but it wasn't much. Just a graze.

To his six, he heard a flurry of shots being exchanged. Sam rolled onto his stomach and low-crawled to the end of the log. Sliding his weapon, he eased into position. Traced the wash of illuminated terrain for the targets.

A head peeked out.

Sam took his time lining up the sights. "Target sighted," he spoke quietly against the mic.

"Take the shot," the colonel said.

Sam fired. The man pitched backward. "Target down."

"Tango at your eleven, Squid," came the near twang of the big guy, Boone.

"Copy," Sam said, spotting the shooter. He wasn't a sniper, but the men chasing Ashland were reckless. It was like picking cans off a line at a fair. "Target acquired." He pulled the trigger back and, "Target down."

Patiently, he waited, eyeing the terrain. Watching for more unfriendlies.

"Clear. Let's move," the colonel said.

They picked their way with stealth and deliberation toward the rocky cleft where they'd spotted the person. He'd worked contract gigs in the jungles of South America and the Middle East, but there was something about being part of a team. Having an objective you believed in. A purpose you'd die for.

He'd die for Ashland every day of the year.

Twenty minutes later, Sam grew wary. They'd gone too far. Should've come across the person by now. *Unless the person is evading. . .*

How would Ashland know they were friendly?

He nodded, sorting the thought. He reached for his mic to ask the colonel when a whistle sailed through the air. "Col—"

A weight slammed into Sam's back. Pain detonated across the back of his head.

"Augh!" He pitched forward but had enough presence of mind to know if he went down, he was probably dead. He went to a knee to break his fall, coiled to strike. He swung out his arm.

Something flew at him.

Slammed him backward. He struggled against the person, wrestling with them. He swung a hard right. It barely glanced off the person's jaw, but their legs were locked against his chest, squeezing.

Beams of light bobbed around them.

Blinding. Confusing.

Only in that chaos, Sam saw the glint of a gold curl.

"Stand down, stand down!" Heart thudding, Sam rammed out a hand against the chest of his attacker, holding them back so he could see the face.

Hands raised over their head, a large rock braced between their fingers, the person looked down at him. Blue eyes registered wild rage.

Then shock.

"Sam?!"

Francesca
Alexandria, Virginia
2 June – 1815 Hours EST

Having her job back, having her access returned, Frankie hesitantly made her way through the first few days. If she retrieved the wrong file or made the wrong call, everything could come crashing down on her. Again. The bitter taste of that defeat hung fresh in her mind, a strong warning. Tomorrow she would go back to work and throw herself into the job. Prove to her father and her boss that she could play by the rules.

Oh, she wasn't quitting. That wasn't in her genes.

She just had to be more careful. Play by their rules—and not get caught. She'd grown up with three brothers who treated her like their father's fourth son. She could play with the big boys and not get hurt.

Tucking her legs up under her, she sat down on her sofa. After a quick glance around the living room she'd spent too much time fixing back up, she tugged her laptop over the cushion. She thumbed through the file from the accident and searched for the report from the EMT. Scanning, she dropped her gaze to the bottom. The signature was about as legible as a doctor's. "Okay, so not much help yet."

Frankie went to the laptop. Typed in *Luckett's Volunteer Fire Department*. She found a handful of results and images but no EMTs. At least, not the one she was looking for.

Wait. . .wait. . . She forced herself to recall the lettering on the side of the ambulance. *Loudoun County*. She typed that in along with *EMT*.

"And voilà!" Frankie smiled down at the image of the EMT with a group of others. A feature from *Leesburg Today* with a picture of the men—and a caption. "God loves me," Frankie muttered as she read the names. ". . .and one Landon Ramage."

Ramage. According to the article, the Ramages were fixtures in Loudoun County since the early 1800s, having owned land and horses dating back to almost as late.

Frankie's grin widened as she typed in his name and city. A half-dozen pictures from local events erupted. Including one with Landon and his older brother, former Army Special Forces sniper—*sniper?* The back of her neck prickled—"Boone Ramage."

A wild tendril of an idea rushed through her. She went to land records. Searched.

No Matches Found.

Frankie frowned. "How can there be no matches?" The article had explicitly stated the family owned land there in Loudoun, had for nearly two hundred years. Maybe she typed it wrong. She tried again.

No Matches Found.

Despite attempts to locate other records, she came up empty. Frustration tightened a noose around her neck. If she kept pushing—this is what got her in trouble last time.

"I am not easily scared off," she murmured.

But she *hated* losing.

Curiosity caught her by the throat. She accessed her work login and navigated into the secure databases. A strange squirreling wormed through her belly. He had to have a driver's license. Did he even own a vehicle? Or have a credit card?

If she didn't know better, she'd say Boone Ramage and his family didn't exist. But she'd met the man. She'd seen him. There were photos on the Internet of him and his younger brother. Frankie glanced at the screen from the local paper. She had to admit—the Ramages bred well. Both sons were striking, handsome. "Well built, too," she murmured around a smile. "And not married."

The page automatically refreshed—and Frankie froze. She tilted her head. "Wha. . .?" She hit the manual refresh icon. But the page was blank. "I was just there. How can it be blank?" After verifying she still had Internet access, she refreshed again. This time, a single line of text vaulted her stomach into her throat.

The page you have requested has been removed.

Nausea swirled. Fingertips to her temples, she tried to weigh what this meant. It wasn't a coincidence that she'd just looked up Ramage and suddenly he disappeared from the face of the planet.

When her phone rang, she yelped. Glanced at it as if it had the plague. Carefully, as if they could remotely see her through it somehow—she peered at the caller ID.

Unknown Name.

Right. No way would she answer that.

It went to voice mail. A few minutes later, her phone signaled a message had been received. Frankie played it.

"Contact Leland Marlowe. He can help." It'd come from Varden. No wonder the identity didn't show up.

Frankie's breath rushed out of her. Leland Marlowe? As in General Leland "Freeland" Marlowe, the firebrand general who'd swept the military clean as one of the joint chiefs last year?

Annie
Athens, Greece
2 June – 0615 Hours EEST

Annie rolled off him, careful of her injured ankle, and slumped to the ground. *Sam?* Sam was here? How was that even possible?

He shifted toward her, the predawn hour barely providing enough light to see his face. "Ash, you okay?"

Ash.

He was on his knees.

Numbness rolled through her, soaking her muscles. Drenching her brain. What was he doing here? Sam didn't belong here.

"Ash—you okay?" he said, more urgently, cupping her face.

His deep, rich brown eyes broke through the daze that fogged her mind. "Sam. Why. . . ?"

"I'm here. It's okay," he said, his voice. . .weird.

Annie drew back, a strange spike of anger bursting through her. Get off. But that was rude. And he was Sam. But why was he here?

He tried to pull her closer.

With both hands, she shoved him backward. "Stop."

Boots thudded closer.

"One, you hurt?"

Annie glanced up. Trace stood over her, his face unreadable. But perfect. Exactly what she needed. "My ankle."

He offered his hand and she reached up, clasping his forearm. His strong fingers tightened around her arm and pulled her up. Hissing through the pain, she struggled to stay balanced. "What happened?"

"Dogs." A shiver traced her spine, the morning cooler than she'd realized.

Trace nodded. "Chopper's on the way back. But we have almost a full klick to cover."

At their side, Boone communicated with the chopper, shedding his pack then removing his tactical jacket. He wrapped it around Annie's shoulders, and she shuddered in the cradle of its warmth. "Thanks, Boone."

He gave a nod and lifted his gear and weapon again. "Two mikes to rendezvous."

This was better. The precision, the strategy, the focus. "Okay," she said with a single nod.

Trace's arm slipped under hers and hooked around her waist. "Other injuries?"

Annie gave a quick shake, her gaze skirting to Sam.

He stood to the side, his expression dark. Stricken.

Unable to sort what she felt, the confusion, the anger, the. . .she didn't know what. It was a tangled mess like a plate of spaghetti.

I hate spaghetti.

"Squid, give a hand," Trace said.

Without hesitation, Sam trudged over to Annie's right and hooked an arm beneath hers. The two men formed a cradle and supported her. They hurried up the hillside to a clearing. They'd no sooner gotten there and the chopper, still blacked out, hovered over them. Ropes snaked down.

Trace quickly worked a rope into a harness and helped her into it, creating an awkward and unladylike mess of her dress. Annie no longer cared. She just wanted to get out of here. Once the men were on board, the chopper veered away from the estate.

Sam took the seat beside her, and Trace remained in the jump seat, eyes trained out. Weapon ready. Boone sat on the other side, watching as well.

Guilt choked Annie. She could feel the tension she'd created between Sam and her. It was palpable. But he—it didn't make sense for him to be here. He had no business entering her life like this.

Does he know who I really am? That I lied to him for two years?

She thanked God a thousand times on the twenty-minute flight to the airstrip that the rotor wash and engine noise were too loud for any conversation to take place. Mostly because she had no idea what to say.

Before the wheels touched down, Trace hopped to the ground. He shifted the sling so his weapon was against his back. He turned and looked into the chopper at her. It was crazy. Really crazy how much she just wanted Trace to be here. Only Trace. It made no sense. Made her feel like a traitor. Unfaithful.

"Will your leg hold?" Trace hollered as the chopper whined down. He held out a hand.

Terrified to face Sam, to face the hurt she'd inflicted, to face the deep, bewildering confusion she felt, Annie scooted across the strap seats toward Trace, keeping her leg elevated.

She reached for his hand.

"Here," he said, tugging her into his arms.

Annie tumbled, her foot jarring against the chopper. She tensed at the burst of pain but relaxed as she felt Trace's firm hold tighten. He carried her to the SUV where Boone had a door open. Inside the vehicle—that's when Annie finally felt safe. When the terror she'd felt, the hypervigilance she'd needed to survive began to melt away.

Sam climbed in next to her.

The doors shut and Annie realized they were alone. Her conscience pricked, warned her she should apologize.

For what?

For shoving him away. With both hands. In front of Trace.

But she wasn't sorry.

"You're mad." His voice poured over her like warm chocolate. As always.

Annie steeled herself. Told herself to talk to him. Explain what she felt. Why she was angry—and that it was so weird to be angry with him. Hadn't she spent the last five weeks pining over the fact that Trace wouldn't let her see or talk to him?

The doors opened and the vehicle rocked as Boone and Trace climbed into the front seats.

Trace looked over his shoulder at her. "We'll have a doctor at the hotel waiting."

She nodded. Had all but forgotten about her ankle.

But her mouth was dry. Her body exhausted. Sam's strong hands wrapped around hers. Her heart. . .jammed. She wanted to snatch her hands free.

What's going on with me? What's with the anger? The animosity churning in her chest stunned her. Sharing the passionate kiss with Sam on the deck in Manson felt like a lifetime ago. Why? Didn't she want him? Want the hope of the life they'd taken the tentative steps toward starting?

One question gaped at her more than any other. *Why am I not happy to see Sam?*

Trace
Athens, Greece
2 June – 1020 Hours EEST

With Annie huddled between him and Sam again, Trace hustled her into the hotel room. A million alarms blazed when he registered a man and two children sitting at the small dining table in the far corner of the room. He nearly dropped Annie.

"Uh," Houston punched to his feet and pointed to another man. "Dr. Foster is here."

317

"Got it," Boone said, nodding Trace toward the others with a "take care of it" look as he slipped in and aided Sam in delivering Annie to the bedroom.

A short, stout man with dark hair and a medical bag rushed after them.

Trace closed the door and locked it then turned to face the others. He rested his hand on his Glock.

The side door opened and Téya emerged with a middle-aged woman with wet brown hair. She wore clothes that didn't quite fit her short frame.

Téya's eyes widened. "Commander." She waved the woman to the table then went and passed the woman a bowl from a room service dining cart.

"Anyone want to fill me in?" he asked as he watched the woman cast nervous glances at the man.

"Commander," Téya said in a voice that was entirely too calm, "this is Carl Loring and his wife, Sharlene."

Stunned, he stared at the couple. The children. So, Zulu had accomplished their objective. "What took so long to find them?"

Nuala rose from a chair where she'd sat undetected until now. "The slums—it's like its own small city. It's a"—Noodle's gaze darted to Téya's—"miracle, really, that we found them at all."

"We were hiding," Carl Loring said. "And when you don't want to be found in a place like that, it's possible to stay hidden for"—he shrugged—"probably forever."

Something smelled rotten. Trace stared at Téya. Then Nuala. They wouldn't look at him. Or at each other.

"I can help you," Loring said. "I was the financial officer for HOMe for the last eight years."

"So why are you living in the slums?" Trace folded his arms.

"*Hiding* in the slums," Loring corrected then glanced at his wife. "We aren't sure what changed, but about two months ago, a man came to our door. He said some things were going to come to light, but if I'd help him, he'd make sure my family and I were safe."

"What things?"

"Financial statements. Black market transactions between HOMe and various organizations."

Trace scowled and searched their faces. "You have this proof?"

"N–no," Loring muttered, looking to his wife. "I was in the process of uncovering the information when everything went crazy."

"Someone burned down our home," Mrs. Loring said, her eyes glossy.

"He got us into the slum and told us to stay there. Then he came to me early this morning and said you would help."

"Who are you talking about?" Trace asked. "Who told you we'd help?"

"Not you. He said *she* would." Mr. Loring pointed to Téya. "Miss Reiker."

Trace unfolded his arms and pulled straight. "Who gave you her name?"

"The man," he said, flicking a finger in the air around his cheekbone. "He said you saved his life, so he owed you."

Téya darted her gaze around nervously, swallowing.

"Who?" Trace demanded.

Wetting her lips, Téya drew up her shoulders. Let out a long breath. "The Turk."

"You *saw The Turk* and didn't tell me?"

"I shot him." She said it so plainly as if she were telling him about a doughnut she ate. "It was a mistake. He was going to die, so—"

"You should've let him!"

Téya's eyes flashed. "I wanted answers."

"You only needed one—that he was dead!"

Trace's phone buzzed. "We'll sort this out in Virginia." He pivoted to Houston, who sat with his head down, hand over his mouth. "Get us back there, Houston. ASAP."

The geek nodded and went to work.

Livid and boiling, Trace moved to the private suite. His phone buzzed again and he lifted it, checked the caller ID, and answered. "General, how are you?"

"Trace, sit down."

Stilled by those words, Trace felt as he had the night of the warehouse disaster. "What's wrong?"

"Know I'd rather spit on this than tell you, but—"

"Just say it," Trace bit out.

"You are being ordered back to DC. General Leland Marlowe has given orders for you to stand down all operations and return to DC at once to stand before a full congressional hearing regarding Misrata."

The world *whooshed* out from under Trace's feet. "They can't do this. I was already cleared."

"Separate charge, Trace. They can and they are. You are temporarily relieved of duty until this matter is settled."

IX

The mood had shifted among the team, weighted by exhaustion. Dim lights provided a serene atmosphere in the cabin of a hired private jet ferrying them back to Virginia. The Lorings were tucked away at the back, resting. Trace had opted for the quicker route rather than the predictable one. He wanted the Lorings on U.S. soil as soon as possible. Boone couldn't blame him, especially now that there was a chance Misrata could get laid to rest with a healthy dose of truth.

Across and one group up from the Squid the girls sat, mostly quiet. On second thought—Téya and Noodle were in animated conversation. Annie sat with her hands in her lap, looking down. Boone could see from his seat that every now and then her gaze slid toward the Squid. Now, wasn't that interesting that she wasn't sitting *with* him? Wasn't talking *to* him? She'd given them grief over not being able to talk to the guy, and now that he was here, she wouldn't give him the time of day.

Renewed focus surrounded Zulu and propelled them to action. Along with that came a new level of tension and agitation, partially laid at the feet of Téya Reiker for her unwilling connection to The Turk. Having that type of breathing down your neck was the equivalent of a nuke's skin-melting fire. Especially with the fury rolling off Trace.

Trace dropped into the chair across from Boone and ran his hand along his closely shorn hair with a heavy sigh.

"Things a'right?" Boone asked as the plane seemed to level off to make its trek back to the States.

Shaking his head, Trace leaned back against the headrest. "Couldn't be worse."

Boone adjusted in the chair. Concern knotted his shoulder muscles. He knew things had gone a bit crazy with Téya making contact again with The Turk. And with the addition of the Squid. But Trace. . .he'd been a storm brewing since they started packing up. "Something I don't know about?"

After another long sigh, Trace leaned closer, his elbow resting on the arm of the seat and his hand hovering near his mouth. "They're launching another hearing about Misrata."

"What?" Boone angled toward Trace and kept his voice down so the others didn't hear them. "Why would they open that thing up again? There's nothing to prove."

Trace shrugged. "I've been ordered to stand down. Cease all operations."

Boone went still and eyed the man he considered both a friend and a confidant. Shutting down Zulu now. . . "We must be getting close."

Jaw out, Trace gave a slow nod. "That's one way of looking at it."

"Do the girls know?"

"No, and they won't. We're making progress, but we need to speed things up." Trace stretched his neck. "We need to get the Lorings back to the bunker and get every mote of dust out of their brains about Misrata."

"Still don't get why they weren't listed among the survivors."

"There was a lot wrong with the information provided," Trace countered.

"True." Boone nodded, lips pursed as he seemed to think through things. He sighed and met Trace's gaze. "Kinda strange, the way The Turk sent Mr. Loring to Téya, don't you think?"

"Definitely. She's going to answer for that," Trace said, a warning in his words.

"Think The Turk will be a problem?"

"*I'm* going to be a problem. She broke the rules. She stepped outside to do what she wanted. She put everyone in jeopardy," Trace said.

"And if she hadn't, we wouldn't have found Loring."

After shooting him a look, Trace pinched the bridge of his nose. "I'm getting too old for this stuff, Boone-Dawg. I feel like I'm trying to corral second graders."

Up the aisle a bit, the Squid scooted across the seat. Angled around to face Annie. He said something softly to her, and she slowly met his gaze. She seemed to be considering something. Maybe he'd asked a question. Or commented on something. Her expression seemed pained, what with her knotted eyebrows and tormented eyes. That's when she finally shook her head and looked away.

"What about the Squid?" Boone asked as the Squid sat straight and pushed his gaze out the night-darkened window. "Annie didn't give him the reception he expected."

"She never does," Trace muttered.

"What's that about anyway?" Boone muttered. "Why's she ignoring him?"

"Annie compartmentalizes. She's an ace at it, which is why she's good at ops." Closing his eyes, Trace leaned back against the white leather seat.

"He stepped into the wrong box, and she can't cope with him being in this part of her world."

"So, what? They're over?"

Without a word, Trace pushed out of his seat. Away from the Squid. Away from the girls who sat two seating groups up from Boone. Away from Boone and this conversation.

It didn't take a genius to see the pleasure Trace took in Annie's cold shoulder toward the SEAL. But Boone struggled to figure out why his buddy didn't make the move he so clearly wanted to make. To fix that bridge he'd wrecked five years ago.

Maybe that's what perturbed Annie, too. Not so much the compartmentalization but the fact that with Squid back in the picture, the chances were rickety that she could figure things out with Trace. Even now, her gaze trailed Trace to the rear of the plane.

They'd set the girls loose on an unsuspecting populace five years ago, and each of them had found a romantic interest at one time or another—well, all except Noodle. The pretty little thing didn't lack for looks or sweetness, so he wasn't sure why she stayed single. Maybe the men she met were afraid of the siren who could slay with looks and a Remington 700. Boone found himself grinning. Noodle's pale blue eyes came to his, and something in his chest knocked funny.

Annie

Annie saw Trace stalk to the back of the plane and hurried after him, careful to slide by Sam without looking. She hated herself. Hated being *right here* with him and wanting nothing more than to jump out the nearest emergency exit. He confused her. Mixed her up too much by being on this mission.

With his back to her, Trace stood at the small galley fridge guzzling a bottle of water. He lowered the bottle and met her gaze, lowering it the rest of the way slowly.

In her periphery, she could still see Sam, so she took a step forward, though it put her almost toe-to-toe with Trace. "*What* is he doing here?" she demanded.

After swallowing the rest of the water, Trace tossed the bottle in a small trash bag, his gaze never leaving hers. "I needed him where I could see and control him."

"What does that mean?"

"That he plastered your name and likeness all over the Internet. He ran your fingerprints through databases."

"Fingerprints? Where'd he get those?"

"Doesn't matter," Trace said, hooking his hands on a thin counter behind him. "He had them, and we couldn't afford you popping back up on the grid when you're supposed to be dead."

"But here?"

Trace said nothing, just gave her that look. The one that said he didn't have a regret. That he made the right decision.

"Just like Albuquerque."

He flinched.

"This is just like that because you think it's the right thing."

Remaining tight-lipped, he didn't move.

Annie scooted in till she stood wedged between him and the counter. "Trace, I can't do this. I can't operate with him here."

"Fine."

She breathed a little easier.

"I'll send him to max-sec."

"*Prison?* Are you serious?"

Again, he went tight-lipped.

"You'd like that, wouldn't you? Sending him away, where I can't speak to him."

"I want him where he can't do any more harm to you or the others. It's not just about you, Annie."

She leaned in, her heart thundering. "Isn't it, Trace?"

"What does that mean?"

"You brought him here because you knew I wouldn't like it. You wanted him to see that. To see me blow him off."

"I wanted his hands out of the fire. Do you realize, have any idea, what his hunting you almost did to this entire team? Do you know what it's done to me?"

"To you?" She scoffed. "You did this because you couldn't have me, so you didn't want him to have me."

"It was five years ago, Annie. I got over it."

"Yeah?" she said, her lungs squeezing tight. "Well, I haven't."

Trace went still, his green eyes probing hers.

The heat rushed through Annie's face, disbelieving she'd said that out loud.

His frown deepened, digging a deep groove between his eyes. That look is what darkened the intensity around his eyes. What had drawn her in. . .every time. She could smell him. Smell the woodsy scent that mingled with the smell that was uniquely Trace.

His hand came to her cheek, smelling of antiseptic soap—probably from the onboard bathrooms. Despite calloused fingers, his touch was light. Soft as he traced his thumb along her jaw.

Annie felt her body responding to his touch as it had all those years ago. The tremor in her chest strangled the hope of a steady breath.

He leaned closer, his gaze on her mouth.

Breath backed into her throat.

"Need something, Squid?" Trace said, his breath skidding across her cheek, then he eased away.

Annie jerked, realizing Trace was actually looking over her shoulder. She glanced that way and froze. Darkening what served as a doorway, Sam stood there, a wicked storm brewing in his expression. When she moved backward, she bumped the counter, so she sidestepped and turned. "Sam."

His upper lip curled. "This how you keep her loyalty, Colonel?"

Trace moved toward Sam, and Annie planted her hands against Trace's abs. "Trace, don't."

Eyes on Sam, Trace touched Annie's shoulder. "It's okay." Trace almost looked ambivalent. He moved past Sam, every taut second it took him to move past him filled with crackling tension.

Fists balled, Sam gave her commander a look that could kill.

Annie breathed a cold, painful breath as Trace returned to his seat. Then slapped Sam's gut. "*What was that?* Do you really have a death wish?"

This time, Sam seemed ambivalent. "Talking to me now?"

Fingers to her forehead, Annie slumped against the wall of cabinets. "Sam. . .I'm sorry."

"For what?" He stepped into the clogged space. Arms folded, he looked much larger than she remembered. "For lying to me for two years? For faking your attraction to me? Or for attacking me in Greece?"

"That's not fair."

He smirked. "You're right. It's not. None of it. But here we are."

Heart aching, Annie lowered her head. It was too much to take in. Too much to process. That he was here. That she had a lot of truth-catching-up to do.

Sam edged in closer, his hands catching her arms and holding her in place. He peered down at her with those rich, dark eyes of his. The last few days had to have been rough on him, because his five o'clock shadow looked closer to midnight now. "Just tell me what happened between us was real."

"Sam. . ."

"Just tell me that, and we can sort out the rest later."

"Ye—" The word caught in her throat, forcing her to swallow.

"Hesitating? Seriously?"

"Sam, there's a lot happening. A lot of deadly things."

"Yeah, I know. My car was rammed off the road. I was there the night—shortly after a heavy make-out session with you, if I remember correctly—that a sniper tried to take our heads off. I get stress. I get combat." His eyes darkened. "I don't get your reticence about us. Was I just convenient?"

Annie stepped back, flaring her nostrils. "Don't do this to me." She set her jaw. "Give me time, Sam. I can't sort through anything right now. I haven't had time to think, and being sarcastic about us doesn't help."

"But you want to work it out?"

"Yes." Annie blinked, not at his smile that ensued but at the doubts that lingered in her mind. *I think so.*

Nuala
Lucketts, Virginia
4 June – 0930 Hours

Being an introvert always put her on the outside of conversations and goings-on. But it also left Nuala very intuitive and perceptive of others' feelings. Rarely did people ask what she thought—not that she'd volunteer her inner workings because she'd never forgive herself for hurting someone, and she'd die inside a little if she was wrong and humiliated herself. They viewed her as quiet, maybe even demure. Thankfully, at least one person in this underground bunker saw her strength. It wasn't the six-pack abs or bulging bicep strength, but one at the center of her being. A strength that wouldn't let her quit or give up. It challenged her and pushed her to do better, be better.

Maybe if she'd been better or stronger Boone might've chosen her instead of Keeley.

Which wasn't a fair thought. Because Keeley had everything Nuala didn't—confidence, humor, an outgoing personality, and. . .Boone.

An old, familiar ache wormed through Nuala's chest.

Stop.

He'd made his choice. And they were a happy couple. Everyone involved with Zulu knew that. Though it went against regs, nobody opposed them dating. It was a tough gig. Much like it must be for Carl and Sharlene Loring, who sat at the table with Téya. Their single-digit kiddos were on the floor of the lounge area, watching TV. The little girl multitasked between the cartoon and the coloring pages Houston had printed out and turned over to her with his array of colored pens. How did two people work in a missionary setting with two children and come out of it happy?

But. . .were they happy? Nuala eyed the two. Mrs. Loring had brown hair and matching brown eyes. Her husband had a Swiss appearance with his blond hair and blue eyes. Tall and lanky, he was taller than his wife even when seated. Right next to each other. And yet his hands were on the table.

Though Mrs. Loring looked distressed, Mr. Loring offered no sympathy. Nuala wouldn't deal with that. She needed a man who would devote time and concern for her. Understand her idiosyncrasies and fears then offer encouragement. Strength.

Boone often did that.

Stop. It!

Nuala shifted in her seat suddenly, drawing the attention of the Lorings and Téya, who sat at the other end. With a fake smile plastered on her face, Nuala met their curious gazes. "Anyone want a glass of water or tea?"

"Water, please." Mrs. Loring gave a relieved smile.

"Look," Mr. Loring said, not taking his gaze from Téya and Trace. "I'm telling you, Chandler and Hollister are a waste of time."

"How's that?" Trace seemed agitated. And not necessarily about the Lorings. Or maybe it was.

Nuala wasn't sure she trusted her assessments right now since her emotions were too tangled up in the nightmares and the events in the Roma slums. Though she had the same combat medic skills Téya had— they all did, in fact; it was part of their training—Nuala had never put them to use to extract a bullet and sew up someone. Especially not a notorious assassin who'd put their lives in jeopardy.

"Ballenger," Mr. Loring said. "You need to talk to Berg Ballenger."

Nuala poured two glasses of ice water, her attention trained on the conversation.

Téya gave a soft laugh. "We met with him in Paris. He blamed HOMe. He basically said Chandler and Hollister were trying to kill him."

Loring shook his head and looked at his wife. "Those ladies don't have it in them to hire a hit man, but I wouldn't blame them if they had."

A commotion to the side drew everyone's attention and silence. The eight-year-old girl and her brother were arguing under their breath. The girl, Cora, seemed distressed and insistent upon something Charles refused. He caught her hand and whispered something quite harshly to her.

Nuala slid her gaze to the parents, who watched but hadn't moved.

Why isn't the mother going to her children?

Just then, Sharlene Loring rose from her chair and went to the lounge area. She squatted with her back to Nuala and the others. Quiet words were spoken, then Sharlene returned with a weary smile. "They are tired of being on the run, of not having their own space."

Back at the table, Nuala handed Mrs. Loring the water then slid into her own chair.

Trace's arms were folded. "Back to Ballenger," he said. "Why wouldn't you blame HOMe if they wanted to hurt him?"

Mr. Loring nodded to his wife, who gave him a reticent look. "Go on," he said. "Tell them."

She hesitated again.

Trace leaned forward and rested his arms on the table. "Mrs. Loring, I promise we are only after the truth here."

"It's disconcerting," she admitted, "with the way you're keeping us here. Won't allow us to go outside."

"My superiors are working on setting up a home for you and your children as we speak," Trace said. "You will all be safe. You can start over. But we also need whatever you can give us to settle what happened in Misrata."

She swallowed and gave Nuala a smile then Téya. Took a sip of water. Set the glass down. Turned it. Then let her hands rest back in her lap. "It was Berg."

Trace—and in fact, all of Zulu—blinked. "What was Berg?"

"He's the one who told Miss Hollister about the warehouse." Sharlene tucked a strand of hair behind her ear and gave a shaky smile. "I'd been out walking in the small garden outside the building we were being evicted from. When I came back in, I heard them arguing. He told her he'd found a place for us to go till the new permits came through for the other building. But she said she wouldn't move us to a rundown warehouse in what was basically the slums. He told her there wasn't a choice and reassured her it was safe."

Téya and Trace shared a long, meaningful look.

Expression taut, Trace got that knotted-up look that clouded his handsome features when he wasn't happy. Nuala could practically smell the fury burning through him. "You're sure? You are absolutely sure Ballenger is the one who sent you there?"

"I am," Mrs. Loring said.

"I need to make some calls," Trace said as he pushed out of his chair. "I'll find out about your house, but I'm sure we're going to have more questions."

The Lorings gave a mute nod before moving to join their children.

Nuala and Téya huddled by Houston's workstation. "That was interesting," Nuala said.

"Right?" Téya chewed her lower lip. "But it sure explains a lot."

Though she had her own ideas, Nuala wanted to hear what her friend was thinking. "Like?"

"Like why the man disappeared after Misrata. Like why I got the snot beat out of me in Denver." Téya's nostrils flared. "And why The Turk was there in Paris. It wasn't an accident. He was after Ballenger, saw me, and then I became a soft target."

"Maybe not so soft," Nuala said. "But I have a question."

Téya eyed her.

"Why aren't the Lorings acting like parents?"

"What?"

Nuala stole a peek at the family, noting that once again the Lorings were sitting apart from the children and talking in hushed tones. "For two people who are supposed to be very loving, why don't they touch?"

Téya frowned. "Not everyone is a softie like you."

The words stung, but Nuala buried it, as she always did. "They just don't seem keyed into each other. They seem. . .separate."

"They've been through a lot. Maybe that's what you're seeing."

Nuala gave a halfhearted, one-shouldered shrug. "Maybe." She hated thinking the worst of people, and it was true. The Lorings had been through a lot, having endured Misrata years ago. "They've been hiding all this time?" Her gaze struck the children. That didn't make sense.

Téya nodded, a frown creeping into her tawny features. "What now?"

The tone, the expression, even her stance bespoke Téya's irritation. Téya wanted her to let it go. And she would. "Nothing." But . . .

Boone sprinted through the warehouse, his face pale.

Heart in her throat, Nuala rushed after him. "What's wrong?"

But he said nothing, only sprinted out and up the darkened steps out of the bunker. Nuala turned, searching for an answer.

"Houston," Téya barked as she stalked toward him. "What happened?"

The geek lowered his head, his mouth set in a grim line. "The hospital called. Something's wrong. Keeley's vitals are all dropping. Her organs are shutting down."

Nuala felt a bitter, metallic taste in her mouth. "But. . .but she was better." This couldn't happen. It'd shatter Boone. "They were just waiting for her to wake up."

"And now," Houston said softly, gently, "she may never wake up."

Trace
Fort Belvoir, Virginia
4 June – 0945 Hours

"I gotta tell you—it looks bad, Trace." General Haym Solomon clicked a pen and set it on the desk in front of him. The pen doubled as a jamming device to block the inevitable listening devices that picked up chatter. They'd have a few minutes before it clicked off and their conversation would resume being recorded.

"When doesn't it look bad?" Trace lowered himself into the seat across the desk from General Solomon. There were few days Trace felt more choked and awkward than in his uniform, but today—coming here, addressing the topic at hand—he was sure the collar had taken the form of a noose. "And just when progress is on the other side of the door."

Solomon's salt-and-pepper eyebrows rose, creasing his forehead. "The Lorings?"

Trace nodded. "We have them. And while they don't have a full road map, they've given us a pretty decent tip."

Solomon's bushy eyebrows rose again, this time in impatient expectation.

"The wife says Ballenger is the one who sent the orphans and staff to the warehouse that night."

"Ballenger?" Haym pushed back in his chair and rubbed his lower lip. "How would he know anything? He was supposed to be a cradle-robbing loser."

"The cradle was robbed," Trace said with no hint of the humor his words begged. "But I think we need to talk to Ballenger again."

"Agreed," Haym said.

"I've got Houston hunting him down. After what happened in Paris, it might be tricky getting him to talk to us again."

"Speaking of Paris—what about Two?"

Trace gave a hefty sigh. He knew this would come up. "We've had a complication there, too."

"You do know you're supposed to avoid complications, right?" The wry smile on Haym's face did nothing to appease the guilt and frustration Trace felt.

"When she was in Athens, she got ganged up on in the slums.

Someone burned The Turk's mark into her hand. Then she shot him in an alley—"

"Shot *The Turk?*"

Trace stilled, measuring the general's response to that statement, then gave a slow nod. "She didn't realize who he was when she pulled the trigger. She'd been trying to protect a boy she believed had information on the Lorings' location."

"Is he dead?"

Trace snorted. "You forgot the part where things are complicated."

"So, he's alive. And he knows she shot him?"

"And that she sewed him up and put him back on his feet."

Haym's expression went from wide-eyed disbelief to scowling fury. "You realize—"

"Fully. She and I will be having a long talk. The only good thing that came out of her foolishness was that The Turk sent the Lorings to her."

Haym muttered something, shaking his head. "We do *not* need to owe that cold-blooded assassin anything."

"Agreed. I'm hoping that Téya's moment of weakness in having compassion on that murderer will even the score, that The Turk will call it even and walk away."

With a loud, long guffaw, Haym held a hand over his chest. "You aren't that naive, Trace."

"No, sir, but I'm feeling that desperate."

Thumbing away moisture from the corner of his eye, Haym shook his head. "All right. Back to the hearing."

Trace nodded. There wasn't much else to say or do. He was at the mercy of those who held more power than they should and made more money in one month wearing silk suits and ties than he made in a year running operations in the desert. When those suits got raises, he and his men went without a warm breakfast.

"I'm going to tell you something you won't like."

Again, Trace nodded. Waited.

Solomon's gaze moved to the wall of bookcases where a framed print—*Is that new?* Trace hadn't seen that before—smiled back. Make that, two dark-haired beauties smiled back. One, clearly older, the other— *Francesca Solomon?* Trace frowned. She had her hair down and makeup expertly applied. They both did. But Trace's mind snagged on the younger woman. Francesca. She could easily be a model or actress. But. . .where was *that* Francesca Solomon, the softer one, the one with a warm smile and rare beauty? He'd only met the hard-as-nails one, the one who wore her hair tied back and skipped the makeup. The one who had steel in place of the Italian femininity evident in the picture.

"Hard to believe she's mine sometimes—like that picture. Taken at my niece's wedding. Frankie and her mother looked like angels. I was the luckiest man on earth that day." He sighed.

Trace shifted uncomfortably. The general's daughter might be able to dress up and play pretty, but she couldn't fool him into believing she was anything other than a demon in disguise.

All that aside, what was the general's point?

"I think Frankie's behind this."

"Sir?"

Haym slid something across the desk.

Trace lifted it and opened the file. A dialogue transcript. He scanned it and asked, "What is it?"

"Surveillance transcript of a meeting between Francesca and a man named Elijah Varden." Trace heard the sneer in the general's voice as he scanned the document. "He's a major, serving under—"

"Marlowe." Trace's gaze stuck to the name at the bottom.

"Afraid so."

Slapping the folder shut and tossing it on the desk did nothing to appease the burn in Trace's chest. "It'd be too much to ask them to stand down and let me get this solved, wouldn't it?"

"They'd blow you off, say you've had the last five years."

"What about when they learn of the deaths?"

"You mean the Three, Four, and Five?"

Who else would he mean? "Five's not dead."

"Honestly," Haym said, "I don't think it will matter to them. In fact, they may try to blame you for their deaths."

Figured as much.

"And Frankie knows you've been to Vegas, not to mention Marlowe and Perrault both know you were in Alaska for the TALOS demonstration."

"Which is when I found out about the hits." And rushed to save them. "You know, I'm tired of this fight. Maybe it's better if I step aside and they put a full task force on this."

"Trace," Haym said, his words filled with sympathy as well as chastisement. "You know they're just looking for a fall guy. Pin the blame on you and they can wash their hands, tell the public Misrata finally has justice."

Click!

"Justice," Trace spat, his gaze flicking to the pen and realizing the conversation was now recording. "They wouldn't know the meaning."

"Easy. I know you're mad—"

"You really don't have the first clue what I'm feeling. No disrespect, sir, but someone up that chain of command gave you the order to have me select, train, and deploy Zulu. Now my mission entails protection against the very people who gave those orders, to find out who sabotaged us, who wanted those girls dead or arrested. It didn't make sense then and it doesn't now. And I'm certainly not giving up, not when this person has now stepped into the arena of premeditated murder."

"You've been ordered to stand down. Your clearances are being revoked, pending this investigation." General Solomon reached to the side and lifted a small paperweight and set it in front of him.

Trace recognized the resin piece with the inlaid gold-embossed gryphon. They both had one, a symbol of the ultrasecretive team they'd put together: Zulu. And with that gesture the general had just given, Trace mulled the last few words. Was that the general's way of saying one thing but feeling another?

Defiance and rebellion had never been his SOP, but they were imperative now, and that's exactly what the general inferred in his doublespeak. "So I hear."

"You understand, Trace, that I can't help you. If I—"

"Understood, sir."

"Being vague with the committee will only cost you time."

"Yes, sir."

General Solomon huffed. "You've gone stiff on me, son."

"Protocol, sir." Tensing his jaw helped him sound angry and agitated, the way he believed the general wanted. "I'm here at your request regarding an investigation. You've informed me I'm stripped of my duties and security pending the outcome. What is there to talk about, sir?" Tension coiled in his gut, ready to erupt.

"I'm not your enemy, Trace. I'm just—"

"Doing your job, sir." Trace stood. "You've made yourself clear, sir. Thank you for taking the time to refresh my memory."

Solomon tapped the gryphon paperweight twice.

Trace nodded. He understood. All too well. The general was in a position to lose a lot if things went south, but he also wasn't a coward who'd hide under his desk until the storm blew over. That double tap on the gryphon was all the encouragement Trace needed to keep moving forward with their investigation.

Boone
Reston Hospital, Virginia
4 June – 1045 Hours

Boone sprinted from the parking lot into the hospital. He punched the button for the elevator and shoved back, watching the light. "C'mon, c'mon," he muttered. His pulse hadn't slowed since Rusty's call an hour ago. Stupid traffic coming down Route 7 killed his timing. That and the cop who pulled him over.

With a *ding*, the elevator door slid open.

Boone threw himself forward—and skidded to a stop. An elderly woman shuffled forward. He slapped out a hand to keep the door open and secretly wanted to lift the woman and place her outside. Would've been faster.

"Thank you," the woman said in a shaky, frail voice.

Hitting the third-floor button, he stepped back. Clasped his hands. Glanced at the numbers above the door. Then to the still-open door. *Why isn't it closing already?*

Finally, it slid shut. And the elevator slowly lifted.

Should've taken the stairs.

The lift alighted and the door took its time opening again. Boone shoved himself through the space as soon as he'd fit. Free of the box and its confinements, he jogged to the end of the hall.

Rusty stood outside, arms folded, pinching his lips as he stared through the wire-beveled glass.

"Rus," Boone gruffed as he approached.

Off the wall, Rusty gave him an "I'm really sorry" expression.

"What's happening?"

Rusty jutted his jaw in the direction of the room. A half-dozen doctors and medical staff were crowded around. An annoying noise rattled across Boone's hearing, but he was focused on Keeley's form. Almost as frail as the old woman from the elevator.

"They're not sure," Rusty said. "She's been flatlining on and off for the last thirty minutes."

"Why?" Boone growled. "She was almost ready to come home."

"They're running tests. Checking for an internal bleed or injury they missed. . ." Rusty folded his arms. "I'm sorry, man."

"Not your fault," Boone muttered as he moved to the window. He planted his hands on the blue-painted steel frame. His breath, warm against the cool glass, bloomed in a fog.

Too many scrubs-covered bodies blocked his view. He leaned to the side, trying to see around them, but it was no good. Boone pushed off and went to the door.

A doctor stepped out, a hand going to Boone's chest.

Though everything in him wanted to take that hand and secure it behind the doc's shoulder blade, Boone restrained himself. "What's wrong? What happened to her?"

"Mr. Ramage, that's what we're working to figure out." He pointed with a clipboard to a corner of the hall then walked that way. Once they were out of traffic and earshot of the others in the corridor, the doctor sighed.

"She was fine. You told me she would be waking up any day. I'm gone for four days, and I get a call that she's on the verge of death. *What* happened?" Boone demanded, glancing to the room as another nurse exited. As the door slid shut, two nurses moved in opposite directions, and for a split second Boone saw Keeley.

Or rather, a ghost of Keeley. A strange tinge colored her face and made her look drawn. Aged. Her lips were almost blue.

"Look, I. . ." The doctor scrubbed the back of his head.

"What aren't you telling me? You have a theory, don't you?"

Again, the doc sighed. "I don't. I wish I did, because then we could attempt to be proactive, but. . .I'm confounded. It makes no sense."

Eyes on where Keeley's toes pushed up the blanket, Boone willed her not to leave him. "I just don't understand how we went from 'she's coming home soon' to 'she's on the brink of death.'"

"I don't either," the doc admitted. "Excuse me. I need to study the labs again, compare them to new labs. I'll keep you posted."

After the doctor and most of the staff left, Keeley's heart rate and blood pressure moderately stabilized, Boone slipped into the room. He went to her side and took her hand, cringing at the tubing that snaked down her throat and the thinner tubes anchored into the top of her hand.

"Keeley," he whispered, lifting her hand gently to his lips and kissing the spot by her thumb where the IV didn't interfere. "Please come on, baby. Don't do this to me. Don't leave me." His throat felt raw and thick. "I need you."

Annie
Lucketts, Virginia
4 June – 1315 Hours

What was wrong with her? The one man she'd wanted a relationship with was here, waiting on her. Right outside the showers in the lounge. Waiting to talk. Waiting to pick up where they'd left off. Sam was everything she wanted in a guy—kind, romantic, tenacious, handsome, honest, full of integrity. And he liked her. A lot, obviously, considering all he'd done to find her.

I should be flattered.

Showered, dressed, and sitting on the floor, she hugged her knees to her chest. Rested her head against the tiled wall and willed herself to go out there. Face the music. Stop being ridiculous.

And yet here she sat.

Maybe it was Trace's fault. What he said, what he did—his touch against her jaw that she could still feel—reignited all the old feelings. Old promises. *Broken* promises. Promises she'd begged God for the first two years after Misrata to fulfill.

"Annie?" Téya's voice echoed in the room seconds before her leggy friend rounded the corner and stopped short. "Sam's waiting for you."

Annie nodded but didn't move.

Téya tossed her towel and change of clothes on the counter by one of the showers. "And why are we avoiding the hot-n-hunky Mr. SEAL?" She crossed her legs at the ankle and sat. "What am I missing?"

"The same thing I am, apparently." Annie sighed and peeled herself off the wall.

"What's wrong?"

"He doesn't belong here."

"Do any of us?"

"We do—you and I. Trace and Boone, Noodle. But not Sam," Annie said, her words cracking on raw emotion. "This, what we're going through, what we've done, what happened in Misrata—it's a nightmare. Half our team is dead or dying, and I don't want Sam to end up like that."

Téya considered her.

Annie slumped back against the wall. She knew those words were more like the wrapper on a burger and not the meat itself. "What?"

"Well," Téya said as she pushed to her feet. "If David walked in here right now, I sure wouldn't be moping in the shower. *Especially* knowing what we're facing, what's out there trying to kill us. I'd be all over him— well, not *literally*—to make sure we had every moment we could get."

"Would you? Really?" Annie felt worse. Guiltier. "But it'd put David in danger."

"Girl, please." Téya went to the shower and twisted the knobs. "You are so not getting that over on me. That hunk out there is a SEAL, Annie. He knows how to handle himself. So, I know that's not the problem behind you hiding in here. No." She wagged her fingers at Annie, motioning her to get off the floor. "Stand and tell the truth."

"That is the truth." Annie stood.

"No." Téya folded her arms. "That's what you're telling yourself so you don't have to face the truth."

"Yeah, and what truth is that?"

"Your feelings for Trace are still too strong. And you can't decide between the two." Téya smiled, took hold of Annie's shoulders, then aimed her toward the lounge. "To be honest, I'm not sure who I'd pick either. But staying in here is only going to make that hair of yours frizzy."

A shove pushed Annie into the open.

Sam looked up, his eyes widening for a fraction of a second. He started to push to his feet then slowly finished the movement. And man! Téya was right—Sam was a hunk. Wearing a navy T-shirt and a faded pair of jeans only made him look more *GQ*. "Still hate me?" His rich baritone voice still smoothed her tension and made her relax.

"I don't hate you." Annie sagged as she released her frustration. "I just. . ."

"You don't want me here."

She sighed and closed the distance between them. Easing onto the sofa, she tucked a foot beneath her as she sat. "It's dangerous, Sam."

He smirked, angling his torso toward her. "You do realize I've run plenty of combat operations. I've shot people and been shot, Annie."

Her heart spasmed, hearing him use her real name. Guilt tugged at her. "That's weird. . ."

"It is for me, too. But I'm in. Whatever it takes."

And that frustrated her. Why, she couldn't explain because she didn't know. He was nice. *Too nice.* Too understanding.

"What's wrong?" Sam asked.

Annie gave a halfhearted shake of her head.

"I feel like I've lost you again."

She sighed. "Sam—" she met his gaze and felt the walls around her heart stagger, so she looked down "—things are really messed up right now. There's so much you don't know—"

"Then tell me."

"I can't." This time, she saw disbelief and hurt in his chocolate eyes.

"Annie, I'm here. I've been on a mission with you and your team. I've seen them."

"But you don't know—" She snapped her mouth shut. What would he think when he found out she'd been the team leader responsible for the deaths of twenty-two innocent lives? Would his resolute belief in her waiver? She believed it would. Sam was too good a person to accept something so heinous. "Sam, it's so complicated. So dangerous for you to know, even though you're here. Even though *we* are here, there are men still trying to kill us. Men resolved to make sure we stay out of the way or silent."

"Fill me in. I've got the clearance level, Annie. I'm here. I'm not going anywhere. I fought to find out, and I'm not just walking away."

"Sam, you don't belong here." Something about his resolution to stay involved made her feel like a heavy blanket had been thrown over her face. Breathing grew harder.

"I belong with you."

Annie met his gaze. Yes, she wanted that. Believed that. But with her, not with her *here*.

Sam touched her face, and she leaned into the warmth of his caress, closing her eyes. He tugged her closer, and she let her temple rest against his shoulder. "Why does it scare you that I'm here, Annie?"

Eyes closed, she thought about how to answer that. Truth was, she didn't know. Was it as simple as not wanting him to get hurt? Yes, a big part—she'd killed twenty-two people. She didn't want to make it twenty-three.

But Sam was a SEAL. He knew how to fight. Knew how to operate.

But if he saw *her operate*. . .what would he think? When he found out she'd killed children and women. . .? "I don't know," she whispered.

He held her close, his chin resting atop her head. "Take your time figuring it out. I'm not going anywhere. Weston has made that clear."

Annie lifted her head. Met his gaze. Their noses almost touched, and she could feel his breath fanning across her cheek.

He homed in on her mouth.

Her heart hammered. But instead of kissing him, she pulled back. Then hated herself because she saw the hurt in his eyes again. "Sorry," she whispered. Telling herself she should just kiss him now, let him know she still liked him. Still wanted to figure things out. "I—"

"Annie!"

Her breath backed into her throat. She turned just as Trace stalked past the oddly angled walls that provided a bit of privacy in the lounge. His expression went from stern to anger in a heartbeat. He and Sam shared a long, hateful look.

Annie stood, intentionally blocking their glare-off. "What's wrong?"

"Need you and Téya out here."

Sam had come to his feet now, standing behind her possessively. And she couldn't deny the jealous rage that spread through Trace's face did her wounded heart a lot of good. But she didn't want them at odds just for her thirst for revenge against Trace. She didn't have a thirst for vengeance, truth be told.

"I'll let her know," she said, then turned to Sam and slid her hand along his arm until she clasped his fingers. "We can finish this later."

Sam nodded.

Annie toyed with giving him a quick kiss, but they hadn't really moved to that level. Or past the obvious rift between them. She squeezed his fingers then went to the showers.

"Give her room and time to figure this out." Trace didn't sound confrontational with that warning to Sam, but Annie knew better. She also knew what Sam would say.

"You mean, give her room so you can step back in."

Yeah. *About like that.* . . She hated the tension between them, but she lingered within earshot to hear what Trace would say.

"What Annie and I had ended five years ago."

Trace's words were like a hot branding iron through her heart, searing any hope she had that they'd get back together. And that was it. That was why she didn't want Sam here. She *hadn't* given up on Trace. Even though he'd ripped her heart out. And now. . .he'd done it again.

"So there was a 'you and her' then?"

Sam sounded furious but also enjoyed getting the dig in.

"If you know anything about her, you'd be smart to bury that and give her the room she needs. Annie can't be forced to do anything she doesn't want to do. And if you try, you'll only tick her off."

Trace
Pentagon, Arlington County, Virginia
5 June – 0910 Hours

Not only had he lost her, but he'd lost her to a squid. For two minutes on the plane, he'd imagined she might actually let him back into her life, forgive him for what he'd done. Being that close to her, smelling that lavender body wash she'd used years ago, he'd nearly given in to those desires. Nearly kissed her.

Call him crazy, but he was pretty sure she would've let him.

Then the SEAL came around the corner.

Trace tucked his cover in his right leg pocket and strode down the hall of the Pentagon with General Solomon to the office of the Army's service chief, General Barry Cantor. They stepped into the office area and were met by a young lieutenant seated behind a desk. His name patch read HOLLINGS.

"Morning," Solomon said. "We have an appointment with Barry."

"Yes, sir," Hollings responded as he stood. "He's waiting, sirs." He led them down a short hall and past three additional doors to one that had the black name plate with CANTOR stamped in white. After two firm raps, he pushed into the room.

"General Solomon and Lieutenant Colonel Weston are here, sir."

"Good, good." Cantor came around his massive desk and crossed the office. "Come in, Haym." The two greeted each other like long-lost brothers with a firm handshake that pulled into a back-slapping fest. "How's Vivienne doing since her surgery?"

"Oh, that was six months ago. She's fine."

"And that beautiful daughter of yours? How's she? Found a good Ranger or Green Beret to run off with?" Cantor's eyes crinkled in a deep smile as he turned to Trace. "You didn't steal her away from him, did you?"

Heat rushed up past the tan shirt collar and up his neck. "No, sir." Francesca would rather gut him than date him. And the feeling was mutual.

Cantor slapped his shoulder. "Oh, don't be embarrassed to admit you noticed how beautiful she is—in fact, Hollings out there has been trying to get her phone number since he met her at the Christmas gala."

"I'm not sure Francesca would date Army," Haym said. "Seems quite determined to do everything opposite me."

"At least she's in the military like her brothers, eh?" Cantor pointed them to where a black leather sofa and two chairs sat huddled in a conversation area. He offered coffee and water, and when they refused, he steered them right into the reason for the meeting. "How are those boys?"

"Grown fighters," Haym said, his words drenched with the pride that drew up his shoulders. "However, I think you know more about Paolo than I do, I believe."

Appreciation for the words colored Cantor's face. "Imagine that's right," he said with a laugh.

Trace might not be privy to the facts of these men's lives, but he could read between the lines as well as the best. Clearly, Haym's eldest son had gone into an intelligence-related field that put him under the direction of Cantor. The knowledge made Trace a little more ill at ease. He had Haym on his side, but the man's daughter enjoyed breathing fire down his neck. Would the eldest son do the same?

"So, she might not be trying to date you, but it seems our dear

Francesca is trying to slice open your old wounds."

Trace blinked, the general's ability to switch topics so fast it left a soldier with whiplash no less sharp today as they sat here. He cleared his throat. "Apparently, sir." A quick look to Haym told Trace there were no ill feelings.

"Well, I'll tell you—Marlowe is out for blood."

Trace nodded.

"Namely, yours."

Another nod. "Yes, sir. I believe he's been after it for the last five years."

"What about the girls?"

Trace hesitated, wishing now he'd accepted the offer for a glass of water. He didn't talk openly about Zulu.

"I have reports the one in the hospital isn't doing well."

Something about this man having such credible, up-to-date information unsettled Trace.

"And The Turk!" He guffawed. "Heavens have mercy—how on earth are you getting so tangled up in everything?"

Trace shifted on the leather chair. Wasn't this meeting to discuss the investigation? To prep Trace for what was to come? To warn him to keep his lips tight and his information tighter?

"And what about that SEAL you had to wrangle into submission?" the general asked, snickering. "I would've paid money to see that go down."

"Holding his own, sir." Irritation clawed its way up Trace's spine and kept him from looking the general in the eye and giving away his anger.

"And you?"

Trace snapped his gaze to the general. "Sir?"

"How are you holding up? It's been one brutal mess."

"It has, sir."

"You have no family?"

"Parents in an assisted living home." Even if he'd told them, they'd never remember if he existed outside their confusion-trapped minds. "My sister makes sure they're taken care of. My younger brother is in the military."

"But what about a love life? A dog? Best friend?"

Trace frowned. Looked at Solomon then back to the Army service chief. "Sir, I'm not sure that's relevant."

"Of course it is," Cantor barked, his amusement and lighthearted banter gone. "You just told me you have no family connections. Psychologist will tell the counsel that means you're disconnected and have trouble forming healthy relationships. That information will turn you into a soldier with a thirst for blood to avenge the bad upbringing you had."

"I didn't have a bad upbringing," Trace snarled.

"And your inability to form bonds also affects your leadership of the ultrasecret black ops team named Zulu."

Anger rising, Trace fought the tug of those demons. What was this? A trap?

"Tell me, Colonel Weston, when was the last time you were with a woman?"

Fury colored his world red. He punched to his feet. "That's none of your concern."

"Of course it is. I need to know her name so I can talk to her, determine what kind of relationship you had. Determine how it ended—assuming it did end." His gaze lingered on Trace, then he snorted. "Good. You don't need to be dating right now anyway."

Heart crashing into his ribs, Trace fought to maintain his hold on the ultrathin line of control.

"Do you make it a habit to be involved with women, potentially compromising the safety of classified information you've been trusted with? How many women have you slept with, Colonel?"

"If it were any of your business, I'd tell you I hold marriage sacred, and when I utter those vows before God, it will be for one woman for the rest of my life."

"God." His hazel eyes flashed. "So, you're a religious zealot." Cantor hadn't slowed down. "You do realize that the military and government classify religious zealots as domestic terrorists."

Trace cursed.

Cantor rose and met his gaze, steel to steel, his expression fierce. "Sit down, Mister Weston."

Trace couldn't move. Didn't trust himself to move.

"You need to realize, Trace, that Marlowe is going to throw everything at you that he can. He'll play dumb, play nice, then he'll rip your heart out." He pointed to the chair. "Sit down. Let me tell you what you've already revealed to me."

He didn't dare ball his fists in front of the Army service chief, but every muscle in Trace trembled with rage. Slowly, gaze still on Cantor, he lowered himself to the seat again.

"You've just told me that you are alone. That you have nobody you go to for counsel. That your relationship with a woman ended poorly, and that your anger is easily aroused. All points the counsel will use against you in determining whether your duties and your job should be returned to you."

Trace said nothing. Did nothing. He remained frozen, convinced one wrong breath would detonate the rage within him.

"You're heading into a maelstrom, Trace," Cantor said, his voice more friendly, less accusatory.

"That's been my life the last five years."

"No," Cantor said. "You've been at the eye of this storm for the last five years. You're about to feel the full intensity."

"Good to know, sir." Trace gritted his teeth, maintaining a civil tongue almost impossible.

Cantor's left eye squinted as he looked at him. "Trace, you should know something."

He waited.

"I'm not your enemy."

"Forgive me, sir, but if this is friendly conversation—"

"Consider it friendly fire, iron sharpening iron."

Trace lifted his chin. He reserved phrases like that for friends. "Why would I do that, sir?"

"Because I'm the one who tapped you to assemble Zulu."

Nuala

Lucketts, Virginia

5 June – 1140 Hours

It hurt Nuala's heart to see Boone in such misery. And it killed her to know that he was in such shape because the woman he loved—which wasn't her—lay in a hospital mysteriously failing. Of course, that made her feel worse because she shouldn't begrudge him. He had no idea how she felt. She'd never given him any indication that he held the moon and stars in her world. Even if she had, he would've rejected her. Nuala King wasn't the type of girl guys fell in love with.

Now, Annie. . .and Téya . . .and Keeley. . .yeah. Guys tripped over themselves trying to get a date with them. But Noodle? The nickname alone told her what they thought of her.

But Boone. Like Rock of Gibraltar. Impenetrable. Solid. That he had enough muscle to make up two humans meant little to her.

Oh, who was she kidding? He was as physically attractive as he was kind. As bulked up as he was compassionate. Which is why it hurt all the more to see him in pain like this.

She poured a cup of coffee, added cream—oops. Not too much. Nuala carried it over to the workstations where Boone sat in a chair, staring at the computer. Which she knew from the blank look on his face either wasn't on or he wasn't paying attention. "Here," she said softly as she set the mug before him.

Boone glanced down at it but seemed as if he didn't see it. Then shifted. "Did I ask for that?"

Heat crept into her cheeks, but not enough—she hoped—to make the blush evident. "No, you looked like you needed it."

Boone's gray eyes came to hers, a shade of disbelief coloring them. "Thanks, Noodle."

Would he call her anything else but that stupid name? Something with respect? Something with meaning? But she had no meaning to him, other than being a member of Zulu. And a top sniper.

They had that in common. And she loved to talk shop with him. Really, she'd talk about anything with him. *Am I pathetic?*

"Wow, I sure would love someone to bring me coffee without having to ask," Téya murmured loudly from the dais, where she sat studying the wall. "Must be nice, Boone."

Again, his mind seemed jogged back to the present. "Maybe you should try being nice to someone," he said, almost not missing a beat. But then he glanced at Nuala and lifted the cup and nodded. "Thanks."

She smiled.

"You think you're nice to Nuala?"

Oh no. This wouldn't end well. Nuala knew where this was going. And suddenly knew what Téya was up to. She swept across the room and stood over her friend, glaring deliberately at her, warning her to stop.

Téya, unrepentant as always, just shrugged. "I'm just saying—he should be more grateful."

Okay, time to clear out before this got really embarrassing. Nuala headed for the bunk room. Maybe she'd journal. Work on a scene in her space opera. Pluck out her fingernails. Anything less painful than being humiliated by Téya, who had somehow figured out Nuala's feelings for Boone.

Hushed, harsh whispers skated out of the corner bunk room, slowing Nuala. Holding the swirl necklace her mother had given her as a teen, she stood outside the room she shared with Téya, listening.

The whispers continued, stiff and hurried. The Lorings were in there, their children visible on the lower bunk and napping. How'd they get older children like that to nap during the daytime? When Nuala had been that age, she wanted to be with the adults. Didn't want to miss anything.

"No. . .you don't. . ."

The broken pieces didn't make sense. What was going on? They sounded pretty upset. With each other? Or with the team?

"...they'll know."

"...no choice."

"...keep doing this...what if..."

"...figure it out."

Nuala edged closer, putting her stealth sniper skills to use, but even with her straining to hear, she couldn't make out the conversation. What she wouldn't do for her long-range microphone. Or a well-placed listening device.

Footsteps came toward her from their room.

Hurrying into her room, Nuala forced her heart to slow. Bring her breathing under control.

"Hey."

Nuala pivoted, surprised to find Annie on the upper bunk. "Oh. I didn't know you were there."

Annie wrinkled a brow. "You okay?"

"Sure. Yeah." She shrugged.

"You're a bad liar."

Should she tell Annie? Téya hadn't believed her. Why would Annie?

Because Annie had a stronger balance in terms of weighing pros and cons. She didn't go on gut reaction alone the way Téya often did.

Nuala wanted affirmation that she was as vital to the team as the others. That her assessments were just as valid. She had to make judgment calls in the field with a sniper rifle pressed to her shoulder. They trusted her to do that. Why not listen to her now? "I just—"

"Oh, hey. Glad you are in here," Sharlene Loring said as she stepped into the room, freezing Nuala's words in her mouth.

Annie sat up. "Need something?"

"Carl and I were talking."

Arguing was more like it.

"It's probably nothing," came Carl's voice from the hall.

Annie and Sharlene moved out there. In order to keep up with the conversation, Nuala had to follow them.

The Lorings wrapped their arms around each other. Carl pressed a kiss to Sharlene's temple. And though Nuala wasn't sure, she thought she saw a grimace. A split-second tweak of Sharlene's lips. But their arms were around each other.

"We both think that there is a connection between Giles Stoffel and Titus Batsakis that cannot be overlooked," Carl said firmly.

"We pretty much figured that out," came Trace's deep, firm voice as they all gathered by the computer stations. "Stoffel's sister married Titus Batsakis."

"That's not illegal," Téya mumbled. When everyone looked at her, Téya shrugged. "What? It's not!"

"Not to disappoint you," Trace said, arms folded over his chest as he leaned against the tables, "but Annie and I got into the bank. Houston went through their systems and found nothing out of the ordinary."

"So, you think they're innocent?" Sharlene said, her voice pitching.

"No way," Annie said. "They kidnapped me. We know they're dirty, but we have no way to prove it."

"We might," Carl said, looking at his wife in a sickeningly adoring fashion. "We believe they keep their secrets on their yacht."

Trace straightened. "Yacht?"

"*Aegean Mercy,*" Sharlene said. "Named after—"

"Mercy Chandler," Annie put in. "Stoffel's wife."

Sam

Lukewarm. Jesus threatened to spew those who were lukewarm out of his mouth, but Sam couldn't quite bring himself to that point regarding Annie. She hadn't been nearly as warm with him as she had been that night on the deck. Then again, Trace Weston hadn't been there.

Was the guy as tripped up on power and as dangerous as Francesca Solomon had said? Sam hadn't seen proof of that, even if his own jealous streak over the way the guy looked at Annie bordered on ballistic. They had history.

"A yacht," Trace muttered again. "That's tricky."

Sam edged into the room, listening. Yacht meant water. He was trained on water. Would they let him run another op? Would that prove to Annie that he could hold his own? Crazy how she felt the need to protect him when he'd vowed back in Manson to do that very thing for her. If it hadn't been so ridiculous, he might be offended that she tried to do that.

"Houston," Boone asked from the station. "What've you got on that boat?"

"Almost got it," Houston muttered, his fingers working quickly. "Okay—it left port. . .ha! Left port the night of Annie's escape."

"Running."

When the eyes in the room turned to Sam, he realized he'd said that out loud.

Trace nodded. "Agreed."

"Makes it more challenging to get on board," Boone said.

Sam grinned. "Not for me."

The team commander's green eyes held his. For a long time. Silence chilled the room.

"No," Annie finally said, moving not to Sam but to Trace. "You can't do this. We can't ask Sam to do this."

He scowled. "Nobody asked me." Had to admit, she'd dented his pride with a sledgehammer this time. "I volunteered." He met Trace's assessing gaze. "You know this makes sense."

"Can you get on board with it moving?"

Not without killing myself. "Yes."

"And without being seen?"

If I have an invisibility cloak. "Yes."

Trace just stared.

Sam took the leap. "When do I leave?"

Sam
Mediterranean Sea
7 June – 0120 Hours

Sam stretched out on the roof of the ultrafast patrol boat beside Annie's friend with the weird name. It was easier for him to call her Noodle, but somehow, that felt a bit insulting. She had a sniper rifle snug against her and long-range binoculars pressed to her eyes.

"What've you got?" Sam asked quietly, waiting for his turn.

She handed over the nocs. "Two armed guards walking the boat. Four passengers inside—the Stoffels and Batsakis plus one."

Sam verified what she reported with his own assessment. He lowered the binoculars and stared out with his bare eyes, unable to see anything but the glint of moonlight off the dark sea. "You can take out the patrols."

"Can but won't," she said, her voice sweet, soft, and confident.

Sam glanced at her.

She met his gaze, looked away, then jerked her gaze back. "If I hit him from this distance, there won't be much left of his chest or head. If I do that, they'll know it was long-range, and every boat in the area will be searched."

Sam nodded. "Good, good."

"What?"

"Thinking it through." He sighed, his mind whiplashing back to two nights ago when he volunteered for this gig. "How many were on your team?"

Nuala glanced down. "You know I can't answer that."

"Can you answer why Ashland hates me?"

"Oh, she doesn't hate you," Nuala said. "In fact, I'd just about say she loved you with the way she doesn't want you out here."

"That makes no sense. Explain that to me."

Nuala smiled. "You have a lot to learn about women."

"Apparently." He borrowed the nocs again and stared at the yacht he'd board in the next hour. "She makes out with me like a fiend one night, then the next time we see each other, I'd swear she'd rather kill me."

"She doesn't want to kill you," Nuala said softly. "She wants you alive."

Sam considered her with a sigh. "I'm going to guess something really bad went down with your team."

Her wide, pale eyes came to his. "Why would you say that?"

"Because both of you said the same thing. That tells me there's probably a pretty significant loss that occurred for her to think she has to protect a Navy SEAL and for you to believe that's what she's doing."

The roof of the wheelhouse banged, his signal from Leo that they were in position and ready. Sam clambered down and paused at the rail, watching the waves that churned beneath the ultrafast patrol boat, but his mind was on the mission. Getting on board the yacht without being detected. Retrieving the necessary information. Returning to the dive prop, which would get him back to the boat and Annie.

She hadn't spoken much to him since he ignored her protests regarding his doing this. What would it take to convince her this was what he did, that she didn't need to protect him, that he'd do this and more just for her? Just to convince her of his feelings for her.

He glanced at the gear he'd already prepped and checked. The vest, the regulator, the tank valve, the air pressure. All good. Any number of things could go wrong with a water insertion, but this is what he knew better than anything.

Two men, associates of his Navy buddy who owned this boat, emerged from the wheelhouse. Leo, the older, balding diver, nodded. "Harry said it's time."

Fins on, Sam shouldered into the vest, hoisting the tank onto his back. Leo double-checked his weight belt for right-hand release, tangles, and trapped equipment, as Sam verified the coms device strapped to his arm. He'd relay information through that to the team during the mission.

Leo patted his shoulder, giving Sam the okay. Strapped to his leg, his gun would provide an extra layer of assurance should he get into trouble. Sitting on the side of the boat, Sam reached for his mask.

Annie's white-blond hair anchored his attention to where she stood.

The interior lights of the wheelhouse behind her haloed around her curls. They needed to have a talk. About this whole mess. About them. About the future.

But did she even want that?

Arms wrapped around her midsection, she eased away from the safety of that lit area and stepped into his darkness. A kiss for good luck? Is that what she was coming to do?

"You don't have to prove anything," she said softly—but loud enough to be heard over the ripping wind and the engine noise.

Sam gave a snort. "I'm not *proving* anything." He took hold of her waist, pulling her closer. "This is what I do. I'm a SEAL. I dive."

"You got out."

"I contract now. You know that."

"But this," she said, hesitating. "What you're involved in is crazy dangerous, Sam. Those people will kill you if they catch you."

He couldn't help the grin, squeezing the hold he had on her waist and tugging her closer. "Most enemies will."

She scowled at him.

"Annie, if you expected me to just be a doting house-husband, you picked the wrong guy."

"I never expected—that's not—" Her nostrils flared.

Sam smiled. "There's a lot of mystery surrounding your past, and if you aren't going to let me in, then I can't establish my place. Especially if you want me to be some weak-kneed—"

"I want you *alive*."

"What happened back then, Annie? What did this to you, made you terrified of caring about someone because they'll die?"

She visibly flinched and snapped her gaze down. "This is wrong. It's not your fight."

"Are you dive qualified?"

She pressed her lips together.

"Are either of your handlers dive qualified?"

She flared her nostrils again.

"And your team members?"

"Sam, this isn't fair."

"That's how I felt when you walked out of my life the night I kissed you."

"I had no choice."

"We always have a choice, Ash." He cringed. The nickname he'd grown fond of wasn't even really her name. "And my choice is to make this dive because it will help you."

"We *don't* know that. It's not clear-cut."

"Life doesn't have guarantees, I get that. But if this can cut the anchors from your life that have held you back, scared you from making good on what I see in your eyes when you look at me, then it's worth it."

"There's more at stake than whether I've slept with you."

Stunned, Sam winged up his eyebrows. "Never said anything of the sort."

Annie stepped back. "You shouldn't be doing this. It's our mess—my team's," she said. "I don't want you dying for a mistake we made."

That was interesting. "What mistake?"

Annie let her hand fall away. "*This*. Trace and Boone letting you do this." No. . .no, that wasn't the mistake she meant, but she'd covered her real intention with a well-placed lie. "You shouldn't be here."

"You want me to leave?" When she didn't say anything, Sam tensed. "You were okay with me being a SEAL back in Manson."

"Back in Manson, we were safe."

"Is that what you call that sniper?"

"Don't twist my words."

"You're doing a pretty good job of that yourself." Even as he sat there, powerless as she grew angrier with each word they spoke, Sam wondered if he'd made a mistake to find her.

"Time," Leo shouted from the door of the wheelhouse.

Eyes on Annie, who moved away from him, her expression livid, Sam slipped in his regulator then shoved over the back of the boat. He had to end that conversation because things were shifting southward fast. If they'd kept talking, Annie would've ended up mad. He would've been, too.

The water cocooned him and dragged him down. He righted himself and kicked back to the surface. Leo leaned over, setting the dive propulsion vehicle in the water. Sam gave a thumbs-up, indicating his gear was fine. After one more look to Annie—he saw her return to the wheelhouse—he caught the prop, released the tether, and rolled onto it. He aimed it downward, once more enveloped by the water. The Fusion dry suit not only kept him dry but eliminated unnecessary drag as he drove the two miles toward the yacht.

Annie and Boone would wait for him on the patrol boat with Leo and his crew. They'd monitor his position and progress but remain a safe distance away so they didn't alert or alarm the *Aegean Mercy*. As he closed in on the luxury ship, Sam tethered the prop to the underbelly, removed his regulator, then swam to the stern. Slow and with as much incredible stealth so he barely disturbed the water, Sam eased upward. He let his forehead break the surface only until he could see. On the water, even with the lights moderately dimmed, the ship seemed well lit. He eased up to the yacht's swim ladder and took hold. Awareness spread through him of being alone. Of not having his team, his SEAL brothers working in unison and synchronicity. One shooting, another catching the target before he hit the water or ground. Softening the landing.

Sam hauled himself up over the back and crouched. As he pushed himself upright, he heard the thump of the guard's boots. Sam shoved himself down, waiting. The guard came right past where he crouched, yawning, and started away.

Aiming, Sam sent a drugged dart into the guy's neck. The guard stumbled and Sam rushed up behind him, catching him before he could make a loud noise. He eased him to the deck and rushed on, toward the front, where he knew the other guard should be. Spine against the hull, he slid toward the bow. Peeked out. Spotted the guy sitting on a padded bench, smoking a cigarette.

Sam steadied his breathing and stepped out. Fired a dart straight into the guy's neck, just like the first one.

Only, the guard had lifted his hand. Accidentally deflected the dart.

Confusion bled into the man's face as he stared at the feathered tail sticking out of his hand. In a split second, he went from a frown to alarm. He punched to his feet with a strangled shout.

Sam fired another dart. And a third. But the man was punch-drunk on adrenaline now. The dart would take longer. Sam rushed him, knowing he had to silence him or the whole mission was shot.

Eyes wide, the man shoved away from Sam. Drew a weapon. Aimed. Seconds took on the weight of death.

Sam knew the guy would shoot him before he could.

Annie
Mediterranean Sea
7 June – 0220 Hours

"Do you have the shot?"

A golf ball–sized lump lodged in Annie's throat. She couldn't swallow. Couldn't breathe. Sam wore a shoulder-mounted camera so she and Boone could see in real time what was happening. Right now he was staring down the barrel of a weapon.

"I have joy," came Nuala's unnaturally calm voice.

"Take the shot."

Annie held her breath, her gaze tempting her to look to the roof where Nuala lay nested for high, unobstructed vision. *C'mon, c'mon.* Time felt anchored in death, waiting for the kill shot.

"Target down," Nuala said quietly even as Annie watched the guy tumble over the side of the boat.

She covered her mouth as Sam rushed to the rail.

"Copy," Boone said. "Moving to a safe distance."

The patrol boat eased away from the yacht so they wouldn't be seen but close enough to help Sam if trouble reared its ugly head again. Annie remained focused on Sam and what he was seeing.

"Houston, you reading us?"

"Loud and clear." Houston's voice came through as if he sat in the galley, not in a country across the Atlantic. "The feed is a bit grainy, but it'll do."

Most likely Trace, the Lorings, and Téya were watching via the live feed as well. Trace had opted out of going, saying he had commitments to take care of. What could be more important than the mission at hand? Than clearing Zulu's name? Truth was, Annie was mad at him. For not coming. For sending Sam. For confusing the tar out of her with that near kiss on the plane. What was she supposed to do with that?

She cared deeply for Sam. Had they been given the chance, she might've loved him—maybe. She didn't know.

Trace, on the other hand, she *had* loved. Maybe she still did. She didn't know.

That was just it—she didn't know what she felt. And having Sam in front of her only mangled things. Made it harder to sort out. She ached for that night on her deck overlooking Wapato Lake. Things were simple then. She was falling in love. He loved her back. For the first time in years, she felt like the sun had found her once more.

"He's in," Boone said.

Annie straightened, her mind whipping back to the present. To the black-and-white feed with Sam easing down a narrow hall on the yacht. They would maintain radio silence as much as possible while he was on board. That luxury boat had more technology and satellites spinning than they had at the bunker.

"Copy," Houston said. "I'm in the yacht's security system." Thanks to a transmitter Sam had on him. "Baby, what I wouldn't do for a ship like this. Then again, I'd go for a super-yacht—"

"Houston." Trace's impatience was evident.

Relief filled Annie as quiet once more fell over the mission. Strange, deafening silence. They couldn't hear anything Sam heard or did, but they could see it. Making his way down a narrow corridor—weren't they all narrow on a ship?—Sam moved decisively and stealthily. At a corner, he slowed, the camera seeming to hesitate on a dark-paneled wall. Then he went left. The angle swung around and Sam was in a small, tight room. The office. Which seemed more like a small walk-in closet than an office. But the wall of books and the glass desk verified the setting.

Hands gloved, Sam searched the desk. Ran his hands along the edges. Turned to the wall of shelves.

Annie's palms grew sweaty, thinking of how much time he was in there. The minutes falling off the clock, each one more opportunity for someone to wake up and discover him. What was taking him so long?

"There's no computer," Houston said, practically reading her mind.

No computer? That was the whole point of the mission, for him to install the USB that would upload Houston's program.

"He needs to find at least a laptop or get to the engine room."

"Engine room?"

"That ship has a lot of technology. Something has to be driving it. Maybe we can find something for him to plug into there."

"Okay, all quiet. I'm going to tell him,"Trace said. "Squid, Lighthouse."

"Copy," came Sam's deep but quiet voice. He moved to a wall and angled the camera around. "You see my problem?"

"Roger."

"Going below. Looking for portable device."

Annie glanced at Boone. "Portable?"

"Laptop."

"Negative,"Trace ordered. "Stay—"

But Sam was still moving out of the office and now headed for a set of stairs. "He's not listening," Annie muttered, her stress level skyrocketing. Stomach clenched, she covered her mouth.

"Squid, you are ordered—"

Sam stopped. Lifted the camera and shone it on his face. "Trust me."

Silence gaped, and while Annie's heart thundered in protest, she had a feeling Trace's was probably doing the same. If Sam was caught or got hurt. . .or died. . .

She turned away, sick at the thought of anything happening to him. "Ten mikes."

Without another word, Sam reattached the camera and proceeded down the hall. Darkness pressed in on the camera, gray and white graininess that felt more like the *Blair Witch Project* than an orchestrated mission. Shadows tested her ability to make out anything and forced Annie to hold her breath with each step Sam took.

"Bedroom," Houston whispered, apparently feeling the strain of seeing Sam open a door.

Annie covered her mouth, but not before she sucked in a breath.

Boone slid a glance toward her but didn't meet her gaze before refocusing on the feed. "He only has three darts left, if I've counted right."

Three darts. But four passengers. Annie's breath climbed up into her throat. "But he has his weapon," Annie said. Hoping that would be enough. "He knows what he's doing." Her words had conviction she didn't feel. But she was right. Sam *did* know, had been trained to do this.

"He better." Boone shifted in his seat and cracked his knuckles. He keyed his mic. "Noodle, stay alert."

"Roger."

None of it comforted Annie.

Sam slid into a room, darkness harboring the passengers. Though thermal imaging showed two forms, there was no telling if it was the Stoffels or Batsakis.

But Sam must've noticed something, because he backed out and closed the door. He moved deeper into the darkness. Swells of light along the corridor only made the feed wash out then back in, rather than lighting the passage. It might, for Sam, be working out okay, but every blinding glare knotted her stomach.

He neared another room, light glowing around the partially open door. Sam's hand reached into view to push it open.

Suddenly, he swung in the opposite direction.

Sam's weapon snapped up at a dark form. Movement blurred.

Annie's pulse flung through the roof. "What happened?"

Attention rapt, Boone watched silently. The video answered her question when they could make out Sam hauling a body back into a room. He shifted and turned, and Annie caught a reflection—Sam's reflection. *Bathroom.* He moved backward and closed the door. Someone had come out of a bathroom and Sam had tranqed her.

"Two darts," Boone muttered, counting down the number of tranquilizers left.

"He's fine," she said. "He's fine." Somehow saying it twice gave her little comfort. It was ridiculous to worry like this. Sam was a SEAL. They endured brutal training, far more rigorous than what Trace put her and the rest of Zulu through. Sam had probably carried out innumerable missions that she could never know about. This was probably a walk in the park for him.

The camera panned and Sam entered the room he'd reached before knocking the woman out with the tranq. She imagined the door creaking as he opened it. The soft pad of his feet, soundless with his training. Sam moved toward the bed where a man lay partially propped up with a pillow beneath his head. Beside him, a woman slept on her side.

Sam eased around the room and moved in deeper. Farther from the exit. Closer to trouble.

The camera angled toward the bedside table. *There!* Her heart jogged in her chest at the sight of a laptop sitting there. The camera went lower and lower, the room seeming to shrink. *He's sitting.* But why?

"What is he doing?" Boone asked, his voice quiet and thoughtful.

"Sitting," Annie muttered.

"Why is he sitting?"

Annie flicked Boone, urging him to be quiet. Truth be told, she had no idea why Sam was sitting. What if he wasn't *sitting*? What if something had happened to him in the hall with the bathroom lady? What if he was injured?

"Annie," Houston's voice crackled through the coms, making her jump.

She turned away, her hands trembling. "What?"

"He plugged the USB in, but the laptop's not on. Tell him to power it on."

"How do you know he did that?"

"The USB sent a signal, but it's stalling."

Annie nodded to Boone, who sat up and leaned toward the monitor, keying his mic. "Squid, this is Lighthouse."

Two staticky taps. He couldn't talk. That was Sam's signal that he heard Boone.

"Bunker needs power."

Chewing her thumbnail, Annie waited. Would Sam understand what that meant? It felt like minutes ticked by without a response.

"Maybe he didn't—"

Two staticky taps.

She blew out a breath and watched as the camera seemed to jiggle. A hand stretched out then froze. And beyond it, Annie saw the man shifting in his sleep. Turning over. Turning into the direction of the camera.

Annie held her breath, willing the man to stay asleep.

"He's running out of time," Boone said.

Sam's hand extended farther. His fingers pried open the laptop. Another inch. Sam must be huddled in the corner, out of sight, but within reach of the nightstand.

"Why doesn't he just take it?" Annie silently begged him to get out of there.

"Number of reasons," Boone said. "If Batsakis wakes up and finds it gone, he'll know someone messed with it."

"He could unplug it and bring it back."

"Greater chance of getting caught."

"What if the laptop is dead?" Annie asked.

"That would be a problem."

Sam eased closer, pressed a button.

Light exploded from the laptop, the screen coming to life apparently. It illuminated the man's face. Batsakis grimaced in his sleep, slapped the laptop shut, then rolled over in the other direction.

Annie shook her head. "It's still on, though. Right?"

Boone shrugged.

"We're good," Houston spoke through the coms. "The program is uploading. Just a few more minutes."

But even as the words were spoken, Annie saw the shape of Batsakis shift again. His feet swung over the edge of the bed. Frozen, wondering if Sam would be discovered, Annie stared. Gripped Boone's shoulder.

The camera edged away. Slowly. Very slowly. *Too slowly.* Even as Batsakis, head down, and scratching his bare chest, made his way across the room, the camera angle darkened. Light exploded through the room again then collapsed as a door was shut.

Bathroom. "He's in the bathroom."

Sam had a minute, three at most.

"How much longer?" Annie asked, bending forward, as if gripping the monitor would give her more control over this situation. Give her a better chance of getting Sam back safely. "C'mon, Sam, c'mon. Move..."

But Sam seemed to be investigating. Looking around.

Annie's stomach squeezed. She felt sick. *Get out of there, Sam.*

And then he was in motion. He retrieved the USB and went for the door.

But brightness flooded the hall.

Bouncing hard, the camera went jerky. Bobbing rapidly. Up and down.

"What...what's happening?"

It went down and right suddenly. Then seemed to scan the floor then veered up and blurred.

"What's going on?" Annie asked, her voice more frantic.

"Easy, easy," Boone said, though his tone didn't comfort her. "He's just moving fast. Job's done. He's getting out of there."

"Oh..." Annie didn't buy it. Was she worrying for nothing? But he was still racing up the stairs. Across the living area. "He's not slowing down."

"Guys," Houston said. "Guys, he's got company."

"What do you mean?" Boone came out of his chair.

"Another yacht is on approach."

Annie stayed glued to the camera feed. He'd almost made it to the top level. He was in a dead run. He ducked to one side, coming to a quick stop. The camera wobbled up and down. He shifted outward, and the camera swept the darkness and revealed a boat coming alongside.

Men were hopping over the rail onto the *Aegean Mercy*.

Sam sprinted toward the front. Skidded to a stop. The camera took in the full form of Titus Batsakis with a weapon. He aimed it at Sam.

Annie froze.

A tiny burst of light.

Then blackness.

Wait. No, not blackness. Stars! Annie's mind aligned the camera with Sam's body. Realized he would have to be lying down to get that angle of the starry sky. Which meant. . .he was flying backward.

Then pitch black.

Boone lunged. "He's shot!"

Boone
Mediterranean Sea
7 June – 0320 Hours

They'd searched for an hour and still nothing. Boone could not face the failure of losing Sam, not with Annie right here.

"Keep searching," Trace said. "He's got the skills to survive. Don't leave that water without him."

Though Trace didn't say it, Boone knew he meant dead or alive.

"He's a squid," Leo said. "He knows how to beat this."

Nuala lifted the thermals and scanned the choppy sea. "What do you think?" she asked quietly. "Is he out there? Alive?"

Boone stood at the rail, gripping it tightly as he stood with Nuala. "Out there, yes. Alive"—he cocked his head—"if he got shot. . ."

At the bow, Annie stood with a jacket wrapped around her shoulders, watching. Silent. Devastated.

"She'll crack," Nuala whispered. "She's held it together, but Sam. . ."

"She was pretty cold toward him when we rescued her in the forest. I didn't think she wanted him around," Boone said, his gaze never leaving the water.

"He thought so, too. Y'all haven't figured out women yet? You have a lot to learn about women," Nuala teased. "Annie loves Sam. She might not know it yet, but when we first came to the bunker, she talked about nothing but getting back to him. She pushed him away because she was afraid of losing him."

"So, in other words, if I don't want her to hate me for the rest of my life, I better find this Squid—alive."

"Alive would be preferable." Nuala gave him a smile without looking.

"He's a SEAL," Boone said with a fake sneer.

"He's handsome. He pursued her. He never gave up on her. A girl likes that."

"All girls?"

Nuala drew back from the nocs and met Boone's gaze. She stood a head shorter than him, but she had the chutzpah to be a sniper and face down many a deadly foe. "Yeah," she said, her words even softer than normal.

Boone stilled. Something just happened there, with Nuala. He wasn't sure what. Somehow, he had this feeling something he'd said held an entirely different meaning to her. That look meant something. He recalled the hints Téya and Annie had dropped about Nuala having a thing for him.

He winced. Never meant to lead her on. He'd asked the question with Keeley in mind.

She returned to the watch. "Keeley will get better, then you can be the gallant hero you always are, and you'll know then that I'm right."

The gallant hero you always are. . .

Is that how Noodle really saw him? Not as some messed-up country hick?

"Boone." Her breathy declaration of his name came only seconds before she touched his arm. "Boone, I see something." She handed the nocs to him. "Four o'clock."

"Send the signal." He took the thermal binoculars and searched the area she'd pointed out as Nuala used the SureFire to flick the rescue code. "I'm not seeing any—" A dark huddle bobbed on the water. "I'm not seeing a response."

"What if he's"—*dead?*—"unconscious?"

"Leo," Boone shouted. "We have something."

The ultrafast patrol boat swung in the direction, churning a foamy wake as they raced toward the dark huddle.

They were within twenty yards when Nuala called out. "It's him! He's not conscious."

Boone grabbed a hook and hurried to the side of the boat. With him were Leo's two men, who leaned over and helped drag Sam's body onto the boat. "Easy, easy." Hauling him up over the side was about like trying to hoist an anchor with his bare hands.

Sam was limp. Dead weight. His head hung and his arms dangled like seaweed. Water dribbled down his face and hair.

They fumbled him up and over and laid him in the back. Even as he sliced away the Squid's dive vest and equipment, Boone felt the patrol boat roaring toward safety. Away from the *Aegean Mercy*. Away from the sea that may have taken Sam Caliguari's life.

X

Annie
Mediterranean Sea
7 June – 0320 Hours

Dread dripped heavy and black as Annie watched the three men lower Sam's limp body to the deck of the high-powered boat. The constant *slap-slap* of the hull against the choppy waters only agitated her nerves and Boone's dark mood as he assessed Sam.

"Move, move!" another man shouted from behind her, pushing into the fray. He dropped a large red-and-white box on the deck as he went to a knee. He lifted Sam's arm and held his wrist as he dug through the kit.

"Anything, Nigel?" Boone cut away the vest that had the oxygen tank and the inflated life vest. Sam had clearly pulled the emergency cord on the vest. If he hadn't, would they ever have found him?

"What can I do?" Annie asked.

"Stay out of the way," Nigel barked without looking at her. "Nothing." He shook his head. "No pulse, no circulation. Start compressions. Leo, get the oxygen."

Immediately, Boone went to work pumping and counting off the compressions. It hurt to breathe, to watch them trying to save Sam, to know that Sam might not survive this. Why had he volunteered for this mission? Why did he think he could do it?

"You." Nigel's gaze hit Annie as he held up a trauma sponge. "Hold that on the wound."

Grateful to be useful rather than standing around watching Sam die in front of her, Annie cut away the dive suit from the wound and pressed the quick-clot sponge to Sam's wound, which was partially sitting in his chest and part on his shoulder.

Leo had high-flow oxygen going as Nigel slid a needle into Sam's arm and attached a tube to a bag marked SALINE.

"C'mon, Squid," Boone said as he pumped his hands against Sam's chest. Each time Boone compressed, blood seeped around her fingers.

Annie grunted, furious that she couldn't stop it.

"Press harder!" Nigel barked.

Pump.

Squirt.

She pressed even harder, straightening so she knelt over his body, her arms fully extended.

"Harder! If you want him to live, get that bleeding stopped."

Pressing with both hands to stop the bleeding, she glanced from Boone's much-larger hands to Leo holding the oxygen mask. . .to Sam's slack, gray face.

No, he couldn't do this. He couldn't die. "Sam, c'mon!" Annie ground out, shoving back tears and panic. "C'mon, Calamari—*breathe!*"

"Got a pulse," Nigel said, holding a hand to Boone, who eased off the compressions. "His pulse is thready, but he's still not breathing—probably has water in his lungs. Keep the O_2 going."

Water in his lungs? As in. . .drowned.

As in might not live.

As in died trying to prove to me that he belonged here. Because that's why he'd volunteered for this mission, right? Because she'd said he shouldn't be with them. And thick-headed SEAL that he was, he wanted to prove he *should*. She just wanted him to return to Manson.

Now, he might not return at all. To Manson. To her. "Sam. . ." Tears slid from Annie's eyes, a mixture of anger and panic. "Please. . ."

"Maybe he's been gone too long," Leo said. "Who knows how long he was like that before we found him. He could be brain dead—"

"No!" Annie ground out, hot tears spilling over her cheeks. "He's not! Save him. Keep pumping that oxygen." She bent toward Sam's head and ran a hand over his dry hair. Oddly dry thanks to the hood he'd worn. "Hey—" Her throat constricted as that lone word trembled, forcing her to clear her throat. "Calamari, please. . .fight!"

"Losing his heartbeat again," Nigel said. "Boone."

And immediately the big guy started compressions again.

"Sam," Annie said with a half whimper. "C'mon," she growled. "Fight. Breathe!"

Boone pounded Sam's chest with the heel of his fist. "Fight, you worthless squid!" He pounded again, Sam's body bouncing from the force.

"It's no good," Leo said.

Annie wanted to punch the guy. "You can't stop. His heart was just going."

"But if he's been without oxygen, he—"

"Keep. Going." Annie heard her words bounce back to her in a hollow echo on the sea.

A gurgle snagged her attention back to Sam. Water spurted up. He coughed.

"Roll him over—*easy!*" Nigel lifted Sam's wounded shoulder and moved him onto his side, thumping his back as Boone steadied Sam.

With another cough, Sam hurled water and vomit all over the deck. He vomited again, gagging and coughing.

"Easy, easy," Nigel intoned, lowering him back to the deck.

Shaking his head, Sam coughed more, his eyes clenched in pain. Then the shakes started.

"I need to take care of that wound," Nigel said.

"Inside." Boone, Leo, and Nigel hoisted Sam off the deck, and Annie grabbed the med kit, knowing they'd need that for the surgery. They ushered Sam into the belly of the patrol boat that had a too-short galley table.

Annie set the med kit on a counter behind where Nigel stood. When she turned, rich dark eyes—still weighted with pain—held hers. She moved around to the other side and placed her hand over his, surprised when his cold fingers coiled around hers.

Boone

"Will he live?"

Boone sat in a cuddy, phone pressed to his ear, the boat racing back to shore, bent nearly in half as he pinched the bridge of his nose. "Probably, but he'll be out of commission for a while with that shoulder wound." The space was confined and would work well to sleep, but not necessarily decompress. At least, not for him. Maybe for the Squid. "What about the Lorings? Did they see or say anything while he was in the yacht?"

"Nothing. They're pretty quiet."

"Guess it was too much to hope that they'd see something. . ."

"Boone. . ." Trace's voice went quiet. Stiff.

And so did Boone's spine. *Keeley.* He straightened. His head thunked against the hull, so he moved into the stairwell. "How is she?"

Trace let out a heavy sigh. "It's not good. Her organs are shutting down. She's on full dialysis—"

"I told you I had to stay there. I told you this was a bad—"

"No choice, Boone. You know that. With the hearing, I couldn't leave the country. We needed someone out there. You're all I had."

"Quade could've come."

"Annie would've killed him."

Boone almost smiled. Instead, his mind swung toward the woman lying on her deathbed, it seemed. He closed his eyes and leaned against the wall, letting everything in him go silent. "I can't lose her. . ."

"First things first. Let's get Zulu and you stateside first."

"Sam is immobile."

"For how long?"

"Unknown. Nigel's sewing him up. We might have trouble leaving the country with the way that tactical team hit the yacht and Sam," Boone said, harnessing his emotions and focusing on the mission again. He wasn't forgetting about Keeley; he was operating in a manner that would get him back to her the fastest.

"Already worked out. You'll have an escort waiting when you make land."

After the call, Boone moved out into the salty sea air. He gripped the rails, knowing he wouldn't be any use down with Sam. Besides, he needed the sea air to clear his mind. His heart. Keeley was dying. There was no other way around it. No use pretending it wasn't happening. No use clinging to false hopes that she'd miraculously pull out of organ failure. What happened? What had changed that she'd go downhill so fast and so completely?

And Sam. Though he'd started breathing on his own, was there brain damage? How long had he been dead? Because that's what it was—right?—when someone wasn't breathing and their heart wasn't beating? Yeah, Boone would call that dead.

And Trace. Back there in DC fighting for his life—*again*. Thanks to the meddling of a tenacious intelligence analyst with a vested interest in the outcome: revenge. How many times had he wanted to go deliver some hard truth to her, get her off Trace's back. Off Zulu's.

The team. The girls. Sometimes he felt bad for calling them that, but there was a level of affection—not in a romantic or perverted way. As if he were their big brother, watching over them. Training them. Protecting them.

Failing them. Jessie. Candice. Now Keeley.

He leaned on the rails and pressed his face into his hands. About now he wished he'd been more of a praying man like his dad. Resting his forearms on the metal rail, he stared out over the choppy waters and wondered if God would listen to him now.

That was stupid. He knew He would. Dad had always said God wasn't just waiting for us to talk to Him, but that He actively searched the earth for someone with a heart willing to serve. Did God barter? Could Boone promise to serve God if He let Keeley live?

But wasn't that an empty promise? Just like the soldier who promised to do his best if. . . Well, the scenario didn't matter. You either did your best or you didn't. If your best depended on circumstances, then that meant you weren't dependable. Who'd want to put their lives in the hands of someone who evaluated whether or not to give their best on what they'd get in return? What cowardice.

Boone sighed. Maybe it did make him a coward, but... "God, please—do something for her."

"Think He hears?"

Angling to the side, Boone looked at Annie as she closed the gap between them. "My dad says He does, but I. . .religion and I didn't get along when I was high school. Too many rules."

Annie snorted. "Right, so you joined the Army."

He grinned and bent forward, resting his arms on the rail again. "Yeah, but it was physical. I needed to be *doing*."

"I believe He hears us. I'd just like to know why He doesn't answer." Annie's small hands wrapped around the metal bar.

"Are we talking about God, or Trace?"

Annie gave him a startled look then opened her mouth to respond. But nothing came out. She pressed her lips together as she pushed her gaze to the moon. "He told you?"

With a shake of his head, Boone pulled himself straight. "Trace talks to me about pretty much everything. We hit it off the first day we were teamed. I could look at him and know what he was thinking. And vice versa. I respect him. A lot. And I'd like to think he feels the same. We don't really have any secrets—even when we try to keep them. He knew from day one about Keeley."

"How is she?"

"Dying." The word felt cold and hollow. Boone picked up the roughed-up edges of his thoughts and plowed on. "My point being—Trace and I know each other. We don't keep secrets." He met her gaze. "Except when it comes to you."

Her wide blue eyes searched his, as if looking for his meaning.

"Trace won't talk about what happened."

Tucking some of that wild blond hair behind her ear, she once more pushed her gaze outward. "You mean. . .what happened after Misrata?"

"I mean *between you two*. He's never spoken of it."

"Oh." Her voice was small, her sagging shoulders smaller. Even with the limited light from the moon, he saw her chin puckering as if she were about to cry. "I guess I shouldn't be too surprised." She scraped together a brave, fake smile. "Trace has always been about the mission."

"That's not quite what I meant."

Uncertainty creased her brow as she turned to him. "What did you mean, Boone? Because I'll be honest—if you're going to tell me Trace has put his feelings for me aside—"

Boone touched her back gently. "The only time Trace Weston goes dark, goes silent, is when he doesn't know what to do." He gave her a soft smile. "That tells me how much you mean to him. How much whatever happened affected him."

Quiet lapping of the waters danced between them, Annie seeming to ruminate over his words. Over lines he may have crossed. He was sure Trace would run him up the flagpole for what he'd just told Annie.

"Maybe he's too late, Boone."

He gave a slow nod. "Reckon I guessed that with the Squid showing up. And truth be told, I think Trace knows, too."

Rubbing her fingers together, Annie chewed her lower lip. The tension that crept into her soft features reminded Boone of the way Keeley acted when she was fighting back something. A truth, a painful realization, or a secret.

"Ya okay?"

"I. . ." Her voice cracked. She took in a shuddering breath then brushed back some curls the sea breeze tossed into her face. "It's hard to know what the right thing is."

"About. . . ?"

With an apologetic smile she worked to fight the tears glossing her eyes. "Sam. . . Trace. . ." She bunched up her shoulders. "A part of me wants to punish Trace. Make him hurt the way he hurt me. But that's not why Sam and I. . .that's not why I like Sam."

"Trace and Sam are a lot alike."

"Too much." Annie gave a soft snort. "I know how to pick them, don't I?"

"You do," Boone said with a laugh. "I can't say the Squid is worth your breath. I mean, he is a Navy SEAL after all."

"Was," Annie corrected.

"No, once that's in your blood, it's in for good. Just like SF."

Annie bounced her legs. "I don't want to hurt Trace, Boone."

"Especially now."

She turned to him, frowning. "What do you mean? Because of Sam? Or because of what's happening with Zulu?"

Boone straightened, cursing himself for letting that one slip. "Because of Zulu." It wasn't a whole lie.

Shoot. He shouldn't be lying at all if he wanted God to answer his prayer about Keeley, but Trace would skin him alive if she found out. "I'd better check on the Squid."

Trace
Capitol Hill, Washington DC
8 June – 0900 Hours

The cherry blossoms had long since bloomed down on the Mall, and the streets were now crowded with tourists, flocking to the nation's capital to visit the museums, historic locations, and the seat of power. Halls of the Capitol teemed with overpaid suits and power-hungry politicos, who had too often turned their backs on the military volunteers fighting fierce, brutal wars while those same politicians sat comfy before a fireplace, feet up, drink in hand, as they cut benefits and dug into the heart of the warriors defending their country with their very lives.

The same was true now as Trace sat stiff-backed at a table with General Haym Solomon before a select committee assembled by the Permanent Select Committee on Intelligence. Seated at the elevated area was Chairman Steve Moller, who had called the assembly at the behest of General Marlowe. Also among the committee members was Mike Souza, the chairman of the Subcommittee on Oversight and Investigations. Souza, a former Army Ranger, had stepped into politics after his team suffered a deadly blow because of budget cuts that sliced right into the supply of equipment to defend themselves. But Trace knew it'd be a mistake to consider Souza an ally; the man would be harder on Trace simply because they both served. Because neither wanted anyone else to see them as allies in what should be a neutral, fact-finding mission.

"It's been five years," Chairman Moller began once the meeting had been called to order, "since the Permanent Select Committee on Intelligence and the select committee on the Misrata incident found no proof that Trace Weston had willingly or knowingly endangered the lives of twenty-two innocent civilians there in Libya."

Yes, five years ago he'd been in this same position, having his career and every decision dissected. Now Trace sat here again.

"We'll move to United States Representative Mike Souza, the chairman of PSCI to begin," Moller said.

Souza sat forward, his salt-and-pepper hair cropped short as if he still served in the Army. His bearing, his tenacity, and his sharp wit had given him the nickname, The Wolf. "Thank you, Senator Moller," Souza said as he adjusted his microphone and opened his folder. "In the last six weeks, it seems the lid has blown off the Misrata incident." He peered over his invisible-frame glasses at Trace. "Including the deaths of three soldiers involved in the strike on the warehouse. Is that right, Colonel Weston?"

Trace eased toward the table and turned on his microphone. "It is."

"The Subcommittee on Oversight and Investigations has received the testimony in a classified briefing from eight individuals, two of whom investigated each of the three murders. Chairman Moller has asked for a detailed timeline of the events, and the Honorable Ellen Dunne will respond to that." Souza turned a page and scanned it. "We will hear from Colonel Weston, General Haym Solomon, General Marlowe, and Lieutenant Francesca Solomon in the course of this investigation. Our purpose here is to determine once and for all whether Colonel Weston, then a captain, was directly responsible and therefore negligent in attacking a civilian warehouse in Misrata.

"Briefly," Souza said, meeting Trace's gaze again, "Colonel Weston, please relate the events of 29 April as you recall them."

As I recall... Trace gritted his teeth. As if what he recalled wasn't the truth. But Souza knew how to play the pundit game. "Five days before arriving in Misrata, I was contacted by General Haym Solomon. SOCOM had been tracking a shipment of weapons that were slated for destruction but were rerouted from the location where they would be disposed of. Due to previous caches of weapons being stolen in this manner, SOCOM had tagged these. They were in Libya, being prepped for a shipment, they believed. My team was tasked with inserting, locating, and destroying said cache.

"We arrived in Misrata on 27 April at 2200 hours. The team made quick progress of locating the warehouse. After a two-day stint of surveilling the location, it was determined through communication with SOCOM and the opinions of my team that we destroy the weapons with explosive charges, since the warehouse was abandoned."

Trace spent the next forty-five minutes going over minute details and carefully protecting the identities of Zulu and wording his explanation in a way that would not condemn himself or anyone else involved.

"Would it be fair," Chairman Souza began, "to say that your team was confident the warehouse was a safe target in terms of casualties?"

"We had every confidence as the charges were set that the warehouse was abandoned and there were no civilians nearby."

"And yet," Chairman Moller of the Oversight and Intelligence subcommittee interjected, "the warehouse wasn't empty. Was it, Colonel?"

"It was not, sir," Trace said in a stiff, decisive manner.

"What happened, Colonel?" Moller looked at him, lifting a file. "We have an update from you on how that warehouse came to be occupied that night. Would you share its contents with the committee, please?"

Trace nodded, moving to the file in front of him, the one that detailed

Berg Ballenger's involvement. He spent the next five minutes explaining about the newest discovery. Tedious stuff, considering they had a full, fifty-something page report detailing every fact and nuance. Trace had been meticulous in crafting that report. But it was a sad fact that many in this room would not read it. He'd seen it too many times—senators or representatives out for someone's throat, out to advance their careers, and they plunged ahead with their machetes to hack their way to success on the lives and backs of those who did nothing but their duty.

"So, why didn't you find Ballenger and question him before now?" Senator Hastings, a member of the SOI asked.

"He didn't want to be found, sir. We searched. I've been searching for the last five years."

"Why do you think you found him now?"

"He wanted to be found, sir. He came to us, asked to meet."

"What do you think spurred that contact?"

Maybe Ballenger has a hand in the hand of someone's pocket in this room. But Trace knew saying that would only tighten the noose Marlowe wanted to hang him with. "I have no idea, sir."

"Do you think he knew about the recent assassination of your team members?"

"I'm not sure how he could, sir. Their names were not nor have they ever been known, because their hands were clean."

"But yours weren't," Hastings said.

"That's what some in this room would have you believe," Trace said.

"So, you don't believe you're responsible?"

"I am responsible to carry out my duty and lead my team to the best of my ability. I did that, sir, and I have no regrets."

"No regrets?" Hastings' voice pitched. "Twenty-two innocents are dead at your hand!"

Trace had handled worse accusations and more testy politicians than Hastings. "They are dead, sir, because of a tragic mistake—Ballenger moved those people into the warehouse that night. The charges were already in place."

Questions came and went. A few more accusations were tossed out and quickly doused with truth and fact.

"Colonel Weston," Souza interrupted. "Let's get back on track here. Your team—where are they now?"

"Two are dead, one is nearly dead."

"And the other three, plus"—Moller glanced at his notes—"Sergeant Gray and then–Staff Sergeant Ramage?"

"Location unknown of the three," Trace said, citing the only information he'd give of One, Two, and Six. "Gray and Ramage maintain vigil over the dying member in an undisclosed hospital."

The monotony of the next several hours that involved questions about him and Haym nearly did Trace in. Though he'd been trained to withstand torture, they ought to consider placing recruits in a hearing like this and make them endure the ridiculous claims of men who'd never served. Men who would have an income for the rest of their lives regardless of whether they worked. Men who made three and four times as much as the average soldier.

And where was the justice they always harped about?

"We'll adjourn for today and pick up next time with the Honorable Ellen Dunne, General Marlowe, and Lieutenant Francesca Solomon."

Funny how only one name on that list bothered and stressed Trace—the last one.

Released for the day, Trace walked with Solomon out of the hearing room. As they rounded a corner, Trace felt his gut cinch. At the end of the hall, backlit by the early evening sun, Francesca Solomon stood talking with a group of uniforms. She wore a skirt with her dress blues. Hair tightly secured at the back of her neck, she possessed the same fire in her eyes as her father.

"When I taught her to fight for what she believed in, I didn't expect to be fighting against her."

Trace said nothing, noting who she stood with. Not just soldiers. General Marlowe. Secretary Dunne. His gaze met hers and he had to admit—she was pretty. Beautiful, if you wanted to be technical. But it was a lot like Delilah. Her attention shifted to her father then back to Trace. Finally, she broke away from the huddle and started toward them with what he could only describe as a smug, satisfied expression.

Right, because ruining someone's life and career was satisfying.

"I'll see you," Trace muttered to Haym.

"Wait," Haym said, catching his arm and striding right past his own daughter without so much as a glance.

In his periphery, Trace noted that she slowed, looked to him, and almost acted like she expected him to say something.

He had nothing to say. This hearing, this fiasco, was her fault. She'd gone digging. She'd fueled a fire that should've been smothered. Now his time and efforts were divided from protecting Annie, Téya, and Nuala. He made his way to the parking garage, grateful for the temporary pass so he could avoid reporters and the like. In his car, he started the engine then backed out and left Capitol Hill. At the first light, he looked up.

In his rearview mirror, a foreign face appeared in the backseat. Trace's heart jammed. He reached for the weapon beneath his seat.

"It is not there," the man said, holding Trace's gaze steady and firm. "And I am not here to harm you or endanger you."

Someone behind honked, and Trace's gaze flipped to the light. Green. He eased through the intersection, pulse thrumming. "Who are you?"

"Please, just drive. I promise it will be worth your time."

Francesca
Capitol Hill, Washington, DC
08 June – 1618 Hours

In her dress uniform, Frankie closed the gap and met her father in the foyer. She placed a kiss on his cheek, all too aware of the anger emanating off him.

"What are you doing?" he hissed at her.

"My job." She bristled, hating that he never gave her the benefit of the doubt. Just like her brothers. "You taught me not to simply look the other way because it might be easier."

"Looking the other way is different than actively working to destroy a man's life." He pushed a thick hand through his short, curly hair. "We've been here, Francesca. He's been here. He's proven his innocence."

"Has he?"

"Yes! Or haven't you read the transcripts from the last hearing?"

"Don't patronize me, Dad. I'm doing my job. I believe Trace was more involved in what happened than he admits."

"I beg you, Frankie," he said, catching her arm and holding it tightly. "Don't do this."

Confused and surprised at his vehemence, she tugged free.

"There are things you do not know. *Cannot* know."

"Are you protecting him now?"

"I am protecting the truth. Protecting those who cannot come forward. Protecting scenarios and assets that you will never know about. It's not just about you, Francesca." He scowled at her, his bushy eyebrows knotted. "For once in your life, think about someone else besides yourself."

Frankie shook her head. Why was he so adamantly on Trace's side? It hurt. A lot. To think that he stood with Trace on this. It was just like all those times growing up, when he took sides with Paolo. Or told her to go play with her Barbies when she wanted to be with her family, doing what they were doing. If he knew the truth about the things she'd seen and done, he'd think differently.

369

"Your affinity for this soldier is blinding you, Dad."

"Your determination that he is guilty is blinding you to the truth."

"Why are you fighting for him so hard? It makes no sense."

"Because if Trace Weston goes down, he's not going down alone."

Frankie frowned. "What does that mean?"

He gave her a kiss on the cheek. "Your mother wants you to stop by tomorrow." And with that, he left her standing in the hall, alone. Confused.

He's not going down alone.

What did that mean? It didn't sound like a threat. It felt more like. . .fear. Her father had been Trace's commanding officer. He'd given the order for Trace to go into Misrata. But had her father been in collusion with something else related to Misrata?

A strange, awful feeling spilled down her spine and into her stomach.

Téya

Lucketts, Virginia

8 June – 1800 Hours

Towel-drying her hair after a long workout, Téya entered the bunk room she shared with Annie and Nuala now that the Lorings occupied one and Sam had taken up residence in another. She dressed, donned her boots, and then headed out to the command area.

Annie lay stretched out on the sofa in their lounge area, her face twisted with concern.

"How's he doing?" Téya asked as she eased onto the arm of an oversized chair.

"Resting," Annie said wearily and pulled herself off the leather sofa. "Though he won't admit it, the pain is pretty intense. I can see it on his face. Doctor said he tore the muscles around the bullet wound, swimming to stay afloat. He'll be out of commission for a while."

"So, why aren't you in there with him?"

A crimson blush filled Annie's face. "I needed to think."

"And you can't think in there?"

"He's a loud breather," she managed with a weak smile.

"You mean he snores." Téya laughed. "What are you thinking about?"

Annie breathed long and hard, her shoulders bunched, then slowly released as she sagged deeper into the leather sofa. "I was so angry when I realized Sam was there, in Greece. Then even more angry when I realized he was with us here."

"You didn't want him here?"

370

"It wasn't that. It was more..." Again, she bunched her shoulders. "It's hard to sort out. But in Manson, Sam was my lifeline. Safe. Handsome. And good." She held her hair away from her face. "But here? He's right in the middle of it like the rest of us. He jumped into that mission without a thought for getting hurt and what that might mean to me."

"To you?" Téya couldn't help the surprise she felt. "What about to himself? He was shot. He was pretty much dead."

"Exactly. And that would've been my fault."

"How?"

"Because he went out there to prove he could. That he'd be fine. Only he wasn't."

"You give yourself too much credit," Téya said with a snicker. "Sam went out there—at least, it seemed to me that he went out there because he had the training. He recognized a need and stepped up to the plate. He's a warrior. It's what they do."

Annie glanced down, lifting her fingers out and checking her nails. Classic avoidance right there. Téya must've hit a nerve and had a theory formulating in her head. One that wasn't very complimentary toward her best friend. But one that held a heaping dose of truth.

"Go on," Annie said. "Your thoughts are screaming through your face."

Téya smothered the smile. "I think this is about you protecting yourself."

"Yes, I don't want Sam getting hurt—"

"Close," Téya said, "but not quite on target. *You* don't want to get hurt. *You* don't want Sam here to end up hurting you the way Trace did."

"That's insane. You don't even know what happened between me and Trace."

"You're right. But I do know something happened." Téya took her time, knowing this soft spot was very sensitive for Annie. "I know he devastated you, because there was a day not too long before Misrata that you had stars in your eyes and could see no wrong that Trace Weston did."

"I'm not doing this," Annie said, pushing to her feet.

"Annie," Téya came up out of the chair to stop her. "I—"

"No. It's okay. I just need...space."

She closed the door to the bunk room and the conversation.

Téya puffed her cheeks and blew out an exasperated breath. She was glad her life was, comparatively uncomplicated. They'd fix this Misrata stuff, find out who killed them and deal with them, then she'd go back to David, if he'd have her, and his simple Amish life. With its 6:00 a.m. early risers to get chores done.

Chores. Here she was running around the world saving lives, fighting. And she'd go back to Bleak Pond to do. . .chores.

"Téya!"

She snapped around, glancing toward the command area. Boone stood waving her over to him. "What's up?"

He handed the phone to her. "Trace."

"Where is he?" Téya put the phone to her ear. "Hey."

"I need you to take the car," Trace said calmly—right as Boone held up a black key fob.

Car? They wanted her to take the car? She hadn't been allowed to drive since her last adventure to see David.

"The address will be in the phone by the time you get in the car."

"And where am I going?"

"Get in the car, plug it in, and head out. Stick to the speed limit."

Téya gave a nervous laugh, disbelieving all the smoke and mirrors. Then the call disconnected. "Is this legit?"

Something in Boone's expression made her pause. Made her smile vanish. "What?"

"Go. Now."

"What's wrong? Don't do this—"

"When was the last time Trace asked you to do something like this?"

"Uh. . ." Her brain blanked. "Never."

Boone thrust his jaw toward the door. "Exactly. Go."

The trip took forty-five minutes, delivering her to a business park in Reston and into the empty parking lot of a building still under construction. Uncertainty chugged through her as she parked then climbed out. Glancing around, Téya had a nauseating feeling. Phone in hand, she dialed the bunker.

But a text came through before she could finish.

Third floor.

Téya repeated the words of the text in a mutter then glanced up at the building. "Right," she whispered and started for the stairs she spied already completed and tucked into one of the main corner supports. Gypsum board, nails, and chunks of wood littered the stairs. As she stepped onto level three, she found a wide open space as big as a Super Walmart. In the opposite corner, Trace sat against a cement barrier. Beside him stood a man. Holding a weapon.

Téya's hackles went up as she closed the distance between them. She mentally cursed herself for not being more thorough, for not demanding Boone give her a weapon. But she hadn't expected trouble. The guy wasn't holding the weapon on Trace, but it was clear Trace was annoyed.

Yet. . .Trace had the know-how to take down this attacker.

She thought of Boone's expression. His terse behavior. He knew. Boone knew something was wrong.

Lifting his eyes, Trace met her gaze. There was so much in that simple move. His head didn't move. His body didn't. Just his eyes. Crowded with wariness. With determination. They were in this together. Somehow.

Téya had fighting skills. So did Trace. He hadn't used his. So she wouldn't use hers. She'd wait. Threading her fingers, she came to a stop a yard in front of Trace and the man.

"Your hands," the man demanded, his words thickened by an accent she couldn't quite determine.

My hands? What did he want with her hands? She gave Trace a look and he responded with an imperceptible nod.

"Your hands!" the man shouted now.

Lifting her hands up, she offered them to him, palms up.

He stomped forward, the gun aimed at Trace as he did, a move that pulled Téya up straight, but she saw Trace out of the corner of her eyes give a quick nod.

Scowling, he gripped her left hand and flipped it over. The scowl in his dark features dug deeper as he met her gaze fiercely. Then turned over her other hand. His thumb swiped over the burn mark and the scowl washed away. He smiled and gave a breathy laugh as he stepped back. "Forgive me." He bent his torso toward her.

Did he just bow to me?

"I had to be certain," he said as he offered another quasi-bow then holstered the weapon at his hip. He motioned Trace closer. "You may call me Nesim."

"Why would we call you anything?" Téya finally asked, her disbelief thick in her words.

"It would help since you are going to work with me."

Trace hadn't spoken. Hadn't smiled. Laughed. Nothing.

"Sorry, I don't work for you," she said.

"That mark says you work with me," he countered, tugging down the corner of his shirt. There on his collarbone was a tattoo of the star-crescent. "He marked you."

Téya folded her arms over her chest, effectively hiding the brand The Turk had given her.

"What do you want, Nesim?" Trace asked. "You've gone through a lot of trouble, breaking into my car, bringing me here, having me call her out. You have snipers watching us."

Fear scraped Téya's courage, ordering her to search her surroundings.

But she couldn't. Wouldn't.

"What do you need?" Trace asked.

"I need Téya to come with me."

"No way—"

"For what?" Trace asked at the same time she refused.

"To find Majid Badem."

Her mind bungeed. "Who is that?" She slapped her hair away from her face. "You know what? Never mind. I don't care. I am not helping you."

Nesim's confidence never wavered. "But you will, Miss Reiker."

"Yeah," she said, her gaze bouncing from Nesim to Trace—why wasn't he saying anything? "Why would I do that?"

"Unmöglich Festung."

Warm dread spilled down her spine. She knew with those two simple words, this man had her. She'd do whatever he wanted.

Téya

Reston, Virginia

8 June – 1900 Hours

"How do you know about that?" Téya's mouth went dry, painful buried memories from the past roaring to the present. "Nobody knows about that." She tried to swallow. Tried to ignore the probing look from Trace.

"It is not important—"

"It is important!" Téya's heart hammered. "That. . .that was buried. Erased from records." *From my life.*

"What's it mean?" Question low and even, Trace locked gazes with her.

She couldn't breathe. No, no. She couldn't go back there. Back to her stupid teenage years when she sought affirmation over conviction. Acceptance over morality. Téya turned away and paced, holding her stomach, willing the contents of her breakfast to stay there. *They promised. Vowed it'd be redacted.*

Panic clawed at her, threatened her with tears. *Tears!* She hadn't cried in she didn't know how long. She'd survived on adrenaline. On being tough.

She jerked to Nesim. "You can't know about that. They erased every trace of it."

"Not every," he said with a smirk. "We are good at finding what cannot be found, what does not want to be found. Would you like to tell

374

your colonel what we know? Or shall I?"

"Téya." Trace's tone warned her he wasn't going to be patient much longer.

She whipped back to him, angry. But not at him. At this man—Nesim, who'd thrown this massive curveball into her life. Oh that the heavens would open and suck her out of this miserable existence. She just wanted to go back to Bleak Pond. Back to the simplicity of just being David Augsburger's love interest.

"You don't need to know this," Téya said, the growl in her voice evidence of her panic, of her need to protect the one thing she'd never told anyone about. "What does this have to do with anything?"

Nesim's smile only became more sinister. "Trust me—you do not want me to go forward without your explaining a few things to your colonel."

"Téya," Trace said, coming closer and lowering his tone and head. "The analyst who's been coming after us—he can help us stop her."

Téya struggled to keep back the tears. Fought the bouncing of her chin. The weakening of her defenses. "I promised I'd never talk about it. I sold my soul to make it go away, Trace." Tears blurring her vision, she shook her head. "If I open this can. . ."

He touched her shoulder. "It stays here, between us. He already knows. I need to know. Nesim said it's directly connected to why he's here."

Gaze down, Téya nodded. The silence in the unfinished building gaped at her. Téya surrendered. She had to. "I was seventeen, living in Germany with my mom and stepfather, who was in the Air Force. There was this base built into the side of the mountain near our neighborhood. The teens hung out on the mountain, having drinking parties and. . .other things. It was like this challenge between the guys to try to sneak onto the base. We called it *Unmöglich Festung*—the Impossible Fortress—because it was impossible to get into. It'd been a Nazi stronghold or something." Téya shook her head. "This new guy showed up at school. I was stupid and wanted him to like me. He dared me to break into the facility."

"So you did."

Téya swallowed. "Kids had tried it for years. I was the only one who succeeded." Telling this story was like standing before a tidal wave and trying to hold it back with her bare hands. "What I didn't know was one of the other girls had followed me." She'd never forget. . . "She triggered the alarm. The authorities came. She panicked and ran." Oh man, the guilt. . . "It gave me the chance to escape. I took it. She was arrested and ratted me out."

"That's it?"

Téya lifted her gaze to his finally. "The new guy and I hooked up, and the girl. . .she was a lot like Nuala. Getting caught and arrested shattered her pristine record and reputation. She'd only done it for the new guy, trying to get his attention. She hated it because he liked me. To her, I had it all—broke into the facility. Got away. Got the guy. She committed suicide a few days later."

Trace winced. "How'd they make it go away? What was the deal?"

"My stepfather was base commander," Téya said. "He made a deal to keep my name out of it if I'd agree to return to the States and never mention it. My mom and stepfather were more than glad to send me back to my grandparents, but I only lasted a summer as an Amish teen. I went to live with my dad's parents then."

Trace acknowledged the story with a nod. Or maybe he was nodding because he understood her parents didn't want her around. But it felt more like a nod indicating he wasn't convinced she told him everything. Which would be smart of him. Because she hadn't.

He pivoted to Nesim. "What do you want with her?"

"We need her to go to the Impossible Fortress."

Stomach churning, Téya shook her head. "No way."

"You will if you want to help your colonel walk away clean from the hearing."

Trace cringed. Jaw muscle popping, he flared his nostrils.

"What hearing?"

"Never mind," Trace said.

"You have no idea what I'm being asked to sacrifice, and you're going to withhold information from me?" A hint of a shriek infected her words. "And Zulu, obviously, if this is a congressional hearing."

"They're investigating Misrata again, threatening to strip me of rank and career. It's not going to happen."

Téya widened her eyes. "How can you know that?"

"Because they don't have the evidence needed, and if you help Nesim get this Badem back, they will give me information that will silence this forever."

"What on earth makes you think you can trust him?"

"The same thing that has him here, trusting us—experience and reputation."

"What reputation?"

"Majid Badem's."

"Who?"

Trace took her hand. Held it up. "The Turk."

Brandishing a photo, Nesim smiled at her.

Téya's worlds collided—Majid Badem was The Turk. "No. . ." Slowly, she shook her head. Then more fervently. "No way. I am not having anything do with him."

Like a flash, Trace stepped between her and Nesim. "Téya, think about it."

"No. He tried to kill me! Beat me to a pulp. Then tried to get others to kill me."

"Majid was testing you," Nesim said.

"All the more reason to say no." Téya backed up. Wanted to sprint back to the sedan and race back to the bunker. The foolishness of that desire wasn't lost on her, but she didn't care. "He's a killer!"

"According to your own testimony," Nesim said, "so are you."

"How did they not bring charges about the girl at the fortress?" Trace just had to ask. It didn't surprise her that he hadn't missed that.

"That girl was my half sister." Téya put a hand to her forehead, hating how this afternoon had turned against her. "This doesn't make sense. You're marked by him, but you want to find and kill him? And you want me to help you—because of something I did when I was seventeen, you think I'll help you kill him?"

He laughed. A long, belly-jiggling laugh, though the man had solid abs if his biceps were any clue. "Not kill him. *Rescue* him."

Téya stepped back. Memories of how the Turk had chased her in Paris. Beat her crazy. Threatened to kill her. Burned her hand. Now it was her turn to laugh. And she couldn't help it, but she did. "You really think I'd do this, just because he burned my hand and dug into my past? Sorry. It's not happening."

"We did not want you to go, only to train one of our assets," Nesim said.

"Train? For what?"

"How to get into the Impossible Fortress."

"I can't."

"You must!"

"I can't," she ground out, relieved that this mission wouldn't happen. "I did it at night. It was so dark on the mountain, I might as well have had my eyes closed." She hugged herself. "Getting in was blind luck."

"For your sake, I hope not. And for your commander."

Holding her arm, Trace tugged her aside. "You *do not* have to do this, Téya."

He could tell what this was doing to her, couldn't he? The terror it struck at the core of her being. "Isn't it the least bit suspect that The Turk needs my help?"

"It's completely suspect."

"Why would they come to me?"

"I can't answer that."

"But you have ideas."

"Too many and too violent to sort through. Which is why I'm telling you, we can walk away."

"I can walk away from this," she said, holding his intense green-eyed gaze, "but then you can't walk away from the hearing."

"They don't have proof because it doesn't exist."

"But you and I know they can twist the truth into some perverted angle to make you look guilty."

"Guilty as sin," he said with a nod. "But that's not yours to worry about."

"Baloney! You're my commander. If you get removed, if you get arrested, where does that leave Zulu?"

Trace hesitated for a second. "Don't borrow trouble. If anything happened to me, Boone would take over."

"I adore the big guy," Téya said. "But he's not you. And if I have a chance to make sure you walk away with your integrity intact, then I need to do that. You've protected us for the last five years. We need resolution, and we can't get that with you behind bars."

Trace

Lucketts, Virginia

8 June – 2020 Hours

"Rough day?"

Trace glanced over his shoulder from where he leaned against the table in the briefing room. Slipping into the room, Annie looked as frazzled as he felt. The sight of her beautiful face and caring eyes shifted something in him. Something he'd locked away five years ago.

And it needs to stay there, Weston. She's not yours anymore.

"How's Sam?" Trace forced himself to ask the question. To get Sam on the table, figuratively, so there would be no mistaking what they were to each other—coworkers.

"Weak and in pain. He's resting." Annie came around to the far corner where he waited. She stood a half-dozen inches shorter than him, but as far as he'd always been concerned, she was perfect. Perfect height. Perfect everything. "You okay, Trace?"

She had to go all soft on him with that question, didn't she?

"Yeah. Fine." He straightened and turned, facing the door.

Her smile brightened those blue eyes he loved. "You're a bad liar, Trace Weston."

378

"Only when it's you," he said, but immediately regretted it. That was stepping into territory he had no business being in.

"What's going on?"

Trace sighed. Talking would be better than thinking about what he wanted—to kiss her. Kiss her and forget everything crashing around him. "A lot of stress. Trying to sort through the chaos and determine the best course of action."

"That sounds a lot like, 'It's classified and I can't tell you.' Close?"

Trace shook his head and looked away. He couldn't tell her about Téya and The Turk, and he didn't want her worrying about the hearing. The weight of responsibility in protecting Zulu was almost too much for him. But the ache that hurt the worst was standing right in front of him. In his effort to protect her, he'd crushed her and any hope of a "them" ever happening again.

"Hey," Annie said, touching his face.

Trace felt the remnants of his resistance crumbling and stiffened. Caught her hand to keep the tempest at bay. "Annie. . ."

Only a few inches away, she frowned. "I've never seen you like this."

She was here. Right here. He could wrap her in his arms and kiss her. But she didn't belong to him anymore.

But there was this crazy voice in his head that pointed out she was in here with him and not with Sam. Did that mean something? His hand slid onto her waist and he straightened. But still couldn't bring himself to look at her. To peer into those eyes and see the rejection he anticipated. Then he finally did.

And what he saw. . .it wasn't rejection.

Confusion. Uncertainty.

She'd been the most precious and fragile step he'd ever taken. Did she know that? Did she know what she meant to him? Trace caressed her cheek, testing her reaction. When her eyes half slid closed and her lips parted, he slipped his hand around to the back of her neck, which was warm from her hair.

Annie wet her lips.

An invitation to kiss her? Trace eased in, slowly, afraid to scare her off. Anticipating the moment she'd pull away or shove him back. Each second without that rejection heightened the pull of the kiss he desperately wanted.

She took in a breath, frozen in the same anticipation he felt.

Trace captured her mouth with his. Her lips were soft beneath his, supple. Willing. Though he wanted to pull her closer, deepen the kiss, he knew this was treacherous ground. Any minute, she'd break off.

But she didn't. When her hands pressed against his chest, Trace surrendered. Tugged her closer, held her firmly against him. Her little moan of satisfaction pushed him to deepen the kiss. One she returned and leaned into. To have her back in his arms—

Salt mingled with the sweetness.

Salt?

That word triggered awareness. Her shuddering. Her heaving chest. Trace drew back, startled to see a tear slip down her cheek. Heart racing and passion still roaring, he shifted his gaze to her eyes. "Hey..."

Shaking her head, she pressed her gaze down. Rested her forehead against his chest as her fingers coiled into his shirt.

Trace encircled her with his arms. Held her as she cried. *What have I done?* "Annie—"

"No," she said, straightening and stepped back. Out of his touch. "This is my fault."

"Fault?" His hopes detonated against the single word.

Cupping his face and rising on her tiptoes, she planted a kiss on his lips again.

"I—I don't understand."

Sorrow lined her pretty, tearstained face. "I don't either, Trace. I've wanted you, missed you, for the last five years."

The warhead filled with her meaning struck him center mass. "Sam."

"Yes...no..." Annie gave a confused shrug. "I don't...know."

Trace snorted and pinched the bridge of his nose. At the rate he was going, he was primed to lose the hearing and his career. He'd now lost Annie. Zulu would probably be next.

"What you did to me—"

"Was to protect you."

"What you did—" defiance blazed in her blue eyes "—devastated me. I—"

Two raps on the door pushed Trace's gaze to the door then to the half-windowed walls. The bunker was lit but not bustling. He could only pray nobody saw them. He considered her again but saw the distance in her expression, in her posture. "Enter." This conversation was over anyway. And so was their relationship.

Nuala gently opened the door, her face crimson.

So, she'd seen. Had anyone else? His gaze skidded around the main hub. Houston had his nose in a monitor, but his head hung lower than normal. *Avoiding my gaze?* "Hey, Noodle. What's up?"

Annie always hated the way he could sound normal and unaffected after one of their liaisons got interrupted. She was already moving around the table and out the door as Nuala came farther in. "Um, Boone called."

Trace glanced at his watch, his mental gears quickly shifting.

"Keeley's on life support. He's not coming back tonight. He asked if you—"

"I'll stay." In his periphery, he noted Annie head off the dais and toward the back of the bunker. Back to Sam.

Nuala nodded but didn't leave.

"Anything else?" He wanted to be alone with his thoughts and the realization that he had lost Annie for good. He'd let himself believe he could win her back. Convince her about his justifications for his actions. If Sam hadn't been in the picture, would he have succeeded? She sure hadn't held back on that kiss.

Make out with me then run back to the Squid. Nice.

"I. . .I think Boone has been pretty distracted."

Trace cleared his mind, automatically defensive of his buddy. "Shay is dying. It's expected."

"Yes. . ." Nuala wrung her fingers. Twisted her ankles.

The girl had killer instincts. It's what made her a fantastic soldier and a top-notch sniper. "What?"

"I think he missed some things while worrying about Keeley."

"Like?"

She chewed the inside of her lower lip. "Look. He's a smart man. He doesn't miss things. I'm not accusing him. It's just a concern—well, more a feeling. . .maybe I'm imagining things—"

"Just say it. I trust you."

Noodle bobbed her head. "Right. Okay, I'm just having misgivings about our guests."

"The Squid?"

"No, the Lorings."

He wouldn't exactly call them guests. "They're assets, Nuala."

"They're perfect assets."

"Yes."

"No," she said, her blue eyes bright beneath her dark bangs. "I mean, maybe too perfect. Have you watched them? I've seen a lot of married couples, but they. . ." She shrugged, stuffing her hands in her jeans pockets. "I don't know, sir. I just think something's off."

"Excuse us," came a firm, masculine voice.

In the doorway stood Carl and Sharlene Loring.

Nuala's shock was palpable.

"Noted." Trace didn't need suspicions cast on the one good thing that had happened to them—the Lorings. But he couldn't shirk off Nuala's instinct. She'd never been wrong. But General Solomon had given the intel about them. At the same time, the two people standing in the doorway did seem awfully convenient. Hadn't they provided the straw that broke the back of the camel sitting on Trace's life? "Thank you," he said to Nuala, dismissing her. Giving her a chance to escape the awkward situation.

The Lorings came in farther. "We wanted to ask if it was possible for us to find a place to live. This place is safe, but the children are cut off from everything."

I thought they'd want to live, Trace couldn't help but think.

"Really," Sharlene said, looking demure. "The children need fresh air. They need friends."

"I thought they needed shelter and safety." Priorities seemed to have shifted. "In Greece—did they have fresh air and friends in the slums?"

"I know you don't have children, so it might be hard to understand, but if you can make it happen, we'd like to move to a safe house." Carl Loring reached across and held his wife's hand. "A real one."

Trace hated that his suspicions were now aroused because he suddenly noted several things that could be nothing. Or could be everything. Maybe it was better to get them out of here.

"We know you're under a lot of stress," Sharlene put in. "What with the people here, Berg Ballenger hunt, and the hearing. Really, letting us go would be one less stressor for you."

With a nod, Trace said, "True." That'd be true if he suddenly believed Nuala's theory. "Done. I'll have Houston get to work on transferring you."

Carl smiled and Sharlene gushed, but Trace blocked it out. Would anything else come tumbling down on him? He stalked out of the briefing room after them and spotted Téya. "A word?"

She came closer.

"Let's not talk missions around the Lorings," he said, his gaze tracking the family who returned to the back of the bunker.

"I haven't."

He snapped his gaze to hers. "The hearing."

"Not a word," Téya said, crisscrossing her chest with her finger. "Scout's honor."

If Téya hadn't told them about the hearing, who had? Boone? No way. He knew better than to discuss anything with them. Especially about the hearing.

So the question remained: How did the Lorings know about the hearing?

Téya
9 June – 0710 Hours
Dulles International Airport

Waiting at a private airstrip abutting Dulles International Airport
provided ample opportunity for doubts to breed on the fertile soil of fear.
Rubbing her knuckles as they waited for the Leer jet, Téya reminded
herself that she couldn't trust The Turk. Which meant this was probably
a trap. But she had to take one for the team, for Trace and for Zulu.

What if I die on this mission?

She'd asked that on every deployment, but this was different. This
had her deliberately walking into a booby-trapped mission.

"This is insane," Nuala hissed as she sidled up to her in front of the
bank of windows overlooking the airstrip. "You realize this is probably a
trap."

Of course it was a trap. Why else would The Turk's people ask *her*
to break into a facility when they clearly had the skill, manpower, and
know-how to become a notorious organization? If they could find out
about her past, a record that Houston confirmed did not exist in her
permanent file. . .then why her?

"You realize they're probably going to try to kill you."

There are easier ways to kill me.

Nuala's frantic pacing rubbed the raw edges of Téya's nerves. "No. No,
they won't kill you. There are easier ways to get rid of you—a Remington
700 among them."

"Plane just landed," Rusty Gray said as he came toward them.

"It's nice to work with you again." Téya smiled at the former Special
Forces operator. "Surprised Boone convinced you."

"They're paying me well." Rusty lifted a rucksack from a vinyl chair.
"Ready?"

They were paying him. But not well. Rusty was here because Boone
wouldn't leave Keeley's side, and most likely, Rusty offered to come in
Boone's place. "You're a good man, Rusty Gray."

The guy had a Stephen Amell look happening that totally worked for
him, especially with the brooding soldier attitude. Hoisting the ruck onto
his shoulder, he started for the door. "Let's go."

She followed him across the tarmac and up into the belly of the Leer.
He hesitated just inside the door, and Téya saw why. Two of the six seats
were already occupied. Behind her, she felt Nuala crowding to get a view.

"Have a seat, Mr. Gray," said the woman wearing a hijab.

Beside her sat a man in an untucked, pin-striped button-down shirt and skinny jeans. He grinned unabashedly at them. His dark brown eyes met hers. "Let's get this party started, Miss Reiker."

Did they have a choice? They'd already stepped inside, not only in the jet, but in the trap. They'd had it set, fully coiled, and now they'd sprung it.

Téya restrained the sigh that wanted to escape, grateful when Rusty moved past them and let Téya find a seat. Was it intentional on Rusty's part that he took the aisle seat, leaving her and Nuala by the windows? Protected. As if seat position alone could guarantee that.

No, Téya was quite aware that she had been at the mercy of The Turk's organization since the Roma slums. Maybe even before. They had her ticket, her entire life's itinerary planned. She was merely the pawn.

"I do not like this," Nuala whispered loudly.

Rusty said nothing. Neither did Téya. She wanted to sleep. Wanted to be unconscious so she didn't spend the next umpteen hours stressing over which would be her last. When they'd decide they'd had enough fun and kill her.

For Trace. For Zulu. She'd do this for them.

What guarantee did she have that they would make good on their promise to write that Get Out of Jail Free card for Trace?

None. I just have to believe they will. He'd done so much for Zulu, for each team member, sacrificing years to protect them. Attempting this was the least she could do, especially in light of the fact that someone was trying to take him down again.

Téya buckled in, pressed her head against the rest, and closed her eyes. Somehow, she dozed off quickly until a steady drone of quiet conversation lured her out of sleep's strong grip.

". . .yes, but without a cold zero, you can't be sure of the trajectory," Nuala was saying.

Opposite her, the gregarious guy was angled toward Nuala, chatting. He shifted toward Téya and his eyes widened. "Ah, you're awake."

Straightening in her seat, she rubbed the back of her neck, eyeing the two of them. How long had she slept? "Where's Rusty?"

"Went to the loo," the man said. He then laughed. "And no, I'm not British. I think that's just a better word than saying toilet."

Téya crossed her legs and tucked her hands there, hating the chill that seeped through the artificially cooled and oxygenated cabin. Hating that she had no idea who this man was or why he was with them.

Nuala rolled her eyes, careful to make sure the man didn't see her as she shifted toward the window.

"I'm afraid I've chatted her ears clean off," the man said. He was way too happy. Way too chatty. "I'm sure she's glad you woke up so she doesn't have to talk to me anymore."

Téya would not let him dictate their feelings or situations. "Why aren't you going after your master?"

"It's far more fun to have you do it," he said. Then laughed again. "I'm not going to risk my life breaking into a facility like that."

"Like what?"

The man gave her a knowing but superior look. "No doubt you did research on the Impossible Fortress before you boarded this jet."

She held his gaze but did not affirm his supposition, even though he was right. Of course they researched it. Who wouldn't do their homework on a mission like this?

"What your research didn't tell you, I'm sure, is that the Impossible Fortress has been an underground base for a group known as Red Wing."

Téya's nerves tightened. Red Wing. Jessie had that on her data wall.

"Yes," the man said with quiet confidence. "You've heard that name, haven't you?" When she didn't answer, he scooted forward in his seat, elbows on his knees. "I can see why he let you live. You have a will of iron and a spine of steel. Do not be afraid that you will be giving away secrets, Miss Reiker. I know that you have an information wall that bears the words *Red Wing*. I know it has come up before."

"Telling me things like that does nothing for breeding confidence."

He chuckled then accepted a snifter of amber liquid the flight attendant handed him. He tossed back a swallow and leaned into the leather seat. "I do not seek to breed confidence. It is understandable that you do not trust us." He shrugged, looking over his shoulder at the woman, who worked on a laptop, her small lips and stern brow giving her a severe aura. Or maybe that was just the woman herself. He slumped back against the chair, slouching slightly, as he lifted the snifter. "We do not need your trust. Only your raw skill."

"For what? You have everything you need. Your organization is well known—"

"No." His lighthearted, annoying attitude diminished as he came forward again. Ferocity filled his brown eyes. "No, that is where you are wrong. We do not have everything we need." Then a one-shouldered shrug as he tipped his snifter toward her. "Unless you are speaking of yourself in that context." His arms went wide. "For this mission, the vital, integral aspect is singular. It's you. There is no one on this planet with the experience you have."

"I was seventeen. I snuck in, blindly following nothing but luck."

"No." He shook his head with a laugh. "You are wrong again. It was not luck, Miss Reiker, but instinct. And we need those instincts."

"Have you tried already to get in?" Nuala asked. "Is that why you're coming to Téya now? Because you tried and failed?"

A soft noise came from the woman who sat up one seating group. She was shaking her head gently, and while she never joined the conversation or looked over at them, Téya knew that the theory Nuala put forward, while sound, wasn't what was happening here.

"Good, Miss King," he said. "You are considering everything. That will serve you well." His gaze returned to Téya, and though he'd given Nuala a nod of encouragement over her idea, his gaze now was filled with. . .derision.

Annoyance.

Rusty dropped hard into the chair beside Téya, the leather hissing loudly as he adjusted.

The noisy intrusion had been intentional on his part. "Trying to steal national secrets, Nesim?"

"Nesim?"Téya repeated. But the man in the garage was named Nesim.

The chatty operative gave her a nod and lifted his snifter to her. "At your service, Miss Reiker."

"How many people are named Nesim?"

He grinned. "She's not," he said pointing to the stern-faced woman, then pushed out of his seat and returned to his compatriot.

"Why exactly are we going to this place?" Rusty asked, folding his arms over his chest.

"Because they want us to." For whatever reason, she didn't know. But they were going. She just prayed they'd come out of it alive.

Téya
Frankfurt, Germany
9 June – 2215 Hours

Tucked in a van two miles from the bottom of the cliff-like setting, Téya had donned a black tek-insulated jacket and jeans. In her hand, she held a hood that would conceal her identity, as the initial recon of the fortress showed an incredible increase in the number of security cameras.

"Houston, you up?" Rusty asked as he accessed remote feeds.

"Copy that," Houston said, his voice tickling in the tiny wire planted just inside her ear canal. Tiny enough to work but not to be seen. "I'll be with you the whole time, lucky duckling."

Téya rolled her eyes. "Guessing Nesim was right," Téya muttered, watching as the small drone camera zoomed in and zipped up the cliff.

"What's that?" Rusty asked as he manned the drone and recorded it on the small laptop he'd brought, compliments of Houston.

"He said the fortress was an underground base for some group."

"Red Wing," Nuala put in.

Téya nodded. Memories of this place were as dark and forbidding as the ominous image streaming through the live feed. Little vegetation aside from the small shoots that jutted out of the rocks. Almost no grass. Her mind skipped to the cemetery a mile north of the fortress. That's where everyone hung out. Partied. Did other things teens shouldn't be doing but thrived on because it drove parents insane and made the teens feel invincible.

At least a hundred feet, almost straight up. She'd never been daunted by heights and it wasn't the height that bothered her. It was what lay at the top. The Turk. Was he really up there? She had more than an inkling of doubt.

He couldn't want to capture her—too elaborate of a ruse. No, she had a distinct feeling he wanted her here for a reason. Not Annie. Not Nuala. Her. Téya Reiker.

And it still rattled her cage—how had he known she'd broken in here?

A light rap against the van's hull came, and Téya knew she had no more time to think through it all. It was time.

The rear door opened and Rusty stiffened. Darkness swallowed the man who stood there, dressed in black from head to toe. Nesim II, she nicknamed him. The late hour made him appear larger and more ominous than he really was.

He wagged his fingers at her, motioning her from the van.

Rusty hopped out, crowding into Nesim's space as he whispered something. Nesim patted Rusty's chest and gave him a thumbs-up. "Ready?" he asked Téya as she stepped into the night. They jogged to the base of the incline. It was her responsibility to lead Nesim inside and help him get back out alive.

But things had changed. Like the electric fence that had replaced the aged, holey chain-link fence she'd crawled through as a teen.

Nesim had come prepared. He crouched at the fence and shifted a small box around in front of him. He connected something to the fence. After a small hiss of electricity, he started cutting up the fence, one piece at a time.

"You knew that was electrified."

He said nothing but finished working, creating a hole. Enough for them to crawl through. He gave her a nod, and she slipped through. Maybe once Nesim got focused on a mission, he wasn't as chatty. She was grateful for that. When he talked, no more than a couple of minutes ticked by before he shattered some misconception she'd held. And right now, she didn't need any more shattering.

They climbed over a bed of boulders that lined the bottom of the sheer rock face. Téya took a second to scan up along the steep incline. Moonlight spotlighted the craggy face of the hill, daring her to try. Warning her she'd fail. *Was I crazy when I did this at seventeen?*

"Second thoughts?"

Téya shifted. Swung her gaze to Nesim, her mind ricocheting off his words. Her boyfriend had said the same thing to her ten years ago. Back then, she'd flashed a smile at Ruzgar, who stood by the cemetery with the others, and grabbed the first hold, placing her foot on a flat-topped boulder. And the one beside her had a nice, swollen curve.

Wrong place. Téya glanced around and moved down three feet, finally locating the right one. Nesim watched her intently, probably second-guessing her change in position. That was fine. He could second-guess all he wanted. When they made it topside, he'd know. She climbed up on the rock and immediately found the first hold. Just like before.

So that was easy. She didn't dare believe the rest would be. If it went easily, then she was in more trouble than she realized. The trap was bigger. The fall would be harder.

Okay, God. . .this is where I could use some help. But would He help?

She'd prayed more in the last several years thanks to the simplification of life in Bleak Pond and the faith that helped the people she loved. But since Trace had yanked her back into the life of a soldier, she'd done things that went against the faith. Would God forgive her? Would He help her as she did something that broke laws?

Téya shoved the thoughts aside and focused on getting solid holds. Digging her fingernails into dirt and clinging on for dear life. Behind her, Nesim did the same, following her lead, gripping the same places she did. Her arms and thighs ached as she climbed. It took more than thirty minutes to make it to the top. She dragged herself over the ledge, experiencing the same exhilaration she had ten years ago that she hadn't inadvertently committed suicide that night.

"Phew," Houston's voice tickled in her ear. "I've got the fly drone hovering above you, and I'm telling you—if I were on the rock, I'd have to change my pants by now."

Téya wanted to groan, but then Nesim would know she was bugged.

"Twice," Houston clarified. "Heights and I have a love-hate

relationship. I'd rather throw them off a cliff."

His humor was as bad as his flirting.

Téya glanced over the side and watched the agile Nesim scaling the rock as if he were a spider. And it struck her then, her sedated pleasure fading, as her mind slid into the past—why hadn't she seen Tara following her?

Because I wasn't looking at Tara. She glanced to the cemetery where Ruzgar had watched.

Returning to the present, Téya rolled onto her back and then onto all fours, moving out of the way as Nesim came over the ledge. Téya crouched to the side as he sat on the ledge, huffing.

She swatted his shoulder, silently telling him they should get moving, and stood. When he grunted, as if pained, she frowned at him.

Nesim pulled to his feet awkwardly.

Was he clumsy? Already exhausted? "Maybe you should've sent Nesim the First, if this is too much for you."

Even in the dark, she saw the glare in the whites of his eyes as he flattened himself to her right. "Up?" He said pointing to a pipe that protruded from what looked like a blasted section of the granite.

"This way," she said, pressing the front of her body against the rock and shimmying around an outcropping that could easily toss them to their deaths if a piece broke away.

His fingers grazed her as she cleared the curve.

Téya made it, glancing down to verify she was in the right spot. The ledge was much narrower than she remembered. In fact, as she looked at the rock beneath her feet, she realized it'd broken. No, it was too clean of a break. That had been—blasted. They'd set charges and destroyed the space. Probably right after she'd broken in.

The moonlight caressed the ledge, seeming to highlight a vein. A deep one.

Crack.

Her heart vaulted into her throat. "Wait."

Nesim froze.

"There's a crack." She pushed her spine against the cold granite. "I'm not sure it can hold us both."

"Where's the entrance?" he asked.

Téya glanced up and over her shoulder. "Oh no," she groaned. She'd used a sewer grate to haul herself up, then pried it open and crawled into the reeking space. But now, the grate was gone. In its place, a steel door.

Trace
Lucketts, Virginia
9 June –1715 Hours EST

"Téya, just hold your position."

"I doubt she's going to take any *leaps of faith*," Houston said with a snicker, his fingers flying over the keyboard, guiding his fly drone toward the grate. "Yep, definitely electronic. I'm going to guess that opens to release the floodgates of sewage."

"Can you open it?"

"That I can, Commander."

"Téya," Trace said leaning over Houston's shoulder to get a better view provided by the drone. "Is Nesim wise to your bug? If you think he is, clear your throat."

Only the sound of wind across the microphone came through.

"Good," Trace said.

Beside them, Annie breathed a sigh of relief. "I still can't believe she's doing this. It's insane—a trap!"

Trace shot Annie a glare. One that told her to settle down. He knew how to run an op. She should know that.

"You send her in there alone then abandon her."

This time the look he sent her way had more personal and emotional capital behind it. "Nobody has abandoned her. Rusty and Nuala are there." And other assets he'd put on alert, ones nobody in this room knew about. He and Téya knew this op was a cesspool of trouble, especially when the Turks had told them he needed to stay behind. She could have an escort, but not Trace. Whatever this was, it was personal and involved Téya.

Because of that, they'd gone to extra precautions. Set up contingencies. If Trace could've left the country, he'd have been there. But with Boone at the hospital, that left the bunker unguarded. That's what she felt, wasn't it? That he abandoned her. But he wouldn't argue with her. Not in front of the geek, whose ears were burning as he listened to this conversation.

Sam appeared from the rear bunk room, his arm supported in a sling. He moved slowly, tentatively.

Annie pushed out of her seat and went to him. "Shouldn't you be resting?"

"I've rested enough to have Rip Van Winkle on my headstone when I die," Sam said as he kept moving toward the station's hub. "What's happening?"

Trace would not answer that. And he hoped Annie wouldn't, but she was letting her feelings for the Squid get in the way of everything:

common sense, operational security, and personal relationships. For now, Trace had to focus on making sure Téya stayed alive.

"Have you figured out what they want from you yet?" That's the thing. Everyone knew the Turks were using Téya for something nefarious. What that was. . . "Clear your throat if you know."

Again, only strong wind.

"Do you still feel it's trouble, a trap? Clear for yes."

A rumble boomed through the speakers.

"Uh," Houston said, lifting his head from his task, "that would be a *definite* yes."

"Don't worry," Trace said. "Nuala has eyes on you." He glanced at the second monitor that held a video recording of what Nuala was watching through the scope of her rifle. "And Rusty's there."

"Okay, the grate should release in three. . .two. . ."

Through the feed, they heard a loud, metallic groaning.

"Watch out!" Téya's shout was followed by a whoosh of liquid-sounding noise.

"I'm going to hurl," Houston said. "Heights *and* a pile of sh—"

"Houston," Trace said. "Are there cameras she needs to worry about?"

Houston's curly head never came up, though he'd spouted off. "Already on it." The clicking of the keys mingled with the disgusted grunts of Téya and her escort.

"Disgusting," Téya said, and blew what sounded like a raspberry.

"Yeah, okay, I didn't need to know that," Houston said. "It's one thing to get crapped on." He looked up and waggled eyebrows with a *Get it?* look. "Another to—"

"Just get it shut down," Trace said.

"Aye, aye, Commander."

Grunts filled the feed once more, and Trace knew they were on the move again. "The drone is still operational. Just play it cool. We're right with you, Téya."

Téya
Frankfurt, Germany
9 June – 2335 Hours

Still nauseated at the smell of raw sewage, Téya low-crawled through the tunnel on her belly, using her elbows to advance. Behind her, she heard the soft splashes of Nesim. He'd been surprisingly agile in the climb and stealthy now. She'd underestimated him on the plane, she guessed. He didn't look like the type of guy who could make a climb like that.

Another twenty minutes or so in, following the pattern she'd randomly chosen—left, left, left, right, left. It'd matched the cadence of the ROTC program she'd been in, that her stepfather, Georg, had demanded she do. As a child under his roof, she had no choice. It'd made her mother happy that she didn't argue. It made Téya happy that she learned to shoot weapons and, once she'd climbed up in rank, got to boss the other cadets around. That was enough for her.

As she banked left for the last time, she slowed. It was dark. Very dark. She should've expected this.

A soft tap came to her leg.

She glanced over her shoulder. "Dead end," she whispered. "They barricaded it."

Nesim waved her back. They renegotiated the last passage and went right instead of left. As they moved along, this time with Nesim in the lead because of the narrow space and having backed out, light trickled into the tunnel. They came to an air vent. Blades of a fan whirred rapidly, daring them to put their fingers in and get them chopped off.

Tugging a small pack she hadn't noticed before from his back, Nesim produced a small torch. He burned through the heavy bolts that held the fan vent on. Téya's gut churned at the thought of having to stop that fan. What if it burned out the motor and set off an alarm? What if it slipped while one of them was climbing through?

Like a pro, Nesim freed the vent cover. Once he'd done that, he reached toward the motor at the center, avoiding the blades completely. With a few deft moves he had stopped the fan.

"Not your first rodeo, huh?" Téya said. She hated that she felt impressed. They were forcing her here. *Why?*

Bracing the fan blades so they didn't move, Nesim hauled his legs out from under his body and sat. He nodded to the interior vent. "Hold it." Using both booted feet, he shoved hard.

Téya pitched forward. The vent came loose, and she nearly fell into the room, but Nesim caught her by the waist. He slowly lowered her into the room. She let the encasing rest against the vinyl floor then pressed both palms to the side and did a sort of cartwheel to her feet. Nesim was at her side.

Metal lockers lined the wall, a few plastic-encased steel benches straddled drain holes. Half walls encircled a center tiled area. Showers.

"You're entering what, according to our schematics, is the locker room."

"Outdated," Téya muttered.

"What?" Nesim asked.

"My memories are outdated," she said, covering her mistake. "This used to be a laundry room."

Nesim rushed to the lockers and dug through them. He produced a green jumpsuit and held it out to her, motioning to the showers.

"No," she hissed. "We have to find Majid, right?"

But he was already going through other lockers. "We reek. They'll smell us a mile away." He bent over a lower locker, yanked something out, then straightened. A blue jumpsuit. "Go," he said again, heading in the opposite direction.

This was all kinds of wrong. But she did stink. And they were probably tracking muck—she glanced at her brown footprints on the floor. Yep.

She stripped, showered, and donned the suit, grateful her undergarments weren't soaked. But they were damp enough to have some of the smell. As were her socks and boots. When she stepped around the corner, dressed, she found Nesim walking toward her. He had a gun. Aimed it at her.

Téya froze. "You wanted me clean before you killed me?"

With an apologetic shrug, he said, "Sorry." And fired.

Trace
Lucketts, Virginia
9 June – 1745 Hours EST

"What just happened?"

Mouth open, eyes wide, Houston stared at his systems. His *silent* systems. "I. . ."

"Téya," Trace called through the coms. "Téya can you hear me?" He spun to Houston. "But we can still hear what's going on, right?"

"Her piece is dead," Houston said, a stunned, bewildered expression plastered to his face. "I don't know how. It's waterproof. That shower shouldn't have affected it."

"The shower didn't," Trace said.

"Is she dead?" Houston asked, his voice squeaking on the last word.

"Negative." Trace would not accept that. "If she was dead, we should still be able to hear, right?"

"Uh. . .yeah." Houston sat a bit straighter. "Yes. If she died, the piece wouldn't."

"Only an electrical surge can shut those down, right?"

Houston nodded but said nothing.

"Can anything else? Think, Houston!"

393

"No, nothing. I mean, they can fluke on us. Something goes haywire and it stops working, but that's rare. It's more likely that there was a surge somehow."

"Stun gun," Sam offered from the lounge area.

"Yes." Houston blinked. "Yes, yes. The Squid is a genius—a stun gun. That's why it died. It's not because my technology is shoddy."

Trace covered his mouth. He didn't want to go there. Didn't want to consider that option.

"Wait—wait. But that's bad, right?" Houston swung another stupefied expression his way. "Because that means he shocked her. And that means he knows she was bugged."

A direct violation of the agreement.

"Would he kill her?"

"Why stun her then kill her?" Sam said.

Trace grouped up what he had left of his nerves and shifted his focus to a recovery mission. "Rusty."

"I'm on my way in," Rusty said without hesitation.

"Noodle."

"I have no joy," she said.

"Stay eyes out. Keep me posted."

"Roger, eyes out," Nuala repeated.

Whatever had just gone down in that facility, Téya was in trouble. The Turk had her. The skilled, trained assassin who had targeted her for the last month had caught up with her. Played chess with her life. Now, was he calling checkmate?

Téya
Frankfurt, Germany
9 June – 2345 Hours

Téya blinked and found herself in a small, dimly lit room. Fire licked through her veins, through every tendril of her flesh. Every hair follicle. Confused, disoriented, she tried to remember how she'd gotten here. In a flash, she remembered the claws of the Taser grabbing her in the chest and pumping voltage through her body. Her heart had seized. Her lungs squeezed, forbidding a breath.

She dragged herself upright and looked around.

Nesim stood against the wall, arms folded and one leg crossed over the other at the ankle. As if this were a casual day and meeting.

"I knew you'd try to kill me," she gritted, rubbing the spot on her chest that still tingled from the tiny charges. "Why not just put a sniper bullet through my gray matter? It would have saved us both some time." She held her palm to her forehead, begging for a breath and heartbeat that didn't hurt.

He came closer. "I was not trying to kill you," he said as he reached for the black hood.

Téya shoved to her feet. Used her palm and struck upward, aiming for his nose.

Skilled and swift, he caught her hand. Jerked it behind her back then dropped to the floor, forcing her down. Her cheek hit hard. "Try that again, and I will kill you."

"What do you want with me?"

"That is my concern. Your concern is compliance." He released her and hopped up, standing over her.

Téya pulled her throbbing head and wounded pride off the floor.

Lowering his head, Nesim reached for the top of his hood again. He pulled it off and scrubbed his still-wet hair. Only then did she realize, he didn't have Nesim's jet-black hair.

He lifted his gaze.

Mentally, Téya threw herself backward, screaming. But a split-second defiance zipped through her. She went perfectly still. However, she could not fend off the terror clawing her courage. She tried to make sense of what she saw. The tattoo on his left cheekbone.

He said he hadn't come to kill her. This time. Then. . .what? Was she to be a captive? His prisoner? Even as she locked gazes with him, she let herself take in her periphery. It sure looked like a cell. Gray cement walls. A lone bed.

He held out his hand, something small in his palm—the device she'd tucked in her ear before making the climb with him. "You were bugged, and that was expressly forbidden."

Téya said nothing. She stared at him. Hard.

"You are smart not to tempt my anger further. I could've used this"— he showed her a Glock—"instead of the taser."

"But killing me would've defeated the reason you brought me here." She hoped it'd induce him to tell her what that reason was.

He almost seemed to smile, the star-crescent dancing. "Still, you do not remember."

Téya frowned. What was she supposed to remember? "What, that you tried to kill me in Paris? Or are you talking about Greece?" She held up the brand.

"Come." The almost light tenor of his voice and his amusement vanished. "On your feet."

"What? I thought I was to be your prisoner."

"Do you remember what Nesim told you about this place?" He stood at the door, gripping the handle.

She did not want to cooperate. But what choice did she have? She couldn't fight him. He was stronger. Faster.

"You may believe me to be the biggest threat to your safety here, but you could not be more wrong." He cocked his head toward the door. "Ready?"

"What are we doing here?"

Light flicked into the room. "Quiet," he hissed at her, grabbing her arm.

Téya flinched at his tight hold. She was about to cry out when she saw two men in black tactical gear stalking down the hall ahead of them. Heavily armed. Intent on something. Had they discovered the fan where she and Nesim—The Turk—had entered?

The realization that she was with The Turk made her head spin. What if he planned to kill someone and frame her for it? It was the only thought that made sense. Why he'd drag her through this facility and not tell her where they were going.

Téya jerked back, planting a foot hard so she could break free of him.

The Turk, again, had lightning fast reflexes. Before her hand could even come up, he held her in a stranglehold from behind. "Stop!" he hissed as he manhandled her over into a shadowed alcove.

"Why? Why me? What do you want with me here?" she squeezed out, her pulse whooshing in her ears.

"There are cameras here. Security officers more than double the staff. Do you want to alert them to your presence?"

Téya considered that. Would it be so bad if she were caught? That would mean he was caught, too, right?

No, he'd escape. If he could outmaneuver her so easily, he'd be gone in a heartbeat.

"You want to know why? I will show you why," he said, loosening his hold then nudging her into the corner, his forearm against her throat. "You must do exactly as I say, or the guards will see you. And they will not hesitate to give you that bullet you asked about earlier." His eyes bored into her, but the tattoo was peculiarly distracting. "Clear?"

Téya swallowed around the pressure of his arm then nodded.

Slowly, he released her. "Come." Again, he took her by the arm. Led her hurriedly down a series of doors and passages.

As they navigated the facility, Téya realized something. It was terrifying and yet reassuring at the same time—he knew where he was going. Which meant he didn't need her to lead him in the back door.

What is going on?

They rounded a corner, and a single door stared back. It was marked Security. It was the same door she'd been herded into the night they'd caught her.

"Wait," she hissed.

But the Turk rushed into the room. In the time it took her to shut the door, he had incapacitated the two security officers sitting at the monitors.

"What—"

"Quiet," he hissed and leaned over the keyboard. He took control of a security camera. Made a few clicks. "Come."

She hated the way he commanded her. The way he assumed she'd do what he said. She toyed with grabbing one of the weapons from the guards.

"Reiker," he growled.

And something twisted sideways in Téya. A chill raced up her spine. She joined him at the desk, feeling unsettled. Unnerved. Her mind struggling to catch up with whatever had triggered the weird feeling.

"Look," he said, one hand on the desk, the other pointing to the monitor.

"That's Red Wing."

Téya's breath caught. "I thought it was an organization. Nesim said it belonged to Red Wing."

"Red Wing is a man, *that* man."

The man stood with his back to the camera, poised as he spoke with a group of guards. Several other guards ran in. Red Wing's body language changed from composed to enraged. Arms flailing. Pointing.

"Why didn't you just tell us where he was? Why bring me—"

Red Wing turned, exposing his face to the camera. To Téya.

Téya went ice cold. No. "Not possible," she whispered, tears blurring her vision. Her heart went from dangerously slow to a rapid-fire beat that made it feel like it'd climb out of her chest. She couldn't breathe. Couldn't think. "He—that can't be. . .he's. . .he's *dead.*

Part 4:
Act of Treason

XI

Téya glanced at The Turk, stunned and confused. Slowly, she swung her gaze back to the monitor. Every nerve ending buzzed. The man in the video was her stepfather. "How. . . ?"

The Turk watched her in silence, holding her gaze but saying nothing.

"How is this possible? He died—six years ago."

"His death was faked."

Téya straightened, feeling as if a tidal wave of unbelievable information pummeled her. "Faked?" Mind ablaze with that revelation, her brain immediately leaped to—"My mom."

The Turk's expression didn't change. "She died in that accident."

"If he survived, then she—"

He took a step forward and squared his shoulders. "Your perceptions about the man who married your mother were borne of a cover story he fed your mother and you."

"Cover story?" Téya felt as if a bucket of ice had been dumped down her back. "What are you—" She severed the question and her thought. Did he seriously expect her to believe anything he said? "You lure me in here, you deceive and lie to me—why would I believe you?"

Again, The Turk said nothing.

Téya's heart still beat wildly, scrambling to iron out the truth. Sort the deluge of shattered facts about her life. "My sister. . ." Her mom married Georg Hostetler when Téya was only four. "All those years. . ."

The Turk took a step back. "We need to leave."

Téya flinched, looking at him. His eyes weren't brown as she'd thought. They had tinges of green and gold. And they were intense. And he wasn't looking at her. She followed his gaze to a monitor that showed a throng of guards racing through the halls.

Alarms shrieked through the cement halls, screaming about their intrusion. Alerting everyone here and around the mountain.

A sharp hiss snapped her back to him. He stood out in the hall. When had he even opened the door? The dude was lightning fast. Téya bolted into the cement corridor after him. He moved fast, not waiting for her. Not checking on her. Téya told herself to stick close. She wouldn't put it past him to leave her to the wolves.

What bothered her more was his skill in navigating the passages. He knew them. Knew them well.

Uncertainty poured through her as they banked right. Téya used the opposite wall to rebound and keep moving, propelling herself faster. She toyed with the idea of tackling him. Demanding information, an explanation. But those instincts were muddied by the out-of-left-field reappearance of her stepfather.

He's here. I'm here. And I'm running.

She would love to go back and hammer the answers out of him, the explanation of how he survived. But something about the way The Turk stared at her. . .left her sick to her stomach and uncertain those answers would provide closure.

No. Right now, she had to get out of here. And her ticket to escape just vanished into a room. A dart of panic threw her forward, narrowly catching the door before it slapped shut, dulling the blaring alarms. She rolled around to avoid getting hit by the door. Four steps in and she saw shadows flying toward her.

Hands up, she braced as the first attacker rushed her. She avoided his initial strike, but her ears rang with the meaty thuds and crack of punches and hits behind her. Fighting hand to hand was hard enough. In a room lit only by dim emergency lights, it was next to impossible.

She missed a block and the guy's fist connected hard. Téya stumbled. He came at her. Rammed his boot into her side. Knocked her to the ground. She grunted and rolled to get back on her feet.

He pounced. Hands around her neck. Choking.

Flailing panic seared her mind. She gripped his wrists. Then the training Quade had thrown at her came rushing back. Téya dug her knee up under him. Oxygen deprivation thumped against her temples. She strained. Pushed. If she didn't succeed, she'd die. Right here. Without answers. And Trace. . .

With a primal growl, Téya rotated her hip. Her knee went up under him. She used her other leg and swung it up around his neck. She arched her back and snapped her hips, effectively bringing him to the ground, his neck between her legs.

Something slid across the cement and bumped against her hand. But Téya focused on incapacitating the man.

"The gun!" someone hissed—The Turk.

Téya glanced down. Saw the Glock at her fingertips. She grabbed it by the barrel and rammed it over the guy's temple. He went limp. Extricating herself quickly, she shoved her foot against his side. Held on to the gun.

Scrambled to her feet.

"Here," The Turk said. Robed in darkness and shadows, he waved to her.

She barely saw the motion before she sprang into action. Téya sprinted toward him. Out a door. When they rounded a corner, he slowed. Hesitated at a corner.

She saw then the damage of the fight on his face. His left eye was swelling shut. His lip was busted. A cut on his temple dribbled blood.

His lips quirked up, and the hint of a smile crinkled the edges of his other eye. "You don't look so bad yourself," he said through heavy breaths after a hard fight. He handed her something. "Here."

She took it then frowned. "It's a twig."

The Turk huffed, turning it over, as if that made a difference. "It's a rose."

Téya held it up. "A twig."

"You are seriously lacking in imagination."

Was he losing it? Only then did the pain in her own lip and temple register. She reached toward the spot and regretted it. "Why are we stopping?"

He thrust his jaw toward the other hall. "C'mere." He tugged her closer, so her back was pressed against his chest. Awareness flared through Téya, but she shut it out. At least, she tried. More well-muscled than she remembered, The Turk exuded power.

She chided herself, told herself to grow up. Pay attention.

"Shadow," he breathed against her ear.

Heat skidded down her neck, eliciting too much response from her betraying body.

But then her mind snagged on what he meant. Against the wall, which wasn't in view when she'd stood behind him, a subtle shift in color—a shadow hung on the wall. She took in a breath, realizing someone stood out of sight, lying in wait.

Had she rushed ahead, she wouldn't have noticed and might've ended up dead. But The Turk had seen it.

Did he miss anything?

His hand covered hers. Not for romance. But to remind her of what she held—the gun. Did he want her to give it to him? Nervous jitters squirreled through her. Give him the gun and she was defenseless. Powerless.

But he'd been in a place to kill her twice now, and hadn't.

Even as she acknowledged that fact, she felt his other arm moving. Saw a dark object and knew he had a gun of his own. She shouldn't be surprised. And she wasn't. Not really. She doubted a man like him was ever unarmed, whether with a gun or some other type of weapon. And he probably didn't need anything to kill. The time he'd pressed her against the wall and rammed his forearm into her throat told her that. One more thrust against her skinny neck and she would've been dead.

He touched her shoulder then slid out from behind her, shimmying along the wall like some type of spider. Crazy fast. Crazy quiet. He had to be half ninja or something.

As he closed in on the person waiting, she realized he had never looked back. Never verified that she'd stay with him. But where else would she go? They were in this together.

Unless he was part of this.

Unless he was the mastermind.

How else would he know the passages so well?

How else would he know Georg was here?

Sidling up against the juncture that held the attacker, he pressed his back to the wall. Téya scuttled up right behind him, breath jammed into her throat. He lunged around the corner.

A shot cracked through the deafening blaze of alarms. Téya sidestepped out, weapon ready. She took aim. Tangles of arms and bodies made it impossible to sort out who was who.

"Shoot!"

The voice, even in the thickly padded noise of the alarms, was distinctly The Turk's.

Shoot. Right? But who? She couldn't—

In a split second she saw The Turk's profile. Instinctively, she fired at the other man. He thumped back against the wall. Turned to her. Angry.

He wore a vest beneath that security shirt.

Téya fired again—this time at the guy's leg to at least slow him down. The Turk spun around and retrieved his gun from the floor. He snapped it up. Fired at the guy. About to object to the brutality, Téya froze when she saw the serrated fighting knife in the man's other hand.

He was going to kill her one way or another. The Turk had saved her.

She pushed her gaze to The Turk. He grinned. "You can't be the hero all the time." He caught her hand and jerked her around the corner, then down the long corridor. Ahead, a door beckoned, a glowing sign above it declared it an exit. They ran toward it for all they were worth.

Out. They were almost out. Téya felt a little giddy.

The Turk pitched toward the door.

Yes. Out. Home free…

Only, The Turk's legs buckled. A dark stain spread over his shoulder.

The door flung open. The Turk clung to it, using it to pull himself around.

Téya nearly tripped over his legs. Like a pileup on the highway. Her legs tangled over his. She flew forward. Rolled against the fall and came back to her feet.

She jerked toward The Turk.

He hauled himself up as he shut the door. Dropped hard against it. Holding his right arm.

Téya lifted his arm and hooked hers around his waist. Then they were rushing on.

"The guard hut on the south," he said as they broke out across the parking lot.

She knew exactly what he meant and headed there. They came to a small overpass, the tunnel below part of a rail system.

"There." He huffed and stumbled toward the rail.

"No, it's—"

His legs were over the edge.

Téya gasped. Then saw the open-bed truck waiting below. Only a dozen feet, but it'd hurt if they landed wrong. Behind them shouts erupted.

Time for a leap of faith.

Téya climbed over the rail, feet perched precariously on the ledge. She looked at The Turk. Sweat dotted his brow in the lights of the facility. With a nod, he took her hand then stepped off the ledge.

They dropped like a sack of potatoes into the truck. Téya's legs crumpled, and she pitched to the side. Their heads collided. It felt as if a hammer hit her and knocked her sideways into the bed of the truck. Pain darted down her cheekbone and neck.

And even before she could untangle herself from The Turk, the truck lurched into motion, barreling into the darkness of the tunnel.

Hands hooked beneath her arms, startling her.

"Easy," someone said, hauling her backward, up against the hull of the cab.

The deafening, windy roar of the tunnel gave way to the intermittent streetlights. Swerving right, the truck sailed over the track and onto the street. The high rate of speed made conversation impossible, wind whipping her hair in her face like tiny snapping needles.

They'd made it. They'd actually escaped.

She turned to The Turk to share her excitement. And found him slumped against a wheel well, someone tending his wound. But The Turk was watching her. Smiling.

A silent message telegraphed through that moment. What it said, she didn't want to think about. She didn't want to read that message right now. Guilt rushed in. Reminded her she was only working with Zulu to get Misrata resolved. To get back home to David. Not to fall for an assassin. Especially one who clearly had no compunction against beating her up, one who'd tried to kill her.

Was she really that stupid?

Annie
Lucketts, Virginia
10 June – 0800 Hours EST

"Téya and the others are back on U.S. soil," Houston announced. "She'll head this way in about an hour."

Annie nodded, sitting at one of the computer terminals in the bunker, working on threads to the mystery with Misrata, but her thoughts kept bouncing back to Téya, Nuala, and Rusty. Were they okay? How had the mission gone? Mostly, she wondered if The Turk had betrayed them. Killed them all.

A ridiculous thought. Had to be. Trace wouldn't have let them go if he had doubts about their security. Then again, Trace hadn't exactly been himself lately. A bit terse, distant—well, except when he wasn't kissing her.

Yeah. . . She couldn't deny how much she'd wanted that to happen or how many times she'd dreamed of it since he'd broken her heart five years ago. Kissing him was every bit as good as it had been when they'd started seeing each other secretly. He'd said she was too young for him. Maybe he'd been right, but she fell head over heels for him. She adored Trace Weston. Admired him. Respected him. Slept with him.

Annie lowered her head, still a bit ashamed at how far their relationship had gone. But there was more guilt at how much she'd wanted it back over those years since their paths diverged. How much she'd wanted the warm comfort of his arms around her. The passion of his kisses. The reassurance of his love.

But he'd left her. High and dry.

She could forgive him. Had forgiven him. But that didn't mean they could just pick up where they'd left off.

"Can we talk?"

Annie blinked and looked up, startled to find Sam standing there thumbing over his shoulder toward the lounge. Coming out of her chair, she nodded. "Uh, yeah." This certainly didn't sound good. Had he read her thoughts, known she was thinking about Trace? Or worse—had he somehow seen her kiss Trace? "Should you be up?"

"A long time ago," he said as they took positions on the seating group.

She tucked herself into a chair, hands in her lap, feeling every bit as if she'd been called to the dean's office.

Sam sat there for a while, rubbing his hands. The bandages around his shoulder poked up against the fabric of his T-shirt. Finally, he brought his dark eyes to hers. "I'm going back to Manson."

She came forward. "What? No, you—"

"With my shoulder messed up, I'm out of commission for a good three, maybe five weeks. I'm not going to be able to help here."

"You can! You can research, do computer stuff with Houston." Her heart thundered as she realized the last thing she wanted was for him to leave.

"Annie, I need to leave. . .you."

She stopped breathing. Tears stung her eyes.

"I think you need to figure out what you want."

The tears spilled over, rushing down her cheeks, hot and fast. That's when she knew. "You saw us."

A pained expression streaked across his face. "No, but I had a feeling. It's all over your face."

"I'm sorry, Sam." She scooted forward in the seat. "You're right—I have to figure out some things, but I don't want to do it without you."

"That sounds good, in theory," he said with a smile. "But in real life, with us here, I don't think it'll work." When she opened her mouth to object, he held up a hand. "If you go forward, I want you to know my intention up front. I want a future with you. I'm not going to yank you around. I'm not going to leave you." He drew something from his pocket. A gold solitaire lay in his palm.

She swallowed a sob. How long had she ached for someone to say those words to her? And to have Sam. . . "Oh, Calamari," she sighed. Her gaze landed on the ring, and Annie knew what she wanted. "I want that life, Sam. I want it with you."

"Yes, but do you want it because it'll hurt Trace? Or do you want it because you love me?"

"Because—"Annie froze, realizing she didn't know the answer to that question. She *did* want to hurt Trace. He'd devastated her. Left her with more than just a broken promise, but she'd never exposed *that* secret to the light of day. And she never would. Truth was, she had strong feelings for both Sam and Trace. In different ways that she couldn't sort out.

"Yeah," he said with a nod that made her aware she hadn't answered. "You have some things to work out. Because if 'us' is just about hurting him, what happens when your anger wears off?"

"It hasn't worn off in five years." She batted her golden curls out of her face. "Look, yes—I have to sort this. Trace devastated me. He left me when he'd promised to be there for me. I gave him *everything*." She paused intentionally to make sure he caught her meaning.

Understanding spread through his features, and he got up from the seating group. Paced. Though she wasn't sure and she'd never heard Sam utter an oath, she was pretty sure one seared the air.

He started for the bunk rooms then pivoted back. Stood there. Came toward her. Shook his head.

He wanted to leave. But Sam, in his intense desire to be honorable, refused to break the promise he'd just made—he wouldn't leave her.

Annie didn't move, because he had every right to be angry. "I trusted him. Believed him. And he left me on an airstrip, alone and—" She bit off the rest of that dark jungle of her life. "It was to protect me, he says. But. . ."

"Annie," Sam said, his tone tight, tense. "You're not over him."

She swallowed. Hard.

Nostrils flared, Sam shook his head, clearly ticked.

"Sam, I—"

A sharp gasp came from the command station. "Oh man." Houston's grave tone of voice spiraled through the open station. "Dude, I'm so sorry."

Annie pushed to her feet and looked toward Houston. "What's wrong?"

Jaw slack, Houston met her gaze and touched the Bluetooth in his ear. "All right, man," he spoke to someone. "See you—and. . .and I'm sorry." He pressed his earpiece, ending the call with a heavy shake of his head. "Keeley died."

The world suddenly felt a lot less bright and cheery. Annie couldn't process it—she was gone. They'd won. . .again.

Thunk! The massive locks of the main door disengaged. With a heavy groan, the steel barrier swung inward. Téya rushed in wearing battle scars—a busted lip, a cut on her temple that made the bruise around her eye seem like a bad makeup job. She lifted a hand to them but started immediately for the back.

"Téya—"

"Not yet," she said tightly.

"Keeley's dead," Annie snapped.

Téya stopped, facing sideways in her trek to the bunk rooms. Lowered her head. Then continued to the back. A couple of minutes later, Nuala and Rusty entered the underground bunker, both worn and weary.

Perceptive Nuala keyed into the problem immediately. "What's happened?"

Something in Annie finally broke loose. "It's Keeley," she said, her throat raw. "She's gone."

Nuala's eyes widened. She covered her mouth and turned, looking for something or someone. Then she came back around to Annie, eyes dribbling tears. "Boone—how's Boone? Where is he?"

"On his way," Houston said, removing his headset.

"What happened?" Annie asked, nodding in the direction Téya fled. "Did The Turk burn her?"

Rusty moved forward. "The mission had complications. We lost coms with Téya after the first twenty minutes in—as I'm sure Houston told you."

"Indeed I did," Houston said, cracking his knuckles. "And I might not be a black ops soldier, but even I know something else went on after all that."

"Téya and The Turk fled the facility. She was missing for two hours. We got a call from The Turk's people, who promised to deliver Téya to the airstrip. She showed up and hasn't spoken a word since."

A phone line tweedled. Houston rolled his chair back to his monitors and caught the call. "What can I do for you, sir?"

Annie knew who it was. Houston only gave that deference to one man—Trace. Out of the corner of her eye, she detected Sam moving toward the bunk room. She met his gaze, briefly. His anger still hung like a neon sign around his neck. She'd failed him. While the intimacy she'd shared with Trace happened prior to meeting Sam, the kiss they'd shared hadn't. And Annie had admitted she was confused. What a great way to ruin one of the best things that had happened to her.

Then again, she'd once said that about Trace.

Maybe Annie just couldn't trust herself where love was concerned. Maybe she didn't have the ability to rightly discern love from loyalty.

"Trace has called an AHOD."

Great. More bad news coming. She could feel it. Sense it in the air. Feel it digging into the pores of her flesh.

Boone
Lucketts, Virginia
10 June – 0900 Hours

The sun had fallen from the heavens. That's how the world felt without Keeley in it. The cloudy sky seemed apropos, as if ready to birth grieving. Boone trudged into the bunker. Though he wanted to keep his head down so he didn't have to see the glum, sympathetic looks cast his way, he walked across the open area with his head up.

Yeah, he noticed the way everything froze, as if breathing or talking might upset him. As if not acknowledging Keeley's death would keep it from being true. He didn't want or need sympathy. What he needed was vengeance. He wanted to be the justice-bringer to those who'd done this to them.

He met Annie's gaze. As Zulu's leader, it was only right he addressed her first. "The commander here?"

"No," she said, her voice soft.

"He's on his way," Houston offered. "How ya doing, Big Guy?"

Right, because small talk right now would fix everything. Because how he was doing mattered. *Nothing* mattered except giving Keeley's death meaning. Bringing honor to the woman who fought so courageously on the battlefield. And who brought even the stoutest to their knees. Even him. In a different way.

"I'll be in the briefing room. Let me know when he's here."

He shut the door and dropped into a chair, his back to the team. Sat straight and tall, remembering his dad's admonishments to never let them see your pain. He didn't want their apologies and offer of prayers or positive energy or whatever they had to offer. He wanted a plan. One to bring down this group behind the killings.

They killed her. That was the only explanation for her sudden decline. He might not have a PhD, but Boone had seen enough to recognize poisoning. Somehow, despite their efforts, despite Rusty being on watch 24-7, they'd slipped her a lethal cocktail of some kind. He'd asked the doctors to run panels, but the results hadn't come back yet. But Boone knew in his gut what happened. They'd won. Again.

And the brightest lights in his universe winked out. *"My shoes are sparkly."* The last words she'd spoken to him. Over a pair of silly, clear sequined shoes. A ridiculous purchase. But that was Keeley. Bohemian in style. She'd wear cargo shorts and a no-nonsense tank top, then add a pair of pink sparkly shoes.

Or the time she put that stark white streak in her hair. It was from some kids' cartoon she'd seen. Fierce fighter, fiercer friend. She gave everything a hundred percent then went an additional fifty. They hadn't crossed God's commands, but he'd come close to ignoring a few where Keeley was concerned. *"That you stopped,"* Keeley had said as they lay on the sand that night, *"makes me love you more."*

He'd realized in that hour how much he wanted to be a better man just to make her love him more. In fact, he had plans to introduce her to his parents somehow. To convince Trace to let him bring her to Lucketts. Marry her. Finish what they'd started on the beach that night.

Now she and her love were gone.

He'd never hear her laughter again. He'd never hear the lilt of her parents' Irish brogue in her words again. Never feel those soft, full lips on his. Or her small yet strong fingers grip his. Or see her wearing ridiculous earrings.

Laughter was gone from his life.

A triple rap against the glass door dialed up his agitation. Didn't they get that he didn't need company or a pep talk?

"Sorry." It was Rusty. Just maybe the man would have the decency to go away. The door clicked shut.

Boone hoped he was alone. But resisted wiping the hot tear trekking down over his stubble.

Rusty broke into view.

Curling his hand into a fist, Boone gritted his teeth.

His friend took the first chair, sitting on the edge. Cell phone in hand, he wagged it. "I just got a call."

Boone gave him a pointed look.

"It was the hospital. Dr. Gates."

This time, he turned his full attention to Rusty. "What poison?"

Rusty gave a snort-smile. "How do you always know. . .?"

"Cyanide?"

"Ricin."

"How did they miss that?"

"He's investigating right now, also trying to figure out who was behind it."

"We know who it was," Boone said.

"I think he meant how they got in, got past me." Something blazed in Rusty's eyes. And in that moment, Boone saw it. Saw the same thirst in his friend that pumped through his own veins.

"Wasn't your fault."

"I think it was," Rusty said decisively. "At least in part. And don't try to write this off. I had one job—to protect her." Though younger by a half-dozen years, Rusty always had a fighter's spirit. It's what made it possible for the young grunt to make it into the Special Forces so fast. "I failed, Boone-Dawg."

Boone could eat a piece of bitter root of truth. "You and me both, brother. She was my girl, and I let her die on my watch." Hearing those words, living their truth, felt like a KA-BAR to the heart.

Rusty's blue eyes bored into him. Conflict borne of a desire to be done with Zulu and a hunger to sate the beast that wanted revenge roiled through his posture, his gaze, his balled fists. Finally, Rusty hung his head between his shoulders. "This is why I got out. The thirst for blood, the yearning to kill something."

"Trusty," Boone said, using the nickname they'd given the kid when he'd first come to the team, "I think maybe your head's getting a little twisted up. You're a warrior. It's what we do. God doesn't put that drive in many men, but in the ones that He does, it comes with a thirst for justice. Sometimes we might confuse that for a thirst for blood, but if we come back to ourselves, recognize that thin line in the sand, we'll be okay."

"That's just it," Rusty said, his lip curling. "I couldn't see the line anymore. After Misrata, I just wanted anyone and everyone in my way dead. I needed someone to take the blame for what we did."

"It was a mistake."

"No," Rusty ground out, his face reddening. "Somebody set us up. Somebody set Zulu up to take that fall. It wasn't a simple mistake."

"You're going to suggest that someone wanted us to kill twenty-two innocent children and women?"

"I'm saying someone wanted Zulu out of their way." Rusty held his gaze, unwavering. "I know it sounds crazy—"

"It sounds right."

They both turned toward the new voice and found Trace entering the briefing area. He looked more ticked than both of them.

Trace

When Boone pushed out of his seat, Trace waved him back down. He shot a cursory glance to the main area to make sure the others weren't coming yet. "We've got ten minutes before the AHOD."

"What do you know?"

"First—I'm sorry about Shay." Trace said it with authority and strength. Not with pity but with promise. "It won't go unanswered."

It seemed a weight lifted from Boone's chest. He gave Trace a nod of thanks.

"Rusty," he said as he met the other man's gaze. "I'm glad you're here, though I know you'd rather be elsewhere."

"No, sir."

Boone stilled.

"I'm right where I want to be now." Rusty said nothing more, and nothing else needed to be said. They were the handlers of the Zulu team, the trainers, the leaders. They had a job to do. A retaliation to put into effect.

"We have a few more puzzle pieces in place," Trace said. "But each time we walk through a door to a question, two more open." He jabbed his fingers across his short-cropped hair. "I'm getting fed up with the whole thing. It's been like this for five years. Answers were merely more questions in disguise. The more they asked, the more questions bred."

"What about Frankfurt? What was that?" Rusty asked. "And since when are we working with the Turks? Téya was missing for two hours—should we be worried?"

"No." Trace could answer that unequivocally. And he had a theory on the missing two hours. One he didn't really want to think about. One he *couldn't* worry about right now. "I don't think that's a problem, at least—not one connected to Misrata."

The door opened and in filed Nuala, Annie, Téya, and Houston, who had an array of technology on a cart. Trace waited for the remnant of Zulu to find a seat then noted Houston plugging in his machines and getting things working. "Okay, let's get this going. First thing I need you all to be aware of is the Lorings have vanished from protective custody."

Silence slapped through the room.

"How is that possible? Did they miss the part where it's *protective*? Why would they leave it?"

Trace had been through these questions a dozen times on his way over and since Haym had called and warned him.

"Do you think they're in danger?" Annie asked.

"No," Trace said. "I think they willingly left."

"But we got their information, right?" Annie leaned forward, pressing her fingertips to the table. "They gave us Ballenger, that he was the one behind moving the children there."

"That's not much for them to be on the run though, is it?" Rusty scratched the side of his face. "What threat are they running from if they only had information on Ballenger?"

This is why Trace had wished Rusty would've returned to the team weeks ago. This type of dialogue, talking out the problem, kept them safe.

"Unless Ballenger is a bigger threat than we realized," Annie said then looked at Trace. "Is he?"

He considered the question. Ballenger. Danger. Yeah, they seemed to go hand in hand. "We won't rule it out. Each time we've sought him, we've encountered deadly opposition—in Denver and Paris."

"Yeah, but that could've just been us. Someone trying to put us off the trail," Annie said.

"Ballenger could be doing that," Nuala offered. "He plays the victim very well."

"We need to move on. We'll qualify Ballenger as a high threat."

"With the Lorings missing, is the bunker in jeopardy?" Boone asked, arms folded over his thick chest.

"Possibly," Trace said, unwilling to play things safe. "Need to keep our ears and eyes out at all times coming and going." He nodded to Houston. "He's going to catch us up on what came off the yacht computers."

"There wasn't much," Houston said as he aimed a remote at a laptop. "I should say—there was a lot, but not much useful to us. There are innumerable files pertaining to what appear to be shipments. Port records. Munitions sales—"

"Batsakis is in weapons," Annie said. "Aegean Defense Systems."

"Yes. Right. Buuuut," Houston said as he pulled up another file. "The pattern is fairly regular. What I looked for is irregularities." He snickered. "Or I should say, irregular *regular* shipments."

"Houston," Trace bit out.

"Right." Houston's Jheri curl hair bobbed as he nodded. "If you look through this file, ADS has a pattern of shipments going out every few months. Same countries. To the same clients. It's your standard fare, right?"

"Except?"

Houston grinned, a tech geek in his element as he pressed the remote and a series of neon blue panels flashed over the screen, highlighting certain entries in the shipping ladings. "Except these."

Trace wasn't the only one leaning forward. "They're imports."

"Bingo! Score one for the commander!" Houston beamed with exultation. "They're imports."

"Where are they coming from?"

Houston sniggered. "That's the question, isn't it? Because you, of course, noticed there's no origination scan to match these records as there is for every other shipment."

"You're telling me that a world-renown defense contractor is buying illegal weapons, and. . .what?" Annie pressed. She always did. She wanted solid proof. She had to be sure the rabbit they hunted was rabid before putting it down.

"Black market," Boone said.

"Makes sense," Rusty put in.

"How?" Annie's voice pitched. "They're a billion-dollar company! Why would they need to deal in the black market?"

"Because seven years ago, they were on the verge of filing for bankruptcy. Most companies in Greece were," Boone said. "How did a company going under suddenly recover? Not just recover, but soar into the billions with profit returns?"

"Exactly." Trace returned to the head of the table. "Our problem is figuring out who's selling the weapons to them."

"And that is where I'm hitting a brick wall," Houston said. "There is a highly encrypted file on that computer that I have not been able to break into. I believe that file will give us what we need to figure out the coded references attached to each entry."

"That's the jackpot," Boone said. "That person, that company—whatever, they're responsible for murdering three of our team. They're the ones out there right now, trying to lob off the rest of our heads. And with Keeley being poisoned in her hospital room, it's clear they are actively pursuing each of us, still."

"Wait," Nuala said, pushing up in her seat. "If they know who we are to target us, would it follow that they know our families? Is this a game changer?"

Silence fell like an anchor.

"Because while I haven't talked to them, I still have a brother and mom out there." She brushed her long bangs from her face. "I want to know if they're in danger so I can warn them."

"No, I don't believe so," Trace said.

"They hit my family—and David." Arms and legs crossed, Téya held his gaze evenly. "Twice."

"Because you were *living* with them." Trace motioned to Nuala and Annie. "You weren't. You were concealed within your pseudonyms."

Téya's eyes blazed. "So, it's my fault."

"Negative," Trace said. She would not bait him into a confrontation. He had expelled too much energy already on frivolous arguments. He wouldn't engage here on his own turf. "They went to Bleak Pond to find and neutralize you. But you were already gone, so they hit those familiar with you."

"And then they went back, hurt him again. Snatched my grandmother. Because I got away."

"It's true—they were trying to draw you out." Trace pointed around the room. "Don't let these dogs put that guilt on your shoulders. They are the ones murdering. Not us. The others did not and do not live with family. Your true identities are not known."

"They know me," Boone said, knuckling his jaw. "I'll put my parents on an Alaskan cruise. They've been wanting it. Can't get my brother out of the way. If he thinks something's up, he'll be more bullheaded than a dog with a scent."

"You mean, he'll be just like you," Rusty said with a chuckle.

"I'm not bullheaded."

Laughter trickled through the room.

Boone scowled. "I'm determined."

The laughter rose to a roar.

"Hey." Houston's interjection killed the laughter. "Oh wow oh wow." His eyes went wild, the overhead vent rustling his curls. "This. . .look at this. I'd been running various algorithms on Jessie's info wall. Check this out!"

Trace looked at the wall again, this time scanning a series of letters and numbers that slid and dropped over rows like Tetris pieces. It happened faster and faster until they ended with a list of names. "What is this?"

"A list."

"No duh, Curly Locks," Boone said. "What names are those?"

Houston bent forward, scrolling up and down. Going back. "I–I'm not sure."

"I know," Nuala said, pulling Trace's attention to the petite girl. Her face had gone pale. She looked sick to her stomach. "It's the names of the children."

Trace knew what children she meant, and it felt like someone had shoved a dagger into his heart five years ago and just grabbed the hilt again to dig it deeper.

"How do you know that's their names?" Annie asked, her question squeaking as Boone turned back to the image on the wall. "We didn't know their names. Did we?"

"Footage," Nuala said, her voice dull. As if she were in a trance. "I watched the videos and interviews afterward." She met Trace's gaze with a nod. "I know we weren't supposed to, but I needed some closure. Something to stave off the nightmares. I wrote down the names. There were only a few publicly mentioned, three." Her pale blue eyes looked like pools of water. "I memorized them"—she nodded to the wall—"Qayyima, Akifa, and Sawsan. They're on that list."

"Wait," Téya finally spoke up, her hazel eyes wide. "Look." Her complexion paled.

Confused, Trace glanced at the screen. Then back at Téya. "What are you seeing?"

"It's what I'm *not* seeing—the Lorings!" She brushed her hair from her face. "The kids aren't listed there."

"But they didn't die," Annie said.

"That's not a list of the dead. There are too many," Nuala said. "It's a list of the children cared for by HOMe."

Boone came alive. "Think Jessie somehow got this from HOMe?"

Though he didn't want to believe a list actually existed, Trace couldn't discount it. "It came from someone in the know. Hope of Mercy told us a list didn't exist, that the facility was too new."

"Apparently not."

"But still—the Lorings." Téya asked. "Why aren't they on there?"

"And now, they're missing. Mighty convenient." Boone rapped his knuckles on the table. "Ladies and Gentleman, I'm thinking we had the enemy right in our midst."

Trace
Lucketts, Virginia
10 June – 1015 Hours

"May I have a word?"

At the intrusion of Téya's voice, Trace looked up from the table where he was reviewing the files Houston had uncovered. He pinched the bridge of his nose and sat back, tossing his pen down. "Sure. Come in." Whatever she wanted to say, he hoped it brought answers about the two missing hours.

Téya entered and took the seat at the corner next to him. She slid a small flash drive on the table. "What they promised."

He expelled a breath. "I'd started wondering if they pulled a fast one on me." Pocketing it, he noted she hadn't moved. "Heard you had some excitement on the mission."

She almost smiled, her expression taut as she stared at the table, seemingly lost in a memory.

Trace sat forward. Leaned into her. "Téya, I'm on your side. Whatever—"

"Red Wing is my stepfather." She said it so fast and with such little emotion that Trace froze. Processed words he hadn't expected. But then he recalled her military records. He'd studied each dossier in depth. "Hold up—your stepfather was a base commander, right? Records show him dying—"

"In an accident that supposedly killed him and my mother. Apparently, my mother was the only unlucky one in that." The news had hit Téya at the core of her being. Trace knew from her dossier that losing her mother had devastated her to the point of needing a therapist.

Téya sat there, processing.

And Trace took the time to do the same. To also note the cuts, bruises,

417

and swelling on her face. "What happened, T?"

"The mission went bad from the get-go. It'd been too many years since I'd been there. Things had changed. We got in, but we had to crawl through raw sewage. When I got in there, I realized the man I thought to be Nesim was in fact The Turk."

Track jerked forward in his seat. "What? I thought you were rescuing him!"

"That's what they told us," she said with a nod. "But he lured me into that facility for one purpose—I thought it was to kill me once I realized who he was. But then he took me to a security room where I saw the camera feed. My stepfather is in that facility."

"I'm not following."

"Good," she said with a laugh. "Because I wasn't either. I couldn't understand why he didn't just tell me. Majid said that he knew I wouldn't believe him if I didn't see for myself that Georg was still alive." She had this wistful smile now as she talked, and it unnerved Trace. Especially when she sat for several long minutes staring blankly at the time. But the flickering of her eyes, like an awake REM, told him she wasn't here. She was remembering.

"Téya?"

"How much of a coincidence is it, Trace, that my stepfather is Red Wing, the one purported to be highly connected to whatever was happening in Misrata and beyond? What are the odds?"

"Pretty high." In fact, he'd call them contrived. Fake. "You said you saw your stepfather in security footage?"

She gave a lone nod.

"That could've been recorded. Faked."

"Perhaps," she said slowly. "But I don't think so. Even if it was, what would be the point of faking it, of telling me he's alive?"

"To throw us off. Get us on the wrong track?"

"Why? How would that benefit him?"

"He hunted you down in Paris and threatened to kill you to get you out of the way. I wouldn't put it past The Turk to do that now, if something we're doing interferes with his mission."

Téya nodded. Then nodded some more, as if sorting the facts and storing them. Finally, the consternation washed off her face and she straightened. "I want to go to Bleak Pond—no, I *need* to go."

"Té—"

"I need to warn them, Trace. To warn David. I won't go see my grandmother. She was too shaken when we rescued her," Téya explained. "But I have to talk to David. Make him aware of the danger."

There was something else behind her reason, he could feel it. See it in her eyes. Did she want to go back to say good-bye? "Did The Turk make you an offer?"

Téya smiled. "I need to go back, Trace. Please." She touched his hand. "I'll be back by nightfall."

"One condition—Boone goes with you."

"Boone's grief-stricken."

"Rusty then."

Nodding, Téya finally relented.

She hadn't answered his question. She'd referred to The Turk by his given name. And now she wanted to return to Bleak Pond—*and* she'd told him rather than running off like last time. Trace had a sinking feeling Majid Badem was recruiting Téya out from under Trace. Stealing her.

Téya
Bleak Pond, Pennsylvania
10 June – 0230 Hours

With a *kapp* on and the familiar dress of the Amish, Téya stared down Augsburger Lane. David's younger siblings and cousins played in the fields, having completed their chores. The older children were at the school building, though they'd be coming home soon.

"You sure about this?"

Téya flinched at Rusty's voice then flashed him a smile she didn't feel. "Yeah." She tugged on the silver handle and pushed open the door. "Remember—watch for me from down the road."

He nodded.

This could take an hour or it could be over in minutes. She strolled down the country lane, nervous and uncertain. Anxious. She had to warn David. More than that, she had to see him. Had to know that what happened in Frankfurt hadn't changed her or anything else. She'd told Trace that she was worried about her family's safety, but she wasn't. At least, not as much. Majid had promised to put an asset or two in place.

Are they here even now?

The pull to scan the fields and tree line tugged at her, but she resisted. This wasn't about Majid. This was about David Augsburger and Katie Gerig.

Téya slowed to a stop, a nauseating knot tightening in her stomach. She didn't even know who Katie was anymore. The *kapp* strings fluttered in a breeze, smacking her in the face. Stinging. Unfeeling.

419

Just as she'd been when she walked out of Bleak Pond without looking back. So what if she'd cried the whole way? She'd left them. Left those she loved.

"What are you doing here?"

Again caught off-guard, Téya spun on her heels. David stood there in his brown pants, suspenders, and white shirt, leaning on a cane. Her heart clinched at the sight. She forced herself to act happy. "I thought you'd still have to rest."

His eyes bored into hers. "It's boring lying about all day. A man needs to work."

She smiled. So like David—but with an edge. He was mad. At her.

"Like I asked, what are you doing here, Katie?" The wind riffled his dark brown hair that hung longer than the men she was keeping company with lately. Trace and Boone had short-cropped hair. Rusty, a little longer but not by much. And Majid. . .

No, not him. She wouldn't think about him now.

"I hoped we could talk," Téya said as she walked toward him.

"Isn't that what we're doing?"

"David," she said with a nervous laugh, skating a look around to make sure nobody heard them talking, heard his harsh disdain. "I've never heard you talk to friends like that before."

"I *don't* talk to friends like that." His words carried the blade of a dagger, right into her chest.

She wet her lips. She ached for the kindness he'd always shown her. For the reassurance that life would be okay.

"Who was the man in the truck?"

Téya started.

"Maggie saw you ride into town with him," David said, referring to his sister-in-law.

"He's a friend—just a man I work with. I don't own a car, so he agreed to bring me." It wasn't the whole truth, but it was a close variant. As close as she could give to David. And that hurt, too. "David," she said, stepping up to him and taking his hand.

He stiffened, his jaw tightening. "Release me."

Shaken at his tone, at the disgust she saw in his eyes and heard in his voice, she stepped back. "What. . .what is wrong?"

David cut his narrowed eyes to her. "Mrs. Gerig told me you're a soldier."

Téya straightened, her lips parting in surprise as she pulled back.

"It's true, then?"

"Dav—"

"Leave us, Katie! Or whoever you are. Leave and don't come back."

"David, you have to listen to me," she said, abandoning the hope of his love. The hope that he'd still smile at her and tell her everything would be okay. "There are dangerous men after me."

"Yes, they nearly killed your grandmother and me then came back to try to finish me off." He started back to the house, hobbling awkwardly on his still-healing leg.

"David, I'm sorry." Her throat felt raw, thick. "I never thought I'd have to go back."

"It's better this way," David said, stumbling as he moved quicker on his bad leg. "You don't belong here, Katie."

Hurt and anger writhed in her chest. "It wasn't supposed to be like this! This place, my grandmother—*you* were supposed to be my life. I *wanted* that. Can't you see I loved you?"

He stopped, the pebbles crunching angrily beneath his feet. With a shift, the rocks groaning beneath him, he held her gaze. "Loved?"

Had she said that? "No, *love*."

"You said *loved*. Past tense." He squared his jaw. "Go back to your warring. To your fighting, Katie. You don't belong here." His eyes seemed to blur with unshed tears. "I could never marry a woman who killed people."

Those last words thrust the dagger deeper, twisting. Killing any hope of love and happiness she had left. Chin trembling, she backstepped. Tears blurred her vision. She wiped at them angrily, not wanting to lose sight of David. "Take care of her, please—my *grossmammi*. Please promise me that much!"

He slowed but didn't look back. Instead, his gaze went to the ground next to him. "Bleak Pond takes care of its own. Without weapons and violence." His shoulders rose and fell as his voice trembled. "We use a more powerful weapon—love."

Annie
Lucketts, Virginia
11 June – 0900 Hours

Beneath a mighty oak, Zulu had laid Keeley to rest. Annie and Nuala hooked arms with Téya as they stood next to the gaping hole in the earth, the one that mirrored the hole in their lives. In Zulu. Bible in hand, Boone read from the Twenty-Third Psalm, determined to give Keeley a "decent" sending off. He'd chosen to place her remains here on his property to keep her close, but also because she'd been buried once already. In a family plot back in Nebraska. The coffin her parents had placed in the ground was empty. The pine box being placed in the ground now, was not.

A somber mood hung over the group. Boone for having lost Keeley. Zulu for also having lost a sister-in-arms. Something had happened to Téya when she went to check on her family back in Pennsylvania, though she hadn't spoken of it since. And Annie bore a new grief, having witnessed flight 5792 out of Dulles at 4:15 that morning. Seated in seat 5F—Samuel Caliguari.

Boone and Rusty shoveled the dirt over the casket in silence, each thump of dirt hitting the box sounding like a clap of thunder against their souls. She was gone. Keeley was gone. Jessie and Candice, too. Half the team. Annie couldn't help but wonder who would be next. Her?

While Rusty and Boone finished filling the grave site, Annie and the others went in and set up a small brunch. Nobody would send flowers. Nobody would bring meals.

"He blames himself," Nuala said softly as she set out napkins.

"They both do," Annie agreed. "Somehow, even I feel guilty."

"I was so stupid to think being a Special Forces soldier was a good thing. So hung up on myself, I never considered—"

"What was there to consider?" Annie asked. "It was an opportunity. We could not know then what would happen a year later. We could not know how upside down things would become."

"So, that's it? We just live with upside-down lives?" Téya's eyes blazed with anger.

"No, we fight it." She considered her friend, surprised at the outrage in her voice and body language. "Téya, what happened in Bleak Pond?"

Her friend stilled, her chest rising and falling unevenly. "Nothing." She batted her hand. "Where's Trace? Why wasn't he at the funeral?"

Annie shook her head, mostly at the way her friend dismissed her, but also to shed her own surprise that Trace hadn't come. "It's not like him."

"I'm sure he had a good reason." Nuala, ever the optimist.

The vault-like door groaned open and Boone stormed in, a phone pressed to his ear. Behind him came Rusty, dusting off his hands.

Boone said nothing. Didn't look at them. Just stalked to the briefing area and closed the door.

"Someday, they'll actually act in accordance with their words, that we're on equal ground."

"We're all soldiers," Rusty said as he washed his hands at the sink in the little kitchen. "But Boone and the commander are our team leaders. There's a reason the Army has a chain of command."

"We're not in the Army anymore," Téya bit out.

"Actually, we are." Rusty picked up a plate and started piling brisket on it.

"Want to explain that?" Annie folded her arms over her chest, watching him move on as though he had not a care. "We've lived civilian lives for the last five years."

He pointed a fork at her. "Lived a civilian life is one thing. You lived it, but you were and still are owned by the U.S. government. Think about it: Who're you taking orders from?"

"All right," Boone's voice bounced off the cement walls. "Eat up, pack up. We head out late tonight."

"Head out for where?" Annie spun toward him, her mind whirling.

"England. We're going to find Berg Ballenger."

Trace
Capitol Hill, Washington, DC
11 June – 1130 Hours

Yawning into his glass of water, Trace had been ready for a lunch break for the last two hours. Honestly, since he'd arrived. Listening to a recounting of endless hours of testimony felt more like being stuck in a time warp. Or watching that movie *Groundhog Day* over and over and over. And over.

There wasn't anything new here. Nothing new to discover. At least, not about him. He'd been there. He'd led Zulu. But this hearing had nothing on him. Nothing they could pin that would cause the devastation they wanted.

Another yawn pulled at him.

"Are we boring you, Colonel Weston?"

Straightening in his seat, Trace felt the heat of embarrassment reach the tips of his ears. He didn't answer the question. It wasn't meant to be answered.

"We'll take a short recess then return with the testimony of Lieutenant Francesca Solomon."

Trace resisted the urge to look at Haym. Why hadn't the general told him about this? What could his bulldog daughter know about Misrata?

The chairman of the committee called a break, and a hum of conversation and movement blanketed the room. Trace leaned over to the general.

"I have no idea," Haym said before Trace could ask his question. "She conveniently kept this from me."

"Why would they hear her out? She wasn't there."

Haym nodded but didn't reply.

"Sir?" Trace insisted on an answer. He needed reassurance something hadn't come to light to wrongly implicate him.

"I don't know." He pushed up from his seat at the table. "Excuse me."

With a hefty sigh, Trace slumped back against the chair. Rubbed his jaw then stood. Stiff in his uniform jacket, he made his way to the main hall. He used the facilities then walked to the far end of the hall and stood at a bank of windows overlooking the green. Across the grassy area, parking lots gave way to the busy streets of downtown DC. Here careers were made. Or destroyed. Pundits needed a scapegoat and nailed whomever they could get their hands on onto the cross of justice. Trace understood that sometimes happened to help people feel like tragedies weren't being ignored. That the pain of innocents wasn't overlooked.

He'd just never expected to find himself fighting for his career five years later. This was a nightmare that just would not end. A glance at his watch told him it was time to go back. Sit at the table like a target lined up as a sacrificial lamb.

"We're pulling for you, sir," a young lieutenant said as Trace pushed past. Trace gave him a nod of thanks as he broke through the crowd at the door.

Someone rammed into him.

Beautiful gold eyes met his. Widened. And that's when the rest of her facial features registered. "Miss Solomon."

Her cheeks pinked. "Colonel," she said tightly.

He took a step away, told himself to leave her alone, but he couldn't. "Just remember, your lies affect more than me."

"I could say the same to you."

He did ignore that and shuffled down the aisle into his seat at the front. For a closed, confidential meeting, there were a lot of people here.

"Where have you been?" Haym hissed.

"Getting some air," Trace said, frowning at the general.

"We have a problem."

Trace's gaze automatically bounced to Francesca Solomon, who'd taken a seat on the row behind them. Without turning her head, she slid her gaze to him. Arrogant confidence plastered her face.

"She has the identities of your team."

"How the heck did she—"

"I don't know."

"We have to shut that down. She cannot go live with that information."

"I'm working on it, but it's not that simple."

"It *is* that simple." He bent forward, his nose practically in Haym's face. "If she reveals their names, Zulu is crippled. I cannot launch them. I cannot get the answers we need. This has to be shut down—*now*, General."

"They'll only argue that the names are okay to be revealed because they're dead." Haym waved a hand. "It's a closed hearing—they'll say the information is safe."

"There are fifty potential sources of compromise in this room," Trace countered.

"You know that. I know that. But convincing them—"

"Then we need a distraction to end this now. Then you need to drag her butt under a bright light and convince her to stop." Trace did not suggest things lightly. But when a bulldog caught the scent of a bone. . .

An idea began to formulate in Trace's mind. It could put his reputation in more jeopardy, but did he have any other choice? Annie, Téya, and Nuala depended on him.

Trace maintained his peace as Chairman Moller resumed the session. He maintained his peace as a summary was presented. He maintained his peace as the chairman handed over control of the mic to Representative Glick, who then called Francesca Solomon to the table.

She moved to the seat beside her father.

"Please state who you are and why are you here, for the record," Glick said.

"Thank you," she said, resting her hands in her lap as she leaned forward. She had the demure thing down pat. "My name is Francesca Solomon. I'm a lieutenant in the United States Army. I work for INSCOM as an analyst. I've been invited here by General Marlowe to provide testimony regarding the tragic bombing in Misrata, Libya, that took the lives of twenty-two innocents."

"Thank you, Miss Solomon," Chairman Moller intoned, taking back control of the microphone. "Can you please explain why we are hearing from you again? The Permanent Select Committee on Intelligence heard from you more than four years ago during the first hearing and your information, I'm afraid, was scant at best.",

"I would agree with you, Senator Moller," she said, her tone respectful and placating.

Oh she was good. Very good. She knew this game better than most. Maybe that was it—she had an agenda to get her foot in the door and secure a place on Capitol Hill with all the other snakes and sharks.

"But the last six months have delivered not just an uptick in valuable intel but also some very disturbing and alarming information on Colonel Weston." Francesca turned off her mic.

"I have here," Chairman Moller said, "a police report from an accident you were involved in a few weeks ago, Miss Solomon."

Poised and composed, she gave no indication of her emotional state. At least not from Moller's viewpoint, but Trace could see her fingers twisting knots under the table.

"It's come to my attention that you have harbored an intense and perhaps perverted sense of vengeance against Colonel Weston," Moller said, removing his glasses and looking up at her. "Is that true?"

"It's what some have claimed when they did not like my investigation efforts."

Moller pointed his glasses to the far left of the room, near the doors. "So, you're going to tell me that these two gentlemen—please stand—are just exaggerating?"

Trace glanced in that direction. Dressed in a pristine white uniform was Solomon's eldest son, the one Trace had met in the office. Paul? Paolo. But the man beside him—the one that made Trace's heart slow—"Brent," Trace whispered. His little brother.

What? When had Brent ever met Solomon? Had she been to his family? Drilled them full of questions?

"I would say that my brother felt I was on the wrong track and wanted to embarrass me, sir."

Moller's face reddened. "You're going to tell this committee that a highly decorated Navy SEAL with multiple tours has nothing better to do on this Tuesday morning than harass his *little sister*?"

Solomon lowered her gaze.

"Thank you, gentlemen," Moller said, as he glowered at Francesca. "Now, I hope to God you have more solid information for us, that you are not wasting our time or recklessly attacking the reputation and career of another highly decorated service member."

Francesca wet her lips, slowly bringing her gaze up. "I have credible information to present, if you would hear it." The tension and anger in her words were palpable.

"Go ahead," Chairman Moller said.

"Thank you," Francesca said, adjusting in her chair and shifting papers in front of her. "As an analyst with INSCOM, I had access to information and key assets on the ground in Libya at the time of the attack. It was my responsibility—"

"Miss Solomon, we've already heard this," Moller growled. "If you do not have new material—"

"I do, sir," she said.

He huffed.

She traced a finger down the page, looking for the right place to pick up. "Roughly two months ago, two women were murdered."

Trace clicked his mic on. Steadied the ramming of his heart against his pulse. This could end his career. This could devastate his life. This could destroy Annie, Téya, and Nuala. So, he began. "I am an American Special Forces Soldier! I will do all that my nation requires of me."

"Colonel Weston, you do not have the microphone," he could hear Chairman Moller saying.

But Trace continued. Never stopped. "I am a volunteer, knowing well the hazards of my profession." Which might include getting arrested today. "I serve with the memory of those who have gone before me." Jessie. Candice. Keeley. "I pledge to uphold the honor and integrity of their legacy in all that I am—"

"Colonel Weston," Moller shouted, his voice mingling the noisy thrum rippling through the courtroom. "Colonel Weston, if you do not stop—"

"Just cut his mic," General Marlowe said.

And Trace's mic died. So Trace lifted his voice, unwilling to let Francesca Solomon in her insane quest to destroy him put the lives of Annie, Téya, and Nuala on the line, too.

"I am a warrior. I will teach and fight whenever and wherever my nation requires." Even with civil disobedience right now. "I will strive always to excel in every art and artifice of war. I know that I will be called upon—"

"Security!"

"—to perform tasks in isolation far from familiar faces and voices."

"Trace," Haym said, his face strangely pale for an Italian. "What are you doing?"

"With the help and guidance of my faith, I will conquer my fears and succeed. I will keep my mind and body clean, alert, and strong. I will maintain my arms—"

Two Capitol Hill police entered the room, and before the door shut, Trace saw two more jogging down the hall.

They hauled Trace to his feet, but he never stopped reciting the Special Forces creed. And he didn't struggle against the authorities. It'd only go worse later. Cuffs tight against his wrists, he was hauled out of the room. As he passed Francesca, Trace broke free. Shoved his face in hers. "Remember, those names—they're lives you're playing with. More innocent people will die because of your vendetta against me. Can you live with that, Francesca?"

Annie
En Route to Dover, England
12 June – 0100 Hours

As the cabin door shut, Annie eyed Boone. "Where's Trace?"

"Not coming," Boone muttered as he took the seat across the aisle next to Rusty.

Why wasn't Trace flying out with them? It was weird, honestly, to have Rusty back in the game, though the guy had sworn he wanted nothing to do with this. Annie guessed that knowing someone had slipped poison into Keeley on Rusty's watch had been the catalyst. But for Trace not to come when they had yet another arrow pointing toward Ballenger didn't make sense.

Was Ballenger leading them? If so, for what reason?

The indiscriminant din of rock music, suppressed by ear buds, drew Annie's gaze to the row behind her. Eyes closed, feet on Rusty's seat, Téya looked like she might be asleep. She'd been distant and moody since returning from Frankfurt and even worse after visiting Bleak Pond.

Nuala had the window seat next to Annie and held an e-reader, devouring the latest novel by a James Rubarb or some other. Annie hadn't listened very closely because, if she were going to read, she'd select something from James Rollins or Brad Thor. Or Lis Wiehl—especially Lis because her novels were relevant and often ripped straight from the headlines.

So, here they were. All but Trace. On their way to Dover to track down the elusive, cryptic Berg Ballenger.

Though the remnant of Zulu was together, they were anything but. Hearts and minds divided meant efforts would be limited. That wouldn't be good trying to find Ballenger and getting him to cough up what he knew.

But it felt silly and almost redundant to track him down. To fly all of them to Dover. What was Trace thinking?

There were no answers and no way to drill Trace with questions, so Annie drifted off to sleep, anticipating the jet lag she'd suffer before this was said and done. Six hours after wheels-up at Dulles, when the plane landed, she had a crick in her neck and a kink in her mood. Rubbing out the knot, she yawned.

They disembarked and immediately grabbed a taxi to get them to the ferry that would deliver them to Dover. Even as they crossed the sea, Annie wished Sam was with her to see the white cliffs. The Dover Castle on the rolling hills. Beautiful, stunning.

"And I get to see it alone," she mumbled as they left the ferry.

"With me," Nuala said, sidling up next to her as she gave a backward glance to Téya, who lagged a few feet behind. Nuala had an infectious smile. The only one of their crew not affected by some recent morbid tragedy.

Not true. Though Nuala hadn't suffered a direct loss, she felt deeply. Annie knew that much. To the side, she noted Boone and Rusty striding confidently up the street toward the town. They'd split up to avoid attracting attention. If Ballenger was here, they didn't need to alert him.

"He's not in a good way," Nuala said, her eyes locking onto Boone. "I'm concerned."

"Well, right now we need to be concerned about finding the Black Lion," Annie said, tugging out a page she'd ripped from a tourist book. That's where they'd stay. Supposedly, it had a decent shot of the water. But more importantly, of Ballenger's flat. "Just can't understand how he could afford a flat here."

"The apartments on the north side are run-down."

"Yes, but they're still by the water," Annie said.

Soon the paved road gave way to the bricked road, which somehow felt better on Annie's feet and back. Halfway up the street, they spotted the white awning with the black pawing lion. Lettering below it announced their destination.

Annie glanced back to let Téya know but found the road cluttered with foot traffic. Loads of people but no Téya. Stowing her irritation at her friend's moodiness, she smiled at Nuala. "Let's check in then come down for a scone and some tea."

"*Mmm*, delicious," Nuala said with a giggle.

Armed with a room key ten minutes later, they made it to the second-floor suite and let themselves in. They each claimed a bed, then Annie walked the room, checking out the bathroom, vanity, closet, and—

The door in the wall swung open. An adjoining door admitted Boone and Rusty. "Where's Two?" Boone asked.

"Sightseeing, I guess," Annie said. "She was gone when I turned around. She'll show."

As if on cue, the door opened.

Annie turned, heart in her throat as Téya entered, casually aloof. "How'd you get in?"

Between two fingers, lifted a key card. "Cleaning lady set it down." She glanced around the room then slung her backpack on a bed. "When are we heading over?"

"How did you know what room we were in?" Annie demanded.

"You weren't exactly trying to hide that," Téya said.

"Where were you?"

"Are you my mother now?"

"What is your problem, Téya? We're a team. We need to have our heads in the game."

"My head is in the game," Téya said. "I was able to ascertain your location and access to your room without arousing suspicion or trouble."

"You should have been with us."

"Well, I wasn't."

Annie shoved her hands into her curly hair. "What is your problem?"

"My problem is we have an assassin trying to take us out and we're running all over the world, and being careless at that." She snatched up her pack and stalked toward the door. "*I* want to stay alive."

"Where are you going now?"

"To recon. To make sure you don't get us killed."

Annie felt a primal growl rolling up her throat. But the hurt that came with Téya's sharp words cut it short. *What did I do to deserve that?*

"Hey." Boone's gruff voice pulled Annie around. "Focus on the mission. We need Ballenger. Need to know what he knows. Got it?"

"I need her to be with me."

Boone pointed to Nuala. "You have her. That's more than enough." He went back to work setting up the surveillance equipment.

Annie met Nuala's gaze, not surprised to see the flush filling her face. "Sorry," Annie said. "I didn't mean to discount you."

"Oh, you didn't," Nuala said, lifting the Do Not Disturb sign from the door and putting it on the outside.

Nuala was beaming. Positively beaming that Boone had noticed and affirmed her. Annie couldn't help but smile that in the middle of what felt like a crumbling mission and team, there was the innocence of Nuala's attraction to Boone. At the same time, Annie found it irritating. Lives were at stake.

But Annie knew what it felt like to be a girl looking up to her handler. That's how it had started with Trace—her desire to make him proud. Make him notice her.

With two earpieces, Rusty came toward them. "Okay, we're ready for you to head out." He nodded toward the window, where a sheer curtain muted the sunlight. Two large devices were aimed out the window. One was a long-range scope, the other a powerful microphone receiver.

If finding and meeting with Ballenger had gone simply and effectively last time, they wouldn't be here in a surreptitious manner or skulking about a gorgeous British tourist hot spot.

"Remember, we're not here for anything other than to find him, talk to him, and get information," Boone said, his expression dark. "Nuala, you got a nose for trouble. You sniff it, bail."

The girl breathed in his praise once more, lifting her shoulders and nodding with a thrust of her chin. How could Boone not see this beautiful girl? Of course, his mind was still weighted with the death of the girl he loved.

Did he love her? Or was it like it was with Trace, where he could get what he wanted then—to borrow Boone's word—bail?

Annie hated herself for thinking that. The thought was birthed from her own pain. Her own tragedy. The one she'd carry alone and to her grave. He didn't need to know. Wouldn't know.

"I'll want a high vantage," Nuala said. "Down by the pier, I saw some sidewalk cafés that had balconies. I think we'd be able to see the apartment building. Watch for him to come or go."

"Good," Boone said. "Go with it."

Impressed with Nuala's uncanny ability to act natural and scope a place at the same time, Annie made her way down to the lobby with Nuala. When they stepped back onto the bricked path bustling with tourists, Annie hesitated.

Nuala didn't—she headed to the right and snapped photos as she went.

With a hop-step to keep up, Annie chided herself. She was letting herself get distracted with heart matters. Time to get her head in the game. Put her heart on the shelf.

Nuala had them seated at a wrought-iron table in less than ten minutes, with the narrowest part of the English Channel to their right, which faced France, and the building that housed Ballenger's flat looming to the left. Cantilevered windows allowed fresh air into the apartments but also dated the structure. It was older, a throwback to the '70s with its sleek, harsh lines and lots of steel and glass. They ordered orange marmalade scones and tea. Soaking up the sun was a nice benefit of working a mission, but after a full lunch their skin was turning pink—okay, Annie's was turning pink. Nuala had this gorgeous, enviable bronze glow that went well with her almost olive complexion.

"Okay," Nuala said. "Ballenger's flat, supposedly, is on the third floor, end closest to the channel."

Annie cautiously sipped the steaming tea as she let her gaze hit the spot. And realized a fatal flaw in their plan. From this angle, Boone and Rusty couldn't see it, right? "The view is blocked," Annie said, glancing at the apartments then the water so a passerby would think she was referring to the building.

"Negative," Boone said. "We're clear."

The corner of Nuala's lips curled up. "My measurements were right then?" Her tone was a bit audacious. Almost saucy.

"Copy that, Noodle." Surprisingly, there was a smile in Boone's voice.

She smiled at Annie. "I found the one hotel that had a perfect line of sight on the corner apartment. Boone thought the bank would block it."

"Show off," Boone said.

Nuala glowed, not from the midafternoon sun, but from Boone's praise.

"Okay." Boone's voice tickled through the earpiece. "Just heard from Téya. Landlady said the flat's been leased for years, but she can't remember the last time she saw the tenant."

"Copy," Annie said as she lifted her napkin to wipe her lips.

"Let's check it out," Boone said.

Nuala

After paying their bill, Nuala headed down the brick path to the sidewalk skirting the English Channel with Annie, a good compatriot, if she could keep her head in the game. Which she hadn't. Not since she'd been lip-locked with the commander. Nuala had to admit, it was weird but good to see them like that. They'd been an item before Misrata, and stumbling upon them together again gave her hope for a bright future, where the team fought terrorists and evil the way they had six years ago.

Choppy waters of the channel churned and writhed, as if in agony. Nuala could only pray this wasn't a portent of doom—what with the stormy sky adding its gloomy touch.

They stepped into the scant shade of the building, and Nuala said, "Entering now." It was protocol, but it also meant she was talking to Boone. She ached for him, for his loss. Nuala hated seeing him grieve, hated that Keeley had been taken from him. Some people might call her dishonest because of how much she cared for him for saying that, but she truly just wanted Boone happy. He was a good man, and he deserved to be happy.

They made it through the nondescript lobby. Her sniper training had her itching for a high elevation or vantage point, but that wasn't possible. She'd have to make do. She spotted the door marked STAIRS and pointed it out to Annie then pushed it open.

Téya, who'd been sitting on the cement steps, pushed to her feet, without so much as a greeting. She climbed the steps one ahead of Nuala and Annie. "I thought he wanted to talk to us."

"Seems a common problem," Annie said, her words no doubt targeted toward Téya, who didn't bat an eye or miss a step at the rebuke. She also didn't spout off a comeback, contrary to her character.

And that made Nuala wonder. There was a lot about a person that changed during trying or difficult times, but Téya seemed like a completely different person.

"Third floor," Nuala said into her coms as they stepped into a long, narrow corridor that only offered doors and no other view save the anemic, barred window at the end.

They moved down the hall that had been recently renovated—well, painted over was more accurate. Previous peeling spots left impressions beneath the new gray paint. The carpet smelled musty and of pet urine.

"Copy that. We have you on thermals," Boone's calm, deep voice relayed. "Looking good, Zulu."

Eyes out. That's what he'd say next.

"Eyes out. Stay alert."

Nuala smiled as she made her way down to the apartment. On the right. Because odds were on the right. "Copy. Entering now." She lifted the tool from her back pocket and easily picked her way into the door. Benefit of old, rundown apartments, thankyouverymuch. "We're in," she said.

"Roger," Boone said. "We have you on the scope."

Some might find it creepy that they were being watched from a half mile away. She found it comforting. An added layer of protection.

"The place is messed up," Téya said.

"How so?" Rusty asked.

"It's old. . ." Annie wrinkled her nose then swept her hand over it. "Musty and dusty."

Nuala walked the perimeter of the living room, taking in the moth-eaten sofa and its pillows. The rug that had a thick layer of dust. Probably mites, too. A crunch beneath her boot made her wince when she saw the droppings. Rats. She shuddered.

Keeping her arms close to her side, she dreaded the thought of touching anything. "Alpha One, this is. . .wrong," she said.

Annie started for the bedrooms.

"Explain," Boone said.

"I don't think anyone's been here in years," she said.

"She's right," Téya said with a gruff tone. "He set this place up and left it so there'd be a record, but nobody's been in here in ages."

"This means he lied to us in Paris, too."

"When *hasn't* he lied to us?" Téya said. "I'm out of here."

433

"Do you think we should look for—"

"Planted evidence? Fake trails? That's all we'll find here," Téya said and strode toward the door.

Defeat clung to Nuala as she had to agree with Téya's conclusion. This place was a front for the lies Berg Ballenger wanted them to believe. "She's right," Nuala conceded. "We won't find anything here."

"It feels wrong to just leave without looking." Annie stood in the living room, glancing around.

"If you want to dig through rat droppings, be my guest," Téya said as she left the apartment.

"There she goes again," Annie said with a huff. "What is wrong with her? You know what? I'm sick of this. She's going to answer some questions!" And with that Annie burst out of the apartment, too.

"Alpha One," Nuala spoke to Boone, with a long sigh of resignation. "Do I stay and investigate?"

"Negative. We'll have a team sweep it and box everything up—except the droppings. Pull out. RTB. We have more important things to worry about right now than finding rats."

"Finding the big rat," Nuala muttered. Berg Ballenger.

"Roger that. See you back here."

Nuala made her way back down to the street, where she found Téya and Annie arguing by the roped-off barrier that provided little protection against someone falling into the channel.

"You don't leave your team."

"Do I have a team?" Téya snapped back. "Because all we seem to be doing is chasing rats and pigs, and getting nowhere. We sit in a bunker and drive each other crazy. You and Trace can't behave like adults in front of us—and even in front of the hunky SEAL you were so gung-ho about when you showed up at the bunker two months ago. Nuala is crazy about Boone and giving him doe eyes all the time, but really—are we a team?"

Nuala's stomach dropped to her toes. The words hurt. Deeply. But it hurt even more that Boone probably heard them.

"We're trying. At least some of us are!"

A glint north of their location snagged Nuala's attention. Seemed like a rifle scope. But that wouldn't—there! It hit her gaze again. Where was it? If she didn't know better... "Alpha One..." Maybe it was nothing.

"RTB. All of you," Boone barked.

The glint glared directly in her eyes this time. Nuala squinted and jerked away. This time, she'd spotted him atop a building. "Shooter! Rooftop!"

Téya

Annie pitched forward, right into Téya as Nuala's words seared the air. A scream closely followed. Then a splash. Glass nearby exploded. Frenzied shouts and running tourists created upheaval in the setting that had only moments before been the epitome of calm.

"Nuala!" Annie shouted, diving behind a trash can with Téya. They scanned the waters, waiting for the girl to surface.

"Was she shot?" Téya asked.

"I don't know. She just went in." Annie's voice carried the same panic that thumped in Téya's chest.

A head broke the surface. Nuala gasped, her face screwed tight in pain.

"What's going on?" Boone shouted through the coms.

"Active shooter," Téya said, scanning the direction of the shots. She had to try to move to draw fire in order to locate the shooter. She scurried to a metal table and flung it on its side. She dropped behind it, disappointed when there'd been no shots. That meant finding the shooter would be more difficult.

Téya worked through the angles. Through the trajectory of the shots. Determined they had to be either in the bakery building or the lighthouse. Any farther would be too far for accuracy. Any closer. . .well, that'd be too easy, because then Zulu would've seen him.

A man emerged from the bakery with a pastry in hand.

"I think I see him," Téya said.

"Berg! That's Berg Ballenger," Annie yelled, pointing in the opposite direction.

Téya whipped around, scanning the others. "Where?"

"Brown jacket. Running up the street."

Téya caught sight of him. "Got him. I'm going." But then she remembered Nuala and looked back. "Are you okay?"

Annie was leaning over the embankment, reaching for Nuala. "Yes. Go!"

"In pursuit," Téya called through the coms. "He's heading east through the town."

"Alpha Two is en route," Boone said, indicating Rusty was leaving the nest to assist. "I have eyes on the target."

Good. Because once he'd rounded that corner, she lost him for the few seconds it took her to break into the open. She kept moving, but having lost him, she slowed.

"Ahead, twenty yards. Blue shirt now."

Blue shirt. Great. Not like that would blend in or anything. But then Téya had him. "Got him!" Téya sprinted, darting around a jewelry vendor in the middle of the street. A cart of delicious-looking candies. She narrowly avoided a collision with a small girl who darted away from her mother. Téya spun around her but never took her eyes off Ballenger. Spry for a guy with a paunch.

He'd reached the fountain. Skirted it.

Téya leaped onto the three-foot wall around the fountain. Sailed over a little boy bending forward, splashing the water. Landed.

Berg dodged a family with ice cream. Pushing him closer to the fountain.

Téya threw herself at him. A man ducked with a shout as she sailed over him, too. Straight into Ballenger. They collided. He let out what sounded like a gargled scream. Before he could react, Téya flipped him onto his stomach. Pressed her shoulder into his. Grabbed his arm and swung it behind his back and up.

He cried out.

All too aware of the crowd of onlookers, Téya knew she had to get out of the open. "We're getting up," she hissed into his ear. "If you try anything, I will end you."

He groaned in pain.

"Clear?"

He nodded and grimaced again.

She hauled him to his feet just as Rusty arrived and used some zip cuffs to secure him. They turned him around, and Téya froze. "It's not him," she breathed, disbelief choking off clear thought. The man had the same hair color and build as Ballenger, but this definitely wasn't him.

"What'd you mean?" Rusty still held the look-alike.

"Where is he?" Téya demanded.

The man sneered. Gave a breathy laugh, still winded from the escape attempt. Which—was it even an attempt to escape? Or an attempt to draw them away from something else?

"Boone—you still have eyes on One and Six?" she asked into her coms piece.

"Roger. They're en route. Bring him back here," Boone said. "We'll sort it here."

They herded him out of the square and up into the hotel, chewing on the fact Ballenger had not just tricked them, but put energy and resources into luring them away. Making them look and feel stupid.

The door opened, and Téya saw Nuala sitting on the dinette table with her shirt removed and her tank affording Boone a good angle to mend the wound. Boone shoved to his feet and stalked toward them. "Who are you?"

"Nobody," the man said with a cocky chip on his shoulder. One Téya really wanted to punch off.

Boone did it for her. He threw a hard right, straight into the guy's face. He grabbed him and pinned him against the wall. "Okay, Nobody, you're going to answer questions."

A crooked, bloody smile crept into his arrogance. "I'm not, actually."

Hauling back for another punch, Boone looked ready to kill the guy.

"Wait," Téya said as she caught Boone's arm. She pushed him back. Slapped her hands against the guy's chest. "Ballenger sent you."

Something...wrong, something dark glinted in the man's eyes. "I was sent."

"Why are you here?" Téya asked.

"I live here."

"Why were you at Ballenger's flat? You don't live there. That place had more droppings than slum alleys."

His eyes widened. "You went to the flat?"

Téya didn't like that look. "Why?"

He shook his head. "It's been rigged for years. If anyone enters it, they're alerted."

"Who?"

"HOMe, their lackeys! I'm to deliver a message. He said you'd come." That greedy gleam replaced the man's momentary shock.

"What message?" Boone demanded, hovering behind Téya.

"He says you need to focus on a man named Varden."

Boone stiffened.

Téya glanced at the big guy. "That mean something to you?"

With a lunge, Boone shoved the man toward the door.

"Wait, wait!" the man shouted. "I'm not done."

"You're more than done!"

"He said to warn you to stay out of his way. He's going to finish HOMe no matter what it takes."

Boone shoved the man out into the hall and closed the door. He secured the locks and turned around, rubbing his jaw.

"Who's Varden?" Téya asked, hands stiff on her hips.

"Ran into him on a couple of tours."

"He's Army?" Téya hated the squeak in her voice. "As in—United States

Army? As in, a citizen of the U.S.? Someone who should be our ally?"

"Varden's only ally is either his bank account or scum like Ballenger who help him get more money." Boone motioned around the room, gave a nod to Rusty, who was finishing sewing Nuala's shoulder. "Pack up. We need to clear out immediately."

"So, we're not worried about Ballenger?" Nuala asked quietly.

"More than worried," Boone said. "We need to stop him or take him down."

Téya held up her hands. "What am I missing? That stranger says Ballenger is warning us, and you just go all lame duck on us?"

Boone rounded on Téya, his strong brow knotting. "Notice his tattoo?" He pointed to a spot at the base of his neck. "Italian Carabinieri Special Intervention Group. The GIS are specially trained in counterterrorism operations with an emphasis on *marksmanship*."

"He's the one who shot me," Nuala said quietly.

"We need to clear out." Boone met her gaze firmly. "Now."

Trace
Reston, Virginia
12 June – 2100 Hours EST

Trace sat at Magianno's, lips resting on his knuckles. Having Zulu out of the country assured him they'd be safe—for now. The scene he'd made at the hearing had left him on disciplinary leave with the threat of being discharged, "other than honorably."

It's what Marlowe had wanted from the beginning. And maybe Trace had finally handed him the golden ticket to accomplishing that.

He didn't know. The only thing he did know is that he had to impress upon the senators and representatives that those names could not be made public. Even a closed hearing wasn't good enough. The names would leak. Lives would be in danger. It wouldn't end.

Trace lifted the USB drive from his pocket. Set it on the table and took a bite of his Hawaiian BBQ pizza. Téya had given the drive to him. But he just had this sinking feeling that the moment he plugged it into one of his systems, The Turk and his people would have access to everything. They could decimate him. More than Marlowe. They could get into secure military files.

He gulped some water, eyeing the drive. Tapping it against the metal table. He felt like Eve must've in the Garden of Eden—the USB drive being the apple tempting him to take a bite. Free himself.

Nothing is free.

He sighed and took another bite of his pizza. This late at night and the eatery was still crowded. Gave him a place to be alone with his thoughts but not alone to be killed. Not that anyone had tried.

Why not?

Why hadn't they tried to kill him? He'd been open and available numerous times.

He roughed his hand over his face and groaned. *God. . .* Had it come to that? *God, I need help.* And he meant it as a prayer, not just an oath. Though, maybe his desperation made it some of that, too.

Air shifted around him. Trace lowered his hands, and an explosion of warm dread erupted in his gut as he found himself staring at a woman. She wore a hijab and had vibrant brown eyes that were impossibly large around a small nose and mouth. Mentally, he reached for his weapon. He always had one on him.

"My name is Badriyya Kanoun."

Oh crap. Turkish. "What can I do for you?"

The left side of her face pulled upward in a half smile. "You have not used the USB."

"Felt risky."

She smiled fully this time, revealing perfect, white teeth. The smile reached her eyes. "Smart man." She reached into her purse.

Trace moved his hand toward his weapon.

"You should know that I never travel with less than four bodyguards." She gave him a devilish smile. "Now, you are smart, but can you figure out who they are in time?" She slid a small white envelope across the table. "The USB is empty. If you want to use it later, go right ahead."

"Or not." No way would he use that thing.

"It was a homing beacon so we could have this conversation." Perfectly manicured nails nudged the envelope toward him. "In that is the evidence you need to stop this vilification of your character and work. Go on."

Trace kept his eyes on her and slid the envelope closer. He lifted it and opened it. Four photographs dumped onto the table. "Why give this to me?"

"Majid is a man of his word."

"And of a hundred deaths." Trace still wasn't happy with the arrangement, especially knowing The Turk was most likely trying to recruit Téya into his organization.

Badriyya gave a one-shouldered shrug with a pound of cockiness. "We all have our strengths, Colonel."

"Why give me this? You could've just killed my asset and stiffed me."

"The man in those photos is still smuggling weapons into our country, and though we know who he is, we have been unable to find who's controlling him. Giving him the information and access. We want that. When you discover it, we could consider it a favor if you'd share." She motioned with her dark red nails to the USB. "When you use it, the connect button will signal us. We'll find you." And with that, she walked out of the restaurant, knowing her guards would make sure she stayed alive.

Trace turned his attention to the photographs. He thumbed them into an arc around his plate of pizza. The man was Varden. Trace knew him. Boone knew him. He wasn't a stranger. The first picture showed him with three different men. The second was a bit too blurry. But they were all centered around weapons caches. Proof positive that Varden was guilty as sin. Trace would love to run his butt up the pole now, but they needed the same information Badriyya needed—the source.

However, it was the last picture. . .the last one that had Trace shoving out of the seat and hurrying to his car. Phone to his ear, he waited for the call to connect, his chest pumping hard and angry.

"Yo, Boss-man."

"Houston, I need an address."

XII

Frankie pulled into her one-car garage attached to the rear of her townhome. Limbs weighted with exhaustion and mind loaded with defeat, she made her way inside. She hated this part of her day, walking into an empty, dark home. . .alone. After flicking on the light, she immediately secured the locks on the back door then dropped her satchel onto the counter and tossed her keys on top.

She glanced at the clock on her phone one last time and gave a considerable groan. Staying at the office, catching up on the mound of paperwork left after her bout of insanity and the hearing, she had enough to keep her there late for weeks to come. She grabbed a bottle of SOBE water from the fridge along with leftover Chinese and headed into the living room. She'd watch a couple reruns of *Fringe* then get back to the files.

With the living room lamplight on, she turned on the TV and slid in a disc from season two, her favorite. She put her feet up and sat back with her leftovers. Paolo always said she was nasty for eating cold leftovers. But there were some restaurant foods that tasted just as good cold as warm.

Okay, that was a lie. She was just too tired to heat it up.

Leaning her head back, she closed her eyes. Truth be told, she was tired of fighting. Of swimming upstream against everyone else. It left her alone, friendless. For crying out loud, even Walter on *Fringe* had a cow for a pet. What did she have? What did her pursuit of justice, of making sure the right thing was done, get her but cold Chinese, old reruns, and a lonely apartment?

Depression had crept in. No denying it anymore. That plus a sizable amount of defeat. She just couldn't win. Sitting there, she felt the tug of sleep and promised herself a few minutes of rest. She deserved it after the week she'd had.

Frankie found herself standing in a park. It looked like Central Park, but she hadn't ever been there, so she couldn't be sure. She stumbled around, her legs feeling like they weighed a hundred pounds each. A low-hanging branch reached toward her. She pushed it away, but the craggy sticklike fingers coiled around hers. Startled, Frankie tried to pull free.

She turned to extricate herself when she realized the brown branches had suddenly become delicate fingers.

Frankie looked up. And froze. The woman—she recognized her—stared back. Her eyes were hollow, lifeless. Her lips blue. What was she—some Goth or Emo punk?

"My family," she said. "I can't find my family."

"S–sorry," Frankie stammered, tugging against the woman's hold. "I can't help you."

"But they don't know. They don't know what happened. Help me."

Panic ripped through Frankie. "Let me go!"

And like that, the woman was gone. Frankie didn't know where she went or why she'd even talked to her, but when Frankie looked around, the greenery of the park had taken on a darker, creepier feel.

She stood in the center of a hedgerow that formed a circle. Turning, she searched for a way out. "I can't find you!" she shouted then remembered she was supposed to be looking for him. "Don't leave me. You can't do this."

She blinked and turned, the branches tussling apart and creating an opening. Frankie threw herself toward him, frantic. Though it was only a very short distance, it took her dozens of steps. Countless steps. She couldn't get there. No matter how much she ran, that opening stayed just out of reach.

A thud behind her sent her pulse racing.

She looked back but only saw more branches. Waving—no, no. Not waving. Reaching. Trying to capture her. Unable to breathe, legs stuck in what felt like cement, she scrambled for the opening.

It was closing! "No!" She cried out and threw herself at the opening. She landed with a thud and scrabbled out of reach of the vines as they cleaved together, leaving not even a breath of space between the leaves.

Pulling to her feet, she dusted herself off, leaning against a large stone as she untangled a vine that had wrapped around her boot. But as she did, she noticed markings on the boulder. She angled away, hand still on the rock for balance.

Though she brushed away dirt and grime, it did no good. So she wiped more. And kept wiping. Until her heart jammed into her throat. It wasn't a boulder but a headstone.

The lettering was strange, broken. But she knew instantly it was the marker for the Children of Misrata. And like a lasso, the vine she'd pulled off her boot snaked from her hand, growing, spinning, curling, and twisting until it finally latched onto the headstone. Then coiled around it. One time. Two times. Ten times. It pulled until she was pressed against the cold stone, hugging it. Then, the vine hauled harder, crushing Frankie against the stone. Face against the cold stone, the moonlight caught something. A glint. She saw silver. Silver oak leaf. What. . . ? She strained to pull away to get a better view. That's when she saw the boulder wasn't a headstone anymore. It was the broad shoulders of a man in uniform. And not just any man, but Colonel Weston.

Two loud booms rocked through the cemetery.

Frankie jerked. Then blinked. And sat up. On the floor in her living room, she groped for coherency. What happened? A dream. . .it was only a—

Thud! Thud-thud!

Her heart beat in cadence with the banging at the front door.

On adrenaline-weak legs, she made her way to the foyer. She squinted back into the living room and blinked sleep from her eyes that blurred her vision. 11:00? Who would be here this late?

"Who is it?" Frankie called through the door, then reached for the weapon she kept in the front closet.

The door crashed inward.

Frankie froze, realized her mistake, then made a last-second attempt to grab the weapon.

The man rammed into her. Shoved her backward. She screamed, but he thrust his forearm into her throat, severing her air. Frankie's shock shifted to panic.

"What were you doing there?"

Struggling for oxygen, she tried every street fighting tactic she knew, including jabbing him in the side. But he had a vest on. That's when her mind let in the small fact that her attacker was none other than Trace Weston. She blinked again.

In the distant thunder of her pulse against her temple, she heard him slam the door shut.

"Why. Were. You. There?" he growled, his face red, his eyes a torrent of rage and anger.

Air. She had to breathe. Her head felt like it'd explode. She batted his arm, trying to signal him to release her. But her eyes started rolling. He was going to kill her. Just like the others.

Then the force against her throat was gone.

Frankie cough-gasped, greedily hauling in air, still pinned to the wall.

"I'll ask you one more time," he said, his voice dead serious, "then I'm done talking—why were you there?"

She kept both hands on his arm in case he decided to follow through with killing her. "Wher—"

He slapped a picture at her. "Talk!"

It took a moment for her eyes to focus on the image. But when they did, Frankie knew she was in a lot of trouble, and that was only if Trace Weston didn't kill her first. She snapped her gaze to him.

"Yeah," he breathed into her face. "I know."

"It's not what you think."

He sneered at her. "You have no idea what I think." And he brought up the handgun.

"Now, wait," Frankie said, her heart jostling against her ribs. "You can't just kill me when—"

"Quiet!"

Trace Weston was formidable in court, but in a confrontation like this. . .well, the courtroom version was tame. The man standing before her let Frankie know he meant business. He had the muscle, the skill, the determination. That last one burned through his irises, making those green eyes even more prominent. "On the couch."

Frankie obeyed the order.

"Hands on your knees."

She complied with that one, too.

"Talk!"

Frankie raised her hands. "Okay, okay." She was breaking a dozen agency rules. She would lose her clearance. "I could lose everything if I tell you—"

"How do you think I feel, with you trying to pin your mess on my team?"

"My mess?" Frankie's words came out shrill. "You don't think I—"

He stood there, his back to the wall, arms extended but not straight. He was comfortable in that position. Though he was intent on his mission, he wasn't stressed. This wasn't new to him.

"I was recruited very quickly into Army intelligence. Quick thinking and tenacious, I was then put on assignment as an operative."

"A spy."

Frankie bit her tongue. Last thing she needed was to set off this man.

"Misrata." He had thin lips that pulled into a flat, straight line, emphasizing his anger. That and his thick brow line that creased fiercely around those green eyes. "That's all I care about."

Reticent to unlock that vault, she let out a breath. "I will lose my job."

"Three of mine lost their lives. Think I care about your career?"

She couldn't argue that. But as she sat there, Frankie started riffling through the information, the facts, Trace being here. . .her dream. Being entangled with him in that cemetery. Both of them laid at the headstone.

"INSCOM had been tracking weapons that were supposed to be disposed of through proper channels but were, instead, showing up in skirmishes and in the hands of our enemies. We had credible intel that Misrata was a weigh station."

His jaw muscle jounced.

"They said they needed a fresh face, someone their assets wouldn't recognize, to go in and talk with the locals. Since I have darker than average skin and hair, I was tapped."

"*Bull.*"

She looked at him in surprise.

"Missions like that don't get filled with newbs. Too high value."

Frankie swallowed. "I wasn't a newb."

He eyed her. "How many missions?"

She licked her lips. Hated admitting anything to this man. "My second."

He snorted. Shook his head. "If you were there, if you were so keyed into HUMINT, how can you possibly think I'm behind what happened there?"

"What? You think just because you have a photo of me there, that this gets you off?"

"I did my job. My team went in. They blew the warehouse. That those kids were there was a mistake. A tragedy. Nothing else." He hadn't lowered the weapon. "But you. . ."

Frankie scowled at him. "What about me?"

"I have this photograph of a man known to be dealing with shady people."

"Varden?"

He gave her a look, one that somehow showed she'd just revealed her hand. "Why was Varden there?"

"To oversee the operation."

Trace hadn't so much as flinched or relaxed. "Your father says you're an intelligent young woman."

"Do *not* bring him into this," she snapped, the heat of anger rushing through her. "I will not let you bring him down—"

"Me?" He held up the picture. "You go forward with this insane trip to crucify me for something I haven't done. . ." His jaw muscle flexed. "I can take it. You've dogged my steps, harassed me for five years, but so help me—if you go forward with those names, if you put the rest of my team in jeopardy"—his nostrils flared as he shook his head—"then I will make sure this makes it into the hands of some very well-known, powerful journalists. They'll know you were there." He rubbed his jaw, a glimmer of arrogance infiltrating the anger she noticed a second ago. "I might even suggest you're trying to cover up your own actions by targeting me."

Frankie punched to her feet. "You can't do that!"

He snapped his weapon up, firming his posture. "You've done it to me for five years, saying I'm letting your father take the blame for something I did."

She held up her hands. "Going to kill me?"

"I can. And I will, so help me." He meant it. That much was evident in his posture, words, and gaze.

"Just like you did Reyna in Alaska and Herring in Vegas?"

Weston scowled. Seemed to deflate, but then surged again. "I have three team members I've fought to keep safe for sixty-two months. Now your insane vendetta against me is putting them at risk."

"Then come clean!"

He took a step forward, the weapon nearly touching her chest.

Frankie drew up short, her breathing going shallow.

"You are endangering their lives." He flared his nostrils. "I can't let that happen. No more are dying on my watch."

"So, what? You want me to just—"

"Your own father told you I wasn't guilty."

"My father tells me what he thinks I need to hear." It hurt to admit that, but Frankie had grown up as a general's daughter with pampered information. "He still thinks of me as a fifteen-year-old."

"Then maybe you should start acting your age."

She gaped at him.

"You have a good brain. I've seen it. You're dangerous only because you are on the wrong warpath."

Frankie propped her hands on her hips. "What warpath should I be on, Weston? Because if you think I'm walking away just because you roughed me up and put a gun in my face—"

"Help me."

Frozen by his words, Frankie stared at him. He seriously did not just say that. "Help you what? Help you get out of jail? Help you frame someone else?"

"Help me and my team—your father—find who's funding and controlling Varden. His name keeps coming up as my team fights to find the truth." He held the picture up next to his face again. "You know him."

Her heart gave a crazy thump at the thought. She could get into Trace's network. Get his information. "He was my handler!"

"Then maybe it's time for you to handle him."

"No." Frankie breathed deeply. "Kill me if you have to, but I'm not doing this."

"How can you be so smart and so stupid at the same time? I'm not the enemy."

"Pointing a weapon at me isn't exactly working in your favor."

Weston snorted and lowered the weapon. Holstered it. Raised his hands to her. "Fine." He touched his temples then flicked his hands out in an irritated way. "Bury me. But leave them out." He inched forward, his bearing raw and powerful. Torment hovered in those intense eyes. "If you believe this, if you really think I'm guilty, then lay that at my feet. They were part of a horrible mistake. If saying I'm to blame helps you, great." He placed a hand on his chest. "I'm to blame. Just leave. Them. Out."

The air thickened with tension and his plea.

"Too many have died already because of Misrata. Don't add to that number, Francesca. Please. Not with more innocent lives."

Francesca
Alexandria, Virginia
12 June – 2330 Hours

Note to self: Get a dog. A big one—like a German Shepherd. No—a Belgian Malinois like the military working dogs down at the base. Something big and unafraid of protecting her from predators like Trace Weston. Lying on her bed, she rested her arm over her eyes, trying to force herself to sleep.

His invasion of her home and life felt like a massive breach of protocol. And it was. Surely he knew what kind of trouble he'd be in if she reported his actions. He'd be arrested, if not court-martialed, not only for trying to forcefully sway her testimony but for assaulting her.

Okay. It wasn't technically assault. He never hit her.

But was the man out of his ever-loving mind to come in here and do that? He had to have a really big chip on his shoulder. *"I'm to blame. Just leave. Them. Out."*

Frankie flopped onto her side and sandwiched her hands between her face and pillow. All this time, all these years, Weston hadn't gotten riled up about anything—not like what she saw tonight—no matter what she or the committees threw at him. He'd been like this massive wall of granite, impenetrable and unmovable.

Until I'm about to go public about his team.

Was it because they were all women? Was he watching out for the girls, afraid they might get hurt?

Right. Because he puts them on an elite black ops team to keep them safe.

With a growl of frustration, Frankie grabbed her pillow and bent it over her head as if she could block out the thoughts. Really, it only kept them in. She threw herself back on the bed.

Trace Weston goes to Misrata. He's involved in a mission through which twenty-two innocents die. And he walks away scot-free. How was that right or fair to the children and staff who died?

It wasn't. Not at all. That's why Frankie had to do this, had to press for justice—because nobody else would.

In his testimony that she'd read and heard, he vowed that his team had been sent in by approval of a senatorial committee. That authorization was conveniently missing.

Because it never existed. Frankie huffed with exultation.

Or maybe. . .maybe it did exist and someone buried it.

No, that was thinking too hard.

Weston said he believed someone up the chain chose his team and hung them out to dry. Not his exact words, but she read between the lines and remembered how angry her father was over the whole debacle.

Why was Daddy so angry?

Because he tapped Weston for the mission. Which meant—was it Daddy's idea to put together an all-female team? Did they realize they had made U.S. military history with the creation of that team, Zulu?

What a boon that would've been for Weston, had things gone right.

Why would Weston deliberately sabotage it?

So this all-female team would take the blame for a tragedy. So the public would sit up and think women didn't belong in combat.

She'd seen that attitude herself. Not from her father. More from her brothers, but only because she was their little sister.

"I'm to blame. Just leave. Them. Out."

Why would Weston set up the team, kill the innocents, then fight so hard to protect the very women he'd sabotaged?

Frankie curled onto her side, her stomach knotted with the sickening question. It made no sense. *What if I'm wrong?* She reached over onto her night table and lifted her laptop. She pushed up in the bed and propped herself against the headboard. Once it powered up, Frankie dug into the files embedded deeply within a ton of security. She pulled up the dossiers of the three remaining Zulu members.

A hodgepodge of skills. Made sense. Get six team members in various fields of expertise and the breadth of missions possible increased exponentially. In that regard, sex of the operatives didn't matter.

Attractive. The three remaining were as diverse as the other three were alike. Annie Palermo—blond, curly hair, fair-skinned. Téya Reiker—long, sandy-brown hair, freckled. Nuala King—dark brown hair, olive skin, pale blue eyes. Sniper.

Frankie grunted. "Remind me to stay behind you."

She scanned their histories. Annie had a big family—brothers and intact parents. Téya had lost both her parents and a stepfather before ever joining Zulu. Nuala had a brother and mother back home, but no father in the picture.

So, basically Annie and Nuala not only lost their careers in Misrata, they lost their families because Trace Weston had put them into hiding. Nobody could locate them. They were presumed dead by the military. But not by Frankie. She'd researched the families. Did Annie know her younger brother was still alive and well, married and in the Coast Guard? Did Nuala know her mom was dying of leukemia? Or that her brother had been arrested for dealing—he said to pay for his mom's treatments?

The point—they had families. They were young, attractive women who had strong careers in the military.

They're just like me.

Trace
Lucketts, Virginia
13 June – 0730 Hours EST

"One hour of life, crowded to the full with glorious action, and filled with noble risks, is worth whole years of those mean observances of paltry decorum." Sir Walter Scott had a point. Going to Francesca may have been the stupidest move of his career, but Trace had colored inside the lines long enough. He'd rather live one hour to the fullest, taking risks in the pursuit of what he believed to be right, than to live with the way things were now.

He strode into the bunker, surprised to find Houston at work. "Starting early?"

Houston had a powdered doughnut halfway to his mouth. He met Trace's gaze then stuffed it in. "Never stopped," he muffled around the fat pill. He chewed then swallowed, holding up a finger.

Trace didn't bother shaking his head. Houston was not rehabilitable in terms of social conventions. And Trace didn't care. The guy got the work done the way nobody else could. "I have pictures I need you to analyze." He handed them over.

"Sure thing, Boss-man." He plucked one of the photos, lifted a thin plastic lid on what looked like a scanner, and pressed a button before he shoved another doughnut in his mouth. "Oh!" Powdered dust plumed out, right in Trace's face. Houston widened his eyes at blowing doughnut powder over Trace's arm and sucked in a breath.

Then started coughing hard. Choking. He thumped his chest.

Trace dusted off his sleeve, trying to stow both his agitation and the amusement. "Easy, chief. Don't kill yourself."

Taking a swig of a blue sports drink, Houston held up a hand. He cleared his throat. And cleared it again, his eyes watering. "Sorry." He thumped his chest. "Went down the wrong hole."

"Houston, did you have something you wanted to tell me?"

"Yes!" He swigged more of his drink as he reached for something. "I got that last file decoded."

Trace resisted the urge to lean in lest he end up with powdered sugar in his face. "What'd you find?"

Houston's fingers flew over the keyboard. "Several files, exchanges between Stoffel and Batsakis, and some person named Red Wing."

"Georg Hostetler."

Houston stopped and cut his gaze to Trace. "Do what?"

"Red Wing is Georg Hostetler," Trace said as Houston's fingers kept moving, though his gaze was still locked onto Trace. "Isn't that—"

"Téya's stepfather."

"Isn't he—"

"Dead? No," Trace said. "He's in Frankfurt at an underground facility."

"Whoa. Wait." Houston lifted another doughnut.

Trace pushed the tech geek's hand back down.

"Dude," Houston said. "Step away from the doughnut."

Trace almost laughed.

"Underground facility in Frankfurt. . .which—I mean, I know I'm not the super-secret agent or black ops operator like you, but you *do* know that Téya was in an underground facility in Frankfurt, right?"

"Houston, you have a way with sarcasm."

He held up his hands "I'm just sayin'. . ."

"I know what you're saying." That this tidbit made Téya look like a traitor. Trace shook his head. "Téya's not part of it."

"And we know this how?"

"Because as soon as she found out, she came directly to me."

"But Boss-man," Houston said, sliding the doughnuts to the side, apparently having lost his appetite, a miracle for the boy-wonder with an amazing metabolism. "She was missing for two hours. How do we know—"

"Houston, we're not going to second-guess our team. Got it?" He met the geek's gaze till Houston crumbled beneath the stare with a quick nod. "Téya came to me. Told me what happened. I'm satisfied. Trust me to do my job."

Something to the side beeped. "And trust me...," Houston said, his voice taking on that drugged sound as his mind whirled a thousand miles an hour and his fingers went almost as fast. "...Oh dude. We have some trouble."

Trace glanced down at the monitor and saw a rectangle with a grayscale version of the photograph Houston had handed him. Houston must've been running facial recognition software on the photo. A weird grid flickered over the various features of the first face. "What?"

"Just hold on to your horses, big T."

Arching an eyebrow at the geek, Trace glanced at the other photos sitting in the scanner tray, which sucked another into its feed.

"Okay, yeah," Houston said more firmly. "We have a problem."

"Fill me in."

"The photo"—Houston clicked and it popped up on the screen— "shows Varden."

Nothing new there. He'd given him that photo just so the software would have a match from which to compare. Not just the person in front but the individual beside him. "Who's with him?" But Trace already knew the answer.

"Well, that's Francesca Solomon," Houston said.

That photo had been iffy. It'd been more proof that she'd been in Misrata long enough to be involved in whatever went down. What if she was really the problem? What if she was turning the tables on them, trying to drown Zulu?

"Thank you," Trace said as he stood and started for the briefing room, which doubled as his office at the bunker.

Having her presence verified didn't give him anything he didn't already know, but Trace needed to hear someone else confirm the grainy image on the second photo. He'd somehow stood in her apartment and found himself asking her to help. Thank the good Lord she'd been stunned silent. She hadn't answered. And he didn't ask again. The more he'd talked, the more stupid his suggestion sounded. He left in the same shape he'd arrived.

Not true. Walking out of her home, driving home, he realized the last shred of dignity he had lay on the floral area rug in her living room. He'd laid himself bare there. And she'd walked all over him.

"But that's not the problem."

Hand on the knob, Trace stopped, pivoted.

"There's another face—the scanner almost missed it, I think, but. . ." He leaned forward. "Yeah. Someone's looking through a window."

How had he missed that? Trace returned to the command station. "Who?"

Houston sat back. "I hope our team is already on their way back."

Gut tight, shoulders square, Trace waited. "Why?"

"Have you talked with Boone or Annie yet?"

"No. Why?"

"Ballenger set them up. Sent some dude from some Italian special forces or something to deliver a message." Houston tapped his monitor. "And dude, that person in the window with your sexy but pain-in-the-butt INSCOM operative?"

Houston waggled his eyebrows. "That's Berg Ballenger."

Unknown Location
13 June – 1130 Hours EST

"Still feeding her information?"

"I am."

"Think it's working?"

"She's like a rabid dog on a scent," he said with a snicker. "I couldn't pull her off it if I wanted to."

"Now don't get all cocky on me, Varden."

"Oh I'm not. I'm confident." He took a long puff on his Cuban and let the hazy smoke ring into the air. "Solomon is so hungry to nail someone to the cross her own father built with his bare hands, her eyes are crossed. She's not seeing straight."

"Good. We want her focused on this." The gravelly voice grated on Varden's nerves. "The more she hassles them, the more his attention is divided—and it's the only way to stay one step ahead of this bulldog."

"You're overestimating the good colonel. He's had five years to figure this out, and he's still walking around scratching his head."

"But you've killed three of his team. He's ticked off, so we have to keep him busy."

Varden sat forward, setting the stogie on the edge of the crystal tray. He looked across the club where lights and bodies pulsed. "You want another hit?"

"Don't you think it's time?"

"I just got rid of hospital girl. If I do too much too soon, he'll—"

"The hearing is running interference for your slow pace. Don't mistake that for your usefulness or effectiveness."

Varden narrowed his eyes, resenting the words. "I've done what you didn't have the stomach to do."

Again, the gravelly voice grated along his spine: "You keep thinking that, if it makes you feel more confident and secure. Just remember who's footing the bill for those stale cigars and raunchy clubs you frequent."

The words irritated him. The man's disregard for the work Varden had carried out. The lengths he'd gone to so the authorities would look elsewhere. . .and he was blowing him off?

"Now, listen—we've got some things shifting in our direction."

Varden chewed the end of the cigar, stewing.

"Weston made a mess of things at the hearing when Solomon started testifying. She'll be back, giving the names of Weston's team."

"So?"

"So, it'll put these women on the radar. It'll make them high-profile targets. Media outlets will start running pictures of them. Talking about them. Wherever Weston is hiding them, we'll find them."

"You're forgetting it's a closed hearing. No reporters. No press."

The man laughed. Hard and long, ending up in a choking fit. "You idiot. How do you think the press finds anything out? Unnamed sources talk to the press all the time." He coughed and cleared his throat, the telltale rumble of a smoker's cough. "And don't worry. They'll find out. You just be ready. I want them dead. A traffic fatality would be great."

"Don't tell me how to do my job. You just make sure this can't come back on me."

"Just get it done, Varden."

The call disconnected, and Varden stared at the phone in his hand then hit the STOP button. The software he'd installed showed a call duration of 2:38—two minutes, thirty-eight seconds.

He smirked and sent the file to a dummy e-mail account. One not easily found but not too hidden that it'd be missed by experts. . .should Varden meet with an untimely death. Something, he was almost certain the colonel had planned. Especially since he, again, offered no reassurance that this wouldn't fall back on him. When things went south, how long would it take the general to sacrifice him under interrogation?

No problem. Varden had his contingencies. After all, everyone knew what they said about payback.

Trace
Lucketts, Virginia
14 June – 0830 Hours

Trace walked into the three bunk rooms and hit the lights. "Let's go! Rise and shine, Zulu!" He banged on the doors. "In the briefing room in fifteen."

Téya threw a shoe at him. Trace dodged it. "I'll have you work that out under Quade's gentle care later."

Téya groaned as Annie rolled over and squinted at him. In the other room, Nuala was gathering her stuff for the shower. "C'mon," Trace said. "Noodle's on her feet, and she's the only one with an excuse to move slow."

As Nuala walked past him, he touched her arm. "How you holding up?"

"Fine," she said then gave a shrug. "Nothing a hot shower won't loosen up."

He nodded. Glanced back at Annie, who was shuffling around her room now. She'd been civil to him since taking a hatchet to his hopes of picking up where they'd left off before Misrata. With Sam gone, she probably blamed Trace for that. *Figures.*

He glanced back into Téya's room and noticed her lying back down, arm slung over her eyes. He banged on her door. "Move it, Two!"

"I'm not a number," Téya ground out.

"Then prove it and get on your feet. Fifteen in the briefing area." Trace headed back to the command area of the bunker, where Houston was digging through the two dozen doughnuts Trace had brought. "Leave some for the others."

Houston turned, doughnut glaze on his chin. "It's your fault."

"Okay," Rusty said, emerging from the fourth room and sliding his hands through a black T-shirt, "this ought to be good." He smirked at Trace. "Can I watch as you kill him?" Rusty slapped Houston. "Go ahead, tell him how—whatever it is—is Trace's fault."

Trace had to admit—it was really great to have Rusty back, especially watching the cocky tech geek squirm.

Houston shrugged. Swept a hand that held a Boston cream–filled doughnut over the boxes. "You left me alone with them."

"Self-control ever enter your mind, Glaze?"

Houston blinked. "Glaze?"

Trace looked at his chin and bobbed his head.

"Yes!" Rusty snapped his fingers and pointed to Houston. "That's his new name." He grinned. "I like it."

"No no no," Houston said. "You are not giving me a name like that. I need a superhero-sounding name. Something like—Techtro. Or Cere—"

"Sorry, Glaze." Rusty snagged a banana from the kitchen area. "You don't get a vote."

"That's some seriously messed up stuff there," Houston argued. "Especially since I have to answer to it."

"If you lay off the doughnuts, you might get another name," Rusty laughed.

"Dude, there isn't enough power in the 'verse to keep me from these amazing confections." He stuffed a chocolate cake one into his mouth, hooked two more on his pointer finger, then headed back to his computer.

Trace gave a snort. "You got everything ready like we talked about last night?"

"Worphin' on it," Houston said in doughnut speak.

"Get your gear in here. We need to start soon." Trace hesitated. Looked around. "Where's Boone?"

"Beaphs me," Houston muffled around his food.

Trace entered the briefing area and planted his hands on either side of the notes he'd scribbled during the all-night marathon session he'd had with a few key individuals. Ones who would keep this between them, him, and God. Well, and the team in about—Trace looked at his watch— "Five minutes!"

Less than thirty seconds later, Téya trudged into the room and tossed a plain doughnut on the table. "Need coffee." She shuffled back out, but not before bumping into Annie, who had tucked her hair up and wore a coral-colored top that made her skin look soft and her lips—

He shoved his gaze to the papers on the table. Down. Away from her. *Haul it up, Weston.* He'd have to reassign her or something after this, assuming she wanted to keep working. She'd never been one to quit, though.

He focused on the plans. The calculated risks forbidding him from entering the arms of sleep last night. He'd made it through the ranks quickly because he hadn't been afraid to take those risks. Sometimes the best solution was unconventional.

Within a few minutes, they were all gathered. Nuala's hair dripped as she sat at the table, legs pulled up on her chair, and instead of a doughnut, she had yogurt.

"I spent thirty dollars on fat pills and you eat yogurt?" he teased.

She bunched up her shoulders. "I eat one of those, I'll be gasping for air when Quade returns."

His gaze skidded around the room. "Speaking of returning...where's Boone?"

"Hey, Boss," Houston said, hauling a squeaky cart into the room with his gear. "I couldn't get the blueprints—"

"Work on it after," Trace said, glancing at the three women and Rusty.

"What's so important that you have to interrupt our sleep? It's not like we weren't out running all over England trying to track down a punk and getting shot at."

"HOMe is getting a fully funded grant along with rent-free facilities in Reston." Trace watched their reactions. Watched the confusion morph into surprise. Then to anger.

"Just like Washington to throw more money at corrupt entities," Téya said with a snarl.

"Are you sure someone's giving them money?" Annie scowled, shifting in her seat. "Their finances are questionable at best. We proved that."

"Yes, but not in a way that can be publicly made known at this time." Trace stuffed his hands on his belt. "A large gala is planned for the Fourth of July. HOMe is the guest of honor."

Annie raised her hands. "Who is stupid enough to give them this benefit and raise money for an organization that is as corrupt—"

"To the outside world, HOMe is a reputable, humanitarian organization," Trace said. "And we want them to believe that."

"Why would we want them to believe that?" Téya asked, mimicking his words.

"Because we're throwing the fund-raiser." Trace had to admit, he was proud of this idea. Felt it was just the lure they needed. "We're inviting them in to honor them."

"We?" Annie's eyebrows winged up. "Are you insane?"

"Information has come to light in the last few days."

"Yes, like threats from Ballenger to stay out of his way," Annie said.

"True."

"He has GIS operatives working for him. We don't want to incur his anger," Annie warned.

"But we also aren't going to lie down and roll over for him," Trace said. "We are in the middle of an active investigation—more active than it's been in the last sixty-two months. We're not backing off."

"What else?" Téya asked.

Trace glanced to her, surprised at the question.

"Well, I mean, you aren't going to just throw this huge event simply because Ballenger threatened us, so what else have you learned?"

"Varden—he's an officer tied to this somehow. I'm still looking into how." Trace nodded. "My contacts at the Pentagon are helping with this ruse—the cover story is that the government is providing a one-year grant to help them build new facilities in countries HOMe has been trying to get into," he said. "Solomon is building the cover and preparing everything. He's got a whole team on this."

"Why?" Annie shoved her hand through the loose curls around her face. "This doesn't make sense."

"Think about it," Rusty said, apparently having already caught on to the game. "Think who'll be there. If this is for HOMe, then not only will Hollister be there, but—"

Understanding washed over Annie's face. "Mercy Chandler." Her face went a little pale. "Won't Batsakis be there, too?"

Trace gritted his teeth, remembering how that man had pawed Annie. "More than likely. Along with Stoffel."

"This is a lot of risk," Annie said, her voice tipping into the realm of fear.

Trace held a hand toward her, trying to stay her complaints and concerns. "If we can make this a big, elaborate event; if we can get Stoffel, Giles, Chandler, and Hollister here, then that will draw the attention of—"

"Ballenger," Téya said with a firm nod. "I like it. Let's do it."

Annie

"No!" Annie sat forward, her mind racing with panic and awareness. "This is insane. Ballenger threatened us. He had a GIS operative in Dover, and you want to lure them into our country? Invite them to take a bead on us? What about Varden?" Annie's head felt like it was splitting open with the flurry of information and names coming to light. "What about the person sourcing him—isn't that who we need to lure into the open?"

"Ballenger is," Téya said. "When will you start paying attention to the facts and not to Trace?"

"Hey," Trace snapped at the out-of-line comment.

Indignation clawed through Annie's chest with a chunk of embarrassment. "Grow up, Téya," Annie said, unable to put up with her friend's snark and moodiness any longer. "I don't know what happened in Bleak Pond—"

"That's right," Téya said, her face darkening. "You *don't*. So *don't* go there."

"I'm sorry," Rusty said as he stood. "I thought I was with a professional team of soldiers, not a WWE cat fight."

Heart on a rampage from the fear, the uncertainty about this new plan, the attitude and meanness from Téya. . .Annie struggled. She was tired. So tired of all of this. She wanted Sam. Wanted him to hold her and reassure her things would be fine. But she couldn't afford a Pollyanna moment right now.

"Easy," Trace said, glaring at both her and Téya. "Listen, we're doing this. It's not up for a vote. We have less than two weeks to get this in play. I've been up all night with Intel analysts and Solomon. This is our prime opp to have everyone in the same place at the same time."

"What about the hearing?" Téya asked, her question filled with defiance.

Trace stilled, stretched his jaw, then looked at Téya.

Annie hated that, once again, Téya knew more. But the look on Trace's face bothered her more. He was an intense soldier and person, but the storm that erupted over his face alarmed her. "What is she talking about?" she asked, bouncing her gaze between the two. "What hearing?"

It would take a machete to hack through the tension in the room.

"There's a hearing," Trace said slowly, definitively, still glowering at Téya. Then looked at Annie. "It's not your concern."

"Wrong," Téya countered. "You were placed under arrest trying to stop that woman from giving up our names."

Trace shifted, his shoulders lifting. Arms out to the side, he was about to detonate.

Annie couldn't move. Her mind galloped through their words as the duel played out.

Trace's face went like stone. "Leave us," he barked.

It took a second for Annie and the others to register that he wanted them to leave. But this—there was no way she'd walk out now. Something big was happening. Trace was hiding something. "No."

He aimed all the ferocity that was the combat soldier and colonel at Annie "*Leave* us. I need—"

"We need openness and transparency," Annie said, tasting the bitterness of the words, knowing she hadn't given him that. Not about. . .everything. Seeing this anger, seeing his fury—she could only imagine how he'd react if he found out the whole truth about their past. But that was different. This was now. They were in a mess that had to be sorted. "We've been operating with half-full files. Put it all on the table, Trace. Enough with the secrets."

Annie couldn't help but notice the way Rusty lowered his head, bouncing his leg. It went against every bit of training they had to question and challenge Trace like this.

Wide-eyed, mouth open, Houston watched.

Trace pinned Annie with a fierce gaze, one that probed down. . . down. . .down. . .into the recesses of her soul. Someday she'd have to tell him. Just not yet.

"Fine," Trace huffed, then touched the table again. "General Marlowe encouraged a committee to reopen the investigation against me regarding Misrata. They are aware of the deaths of Herring, Reyna, and now Shay. Someone—"

"Tell them," Rusty said, and when Trace about punched the guy, he raised his hands. "They should know it all."

"General Solomon's daughter somehow obtained files on your identities."

Annie felt the dagger of those words right between her ribs and straight to the heart.

"She was going to reveal them in the hearing. I. . .intervened." He seared Téya with one of the angriest expressions Annie had seen. "Though I'm not sure how Téya is aware of that."

Dear God, help us. "Is it over?" Annie asked, folding her arms as she took her seat again. "Do they know our names?"

"No," Trace snapped. "I won't let that happen."

Something in his expression bothered Annie. Something about the dark fury in his face. "Wh–what do you mean? What are you going to do?"

Fingertips on the cold surface of the table, Trace tempered his frustration. "Can we get back to the mission? There's a—"

He was going to do something. Anything. Whatever it took to stop someone from exposing them. Annie could see it all over him. "We want to be there," Annie said.

"Not happening." Trace swallowed—hard. "The hearing is closed. I can't get you in without credentials, and that's not possible."

"You get us into other countries but can't get us into a hearing?" Téya once again worked against him.

"It's a case of can't, not won't, right, Trace?" Annie said.

"Commander," Nuala said, clearing her throat.

"Listen!" Trace barked. "You're not going. It's hard enough to keep you safe here. But out in the open"—he shook his head—"impossible. Forget it."

Annie sat forward. "But—"

"Enough! It's not happening. End of story," Trace roared. He snatched up his files then stomped out of the room. "Reconvene at fifteen hundred."

And he was gone.

Stunned, Annie sat there, working through what had just happened. Téya left the room almost immediately. Nuala and Houston departed together. But Annie stayed, thinking. Trying to separate the angry, yelling Trace from the man she knew.

On the other side of the table, Rusty sat there, his chair sideways against the table, forearms on his knees.

"They'll take him down, won't they?" Annie asked quietly, her heart breaking for Trace. He shouldn't be facing this alone.

Rusty said nothing.

Annie moved around the table and sat in front of him. "Is it bad?"

Rusty gave an almost imperceptible nod. Then he dropped back against the chair with a sigh. "Francesca Solomon is driving a Bradley right up Trace's butt. She's relentless, and her information, though wrong, sounds and looks right."

"Rusty, what will happen to him if they find him guilty this time?"

"He'll be buried in the prison system."

"And Zulu?"

His blue eyes held hers. "On your own. Or worse—arrested and tried as well. Assuming they find you."

"So, worst possible."

He bobbed his head. "Worst possible."

"Then, Rusty, I need your help. Would you take me for a drive tomorrow?"

Francesca
Capitol Hill, Washington, DC
15 June – 0830 Hours

She couldn't get those three women out of her head. Seeing their faces, studying them, it. . .

"You all right?"

Frankie looked up at the uniform standing in front of her. Blinked. "Paolo." She glanced around. "Where'd you come from?"

He grinned. "Late night studying how to destroy Weston's life?"

His words stabbed her. Hurt. Wounded. "Not fair," she muttered, lowering her gaze. "W–where's Dad?"

"Inside, I think. Why?" Paolo's dark eyes fastened on her. "Second thoughts?"

Frankie shifted uncomfortably. He didn't seem to be taking pleasure in her doubts, but rather seemed interested. She glanced around the hall.

Remembered the look in Trace Weston's eyes. The torment. Nightmares kept waking her up. Inflicting his torment on her. "What if I've got it wrong, Paolo?"

He took her arm and ushered her to the side. "Frank, what happened?"

She loved when he called her that. It made her feel like one of the boys. But today, it just somehow emphasized that she *wasn't* one of the boys, especially if he found out Trace had come to the house. Pinned her to the wall. Paolo might be on his side politically, but she was his sister. Even she knew that went deeper.

Still, if she told him what happened. . .if someone else heard, Trace would be arrested. Again.

Why did she even care if he did? Why did she suddenly care a whit about Colonel Weston? "He came to my home."

Paolo's eyes widened and he craned his neck down. "Weston? Came to your house?"

She nodded, skating a glance around to be sure nobody else heard that. Now Paolo scowled. "What'd he do?"

Frankie rolled her eyes. "It's what he said." She couldn't bring herself to admit she had been taken off guard. Paolo and Roman would never let her live that down. But she also worried how it'd make Weston look.

Again—why do you care?

"What did he say?" Paolo had gone all big brother on her. But she sensed in him also an intense curiosity.

No—it wasn't curiosity. It was suspicion.

"You don't believe me."

"Never said that." Paolo angled a shoulder toward her. "This is way out of character for Weston, and visiting you would jeopardize this hearing and every bit of credibility he has built up."

Defiance dug through her. She lifted her chin. "He was worried about his team. Insisted I not expose their names." No, it was more like pleading. . .begging. The thought unsettled her. "He said I'd put them in danger."

Paolo's strong suit had always been sarcasm, and she expected him to frost this whole conversation with a thick layer of it. When he didn't say a word, she scrambled not to let him think she'd been swayed by this. If she was so weak she let a guy shoving into her house change her mind, then. . .

"Since I started digging, my house has been ransacked. My credit destroyed. My confidence shaken." Frankie's heart danced a jig when she spotted Colonel Weston walking down the hall in his Class A's. "I was convinced it was him trying to scare me off."

"And now?"

461

Weston shook hands with other officers as he made his way down the short corridor to the hearing room. Nice smile, considering he'd just scowled and frowned at her. Broad shoulders. A chest decorated with ribbons. A half dozen or more gold slices marked his forearm sleeves, indicating his deployments. Clearly, Weston was no stranger to combat. He shook General Cantor's hand, shared a laugh, then pivoted. His gaze rammed into hers. He hesitated for a fraction of a second. Not enough for anyone to really notice. Well, nobody but her. She noticed.

"I'm to blame. Just leave. Them. Out." His plea boomed through her mind.

Paolo touched her elbow and leaned in, cutting off her view of the lieutenant colonel as he made his way into the hearing room. "Frank?"

She flinched, giving herself a mental shake and pulling herself free of Weston's gaze. She turned to her brother. "I. . .I need to talk to Dad."

He pointed toward the double doors. "It's time."

Frankie looked inside and immediately registered Weston sliding down the narrow space between the tables at the front and the chairs of the audience. He clapped a hand on the shoulder of her father, who was already seated inside. The two exchanged a smile and handshake.

"You believe him?" Her question had been for her father, a surprised thought, but her brother thought it was aimed at him.

"Weston?" Paolo said as he guided her into the room. "He's one of the best officers I've ever met. So, yeah, I do."

Frankie pushed into the room and made her way to the table where her father sat. "Do you have a minute?" she asked her dad, avoiding Trace's gaze. She didn't want to look at him. Didn't want to even acknowledge him. His escapade at her home had destroyed her confidence of his guilt.

"Frankie, it's about to start, honey."

"Two minutes, Dad." She put her hand on his arm. "Please."

He nodded and excused himself. She met him by the doors, her heart ricocheting off her ribs. Out of the corner of her eye, she noticed Weston watching.

"What is wrong, Francesca?" her dad asked, straightening his jacket.

"Daddy, will you please promise to answer one question for me?"

His brow dove toward his eyes then rose again. "Okay."

"Promise." It was an old joke with them.

He smiled. "I promise."

She took a measured breath for courage then slowly let it out. "Did Colonel Weston request that I be on his team, on Zulu?"

Her father paled. Slipped a quick glance to the side. Then eased in. "I can't discu—"

"Yes or no. Please."

Her father sighed, his head down. Then he raised his eyes only to her. "He mentioned you in the preliminary list, but I refused him."

Francesca straightened. Expelled the breath she didn't realize she'd held till that moment. *It could've been me. It could've been me.* She pushed her gaze back to the table, where Weston leaned to his left, chatting with someone in a dark suit.

I've got it all wrong.

Or did she?

Regardless, she had too many doubts to go forward. To put the lives of three young women on the line. Especially knowing she could've been on the opposite side of this.

"Franny?"

She met her dad's brown eyes.

"What's this about?"

Just then, the session was called to order.

Annie
Capitol Hill, Washington, DC
15 June – 1030 Hours

"He's going to shoot me," Rusty said as he slid down Pennsylvania Avenue NW.

"I'll take the heat. It's nothing new," Annie said, watching out the window of Trusty's Ford F-150 for sign of the small red SUV.

"Things have changed a lot between y'all," Rusty said as he aimed into what amounted to four rows of parking availability sandwiched between the small body of water that stretched before the Ulysses S. Grant Memorial and Constitution Avenue. They'd already checked the parking spots that lined the roads around the Capitol.

"He changed," Annie muttered.

Rusty snickered.

"What?"

He gave a one-shouldered shrug. "I've known Trace nearly ten years." He cocked his head to the side. "That man hasn't changed at all—except when he was dating you. Now he's as grumpy as before."

Annie looked away.

"Actually," Rusty said, lifting a finger of his hand draped over the steering wheel. "I'd say he's even grumpier."

"There's a lot happening. Three of us are dead." She felt bad for being blunt, but she didn't want this conversation. Mostly because she still hadn't figured out what to do about her and Trace.

"But not a lot between the two of you."

Annie huffed. "What do you want me to say, Trusty?"

"Why'd you break up with him?"

"I didn't." She really had to focus on finding this car. "He left me at an airstrip. Promised he'd come. He never did. I stopped waiting."

"He still loves you."

The thought made her heart ping-pong through her chest. "Well, he's too late."

Rusty applied the brake, drawing her attention. He pointed to a red SUV parked to his left. "That it?"

"Red Ford Escape," Annie said, as she lifted the paper with the registration number on it and compared it to the Virginia plates. "Yep, that's it." She reached for the door handle.

Rusty touched her arm. "You sure about this?"

Annie looked at the SUV. The woman had been a plague. And though Rusty blamed Trace's mood on her, Annie knew it had a lot do to with the lieutenant who'd been applying an indecent amount of pressure against Trace—all based on speculation. "Yeah."

"There's a spot on the other side. We can park there and wait." Rusty drove up the aisle.

As he made the U-turn, Annie spotted a uniformed officer walking down the path from the Capitol. "Hey." It was a woman. Was it Solomon? She peered around the visor to get a better angle. "Is that her?"

"I think so," Rusty gunned the engine and sped down the small parking area, hurrying. He slid to a stop a few cars from Solomon's.

Annie climbed out, tugging the brim of the Nationals ball cap down on her brow. Gaze locked onto Solomon, she waited and timed it so they'd arrive at the red crossover at the same time. But each passing second made Annie's heart thump louder and harder. This woman wanted to put her face, Téya's face, and Nuala's all over the news in her pursuit of taking Trace down. And Annie had to admit, just that the woman wanted to hurt Trace brought out every primal instinct in Annie. She might not be sure about her own feelings for Trace, but he was a good man. An amazing soldier. And a very loyal friend.

Francesca Solomon stood about Téya's height. Leggy in her skirt, she cut a nice figure. One Annie envied with the height and curves. Almost black hair secured in a bun beneath her cover, Francesca strode down the sidewalk. She glanced to the left and to the right, though traffic arrows clearly marked it one-way. She stepped off the curb, cutting between two sedans, and crossed toward her red vehicle. Her dark shades concealed her eyes, but her posture and the way she carried herself seemed to say she hadn't noticed Annie. That, or she wasn't worried about her.

Annie would change that. She slinked between two vehicles to come up on the rear of the Ford Escape. "Francesca Solomon?"

The woman hesitated, shifting her satchel to her left hand. Easier to get to her weapon—one she wasn't carrying—Annie imagined. "Yes?"

Formal. Stiff.

"Do you have a minute to talk?"

She glanced at her silver and gold watch. "Sorry, I'm already late for a meeting."

"Well, you're going to be more late." Annie wished the woman didn't tower over her, giving her a mental edge. She lifted the bill of the cap a little and met the woman's gaze head on.

Solomon stilled.

"Do you recognize me?"

Rigid, Francesca gave a quick nod then glanced around. "It's not really smart for you to be here."

"A lot of things aren't smart," Annie said, glad the woman had given her a segue. "Like you exposing my identity to the world."

"Only to the hearing."

"You and I both know that telling those suits my name and the names of my sisters-in-arms is as good as handing a press release to CNN. By tonight, my picture will be all over the news." Her palms grew sweaty at the thought. "You really have no idea the damage you've done. The danger you've placed our lives in."

"Everyone's telling me that," she murmured, once more looking around. "I just need justice for Misrata."

"No," Annie snapped, her anger vaulting over her fears. "No, you don't get to say that." Her breath came in gulps. "Don't you dare act like your vendetta against Colonel Weston is about the children. Spew your lies in that hearing, but not here. Right here, we're on even ground, Miss Solomon. I was there. I heard those children scream as they died. I watched it while you were probably in a comfy chair in an office. So don't do that. Play it straight."

Brownish-gold eyes held hers. "What do you want?"

"I need you to go back in there and tell them—tell them you were wrong. Your information was wrong. Have our names redacted. Whatever it takes."

"I can't."

"You can!" Annie snapped. "And you will. This campaign against us needs to stop. Three of my very dearest friends are dead—"

"Not my fault—"

"Did you go to Keeley at the hospital?"

Again, the woman said nothing.

"Were you there? Ever?"

Another curt nod.

"Then you bear the blame just as much as whoever poisoned her."

"Are you just here to try to put me on a guilt trip?"

This time, Annie hesitated. Partially because the woman's attitude surprised her. But also because—yeah, she had come here for that reason. Annie removed the baseball cap. "I thought if you put a face with the name you just spread all over the news...if I end up dead..."

"Then maybe you should stop standing around in public."

Building Rooftop, Constitution Avenue

Careless, foolish women. They made his job too easy. They might as well climb up on the cross and nail themselves to it, they made it so simple. Staring down the scope of the military sniper weapon system, he aligned his target. Checked the wind. Dialed the gun. Rechecked the wind.

All while they stood in the open, nice soft targets.

Two birds with one stone.

Two kills with one round.

He smirked as he pressed the stock to his shoulder, braced for the kick.

Wouldn't that be sweet? But he didn't need the ball cap chick. He only needed Solomon. She'd gotten too chatty. Too used to thinking on her own rather than just following orders.

His phone buzzed against his hip. He had time, so he answered. "Yeah?"

"We're coming out. Be ready."

"I have another target in sight."

"Which one?"

"Solomon. Staring at her right now." He dialed and shifted the scope. He tightened up on the blond. "Boss..." His heart thumped a little harder. "I think this is your lucky day, General."

"How?"

"I'm staring down the scope at Solomon—"

"How's that lucky?"

"And Annie Palermo."

"She's here?"

466

"Standing next to Solomon."

"No, focus on the original target."

"I have no joy on that target." He lifted his cheek from the scope and glanced toward the Capitol with his bare eyes. "There's enough distance. Solomon is isolated with Palermo. Nobody will know what's happening by the time I hit Weston."

"I need Weston—"

"I can do it."

"Varden!"

He ended the call. Tucked the phone away. Then again checked the wind and temperature. Slid his finger into the trigger well.

Annie

Stunned at the woman's cruelty and insensitivity, Annie shook her head. "I met your dad the Christmas Colonel Weston tapped me for the team. I was so impressed with him."

"Yeah," Francesca said, removing her cover and setting it and her satchel in her car. "Is this where you—like everyone else—tell me I'm nothing like him? That he and my brothers are much better people than me?"

Annie heard the hurt in those words. Saw the sting on the woman's pretty face. "Actually, I was going to say you were just like him."

Francesca looked down. Rubbed her forehead, with one hand on her hip. "Look, I didn't do it."

Did Annie dare hope that meant what she wanted it to? "Didn't do what?"

Francesca unbuttoned her uniform blouse and removed it, standing in the parking lot in a tank top. She loosed her hair from the tight knot at the base of her neck. Somehow, Annie knew the moves were symbols of her shedding the rules and regulations of the military. "I walked out of the hearing without giving my testimony. Without telling them who you and the others are."

"Why? I mean—I'm glad. Thank you." She could breathe. Feel the air on her face. "But. . .why?"

"I realized I could've been on your team. I could've been one of those girls who died. One of your friends. It's crazy, I know," Francesca said, leaning against her car. "But it changed things for me. When he begged me to leave you all out of it, there was something about the way he said it, the torment in his eyes. It haunted me."

"He?" Annie's stomach squirmed. "Colonel Weston?"

Francesca stood up straight. "I—"

Crack!

A split second carried a bevy of noises and images: the tinkling of shattering glass. The *oof!* of Solomon as she rammed into Annie. Solomon's shouting "Down!" and the crackling sound of the windshield safety glass spider-webbing.

Shots! Someone was shooting at them!

* * *

Annie threw herself at Francesca, knocking them both to the glass-littered pavement. "Shooter!" Head down, she covered it with her arm.

Tink! Thunk!

That was close! Right above her head. Which meant the shooter could see her. She rolled, grabbing Solomon. "Here."

Without hesitation, the woman went with her, and as she did, Annie tried to shift to the side. Her hand slipped on a slick puddle. Nausea churned. Though she wanted it to be oil, she knew better.

Rocks spat at them. Dust plumed in her face. Annie pressed herself harder against the car and road, trying to edge out of view. "You okay?" she shouted to Francesca.

"Where is he?"

"I don't know," Annie shouted.

"Yeah. . .my name is Francesca Solomon," the stiff, formal words of the woman drew Annie around. Solomon had her phone pressed to her ear. "I'm on Pennsylvania Avenue by the Grant Memorial. We have an active shooter." She glanced around, shaking her head. "I can't tell. Across the street, I think—what is that?" Pointing away from the water, Francesca nodded toward another street. "I think. . .it's Constitution, I think."

Sirens wailed in the distance. Someone else must've called in the shooting. All Annie could think was that she had to get out of here. But moving could get her head sniped off.

Tires squalled, and within a matter of seconds, Rusty's large gray and black Ford F-150 backed up into view. "Annie!"

"Here," she said, lifting her hand. She looked up, afraid to lift her head too high. Rusty had the door flung open, leaning out. "Did you see him?"

"No. You okay?"

"Yeah." Annie instinctively glanced back to Francesca, who was on her back staring up at the sky, phone still in hand. Bloody hand.

"Francesca!" Annie scrambled toward the woman. Her white tank wasn't white anymore—a large dark stain spread over her waist and hip.

Her Italian complexion had gone pale. "Francesca!"

She lifted her head to look at them and cried out, throwing herself back down. A sheen of sweat covered her face.

"Apply pressure," Rusty said. "I'll get my med kit."

Annie planted her hands on the wound and pressed.

"We need"—Francesca grimaced, blew out a breath, then continued—"EMS. Y–yes. I'm shot."

Rusty was at her side, kneeling with his gear. He grabbed gauze that would stop the bleeding, lifted Annie's hands, and then pressed her hands back down. "Hold it." He lifted the phone. "My name is Rusty Gray. I'm a trained medic. We have a late twenties female with a single gunshot wound to her abdomen. Both exit and entry wounds. Blood loss is significant." He tucked the phone between his shoulder and chin. "I'm running a wide bore IV. . . ."

Annie dropped back against the car, sagging in relief. The shooter—she couldn't just assume he was gone, but he'd be stupid to stay there now that even she could hear sirens blazing.

Trace

"Colonel Weston," General Marlowe droned on, "has shown contempt for the proceedings of this committee and the Select Intelligence Committee's investigation. He has refused to answer questions, and what little he has volunteered is repetitive or nonissues."

"This is the same complaint that I have personally heard as well," Representative Glick said, his slicked-back hair glossy beneath the lights. He proved to be as slimy as his hair. "I believe Colonel Weston's refusal to be cooperative with this committee and its investigation is proof positive of his hand in the deadly and tragic events of 29 April. Would you agree, General Marlowe?"

Marlowe leaned forward, keyed the microphone. "I would, sir."

Trace sat staring forward. Not only would he refuse to answer those questions, he would refuse to acknowledge these two. Besides, this was nothing more than a scripted attempt to get Trace stripped of rank and duty. Marlowe had been after his oak leaves since before they were pinned on Trace.

Glick tilted his head to look at the chairman a few seats down on the raised dais. "I think we have what we need, Senator Moller. The Select Intelligence Committee is of the mind that Colonel Weston, due to his extreme lack of respect and compliance with this committee, be charged with obstruction of justice. And it would be our recommendation to his superiors that this is not the type of soldier we need leading a younger generation. In fact, he has failed his duty and dishonored the uniform he wears today."

"I would remind you, Representative Glick," Chairman Moller said, "Colonel Weston has not been found guilty, and therefore, the blame and accusation you lay at his feet is premature." With a heavy sigh, Moller turned to Trace.

Trace knew he'd tied the chairman's hands with the stunt the other day. And with his silence and refusal to speak today.

Trace's phone buzzed in his pocket, but he ignored it. The guillotine was coming down on his neck. He wasn't going to answer a phone call while it was happening.

Moller held out his hands, as if pleading with Trace. "Colonel Weston, you haven't said much, and like General Marlowe said, what you've conveyed to us has been a repeat of the earlier hearings. You've heard what my colleague, Representative Glick, has said, what he has recommended." He stared at Trace, and though the message was clear—*please, tell us something, break this silence, don't let them win*—Trace held his peace. "Do you have anything to say, anything that can sway the minds of this committee?"

"I do not"—Trace's mind flicked to Francesca, to her refusal—"except one thing: I would charge each member of this hearing to consider the proceedings. What happened. But more importantly, what didn't happen. Let that speak for itself."

His phone buzzed again. Trace slid it from his pocket, wondering what was so urgent.

"May I speak?" General Solomon asked. "Briefly."

Houston's number showed up with the message: SHOTS FIRED. ANNIE INVOLVED.

Before Trace could register the move, he was pushing to his feet, sucking in a quick breath.

Kneading his brow, Moller hesitated. "Briefly," he agreed.

Solomon cast him a curious gaze and reached for the microphone.

A security guard raced to the front of the room as Solomon started talking about the inherent sensitive nature of black ops missions and teams.

Another Houston text: F SOLOMON INJURED. RUSTY ON SCENE. CALL ASAP.

"Excuse me, General," the chairman cut in, leaning forward, his expression taut. "I've been advised that we are in lockdown. There is an active shooter just outside the building."

Trace rushed toward the door.

"Hey!" the security guard shouted. "Nobody leaves."

But Trace was already out of the courtroom, sprinting now to the foyer as he hit the autodial for Houston then aimed for a side door. "Tell me," he ordered as soon as the call connected.

"Trace!" a shout from behind didn't stop him.

He pushed the door open and stepped into the warm, balmy June afternoon. He sprinted behind a Dumpster, all too aware and too familiar with avoiding eating lead. What he missed was his gear, his M4, and his Glock. Being in the hearing, he was unarmed. Had to get to his Charger.

"EMTs are on the scene."

That stopped Trace. He pulled his shoulder back, gaze skimming the surroundings. "Wait—Annie's there? Why is Annie there? Is she hit?" his mind raced. What was she doing out there? Why wasn't she at the bunker? All the five- and six-story buildings could offer a sweet spot for a shooter. Taller ones made it impossible for him to know if they were up there.

"No, she *was* there," Houston said, "but Rusty got her out of there."

"Rusty's there?" What in blazes was going on?

"On scene. Told them he was driving by when he saw Solomon get hit."

Good, good. Trusty always knew how to think on his feet. Two massive forms of relief right there. Having Annie at an accident and her name being taken in reports would not be good. Even worse would be if she'd been injured.

"What's the situation?" Trace darted to a delivery truck parked a few yards away. "Are you into the satellites or cameras?"

"Me? That's illegal, Colonel Weston," Houston said, a mock in his words.

"Houston," Trace growled as he crouched next to a truck, then sprinted to another.

"Chillax, Boss-man. What do you want to know?"

"What do you see?"

"Using cameras on the poles, I'm seeing a lot of emergency vehicles. Roads around the Capitol are shut down and blocked. Cops are hunting the shooter, according to radio chatter and the SWAT teams racing into two different buildings."

Trace jogged toward his car. "Shooter's still active?"

"Active, no, but out there, yes. I've piggybacked a satellite. Scanning rooftops."

"He's pretty cocky to do this in broad daylight," Trace said. He took a step.

Glass exploded in an older model sedan.

Trace threw himself to the ground, scoring his palms. He bit back a curse. His phone clattered across the parking lot, spinning to a stop under a Volkswagen Bug. He peered beneath the vehicles, eyeballing his Charger three more down. He huffed and pulled himself into a crouch.

"Weston!" someone behind him shouted.

Trace glanced back and saw Haym jogging toward him. "Get down! Get down!"

Face white, Haym went to a knee.

"Still active," Trace shouted to his friend, still thirty feet away. "Stay there." Hand on the bumper of a silver Mercedes, he readied himself to run. He took in two quick breaths and blew them back out then launched himself forward.

Crack! Tsing!

He threw himself at the Bug and retrieved his phone. Shimmying along the side, he made his way to the rear of the vehicle, grateful the parking area had a curve to it. He sighted his Charger. Scanned the rooftops. There were enough trees that if the shooter wasn't high enough, he wouldn't have a good vantage.

"Houston—higher the better. He needs to be able to see over the trees," Trace barked into the phone. "He's got a bead on me."

"You're his target?" Houston asked, his voice unusually high. "That's. . .that's odd."

"Why is that odd?"

"How could he possibly know you and Annie would be there?"

Trace crouched next to the Bug, thinking. "He didn't." Which meant— "Solomon." Why was he after her?

He shoved into the open, sprinting for his car. Within a few feet, he dived for cover.

Fire screamed down his leg. He pitched forward. "Augh!" Trace hit hard. His breath knocked out of him. "Son of a biscuit!" Trace bit out, grabbing his leg, the trail of fire not soggy, but raw.

"Trace! Trace are you shot?" Houston cried.

Gritting his teeth, Trace unlocked his car. Flipped open the door. "Find this piece of crap, Houston. I want him."

"I haven't stopped. You didn't answer if you're shot."

"Just a graze. Won't be so lucky next time." Trace dragged himself into the seat, lying across the console. He started the engine and laid back the seat. "Get me that guy's head on a platter!"

"Roger that," Houston said. "Trace—patching Rusty through."

"Rusty?" It was half repetition, half invitation.

"Trace. Where are you?"

"West side of the Capitol." If he could get a little farther north, he should be out of the shooter's line of sight. With the Capitol in lockdown, the parking lot wasn't busy right now. That worked in his favor. "The shooter has me targeted, but I'm trying to get out of here. Where's Annie? Why was she here?"

"That's why I asked Houston to patch me in. She was here when Solomon got hit—"

"You'll explain that to me when we get back." Trace rammed his shifter into gear and gunned it. Tires pealed. He whipped to the left, keeping his head out of sight.

Glass exploded, peppering his face. The shooter had hit the driver's side. Trace squinted, shielding himself as he turned his head away but kept his gaze forward. Aimed for the exit to Northwest Drive. "Rusty, shooter's on Constitution somewhere. Find him!"

"Working on it. . ."

Trace raced down Northwest then Northeast to Capitol. He flashed his ID to the guard, who gave him a nod and directed him to the south. Routes to the north and west were blocked, he warned Trace.

"Rusty—talk to me. Annie." Trace gunned the engine, racing down First.

"She was supposed to wait at the Grant Memorial."

Trace's gut churned. "Supposed to?" He flicked on his blinker, crawling out of his skin over the traffic clogging the roads. Didn't they know there was a lockdown?

"I can't get over there. Roads are blocked."

"On my way," Trace said then focused on getting to her. "Turning onto Independence now."

He dodged cars, weaving in and out of traffic like a Capitol cabby would.

"She's not at Grant."

Annie. . .Annie. . .what were you thinking?

She got shot at. Or Solomon did. The sniper couldn't have known Annie was there. But if Annie felt the threat was coming from Constitution—just as he did—then she'd head away from it. Put as much distance between him and the shooter. "I have a theory," Trace said, driving as fast as possible while he scanned the sidewalks and pedestrians. The light went yellow.

Trace punched the pedal. Glided through the intersection. *C'mon, c'mon.* Where was she? He passed the botanical gardens. The wall would block a shooter, but it was too open.

Sirens whooped behind him.

He glanced in the mirror. Saw a Capitol Police car.

"For the love of. . ." Trace growled and pulled to the side, wanting to curse. Wanting to gun it and outrun the cop. But that would only get him jail time. Annie would be missing. He eased to the curb.

The cop revved and sped around Trace, hitting the corner hard at Third and squalling his tires.

Trace breathed a sigh of relief and guided his car back into traffic. His gaze tracked the roads. Sidewalks again. His attention hit a copse of trees just past Third. Little grass grew near the sidewalk bench—

Trace's heart vaulted into his throat. "Annie."

He sailed through the intersection and yanked the car to the side of the road. Ignored the No PARKING sign, shoved the gear into PARK, and threw open the door.

A horn blared.

He sprinted to the bench. "Annie!"

She looked over her shoulder. Chalky faced, she gave a weak smile. "You found me."

He went to a knee. "What's wrong?"

She lifted her head and managed another smile. "Two for the price of one."

"Crap," Trace said as he went to a knee, lifting her hand and checking the wound. "What have I told you about eating lead?" he asked, his tone chiding but light.

"Never did listen well," she mumbled.

"Got that right." The bullet hadn't exited, which was good—it limited the amount of blood loss—but that could be dangerous—jarring it could push it into an organ. "Okay, we need to get you back to the bunker."

"Sorry I left."

"We'll talk about it later."

"Sounds ominous."

"Good, I'm finally doing *something* right," he said, helping her to her feet. He slipped his arm around her waist and hooked hers over his shoulder.

"I had to get away from there," Annie said, grunting in pain. "He was still shooting. If I stayed— How's Rusty?"

"Fine." Trace guided her into the backseat so she could lie down. But her question nagged at him. Was Trusty doing okay? As he straightened, he heard the whoop of a police warning siren. He glanced back.

The cop was motioning him away from the curb.

Trace held a hand up, praying he didn't have blood on it from Annie, then hurried to the driver's side. He slid behind the wheel. "Stay down. We have a cop behind us."

As he eased back into traffic, his phone rang. He hit the speaker. "Houston—"

"Trace. Trace, it's bad," came Houston's frantic, almost shouted words.

"Slow down," Trace said, heading back to Independence so he could catch 50 up to 66 and then fight the insanity of Route 7. "I'm on my way back with Annie. We need a doctor."

"You're not listening!" Houston shouted.

Trace drew up short at the terse, angry words. The laidback guy had a rocket up his rear end. This wasn't like him. "Okay," he said calmly. Very calmly, though his pulse probably registered on the Richter. "I'm listening. Talk to me. What's wrong?"

"It's Rusty!" Houston's voice cracked. "Oh my gosh, Trace. He's dead. The shooter hit him. Rusty is dead!"

Nuala
Lucketts, Virginia
15 June – 1430 Hours

With Houston's help, Nuala had converted the isolated workout room into a sterile surgical environment with draped industrial-grade plastic enclosing one-third of the space. Within that enclosure were heavy lamps, metal trays, a metal table, and a complete surgical care system. All sanitized as they had waited for Trace to show up with Annie.

It was strange, watching Annie lie there, silent. Still. Sleeping death. That's the only way Nuala had been able to cope over the years with seeing her targets in that position. Of course, they were dead. Annie was only sedated. But the fear that Annie could take a turn for the worse, that the doctor would discover the sniper bullet had punctured an organ, haunted Nuala. Just like knowing the sniper had killed Rusty. She shuddered, hating that their team had once again been affected. Targeted.

"She'll be fine." Houston handed Nuala a cup of water.

"Do you realize how fast a sniper bullet is?" She held the water but kept her eyes on her teammate. "It's designed to kill. It's messy. The speed and trajectory of the bullet create incredible damage..."

He touched her shoulder. "Hey..."

Startled by his tenderness, which made her more aware of how morose she was being, Nuala sipped her water. "Sorry."

"No worries. I'd rather be here hearing about bullet power than sitting by my station listening to Trace and Téya shout it out."

"They're still going at it?"

Houston nodded. "You'd never guess Téya was his subordinate."

"I don't think she sees herself that way," Nuala said. "At least, not since Frankfurt."

"Yeah," Houston said, scratching his curly mop. "I'm still working feeds and surveillance to see if I can find her, figure out where she went and what happened. Sometimes I get lucky. Like today—I spotted him."

Nuala pushed her gaze to his. "The shooter?"

He nodded, his chin lifting as a touch of pride hit his expression. "Saw him on the rooftop of Washington Gas. Missed him first couple of gos, but then finally located him behind one of the big A/C units."

"Did they catch him?"

Houston's face fell. His shoulders sagged as he stuffed his fists into his jean pockets. "No. He was gone by the time the team made it up there. They'd been up there once."

Nuala frowned. That didn't make sense. "How'd a SWAT team and a satellite scan miss him?" A gun that size wasn't easily overlooked, nor a person. "What if he moved?"

"What? From one building to another?" Houston shook his head. "But I'm working the image through facial recognition in the hopes of pinning him down."

Thwap.

Nuala spun, the sound eerily like a silenced shot. Instead, she found Dr. Olson emerging from the sterile environment. Nuala straightened, taking a step forward.

He held up a hand as he removed his surgical gown, cap, and gloves, snapping them into a receptacle. "She'll be fine. Bullet missed her vital organs, thank goodness."

Nuala gave a relieved sigh.

"Is the colonel around?"

With a hesitant glance to the briefing area, where Téya and Trace were visible and in the throes of an argument, Nuala hesitated. "Yeah. Sure. Let me get him."

"No," Dr. Olson said. "My nurse will stay with her for the night to monitor her vitals. I'll call Weston and give him my report."

"If you're sure. . . I don't think he'd mind me interrupting."

"It's okay. I have to get back before questions are asked anyway." Dr. Olson gave a nod to Nuala.

"I'll walk you out." Houston's offer wasn't simply consideration. It was necessity. Dr. Olson couldn't access the security panels. Trace trusted him, had requested a surgeon through General Solomon so they didn't have Annie on the grid with a gunshot wound. That would draw the kind of attention Zulu did not need.

Houston and Dr. Olson had just made it into the tunnel and closed the door when Trace and Téya emerged, still bantering.

"We can't go on with this. Annie's down. Nuala and I can't pull this off alone."

"You won't be alone," Trace said as he came toward her. "Where's Olson?"

"Just left." Nuala thumbed toward the doors. "Said he'd call you. But Annie's going to be fine, he said. Bullet missed vital organs."

Visible relief washed through the commander's face. He swiped a hand over his face and sighed. "Probably slowed because it passed through Francesca first."

"Could be," Nuala said. It wasn't completely implausible that the sniper had hit the two of them, but Nuala didn't want to think about it. "Any word on Miss Solomon?"

"Not 'miss.' *Lieutenant*," Téya corrected with a growl. "That woman got what was coming to her for all she put Trace through and what she almost did to us."

"But she didn't," Trace countered. "She left your names out. That's what mattered."

Nuala noticed Houston return. The guy hated confrontation as much as she did—he shimmied over to his workstation and hid behind the monitors. She joined him, moving away from Téya and Trace. Away from the tension. Sitting beside Houston, she brushed her long, straight brown hair from her face and yawned—hard.

Houston yawned through a "stop that" complaint. He shook his head. "That's...too...." His eyes bugged.

Laughing, Nuala realized he was staring at something on his monitor. "What?"

He clicked a ticker feed. Sucked in a hard breath.

So did Nuala. The ticker was from a news program. Hand over her mouth to cover her gasp, she found herself staring at the image of Boone Ramage. Talking with a reporter. The ticker below the journalist's face read LOWEN MILES, then it switched to SPECIAL FORCES SOLDIER COMES FORWARD ABOUT MISRATA.

"No," she muttered through her hand.

"Commander," Houston said, his voice tinny, stressed. "This is bad.

No, this is cut-your-losses-and-run-as-fast-as-you-can bad."

Trace hurried over to them.

Houston pointed to the wall, where he mirrored the news feature.

". . .and can you tell us why you decided to come forward now?" Lowen Miles asked.

Please please please don't do this, Nuala silently begged the man she loved. The man she held on a pedestal like no other. The man who'd mentored her. Encouraged her. Championed her. Protected her. Trained her. He had never given her a reason to think he saw her as anything other than a soldier, but she didn't care. She got to be with him, near him. Hear his thoughts. Hear his voice.

Now. . .now his voice sailed through a national television show, revealing secrets Zulu had fought—and died—to protect. "Too many people are dying. It's time to stop this. I've had enough."

"But it's been five years," Lowen said.

"Yes, and someone is actively hunting anyone connected to the incident," Boone replied.

"You mean those responsible?" Miles's words were a challenge.

"Did you know about this?" Téya demanded of Trace, who shot her a look.

But he said nothing. Just stared at the screen. Expression blank. But then, Trace's expression, if it wasn't blank, was terse. He had two modes: blank and intense.

"Holy bloody backstabbing, Batman," Houston said as he dropped back and stared at the screen open-mouthed.

"Quiet," Trace warned.

"Are you not seeing—hearing this?" Houston squeaked.

"Shut up!" Trace snapped. He moved closer to the wall, the image of Boone exploding in enormity—not only his visage but his betrayal.

Nuala squeezed her hand over her mouth, afraid her yelp might escape. Why was he doing this? She wouldn't believe he did this to harm them. But why else would he do it? Why go public?

Oh God, please help us.

She couldn't hear the rest of the interview, and she could only pray—and hard—that Boone wasn't giving their names. That he wasn't putting her life, or anyone else's, in danger. But that was vain, dark hope.

"He's betraying us and you're sitting there doing nothing," Téya shouted at Trace.

"No!" To everyone's surprise, including her own, Nuala's voice rang through the bunker. Somehow she'd come to her feet. Her heart rammed hard against her ribs, threatening to break through. "No," she said, firmer but softer. "Boone is not betraying us."

"Open your eyes, Pollyanna!" Téya said, her words sharp.

"I believed in you when everyone questioned your loyalty."

Téya's eyes widened. "My loyalty?" She scowled. "What do you mean?"

"You were gone for two hours," Nuala said, not backing down. "Then when you return, you're mean and hateful to everyone. To all of us, who have done nothing to deserve your anger and spite. I don't know what your problem is, but I think we've endured it long enough. Give Boone the benefit of the doubt."

"Bene—"Téya choked out a laugh. "You need to get over your lovesick crush and wake up and smell the betrayal, sweetheart." She stabbed a finger toward the news footage, glanced at it, then froze. Her expression went from hatred to shock.

Nuala whipped around, just in time to see a convergence of uniforms covering the screen. She gasped.

"Oh, that is not good," Houston said with a groan.

The screen minimized and another news anchor broke in. "As you can see from the earlier footage, authorities burst into the studio, tackled Mr. Ramage to the ground, and brutally and forcefully dragged him out of our New York studio."

Anguish twisting her heart and mind into knots, Nuala flung herself around to Trace. He watched, emotionless, as Zulu's team daddy, as they'd nicknamed him, had been dragged away. And yet he still said nothing.

"How do we get him back?" Nuala said, her throat feeling raw and thick as she spoke around the silent tears streaming down her face.

Commander Weston's green eyes hit hers. Hard. Cold. Unfeeling.

His phone rang and his hand moved to the holster at his hip. "We don't." He lifted the phone, turned and walked toward the briefing room.

Trace

"Weston." Trace's gut churned.

"D'you see the news?"

"Yes."

"Well," General Solomon said with a hefty sigh. "Have to admit, I haven't seen things go south so bad on someone."

"Welcome to my world," Trace said rubbing his neck. "How's your daughter?"

"Fine. Surgery went well. She's already awake and talking."

Trace lifted his head. "Talking?"

"Oh—not like that. In fact, she said she doesn't know what hit her."

General Solomon snickered. "She'll be laid up for a couple of days."

In a chair, Trace bent forward, his elbows on his knees as he stared at the cement floor. At least one thing went as right as it possibly could. Not right in the man's daughter getting shot, but right in that she was okay and she hadn't talked. He still didn't know what Francesca and Annie were doing together. And that unsettled them, especially with both getting shot.

"Sorry about your man," Haym said. "I liked Gray."

"Me, too," Trace said. "Thanks." Trace massaged his temple, trying to breathe. Trying to believe all he'd fought for wasn't really crumbling and running between his fingers. But even lying to himself about it wouldn't help. Things were seriously messed up.

His dark thoughts parted and he caught a clear thought. The general wasn't talking. And he hadn't hung up. "Sir?" He stood. "I take it this isn't a social call."

"Afraid not, son. The decision was handed down with the committee's recommendation to move against you. Cantor's hands are tied."

Trace felt the room sway. His knees buckled.

"I'm sorry, son, but you're to be discharged, other than honorably, effective immediately."

XIII

Trace
Lucketts, Virginia
18 June – 0945 Hours EST

Sixty-two months of protecting and fighting to make sure Zulu remained alive. Sixty-two months of going without the one element in life that made it worth living—Annie. Countless lies, though they'd all been done in the name of competing harms. Watching the families of the team burying an empty box and clinging to the memories of girls who were still alive.

He hated it. Hated the deception. But he'd done the right thing.

Did I?

Sitting at the table in the briefing room, Trace cradled his head in his hands. Six funerals five years ago. Four in the last two months. He hadn't been able to stop any of them. He bore the guilt of that heavily and fully, and felt it now that Rusty had been buried with full honors. Trace shook his head. He wanted to rage and say he'd get who'd done this, but he'd said that for five years. Now he seemed further from resolution and justice than ever before.

He'd stayed here with the remnant of Zulu who were divided and struggling with the latest events. Nobody wanted to do the mission to capture whoever was behind this. Their focus had collapsed. Their will died. As their team commander, he should encourage them. Challenge them.

But there was nothing left to say. Nothing in his defense—he was to blame. Completely. He'd been given one task: lead and protect Zulu. With half the team dead. . .yeah, he'd call that a failure.

And the decision, the one he'd narrowly avoided four years ago in the first hearing—a year after Misrata—finally came down. Fourteen years committed to the art and craft of warfare. . .gone. Forever.

Now, I'm nothing.

Not a soldier. Not a leader.

Where did Zulu stand? What would happen to the girls when Solomon was forced to hand over the reins of leadership to someone else? What would he do?

Nothing like returning home to hang his head in shame.

A light rap on the door made him grit his teeth. "Come in," he said

481

without looking, without lowering his hands.

Once the door opened then closed, he sat up, rubbed his hands over his face, and sat back again. His heart kick-started at who stood there. "Annie," he said, coming out of his seat.

"No," she said holding out a hand as she came forward. "Let's sit. Talk."

"You should be resting."

She smiled. "I'm fine. A few days to heal and I'm as good as new."

He arched an eyebrow.

"Okay," she said with a smile. "Maybe not new. Probably lightly used."

"It's good to see you up and around," he admitted as he took his seat again, watching how she lowered herself gingerly into the chair beside his.

"I confess, I was sure sitting on that bench that I might not ever get up again." She brushed a few curls from her eyes. "But"—she nodded—"being there helped me get some things sorted. I've been thinking about us."

Trace felt his gut tighten. He'd had a conversation or two like this before. And considering his track record the last few weeks. . . Weary, he resisted the urge to shake his head. It wouldn't end well, this conversation. Just wouldn't. Nothing ended well for him these days. "Glad you had that time to think."

"Trace, I have to let you go."

With a quiet snort he nodded. Raw. Bleeding raw. That was how he felt. That's what his heart felt like. As if it'd been skinned alive. Everything he'd done, all the fighting and searching and hunting and tracking. . .all so the team could be free. So he could be free to go to Annie. Be with her the way he'd wanted.

And he got the kiss-off.

Couldn't say he didn't see this coming. "Sam's a lucky guy," he managed and pushed to his feet. He started for the door.

Annie leaped up, grimacing as she clutched her side, and caught his arm. "Trace, please."

He held his hands out to the side in surrender. There was no fight in him. "It's okay, Annie. I get it. I deserve it."

Her grip tightened. "That's not why I'm doing this."

"Isn't it?" Trace pivoted to her. "If I'd stayed with you, gone to Manson with you, I can't help but think you and I would be together, and I'd trade war stories with Sam. You'd trust me and believe in me. You'd love me."

Annie's eyes widened. "Trace, I do believe in you. And I do love you—"

"No." He held up a finger. "No, you don't." He shook his head. "And honestly, at this point in the game, I don't blame you." Considering everything that had been happening. . . "Maybe Zulu would be better off if I'd let the chips fall five years ago."

"Let the chips fall?" Téya's voice cut into their argument. When they looked at her, she shrugged. "If you want a lover's quarrel, try doing it in private." Téya stepped into the room. "As for letting the chips fall, Trace—seriously. Grow a brain. If you'd done that, we'd all be in jail or dead. Because whoever set us up wanted us out of the picture."

"There are things you don't know about," Trace said, irritated with Téya's sudden alpha behavior.

"Right. The investigation. How about Boone going off and betraying us—and speaking of, shouldn't we be clearing out?"

"No, we're fine here."

"How can you say that? He went live—"

"If Boone wanted us harmed, authorities would be crawling all over this place already. We wouldn't be sitting here having this conversation."

"Okay, fine. I don't agree, but moving on. What about Francesca Solomon and the hearing?" Téya crossed her arms. "Why don't you enlighten us?"

"She said she didn't reveal us," Annie said. "I think, in this case, we're clear."

Téya shook her head with a huff. "But the hearing. Why hasn't the commander told us anything about the hearing?"

"What's going on?" This time, it was Nuala who came into the conversation with her soft voice and innocent eyes.

"Our dear commander was going to enlighten us—"

"I'm out," Trace said, his anger rising. "I've been relieved of command and discharged. You'll have a new leader. In fact, Solomon said to expect them today."

Silence roared through the room.

"What?" Trace spat at Téya. "Nothing to say now?"

"Yeah, I have something to say," Téya bit back. "Show us what you've got. You've protected us for five years. Don't back down now."

"*Protected* you? Reyna, Herring, and Shay are dead! Dead because I didn't *protect* them."

"Guys."

"You have a god complex."

"You have an attitude."

"Guys!"

"I think we all need to—"

"What is your problem, Reiker? What really happened those two hours with The Turk? I think you need to enlighten the rest of us," Trace said.

"GUYS!"

"What?" Trace and Téya demanded, spinning toward Houston, who stood outside the door.

Eyes wide, Houston took a step back. It seemed even his hair trembled. He pointed to the side, to his station. "We"—his voice cracked—"we have company."

Trace stomped out of the room, more than grateful to leave the nest of stinging hornets in there. "What kind of vehicle?"

Houston was back at his station, pecking on the keys. "Black SUV. Looks armored."

A few more steps placed Trace behind Houston's chair. He leaned forward, a hand on the back of Houston's chair and one on the desk. They watched the grainy, black-and-white feed as the Suburban pulled up to the access gate, a mile out from the main road. Heavy tinting protected the occupants from view. The driver's side window rolled down.

"Can you see the face?" Trace asked, subconsciously craning his neck forward as if that would help him peer into the truck.

"Yeah, different camera." Houston pointed to another screen. "There."

The older, wizened face peeked back.

Trace touched his shoulder. "That's Solomon. Let them in."

"Uh," Houston said with a grunt. "I don't have to—he has the access code." Houston shifted and let his mouth hang open. "How does he have our access code?"

"Easy," Trace said, but he'd like to know, too. His phone buzzed and he lifted it from the holster. Glanced at the caller ID then answered the phone. "Sir, welcome to the bunker."

"Going to need some help."

Trace frowned, watching from another camera, mounted in a tree if the leaves and branches cutting slightly into the view were any indication. "How so?" The general aimed into the barn with the SUV.

"Meet me."

Trace sighed. "Be there in two." He ended the call. "Okay, people. Look alive. We have guests."

Though Téya and Annie and Houston all peppered him with questions, Trace stalked out of the bunker, up the cement stairs, and down the narrow tunnel Boone had burrowed up into the barn. He emerged from the secret door at the back of a stall when Haym climbed out of the SUV. Trace met him at the front end and extended his hand. "Sir."

"Sorry for the sudden appearance."

Trace ignored the apology. It wasn't sincere. The general had arrived here suddenly on purpose. "Who's with you?"

"Three people—they're hooded."

"Prisoners?" Trace frowned. "Did you capture someone connected to the shooting?"

"No. Better." Haym gave him a smart-aleck grin. "Help me get them inside and I'll explain."

Trace didn't move. Taking three strangers into the Zulu bunker where the girls were would expose them. Put them in more danger. He didn't trust his instincts on this, but even more, he didn't trust anyone else.

"Son, I know. . .but you have to trust me on this one. I promise, you'll want to talk to them."

After another long pause, Trace finally consented. Gave a curt nod. Haym smiled as he started back toward the door and motioned Trace to the other side.

Trace complied. He lifted the handle and tugged it open. And stopped short, his gaze snapping to Haym's on the driver's side. Of the three in the middle row, two were females. One a male.

"Okay," Haym said, his voice light and almost merry. "This way," he said, taking the arm of the man who sat by the door. "Step out then wait."

Trace touched the elbow of the woman on his side. She flinched but then tentatively reached out. He caught her hand and provided support and direction. Best way to do this was to have her hold his sides. He eased in front of her and placed her hands on his sides. "Take your lead from the way I move," he said.

She hesitated, her fingers lifting off his shirt.

Trace pressed his hands against hers, forcing her to hold on. "This way or you injure yourself."

Her hold took on more strength. Trace walked to the secret door, accessed it, then let the general, who did the same with his two charges, guiding them down the ever-sloping tunnel to the cement steps. Once they'd descended, Trace edged along the others, his hooded woman hesitating and gripping tighter when her steps grew uncertain.

He punched in the code. The steel groaned as the door hissed inward. Trace waited as the four entered the room. Zulu stood around, watching, curious. Concerned.

Trace motioned them away, mouthing "out of sight," as he moved his hooded charge toward the briefing room, the most confined space and the only one with a door. The woman missed the first step and tripped into him, face-planting against his side. She yelped, clenched her fingers in his shirt, and gave a nervous laugh.

Once inside, Trace secured the door, turned, and folded his arms over his chest. Nodded to the general, who looked like a mad scientist, anxious to reveal his exciting experiment. And this was an experiment, though not exciting. More like threatening. Had he made yet another mistake?

Haym pulled off the first hood. Then the second. Each shock more incredible than the first. When the last hood came off, Trace tensed. Came unglued. "You son of a—what is *she* doing here?"

Annie
Lucketts, Virginia
18 June – 1015 Hours EST

At the roar of Trace's voice, Annie stalked back toward the briefing room, Téya and Nuala at her side.

"You are risking their lives, their existence! How could you even think this was okay?" Trace shouted at General Solomon.

But Annie couldn't tear her gaze from the couple standing calm and unaffected—the Lorings. What were they doing here? Why was Trace so upset over them returning? Did they need more protection?

"Who's the other woman?" Nuala whispered, pointing to the woman with her back to them.

"Let's find out," Annie said. But when she took the first step, the woman turned, and Annie froze. "No. . ."

Téya bumped into her. Glanced at her. Then to the room.

Nuala gasped. "That's—"

"Francesca Solomon." So, she didn't die. Annie hadn't wanted to ask. Even seeing the woman now, she wasn't sure what to feel after all the woman had done to expose Zulu and decimate Trace.

"Please," General Solomon said. "Hear us out." He waved Annie, Téya, and Nuala into the room. "All of you."

"No." Trace swung around, stilling when he saw them there. His shoulders slumped and he pinched the pressure point between his eyes.

Annie gave Francesca Solomon a hard glare as she moved into the room and took a seat. She wasn't wearing a uniform today. Instead, Francesca wore a pair of capri jeans and a cream-colored sweater that accented her olive complexion and curves. Truth be told, Francesca looked as annoyed as Annie felt at seeing her.

"First, I must beg your forgiveness," Haym said. "Francesca did not know she was coming, but I felt—for reasons I will soon explain—that she needed to be here." With that, he directed her into a chair. "And well, I think the rest should be explained by these two." Now, he sat down.

Trace folded his arms over his chest. His brow knitted tight. His jaw muscle bouncing. Ticked off.

"First," Sharlene Loring said as she took a step forward and reached up to her brunette crop. She tugged, and the hair fell away, revealing a mop of blond hair. "My name is Elizabeth Olmedo." She motioned to her right, where Carl Loring stood. "And this is my partner, Amato Aznar. We're with the CIA. We apologize for the deception, but it was necessary."

Stomach roiling, Annie braced herself. "Necessary for what?"

"To gain your confidence," Amato said, "but also in the hopes that our story, the potential of a witness to Misrata, would bring Berg Ballenger into the open."

"That didn't happen, though," Nuala said, then drew in on herself. "Did it? I mean—he gave us the shaft in Dover."

"Unfortunately," Elizabeth said, "no, it didn't."

"Because you weren't really there the night we hit the warehouse," Annie said. "Your names weren't on the list of the occupants. He knows that because he was there."

"You're right. We weren't, but you shouldn't have known that," Elizabeth said. "The agency back-filed all records pertaining to those in the warehouse. We'd like to know how you were aware that our names weren't there."

"Don't answer," Trace said without moving.

Startled by his response, Annie glanced at him then back to the operatives. "I don't understand—if you weren't there, why would you fake your names? He'd know that. Right? Is he the one you're after? Is he somehow involved—is that how he knew to go to the warehouse?"

"No, whoever gave him the info on the warehouse is who we're after," Elizabeth said. "As far as we're concerned, Ballenger is nothing more than a grieving widower."

Téya snorted. "One who has had five years to nurture that grief to become a violent vigilante."

"Possibly, but we aren't convinced."

"He set us up in Dover," Nuala said.

"We hoped our names on the map would get him curious enough to investigate, to tip his hand—and that's another reason for the gala. We need Berg Ballenger. Need to talk to him."

That was dangerous information, and the CIA didn't openly cooperate with rogue organizations like theirs, which made Annie more uncomfortable and irritated with this whole setup. "Why are you telling us this?" Her head hurt, thinking of the implications. "Why is Zulu being read in on this? Why now, after you'd effectively stepped out of our attention?"

"The gala," Téya muttered quietly. "This is about the gala." She turned

487

to their commander. "You were in on this."

"It was my idea," Trace began, "but not my idea to bring in the CIA or *her*."

Annie took a bit of perverse pleasure in the way Trace referred to Solomon's beautiful daughter. And that curl in his lip only added to the meaning and her pleasure.

"That's right," Amato said. "Since time is short, we'll just lay it all out. We have scheduled a weapons cache of high value on the black market to be destroyed. Rumor will only be started once the gala is in play."

"Why the gala?" Nuala asked. "I mean—there will be innocent people there. Why put their lives in danger?"

"It is our only opportunity to have all the players on one chessboard, so to speak," Amato said. "We have five suspects as to who may have been the leader of this weapons-stealing ring. We've invited all five."

"Wait," Annie said sitting forward in her chair. "You know who's behind it?"

"Suspicions only," Amato said, glancing at his partner, "and only because of recent activity—including connections with Ballenger. That and clearance levels—what we're destroying isn't readily known, so that limits who could get their hands on that information."

"The shooting—that's the recent activity you're talking about," Francesca said. "The person who shot me is on that list?"

"You weren't the only person shot that day," Téya said evenly, drawing attention to Annie.

Annie glared at the general's daughter. She really had no business joining this conversation or being in the bunker. She'd put them all, especially Trace, through so much. But the fact she'd kept their identities out of the hearing was the only thing saving her from a tongue-lashing.

"We believe the shooter is named," Amato said. "Which is why it's important for you to be there."

"You?" Téya moved her hands to her hips. "Who?"

"Zulu," Trace said.

"I'm sorry," Téya said, with an exasperated sigh, "then why is she here again?"

General Solomon straightened. "Because she is going to work with you."

"Isn't she medically fragile right now?" Téya asked. "Bullet in, bullet out. I'd call that fragile. Commander, you made us train with Quade till our eyes were bleeding, and you're going to let a soggy recruit in?"

"I'm fine." A nervous expression flared through Francesca's expression as she glanced at her father then Trace.

"Never said I was letting her in."

Francesca

She deserved this. That much she knew. But it still didn't make it any easier to swallow the bitter pill of resentment this team doled out in bulk. Frankie ignored the nagging pain in her side, ignored the anger at her father for luring her into this mess. She'd never have come if she'd known this would involve Trace Weston.

Guilt also came in bulk this morning, with the operatives making it very clear Frankie had been wrong all along in her assumption about the colonel. Regret coiled around her stomach and squeezed hard. Imagine if she'd succeeded.

Well, she had, actually. They'd stripped him of rank. She'd heard that news floating around work. The blame for that rested on her shoulders.

Frankie rubbed the knot at the base of her neck as the agents talked and gave her the opportunity to avoid looking into the eyes of spite and hatred.

"But then," Trace said, "I'm not in charge anymore."

Frankie didn't miss the way the Zulu team reacted to his words. Or the daggers they shot in her direction.

"Later," Frankie's father said, shifting awkwardly as the tension roiled through the room. Another relationship her actions had poisoned. "For now, I need you to go with me on this, Weston."

"Fine," Trace said. "But we will *talk* after this."

"Mr. Weston," Ms. Olmedo said, interrupting the tension, "your team has been to hell and back in the days since the bombing. You went in as instructed, located the weapons, set the charges. You executed your orders with precision and stealth. I think we all know, including Miss Solomon, that you were not guilty in the murder of those twenty-two civilians. We need to move beyond that. Put our adult hats on."

Trace straightened. "How do you know so much about that?"

Elizabeth said nothing but stared down Trace, who glanced to the general. A silent conversation vibrated between their heated expressions. Then Trace's brows rose, wrinkling his forehead. "Them? Our orders came from *them*?"

"The intel came from us," Amato said. "But it was corrupted or sabotaged. Olmedo and I are here because we need to get these weapons stopped. Batsakis has made a fortune on stolen U.S. military weapons, but they're always one step ahead. This time, we want to be ahead. We want to know who got in the middle of the mission."

"So, this is about Berg Ballenger?" Annie asked, her head spinning. So much happening. So many tensions emanating through the room. "Was he the sniper who hit Francesca and me?"

"Remember," Téya, the one woman in this room Frankie would not want to have a confrontation with, said with no small amount of sarcasm, "he's just a grieving widower."

"Then why do we care about him?" Annie asked, trying to keep up with the reasoning.

Elizabeth nodded. "Ultimately, someone fed Ballenger that information about the warehouse. We do not believe it was coincidence that he moved the orphans there that night. Someone knew your team was there to destroy the weapons. We believe they wanted you out of the way so they could get the weapons to Batsakis, who paid them a hefty sum. It's our theory that they intended to kill Ballenger that night as well so they could cover their tracks. We want them to find out about this gala so they'll show up."

"Kill him and the kids but leave the team alone?"

"Oh," Amato said with a dark laugh. "They had no intention of leaving Zulu alone. We have evidence that a response unit had been dispatched to the area—before the explosion."

Weston straightened, his tactical shirt pulling taut as he balled his hands into fists. "They targeted us?"

"If you hadn't extracted Zulu and hidden them—they would all be dead right now."

Surprise spiraled through Frankie. She watched the news impact Weston, and once more, she saw the depth of concern the man had for his team. His dedication to them. She'd been wrong.

"You said the rumor would be started once the gala is in play?" Trace said, his hands on his trim waist.

Amato nodded. "Yes, we'll get it circulated. Miss Solomon will be the person who'll mention it."

Once more, she watched Weston's reaction. His green eyes rammed into hers. She expected to see a hint of glee that she might end up dead. Instead, more of that concern.

"Is that a good idea?" he asked Amato.

"It's the best we have."

"I'm capable," Frankie said, hating the way they talked around her. She felt her father at her side and met his concerned gaze. Yeah, she wasn't going to play into his fears.

"What about Zulu?" Weston had completely ignored her. Again.

"They'll mingle," Amato said.

"No way," Trace snapped.

"I understand your reticence, but—"

"I don't think you do."

"You're not the only leader to lose soldiers in the field, Colonel Weston."

"*Mister* Weston. And I don't care who you've lost. I care about not losing these three."

"You won't lose them," Olmedo said. "We have more than twenty operatives who will be in attendance, along with a SWAT team on standby."

"If they are seen—"

"We'll know," Téya said. "We'll know if someone recognizes us."

Weston grew more agitated. "Batsakis knows Annie—he kidnapped her when we were in Greece!"

They were in Greece? When was that?

"Annie will be in the task force room with us," Olmedo said. "You can guide us."

"I'm not hiding in a room while my team is out there in the open."

"He can be my escort," Frankie said. Her heart beat hard as Weston's gaze snapped to hers. "My date."

"Won't Trace be too recognizable?" Téya asked. "Whoever is selling the weapons will probably know that he's been stripped of rank."

"Which is why he's running private security. We all know the colonel is a man of action. He's not a desk jockey," Frankie said, bolstered by her idea. "After the shooting"—she looked to her father—"my father wasn't comfortable with me attending alone—"

"No. Two is right. Trace is too easily recognized. He needs to be in the command center with Aznar and Olmedo. Frankie, you'll be down with the others."

Téya's hazel eyes held hers. "Nuala will be on the rooftop with her sniper rifle monitoring your every move."

Was it a promise? Or a threat?

Annie
Reston Town Center, Reston, Virginia
July 4 – 1900 Hours

"Okay, just like we practiced." It'd been two weeks since that day in the bunker when the Lorings revealed themselves as CIA operatives. Since Francesca Solomon entered their lives and bunker. . .and stayed. Tension high and resentment higher, Annie and her sisters had done their best to steer clear of the troublemaker.

Annie stepped out of the hotel lobby and into the warm, Northern Virginia air. Lights sprinkled through the trees abutting the One and Two Fountain Square buildings threw a romantic aura over the cozy setting. Mercury Fountain, whose water danced in the glistening lights, made the area feel more festive for the celebration that wasn't really a celebration but a dupe. A fake to lure murderers into the open.

This is it. The night Zulu would break free of the chains tethering them to the past.

Annie's heels clicked on the pavement as she headed toward the tented pavilion, feeling the throb of loud music against her chest. She caught her reflection in the window of Clyde's, a restaurant. The navy satin gown would've cost more than a month's salary—if she had a salary. Or a job.

"Looking good, One," came Trace's firm, calm voice through the small device embedded in her ear. He monitored the event from the third-floor room in the Hyatt Regency. "Two, your position is good."

Annie furtively swung around until she spotted Téya by the fountain on the other side of Market Street. Their gazes met then moved on, unwilling to draw attention or give away that they knew each other. Tonight, the only people who should recognize Zulu would be the team behind this trap. And the ones trying to kill Zulu. "Six, how's your view?" Trace asked quietly.

"Flying high. Should have a great view of the fireworks down on the Mall."

"Not exactly how I wanted to spend the Fourth of July," Téya muttered.

Annie's favorite celebration included a very handsome Navy SEAL. And when this night was over, she'd go back and get her life on track with Sam. If he'd forgive her. She wasn't sure, not after the way he'd handled her, pushed back and called her on her feelings for Trace.

But getting shot, sitting on that bench, Annie's biggest regret was not seeing sooner how much she loved Sam. Thinking of dying without him knowing how important he was to her. . .

Annie floated around the other suits filing into the pavilion. Smiled at the plastic-fest of trophy wives and girlfriends.

Sam and Jeff would be out at the lake watching the biggest fireworks celebration in Washington. She ached to be there with Sam. Laughing with Jeff and his wife. Eating sandwiches from the Green Dot.

"Nice setup, but it doesn't have anything on Manson," came teasing, husky words.

Annie froze, her eyes widening as she swirled around to find Sam before her. She opened her mouth to ask what he was doing there, but her mind got log-jammed with the million other questions. How did he know? He was wearing a suit. Heavenly days, he looked good. Smelled good.

He smirked at her. "Speechless for once, eh? Glad I have that effect on you." He took her hand, stepped back and let his rich, brown eyes take her in. He lingered a little too long on her curves.

"Hey, sailor," she said with a tease in her voice. "Eyes up here."

Sam slid his arm around her waist, inching closer.

"What are you doing here?"

Sam smiled down at her, his gaze taking her in. As if he didn't want to miss anything. "I came to save the day."

"I asked him to come," Trace corrected quietly, effectively reminding Annie that the coms were still live. That he could hear the conversation. "With Boone MIA, we needed the extra hand."

"You mean," Annie said to Trace, though she held Sam's eyes, "you wanted someone watching over me since you knew you'd be up there and not at my side."

Eyebrow quirked, Sam leaned in. "Evening, Weston," his whispered words tickled down the side of Annie's neck. When she shivered, Sam's smile grew. He leaned in and kissed her.

Knowing they were being watched, having Trace in her head, for all intents and purposes, Annie blushed. She gave his arm a gentle squeeze. "I'm glad you came."

"Look alive, people," Trace said, his voice all business. "Batsakis and Stoffel are here."

Annie hooked her arm through Sam's and aimed them toward Democracy Drive, where the limousines were delivering guests to the event. Titus Batsakis stepped from the armored SUV limo. A different kind of shiver traced Annie's spine.

Sam gave her a look.

She squeezed his arm, warning him not to say anything.

"Annie, stay low for now," Trace said.

She immediately turned and guided them toward a crowd of suits and uniforms but kept her eye on the two Greeks who walked tall. The interesting addition was Mercy Chandler. Attractive and young, the woman exuded confidence and wealth. Chin lifted, shoulders relaxed but spine straight, she knew who she was and what crowd she walked in. The one who'd come to her, offering to honor her and give her more money.

So she thought.

Annie couldn't help but wonder if the woman knew what her husband was doing, how he was funding their lives, using the orphanages as covers for the weapons smuggling.

Bulbs flashed as the Greeks posed for photos before entering the roped-off area for the event. Batsakis, who towered over his brother-in-law, let his gaze surf the crowd.

That man was as slimy as they came. He stood arrogantly, strutting his stuff. Then his gaze hit something he didn't like. His brows knitted. Nostrils flared.

"What's he looking at?" Trace asked.

Annie turned subtly to identify the subject.

"Anyone?"

"No joy," Nuala said softly, meaning she couldn't tell what he was looking at.

Annie tried to line up his gaze with the crowd. "Lots of Brass and suits over there."

"Houston's working on it. Okay, Cantor and Solomon are in play," Trace said. "Anyone seen Ballenger yet?"

"Negative," Téya said.

"No." Annie gave Sam a smile when he shot her a questioning look. Clearly Trace invited him, but he didn't have a coms piece? His gaze slid to her ear, and she could tell he was questioning the very thing she had just then.

"Miss Palermo," General Solomon extended a hand as he and General Cantor joined them. In dress blues, Solomon cut an impressive figure, whereas Cantor struck an imposing one.

Annie greeted them then introduced Sam. "This is Mr. Calamari."

"Caliguari," Sam corrected without missing a beat as he shook their hands.

Cantor shot a look up and down Sam. "You're the SEAL."

Sam started then nodded. "Yes, sir."

"Good work in Greece," Cantor said.

"Thank you, sir. Took home a souvenir, but I'm glad to have been able to help."

"Oh, you helped all right," Cantor said with a grin. Then elbowed Solomon, who grimaced. "Wouldn't you agree, Haym?"

Rubbing his side, General Solomon nodded and flashed a smile. "Of course." But his smile vanished as quickly as it'd come.

"You okay, general?" Annie asked.

"Of course." Then he frowned at her. "Lot at stake tonight."

"Annie," Trace said, his voice thick with warning, "move on. If you stay near him, it'll draw attention."

Happy to comply, Annie smiled at them. "I think it'll be a great, memorable night, General Solomon." She nodded as she took Sam's arm again. "If you'll excuse us. . ."

But even as she moved past him, she couldn't help but feel something was off with the general tonight.

"Uptight," Sam muttered.

"Yeah." Which wasn't like the general. "Must be really stressed about tonight."

"He has as much to lose as the rest of us," Trace said.

"True," Annie replied.

"True what?" Sam scowled at her then at her ear. Resolution carved a hard line through his face. "I'll be right back." He stalked across the pavilion then into the door of the Hyatt Regency.

Trace
Reston Town Center, Reston, Virginia
July 4 – 1930 Hours

The command center thrummed with tension and activity. Aznar and Olmedo sat at folding tables with laptops that showed a quad-split screen of different camera angles. Trace stood by the one-way glass, hovering over the scene, wishing he was down there in the fray. Closer to the fight. Closer so he could protect Téya and Annie.

The tented area only hosted the food and entertainment. Everything else had been deliberately set up so they had a bird's-eye view of every attendee. Annie stood alone, sipping a drink. Water. She'd never compromise her state of mind for alcohol. She was too stringent with the rules to bend them. It's what he'd liked about her.

A cluster of uniformed officers drew his attention. He considered their placement. The analysts said Batsakis had been looking in their direction when he reacted. Trace scratched the side of his face, thinking.

"Boss-man?"

Trace shifted and glanced over his shoulder.

At his own workstation, Houston waved him over.

The door to the suite clicked and opened. In stormed Samuel Caliguari. An agent stopped him, but Trace lifted a hand. "He's with me."

Caliguari crossed the room. "You wanted me here."

"I did."

The Squid nodded. "Good. I came to get the mic you forgot to give me."

The guy had some chutzpah.

"I mean, I know you meant to. You wouldn't want me on the ground during a mission without being able to communicate possible threats. I know you want to protect Annie, and I need a piece"—he thumbed toward his ear—"to do that."

"You know that, do you?" Admirable that the fish out of water presented this in the best possible light for everyone. He'd put Trace in a corner.

"I do. Because I know you're an honorable type of guy. You wouldn't let personal feelings get in the way of doing the right thing."

Grinding his teeth, Trace lifted a coms box from the table and held it out.

Sam took it without a word.

"Uh, Boss-man. . .I think you'll want to see this," Houston said.

Trace turned, pulling his anger and attention from the SEAL. He lifted his chin in a "go-ahead" to Houston.

"It's that trajectory analysis you wanted."

"The what?"

"The trajectory of Batsakis's gaze."

Trace made his way back to Houston near the windows. As he reached for the table, he noted Caliguari with him. Trace scowled at him.

"What? I need to know threats on the ground, right?"

With a huff, Trace nodded to Houston.

"Well, I have been working with the feed from Batsakis. . ." Houston's wiry hair seemed especially frizzed today, and Trace had to shift to see around the mop.

Caliguari adjusted, too, watching the video.

Houston's fingers sailed over the keyboard. "So, I—"

"Weston! Weston, your girl's in trouble!" Aznar shouted, and flipped a switch. The audio went live through all speakers.

"What do you want?" It was Annie's voice. Her trembling voice.

"You did this little event, so I would imagine you know what I want, Miss Palermo."

Trace stilled. "That's Ballenger. He knows her name. Her real name."

"He also knows this gig is a setup," Caliguari added.

With a pat on Caliguari's chest, Trace nodded. "Get down there now."

Sam darted for the door.

"Anyone got a twenty on One?" Trace demanded. "Six, do you have Annie?"

"Copy that," Nuala said. "She's directly below your suite. Out of your sight."

"The man with her—"

"No joy," Nuala said. "He's hidden. Perfectly. Hotel pillar covering from the south. Large planter from the north. Annie's shielding him. Repeat, I have no joy."

Trace cursed but heard Aznar ordering one of the SWAT teams to the roof of an adjacent building. Security camera angled in and caught Annie, standing rigid and wide-eyed. Not moving anything but her eyes and lips. Ballenger could kill her right there, right in front of him. Retaliation?

"Two," Trace said.

"Moving in now," Téya replied softly. "I only see a shadow. He's smart. And good."

"We need to be better!" Trace shouted.

"You understand," Ballenger said, "that I couldn't just stay in the shadows. I couldn't let those responsible continue to profit year after year."

"Who are you after?" Annie asked.

Yes, keep him talking. Good girl.

"Oh, the wisest man in the world." Ballenger snickered. "Which, obviously is nobody on your team. It has been so easy to get around you."

"Why would you want to target us?" Annie's voice shook. "We were only—"

"No. No! You do not get to do that," Ballenger's voice growled through the coms. "Let them sit in their temple and palace, built on the blood of my daughter and wife."

"Almost there," came Sam's breathy grunt through the coms.

"Be ready, Miss Palermo. The fireworks start soon."

"Who are you targeting?" she asked. "There are a lot of innocent people here who will get hurt. Think this through, Berg."

But he didn't answer.

The camera captured Téya scurrying up to Annie. Trace bent forward, waiting for the confrontation.

"He's gone," Téya panted out the words. "Ballenger is gone."

"Find him!" Trace shouted, his heart pounding.

"Boss-man."

"Not now, Houston."

"No, really. You need to see this now."

"Colonel Weston?"

Trace pivoted toward the voice. A man stood in the corner of the room, being checked by security. He stepped forward and Trace frowned. "General Cantor." Another man loomed behind the Army chief of staff. "Do I know you?"

Cantor motioned to the man. "Colonel Weston, this is my future son-in-law, Eric Goff."

The young captain shifted but gave Trace a firm handshake.

"Sir, I'm sorry, but this is a bad time," Trace said, irritated the man would bring his future son-in-law up here to show off. It didn't seem within character for Cantor either, but Trace couldn't focus on them. "If you'll excu—"

"Actually, Colonel, this"—Cantor bobbed his head around the room—"is why I came up here."

"Sir?"

"I'd like you to keep a close eye on Solomon."

Trace blinked. The general? No, he must mean the daughter. "She's fine, sir. I have—"

"*General* Solomon," Cantor clarified.

Again, Trace blinked. "I. . .we—am I missing something, sir?"

Cantor exchanged a look with Goff then sighed. "We have reason to believe Haym may be in danger."

"You think he's a target?"

"I think he *is* danger."

Trace's mind was starting to feel like a pretzel. "Ballenger knows he's the one who sent Zulu in?"

"Just keep your eyes on Solomon, Colonel." Cantor gave a firm nod then turned and started for the door. Trace watched the two leave without another word and closed the door behind them.

That was bizarre, to say the least. Trace shook off the scowl and confusion. Insanity.

"Boss-man?"

"Right," Trace said, turning. "Sorry. What did you want to show me?"

"I think Cantor might be right."

Trace frowned. "How's that?"

"The trajectory lines of Batsakis's reaction. . .he was looking at the officers."

"We know that—the five Aznar warned us about."

"Yes, but when I used other videos and footage," Houston said as he moved the mouse and clicked a few screens. "I figured out *who* he reacted to."

Trace would kill the guy if he didn't get to his point soon.

"Sir, it was General Solomon." Houston's eyes were wide. "What if Cantor is right—what if Batsakis is going to kill Solomon?"

Téya
Reston Town Center, Reston, Virginia
July 4 – 1945 Hours

"Why are you doing this"

Francesca Solomon glided around in her tight black evening gown. She gave a cool, unaffected air as she smiled at Téya. "Doing what?"

"Getting under our skin," Téya said with an even smile. "Being a pain in the backside."

"Maybe it's what I do best," the woman replied, unfazed by the confrontation.

"That's for sure," Téya said. "That and destroy lives."

"Sorry, dear. You did that on your own."

"Mm, perhaps, but did Trace?"

"Dial it down, ladies," Trace's voice cut into the coms. "Focus on the task at hand."

"Yes, and let's be grateful we weren't forced to wear formal dress uniforms," Francesca said. "We'd stick out like sore thumbs."

"More like gaudy targets," Téya said.

Francesca laughed. "At least we can die in the company of good-looking men." She nodded to a well-muscled man in a suit. "I didn't know they grew the charity types so brawny."

Téya had to admit Solomon was right. She'd seen a handful of hunks wandering the event. One had flirted with her at the fountain.

"Now, there's a sound I haven't heard in a while," General Solomon said as he and Cantor joined them, flanked by two others: one a colonel and a peer to the first two. The younger, however...Tall, handsome, a little on the lanky side. But not hard on the eyes.

"Ladies, this is Sergeant First Class Goff and his father, Colonel Goff."

Téya and Francesca greeted them, Téya taking in the newcomers' uniforms. The younger Goff had an air of determination she'd often seen in men like Trace and Boone. Colonel Goff bore the full bird, being a rank higher than Trace. But at the man's age, she'd have expected him to have attained a higher rank. Maybe he hadn't entered service young like his son, who had enough medals and recognition pins to serve as a Kevlar vest.

Téya tilted her head, eyeing his left shoulder. Over the Airborne patch, he wore the blue Ranger tab. Ah. That explained the no-mess attitude. She wanted to trade stories with him, but she'd tip her hand if she did.

"Keep up the casual banter," Trace intoned in their ears. "But stay eyes and ears out."

Right. Because in fifteen minutes the fireworks display would start. That would be the prime opportunity to shoot someone or blow something up and attract not a lot of attention. So, basically, she had fifteen minutes to live.

Music drifted into the night. Attendees grouped up and headed for the wooden dance floor covering the center of the pavilion. Cantor extended his hand to Francesca, who graciously accepted.

Téya hated dancing but couldn't exactly say that when the younger Goff offered his hand. She smiled and accepted. He led her onto the dance floor.

"You're not wearing your uniform," he said.

Téya's heart thudded hard.

"Don't worry," he said, easing in and holding her close. "I'm not the threat. I'm part of the protection detail. My team is here."

"Rangers?" she asked, leaning back to eye his uniform again.

"5th Group."

Arching an eyebrow, Téya appreciated the news. "Special Forces. With a Ranger tab."

"What can I say?" He grinned. "I'm just that good."

"Téya, he knows you're the asset. That's all," Trace's warning came through the coms quiet but strong. In other words, don't give him more info than he needs.

Goff talked casually and laughed a lot, but she noticed his gaze never stopped roaming. Neither did hers. Any second she expected to feel heat and pain explode through her back.

"You here?"

Téya flinched. "What?"

"You zoned."

"Sorry."

"Guess you can take the girl out of the uniform, but not the uniform out of the girl."

"Something like—"

A familiar face bobbed between two dancers in the crowd. Familiar. Very familiar. She followed with her gaze, her breath jacked up into her throat. She saw— Téya sucked in a hard breath.

"Hey." Goff tightened his arm around her. "You okay?"

"He's here," she breathed, frantic.

"Téya?" Trace's voice was clear, distinct. Terse. "Who'd you see?"

Her mouth went dry. She realized she wasn't dancing anymore, but she didn't care. She pushed through the crowd, plunging in the direction she'd seen him. It was like trying to swim up a raging river, the throng of partyers unyielding as she tried to push past them.

"Téya, what's happening?" Trace asked. "What'd you see?"

Him. She saw *him*. Her mind raged, demanding she verify who she'd seen. Demanding she find him. Téya sprinted around a corner. Saw a door close. She raced after it.

"Téya! You're out of line of sight."

She sprinted for the door.

"Téya!"

She jerked open the door and stepped in. The door slammed shut behind her. She stopped short.

Felt a poke against her back.

"Thank you," a man's voice breathed down her neck. "Thank you for helping me avoid listening ears."

Her coms was still in place. She could still hear Trace shouting for someone to find her. Go after her.

"You and your sisters—how foolish to come here. To set a trap for me. You see? The one for whom you set the traps has sprung the traps." He chuckled.

Téya shifted.

He pressed the gun harder into her back. "Uh-uh-uh," he grunted. "Keep your hands where I can see them, or I'll be sure you can't lift another finger ever again."

"What do you want, Ballenger?"

"I want to know why you're with Queen of Sheba? Why would the angels of Zulu taint themselves with the blood of the pagan queen?"

Téya scowled. What was he talking about? "She's helping us find you."

He laughed loud and hard. "Helping you? Find me? But dearest, I'm right here. And where is she? Dancing with a soldier."

"Téya, stay cool," Trace said. "We're coming for you."

"Ah, my good Colonel," Ballenger said. "No need to treat me like the enemy. We are on the same side, you and me. We want the same person dead."

Téya's heart thudded. He knew Trace was listening. And if he knew that—would he kill her?

"Tell him I hear him," Trace said.

Wetting her lips, Téya gathered her courage. "He heard you."

"Oh, I know he does." Ballenger chuckled again. "He should be asking himself how I know that. I've given him the clues he'll need to end what he's been trying to end for five years. But I'm not convinced he's paying attention."

"I am!" Trace shouted, his voice panicked. "I'm listening, Ballenger."

"He said he's listening," Téya said, her breaths coming in gulps.

"Oh, I'm sure he is. I have his girl here. Though, not his favorite. That'd be Palermo, wouldn't it? Or maybe he now likes the Queen of Sheba." Ballenger caught Téya's hair in his hand and jerked her head backward.

She yelped but quickly braced herself.

"See, he's not interested in you because you belong to another."

"No," Téya said. "I belong to no man."

"Tsk, tsk," Ballenger said as he drove the gun into her cheek and then grabbed her hand. "This mark says differently." He leered down at her. "Do you know what this scar, this burn means?"

"I need plastic surgery," Téya ground out, focusing her energy. Focusing on how to disarm him without getting her head blown off.

He guffawed. "No wonder he claimed you." He grabbed her hair again and tugged her toward the door. "No, this mark means if I kill you, he will kill me. It guarantees your death will only come at the hand of one man—The Turk. And if it doesn't, then there will be hell to pay for whoever robbed him of the pleasure."

"What do you care?" Téya growled.

"Oh, I don—"

Téya snapped around. Flicked her hand in a palm-strike against the weapon, knocking it out of his hand. She drove the heel of her other hand into his chin. But he deflected just in time.

Ballenger stumbled. Reared back with the butt of the weapon.

Clink. Clink. Clink!

Téya saw the gray canister tumbling toward them. She threw herself around, opened her mouth, held her breath, and closed her eyes.

Booom!

White light exploded through her thin eyelids, searing her vision. She squeezed her eyes tighter.

Trace
Reston Town Center, Reston, Virginia
July 4 – 1955 Hours

"Where's Téya? Anyone got the twenty—"

"Got her, got her," Sam's voice carried through the coms. "She's okay. Came out the south side of the Hyatt."

"Flash bang," Téya breathed.

"Who threw it?" Trace demanded, feeling powerless up in the suite with the analysts and not on the ground protecting his team. Anger churned through him. Ballenger had gotten to one of the girls again. And again he hadn't killed her. He was toying with Zulu, but Trace wasn't sure why. What the point was.

And Ballenger had a point.

"Trace," Téya coughed out his name. "He was here."

"Who? Ballenger? Yeah, we figured that—"

"No," Téya croaked out with another cough. "The Turk."

Trace hung his head. The night could not get any worse. "Okay." No it wasn't okay, but what could he do? He needed time to think. "Come up here and—"

"No." Téya's voice was suddenly clear. But then she barked, her throat no doubt burning from the gas in the flash bang. "No, I'm not leaving the ground. He's here. That means he wants something."

"You in a casket?" Annie said.

"If he wanted that, he wouldn't have saved me from Ballenger."

"Maybe that's why he did save you—so he could kill you."

"Enough," Trace said. "Get out there. Eyes open, everyone. Showtime—fireworks going off in five."

Planting his hands on the window ledge, Trace bent forward. Pressed his head to the glass. What was Ballenger's game?

"It was so weird," Téya said, "the way he kept calling Francesca the Queen of Sheba." Even as she talked, Téya moved back toward the fountain. "I thought for sure that was going to be it."

"Trace." Annie's voice, clear and precise, broke through the din of chaos in the command center and into his own fried brain.

"Go ahead."

"Something's not right. Ballenger isolated both of us but didn't take the opportunity to kill us."

"Maybe he was distracted by the Queen of Sheba," Téya said.

"I resent that name," Francesca said. "I'm not even Ethiopian. I'm Italian American."

"My favorite food," Téya shot back. "But maybe that's what we can call you now."

"Fine as long as I get the temples."

"The what?" Téya asked.

"Oh come on," Francesca said. "Tell me you don't know Bible history. King Solomon and the Queen of Sheba had a thing. So, if I'm going to be the Queen of Sheba, I want my handsome king and the temple."

Wait. Trace froze. Wait wait wait.

"*. . .wisest man in the world. . .*"

Ballenger said that to Annie. He'd taunted them about the wisest man. Then he'd said something to Annie about palaces and temple.

Queen of Sheba.

King Solomon was considered the wisest man in the world. Solomon's Temple. Solomon and the Queen of Sheba. . .

Trace lifted his head. The data wall! The icy touch of dread filled his gut. "Heads up," Trace snapped. His gaze hit the man in uniform. A man he'd considered a friend. A man who had been his confidant.

Hollow ringing in his ears made Trace feel light-headed. This cannot be true. He couldn't. . .it was circumstantial. Right?

"Just keep your eyes on Solomon. . ." Cantor's concern about the general— it wasn't because he was in danger. It was because he was the danger.

Trace spun to Houston, who was already watching him expectantly. "Can you get me a secure link to Six?"

Houston stared for a second, confused. Then blinked. "Yeah. Sure."

"Do it." Trace hurried to the tech geek's side. Waited as he called up Nuala then handed him the phone. "Six."

"Sir?"

"We are on a secure, isolated channel. I need you to focus on one target. And one target only. Stay on this target no matter what. If he does anything, anything you deem dangerous, you take the shot. Am I clear?"

"Yes, sir." The tense affirmation told him she understood. "But, sir? Who's my target?"

"General Haym Solomon."

Francesca
Reston Town Center, Reston, Virginia
July 4 – 2003 Hours

For the first time in her life, she felt like she fit in. Only she didn't. *Couldn't,* because these ladies, this team, hated her. She had nearly ruined their lives. Had their commander arrested and imprisoned. He'd lost his career because of her. And yet Francesca never felt more at home, never felt more herself than she did with them.

Maybe it was the action. The adrenaline rush of working a live mission. Or maybe it was the buzz of knowing someone targeted this new team who had teased her, shared a few laughs, ridden her butt. . .

"So," Frankie said, wondering if this would be the true test of friendship—would Téya answer this question? "You mentioned The Turk."

Téya's eyes flashed to hers.

"Who is he?" Well, she knew who he was but wanted to know what this woman knew, too.

Something sparked in Téya's eyes that bespoke anger, irritation, and fear. "Look it up when you get home and have nothing better to do." But then Téya straightened as her gaze slid over Frankie's shoulders. She frowned.

Frankie glanced back. Her stomach vaulted into her throat. Trace Weston stormed toward them. His brow was more tightly knotted than she'd ever seen. And that was saying something since he never looked at her without that infamous scowl. But right now, he looked like a tornado setting down on them.

Correction: on her.

She braced herself. "What—"

He took her hand. Tugged her onto the dance floor. Drew her into his arms.

Frankie swallowed hard. The coms piece went strangely quiet. Was the team listening in so closely they weren't talking? Speaking of—he hadn't said a word to her since they started dancing.

"Our coms are muted," he said, his voice tight.

Frankie tried to work that out—why would he mute their coms?— but she came up blank. "Okay."

A high-pitched whistle screamed through the night. *Crack! Boom!* Brilliant red and blue lights exploded across the sky. Dancers scurried to better spots to watch the fireworks. Frankie smiled up at them.

Trace grabbed her wrist, tugged her aside. To a dark spot. He pulled her close. Not to be intimate. But to be heard. "I've got two snipers trained on you."

Frankie widened her eyes and tried to step back.

Trace held her tight. "Tell me what you know!"

Panic pushed her to get free. She shoved him back—or tried. He didn't budge. "I don't know what you're talking about."

His iron grip pressed into her flesh. "You have one more chance, and then this all ends—with you."

Frankie tugged against his grip, frantic. "You're insane! I don't know what you're talking about."

"Your father."

She stilled, scowling at him. "What about him?"

"Your father is the one who set my team up."

Frankie froze. "No." Tried to let those words sink in. "No, that's . . ." Tried to fathom how Weston could even come up with that. "Where did you get that idea? That's insane! My father loves you like a son."

"No, I think he kept me close to keep me under control." He shook her. "Think about it. The whole thing makes sense. He controlled my every move. Kept me hidden from you—why?"

Frankie couldn't take it anymore. Couldn't take the horrible accusations. She lashed out, thrashing against him. Screaming. Shoving. Pushing. Kicking.

Fireworks roared and popped. The crowds cheered.

"Ballenger told me. Ballenger gave me hints that your father was behind Misrata."

"No," Frankie growled. "You're sick, Trace Weston. You're a sick dog."

"Think about it, Francesca. Why did he keep you away from us? Why didn't he help you by showing you the truth? Why did he keep it hidden?"

"Shut up!"

Nuala
Reston Town Center, Reston, Virginia
July 4 – 2008 Hours

A slightly chilled breeze tugged against her tied-back hair as Nuala sat on her perch with the sniper rifle tucked against her shoulder. She had maintained a visual lock on the man they had all come to view as a guardian. A mentor. Though he didn't have direct contact that often with them, General Haym Solomon had earned her respect.

So holding her sights on him, knowing she had orders to take him down, Nuala struggled. Palms sweaty, heart ramming against her ribs pressed to the tarred roof, she worked herself down. Took deep, calming breaths. What she wouldn't give to have Boone here. To hear his voice. To know he—

Nuala's thoughts snapped closed as the events below registered. Haym Solomon was moving away from the pavilion. "Six to Actual," Nuala radioed in.

"Six, this is Command. Actual is offline."

Offline? Why was Trace offline? "I need him online," she said, too aware of the panic, the rapid heartbeat, the trembling fingers. All things that would affect her shot.

"Sorry. We'll do what we can."

The *thump-pop* of a firework warned her of the bright light. A few seconds later, the dahlia bloomed in the sky. Right. That could take forever. She could lose sight of Solomon.

What if she didn't take the shot and he did something awful?

Or worse—what if she took the shot and things had changed? Trace realized how wrong he was?

But if Haym Solomon was responsible for setting them up, for making them kill those children. . .

Nuala drew on courage and strength she did not know she possessed. He'd inflicted her with the nightmares that invaded every breathing moment of her life. And he'd looked her in the eye.

She lowered her cheek to the rifle. Peered down the scope.

Thump. Pop! Crackle!

The night sky gave way to the peppering array of fireworks as Nuala took aim and slid her finger into the trigger well. Worked her calculations.

"Nuala!"

She lifted her head. That sounded close. Behind her. She glanced over her shoulder.

Boone dashed across the rooftop, waving his hands. "Go! Go!"

She scrambled to her feet, surprised. Startled. Confused. Her instincts to obey his orders without hesitation had her coming to her feet. But then her mind caught up with the betrayal. He went on television. "You shouldn't be here!"

He came unyielding. His face a wild mixture of terror and panic.

Nuala back-stepped. Toward the edge of the roof.

He dove at her.

She screamed. His bulk plowed into hers. Knocked the wind from her lungs. They went airborne.

Téya
Reston Town Center, Reston, Virginia
July 4 – 2015 Hours

Téya stood at the fountain, watching the fireworks. Watching Trace and Frankie in a wrestling match. A shouting match from the looks of things.

The fireworks popped, the booms thumping against her chest. A chrysanthemum was quickly followed by crackles. Some in red. Some in blue. She had to admit it was weird to think of it this way, but Téya hated that everyone had someone. Annie and Sam stayed close to each other. Trace had his firebrand in Francesca, though there wasn't anything romantic in that. Mutual disdain and hatred. But the girl was exactly Trace's type, so it was a good thing they wouldn't have anything to do with each other when this was over.

507

BooOOOOooooom!!

Screams and shouts made Téya duck. She felt thumps against her back and scurried to the side. She looked back, stunned to see the building missing its top two floors. Téya went ice cold. That. . .that was where Nuala had been set up. "Oh my—"

"Get back!" Eric Goff shouted to her.

But Téya pushed forward.

As she did, she saw sparks. Not just sparks—the tiny explosion visible at night from a gun. She glanced in that direction. Then an avalanche of partygoers rushed past her, screaming. Shoving. Tossing her aside like she didn't exist. What were they running from in wild panic?

As the crowd cleared, a woman in a gold gown bent over a man. The fireworks show went on, making it impossible to hear what was being said. But she could see. The woman's gut-birthed sobs told Téya what happened.

He's been shot.

She spun around. Where she'd seen the sparks. Tracked movement. The wild, frenzied movement of the crowd.

But one more controlled, more intentional pattern drew her attention. A man was running toward Democracy. Around the barricades, then sprinting down between the buildings.

Ballenger!

Téya kicked off her shoes and sprinted after him. She heard shouts behind her but didn't dare look or take her eyes off Ballenger. He was not getting away with this. What if Nuala was dead? And Annie—where was Annie?

"Zulu! Report," Trace's voice—so smooth and calm—came through the coms.

"One here. I'm fine."

Tugging up her gown, Téya dodged fleeing guests. She felt like a Ping-Pong ball as she made her way down Democracy. Past the cupcake shop. And the theater. Ballenger was past the Starbucks now. Heading toward the small outdoor amphitheater.

"Six, Two, report."

Kinda need to breathe right now. If she took even an ounce of her focus off this mission, she'd fail. Ballenger would get away. And he'd kill again. She would not let that happen.

"Dawg here."

Téya tripped. Her mind skidded right into that voice. Boone? What was Boone doing here?

"Six's injured but alive."

"Copy that, Dawg."

Téya darted across Library Drive, narrowly missing a cabby, who gave her a blaring welcome. But she kept going. Behind her, she heard feet slapping the sidewalk.

"I'll cut him off on Market!"

Goff. Eric Goff was with her.

Téya refocused on the mission—getting Ballenger. She ran past Mon Ami Gabi and PassionFish. She banked right onto Explorer Street. Headed toward the Reston Town Square Park.

Darkness crowded her, making her all too aware that she couldn't see well enough.

Shadows shifted. Coalesced.

A fraction of a second too late, she realized the threat. Her body jolted with adrenaline. The massive form plowed into her. Téya vaulted sideways. Felt herself flying. Unable to control her direction. Her movement. The stone steps rushed up at her. She tumbled down the amphitheater.

Simultaneously, she registered a bright explosion. Felt its concussive boom.

She dropped hard. The stone steps jabbed her side. Punched the breath from her lungs. Téya arched against the pain and rolled onto all fours. Her ears rang. Smoke spiraled through the air, reaching her. She coughed.

Something clattered to the ground and rolled to a stop in front of her. Wincing at the bruised ribs she'd no doubt have, and the fiery pain, she reached for the item. And stilled. A pen? What. . . ?

Another boom tugged her attention toward the street. Flames consumed two cars. Alarms screeched from a BMW, its lights flashing in panic against the intrusion of the explosions. Bombs? Had someone set a bomb?

She stepped up and her legs buckled. Téya steadied herself, her balance and orientation still off because her right ear was still plugged. She pressed her finger to it and felt a warm stickiness. "Great." Pulled away, her finger was tipped in blood.

But the movement pushed her attention back to the pen. She lifted it and the light of a streetlamp caught the white lettering on the shaft. THE ROSE CLUB AND PUB. A single red rose snaked up the black body of the pen.

The Turk. *Majid. . .*

Téya's heart thumped. Hair dangling in her eyes, she lifted her head. Looked up the steps she'd been thrown down. Glanced toward the street, where the large form had barreled into her. Smoke and flames roared into the sky from a burning car. Téya climbed the steps, holding her side. At the top, she scanned the park, searching for him.

She caught sight of a man jogging from Saint Francis onto Market. Téya gripped the pen tightly. She rushed forward, expectation pulsing hard through her veins.

A streetlight exposed the runner—Eric Goff. Panting hard, he shook his head, brow beaded with sweat. "I lost him." He sucked in a loud breath. "I thought he went into the garage, but—" He gripped his knees.

Téya used the back of her hand to brush the hair from her face and look around. Ballenger was still free. And The Turk. . .

She scanned the levels of the parking garage. Most of it was dark. A few scattered lights mottled the darkness with a dull glow. Was he up there? Watching her even now?

Yes. She could almost feel his gaze on her. But was he in the garage or. . . She turned to the buildings. Condos. Office buildings. How did he manage to slip in and out of her life like that, so effortlessly? So stealthily?

Goff scowled as he crossed the green. "You're bleeding."

Somehow, she knew that Goff's presence meant no Turk. He wouldn't expose himself. He wouldn't make his presence known. "It means I'm alive."

Was she insane for wanting to see Majid again? Dangerous ground when she started thinking of a skilled assassin by his first name. Better to keep it business. The Turk. *He's a killer, you idiot!*

A shadow shifted by a parked car. Téya snapped her attention toward it. Was it him?

"D'you see something?" Goff said, coming closer, watching in the same direction.

Téya flinched. She didn't need this Special Forces operator tracking down The Turk. "Uh, no." She pried her gaze from the car and glanced toward the burning car. "What happened over there?"

"Explosion of some kind. I saw it go up but didn't see anything else." He shifted and reached for her head, assessing her injury. "Did it hit you?"

Téya rolled the pen between her fingers. She'd been hit all right. But not by the explosion—well, at least not until after *someone* sent her flying. But if she hadn't been knocked away, the explosion could've seriously injured or killed her. "No, I think. . ." She checked the amphitheater. Remembered tumbling to safety. The pen. She glanced at it. But by the time she'd regained her bearings, she'd been alone again. "I guess I didn't see the first step."

"Never took you for clumsy," Goff teased.

"I like to keep them guessing." Téya gave one more survey of the area, searching for The Turk. For Ballenger. He could easily just shoot her right here. Right now. Secretly, she hoped The Turk was here. That he crossed paths with Ballenger. It was a dark thought that only had one outcome—death.

Trace
Reston Town Center, Reston, Virginia
July 4 – 2022 Hours

Emergency medical services flooded into the square. Firemen checked the building for damage, removing the injured.

Trace stood watch as they loaded Nuala onto a stretcher, her neck in a brace and a strap securing her head so she didn't aggravate whatever injury she sustained when Boone saved her life, plowing off the roof onto the lower balcony of the top floor.

She held Boone's hand as he walked with the EMTs taking her to an ambulance. "I told them you didn't betray us," she whispered.

Boone smiled at her. "You always saw the best in me."

"That's because that's all there is to see."

Trace grunted. "I might lose my cookies," he teased then looked at the EMT. "I think she hit her head harder than she realizes."

As they loaded her up and locked her stretcher into place, Trace patted Boone on the shoulder. "You going with her?"

"No," Nuala said, straining to look down the length of her body at them. "Stay. I'll be back once they X-ray me and realize I'm telling the truth that I'm fine."

Boone hesitated.

"I could use your help here," Trace said.

"I'll go with her," came a female voice from the side.

Trace shifted, surprised to find Téya walking toward them, barefoot and escorted by Eric Goff. Dried blood clung to her sandy-colored hair and down her jawline. "You look like you could use some medical tending."

"Why do you think I offered?" She climbed into the ambulance without a word. She sat and sighed, glancing down at something in her hand. As the doors closed, Trace caught sight of a pen.

"What happened?" he asked Goff.

Goff stood with his hands on his belt. "She took off like a bat out of hell. That's when I saw Ballenger, so I went after her. Chased him all the way down to Saint Francis. An explosion blew up two cars—I think he led her down there intentionally. To kill her. The explosion blew her into the amphitheater. She said it didn't, but I can't see how it didn't. I maintained pursuit of Ballenger. Lost him in a garage. Called in a team;

they're sweeping it now. I went back to find Two. She looked pretty rattled."

"She's tough. She'll be okay."

Goff nodded. "Noticed that." He had an appreciative gleam in his eye. One Trace wasn't sure he liked.

"Thanks for your help." Trace turned away.

"Colonel?"

Trace stilled. Didn't bother to correct the guy. He shot him a sidelong glance.

"If you put the team back together, I'd appreciate it if you'd consider me."

Put the team back together? What was he? Humpty Dumpty? "Noted." Trace couldn't even fathom entering the war game again, not right now. Not as he stared down bloodied operatives, dead agents, and wounded civilians. Again. Trace keyed his mic. "Anyone got a twenty on General Solomon?"

Cantor came toward him. "Solomon's car is missing. Batsakis and Stoffel are dead. Colonel Goff is in critical condition."

Trace slid his gaze to Eric Goff. The man was unfazed by the news. And he wasn't rushing off to be at his father's side. "What don't I know?" Trace asked them then pointed to Cantor. "You didn't want me to protect Solomon. You wanted me to watch him. Because you knew. You knew he was dirty."

Cantor sighed. "I came to you because—"

"It was me, sir," Eric Goff said. "I learned of my father's involvement in the weapons smuggling and approached General Cantor with the news."

"*Learned* of it?" Trace challenged him.

"He paid attention," Cantor said. "Look, Trace, I had information I couldn't prove. I needed tonight to happen. Solomon and Goff made their move—tried to take out Nuala then Téya—right in front of our eyes. If we hadn't had resources in place, this would've been a lot worse. What we weren't counting on was Ballenger's complicity and retaliation."

"He killed them?"

Cantor nodded. "Hit Stoffel then used the panic of the crowd and the explosions to cover Batsakis and Goff."

"Solomon?"

"I have teams hunting him down now."

Over the general's shoulder, Trace spotted Francesca Solomon. Tears made her eyes look like pools of liquid gold. Her dark eyebrows curled against her brown skin. She shook her head.

"Excuse me," Trace said. He made his way over to her.

Francesca

Life imploding had a way of clearly establishing priorities, defining wrongs, and stirring a deep awareness of forgiveness owed. He owed her nothing. In fact, flipped on its head—she owed him everything. An apology. A begging of forgiveness. And eternal servitude. It was an unrealistic, archaic thought, but it just made it very clear to Frankie that Trace Weston had every right to hate her guts.

And yet here he came toward her, wearing a mask of sympathy. Empathy.

Frankie shook her head. She didn't want that. Not from him. She didn't deserve it. She took a step back.

"Hey." His voice was soft in a way she'd never heard it before. He dragged an overturned chair toward them and hefted it upright then set it down. "Sit."

Frankie resisted.

Trace took her by the shoulders and nudged her down. "We need to talk."

Right. Of course. "I. . ." Words tangled amid her grief. She felt numb. Disbelief churned in the wake of her father's betrayal. Frankie had watched Trace move from one injured person to another in the aftermath of the explosion and shoot-out. Talk with the operators. Confer with the emergency personnel. It became so clear to her then. So night-and-day obvious that she had Trace Weston all wrong.

The worst of it? There wasn't anything she could ever do to make up for the way she'd actively torn his life apart.

Rather fitting that it was her life now that was torn apart.

Trace snagged another chair and sat on it, elbows on his knees. His hands were steepled as he sat with her. "You holding up okay?"

She half nodded, half shook her head.

"Yeah, I know that feeling." Trace threaded his large hands, fingers edged with callouses and smeared with dirt from working the scene. "I don't want to be insensitive, but do you have any idea where your father might have gone?"

Frankie heaved a thick breath that had a tinge of smoke and ash. Would he go home? Bring the danger to her mother? "I. . .I don't know. My first thought was home, but I don't think he'd go there because Mom is home." She shoved her hand through her hair—only to have it get tangled. She grimaced. How could she forget she had her hair up? She freed the pins at the back and massaged her scalp. "I'm not sure if I'm the right person to ask. I"—her chin trembled and made it hard to talk—"I never saw this coming. I had no idea he. . ."

Trace nodded. "We have that in common." Then he looked at her with a small smile crinkling the edges of his green eyes. "It's to your credit that you saw the good in him. Loved him enough not to fathom he was capable of that."

"And what does it say of me. . .what I did to you?" She didn't want to look at him. Didn't want to face the music.

Apparently, he didn't want to look at her either. Once again, he steepled his fingers. Flexing them in and out, widening and shrinking the triangle formed. "That you're tenacious and bullheaded?"

Stunned, Frankie stared at him.

Late thirties, a war hero, a warrior, but he had a soft side. He arched an eyebrow and smiled at her.

Frankie laughed. "I deserved that."

He pushed back in his seat. "Yes. Yes, I believe you did."

The laughter, the teasing—she needed it. Needed the chance to breathe in the midst of this avalanche that had swept her perfect, unrealistic notions away. "I'm sorry. Sorry for. . .everything. You didn't deserve what I did to you. I wish I could undo it all—you didn't deserve to lose your job."

"Being uncooperative pushed that envelope over the edge."

"I'll never forget you shouting the Special Forces creed."

"Neither will I," he said, another smile tweaking his lips. "And what about you?"

Frankie frowned at him. "What do you mean?"

"I heard your place was trashed. You lost your job."

She widened her eyes. "He told you?"

Trace nodded. "Not all of it, but I'm still connected to the intelligence community. Word gets around."

The Pentatonix–Lindsey Stirling version of *Radioactive* belted into the night. With a gasp, Frankie dug in the small wristlet and retrieved her phone. Her heart tripped and fell when she saw the caller ID. "It's my father."

"Wait." Trace placed a hand over hers and looked out at the pavilion. "Cantor, Goff!"

The general and captain hustled over to them.

Trace released her hand "Put it on speaker."

Hand trembling, Frankie nodded. She answered it and immediately pressed the speaker option. "Daddy? Are you okay?" She couldn't help but come to her feet. "It's crazy here. . ."

Weston, Goff, and Cantor huddled around her. In minutes, there were more operators gathered, including Annie Palermo and a dark-haired man she'd referred to as Sam.

"Hey, Angel," he said, using the pet name he'd given her. She'd wanted to be an angel for dress-up parties for years. But she could hear in his voice his grief and torment.

"Daddy, where are you?"

"No," he said, his voice thick with emotion but also ferocity. "I know they're there. I know they're listening. But this isn't for them. This is for you, Frankie. This is my apology to you."

Feeling closed in, Francesca turned her back on the others and found herself staring at the brick wall of the Hyatt. "Daddy—"

"Just listen to me, Angel. You were right. All those things you said about Trace."

Frankie froze. Her mind bungeeing through his words.

Trace

Trace held his peace. There was no way Solomon could pin this on him. Right now, Trace needed to be here for Francesca. The girl was taking a mortal blow to her lifetime hero—her father.

Her brownish-gold eyes bounced to him.

Trace didn't react. Would Haym really do this? Shift the blame?

"But they were about me."

Trace had to admit, he released the breath he'd held.

"Hey," Cantor whispered as he touched his sleeve. "Eric called Solomon's wife. She said he's at the house. Showed up a few minutes ago and went to his office by the pool. Locked himself in."

Trace tensed. "Get a team there."

"Already en route," Cantor said. "About four minutes out."

"What you said about Trace—you should've been saying them about me," Haym spoke through the phone. "I arranged for the weapons to be removed from U.S. custody. That warehouse had been our shipping point for years. But it wasn't me, though—I'm not the one who put those kids there. That was Goff. He knew Cantor had gotten wind of it. He wanted the team out of the way. Wanted to send a message."

"Daddy, let me come to you." Tears slipped down Francesca's face as she held Trace's gaze, and he gave her a nod, communicating she was doing good. "We can talk. Turn yourself in."

"No, no, that's not how this will play out." His voice trembled. And even in the din of the cleanup behind them and the shakiness of Francesca's sniffling and words, the unmistakable sound of a slide racking.

Chambering a round.

Unfortunately, Francesca recognized the sound as well. She snapped her gaze to Trace, her mouth hanging open.

"Sir!" Trace bent closer. "Please. Let's talk. It's not worth your life."

"Trace." Haym's voice wobbled through a sob. "I really did see you like a son. I tried—I tried so hard to keep you safe. It's why I fought so hard after Misrata."

"But you didn't tell the truth, sir." Trace figured if he could keep him talking, then the man was still alive. The team would get there and stop him. "You didn't come clean. It would've been better, sir. We could've faced it."

"Trace, you looking at my angel?"

Trace met Francesca's gaze. "I am, sir."

"Coming clean would've destroyed her. And her mother, who was a saint putting up with me. My sons—they're heroes, Trace. I couldn't come clean without destroying all of their lives."

"Daddy, please."

"I love you, Angel. Always have. You make me proud."

"Daddy!"

A loud noise snapped through the line. Shouts came for the general to put down the weapon. Francesca's hope rose that they'd save him.

Crack!

Francesca screamed, her face contorted in agony, as she stared at the phone. "Daddy!" She flung her grief-riddled gaze at Trace.

Shouts carried through the line. A few curses. A woman's scream.

Cantor spoke into a phone, his expression going dark. He met Trace's gaze and shook his head. "A minute too late."

The phone tumbled from Francesca's grip. She stumbled backward, shaking her head in frozen torment.

Trace reached for her. "Fran—"

Her legs buckled.

Lunging, Trace caught her. She curled into his shoulder, her body tremoring as she sobbed.

Trace
Reston Town Center, Reston, Virginia
July 4 – 2330 Hours

The remnant of Zulu sat in the now-disassembled command center, debriefing. Trace leaned against a table along the wall. Nuala had returned a few minutes earlier, cleared of any breaks or internal injuries from the nosedive off the rooftop with Boone. With her, Téya had cleaned up and bore a butterfly stitch over her cheekbone. Annie and Sam sat across from each other in a pair of chairs opposite the sofa. Francesca sat between Nuala and Houston, who seemed to have developed puppy eyes over the attractive lieutenant. Trace wanted to slap the drool off the guy's face. Behind the team, both figuratively and literally, Boone held up a wall behind a seating arrangement.

"Hard to believe," Annie said quietly, glancing at her teammates, "that it's over. That Misrata is settled."

Francesca burrowed into herself, crossing her arms. She shivered, and from the few feet separating them, Trace could see the goose bumps on her arms. Probably leftover shock. He'd tried to get her to go home, but she wouldn't leave. Said she needed some space and time. And yet she was here. With them.

He went into the bedroom and retrieved the soft blanket folded over the foot of the bed. In the living room, he handed it to Francesca then sat on the edge of the sofa arm. "A lot happened tonight. It's going to take time to get it all written up, but yeah—Misrata is settled. It took a colossal effort, but it paid off. I want to apologize for the deception regarding Boone."

"Deception?" Téya asked.

"Boone didn't betray you. It was part of a plan to push the persons behind this into the open. It was a risk, but one we felt was the only way to draw Ballenger into the open, for those behind Varden's illegal actions to think they had to silence us immediately. It was dangerous, but it worked."

"I told you," Nuala said triumphantly, "he'd never betray us."

Téya tossed a couch pillow at her. "You're just glad he's back."

Nuala went crimson, her humiliation screaming. "Of course I'm glad. We're a team. He's part of it."

"Uh-huh," Téya said, but left it alone.

A knock at the door made Trace hesitate. They weren't expecting visitors. He shared a look with Boone then gave his buddy a nod signaling him to answer it.

Weapon held low, Boone called, "Who is it?" through the door.

"Cantor."

Boone gave Trace a startled look as he unlocked and opened the door.

Cantor entered, wearing a pair of slacks and a button-down shirt. By the clean smell wafting off him, he'd showered. His salt-and-pepper hair looked wet still. Eric Goff wore a loose dress shirt and a pair of jeans as he trailed the general into the room. Cantor met Trace in the middle of the room and shook his head. "How's everyone?"

"Beat up but alive," Trace said.

"Well," Cantor continued. "Sorry to interrupt, but I wanted to talk with you."

"Okay," Trace said, motioning to the adjoining room.

"No, actually, I meant to the team. To all of you." Cantor stood at ease as he faced the team. "First—I am truly sorry for the loss of your sisters, Herring, Reyna, and Shay." At the mention of Keeley, Cantor's gaze hit Boone, who gave a small nod. "The loss of their lives cannot be justified, but I hope that tonight's operation and events will give you a sense of vindication."

"Sir," Annie asked, scooting forward a bit. "Can you explain this to us? What happened? How were Solomon and. . ."

He held up a hand. "Glad to. As you might know, Solomon came to me with information about illegal weapons sales of U.S. military-grade weapons. I tasked him with solving the problem—which is exactly what he counted on."

"I just can't believe he'd kill children," Annie whispered.

"That," Eric Goff added, "was not his doing. We have a trail that shows my father was supposed to get the warehouse cleared out before your team hit it so there'd be no evidence. It'd look like a dead end. Instead"—his gaze dipped, marked with disgust and shame—"he wanted to send a message or something, so rather than clearing out the warehouse, we believe he tipped off Ballenger."

A nervous quiet fell over the team. Most likely aware of the price for vindicating their sisters. For not being able to *enjoy* that cost. But appreciating it all the same. A somber, bittersweet thought.

"We are still in pursuit of Berg Ballenger." Cantor glanced at Goff. "We won't give up until he's found, nor will we rest until he answers for what he's done. Colonel Goff will face a full court-martial."

"Doesn't that mean the reverse is true of Ballenger, too?" Téya asked, sitting forward. "I mean—he still wants the rest of us dead, right?"

"I do not believe that's true," Cantor said. "It's our belief that Ballenger was retaliating against those who ran the weapons. That wasn't you."

"Somehow," Téya said, tapping a pen against her lips, "that's not entirely comforting."

"My point tonight is that I don't want this to be the end of Zulu."

Trace pulled straight, glancing at the general. Then at his team. Half his team. Remembering how they'd stripped him of rank. That he wasn't an officer anymore. If he was going to keep Zulu active, then it meant he was doing it without Trace. Maybe that's why Goff was here. *My replacement.*

"It wouldn't make sense," Francesca spoke up from her nested place in the couch, clutching the tan blanket, "to ask a team to continue on when you've stripped their commander of his career."

Surprise at her words spiraled through Trace. He started to look down at her but then stopped. What was she doing? She didn't have anything vested in this fight. Was this her guilt talking? Her regret?

Cantor stepped back and placed a hand on Trace's shoulder. He gave a small, breathy laugh. "You didn't know?"

Trace frowned. Looked at Goff, who looked pleased as punch at this situation. "Sir?"

"I signed off on your discharge for publicity reasons only. The public needed to feel like Misrata got justice."

"So, punish me."

"Son, you need to think bigger." Cantor laughed. "Your name is blacked out from records because I wanted you off the grid to lead Zulu in more missions."

"Sir, respectfully—it doesn't make sense. I have three team members left."

"Actually, you have four." Cantor nodded toward Francesca. "And I've asked Goff and Caliguari to step in as advisers and handlers. We'll get you fully ramped up and ready to go. You have six months to get in shape."

"Sir, again—I appreciate this, but I can't do this. Not again. I thought we had clearance before, and it all went south."

"I understand that." Cantor nodded, undeterred. "But son, I'm it. I'm the top of the line. If Zulu goes out, it's because I or the president has signed off on it." Cantor slapped his shoulder. "This isn't the end, Weston. It's just the beginning."

Téya
Reston Town Center, Reston, Virginia
July 5 – 0115 Hours

Téya stood on the balcony, overlooking the square that had just hours before been a riotous scene of bloodshed and death. She tried to come to grips with the fact General Haym Solomon, the man who'd been like a father to the team, turned out to be smuggling the very weapons they'd been sent to destroy.

She stood in her pajamas, listening as Nuala readied herself for bed in the other room. Cantor had been kind enough to pay for the team to stay here rather than make the hour-long drive back to the bunker.

Tree lights sparkled over the trendy shopping area and gave the little light Téya needed to see the pen's rose.

"It's a twig."

The Turk huffed, turning it over, as if that made a difference. "It's a rose."

Téya held it up. "A twig."

"You are seriously lacking in imagination."

The door opened and gently clicked shut. Téya leaned against the sun-warmed wall, staring up at the night sky. "D'you forget something?" she asked Nuala.

"My pen."

At the sound of the man's voice, Téya lowered her chin, heart rapid-firing. Hid the smile she felt filling her with warmth. She turned her hand, looking at the pen. She angled to the side, now pressing both shoulders to the wall, but her ankles crossed.

Majid Badem, aka The Turk, stepped onto the balcony. He wore a black silk shirt and black slacks. Slick as snot and handsome to boot. His hair hung curly and loose around his face, seeming to accent the tattoo on his left cheekbone.

She held up the pen and gave him a lazy grin. "It's a rose."

He came closer. "It's a pen." He tried to pluck it from her hand.

"You are seriously lacking in imagination."

About the Author

Ronie Kendig is an award-winning, bestselling author who grew up an Army brat. After twenty-plus years of marriage, she and her hunky hero husband have a full life with their four children, a Maltese Menace, and a retired military working dog in Northern Virginia. Author and speaker, Ronie loves engaging readers through her Rapid-Fire Fiction. Ronie can be found at www.roniekendig.com, on Facebook (www.facebook.com/rapidfirefiction), Twitter (@roniekendig), and Goodreads (www.goodreads.com/RonieK).

Other books by Ronie Kendig

QUIET PROFESSIONALS SERIES

Hawk

Falcon

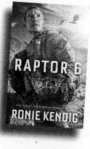

Raptor 6

DISCARDED HEROES SERIES

Nightshade

Digitalis

Wolfsbane

Firethorn

A BREED APART SERIES

Trinity

Talon

Beowulf